SUBTERRANEAN:
Tales of Dark Fantasy 2

SUBTERRANEAN:
Tales of Dark Fantasy 2

EDITED BY WILLIAM SCHAFER

ILLUSTRATIONS IN THE LIMITED EDITION BY J. K. POTTER

Subterranean Press 2011

First Edition

ISBN
978-1-59606-368-6

Subterranean Press
PO Box 190106
Burton, MI 48519

www.subterraneanpress.com

Table of Contents

This is for Yanni Kuznia

Wolverton Station | *Joe Hill*

Saunders saw the first wolf as the train was pulling into Wolverton Station.

He glanced up from his *Financial Times* and there it was, out on the platform, a wolf six feet tall with a scally cap tucked between his bristly, graying ears. The wolf stood on his hind legs, wore a trench coat, and held a briefcase in one paw. A bushy tail whipped impatiently back and forth, presumably poking out from a hole in the seat of his pants. The train was still moving, and in a moment the wolf blinked out of sight.

Saunders laughed, a short, breathless sound that did not quite convey amusement, and did the reasonable thing: looked back at his paper. It didn't surprise him, a wolf waiting on the train platform. The devil would probably be at the next stop. Saunders thought there was a good chance the fucking protestors would be parked in every station between London and Liverpool, parading around in costume, hoping someone would point a camera at them and stick them on the telly.

They had staked out his hotel in London, a raggedy-ass pack of kids, marching back and forth on the sidewalk directly across the street. The management had offered Saunders a room in the rear, so he wouldn't have to see them, but he insisted on a suite up front just so he could look down at them. It was a hell of a lot more entertaining than anything on British TV. He hadn't spotted any wolf-men, but there had been a dude on stilts in an Uncle Sam costume, with a three-foot rubber dong hanging out of his pants. Uncle Sam's features were stern and hateful, but the dong was scrubbed and pink and had some cheerful bounce to it. Slammin' Sammy carried a sign in both hands:

UNCLE SAM *PISSES* IN A CUP
& WE ENGLISH PAY TO *DRINK* IT
NO JIMI COFFEE! NO SLAVE CHILDS!

Saunders had a good laugh at that, had enjoyed how it treaded the line between righteous anger and mental deficiency. "No slave childs?" What had happened to the legendary British educational system?

The other protestors, a gang of self-important hipsters, were hauling signs of their own. Theirs were a little less amusing. They showed photos of barefoot, half-naked black kids, standing by coffee bushes, the children staring bleakly into camera, eyes dewing over with tears, as if they had just felt the foreman's lash. Saunders had seen it before, too often to really get angry, to be anything more than irritated, even if those signs perpetuated an outrageous lie. Jimi Coffee didn't use kids in the field, and never had. In the packing plants, yes, but not in the fields, and the plants were a hell of a lot more sanitary then the shanty towns those kids went home to.

Anyway, Saunders couldn't hate the hot little hipster girls, in their stomach-baring Che Guevara T-shirts, or their fashionably scrungy, sandal-wearing boyfriends. They protested today, but in three years, the hipster girls would be pushing baby carriages, and the half-hour they spent in Jimi Coffee gossiping with their girlfriends would be the best part of their day. The scrungy hipster boys would be shaved and chasing jobs in middle management, and would run into Jimi every morning on the way to work for their all-important double shots of espresso, without which they could not make it through the most boring day of their lives since the day before. By then, if the hipsters allowed themselves to think about the time they had picketed the arrival of Jimi Coffee on British shores, it would be with a flush of embarrassment at their own pointless and misplaced idealism.

There had been a dozen of them in front of the hotel the night before, and two dozen in front of the flagship store in Covent Garden, in the morning, at the grand opening. Not great numbers. Most passersby never so much as glanced at them. The small few who did take note of them always flinched at the sight of Uncle Sam with his rubber prick hanging out, the thing twitching back and forth like the fleshy pendulum of some perverse, surreal grandfather clock (grandfather cock?). That was all anyone would remember—Uncle Sam's strap-on—not what was being protested. Saunders doubted the marchers would register as anything more than a single sentence at the end of a minor story buried in the business section of the *Times*. Possibly someone would be quoted about Jimi's business practices, practices Saunders himself had helped to develop.

The way Jimi worked, they found a neighborhood Mom & Pop coffeehouse that was doing good business, and opened up across the street. A Jimi franchise could operate at a loss for months—years, if necessary—however long it took to put the competition out of business, and claim their customers. And this was looked upon as an outrage, a borderline criminal act, and never mind that the Mom & Pop usually served watery third-rate instant in thimble-sized cups, and couldn't be bothered to keep a clean bathroom. As for child labor, the protestors didn't like it, but were apparently at peace with children starving because there was no work at all.

No. Saunders couldn't hate them. He understood their mindset too well. Once upon a time he had marched himself...marched, smoked weed, danced in his underwear at a Dead concert, and trekked in India. He had gone abroad looking for transcendence, a mantra, *meaning*, and goddamn if he hadn't found it. He had stayed for three weeks in a monastery in the mountains of Kashmir, where the air was sweet and smelled of bamboo and tart orange blossoms. He had walked barefoot on ancient rock, meditated to the ringing drone of the singing bowl, and chanted with all the other potheads who had wound up there. He had given himself over to it all, trying to feel pure, trying to feel love—he even gave himself over to the food, daily servings of a mealy rice that tasted like waterlogged chalk, and bowls of what appeared to be curried twigs. And there came a day when at last Saunders received the wisdom he had come looking for.

It was a scrawny, raven-haired kid from Colorado named John Turner who pointed the way toward a higher purpose. No one prayed longer or more intensely than John, who sat through the guided meditation sessions, stripped to the waist, his ribs showing in his painfully white sides. They were supposed to focus on something beautiful, something that filled them to the brim with happiness. Saunders had tried picturing lotus petals, waterfalls, the ocean, and his San Diego girlfriend naked, without feeling any of it was quite right. John seemed to get it, though, right away—his long, horsey face shone with rapture.

Even his sweat smelled clean and happy. Finally, their third week there, Saunders asked him what he was visualizing.

"Well," Turner said, "He told us to picture somethin' that filled us with happiness. So I been imaginin' the fuckin' Quarter Pounder with cheese I'm going to sink my teeth into when I get home. A couple more days of eating sticks and spiced dirt, I think I might be able to visualize a bag of the flavorful motherfuckers right into existence."

Saunders had gone to India in love with a blonde-haired girl named Deanie, The White Album, and ganja. By the time he got back to San Diego, Deanie was married to a pharmacist, Paul McCartney was touring with Wings, Saunders had smoked his last-ever joint, and he had a plan. Or not a plan, exactly, but a vision, an *understanding*. Reality had briefly slid aside one of its black, opaque panels, to give him a glimpse of the gears that ticked behind it. Saunders had discovered a universal constant, like gravity, or the quantum nature of light. No matter where you went—no matter how ancient the traditions, no matter how grand the history, no matter how awe-inspiring the landscape—there was always a market for a cheap Happy Meal. The Lotus Way might lead to Nirvana, but it was a long trip, and when you had a lot of miles to cover, it was just natural to want some drive-thru along the road.

Three years after he left Kashmir, Saunders owned five Burger Kings, and upper management wanted to know why his restaurants turned a profit 65 percent higher than the national average (his trick: set up shop across from skate parks, beaches, and arcades, and grill with the windows open, so the kids were smelling it all day). Thirteen years later, he was in upper management himself, teaching Dunkin Donuts how to repel Starbucks (his plan: make 'em look like snobs and outsiders, play up the New England angle, total market saturation).

When Jimi Coffee offered him a seven-figure salary to help them restructure and take their franchise international, Saunders agreed after mulling it over for less than twenty-four hours. He especially liked the idea of helping Jimi go global, because it would offer him a chance to travel; he had hardly left the States in the years since India. Maybe they could even open a Jimi Coffee in Kashmir, right across the road from his old monastery. The seekers would probably appreciate the many vegetarian offerings on the Jimi menu, and a vanilla cappuccino would make the sunrise chants a whole lot more palatable. When it came to producing a state of focus, quiet contentment, and inner peace, Zen meditation ran a very distant second to caffeine. The average suburban whitebread Buddhist could manage without their daily yoga class, but take 'em away from their coffee, and they'd be an animal in no time, an absolute—

Saunders folded back one corner of the paper and took another look at the platform.

The train was yanking itself to a stop at last, in little hitches and jerks. He couldn't see the joker in the wolf suit anymore, had left him well behind. Saunders sat in the front-most car in the train, the first class car, and he had a view of one corner of the platform. A metal sign, bolted between two stone pillars, read WOLVERTON STATION. It was a good thing most activists barely had the money for the cardboard, Sharpies, and duct tape they needed to make their protest signs; the last thing Saunders wanted to do was share the otherwise empty first-class car with the crazy son-of-a-bitch dressed like the big bad wolf.

No, thought Saunders. *Fuck that. I hope he comes right in and sits down next to me. He can sit there in his asshole wolf suit and lecture me about all the little black kids who suffer under the baking sun in east Africa picking our coffee beans. And then I can tell him we don't let the kids pick, and that Jimi Coffee offers full scholarships to* ten *children from the third world every year. I can ask him how many kids from the third world his local Mom & Pop place put through college last year, when they were getting their coffee from an outfit of Samoan slavers, no questions asked. I can ask when he's going to start protesting* them.

In his years in management at Burger King, he had earned the nickname "The Woodcutter," because when there was a hatchet job that needed doing, Saunders never shied away from wielding the ax. He had not made his sizable personal fortune (his largest assets being a house on twenty acres in New London, CT, another in the Florida Keys, and a 43' Sportfisher that ferried him between the two) by avoiding confrontation. He had once fired an eight-month pregnant woman, the wife of a close friend, with a two-word text message: *you're toast*. He had closed packing plants, put hundreds out of work, and had stoically endured being called a soulless cocksucker in Yiddish by a red-faced and shaking old woman who had seen her little chain of Kosher coffee shops systematically targeted and taken out by Jimi. But this was, of course, exactly why Jimi hired him—they *needed* a woodcutter, and he had the sharpest hatchet in the forest. Saunders had been all for peace and love in his twenties, and he liked to think he still was, but over the years, he had also developed a hankering for the rusty-salt flavor of blood. It was, like coffee itself, an acquired taste.

The train sat for a long time, long enough so that after a while he put down the paper and looked out at the platform again. For the first time since boarding at Euston Station, he was irritated with himself. He should've hired a fucking car. The journey by train had been an impulsive, sentimental act. He had not been in England since the years right after college, had spent two weeks in the UK, on the first leg of the world tour that would eventually dump him in a decaying heap of stone in the breezy mountains of Kashmir. He had come because the Beatles were there; if not for the Beatles, he believed he would've killed himself in his teens, in the bad days after his father left his mother. He arrived in London with a craving to *feel* the Beatles in some way, a restless need to put his hand against the bricks of The Cavern Club, as if the music they had played there might still resonate in the warm red clay. He rode the rails north, packed into coach, on his feet for hours in the hot stale air, pressed up against an auburn-haired Edinburgh girl in blue jeans, who he didn't know when the trip began, and who he was half-mad for by the time they reached Liverpool. It was maybe the happiest memory of his life, all the reason he needed to go by train now.

Saunders tried to never think about what had happened *after* he got off the train. He and the Edinburgh girl had split up, making a loose plan to meet at The Cavern Club that evening; Saunders had stopped at a Mom & Pop for some fish and chips, but the fish was greasy and spoiled, and he spent the night in a sweat, shaking in a hostel, unable to stand. In the days that followed, there was a continuous sick fizzle in his stomach, as if he had gulped down a cup of especially bitter coffee, and he couldn't go more than half an hour without running for the can. He could not shake the grim conviction that something special had got away from him. When he finally made it to The Cavern, the night following, the Edinburgh girl wasn't there—of course she wasn't—and the house band was playing fucking disco. The branch of Jimi Coffee they were opening in Liverpool was not actually built on the ruin of the Mom & Pop that had served him rancid fish, but Saunders could pretend.

The train platform was lit by fluorescents. He could see nothing of the world beyond. It seemed like they had been sitting there for a long time. Although the train was not quite standing still. It rocked now and then on its steel wheels, as if someone were loading something heavy into one of the rear cars. In the distance he heard someone braying, a man's loud lowing voice—*stop*, he yelled, *stop it.* Saunders imagined two movers trying to lug an oversized dresser onto the train, and being yelled at by a conductor…reasonably enough, this wasn't a freight car. A woman's voice rose in a sob of laughter, then faded away. Saunders half had a mind to get up and walk to the back to see what was happening, but then the train jerked forward with a loud bang, and began to struggle out of the station.

At the same moment, Saunders heard the door of first class open behind him with a smooth steely clack.

Well—that's him, he thought, with a certain grim satisfaction. The protestor. He didn't look back to confirm it and didn't need to. When Saunders glanced sidelong at the window across the aisle, he could see the dim, blurred reflection of the guy: tall fella with the pointed ears of a German Shepherd. Saunders lowered his gaze, fixed it on his newspaper, and pretended to read. When someone dressed in a getup like that, they wanted to be noticed, were hoping for a reaction. Saunders had no intention of giving him one.

The new arrival in first class started down the aisle, his breathing loud and strained, what you would expect from a man stuck in a rubber mask. At the last moment, it came to Saunders that it was a mistake to be occupying the window seat. The chair to his left was open and empty, a kind of invitation. He thought of moving, shifting his ass over to the aisle seat. But no, the protestor would relish the fear such a move indicated. Saunders stayed where he was.

Sure enough, the protestor took the empty seat beside him, heaving himself down with a heavy sigh of satisfaction. Saunders willed himself not to look over, but his peripheral vision filled in a few details: a wolf mask that covered the entire head, furry gloves, and a bushy tail that was apparently controlled by a hidden wire, because it swung to one side when he sat. Saunders exhaled a thin breath through bared teeth, and realized for the first time that he was grinning. It was something he did automatically, when he was in for a fight and knew it. His first wife said it made him look like Jack Nicholson with the ax in that movie. She had called Saunders The Woodcutter too—at first with coy affection, later when she was being bitchy.

The protestor shifted around, getting comfortable, and one hairy gloved hand brushed Saunders's arm. That casual touch was enough to throw the switch on Saunders's well-practiced rage. He snapped down one corner of the newspaper and opened his mouth to tell Lon fucking Chaney to keep his paws to himself…and then Saunders's breath caught in his chest. His lungs seemed to bunch up. He stared. He saw, but couldn't make sense of what he was looking at. He tried to see a protestor as hard as he could, a protestor in a rubber wolf mask and a tan overcoat. He *insisted* on it to himself, for a few desperate moments, trying to make the perfectly reasonable notion in his head match the perfectly unreasonable reality beside him. But it wasn't a protestor. All the wishing in the world wouldn't make it a protestor.

A wolf sat on the seat next to him.

Or if not a wolf, then a creature more wolf than man. He had the body, roughly, of a man, with a broad wedge-shaped chest that swept down to a sunken stomach and narrow waist. But he had paws, not hands, wiry gray hair on them. He held a copy of the *Financial Times* himself, and his hooked yellow nails made audible scratching noises as he turned the pages. Old, stained fangs protruded over his lower lip. His ears were proud, furry, stiff, his scally cap shoved back between them. One of those ears swiveled toward Saunders, like a satellite dish revolving to lock in a signal.

Saunders stared at his own paper. It was the only thing he could think to do.

The wolf didn't look at him directly—he remained behind his paper—but he did lean into him, and spoke in a gravelly bass. "I hope they bring the dinner trolly through. I could do with a bite. 'Course on this line, they'll charge you two quid for a plate of lukewarm dogfood without blinking."

His breath stank; it was dogbreath. Sweat prickled on Saunders's brow and in his armpits, a hot, strange, disagreeable sweat, not at all like the perspiration he worked up jogging on the treadmill. He imagined this sweat as yellow and chemical, a burning carbolic crawling down his sides.

The wolf's snout shriveled and his black lips wrinkled to show the hooked rows of his teeth. He yawned, and a surprisingly bright red tongue lolled from the opening, and if there had been any doubt in Saunders's mind—there hadn't been, really—that was all for it. In the next moment he fought with himself, a desperate, terrible struggle, not to issue a soft sob of fear. It was like fighting a sneeze. Sometimes you could hold it in, sometimes you couldn't. Saunders held it in.

"Are you an American?" asked the wolf.

Don't answer. Don't talk! Saunders thought, in a voice he didn't recognize—it was the shrill, piping voice of panic. But then he did answer, and his tone was his own: level and certain. He even heard himself laugh. "Hah. Got me. 'Scuse, do you mind if I use the bathroom?" As he spoke he half-rose to his feet. He and the wolf were in chairs that faced a spotted Formica table, and he couldn't quite stand all the way up.

"Right," said the wolf. He said it *ro-ight*, had a bit of a Liverpoolian accent. *Liverpudlian*, Saunders corrected himself mentally, randomly. *No, Scouse.* They called it Scouse, which sounded like a disease, something you might die from after being bitten by a wild animal.

The businesswolf turned sideways to allow Saunders by.

Saunders edged past him toward the aisle, leaving behind his briefcase and his eight-hundred dollar overcoat. He wanted to avoid making contact with the thing and of course that was impossible, there wasn't enough space to get by without his knees brushing the wolf's. Their legs touched. Saunders's reaction was involuntary, an all-body twitch. He flashed to a memory of sixth-grade biology, prodding the inside of a dead frog with tweezers, touching the nerves and watching the feet kick. It was like that, a steel edge pressed right to the nerves. He could keep the fear out of his voice, but not his body. Saunders believed one atavistic reaction would be met by another, and the wolf in the suit would lunge, responding to his terror by grabbing him around the waist with his paws, opening his jaws to sink his fangs into his belly, hollowing him out like a skin pumpkin: *trick-or-treat motherfucker*.

But the wolf in the suit only grunted, low in his throat, and twisted even more to the side to let Saunders past.

Then Saunders was in the aisle. He turned left and began to walk—*walk*, not run—for coach. The first part of his plan was to get to other people. He hadn't worked out the second part of the plan yet. He kept his gaze fixed straight ahead and focused on his breathing, just exactly the way he had been taught in Kashmir, way back down the long and winding road. A smooth *in*, drawn through parted lips. A clean *out*, puffed through his nostrils. *I am not going to be killed and eaten by a wolf on an English train*, he thought, quite clearly. Like the Beatles, he had gone to India as a young man to get himself a mantra, and had come home without one. On an unconscious level, though, he supposed he had never stopped hoping to find one, a single statement that resonated with power, hope, and meaning. Now, at sixty-one, he had a mantra he could live by at last. *I am not going to be killed and eaten by a wolf on an English train.*

In and out went his breath, and with every step the door to coach was closer. In eight steps he was there and he pressed the button that opened the door to the next car. The lights around the button turned from yellow to green and the door slid back.

He stood looking into coach. The first thing he saw was the blood. A red handprint had been planted in the center of one window, and then dragged, to leave a long muddy-ochre streak across the Plexiglas. A mess of other red smears and splashes made a Jackson Pollock painting out of a window directly across the aisle. There was a red swipe dragged impossibly down almost the full length of the ceiling.

Saunders saw the blood before he saw the wolves—four in all, sitting in two pairs.

One pair was on the right, in the back. The wolf who sat on the aisle wore a black track suit with blue stripes, honoring a soccer team. Saunders thought it might've been Manchester United. The wolf who sat by the window sported a worn white T-Shirt advertising an album:

WOLFGANG AMADEUS PHOENIX. They were passing something wrapped in a napkin, something brown and circular. A chocolate donut, Saunders decided, because that was what he wanted it to be.

The other pair of wolves was on the left, and much closer, only a couple yards from where Saunders stood. They were businesswolves, but less well-dressed than the gray wolf in first class. These two wore sagging, wrinkled black suits and standard issue red ties. One of them was looking at a newspaper, not a *Financial Times*, but *The Daily Mail*. His great black furry paws left red prints on the cheap paper. The fur around his mouth was stained red, blood streaked back almost to his eyes.

"Sez Kate Winslet has broke up with that bloke of 'ers wot made American Beyootie," said the one with the paper.

"Don't look at me," said the other businesswolf. "I didn't have nuthink to do with it."

And they both yapped—playful, puppy-like yips.

There was a fifth passenger in the car, a woman, a *human* woman, not a wolf. She was sprawled on her side across one of the seats, so all he could see was her right leg, sticking into the aisle. She wore black stockings, a very bad run in the one Saunders could see. It was a nice leg, a handsome leg, a young girl's leg. He couldn't see her face and didn't want to. She had lost her heel—it had dropped in the heap of her entrails that were piled in the center of the aisle. Saunders saw those entrails last, a glistening pile of fatty white coils, lightly basted with blood. A string of gut stretched back out of sight in the direction of her abdomen. One of the woman's high heels rested on that mound of intestines, set there like a single black candle on a grotesque birthday cake. He remembered how they had seemed to wait at Wolverton Station forever, the way the train shook now and then as if something were being forcibly loaded into coach. He remembered hearing a woman's sob of laughter, and a man yelling orders, *stop, stop it*. He had heard it the way he wanted to hear it. He had known what he had wanted to know. Maybe it was always that way for almost everyone.

The businesswolves hadn't noticed him, but the two louts in the back had. The one in the rock T-shirt elbowed Manchester United, and they rolled their eyes meaningfully at one another, and lifted their snouts to the air. Tasting the scent of him, Saunders thought.

One of them, Wolfgang Amadeus Phoenix, called out. "'Ay. 'Ay there mate. Comin' to sit with the lower classes? Goin' to roost with the plebes?"

Manchester United made a choked sound of laughter. He had just had a bite of that glistening chocolate donut that he held in the white napkin and his mouth was full. Only it wasn't a napkin, and it wasn't a donut. Saunders was determined to see and hear things as they were, not as he wanted them to be. His life depended on it now. So. See it and know it: it was a piece of liver in a blood-stained hanky. A woman's hanky—he could see the lace trimming at the edges.

Saunders stood in first class, fixed in place, unable to take another step. As if he were a sorcerer who stood within a magical circle and to cross the line into coach would be to make himself vulnerable to the demons that waited there. He had forgotten about breathing, no clean in-and-out now, just that feeling of paralysis in the lungs again, a muscular tightening that made it difficult to inhale. He wondered if anyone had ever suffocated to death from fear, had been so afraid to breathe they passed out and died.

The door between cars began to slide shut. Just before it closed, the wolf in the Manchester United tracksuit turned his snout toward the ceiling and uttered a derisive howl.

Saunders backed from the door. He had buried both his parents, and his sister too, who had died unexpectedly, when she was just twenty-nine, of meningitis; he had been to a dozen stockholder funerals; he had seen a man collapse and die of a heart attack at a Jets game once. But he had never seen anything like guts on the floor, a whole battered train car painted with blood. Yet he did not feel any nausea, and did not make a sound, not a single peep. The only physical reaction he was aware of was that his hands had gone to sleep, the fingers cold, tingling with pins-and-needles. He wanted to sit down.

The door to the bathroom was on his left. He stared at it in a blank, thoughtless kind of way, then pressed the button, popped the door open. An eye-watering smell hit him, a disheartening human reek. The last person through hadn't bothered to flush. Wet, filthy toilet paper stuck to the floor, and the little trashcan next to the sink was overflowing. He considered going in there and bolting the door shut. He didn't move, though, and when the bathroom door closed on its own, he was still in the first class aisle.

That little bathroom was a coffin—a coffin that stank. If he went in there, he understood he would never come out, that he would die in there. Torn apart by the wolves, while he sat on the toilet, screaming for help that wasn't going to come. A terrible, lonely, squalid ending, in which he would be separated not just from his life, but his dignity. He had no rational explanation for this certainty—how could they get the door open if it was locked? —it was just a thing he knew, the way he knew his birthday or his phone number.

His phone. The thing to do was to call someone, let them know (*I am on a train with wolfmen?*) he was in trouble. His cold, dead hands sank to the pockets of his slacks, already knowing the phone wasn't there. And it wasn't. His phone was in the pocket of his eight-hundred dollar overcoat—a London Fog overcoat, actually. Everything, even clothing, had, in the last few moments, taken on heightened meaning, seemed significant. His phone was lost in a London Fog. To get to it he would have to return to his seat, and squirm past the businesswolf, something even more impossible than hiding in the bathroom.

There was nothing in his pockets he could use: a few twenty-pound notes, his ticket, a map of the train line. The Woodcutter was alone in the deep dark forest without his ax, without even a Swiss army knife, not that a Swiss army knife would do him any good. Saunders was seized by an image of himself knocked flat on his back, the wolf in the scally cap pinning him down, his wretched breath in Saunders's face, and Saunders raking at him frantically with the dull, ridiculous, inch-and-a-half blade of a Swiss army knife. He felt a laugh rise in his throat, and choked it back, understood he was quivering not on the edge of hilarity, but panic. Empty pockets, empty head—no. Wait. The map. He jerked the map out of his pocket and unfolded it. It took an effort of will to focus his eyes…but whatever his other flaws, Saunders had always had will to spare. He looked for the Liverpool line, and began to follow it north from London, wondering about the stop after Wolverton Station, how far away it might be.

He spotted Wolverton Station about two-thirds of the way to Liverpool. Only it wasn't Wolverton Station on the map, it was *Wolverhampton*.

He blinked rapidly, as if trying to clear some grit out of his eyes. He supposed it was possible that he had misread the sign at the last stop, and that it had *always* been Wolverhampton. Which made the next stop Foxham. Maybe there would be foxes waiting on the platform there. He felt another dangerous, panicky laugh rise in his throat—like bile—and swallowed it down. Laughing now would be as bad as screaming.

He had to insist to himself there would be *people* in Foxham, that if he could get off the train, there was a chance he might live. And on his map, Foxham was barely a quarter-inch from the Wolverhampton stop. The train might be almost there, had been rushing along at a hundred-plus miles an hour for at least fifteen minutes (*No. Try three minutes,* said a silky, bemused voice in his mind. *It's only been* three *minutes since you noticed the man sitting beside you wasn't a man at all but some kind of werewolf, and Foxham is still a half an hour away. Your body will be room temperature by the time you get there.*)

Saunders had got turned around and started, unconsciously, to walk back the way he had come, still staring at his map. At the last moment he realized he had pulled abreast of the wolf reading the *Financial Times*. At the sight of the giant dog-faced thing on the periphery of his vision, he felt icy-hot skewers in his chest, needling toward his heart; Saunders, the human pincushion. *You aren't too old for a cardiac arrest, buddy,* he thought…another notion that wouldn't do him any good right now.

Saunders pretended to be lost in the study of his map, and kept walking, wandering down to the next row of seats. He looked up, blinking, then settled into a seat on the opposite side of the aisle. He tried to make it look like an absent-minded act, a thing done by a man so interested in what he was looking at, he had forgotten where he was going. He didn't believe his performance fooled the wolf with the *Financial Times* in the least. Saunders heard him make a deep, woofy-sounding *harrumph* that seemed to express disgust and amusement alike. If he wasn't fooling anyone, Saunders didn't know why he went on playacting interest in his map, except that it felt like the safest thing.

"Did you find the loo?" asked the businesswolf.

"Occupied," Saunders said.

"Right," the wolf said. *Ro-ight.* "You *are* an American."

"Guess you could tell by the accent."

"I knew by the smell of you. You Americans have different accents—your southern accent, your California surfer accent, your New Yawk accent." Affecting an atrocious faux Queens accent as he said it. "But you all smell the same."

Saunders sat very still, facing straight ahead, his pulse thudding in his neck. *I am going to be killed and eaten by a wolf on an English train,* he thought, then realized somewhere in the last few moments his mantra had turned from a statement of negation to one of affirmation. It came to him the time for pretend was well past. He folded his map and put it back in his pocket.

"What do we smell like?" Saunders asked.

"Like cheeseburgers," said the wolf, and he barked with laughter. "And entitlement."

I am going to be killed and eaten by a wolf on an English train, he thought again, and for a moment the idea wasn't the worst notion in the world. It was bad, but even worse would be sitting here, letting himself be taunted before it happened, taking it with his tail between his legs.

"Fuck you," Saunders said. "We smell like money. Which beats the hell out of stinking like wet dog." His voice shaking just slightly when he said it.

He didn't dare turn his head to look at the wolf directly, but he could watch him from the corner of his eye, and he saw one of those erect, bushy ears rotate toward him, tuning in on his signal.

Then the first class businesswolf laughed—another harsh woof. "Don't mind me. My portfolio has taken a beating the last couple months. Too many American stocks. It's left me a bit sore, as much at myself as at you lot. It aggravates me that I bought into the whole thing, like everyone else in this blighted country."

"Bought into what whole thing?" Saunders asked. A part of his mind cried out in alarm, *Shut the fuck up, what are you doing, why are you talking to* it?

Except.

Except the train was slowing, almost imperceptibly. Saunders doubted under normal circumstances he would've noticed, but now he was attuned to fine details. That was how it worked when your life was measured in seconds: you felt your own breath, were aware of the temperature and weight of the air on your own skin, heard the prickling tic-tic of the rain on the windows. The train had hitched, slowed, and hitched again. The night continued to blur past the windows, some rain-splatter sprinkling against the glass, but Saunders thought there was a chance they were closing on Foxham, or whatever was next down the tracks. And if the businesswolf was talking to him, then he wasn't attacking.

"The American fairy tale," the wolf said. "You know the one. That we can all be like you. That we should all *want* to be like you. That you can wave your American Tinkerbell dust over our pathetic countries and abracadabra! A McDonald's here and an American Outfitters there and England will be just like home. *Your* home. I am honestly humiliated to have ever believed it. You would think a bloke like me, of all people, would know it isn't true. You can stick a Disneyland T-shirt on a wolf, but it's still a wolf."

The train hitched and slowed another degree. When Saunders looked out his window, he could see brick townhouses flashing by, some lights on behind a few of the windows, and bare trees, tossing in the wind, clawing at the sky. Even the trees were different in England. They were the same varieties you found in the States, but subtly unlike American trees, more gnarled and bent, as if twisted by colder, harsher winds.

"Everyone is dead in the other car," Saunders said, feeling curiously removed from himself, from his own voice.

The wolf grunted.

"Why not me?"

The wolf didn't look at him, seemed to be losing interest in the conversation. "This is first class. If you can't get civility here, where can you get it? Besides. I'm wearing a Gieves and Hawkes. This suit set me back five hundred quid. Wouldn't do to stain it. And what's the point of riding first class if you have to chase down your own grub? They bring a trolley through for us." He leafed to the next page of his *Times*. "At least they're supposed to. They're taking their fucking time about it, aren't they?" He paused, then added, "Please pardon my language.

The thing about civility—it's hard to maintain when you're barking mad with hunger."

The conductor said something in a choked, wolfish voice over the intercom, but Saunders couldn't hear him over what his own wolf was saying to him, and above the roar of blood in his ears. But he didn't need to hear the conductor anyway, because Saunders knew what he was saying. They had arrived at the station at last. The train was slamming ungently to rest. Saunders grabbed the seat in front of him and lurched to his feet. Outside he had a glimpse of a concrete platform, a brick breezeway, a glowing old-fashioned clock stuck up on the station wall. He began walking swiftly for the front of the car.

"'Ey," laughed the wolf. "Don't you want your coat? Come on back and get it."

Saunders kept walking. He reached the door at the end of the cabin in five long strides and hit the Door Open button. The wolf barked a last laugh at Saunders's back and Saunders dared a final glance over his shoulder. The businesswolf was disappearing behind his paper once more.

"Microsoft shares are down," the wolf said, in a tone that somehow combined disappointment with a certain rueful satisfaction. "Nike shares are down. This isn't a recession, you know. This is reality. You people are finding out the actual worth of the things you make: your sneakers, your software, your coffee, your myths. You people are finding out now what it's like when you push too far into the deep dark woods."

Then Saunders was out the door and on the platform. He had thought it was raining, but what came down was more of a weak, cold mist, a fine-grained moisture suspended in the air. The station exit was across the platform, a flight of stairs to the road below.

He had gone no more than five paces before he heard loud, derisive yipping behind him, and looked back to see two wolves descending from coach. Not the wolves in suits, but the one in the Wolfgang Amadeus T-shirt, and the other dressed for a Manchester United match. Manchester United clapped Wolfgang on the shoulder and jerked his snout in Saunders's direction.

Saunders ran. He had been fast once, on his track team in high school, but that had been fifty years and five thousand Whoppers ago.

He didn't need to look back to know they were behind him, loping across the concrete, and that they were faster than him. He reached the staircase and leaped down it, three, four stairs in each step, a kind of controlled falling. His breath screamed in his throat. He heard one of the wolves make a low, purring growl at the top of the stairs. (And how could they be at the top of the stairs already? It wasn't possible that they could've closed so much distance so quickly, it *wasn't*.)

At the bottom of the steps was the line of gates, and the street beyond, and a taxi waiting, a black English taxi straight out of a Hitchcock movie. Saunders picked a gate and ran straight at it. The gates: a row of chrome dividers, with waist-high black Plexiglas shutters between them. You were supposed to stick your ticket into a slot on the top of the chrome dividers, and the shutters would swing open, but Saunders wasn't going to fuck with it. When he reached the Plexiglas shutters, he went right over them, in a graceless scramble, followed by a tumble to the ground.

He sprawled onto his stomach, facedown on the rain-spattered concrete. Then he was up again. It was like a skip in a piece of film, so it hardly seemed he had gone down at all. He had never in his life imagined he could recover so quickly from a spill.

Someone yelled behind him. Every set of gates in every train station in the UK had an officer to watch over them, and take tickets manually, and Saunders thought this had to be him. He could even see him out of the corner of his left eye, a guy in an orange safety vest, white-haired and bearded. Saunders didn't slow down or look over. A joke floated unbidden to his mind: two hikers in the woods come across a bear. One of them bends over to lace his sneakers. The other hiker says why tie your sneakers, you can't outrun a bear. And the first hiker says, no shit, asshole, I only need to outrun you. Pretty funny. Saunders would remind himself to laugh about it later.

He fell against the back of the taxi, clawed for the door lever, found it, popped it open. He fell in across the black leather seat.

"Go," he said to the driver. "*Go.*"

"Where are we—" said the driver, in a thick west country accent. Scouse.

"Town. Into town. I don't know yet, just go. *Please.*"

"Right then," the driver said. The taxi loosened itself from the curb and pushed off down the avenue.

Saunders twisted in his seat to look out the rear window as they left the train station. Manchester United and Wolfgang Amadeus had stopped at the gate. They crowded around the ticket taker, towering over him. Saunders didn't know why the ticket man just stood there staring back at them, why he didn't recoil and run, why they didn't fall on him. The taxi carried him around the corner and out of sight of the station, before he could see what happened next.

He sat in the darkness, breathing fast and hard, incredulous at his own survival. His legs shook, the big muscles in his thighs bunching up and uncoiling helplessly. He had not shook the whole time he was on the train, but now it was as if he had just climbed out of an ice bath.

The cab glided down a long, gradual hill, past hedges and houses, dipping toward the lights of a town. Saunders found one of his hands feeling in his pocket for the cell phone he knew he didn't have.

"Phone," he said, talking to himself. "Damn phone."

"Need a phone?" said the driver. "I'm sure there was one at the station."

Saunders glanced at the back of the driver's head, peering at him in the dark of the car. A big man with long black hair, tucked down into the collar of his coat.

"There wasn't time to stop and make a call there. Just take me to someplace with a public phone. Someplace else."

"There's one at The Family Arms. That's only a couple blocks."

"Family Arms? What's that? Pub?" Saunders's voice cracked, as if he were a fourteen-year-old in the throes of puberty.

"Best un in town. Also the only un. But if I'd known that's where you wanted me to drive you, I wouldn't have taken the fare. It's easier walking, see?"

"I'll pay you triple your usual rate. I've got plenty of money. I'm the richest man that's ever sat in this fucking cab."

"Isn't this my lucky day," said the driver. The ignorant country moron had no idea Saunders had just almost been torn apart. "So what happened to your regular chauffeur?"

"What?"

Saunders didn't understand the question; in truth, he hardly registered it, was distracted. They had stopped at a light, and Saunders happened to look out the window. Two teenagers stood necking on the corner. They had a couple dogs with them, who stood at their sides, whisking their tails nervously back and forth, waiting for the kids to get done kissing and start walking again. Only there was something wrong with those two kids. The taxi was moving again before Saunders figured out what it was. Those tails, fretfully whisking from side to side—Saunders hadn't actually spotted the dogs attached to them. He wasn't sure there had been any dogs there at all.

"Where is this?" Saunders asked. "Where am I? Is this Foxham?"

"We isn't anywheres near Foxham, sir. Upper Wolverton, this is," said the driver. "Which is what they call it because The Middle of Nowhere don't sound as good. Edge of the known world, really."

He eased the cab to the end of the next block and swung in at the curb. There was a pub on the corner, big plate glass windows, bright squares of gold in the darkness, steamed over with condensation on the inside. Even shut into the backseat of the cab, Saunders could hear the noise from within. It sounded like an animal shelter.

A small knot of people loitered outside the front door. A carved and painted wooden sign, bolted to the stone beside the door, showed a crowd of wolves standing on their hind legs, gathered around a table. In the center of the table was a great silver platter, with an assortment of pale human arms laid upon it.

"Here you go," said the cab driver, turning his head to look into the rear. His snout moved close to the glass that separated the front seat from the back, and breathed a filmy white mist on it. "You can make your call here, I 'spect. Have to fight your way through a bit of a crowd, I'm afraid." He made a low chuckling sound that Saunders supposed was meant to be laughter, although it sounded more like a dog trying to cough up a hairball.

Saunders did not reply. He sat in the black leather seat, staring at the crowd outside the door of The Family Arms. They were staring back. Some of them were walking toward the cab. Saunders decided not to make any sound when they pulled him out. He had learned in Kashmir how to hold onto silence, and if he was strong, he would only need to hold onto it for about a minute and a half, and then it would be holding onto him.

"Good little Mum and Pop place, wot this is," his driver told him. "They serve up a right fine dinner in here, they do. And you know what, mate? I think you're just in time for it."

Note: The first draft of "Wolverton Station" was written entirely while riding English trains…the first part on the rails from London to Liverpool, the second while en route from Liverpool to Manchester, and the conclusion on the Manchester-Nottingham line. The author wishes to thank the people of England for not devouring him while he toured their country.
- Joe Hill, April 15, 2010

THE PASSION OF MOTHER VAJPAI |

Jay Lake and Shannon Page

THE SCENT OF sandalwood cut through the hot, humid Kalimpuri night like a knife through a disgraced courtesan's wrists. Cinnamon trees drooped in the garden below the roof where Shayla waited, and watched. And wondered.

The moon looked back from a pond's mirrored surface three stories below. The silvered face was wrinkled from time to time by the passage of one of the golden carp kept there by the Arbiter of the Woodcock Court. Cinnamon trees bordered that long, narrow water, themselves surrounded by a profusion of hortensia bushes and other, more elaborate plantings bearing the taint of ritual.

Shayla stroked her knives. The weapons had secret names, that she'd never whispered to the other Blade aspirants or dared admit to Mother Meiko. The training mother would have laughed Shayla into the street for her presumption. The woman had a grasp of mockery that was the envy of even the cattiest of the girls in the dormitory.

Her left hand touched the knife she called Remembrance. Her right hand brushed over the haft of Sorrow. They were *her* names, by the Lily Goddess, and she would keep them. She was the fastest aspirant in the Lily Blades, possibly the fastest woman of any rank. She would name her weapons as it pleased her.

The city murmured through this sixth watch of the night. Much like the beating heart and dreaming mind within the human body, some parts of Kalimpura never slept. The docks, where ships unloaded at all hours. The counting houses of Bent Arrow Street, where the day's receipts were tallied and letters of credit balanced and rewritten between dusk and dawn. The gates, where guards stamped their spear butts to signal for bribes from those who would pass after curfew, one thump for a copper paisa, two thumps for a hand of copper paisas, three for a silver paisa if they thought you wealthy or desperate.

Though she'd been born far from the city, Shayla had not been outside the walls since before she could remember. All she'd ever known was this monstrous, uneasy beast that lazed on the edge of the Gulf of Seli, eating up people and rice and chickens, and shitting out silk and teakwood and spices.

But now she sat in the wreathing smoke of sandalwood and studied a certain second story window. A Blade aspirant had to pass through seven Petals before she could don the blacks and run the streets of Kalimpura. The Seventh Petal was usually a killing. As it was the Lily Blades who guarded and enforced the Death Right on behalf of all the guilds and courts and corporations of the city, there was quite often a killing to be done.

Remembrance and Sorrow gave her comfort as she waited and watched. Light yet flickered within the distant window, so late now, the mantle of a lantern fussing with some bit of ash caught upon its web. This was how her Seventh Petal would go. She would watch a window, then at a certain time she would slip within, claim a life already forfeit in law and custom, and turn away from whoever might mourn afterwards.

But not tonight.

Tonight she just watched.

Eventually fine, dark hands reached out to grasp the screened shutters. A fall of hair so black it was almost blue caught both the moonlight and Shayla's breath in the same moment. A face, the curve of breasts bared before the quiet privacy of a courtyard and the final watches of the night.

Umaya.

Shayla would have given much to see those deep brown eyes. She would have given far more to slip through the window and hear breath caught firm and sudden, to see a chest heave, to clasp hands and pull herself into welcoming arms.

But not tonight.

When the light vanished, so did Shayla. She would be far too short of rest already tomorrow. Mercy was not in Mother Meiko's nature.

Its place had been taken up by a wicked ruthlessness of which Shayla knew she would bear the brunt in less than two hours.

Over the rooftops she raced, flying away from the scent of sandal-wood and cinnamon like a windborne mist. She must find her bed, and pray she could give herself enough release before sleep not to spend tomorrow on a wire's edge.

—*C*—

THE CROSSBOW QUARREL grazed her scalp, stinging Shayla as the solid thwock of it hitting wood just behind her echoed too-loud in her ears.

"Notice how Shayla does not flinch," Mother Meiko announced to the dozen Blade aspirants gathered in the training yard.

For this exercise, the Lily Blades borrowed an enclosed square from the Wall Guild, that trained most of the city's guards for their work. They were all turned out in their training leathers, most of the girls proudly bearing bruises or scars from recent sessions fighting with staves and farm implements. The air reeked of rotten straw and the Afternoon Fish Market just beyond the western wall of this courtyard, where the spoiled catch unsold from yesterday or the early morning was being sold off for glue. Or possibly stew.

Meiko's marble-hard eyes bore into Shayla. "Why not flinch?" she asked of her victim.

"Three reasons." Shayla buried anger and the writhing discomfort of speaking before others behind her pride. Only *she* was brave enough to have volunteered first for this exercise. Only Mother Meiko was careless enough of her girls' lives to try it. "If one cannot dodge what comes, one is best to remain in control. And no one can dodge a cross-bow quarrel. Not from half a dozen spans away.

"Secondly, to defeat a crossbow, you must let the shot get off, and rush while they are recocking. If I am rolling this way or that, I will lose time."

She fell silent, regretting that she'd announced three reasons. Her stomach twisted already as she endured the gaze of every aspirant.

"Very good." Meiko's voice was a silky purr, a razor splitting a fruit skin. "What was your last reason?"

Shayla summoned her courage and blurted out, "If you wanted to kill me in truth, it would not matter if I flinched or not. I prefer to retain my dignity."

Meiko's hard eyes locked on hers. Several of the girls sniggered, waiting to see what punishment would come of this insolence. Then the training Mother laughed, a genuine peal like water over rocks. Shayla had heard this perhaps three times in the fourteen years she'd been a Blade aspirant. The formidable older woman never let down her guard.

Mother Meiko bent to slap her knee, then rose with the crossbow cocked and ready. "Rush me now." Her voice was steel that had never known mirth.

Shayla gave the lie to her statement and rolled forward into a fast tumble even as the crossbow twanged again. The quarrel passed over her and she was up into Mother Meiko's face with Sorrow high in her right hand, Remembrance low in the left.

They stopped, so close the two of them could have kissed without stretching their necks.

"I have a blade at your belly." Mother Meiko glanced at the upraised knife.

"I have cut your bowstring," replied Shayla.

That brought a harsh chuckle. A few of the girls applauded, but that died quickly away at a glare from Mother Meiko. "Who will be next?" she demanded. Then, almost whispering, to Shayla, "See me in my office just before the supper hour."

SHAYLA TOOK CARE to bathe well in the great stone tubs. One advantage of living in the Lily Temple was copious hot water. Such hypocausts were a rarity in Kalimpura, she knew, but none of the mothers from any branch of the temple wanted the Blades stiff and difficult as they wandered the halls of this house of women.

Ointments were provided as well, and oils and scrubstones and finer things. The baths always smelled as she'd imagined a wealthy woman's bower might. Shayla, ever shy, had had few lovers, so she had no one right now to rub upon her back and ease the pains in her neck and shoulders. The one she longed for lived above a garden of cinnamon trees, and no amount of dreaming fantasy would bring that beloved walking through these doors.

In time she dressed herself in simple white—a holy color here in the temple, though not reserved for ritual use. The gown fell in easy lines, with a spacious skirt that would still allow her to run and kick as she might need to. She touched at her cheeks with a bit of the colored powders kept before a silvered mirror, then felt foolish and scrubbed them clean again.

Whatever Mother Meiko wanted of her, it would not be summarily brutal. Not in her office. Summary brutality was all too easy to accomplish in the training rooms, or out on the streets.

Had it come time for her to take the Seventh Petal and swear her final oaths as a Lily Blade?

Shayla had figured on another half a dozen moons before that became likely. The girls who'd passed out of aspirancy before her these past few years—Rani who'd become Mother Argai, Little Cotton who'd become Mother Suri, and so forth—had all seemed to know well in advance that their last test was coming.

But surely they had each experienced a first moment of shock at the news?

Realizing she was thinking on this far too much, Shayla did the first three series of crane forms to loosen her body and release her mind from its own chains. Smelling of nothing more than warm water and the simplest soaps of the bath, she went to meet her fate.

"THE SEVENTH PETAL," said Mother Meiko, "is a challenge to the fitness of a Blade aspirant's spirit. You would not have come this far without your martial fitness being proven beyond doubt. As Blades, we are not expected to be so diligent in our duties to the Lily Goddess as the priestesses are, or even the Justiciary Mothers. Still, you bring offerings and bow in prayer and listen to the homilies well enough."

Shayla nodded. She had no idea what target Mother Meiko thrust toward. Listening was far better than speaking.

"It is customary for the Seventh Petal to be earned by a death."

Familiar ground now. Shayla nodded again, and swallowed a smile. Death she could handle.

"But not always."

A silence stretched between them. The tiny office seemed filled with it, as if the absence of sound were laced among the scroll racks and in the little drawers of notes lining the wall behind Mother Meiko; and about the three brown-crusted swords mounted on the wall, that no one ever spoke of. The room carried the scent of paper and women and weapons, which seemed fitting enough.

Finally Shayla spoke. "So there are other ways…"

"Yes. For your Seventh Petal, I believe that I shall set you the problem of attending a banquet."

The air seemed to leave the room. Shayla gasped for breath a moment, then her lungs restarted with a stinging shudder. "I…"

"You'd rather kill, yes?" Meiko smiled, and it seemed to be genuine for once, not an ironic cudgel with which to drive her charges forward. "But killing is easy for you. You've slain men twice already, and you do not show any squeamishness with the pigs and dogs on which we practice. The Seventh Petal is supposed to be a challenge, not a familiar comfort."

She *had* killed twice. The first time has been in self-defense—well, not *self*-defense—when she was eleven. Shayla and Rani had been out to buy spices in the market, as part of their kitchen learnings, when four sailors pulled them into the alley. Shayla had been tossed aside while four men concentrated on the girl with breasts.

They'd been foreigners, they'd had no idea who they'd picked for their little crime. Rani could have taken them all down, except their first blow had been to smack her across the back of the head with a weighted leather strap. Shayla used the knife Remembrance to stab one of the sailors right in the pucker of his ass. He'd screamed and gushed blood; another had turned to her, and she opened him up from nipple to navel before he could strike her down with the strap. The other two fled, abandoning their comrades.

There had been a trial, a ship impounded, all sorts of scandal, but Shayla had not followed all the details at that age as she would now.

The second time had been a mason who worked along the docks as well. He refitted the bollards and mooring rings for the harbormaster, and brought his enormous muscles to other tasks as needed. He'd been slicing open beggar girls for years, and throwing their corpses in the harbor when he was done with them. No one spoke for the children, and beggars were not protected by the Death Right, so no complaint was taken up. Everyone knew it, but none had seen the mason at his bloody work until Shayla began stalking him as an assignment from Mother Puram.

When she *had* seen the mason at his work, she had not hesitated. Onto his back, Remembrance across his throat, then a mad flight to bring the wounded girl to someone, anyone, who would bother to treat such a one with no family or money or standing in the city.

She'd come back to the Temple of the Silver Lily trembling and knot-gutted as she had not been after the assault in the alley, and in a spasm of sorrowful regret tried to put her knife in Mother Puram as the woman sat eating a bowl of clam stew with okra.

That was a painful memory.

"I have killed twice," she said, returning from the reverie. "Once in the heat of self-defense, and once that made me truly ill in mind and body."

Mother Meiko's eyes softened. "And you will kill again. We are the justice in this city, and we are the arm of the Lily Goddess. But you already know you *can* kill. What you do not yet know is that you can walk into a room full of glittering merchants and nobles, eat correctly from their profusion of porcelain and poisonous fish dishes, and whisper the words to move a heart into a heartless man's ear."

Shayla squeaked her next words as fresh terror filled her chest. "I am a Blade, not a courtesan!"

"You *will be* a Blade," Mother Meiko corrected. "But we are much more than violence. Even the simpletons at the Princemarket Fountain know better than that. I am certain you do as well."

Finding her voice again, Shayla said, "You are the Blade Mother. You treat with the Prince of the City at times, and with the courts and guilds. The rest of us run through the night, and do what must be done."

"Where do you think Blade Mothers come from?" Mother Meiko's voice was gentle now. "We were all aspirants once, and we all were forced to learn our hardest lessons in the Seventh Petal."

Shayla took a deep breath, then quelled the shaking in her heart and the clamminess in her hands. She knew her hatred of appearing before people was unreasonable, but it was who she was. A woman on a street was one thing, but stepping forward? She was a Blade because Lily Blades ran in darkness and conducted their work in silence. Not a diplomat. Yet if this was to be her task… "Where is this banquet I must attend? And what will I do there?"

"You will whisper a few words into the ear of the master of the house. You will make yourself known to him as a Lily Blade, though the chamberlain will not admit you dressed in your leathers. I leave the mechanics of your attendance to your undeniable skills and imagination."

"When you give the words, I will have them. But where is this master? And when is his banquet?"

"Upon the new moon hence, at the mansion of Arbiter of the Woodcock Court."

Her heart reeled. Shayla could not possibly face fair Umaya, daughter of that house. Not after all that had—hadn't—happened between them. A girl, glimpsed once on a palanquin in the market. Seen a month later outside a foreigner's temple laughing with pale-skinned tradesmen. Followed home. Loved. Worshipped. Adored.

But to appear before her? And *speak*? She was mortified.

"Now you see the test." Mother Meiko's voice was tinged with her usual wicked irony. Shayla's mortification grew when she realized that even the deepest secrets of her heart were as shouts to this woman.

SHE CROUCHED ON the roof above the cinnamon garden. The household was not burning sandalwood tonight, and so the smell of the trees themselves wafted undiluted. It was subtle now—come harvest, the spice would be almost a reek. Umaya's window was dark this evening, had been so since dusk. The girl was out attending a great masque at the court of the Prince of the City.

That was fine with Shayla. She had enough trouble keeping her eyes off the window as it was. To imagine the bedchamber within, the soft secrets of Umaya's wardrobe, the silken sheets on which the girl lay slicked with sweat in the hot Kalimpuri nights—

Stop! she ordered herself. Focus, focus, focus.

The formal entrance to the Arbiter's mansion was on the far side of this garden, but Shayla had spent enough time watching here to know the routine. Besides, as Mother Meiko had said, the chamberlain would not likely admit her, so she must find her own way into the house.

It would be far easier to assassinate the Arbiter of the Woodcock Court than to deliver him a message. A crossbow bolt from a hidden place above, if the killing was to be bloody and public. A stiletto in a hallway for a quieter death. Poisons on the edge of his water closet seat for a secret death.

But to walk in, amid people and servants and guards, to sit at table, then to address him surrounded by his court—she was no spy.

How to get in, without invitation?

The answer dawned slowly on Shayla. She had watched this garden night after night, not to find a way into the house, but to find a way into Umaya. Even the chamberlain could not bar her if the daughter of the house brought Shayla as an escort. Women were expected to marry men and produce heirs, but it was far from unknown for aristocratic girls to squire one another around town in the years between menses and marriage. No question of an inconvenient heir, and men seemed think their daughters' virtue would still be safe in the company of women.

Men were idiots.

But Shayla had, what, less than two weeks to win the heart of a woman she was so taken with that she had not the least notion how to approach the girl without bursting into tears, or vomiting. No, assassination would be far easier. Killing was what she had trained to do. She had no idea how to court a woman of quality.

But…she certainly knew how to enter darkened rooms in a great house.

With a wicked grin, Shayla set out to meet Umaya on her own terms. Across the eaves, down a drainpipe, along a stand of vines and into the window. It was the work of moments to enter the bedroom of her dreams. How to prepare herself…that was a different matter entirely.

SHAYLA WAS VAGUELY aware that girls such as Umaya had maids. She secreted her leathers and her weapons in the vines outside the window, and donned a simple cotton shift she found among Umaya's clothes presses. Then like a cat she hid herself atop a wardrobe, where she could see the room well enough but would be unlikely to be seen in turn. A sheer black veil served to cover her with shadows. Unless they set lamps all around the room and made a study of the ceiling, Umaya and her maids were very unlikely to espy Shayla at her lurking.

Eventually Umaya did come in, not bustling, but quiet. She turned and dismissed a maid at the door, shaking her head in quiet protest. When the girl lit a lamp, Shayla's heart was caught in her throat once more, blocking all breath and even thought.

Blue-black hair cascaded like a waterfall of mineral oil. Her hands moved like the gentlest of grass doves, soft and brown and fluttering. Umaya's profile, as she turned away from lamp, was even more arresting than Shayla had dreamt it would be. The girl began unclasping the little frogs across the shoulder of her kurti, then stepped out of the silk as it fell like an orange puddle at her feet.

Beneath she wore only velvety skin. Even in the shadows of Umaya's body, Shayla could see the blue-black curls surrounding her sweetpocket. The girl's breasts were perfectly small, perfectly formed, perfectly firm, with great brown aureoles and nipples that looked like thumbs. Shayla's mouth pursed open in sympathetic longing.

She was not here to seduce the skin, but the mind. She needed this girl to get her into the banquet. But she wanted Umaya, so badly, so very badly, so much more than Little Cotton or any of the other girls and women with whom she'd played and learned these past years in the dormitories of the Lily Blades.

Not for Umaya the whipping frames, or the nine-fingered knout. This woman would never show her bruises with pride, or wish as some did for the salty tang of blood in her mouth before the sex was done. No, this was a girl to love with swaddling silks and scented oils and the slow passage of fingers down the long flanks of her body, across the sensuous curves of her ass.

Shayla realized she was touching herself, and that her breath had begun to heave. Umaya stopped brushing her hair, and without turning from her shadowed mirror, said quietly, "My father's guards can be here within a ten count of my first scream."

Now was the moment to declare herself, or be forever a bandit and a burglar and a thief. Shayla tried to speak, but her voice only croaked. She gasped, then blurted, "Never would I make you scream, l-lady."

"Who are you?" Umaya was not asking questions of fear, Shayla realized, but intrigue.

"I-I am one who would keep your f-father safe."

A small smile, ivory teeth flashing in the shadows of the single dim lamp. "I am afraid you have lost your way, then. My father's chambers are the floor below."

Shayla slipped down from atop the wardrobe, landed in the double half-cat pose that makes no more noise than a fleeing feline, then flowed to her feet. "You are the key to his safety."

Umaya turned toward her. All Shayla could scent was her own musk. Did the girl know fear beneath her brave, casual words? Or was the intrigue real?

Oh, Goddess, could this be my time?

"So," the girl said as sarcasm tinged her voice, "if I am the key, are you the lock I should turn?"

Shayla stumbled, literally, at the words, her romantic fantasies collapsing into a realization of how much trouble she would be in if Umaya did scream. She could be out the window well before a ten count, but at the best she'd be running the roofs naked and unarmed, her belongings in a bundle.

Wits, time to keep the wits as sharp as possible.

"It does not matter who is locked," Shayla said, then winced. That was neither clever nor to the point. A smile ghosted across Umaya's face as the girl nodded encouragingly. "I…" Glib wit, never her strong point, deserted Shayla utterly.

"You have loved me from afar for a while," Umaya supplied. "I believe that's what you intended to say. You have watched me from the rooftop across the garden, and followed me through the street."

Shayla emitted a strangled noise. "Um, yes."

"Let's see…" The girl sat in her dressing chair and made a show of counting on her fingers. "Unrequited love, distant longing, my fair face haunting your dreams. You would not believe the number of notes and missives I have received to that effect. Being beautiful has its problems, believe me." Her eyes narrowed. "Tell me the truth. What brought you in to my room? No one has ever had the nerve or courage to cross my windowsill before."

"Or perhaps not the skill," snapped Shayla, stung.

"Skill? To climb through a window?"

"Skill to ascend the south wall of your father's compound in the moments between the passage of the guards." Shayla was caught up in the route of her passion. "Skill to cross the mossy tiles of the roof without slipping. Skill to climb down the drainpipe and vines of the cinnamon courtyard without slipping or creating such a noise as to be noticed. Skill to reach your window and slip within and conceal myself until your arrival." Out of breath, angry, she felt naked clad only in Umaya's cotton shift. Her weapons and leather were too far from her.

Umaya must have shared the thought, because her face tightened. "You are an assassin."

"No!" Shayla shouted, then clamped her hand over her mouth. "No," she whispered urgently through clenched fingers. "I-I am a Lily Blade. We kill only by right."

The other girl took half a step back, but looked more fascinated than horrified. "What do you *want*, then?"

"Only to kn-know you, lady Umaya. I would slay no one." The words 'except at your command' hung unspoken in the air.

Slay no one, but speak to your father.

"Go, then," Umaya said. "If you would know me, come back two nights hence with my favorite fruit on ice."

"What is your favorite fruit?"

"You are the Lily Blade. You will find out, if you want to badly enough."

—⬦—

SHAYLA FOUND THE answer via the expedient of waylaying a kitchen maid of the Arbiter's household on the way to the freshmarket. A combination of threats and bribery revealed a passion for plantains on the part of Umaya. Those were not so hard to find, though the problem of transporting them over the rooftops with sufficient ice to present them chilled was something of an issue.

Two nights later she crouched on her familiar rooftop post above the cinnamon garden. Sandalwood tickled the night air once more. Shayla had brought with her a hammered copper bucket with a tight lid, intended for the storage of butter or cooking fat in a cold room. Ice rattled within, though she was forced to pour out some of the melt that had already settled in the warm night air. It was a matter of moments to use the knife Remembrance to slice the four plantains she'd carried over her shoulder in a string bag.

Leaving her supplies and refuse in that same bag, hooked onto a roofing tile, Shayla waited until the midnight bells, then made the awkward one-handed climb down and over to Umaya's bedroom. Light still glowed, as if the girl read by candleflame.

Shayla slipped within, still in her leathers. "I am here," she whispered.

Umaya sat in her bed, a pale sheet drawn up around her. "I did not think you would come," she replied, also whispering. Something sweet and shy hung in her voice.

"Your favorite fruit." Shayla slid to one knee by Umaya's side and whipped the top off the awkward copper bucket to present sliced plantains over ice.

The girl giggled, then reached out for one of the fruits. "You are more devoted to me than all the boys with their gifts of jewels and silk." Her face glowed in the candlelight—perfect cheekbones, a sweet nose, noble chin, eyes gleaming with the promise of passion. And something in Umaya's scent was giving Shayla an itch she'd not ever known she had.

Her hands trembled as they never had before.

"I would be devoted to you," said Shayla, her tongue thick with passion. "Should you only permit me to do so."

Umaya took Shayla's hand and kissed it. "Bring me a sweet, white kitten two nights hence, already trained to pounce a silver ball, and another part of my heart will be yours."

—⌀—

So it went for the next two weeks, this game of mutual seduction. Delivery of the kitten caused Umaya to clasp Shayla's hand to her breast, the nipple beneath thin silk firm against her fingers as any lover's might be. Then she asked for swordfish samosas fresh from the cart hard by the statue of Maja's Boar, near the waterfront. Though the cart vendor turned off his flame and trundled away his tiny kitchen at dusk, or whenever the food ran out, Shayla pawned her best boots for enough money to bribe him to cook again just before the midnight hour. That escapade earned her an embrace from Umaya, though Shayla's shy attempt at kissing was turned away with a small smile.

After that it was a kangaroo rat from the country around the Fire Lakes. The animal was a bit of a demon, and its bamboo cage seriously awkward for climbing. Besides which, she had to beg money from Mother Meiko to afford it, saying the paisas were to bribe a household servant. In a way, that was almost true. The kangaroo rat netted a close kiss with darting tongues, and another clasp of the hand on a sweet, firm breast, this time beneath cotton so fair that Shayla could see the dusky areola.

The gifts became more challenging still. Thrice Shayla was forced to outright theft, other times misrepresenting her needs to Mother Meiko. Lugging the harmonium over the rooftops nearly cost her a forty-foot fall in the bargain. But each time lips parted, buttons fell open, and eventually they met in skin, the night before Umaya's father's banquet.

Somehow it had never seemed time for Shayla to tell the girl of her heart why she had ever slipped within the bedroom window in the first place. Her mouth tart with the honey of Umaya's sweetpocket, the girl's passion glistening on Shayla's face, Umaya now suckling contented at her breast—this did not now seem to be the moment to admit of her purposes.

Yet she *must* get into the banquet. Delivering this message to Umaya's father was her Seventh Petal, the test for which Shayla had worked all her life thus far. It would be much easier to slip in Umaya's window while the guests were at their feast, but she truly was no assassin. *Not this time.*

In that much she had not lied to Umaya.

Summoning the tatters of her courage—she would quite literally rather fight tigers, or slay a dozen Street Guild enforcers than have this conversation—Shayla spoke up. "I w-would come be-before your father, Umaya, at your side."

Umaya lifted her lips from Shayla's nipple and laughed softly, a look of soft fascination fading from her eyes. "He will never let a Blade into his hall. Not unless they come to the front door with a writ from the Prince of the City or one of the greater courts."

The truth, the truth! shrieked a voice within Shayla's head. But her mouth lied onward, despite her intentions. "May I come as your friend, a girl of your acquaintance? If I could see him as he is among his own kind, I would know you better."

The girl frowned. "He hosts a banquet tomorrow, which I will attend. But—"

Shayla interrupted with a joy she hoped did not sound too forced. "That would be perfect! I will be one face among many, and can see him without being the focus of his attention."

"Why this?" Umaya asked. "Why now?"

The next words burned Shayla's throat, for all that they were the truest of lies. "Because I love you."

THE NEXT MORNING she went to Mother Meiko after the prayers, and just before the first classes of the day. The teaching mother was in her little office, sharpening a bit of wire on a whetstone.

"An interesting weapon," Meiko said before Shayla could ask permission to speak. "Add a bauble or a gem to one end, and any woman may wear this as a hairstick. Yet I can show you half a dozen ways to maim or kill with it so swiftly you have a good chance of not even being spotted by those around you."

"Such as at a crowded banquet?" Shayla asked in mounting horror.

"Well, surely." Mother Meiko smiled. "Will you be there tonight?"

Will you pass your test?

"Yes." Misery tinged her thoughts. Shayla tried to keep it out of her voice. Though she was certain Mother Meiko already knew the truth of both her actions and her feelings. "I need the message, and I need the right clothing to wear, that I might seem a lesser daughter of one of the lesser courts. There is not time to get me on the list to pass the doorway, but I can enter through a window and come to the banquet from within the house."

Enter with me, and the servants will not dare question, Umaya had said. *Dress just poor enough to be no threat or competition, just well off enough to be no shame or disgrace at our table.*

Shayla had a sick feeling Umaya hadn't only been talking about the clothes she'd be wearing. The unlikeliness of the whole love affair gnawed at her. Was she being played the fool all along, from both sides?

"We can clothe you well enough," Mother Meiko said thoughtfully. "See Mother Kuchai in the workshops downstairs. Tell her I said for you to have what you needed. The real stuff, not the festival knockoffs."

"Yes, ma'am," Shayla said, glad for a moment to be back on something like a normal footing in the conversation.

"As for the message, I shall give it to you in a sealed slip. Break the seal just before you speak to the Arbiter of the Woodcock Court. The words must be fresh in your mind and new-fallen from your lips." Mother Meiko took up a quill, dipped it into an inkstone's well which still gleamed obsidian and damp, and scratched a few words on a strip of parchment. This she rolled, then tied with a thin silk cord, before crimping the cord with a wax seal forced into place by strong iron shears. She offered that to Shayla. "Here."

The parchment felt like poison in Shayla's hands. Crisp, small, oddly warm and heavy. How could the Blade Mother be so casual about this? Surely such a message meant to be delivered in this fashion had been debated among the senior mothers of the Lily Temple— priestesses, justiciars, everyone. Not a few words dashed off unthinking to bedevil a nervous aspirant.

"One more thing," Mother Meiko said, though Shayla had made no move to leave. "Have you thought about what your temple name will be, when you have passed the Seventh Petal and stand to take your life vows as a Lily Blade?"

Shayla looked down at the floor. "No. I never have." Which was true. Some aspirants spent years thinking and dreaming of their names.

Others just seemed to arrive at their names when their names arrived at them. Shayla had been much in the latter camp. It had always seemed bad luck to her to look ahead so.

"I have been thinking lately of the woman who trained me when I was a small girl." Mother Meiko smiled in reminiscence. "She took me on my first Death Right kills, and together we fought against the foreign sailors in the Spice Rebellion. Mother Vajpai she was, lost to us since well before you were born. A name with much honor and glory among the Lily Blades, and favored by the Lily Goddess Herself."

"I am neither honorable nor glorious," muttered Shayla, thinking of her lies to Umaya.

"Allow me to judge that," Mother Meiko said. "For surely I will, before you pass the Seventh Petal."

MUCH EARLIER THAN usual that evening, Shayla went up the Arbiter's roof with her dress in a bundle at her back and her message tucked within her leathers, close to her breast. Should some back alley footpad slash at her burden, she could not lose *that*. No sandalwood curled on the air this evening, but rather the mouth-watering scent of whole roast pig, with half a hundred oils and spices behind it.

The Arbiter of the Woodcock Court advertised his banquet to the entire quarter of the city, or at least anyone within it who kept even a portion of their nose in working order.

She slid over the tiled ridge as she always did, only to see a guard just ahead of her, squatting uncomfortably as he faced down into the cinnamon garden. Shayla slid right back and stopped, forcing her breathing to be shallow and quiet as it could possibly be.

How was she to get to Umaya's window? She could not just kill the guard. The man worked for Umaya's father.

Or could she?

Shayla shook off the thought. She was not pursuing a broken Death Right, or avenging a court writ. Eliminating the guard under these circumstances would be murder, pure and simple.

Yet she could not allow one man to stop her from meeting her test at the Seventh Petal.

Distract, do not destroy, as Mother Pinara taught them over and over. *The Lily Blades are not an army, and never will be. You are no soldiers. Just a very well-edged sort of priestess, in truth.*

Shayla breathed a slow prayer to the Lily Goddess, then fished Remembrance from her left sheathe. She was midway along the west roof at this side of the garden—perhaps fifteen paces in each direction from where she currently lay, just below the guard's line of sight, should he choose to stand, turn and crane to peer over the row of tiles at the ridge of the roof.

A sharp, careful flick of her wrist sent the knife Remembrance tumbling to the left. With a sharp clatter, it bounced off the tiles almost at the end of the roof before sliding into the alley behind the Arbiter's mansion. Shayla prayed she'd be able to recover the knife later.

The guard just over the ridge grunted softly, then moved off with unsteady steps to check on the noise. Thankfully he did not first call for help—she hoped he would be more worried about looking foolish for investigating a cat or some such, than cautious in protecting his master's house.

When he shakily climbed over the ridge, facing away from Shayla and toward the source of the noise, she rolled over the ridge toward the courtyard, moving the opposite way. A moment later she dangled from the eaves, swinging for the drainpipe.

Two more men walked among the cinnamon trees below.

Swearing silently, Shayla abandoned her grip on the wall to slip into the first open window she could find. Half a building away from Umaya, and down a corridor and around a corner about which she knew nothing from the inside.

She was in a modest office, lined with scroll racks and long poles from which hung account sheets. The desk was covered with piles of paper slips in several sizes, and a stack of ledgers, along with a plate on which someone had abandoned their meal hours earlier from the looks of things.

This room was too small and busy to be the Arbiter's office, and lacked the sort of artwork and decor she would expect from one of his family. Work got done here, quickly and hard. The chamberlain's, she reasoned.

And as good a place as any to change into her party dress. Roaming *these* halls in her leathers was an invitation to the guards. Shayla stripped off her blacks down to the skin before slipping into a silk undershift and the copper-brown thing the sewing Mothers had pressed upon her. She'd refused as too constraining the more elaborate garments intended to be worn beneath the clothes.

"You'll be the darling of the smart set," Mother Kuchai had said, amid much tittering of her sisters in the temple basement.

Shayla didn't feel very smart now, and she was perforce either barefoot or in her own, second-best working boots. She'd planned to borrow more suitable shoes from Umaya this evening. Wrapping up the boots and her remaining knife in her leathers, she carried them in a bundle under her arm. The message was tucked once more beneath her breasts.

Much to her own surprise, Shayla found her way without incident. A maid passed her in the hall, bowing her head. The stairway down to Umaya's floor was unguarded, and while she heard a handful of guards laughing over dice, no one noticed or cared as she counted doors to reach the one that had to be behind the window of her desire.

She rapped lightly. "Umaya?"

"What?" asked the girl from within.

Relieved at the sound of her voice, Shayla slipped the latch and stepped inside.

"Oh," Umaya gasped, a complex of emotions flickering across her face.

Shayla gasped in return. Her love was resplendent in a gown of pink seed pearls, sewn in their thousands to an underlayer of white silk that lent them a shimmer. Umaya's brown eyes seemed huge in twinned rings of makeup, while some drug or potion had been placed within to make them gleam like firelight seen under water. Her hair flowed in an inky river, highlighted with something silver and frosted as if to foretell a legendary winter that had never come to Selistan except in traveler's tales of the unreasonable lands to the north.

"You look like a goddess," Shayla said softly.

"You look like…like…" Umaya began giggling. "An ungoddessly mess."

Shayla's heart fell, and her face must have fallen with it, because Umaya took her hands. "No, no, dearest. The dress is perfect for who you must pretend to be in this house, but your hair is a mess and your face is sweaty and too, too brown, and your feet have dust on them." She pulled Shayla close into a long embrace. "I have already dismissed my maid, but I can fix these for you. We shall be a bit late descending to the banquet hall, as befits the daughters of a noble house."

Shayla would have much rather slipped in with a crowd than engineer a dramatic entrance, but this was no longer her business. She allowed herself to be taken by the hand and led to the dressing table, where Umaya sat her down, then began tucking and pressing at the seams of the pretty gown, to smooth it out.

"What's this?" Umaya asked as her hands slipped across Shayla's breasts and found Mother Meiko's rolled-up note.

Truth! shrieked a voice within her, before it was too late. Shayla opened her mouth, but could not say the words that would fail her in the Seventh Petal, not even to this girl whom she loved so unreasonably.

"A prayer," she managed to gasp out. "For my luck."

Umaya patted it back into place, her hand lingering a moment longer on Shayla's breasts. "Your luck will change even more tonight, my dear."

Then Umaya set to work with paint pots and oils and brushes, while Shayla let her conscience make of her an ever more arrant coward.

UMAYA TRANSFORMED SHAYLA into a beauty that exceeded the station signaled by her modest yet becoming attire. They descended to the banquet an hour late, entering by the family stairs—conveniently avoiding the chamberlain with his lists, and the herald whose bawling announcements of the guests had been faintly audible even from Umaya's chambers. Shayla tried to assess the area for dangers, for political factors, for lines of fire and distributions of force and the body language of loyalty among half a hundred scattered men and women.

All her learnings deserted her in a blur of unshed tears, and what she mostly saw was the room.

The space was huge, with an unpillared, unsupported ceiling. Walls were hung with tapestries so heavily embroidered with silken cord and gleaming beads that they were practically sculptures—a Selistani style that favored peacock colors, running to rich greens and blues. The teakwood floor was covered with silks and small carpets artfully scattered as if by the random fall of leaves. Tables stretched between them, low in the current mode so the guests sat or lounged upon a collection of poufs and bolsters. Silver fountains poured wine and broth into wide bowls set at the ends of the each table, while a course had already been served of whole-roasted shoats arranged as if dancing upon bakery logs studded with dates and filberts.

All faces turned toward them a moment, a wave of silence in the chatter of this society rippling through the room, until the noise resumed once more like birds settling down after a startlement. Still, Shayla was so very conscious of the eyes upon them, from the chamberlain at the far end of the hall to Umaya's father lounging on a throne-like seat of green velvet and blue silk.

"Let us meet him," she said gaily, "then take our places." Tugging at Shayla's hand, she led them through the room, smiling and waving at this one or that. Shayla's squeak-voiced "Not yet!" went unheard, and she found herself avoiding the daggered eyes of the young men and younger women who seemed so focused on Umaya.

An echo of "Oh, so *she's* the one" rippled through the chatter, leaping from jealous mouth to youthful ear.

Not yet, prayed Shayla. *Please, let me have one more hour with her. I will never be so beautiful again, and neither will any woman I love. One more hour, Goddess, I beg.*

But then they knelt before the Arbiter of the Woodcock Court, and Umaya was chattering about girls and friendship and how wonderful things were.

Now, thought Shayla, *or give up all.* Her hand slipped to her breast.

The Arbiter frowned, but Shayla brought out the little rolled-up paper—a tiny scroll, it must have seemed to him. She smiled falsely at the man and slit the seal with her fingernail, then peeled the paper open.

Umaya looked at her, and Shayla realized she'd missed something important.

"Kiss papa, please," the girl said. "For respect." Her tone added, *if you can*, another painful layer on top of the jealous whisperings of the room. Shayla realized in that moment that she would never fit into this world, no matter how much love—or lust—she might feel.

Shayla kissed Umaya instead, drawing a titter from the people at the head table and those nearest down, then turned to the Arbiter and pulled open the scroll. The words wavered as she read them, as though she was but a mouth for Mother Meiko to speak through.

"I am Mother Vajpai of the Lily Blades, and you would be dead now if we wished it so," she whispered into his left ear, then kissed him there.

He looked shocked, then angry. Shayla turned her back on the Arbiter, smiled at Umaya and left her youth behind with the words, "I will always love you."

Mother Vajpai walked back up the stairs accompanied by the kind of silence only a hundred nervous people can make. As she passed out of sight of the great hall toward the room where her leathers were hidden, she heard a young woman weeping.

The sound followed her through the house until Mother Vajpai realized whose tears wet her cheeks. She did not have to kill to go home, though she wished mightily for the excuse.

CHIVALROUS | *Kelley Armstrong*

FRIDAY NIGHT UNI parties were the reward for a week of hard work. Time to cut loose. Get wasted. Get laid. All of which was hard to do when your mother kept texting you.

As Trevor handed him another beer, Reese texted back, saying he needed to study and he'd call her in the morning.

Am I cramping your style? Can't party while talking 2 your old lady.

He choked on his beer, then replied, insisting he was studying.

ROTFLMAO. Go on. Party. Just B safe. And don't forget 2 run this wknd.

Trevor glanced over Reese's shoulder and read the last text before Reese closed his phone.

"Run?" he said.

"Beer run. Promised my study mates I'd pick up a slab tomorrow."

Trevor slapped Reese's back. "I thought maybe you'd joined the athletic team. Decided footy getting too rough for you. Don't want to mess up that pretty face." Trevor looked around the room, gaze pausing on every girl along the way. "Speaking of which, have you made your choice yet? I know enough to let you pick first or my ego's going to take a beating."

Reese's gaze slid to the dark-haired girl in the corner. She'd been shooting glances at him all night. Shy glances, her pale cheeks flushing when he'd caught her looking, her grip tightening on her glass, gaze ducking away.

She was small and pretty. Looked very sweet. The kind of girl he could take home to Mum, which meant she wasn't the girl for tonight.

He needed a run. Already, the restlessness pulled every tendon as tight as a piano wire. But the kind of run he needed meant driving out of Melbourne, suffering through the torturous change into a wolf and spending hours hunting and working it off. Not something he was eager to do any sooner than necessary.

At home, on his parent's farm, Reese enjoyed his runs. Sure, the transformation was hell, but he'd waited for his first Change the way other kids wait to learn to drive. At uni, though, it was a major pain in the arse, so he postponed it for as long as it was safely possible. And one advantage to letting that restlessness build? Really great sex.

He knew enough not to let it go too far. A werewolf couldn't risk losing control with a lover. He knew, too, that he had to find the right girl, someone who wanted exactly what he wanted—sex straight-up, no guilt chaser when he didn't stick around until morning. The sweet little dark-haired girl wouldn't do.

He scanned the room. Despite what Travis said, Reese didn't have his pick of any girl. He just did better than Travis, who was the soccer team's enforcer and looked like he used his face to do the enforcing. But dark blond hair, a pleasant face and an athletic build usually got Reese what he wanted and it only took him one good scan of the party to decide what he wanted tonight.

She was a redhead. Not naturally, he was sure, but he'd find that out soon enough, if the looks she was giving him were any indication. She sat on a high stool by the makeshift bar with her arm around a blonde friend's waist, hand in her pocket, a fake lesbian show that *wasn't* designed to scare guys off.

When she saw Reese watching, she leaned over and nuzzled her friend's neck, fingers kneading her arse, and Reese felt himself harden at the thought of a threesome. Wishful thinking, he knew, but he could always hope. He headed over.

Twenty minutes later, he was leaving with the redhead. The blonde stayed behind. As usual, the threesome hints had only been bait. Which was fine. Pleasing two girls would take time and patience, and all he wanted was release. Hard and fast release.

When he'd suggested they step outside, the girl—Mandy—was on her feet before he was. They'd made it as far as the back of the building, and he'd put her up against the wall, just for an appetizer, but she seemed quite content to stay there through the main course. He did check, though, asking if she wanted to go to his flat or hers.

She pressed against him, her open shirt falling to her waist, bare breasts pale in the moonlight. "I don't think you'd make it that far," she said as she rubbed his crotch. "In fact, I don't think you're going to make it through the next five minutes."

"Can't help myself." He kissed her hard, and she groaned and pressed against him. "Is that a problem?"

It wasn't. Girls were usually flattered by his eagerness. Flattered and excited, his passion contagious, and when zippers were being yanked down a minute later, it wasn't Reese doing the yanking. That was normal, too. He let the girls set the pace, even if they didn't quite realize they were taking the lead. He always had to be sure he wasn't pushing them into something they didn't want.

But Mandy definitely wanted it. Reese was ripping open a condom packet when a distant crash stopped him. As he looked around, a girl screamed.

"Sounds like someone else is enjoying herself," Mandy said.

It didn't. Werewolf hearing meant he caught the notes of fear in that shriek. Then he heard her protesting, telling the guy to stop. Reese waited. Mistakes happened. Guys go to a party, get drunk, get a little pushy. But a good firm "no" usually smacked their brain out of their pants.

Not this guy. The protests kept coming, getting panicky now. Reese zipped his jeans and stepped back. When Mandy grabbed for him, he moved out of her reach.

"That girl's in trouble," he said.

"And who are you, Bruce Wayne?"

When he started walking away, she caught the back of his shirt. "Forget her. I'm sure she wants it. She just doesn't realize it yet."

Reese spun, knocking her hand from his shirt and giving her a glare that had her stumbling back.

"Go home," he said, then took off in the direction of the voices.

—❦—

THE GIRL WAS a street over, behind another building. She'd gone quiet. Reese picked up speed, hoping she'd escaped, fearing she hadn't. As he drew closer, he heard muffled protests and a guy telling her to shut up. Then another male voice chimed in.

Shit.

Slowing, Reese carefully rounded the building. The first thing he smelled was booze. The air reeked of it, and he could see a smashed bottle lying in a pool of liquid. That booze was all he *could* smell, so he couldn't tell if it was two guys or more. Werewolf strength meant he could manage two. More? It depended on what kind of shape they were in.

As Reese glanced around the corner, he realized he didn't need to worry about that. It was only two thirtyish guys, and they were so drunk they could barely stand upright. One had the girl from behind, hand over her mouth and she was kicking and writhing and punching.

The girl's foot connected with the crotch of the guy in front of her. When he fell back, howling, Reese caught a glimpse of the girl, seeing dark hair and a pale green shirt. The shy girl from the party.

Reese crept forward. The men were too intent on restraining the girl to notice him. He grabbed the man holding her. He yanked him away, threw him aside, then went after the other one.

After Reese blocked a few wobbly swings and sent them flying with ones of his own, the men realized they were outclassed and took off. He chased them for a block, hoping to catch one and hold him for the cops. But those few blows seemed to have knocked the booze from their heads. They made it to the main road just ahead of him, darted through traffic, and hopped into a taxi.

Reese found the girl where he'd left her, still behind the building, tugging absently at her torn shirt as she stared down at her mobile phone.

"Did you call it in?" he said.

She jumped, skittering back, then saw it was him. "I was waiting to see if you'd catch them."

"I didn't."

Her expression wavered between disappointment and relief. She pocketed the phone.

"You really should call—" he began.

"I know."

She looked around, then retrieved a shoe that had fallen off in the struggle. Her fingers trembled as she tried to get it on.

"Here." Reese bent and put it on her.

"I feel like Cinderella," she said, trying for a smile. "Does it fit?"

"It does. About those guys—"

"I should report it. I know that. But my parents—" She stopped and rubbed the back of her neck. "They don't like me going to university here. Big city and all that. If they find out I was jumped by a couple of drunks, they'll cut me off, make me come home. Maybe they wouldn't have to find out, but…"

She looked up at him. "I really don't want to take that chance. Not when nothing happened."

"Something did happen. You got attacked."

"I know." She shoved her hands into her pockets. "But I'm okay. Can you—can you just walk me to the road? Wait while I hail a taxi?"

He didn't offer to escort her home. That might seem like the chivalrous thing to do, but he doubted a girl who'd narrowly escaped rape wanted a stranger near her flat, so he got her into a taxi, realizing only as the car pulled off that he hadn't asked her name. Just as well, he supposed, all things considered.

WHEN REESE GOT back to his flat, it was empty. Not surprising. Niles wasn't around much, which made him the perfect flat-mate.

He kicked off his runners, sat on the couch and picked up the remote. He didn't turn on the TV. Just sat there, staring at his reflection in the blank screen. Then he pulled out his mobile and hit speed dial.

His mother answered, yawning, on the fourth ring. "What's wrong, baby?"

"Nothing. I just—" He glanced at the clock on the DVD player and winced. "Sorry, I didn't realize how late it was. I'll call you in the morning."

He heard his mother get out of bed. His dad mumbled something in the background.

"He's fine," his mother murmured to his dad.

"I am," Reese said. "Go back to bed. I'm sorry. I just—" *I helped this girl tonight, saved her from a couple of guys and it made me think of you.*

Of course he couldn't say that, wouldn't jog those memories. He shouldn't have called.

"One too many beers," he said finally. "I totally lost track of time. I'll call in the morning."

"You sound like you want to talk."

He forced a chuckle. "No, I sound drunk, and when I'm drunk, I like to talk. I'll wake up Niles and make him suffer through it. Payback for eating my leftovers last week."

She didn't let it go that easily. Eventually, though, she accepted the excuse, along with the promise to call in the morning.

Reese hung up, but stayed on the couch, staring at the blank television screen. Twenty years ago, his mother had been the university student leaving a party, the one who'd bumped into the wrong guys. An American, she'd told everyone she just wanted to study abroad, and picked the University of Sydney on a lark. Not true. Going to school abroad was too complicated to ever do "on a lark." She'd picked it because she didn't know anyone in Australia, and it was as far as she could get from a bad family situation.

She'd been at an out-of-town party with her boyfriend. Driving back, they'd fought—she couldn't remember over what. He'd kicked her out of the car ten kilometers from town. A long walk on an empty road. She'd ducked out of sight whenever a car passed. Then came the one that didn't pass. They'd had their windows down. Smelled her. Three young werewolves. She hadn't stood a chance.

Raping her wasn't enough. They decided to hunt her. Kill her. Feed on her. Let the police chalk it up to dingoes. Thinking she was unconscious, they'd gone to Change in the bushes. She snuck the keys from the leader's jacket. Then she took off in their ute.

When she got to the authorities, she had quite a story to tell, about three men who'd raped her, changed into wolves and chased the ute as she'd sped off. Clearly the girl was in shock after her ordeal. She needed help, not the ridicule that would come by making her allegations public. So the police tried to cover it up, but the story hit a few small papers without the scruples to ignore it.

The Australian Pack found out. They sent a delegation to hunt and kill the trio of man-eaters. Then they sent another of their own—Wes Robinson—to take care of the girl. That didn't mean protecting her. Their interest was in protecting the Pack, and the girl posed an exposure threat. She had to die.

Wes didn't carry out his orders. He met the girl, fell in love, and ran away with her. All terribly romantic. Unfortunately, the Pack didn't see it that way.

Most Packs forbid long-term relationships. The Australian one, though, operated more like a wolf pack. The Alpha—and only the Alpha—could take a mate. When Reese's parents ran off together, Wes Robinson wasn't just disobeying a direct order. He'd unwittingly issued a challenge to the Alpha that could not be ignored. So they'd taken on new surnames and spent the last twenty years hiding in the Outback, raising sheep and, then, their son.

Reese had been born nine months after his parents met. Also nine months after his mother had been attacked. They hadn't told him that, of course. He'd figured it out when he'd looked up his mother's story and seen the date.

Born nine months after a brutal gang-rape. He was pretty sure he knew what that meant. He'd confronted his father about it once. His dad had said, "You're my son." That's all he'd say. All he needed to say, Reese supposed. Wes Robinson was his father in every way that counted.

If his parents didn't care, Reese shouldn't. In most ways, he didn't. But he still had his hang-ups, like making absolutely sure sex was consensual. And there were things that would remind him, pull him down into his thoughts and fears. The attack on the dark-haired girl had done that. He'd deal, but this would be a long, sleepless night.

REESE HAD A soccer match the next afternoon. The Pack discouraged their young sons from playing organized sports, knowing that when they came into their powers, they could get into trouble, being too strong, too aggressive. But Reese was home-schooled, so his parents had decided he needed all the social interaction he could get. They'd made the two-hour round trip into town twice a week so he could try out different sports at the community center. Soccer was the one he'd stuck with.

When he'd started coming into his strength, his parents had watched closely for any sign that Reese might need to restrict himself to skirmishes with his father. But they'd taught him well. He avoided fights and relied on speed and agility instead.

Now, of course, his parents weren't there to watch him play. But that afternoon, someone else was: the dark-haired girl.

He didn't see her until near the end of the match, glimpsing her sitting behind a group of middle-aged men. She seemed to be alone. Was her boyfriend on the team? He felt a flicker of disappointment.

It didn't matter. You couldn't save a girl from rape, then ask her out on a date. That was all kinds of wrong.

After the match, when he saw her standing beside the benches, he waved. It was the polite thing to do. She walked over. Also the polite thing to do.

"How're you doing?" he asked, motioning her to a quieter place where they could talk.

"Fine." She made a face. "Well, not really, but I'm holding up. I just…I didn't get a chance to say thank you last night. Not a proper thank you, anyway. If you hadn't come along…" A deep breath. "Well, I'm glad you did."

"You're welcome but, honestly, I think you could have handled it. They were pretty far gone, and you put up a good fight. A damned good fight."

She blushed. "Maybe. I wanted to come by and say thanks, though. A friend from the party didn't know your name, but said you played on this team."

"It's Reese."

She blinked, confused.

"My name," he said. "Reese Wilson."

Her cheeks flushed deeper. "Right. Sorry." She put out her hand. "Daniella DuMaurier."

One of Reese's teammates shouted that they were heading to the pub. "Going out for a beer after the match?" Daniella asked.

He'd planned to. And this would be an easy way to ask her out without really asking her out, just casually invite her to come along. But he had a feeling she'd say no. A rowdy victory party with strangers wouldn't be her idea of a good time.

"Nah. Assignment due tomorrow. I'm just going to grab a bite to eat." He squinted beyond the park. "Do you know any decent places around here?"

"No, but I'm sure we could find one." Another blush. "I mean, if you want. Buying you lunch is the least I can do."

OVER LUNCH, HE smoothly led the conversation, searching for a subtle way to ask her out. He knew he was being overly cautious. She'd obviously wanted to have lunch with him, and by the time they'd found a restaurant, she'd been laughing and chatting, completely relaxed, giving all the signs that said, "I'm interested."

Still, he was careful. When he steered the conversation into recent movie releases, though, she admitted there was one she really wanted to see and, wouldn't you know it, so did he. Or so he said. He suggested they go together. She said yes. And that was that.

REESE HADN'T HAD a girlfriend since high school. There wasn't any reason to get one, not when plenty of uni girls were happy to hook up for a night. If he could get sex without the dangers of a romantic relationship, then he would. Romantic relationships were dangerous for a werewolf. Just too many secrets to hide.

After three dates with Daniella, though, he'd decided he could make an exception. Sex was still off the menu—he wasn't pressuring a girl who'd nearly been raped—but that didn't stop him from wanting to see her as often as he could, which was as sure a sign as any that this was something different.

Daniella was different, too. When he'd first met her, he'd thought she was sweet and shy. He liked that in a girl—or his werewolf instincts did. Someone gentle and delicate, someone he could take care of and protect. And she *was* sweet and shy, but as he'd seen the night of the attack, there was strength there, too. An iron will hid behind her delicate exterior. And passion. When they kissed, she'd always start slow and tentative, but it didn't take long to get her motor running.

Delicate and innocent on the outside, tough and hot-blooded on the inside. That fascinated him. Excited the hell out of him, too. Wherever this relationship was going, he planned to follow.

THEY'D BEEN DATING for a month when a long weekend meant trips home for both of them. Daniella's family lived near Sydney, so he saw her off on the plane Thursday night, then made the long drive home himself right after his Friday morning class.

Before Daniella left, she told him how much she'd miss him, how much she wished she could stay. He felt kind of guilty at that. Though he'd miss her, too, he was looking forward to going home.

Home was the Outback. Home was endless, empty expanses of red soil and scrub brush. Home was the smell of diesel and wet sheep, the whoosh of the windmill and the whine of the wind. It was his dogs, racing up the dirt road when they heard his ute coming. It was his mother, waiting on the porch with a cold beer and a hot meat pie. It was his dad, ambling in from the barn, weathered face brightening in a smile. For the next two days, they wouldn't do much of anything, just hang out together, talking, then going for runs at night, his mother coming along, staying in the ute with picnic baskets of food for an American-style tailgate party afterward.

His home life was damned near perfect. A helluva lot better than Daniella's, as he came to realize during their calls that weekend. By Saturday night her parents were driving her nuts. More than that, she seemed depressed, and that worried him. He told himself she just wanted to get back to school—and back to him—but he couldn't help wondering if there was more to it.

That werewolf streak of possessiveness kept nudging him toward one conclusion—that she had a guy back home, a boyfriend she'd broken up with to go to university, and now was reconsidering that decision. He told himself he was overreacting, but when her plane landed, he met her at the airport with a single red rose.

When she came out, she walked with her gaze down, letting the other passengers elbow and jostle past her, not even seeming to notice. Her hair was pulled back in a tidy ponytail, but it didn't gleam the way it usually did. Her oversized sweatshirt seemed to envelop her tiny frame, weighing her down as she trudged along.

"Daniella!" he called, as she started heading the other way.

When she saw him, her face lit up. As she took the rose, her cheeks turned as red as the petals. She murmured a thank you. Then she noticed what he held in his other hand—a wrapped hamburger.

"That's the romantic gesture," he said, pointing at the rose. "This is the practical one. It's late and you're probably hungry."

She gave a tiny laugh, then threw her arms around his neck. "My hero." She hugged him as she said it, but he didn't miss the catch in her voice and the way she clung to him, as if composing herself before pulling back.

"What's wrong?" he whispered, as he took her laptop bag.

"It's noth—" She stopped. Pulled herself up straight. "No, it *is* something. I need to talk to you, Reese."

"Okay," he said carefully. "Let's get out to my ute and we'll go someplace and—"

"No." She grasped his arm. "Now. If I wait, I'll change my mind. I can't change my mind."

Actually, he had a feeling he'd be fine with that, but he let her lead him to a cluster of empty chairs. She walked to the far corner and sat, hands folded in her lap.

He knew what she was going to say. *There's this guy...We broke up when I came to Melbourne, but I saw him when I went home and...I'm sorry, Reese...*

He steeled himself against the words. He'd fight for her. If there was any hope at all, he'd fight.

"My father is Gavin Wright," she said finally.

He jumped a little at the name, then tried to cover the reaction by shifting, coughing. He'd misheard. He must have misheard.

"You know who that is," Daniella said. "I know you do."

He forced a laugh. "Maybe I'm showing my ignorance, but no, I don't. Is he a politician? A CEO? Local celebrity? Someone who isn't very happy about his daughter dating a kid from the Outback. Is that it?"

Temper flashed in her eyes. "Don't play dumb, Reese."

"Maybe I'm not playing."

She got up and walked to the window. For a moment, she just stared out. Then she wheeled.

"Gavin Wright is the Alpha of the Australian Pack," she said. "And if you pretend you don't know what a Pack is, I'm..." She trailed off and lifted her hands. They were shaking. "Do you see that? Don't play games with me, Reese. Please. This is hard enough already."

He said nothing. He couldn't, and if she really was Wright's daughter, she should know that. He could not let on that he had any idea what she was talking about until she proved who she was and confirmed that she knew what he was.

She sat down again, two chairs away now, and twisted toward him. "Gavin Wright has two daughters. No sons. My older sister is engaged to the Alpha-elect. That's how it works. Only the Alpha can marry. One of his daughters is mated with his successor. The others..." She shrugged. "Aren't."

Any other daughters were expected to devote their lives to the Pack, cooking, cleaning, and taking care of the men. A life of celibate servitude. Reese knew that from his father's stories.

Daniella continued. "I wanted to go to university, but my father laughed at the idea. Then a lone wolf who was in trouble with the Pack gave them a tip. He'd smelled a young werewolf on campus here. My dad knew Wes Robinson was hiding out this way, knew he had a college-aged son. So he decided I could go to Melbourne Uni. To find you."

Reese realized he was gripping the seat. He let go. "Mission accomplished."

"But I didn't *want* to find you. I hoped I could string my father along until I got a degree. Then, with an education, I could..." She glanced away. "Escape"

"Only he expected results, so you had to produce them. You saw me at the party—"

"And figured out who you were. Yes. I could smell you. I'm not a werewolf, obviously, but I have a good sense of smell and I can recognize a werewolf's scent. That's how my dad expected me to find you. Once I was sure who you were, I left the party. But I was so distracted that I walked right into those guys."

She went quiet for a moment, then said, her voice soft, "That would have been ironic, wouldn't it? Your mum gets raped. My dad's trying to kill her because of it and the same thing happens to his daughter. Poetic justice."

"Don't say that."

She shrugged. "I feel that. I know I'm not my father, but I still feel guilty about what he did. And now I feel even guiltier because I ended up doing exactly what he wanted. I should have stayed away from you. I tried. That's why I took off so fast that night. But I couldn't."

"So you told him I'm here. He's coming for me."

"No. Never. I didn't say anything. I just—I had to tell you the truth. I know this means it's over, but I won't put your life in danger."

"And staying with you means it is?"

She nodded.

"What if I disagree?"

"Then you'd be wrong. Your death is my father's idea of the perfect revenge. But you don't need to run. He won't let any of the Pack come here, for fear you'll scent them. So you're safe at school. Just not with me. I'm going to drop out. I'll tell my father I couldn't find you and I'm homesick and—"

"No."

"I have to. As long as I'm here—"

"—your dad and the Pack are up in Sydney. I'm safe from them. You're safe from them. And that's just as important."

He kissed her. It took a moment for her to kiss him back, unsure at first, then heating up until she was in his lap, kissing him deeply and desperately. When she finally pulled back and whispered, "Will you come to my place tonight?" he got the feeling she meant it as a goodbye. He'd make sure it wasn't.

—*∂*—

IF SEX HAD been her goodbye gift, it turned out to be a bigger offering than he expected. She'd been a virgin. They'd been taking things slow, but he'd attributed that to her rape scare. When he'd figured it out, he'd tried to stop. But Daniella hadn't wanted to stop. Really, *really* hadn't wanted to stop. While he'd love to credit that to his sexual prowess, he suspected she'd been so determined because it was, for her, the point of no return.

After they made love, there was no more talk of Daniella going back to Sydney. She'd made her choice, and she'd picked him over the Pack. He understood the magnitude of that choice.

He understood what it meant for him, too. He'd slept with the Pack Alpha's daughter. His father's crime paled beside that.

It wasn't until his mother's next call that Reese realized how much trouble he was in. He didn't tell his mother about Daniella. He'd already had that conversation with Daniella, and even the suggestion had terrified her. His parents could help, but he needed to convince her that his father wasn't like the Pack werewolves. She'd be safe with them. The problem, as he now realized, was that *they* wouldn't be safe with *her*.

How *was* he going to tell his parents that his girlfriend was Gavin Wright's daughter? They'd understand her situation, of course. They'd protect her, help her get away from the Pack. But taking her in meant Wright would double his efforts to find them, and he wouldn't rest until he got Daniella back and slaughtered Reese's family.

So, when Daniella begged him not to tell his parents, he was relieved. That gave him time to figure out how he was going to handle this. In the meantime, he was too caught up in the relationship to think much about the repercussions.

If he thought he'd liked Daniella before, it was nothing compared to how he felt now. For the first time, he could really be himself with a girl. He hadn't realized how much he'd longed for that, how much he'd envied that bond between his parents.

As deeply in love as his parents were, it had been hard for them at first, his mother learning to handle all the things that made her husband different, all the things he had to hide from the world.

Now Reese had a lover who not only knew his secret, but considered it normal. She brought him food when he was dashing between classes. She made sure he got lots of exercise—in and out of bed. She indulged his protective streak and gave him no cause for jealousy. She prodded him to Change, even going with him, staying with him. She figured out his penchant for delaying his run, and taking the edge off with sex, and she accommodated that, too—enthusiastically.

They were in class, three weeks later, when she texted to remind him it was getting close to his "time," and asking if he was "feeling it" yet. When he'd said he was, she'd told him to meet her in a nook behind one of the campus buildings.

As he headed there, knowing what was coming, his blood ran so hot that when he smelled a werewolf, he thought, for one confused moment, that it was her. Luckily, his brain kicked in and stopped him. That and the sound of Daniella's voice.

"I *am* looking for him," she was saying. "But it's a big campus and I have classes—"

"We aren't sending you here to go to classes, Daniella," a man answered.

Reese peered around the corner and saw a dark-haired man. He looked about thirty, which meant, with a werewolf's slow aging, he was probably a decade older. Daniella's father? He was acting like it, towering over her, speaking in a growl that made her press back against the wall, books clutched to her chest.

There was nothing in his scent that suggested they were related, though. And the man's stance was a little too familiar to be familial. He was leaning over Daniella, his body a hairsbreadth from hers. Reese felt his hands clench. He stepped out of hiding.

Daniella sensed him and glanced over. She looked away fast, but he saw the panic in her eyes. She inched to the side, making the werewolf turn his back to Reese. Then she dropped her hand and madly waved Reese back.

It took him a minute to obey. He knew he should. If he went after the guy and didn't kill him, this man would expose their relationship. Protecting Daniella meant backing down, as cowardly as it felt.

He didn't leave, though, only moved out of sight, where he could keep listening. They argued for a few minutes, then she led the man away, in the opposite direction, so he wouldn't cross Reese's scent trail. At the road, Daniella escaped, joining a couple of girls she knew, telling the guy she'd call him later.

Reese followed the werewolf to a visitor's lot, where he climbed into a brand-new four wheel drive and roared off.

—*c*—

TWO HOURS LATER, Reese met Daniella at an off-campus pub. After the encounter, she'd gone straight to a gift store, where she'd bought a bagful of scented candles. Then to her flat, to light them, change the bedding and get rid of any sign—and scent—of Reese.

Now they were alone in the back of the noisy pub, clutching beers they had no intention of drinking.

"His name is Keith Tynes," she said. "He's—"

"The Alpha-elect. I know the name. My father…talked about him."

"Nothing good, I'm sure. My dad isn't the nicest guy, but Keith?" She shivered. "I feel sorry for my sister. The Alpha's mate is treated like a queen, but it's not worth it. Not with Keith."

"Is he sticking around to hunt for me?"

She shook her head. "He wasn't even supposed to be on campus. I can't believe he disobeyed my dad like that. He's starting to throw his weight around, see how far he can push it, but he knows not to push it too far. One call to my dad and he'll get the usual punishment. Dad will make him wait another six months before he gets my sister." A faint sparkle lit her eyes. "Keith was supposed to get her when she turned eighteen almost two years ago, and he's really getting anxious."

"Horny."

She laughed. "Yes, horny. Speaking of which…" Her fingers crept up his leg.

He put his hand on hers. "So Keith will leave?"

"He will."

"And if he doesn't?"

She leaned over and kissed him, whispering, "He will."

—*C*—

KEITH DID LEAVE. But the close call was a wakeup for Reese. This situation wasn't going to resolve itself. Daniella needed to get away from the Pack and he needed to get away from Melbourne. That meant dropping out and going home, and as much as that would hurt his parents, it would hurt them a lot more if the Pack killed their only child.

Step one, though, was getting Daniella to agree to meet his parents. The day after her encounter with Keith, he began his campaign to convince her they wouldn't murder her in her sleep and send her severed head back to her father.

He started taking every opportunity to talk about his family. Before soccer, he'd tell her about skirmishes with his dad. After a run, he'd talk about their tailgate parties. At dinner, he'd tell tales of his mother's disastrous attempts to cook new dishes. Before long, Daniella was the one encouraging him to share his stories. There was a wistfulness in her eyes when he talked about his family, and he could tell her own childhood hadn't been nearly so happy.

Within a week, she was ready to meet them. That's when Reese started having second thoughts.

Was it really wise to take Daniella to his parents, when they'd spent half their lives hiding from her father? He trusted her completely, but he had to think about his parents' safety. Most importantly, was there any *reason* to take Daniella to them? He was an adult. He had enough money to get them to America or England. Maybe he should just do that. Leave and tell his parents after he was gone, as much as that would hurt.

Daniella seemed a little disappointed, but she agreed with his logic. They'd go to England. Then he'd call and break the news to his parents.

—*C*—

TWO DAYS LATER, he was heading to his last class of the day, thinking it was kind of silly to keep going. But he supposed there was still part of him that hoped he wouldn't have to leave, that the situation would miraculously resolve itself. Immature, he knew. Daniella wasn't stalling. She was out emptying her bank account and following up on his lead to get a fake passport.

He was debating skipping class when his phone rang.

"Got it!" Daniella sang when he answered.

"You're a criminal now, you know. Buying fake ID is a criminal offense."

She laughed. "Then I've been a criminal from birth."

True. All her ID was fake, common among werewolves even in the Pack.

"So who am I taking to England?" he asked.

"Gabriella. She's much sexier than Daniella. You'll love— Oh, God."

"Daniella?"

"Keith," she said, her voice going distant, as if she'd yanked the phone down.

"Who are you talking to?" Keith called.

"A friend." A rustle, like she was stuffing the phone into her pocket. "What are you—?"

"Didn't sound like a friend." Keith's voice came closer. "Do you think I'm stupid, Dani? That I don't know what you're up to? That I don't know who that was?"

Oh, shit. Oh, shit! Where was she? Reese looked around, but he had no idea if she was even on campus.

Come on, Daniella. I'm still on the line. Give me a hint, a clue and I'm on my way.

"I don't know what you—" Daniella began.

"Cut the crap, Dani. He's your boyfriend, isn't he?"

"Wh-what? Who? That was a friend."

"Bullshit." The voice came closer still and Reese swore he could hear Daniella shaking. "What would your father say if he found out? A human boyfriend?"

"H-hum—" She stopped. Reese could hear the relief in her voice when she continued. "It's not like that. Just a guy I...kind of like. We went out a few times and—"

"You'd better be telling the truth, because you're mine, Dani."

An edge of steel slid into Daniella's voice. "No, Rose is yours. I'm going to be your sister-in-law. I've warned you already—if you ever touch me again, I'll tell my father and he'll—"

"He'll do nothing. I'm tired of waiting for my turn. I've got half the Pack on my side, plus your sister. It's our turn, and if your parents don't step down gracefully, you're going to be an orphan."

"Rose would never—"

"No? It's her idea. She's sick of waiting. Sick of serving your mother. Sick of watching me serve your father." He chuckled. "And sick of getting her wedding night postponed. Now I'm bringing you home, and if your father complains, that'll give me just the excuse I need. So call your boyfriend and say goodbye, and I hope all you gave him was kisses, because if I find out otherwise..." His voice lowered to a growl. "I owe my Pack brothers for their support. If you're damaged goods, you'll be their reward."

"You're hurting me."

"Oh, believe me, I'm going to hurt you a lot more—"

Reese didn't catch the rest of the threat. He started running, phone gripped to his ear, having no idea where he was going, just running, praying she'd remember he was still on the line and tell him where she was.

Even when he slowed and strained to listen, though, he could barely hear anything. Their voices were muffled now. But he could catch the panic in Daniella's and hear the faint sounds of a struggle. Then Keith said, "Maybe I'll save myself the disappointment and just check those goods now."

Daniella let out a shriek. Reese ran faster, shouting "Daniella!" into the phone.

A smack. Then a gasp of pain. Daniella's gasp. He called her name again, louder, but the fight got louder, too. Then a *whoomph* and a hiss of pain from Keith.

Footsteps pounded.

"You bitch," Keith wheezed, his voice getting distant. "You'd better run. When I catch you..."

He didn't finish the threat. Didn't catch her either.

—*C*—

BY NIGHTFALL, REESE and Daniella were in his ute, roaring out of Melbourne. He'd screwed up—again. He hadn't wanted to leave, so he'd come up with excuses. *Oh, you need ID. And we need to empty our bank accounts. And figure out where we're going to stay...*

Bullshit. He'd been stalling. After Daniella escaped from Keith the first time, they should have packed their bags and driven across the country to Perth, holed up there until they could leave Australia.

Now they were doing exactly what he'd tried to avoid. Taking her to his parents. They had no choice. All her ID—new and old—had been in her purse, which Keith had grabbed as she'd run away. They needed a place to hide and they needed help.

He'd called first. His dad had answered and Reese said he was coming home for the weekend. His father didn't question it, just figured Reese was homesick.

At midnight, Reese called again to tell them not to wait up. He was exhausted and grabbing a motel room for the night. His mum agreed he shouldn't drive while he was tired, but said, "Is something wrong, Reese?"

"Kind of."

Daniella glanced over sharply. They'd agreed not to tell his parents the truth until they got there. She was worried they might tell him to get the hell away from her as fast as he could. Too little experience trusting anyone, especially werewolves.

"I'm okay for now," he said. "I'll explain when I get home."

A pause. A long one. Then, "All right. Call me when you leave the motel and I'll have breakfast ready when you get here."

He hung up and Daniella said, "It's only a couple more hours drive."

He didn't answer, just checked the mirrors for the thousandth time since they'd left Melbourne.

"Keith isn't following us, Reese." She studied his face. "But you're still worried, and I guess I can't blame you. You don't want to risk leading him to your parents."

"I can't."

"I know."

They started looking for a motel.

—*C*—

TEN MINUTES LATER, they were in a room, but it was an hour before they got to sleep. As Daniella joked, it would be a while before they'd get time alone together. That's what cheap motels were for, he'd said. So they'd taken advantage of it, burning off the stress and anxiety of the day.

Afterward, he'd gone into the bathroom to brush his teeth. When he came out, she lay naked on the bed, examining a tourist map from the desk.

"Trying to figure out where the hell we are?" he asked.

She laughed. "Yes. I found the last town we passed. Now I'm trying to guess where we're going." She pointed at a stretch of land marked with sheep. "I know it's not here. It's the right distance, but it's ranch country. No way werewolves would be farming livestock."

When he didn't answer, she looked up and caught his smile.

"Seriously?" she said. "How'd you manage that?"

He shrugged. "Get them while they're lambs and they get used to our smell. A sheep farm is the last place the Pack would look for us."

She let the map slide to the floor. "Smart. Do you have dogs to herd, then?" She grinned. "Or just Change and do it yourselves?"

He laughed and stretched out on top of her. "We have dogs."

"Lucky. I always wanted dogs. Pets of any kind, actually." She put her arms around his neck. "I think I'm going to like it out here. Even if it is a million miles from anywhere."

"That's part of its charm," he said, and kissed her.

—*C*—

HE AWOKE ALONE. The spot beside him had cooled, but the faint smell of shampoo wafted from the bathroom. He stretched and flipped over to check the time—

Shit! It was after nine. He'd set it for six—

No, Daniella had set it. Had she done it wrong? Damned motel clocks. No two ever worked the same.

He rolled out of bed and padded to the bathroom. The door was ajar. He pushed it open.

"Hey, we're running late, so—"

The bathroom was empty. He yanked the shower curtain back. The walls were dry. Only a damp film of soapy water still coated the floor.

He hurried back into the room and looked around. There was a note by the door.

Shit. Oh, shit. Please tell me she didn't get spooked and run.

He snatched it up.

Getting coffee, it said. *Be right back!*

Reese grabbed his jeans and was still zipping them up as he strode out, bare-chested and barefoot, his heart pumping so hard he didn't feel the morning's chill. Didn't notice the sour looks of the elderly couple in the motel restaurant either.

Yes, the server had seen Daniella. She'd ordered coffee, toast and sausage and taken the food back to her room. When? Oh, at least a couple of hours ago.

Reese tore out of the restaurant. His ute was still in the lot, but he noticed that the interior light was on. He ran over to find the driver's door open. The smell of werewolf hit him. Keith Tynes and at least two others. They'd sniffed inside his ute. Smelling him.

The croak of a crow made him jump. He turned to see two fighting over a piece of toast. Two coffee cups lay beside the takeaway box, brown liquid swirling around the battling birds.

Keith had taken Daniella. She'd dropped the tray, maybe tried to run, but there was no place to run, not out here.

But why take her and let him live? Wasn't he their target?

Unless they didn't know who he was. If Reese wasn't Wes Robinson's biological son, these Pack wolves wouldn't smell the connection. Daniella was smart. If they couldn't tell, she'd claim she'd hooked up with another young werewolf, maybe say he'd taken her hostage. They'd get her out of harm's way. Then they'd come back for him. Or, better yet, wait for him to drive off into the Outback, where there'd be no witnesses.

Still, he had to call his parents. Warn them, just in case.

He ran into the motel room and grabbed his mobile. His home number rang through to the answering machine. He tried his mother's mobile. Same thing.

Reese's hands shook so hard it took him a moment to realize his phone had vibrated. He had two text messages. Both were from his mother.

Don't come home. Run, baby. Just run. Please.

The second had been sent a minute later. Three words.

We love you.

Reese took off.

—*⊘*—

HE WENT HOME. There was no way in hell he wouldn't, no matter what his mother's message said.

Any hope that nothing was wrong vanished when he saw their sheep milling about the road. Wandering, confused and lost, some dead, run off the road or just run over. The dogs were dead, too. Matt and Tam. *His* dogs, or so his father had said, bringing the balls of black, grey and white fluff into his bedroom one Christmas morning—

Reese inhaled sharply, tore his gaze away from his dogs and hit the gas, honking and weaving around the sheep.

As he approached the homestead, he could see his father's ute parked in the front yard. Driven right through his mother's garden, the driver's door still open.

Reese smelled the blood first. Then he saw it, a trail leading from the ute to the front door. Bloody drag marks on the veranda. Bloody handprints on the door.

He teetered, then lunged forward, and ran in, calling, "Mum! Dad!" He followed the bloody trail into his parents' bedroom. There was his father, facedown. Dead.

His mother sat on the floor beside him. In one hand, she clenched his father's fingers. In the other, she held the pistol his dad had given her years ago. Her blond hair fell forward. Dried blood tracks ran down her cheek. More blood pooled on the floor around her, mingling with his father's.

The werewolves must have found his father with the sheep. He'd gotten away, managing to stay alive until he'd made it back to warn her. She'd known she couldn't escape. Known they wouldn't kill her quickly. She couldn't—wouldn't—go through that again. She'd sent him the messages. And then…

Reese dropped to his knees beside them. A sob caught in his chest, lodged there, stopping his breath, and he didn't try to let it out, didn't try to breathe, didn't want to breathe. Didn't deserve to breathe.

"It's my fault," he whispered. "My fault."

"Yep, boy, it is."

He grabbed for the gun, but Keith easily wrenched it from his shock-numbed fingers. Reese scrambled to his feet. He saw the gun barrel pointed at him, and he didn't care, just dove at the man, praying he could do some damage before the bullet killed him.

No bullet came. The gun whacked Reese's forehead. He fell back. When he tried to rise, Keith hit him again and again, until he couldn't get up, just crouched on all fours, retching and dizzy.

He heard a voice and lifted his head. His eyes wouldn't focus, but he still recognized the slight figure in the doorway.

"Daniella," he croaked.

Flanking her were two big brutes. Werewolves. He could smell that. There was something else about their scent, too. Something familiar. As his head stopped spinning and he saw their faces, he knew where he'd seen them before.

The night Daniella was attacked. These were the men who'd attacked her. That's why the place had reeked of booze. Splashed around to make their scent so faint that Daniella wouldn't recognize them as werewolves. Outside werewolves Keith had hired to hurt her.

When Daniella stepped forward, the two men did nothing to stop her. There was no sign that she'd struggled against her captors. No sign that she was the least bit concerned for her safety. That was when he knew he'd been wrong. They hadn't splashed around the rum to disguise their scent from *her*.

"No," he whispered. "Daniella…"

Keith put his arm around her neck, one hand toying with her hair. "She's something, isn't she? A worthy mate to the Alpha."

Reese puked, emptying his stomach onto the floor as the werewolves laughed.

When he looked up again, he searched her face for some sign that she was just playing along. But she was clear-eyed, calm and resolute. He remembered how he'd marveled at the dichotomy in her, sweet and gentle on the outside, hot-blooded and passionate on the inside.

Dichotomy? No. The sweet and gentle side had been an act to lure in a young werewolf eager to be chivalrous, needing only a damsel-in-distress to protect.

When her gaze fell on his parents' bodies, he felt a blaze of hate so strong a growl vibrated through him. How many hours had they spent talking about his parents? All the stories he'd told, bringing them to life, showing her what amazing people they were. And now she surveyed their corpses without a spark of emotion.

"It was her idea, you know," Keith said. "Her father wants me to marry her sister. Rose is the sweet one, like her mother. Dani takes after her daddy, and Gavin thinks an Alpha needs a submissive, supportive wife. I was open to the idea of a stronger partner, though. I just needed some convincing."

Reese could figure it out the rest. The Pack had heard he was at Melbourne Uni. Daniella had volunteered to get him. She'd set up that rape scenario in the alley, knowing it would echo his mother's past, draw him to her. Then she'd confessed to being the Alpha's daughter. Make her the victim. Put him in the role of protector. Get him to talk about his parents in hopes he'd give away their location. When that failed, force his hand. Make him take her to them. Only he'd stopped at the motel. Impatient and fearing he'd change his mind, she'd gotten enough information for the Pack to find his parents. Kill them. Wait for him.

"She'll make a fine Alpha female, won't she?" Keith said. "Willing to do anything for her Pack, however unpleasant."

As the others laughed, Reese looked up at Daniella. "Oh, I wouldn't say it was all unpleasant. She sure seemed to be having a good time."

Keith tensed. Daniella opened her mouth, but Reese kept going.

"Gotta hand it to you," he said to Keith. "You're not the bludger my dad said you were. It takes a damned fine leader to put the Pack's interests in front of his own, and a damned big man to let another guy screw his bride before he gets the chance."

Daniella sneered. "Right. Like I'd let you touch me—"

"Oh, I did a lot more than touch. But I don't blame you. You want to be Alpha female, but to do that you need to marry this old guy. Had to get your fun while you could, then fake the wedding night, trust he's dumb enough and horny enough not to notice." He turned to Keith. "Don't worry, though. I was the first. And I broke her in real good."

Daniella lunged at him. Keith caught her by the back of the shirt.

"Tell me he's full of shit, Dani."

"Of course he is. He's just trying—"

"If I'm lying, tell me this," Reese said. "Why'd she shower before she met up with you guys? You could smell the soap on her, I'm sure. What did she need to wash off so badly that she'd risk waking me up to do it?"

Daniella lunged again. This time, Keith whipped her right off her feet, snarling, "He'd better be bullshitting, Dani, or—"

Reese leapt for the gun dangling from Keith's free hand. Keith recovered too fast for him to grab it, but Reese managed to smack it out of his hand. It hit the floor and skidded between the two other werewolves. Reese dove and got it.

One of the werewolves reached for him. Reese kicked him in the jaw, then leapt to his feet and raced into his bedroom. He slapped the lock shut, then grabbed his desk chair and jammed it under the handle.

The hinges groaned as a werewolf threw himself at the door. Reese aimed the gun and waited.

Keith's muffled voice said, "You break that door down and he's going to shoot you."

Not as dumb as he looked. As they conferred, Reese checked the chamber, making sure he had at least four—

There was one bullet left.

No way. No fucking way.

He took a deep breath. One bullet. He burned to use it on Daniella, but knew he'd never manage it before the others got him. And even if he did, would killing her truly avenge his parents?

There was only one way to do this, as much as his gut twisted at the thought.

He lifted the gun, took a deep breath, and yelled, "You want me dead? Here you go." And he pulled the trigger.

The gun fired. As Reese's body hit the floor, the werewolves went silent.

Then, "Shit."

"You want me to break the door—"

"No. We need them to disappear. No signs of forced entry. Find the key."

As Reese slowly rose, he rubbed the hip that had taken the brunt of his fall. He glanced at his bed. The bullet had gone into the mattress, silencing the impact.

Reese took a pocketknife from his dresser and snuck to the window. He climbed out and crept around to the barn. Keith's four wheel drive was hidden behind it. He slashed the tires, then, crawling, got to his dad's ute and did the same. He was just getting into his own ute when he heard Keith inside, saying, "He's got something jamming the door shut."

When they heard his ute roar down the lane, they raced out. Reese forced himself not to look in the rear-view mirror. Forced himself not to think of going back and facing them. Not to feel like a coward for running. He still did the last. But his mother had told him to run, and she'd been right.

Run until he was ready to come back. Until he was ready to take revenge. One day, he would be. No matter what it took, one day, he'd be ready.

Smelling Danger:
A Black Company Story | *Glen Cook*

) The Captain was suffering one of his random infatuations with training and order. The Dark Horse was almost empty. Long days left men too tired to come relax. Markeg Zhorab met me, scowling. I showed him a coin. I had an edge on the troops. They were healthy, lately, except for an odd fungus going round.

Tavern business was so feeble Goblin and Otto were playing tonk three-handed with a kid called Sharps. Sharps was one of the recruits whose need for training had set the Captain off. Sharps being in the tavern instead of learning his trade suggested that he would not last.

Zhorab brought my beer. He took my money. I settled into a chair. "I'm in."

Goblin asked, "You slither out on your belly?" He dealt. And buried me in a pathetic mess.

"I got nothing to do."

"You would have if you bothered to turn up at the free clinic."

Otto observed, "There's always something you can improve." Making mock of the Captain.

"I see you skating yourself."

"I'm teaching young Sharps the nuances of urban intelligence work."

"And your excuse?" I asked Goblin, kissing a fresh hand hopefully.

"I'm like you. I've got nothing to do."

"The standard state of affairs with him," I told Sharps. "To hear him tell. Goblin. I thought you had an apprentice to train."

"The Third? The Old Man sent him and One-Eye out on another livestock census."

Otto said, "The Captain has had a hard-on for One-Eye ever since the Limper was here. How did the little shit piss him off?"

I said, "You remember. You was there. He pulled a One-Eye. He tried to take over the op so he could scam some cash. If we'd gone along we'd all be taking a dirt nap now. That's what he did."

Goblin said, "Don't get all hot, Croaker. It came out all right. We ended up looking sweet to your honey."

I deflected talk from the Lady. "That isn't the problem. The problem is the same as it always is. One-Eye never learns."

Goblin used his soothing voice. "Your deal, Croaker."

I dealt. "This is more like it. I need to be permanent dealer."

—*C*—

"CROAKER." GENTLY OVER my right shoulder, from a man who had fallen out of a tall ugly tree and had hit every branch on the way down.

"Candy?" Why was the number three man of the Company in a dive like the Dark Horse?

"The Captain requests the grace of some of your precious time."

I exchanged looks with Goblin. Otto and Sharps had turned away in hopes of going unrecognized.

For Candy to catch up this quick meant he had left the compound before I'd gotten halfway to the Dark Horse.

I gathered my winnings, passed the deck to Goblin. Headed for the street, I asked, "What's up?"

"You'll find out." Candy did not speak again.

Native building materials were limited, other than a plentiful supply of clay-rich dirt that made a good mud brick. The compound wall, that the Captain wanted heightened and thickened, and every building wall inside, was adobe. Beautiful to those who favored brown.

A hot breeze blew strong enough to toss leaves and dust around and kick up spin devils. One baby whirlwind danced in front of the Admin building. I asked Candy, "Does that look natural?"

"No. And it was there when I left to get you. But Silent says it's harmless."

The spin devil chose that instant to race off across the parade ground. It fell apart before it got a hundred feet.

The Old Man waited behind the massive, crude table he used for a desk. He gestured at a chair facing him.

I sat. We were alone except for Candy. Candy did a fast fade.

The Captain was a bear of a man, none of him gone to fat. Nobody recalls why he was elected. He has been good as Captain. He has kept most of us alive.

He leaned back in a chair as crude as his table, made a steeple with his fingers in front of his mouth. He stared. All part of the routine.

I asked, "What's up?"

"Have Goblin and One-Eye seemed odd, lately?"

"How could anyone tell?"

"An excellent point. But the question stands. Think."

I did. And my answer stood, too. "Unless you count One-Eye developing an honest streak." The little black wizard had not gotten caught cheating at cards, or indulging in black market schemes, for weeks.

"I count it. An honest One-Eye is a One-Eye up to something. He doesn't want to attract attention."

"Sir?" He had me nervous. Once he takes official notice of anything that means he sees a problem in need of addressing.

"I'm thinking back to the Limper's visit. Recall that?"

"I could forget? I'm still trying to get the stains out of my small clothes. But we found the woman for the Lady before he messed us up."

"You men were clever. You managed that slickly. But the truth found its way back to me. Think it might get back to the Limper, too?"

"No way. Who would tell him?"

"He has no friends here. That's true. But that isn't the point. He wouldn't need to be told. He'd know. The information was inherent in your blackmail plan."

"Oh." And I knew who had ratted to the Old Man. Me. I put everything into these Annals. He does look in occasionally.

"Focus. Goblin and One-Eye. Limper took them away. They were gone two days. We forget that."

Not me. Nor Goblin, once I proved that part of his life was missing. He had no recollections of those two days, though.

"Watch them, Croaker. Though with the Limper involved anything could be a diversion. Pass the word. Somebody should be eyeballing them every second."

"They'll figure it out. It'll piss them off."

"I don't care. Maybe they'll behave. Go on. Get out."

I got, lost in wonder. That was an epic conversation for the Captain. What was he up to? Was he really worried about those idiots? Or was he trying to ramp their paranoia, hoping they would keep their chaotic tendencies in check?

We had been in Aloe a long time. One-Eye was the sort who might stir shit just because he was bored.

Then I got it. The Captain made the point but I missed it. One-Eye was not behaving like One-Eye. And that started right after the Limper's flying carpet vanished over the western horizon.

Hagop fell in beside me as I headed back to town. I asked, "You skating out of work?"

"I noticed you never stopped at the infirmary."

The notion had not occurred to me.

"You might have fifteen guys lined up."

"To get out of work, maybe."

"Guys have been complaining about feeling dizzy."

"Not to me. All I see is purple fungus, crabs, or clap. Only no crabs or clap anymore. Those temple girls are cleaner than Elmo's mom. Anybody does come up with the crabs or clap, I'll just let them scratch and squeal when they need to piss."

"That's what sets you apart, Croaker. Your boundless empathy."

THERE WAS SOMETHING wrong. Something strange in the air.

Hagop felt it, too. "Is this Aloe? Where is everybody?"

There were few people in the street. The wind was rising, hot, dry, and dirty. A dead weed, uprooted, rolled with it.

I slowed, hand on my knife, thinking wishful thoughts about weapons with a bigger bite. Hagop drifted out to my right, denying the cluster target. He drew his knife, too.

Another weed bounded in from my left, flying up to chest level. I stabbed it twice, then felt stupid. But I did not relax.

The wind went away. The weeds stopped rolling. A half dozen spin devils formed, then collapsed.

"I don't care what Silent says, that's spooky."

Hagop grunted. He was fight-ready, not thinking.

I grumbled, "There's something off. I'm worried."

"Your problem is you don't believe in Aloe."

Right. Aloe was too damned nice. The people were not determined to kill me first chance they got. They were genuinely grateful when I fixed their kids. They appreciated the peace we brought and the justice we enforced. They reported villainy when they discovered it.

The Captain had men helping with agriculture and civil engineering, not just to win the people over but because busy soldiers get into less mischief.

I confessed, "You're right. The longer this goes on, and the longer the Lady holds off dropping us in the shit, the more I'm sure the big ugly is crawling up behind me. I'm seeing things out of the corners of my eyes." I watched a spin devil cross ahead of us, then fall apart.

Hagop paid it no heed. "Fifty yards and you'll be safe, Croaker."

There it was. The Dark Horse. Almost close enough to touch. And us alone outside... Not really. I did see people when I relaxed and looked.

We hit the door to the tavern. Doom had stayed its hand again. It would gnaw my bones some other day.

"I need a hobby, Hagop."

NEITHER GOBLIN NOR One-Eye were inside. Our third wizard, Silent, was. He was in the tonk game in my usual spot. Hagop's buddy Otto had his usual seat. So did Elmo. Several soldiers watched. "Shirking, Sergeant?" I asked Elmo.

"Damned straight. The Old Man is out of his fucking mind lately."

"Could be this town is getting to him, too."

"Too?"

Hagop said, "Croaker's got the heebie-jeebies because Aloe is peaceful and friendly."

"He is a gift horse mouth-looker kind of guy," Elmo said.

Corey had the cheat seat usually occupied by One-Eye. "I'm tired of losing. Take my place, Croaker."

I must have looked troubled. Silent signed his willingness to move.

I confessed, "I'm going nuts thinking something bad has to happen. It's to where I'm wishing it would instead of piling up the awful nothing."

Elmo said, "He's lost it. He's speaking in tongues."

Otto said, "You think too fucking much, Croaker."

Elmo agreed. "It's all that education. So. What did the Old Man want?"

"He's worried about Goblin and One-Eye. He thinks the Limper did something to them."

Elmo asked, "He mention any messages from out west?"

"No." The Tower would communicate through Goblin if it was an emergency or by airborne courier if it was routine. We had not seen a flying carpet since the Limper left.

"How about from army headquarters?"

That was closer. Messages came by mounted courier.

"No. He didn't say anything about messages. Don't go calling something down on us. Let them forget we're out here."

Silent gave that sentiment a thumbs up. Then he dealt me a hand that failed to qualify as a foot.

The deck moved around the table. Pots came and went. There was little table talk.

Elmo said, "If I was the Lady and wanted to get a secret message to the Captain, I wouldn't send it through Whisper's camp."

"You know something?"

"Just brainstorming."

We all turned to Silent. Not pleased to be on the spot, he signed, *Smelling danger.*

I grumbled, "Why didn't I figure that?"

"Calm down," Elmo said. "Sit. It's your deal." He tipped a finger toward the door.

Goblin had arrived.

—⁂—

THE LITTLE WIZARD looked more like a toad than ever, crouching between Otto and Elmo. He said, "Big storm coming in from the north."

Otto said, "Weather coming in would explain why everything feels strange today."

"North?" Elmo asked. "That don't sound right. Sharps. Storms come down from the north, this time of year?"

"About once every five years. They're bad when they do."

Goblin repeated himself. "Big storm coming. Croaker, I got a sore I need you to check out."

"Now?" I was trying to drink beer, eat fried chicken, and not ruin the cards with greasy fingers.

"I'll bring it to sick call. I'm letting you know so you'll show up."

Elmo and Otto thought that was hilarious.

"I'm the hardest working man in this outfit."

"Definitely in the top six hundred and fifty," Elmo admitted. "How about you stop whining, quit eating, and play?"

The cards goddess spurned me again. "You want my seat, Goblin?"

He made a noncommittal noise. He looked troubled. Was he in pain? This might not be good.

Goblin was older than stone. He might have something really ugly. I asked, "You all right?"

"I am now. But there's a storm coming in from the north."

Otto told me, "Pick up them cards, Croaker. Let us skin you while the skinning is good."

—⁂—

I OPENED THE infirmary after breakfast. The air was heavy, humid, and still. It would be a day when nobody felt good, tempers would be short, and it would be hard to get anything done. In time, though, a hard wind came down from the north.

Three men showed for sick call, all legit. Two sported patches of purplish velvet something on their legs. I saw new cases most every day. The men did not know how they got it, it itched, and most reported having had dizzy spells a day or two before the purple developed. A fifty-fifty mixture of salt and borax, both common locally, cleared the stuff in three treatments.

It was not just a Company problem. The fungus was new to Aloe's physicians, too. It was not dangerous. There were no re-infections.

Goblin showed when I was about to give up on him. He was not comfortable, which was odd. I had been treating him for years. He had no reason to go maidenly.

"You do something you know better than to do?"

"I don't know…I think something might've been done to me."

"You said you have a sore."

He started muttering, two voices talking about him in the third person. I interrupted. "Runt. Can the silly shit. Get undressed."

He shut up. He stripped. The pasty, doughy result would bring no maidens running.

The sore was on his paunch several inches to the right of his belly button. It was an inch and a half across, round, suppurating, and stinky, though it did not smell of gangrene. It made a tricolor target. The outer ring was the hot scarlet of blood poisoning. That faded to black. A three-eighths inch dot in the center was a puddle of pus.

"How long you been letting this slide?"

"A while. It started out like a pimple. I popped it. It came back. Now it's like this."

"Might be a spider bite." There were some nasty fiddlebacks out in the bush. "I'll clean it out and run a test. You try any sorcery?"

"Slowed it down. Made it stop itching. That's all."

"Climb up here." I stretched him out on a table and got busy with a scalpel. I cleared the pus and dead flesh. I treated the hole with distilled spirits. One ounce for the outside of the man, two for his soul. Goblin yelled a lot. I gave him another two ounces for the inner man, then put sulfur and sulfur acid into the wound. I followed that with a water flush. I was about to stuff the hole with fresh lichen when I spotted a black grain down deep in the meat.

"Hang on. I found something." I went after it with scalpel and tweezers, sure it was the cause of his trouble.

I finished him up, bandages and all, and added two more ounces of medicinal spirits. "Sit up. Look at this. It was in the sore."

He scowled. "Don't look like much."

"You been somewhere where you could get stuck with a thorn or a splinter?"

"I never had a splinter fester like that. Give me one of them little bottles to put it in."

"I want you back in the morning. Meantime, find out what that is. Think about did it start when you were off with the Limper."

He gave me the hard eye. "What's going on?"

"The Captain's got you and One-Eye on the suspect list."

"The Limper thing."

"Yes. Mainly One-Eye, though. He's the one acting weird."

"He is?"

"He's stopped cheating."

"Shee-it! You're right. He hasn't tried to… His last dumbfuck idea was that freelance raid on the Temple of Occupoa. Damn! I'm starting to feel the medicine. We need to tie the little shit down and hypnotize him."

"That's an idea." I considered taking Goblin to the Dark Horse so Silent could work on him but the weather demurred.

The north wind was fierce. The sky grumbled in the distance. The air had an electric feel.

Goblin said, "I'll go sleep the storm off." He swiped a long pull of medicine.

"I might prescribe some spirits and a nap for myself."

The sky lords engaged in a savage brawl. The door and shutters rattled furiously. Rain slammed the infirmary. Water came in under the door. Major repairs would be needed. The roof leaked and mud brick walls weather fast once the stucco comes off.

Still, encouraged by self-medication, I considered visiting the Dark Horse.

The Captain flew inside behind a wild swing of the door. He grabbed hold and strained to force it shut. I went to help.

Hailstones bounded in, some an inch in diameter. They stung.

The Old Man treated himself to an uncharacteristic oath. Then, "What the hell? This isn't summer weather."

"Locals say it happens once every five years. Goblin started predicting it yesterday."

"And how did he know?"

"I don't know, boss. I do think that this isn't as bad as it can get."

A jaundiced eye. "It'll take a month to fix what's busted already."

"You wanted something?"

"Two somethings. A report on Goblin. And treatment for the purple stuff." He hoisted his right trouser leg. "It came on fast. I had an itch last night. I got this now."

"Take the pants off."

He complied. "About Goblin. What was it?"

"I thought a spider bite. When I cleaned it out I found a little black something. Maybe a splinter. Maybe a thorn. He's going to examine it. Up on the table. Don't move while the paste is drying. You suffer any dizzy spells lately?"

"Yes. Why?"

"That's the only thing people with the purple have in common."

"They get it in town, too?"

"They do. They use this same treatment."

"That feels good. The itching is gone."

A savage thunder battle broke out. The building shook. Hailstones pounded the roof. New leaks developed.

The Captain grumbled, "All this, and flash floods to come. Not good. I'll call One-Eye in. Give him a complete physical. Understood?"

"No. Am I looking for something?"

"You'll know it when you see it. If it's there."

The air was saturated. The poultice on the Captain's leg was not drying. He sat up, pressed a finger into the paste. "We're being inundated with distractions."

More thunder. Blinding shards of light got in around the shutters. A downpour of legendary violence followed.

Mud was everywhere. Water concealed the horizontal kind, rippling in the wind. Every structure in the compound had a melted look. Those not included in the recent improvement campaign were no longer habitable.

The wind remained strong but had turned dry. That helped some.

Nobody had been killed, Company or in town. Injuries were few. Property damage was terrible. People worked feverishly to save what they could.

The folk of Aloe insisted that their gods had protected them. They claimed that past storms had been much less benign.

One-Eye came back looking like death warmed over. He had left the Third with a pig farmer, unable to travel. The Third had been caught in the open during a hailstorm. He had been hammered badly.

The ugly little black man with the filthy black hat got dragged to the infirmary, struggling. He screamed and swore that he did not need to see me.

My shop had gotten rehabilitated immediately after the mess hall.

"Get naked, One-Eye."

"Croaker? What the hell? No fucking way!"

"Gentlemen, help our brother shed his apparel. Be sure to wash your hands afterward." One-Eye was not fastidious. He wore clothes till they rotted off, or till he stole something he considered fetching. What he wore now would be dangerously infested.

Candy took that beaten old hat. One-Eye tried to groin-kick him. Candy drove a fist into his gut.

One-Eye screamed like a little girl thrown into a fire. Everything stopped. One-Eye collapsed.

Damn! "Gentlemen, please continue."

They finished. They took care not to hurt One-Eye any more. He was careful not to provoke anyone else.

Goblin turned up. He might be useful. "Stand by, runt. Candy, I need him on the table."

The men hoisted One-Eye and stretched him out.

"Gods," somebody muttered.

Because of One-Eye's purple legs? Or the smell? Candy's punch had knocked a crusty bandage off a nasty wound.

"We have to knock him out before I can do anything. Goblin?"

"I got nothing better than you."

I told him what to bring me, mixed in a sweet fig wine. Meantime, One-Eye got his breath and attitude back. We had to make him drink.

Eventually, Goblin declared, "He's under."

"The rest of you guys can go. He'll be out for hours. He won't feel like scrapping when he wakes up."

Candy and crew departed. Somebody wondered why we didn't burn One-Eye's hat and clothes. Entire tribes of creepy-crawlies would be living in there. "Too much," I said. "Just wash them."

The Captain turned up. He had mud all over. He had been out working like everybody else. "What have you got, Croaker?"

"The worst case of purple yet. Both legs, ankles to mid thigh, all the way around. It's turning green and gray where it's been there the longest. He wanted to keep it secret."

"The original case?"

"That's my guess. I'm tempted to let him be so I can see the disease's full course." I scraped graying mold to see what lay beneath.

"And the belly wound?"

"Like Goblin's but farther inboard and farther gone. It looks and smells the same. He'll be a while healing."

"He didn't treat himself."

That was actually a question. One-Eye was my backup as physician. He should have taken better care of himself.

"We'll ask when he comes around."

"Deal with him, Croaker. Goblin and I will be in the corner having a word."

Ouch! Poor Goblin.

I got out more little bottles. I put pus in one and purple scrapings in others. I cleaned One-Eye's wound. I found another something that looked like a bit of thorn. "Here we go. Same thing."

The meeting of the minds took a sabbatical. Goblin was grateful. He looked like an eight-year-old saved from having to go cut a switch. The Captain studied One-Eye's wound. "Can you keep that from going bad?"

"I can. If One-Eye takes care of himself."

The Captain told Goblin, "If he croaks you go in the same hole he does." He stalked out.

I looked at Goblin. "Wow."

"Got pretty intense."

"Yes?"

"The man needs to get a sense of humor."

"He needs a life without hassles like you and One-Eye. He had a sense of humor, once upon a time." That won me no love. "You get anything from that thing I took out of you?"

"It was a spider fang. Venomous. But not a fiddleback. The festering is a diversion. The fang's mission was to carry a spell into my guts. You ruined that when you convinced me that I was missing for two days. It still went on poisoning me till you pulled it out, though."

"That adds up, sort of. To a sorcerer. Was the spell supposed to make you do something?"

"I don't know. We can ask One-Eye. He had the full effect for a whole lot longer."

There was that dim hope. I had a feeling we were caught inside a puppet show.

"Goblin, if you was seeing this with a neutral eye would you say it was Limper's style?" In the past the Limper had been a get a bigger hammer kind of problem solver. This seemed too complicated.

"What do we really know about him? Not much. But who else stands to profit? Nobody since the Battle at Charm. Unless Whisper…"

Uh-oh.

I harkened back to two people in a forest clearing years ago, when Raven and I ambushed and captured the great Rebel commander of the day, Whisper. Now Taken. Now the Lady's proconsul here in the east and our commanding general.

The other person there, then, had been a Taken trying to make a turncoat deal. The Limper. Who had suffered terribly for his treason.

Goblin said, "He might be that clever. We don't know what he hasn't shown us. We only know that he doesn't want to do anything the Lady will notice. Especially since we got hold of that rescript."

I grunted. One-Eye was set to go.

Goblin stuck with his theme. "We've never proven that the Limper is stupid, only that he's so powerful he doesn't need to be smart."

"Maybe." But I wondered.

Goblin growled, "Damn it, Croaker! There you go thinking too much again."

Days passed. Work proceeded. The Old Man kept just two hundred men in to refurbish the compound. He seemed unusually edgy. He did not get enough sleep. Some men, me included, worked in town part time. The rest helped salvage livestock and crops and got fast growing stuff into the driest ground quickly so Company and Aloe alike would not face a hungry winter.

One-Eye did not waken for five days. Goblin kept him in a healing coma.

In normal times Goblin and One-Eye spend a lot of time making like they are deadly enemies but neither one can get by without the other.

I had an epiphany. A teensy one, but an epiphany nonetheless.

One-Eye always started their squabbles. They had not had a serious dust-up since the Limper left. That had been overlooked by everyone but the Captain.

Being a precious Company intellectual resource I indulge in manual labor only when I must. I do not operate shovels or mattocks. I felt for the blacksmiths, armorers, carpenters, and Silent. Silent was draining himself trying to make fields dry faster.

The purple loved the damp. I saw dozens of new cases.

That was true in town, too. We had to hustle to find enough borax.

I staggered into the Dark Horse the evening of the sixth day of the cleanup. I had passed beyond exhaustion. I might never go back to the compound.

"Croaker?" Zhorab was surprised to see me. He had only one customer, himself. He sat at the bar in the light of one feeble lamp.

"Damn. I didn't think it would be this dead."

"Me neither. I thought people would come drown their sorrows. But they're all being civic-minded. Even me. I finish the day too exhausted to come back and pretend. What'll you have?" He oozed off his stool, eased behind the bar. "Beer, of course. With you guys it's always beer."

He drew a flagon. I put a coin down. He pushed it back. "No point." He topped up his own drink, returned to the customer side of the bar. "I blame you."

"Me? For what?"

"Not you personally. The Company. For all your energy and determination to make things right. Instead of busting their asses most folks here would rather drown their sorrows while shaking their fists at the gods."

"The gods help most those who help themselves."

"Right. I'm telling you, you guys set a bad example."

"Sorry about that, Markeg. I got to head out before I pass out."

"Hang on."

I hung, leaning on the bar, as a man struggled with his conscience. I let the battle run.

Markeg Zhorab, barkeep, had been something else, once upon a time. He was a big man with a lot of old scars. His yesterday and today were conflicted.

He had something to tell me. He would give it up, gently, voluntarily, now, or later to men who would not be polite when they asked.

"You people have been good to me, Croaker. You've been good to Aloe. You've been good *for* Aloe."

"That's what we do. We're peacemakers. Bringers of order. Prosperity follows us."

"Some don't see that. Some don't want to see that."

"Uhm?"

"They're stirring trouble because you arrested that temple girl."

"Really?" I had been surprised at the lack of outrage then. The girl had had no family. The indignation focused on our intrusion into a temple.

Zhorab said, "They want me to spy on you guys."

"Go ahead. If that helps keep you safe."

"Damn! You won't force me to be a double agent?"

Yes, Zhorab would be a double agent. But he would not know it. Every word he heard from now on would be designed for Rebel ears.

"We aren't worried. Anyone who looks can see what we're doing and why. The system goes back forever. It works."

Did I believe that? Some. Mostly I do not worry about that stuff.

Zhorag decided. "There's something else."

—◊—

"Bring me some sticks to hold my eyes open," I told Silent. "I'm surprised I stayed awake long enough to make it back." I exaggerated. Operating without sleep is a necessary skill for a soldier.

One-Eye was awake, more or less, shading toward less. I was standing by in case the little shit got overexcited.

I had told the Captain about my visit with Zhorab.

His one comment was, "We're on our own." Then he told me to watch One-Eye. I got the feeling that he considered my news good.

Silent and Goblin wanted to put One-Eye to sleep, but hypnotized. Silent had tried with Goblin before, with unsatisfactory results. They had better hopes for One-Eye.

Goblin whispered, "What was that with the Captain?"

"I came up with confirmation that the weird shit going on is all aimed at us. And we'll be on our own, dealing with it."

He pricked One-Eye with a pin. One-Eye did not respond. "Meaning?"

"Whisper could be involved. Limper, too. A Rebel operator called Cannon Shear has been ordered to destroy us. He's actually been on the job since last fall. He's Whisper's cousin, which might interest them back at the Tower."

"You came up with all that where?"

"In town. Some folks hear all the scuttlebutt."

"Grain of salt?"

"A bucket of salt. But think about this. Where did you go for two days? What did you bring back? Limper was multi-tasking when he came out here before. He was following the Lady's orders, yeah, but he was working on us at the same time. He fixed you and One-Eye so we don't dare report through you. He'd know if we tried. Right?"

Goblin tested One-Eye. "Maybe."

"Maybe his main reason for taking you off somewhere was so the rest of us would distrust you now. We have to honor the threat. But, looking at One-Eye, I'm sure there's more to it." If Company hygiene matched the Limper's abysmal standards the purple would have crippled us all by now.

"I see. I can't yell for mommy direct, we can't go through Whisper's headquarters, and there's no way to get a courier through to the Tower. You set, Silent?"

Silent nodded.

I said, "I think Whisper and Limper mean to let Cannon Shear be their revenge. They don't need to do anything. They can claim ignorance later because we never asked for help. After they eliminate Shear."

"Clever. Though it would mean that Whisper is in it deep. One fly in that ointment, though, Croaker. That rescript with the slurs to the Lady you swiped from Limper when he was here. He'll want that back, bad. It can take him down with us. One-Eye. Sweetheart. Wake up. You've just enjoyed a wonderful night's sleep."

I had tucked a copy of that damning rescript into the shirt of the girl that Limper had had to carry back to the Tower. The Lady might be watching him already. But I could not mention that while Goblin or One-Eye were suspect.

Both wizards signed for silence.

"Cannon Shear is headed our way. His initial strategy was to hit us while we were still scattered and confused by the storm."

The Rebel had expected the bad weather. This was the summer it was due. But they were more than a week late, now.

Goblin and Silent signed for silence. Who knew what ears might be listening?

Shear's force had not assembled when and where it should have. Zhorab did not know why. He reported severe confusion in the underground.

Unexpected shit can screw up the plans of the bad guys, too.

One-Eye's eye was open. He appeared rested, relaxed, amused, and ready to talk. His answers, though, were no more useful than Goblin's had been.

Goblin kept after him from various angles. It did no good.

Goblin said, "More effort went into him than into me."

"Might have to do with perceived character. Maybe we should keep him under."

Silent signed something about the Third.

Goblin nodded, started whispering about spiders. One-Eye had no use for eight-leggers except to deploy as an affliction on someone else. Goblin signed to Silent, told me, "Let's go outside."

It was dark, the sky was clear, moonless, stars in a flood beyond calculation. Goblin whispered, "One-Eye will sense that I'm not there to protect him."

So. Silent would do something with imaginary spiders, going for a backside breakthrough.

"We're past where we might need you, Croaker. Go make love to your cot."

The Captain said, "Not so fast." Great. He was back and determined that I never sleep again.

"Sir?"

"Any headway with One-Eye?"

Goblin said. "No. We were about to..."

"Finish what you're doing, then shut it down. There's something more pressing. Croaker. You said this Cannon Shear is going to come at us from the north."

"Yes, sir. He's late."

"Goblin. Which one of you manages wildlife?"

"We all do, sir."

"Who does it best? Who can send a bird to find Croaker's fabulous Rebel army? I want to know, is it late because it was smashed by the storm, too?"

"You'll want Silent."

"Get him. Now."

"Right." Goblin ducked inside.

The Captain said, "It occurs to me that your witness, though telling you what he believed to be true, may have been deliberately misled."

Goblin let out a howl. The Captain and I rushed inside.

One-Eye had gotten a hand free. He had smacked Goblin. Now he was trying to work some kind of sorcery.

The Old Man punched him in the temple, stepped round so the little wizard could see who was taming him. Then he pressed a hand down on One-Eye's face so he could not breathe.

One-Eye faded into unconsciousness. The Captain said, "Bind him. Put a sack over his head. Stuff him in an empty pickle barrel with some brine still in. Croaker, help Goblin with that, then get some sleep. Silent, you're with me." And he was gone.

I wondered, "What got into him? He don't usually get involved."

Goblin opined that a pickle barrel might be good therapy.

We outfitted One-Eye with said barrel, hammered the top into place, then went off in search of our cots.

IT WAS MIDMORNING before I wakened with what felt like a hangover. I had thirty-some clients waiting at the infirmary. Fourteen had purple in its earliest stage. Word about One-Eye's legs was out. Rumor said we stuffed him into a pickle barrel to preserve him till we discovered a cure for the advanced form of the disease.

There were malingerers, men with bruises and scrapes, and two with bad colds. There was trench foot because of all the wet.

Orders came to assemble, to inspect weapons and commence combat drills. Scuttlebutt said the Old Man wanted a straight up, force to force engagement once he located Cannon Shear.

Not good. We had not seen one of those since the Battle at Charm. Fewer than half of today's Company had seen that epic bloodletting.

Elmo was my last patient. He had a broken pinkie on his left hand. Something to do with a miscreant hammer. I asked what the Old Man was up to. "You got questions, Croaker, take them to him. All I know is, we got today to get our shit together, then we're headed for a badass brawl with a million crazed Rebels."

Master of understatement, the good sergeant. That should motivate the men to hone their blades extra sharp. They would need to cut down thirty or forty Rebels apiece.

There was a more subtle message for me. Need to know.

Sick call concluded, I went out to see what I could contribute. I should have stuck to the infirmary. I needed to get my show ready to hit the road. I had to have everything aboard the hospital wagons and secured before the order to make movement came.

Lots of things were happening at once, all in the open where any keen-eyed spy could see. Men drilled. Archers practiced, testing bows and strings. Wagons loaded. Farriers checked horseshoes. Teamsters checked harnesses, trees, brakes and traces. Wheelwrights and wain-wrights made sure the wagons were fit to roll. And a hundred men went on repairing the compound. They demolished wrecked buildings and used the salvage to strengthen the outer wall.

There were a lot of extra wagons. The Old Man had hired forty from town, with two teamsters to handle each. I am sure he counted on some of those men to be spies.

He materialized behind me. "You ready to go, Croaker?"

"Just about to get started, sir."

"Good. First thing you need to do is roll that pickle barrel into Admin. Park it beside your work table."

That would be the table where I am supposed to record these chronicles. Which I use maybe a quarter of the time. I prefer the privacy of the infirmary. The stuff over there was weeks behind. "Shit! I forgot the Annals over there! The storm..."

"They're fine. All sealed up, waterproof. Thank the clerks when you take the barrel in. You want to fuss, worry about the stuff you got here."

WE DID NOT gag One-Eye before we kegged him. He had unkind things to say as I rolled him over to Admin, stood the barrel up to walk it through the doorway, then tipped it and rolled it on into my corner. The little ingrate kept forgetting that it was me who saved him from having to slosh around in ten gallons of pickle juice. He might have drowned when I was rolling him.

One of the clerks asked, "How about you shove that under the table, out of the way?"

"It won't fit."

"Leave it laying down. Here. I'll help you."

He did. I stepped back. I hoped the Old Man knew what he was doing. Predecessors had tried everything to tame One-Eye, with no success.

I did not feel bad for the little shit. He brought these things on himself.

"About my papers…"

"Taken care of."

"But…" My work table was the usual mess.

"Sir, you need to prepare your wagons. The mounted vedettes are leaving now."

True. I did not have forever to get ready. "But…"

They practically gave me the bum's rush, moving me out of there.

A SOLDIER SHOVED inside the infirmary. He held the door. Two more followed with a litter. "Damn!" If I had to saw a leg off, or anything major, I would have to unpack again. "What's this?"

Silent and Goblin followed the stretcher bearers. The human toad explained, "The Third. We need him waked up so we can ask questions."

The soldiers made themselves scarce. They wanted nothing to do with what happened next. Wizardry would be involved. The stretcher was on the floor. I needed the patient on my examining table. "All right, boys. Time for heavy lifting. What's his problem?"

Goblin said, "Bad case of attempted suicide complicated by advanced stupidity and wanton disregard for personal hygiene."

I saw the slash marks on his wrists. They ran crosswise and were not deep. The blade had not been sharp. He had not been committed.

"Let's get him restrained."

While they handled that and I prepared smelling salts the Captain invited himself to the show. "Why didn't you strip him?"

I frowned.

"You stripped One-Eye and Goblin."

I had had help in one case and cooperation in the other. "You're the boss. Untie him, guys." I pulled clothing off, had the Third tied down again.

I checked his outside. Other than a bad case of the purple and complementary fungi in several places, plus prime herds of livestock, I found nothing unusual. He smelled as bad as One-Eye had but did not have a similar wound.

The Captain asked, "Why did he cut himself?"

I handed over the smelling salts. "You can ask him in a minute." I cleaned and treated.

"Make sure he gets a bath when we're done here."

The Third responded to the salts. Sluggishly. The Old Man slapped his cheeks. "How many fingers, kid?"

"Free?"

"Close enough. Ask questions, gentlemen. Let me know what you get. I have to make sure the Lieutenant has the vanguard moving."

I muttered, "They're really doing it."

Goblin told me, "There's a rumor that Cannon Shear is a hoax. That this is all just an exercise."

"Yeah? I heard one about the Lady being on her way to help."

Goblin grinned at Silent. "Our little boy is maybe gonna get him some nooky."

"You're here to question the kid, runt."

"He's all touchy about it, too."

Sometimes they make me so mad. I missed half the questions. The thrust, though, had to do with what One-Eye was up to while he was out in the country.

I was not surprised to learn that he kept ditching the Third and skating out on doing the livestock inventories. He would have done that in the best of times. The man was bone lazy. He did only what he had to to get by.

The Third thought the runt might have been up to something this time but had no idea what. He knew only that One-Eye never stopped bitching about having to stay away from the compound.

"And that wasn't the usual stuff," the Third said, still groggy. "He didn't whine about missing out on women or drink, or even the tonk games. He just thought he belonged at the compound. But he always looked puzzled when I asked why."

"What about spin devils?" I asked. And harvested baffled looks all round. "You know, wind witches. Little baby whirlwinds."

"They wasn't any that I saw."

Silent shook his head, signed something. Goblin told me, "You only get those where the ground is bare and dry, Croaker. In a lot of direct sun. Not in pasture country. Nowhere now, till the world dries out."

So. Maybe Silent was right about them being harmless. I do get distracted by side issues.

"Do your worst."

Those two rascals worried the boy from nine different angles. An hour later they still had nothing useful. He did not know, or had been made not to know. In the end we had only what everybody always knows about One-Eye. He was up to something. Probably.

I got the Third all cleaned, treated, and bandaged. He would get to skate out of the coming campaign. A racket outside told me the main body was moving out. I had only minutes left. "So why did you try to kill yourself?"

The Third's face went blank, then pruned into a frown. "I didn't."

I lifted a wrist to show the ugly cut.

Goblin said, "The pig farmer said you did that. He admitted that he didn't actually see it happen, though."

A grim thought hung in the following silence.

One-Eye?

The muleteers on my wagons yelled at me to get my lard ass moving if I did not want to walk.

We made a scant nine miles. Evening sick call produced a dozen customers, most with blisters. The Captain strolled through the camp, looking smug as he took reports. Once he visited my station everyone knew new physical fitness requirements would be on the way.

Interesting. The men were less worried about the coming fight than about possible fatigue marches later.

I blame the Old Man. He had them convinced that they were invincible. Of course, what was gospel to them leaked into the broader social environment. The locals believed it, too.

Their blisters treated and my body fed I figured I would see if Goblin had gotten anything more from the Third. I could not find him. The Old Man had him and Silent looking for Cannon Shear using owls. Then I had to go back to work.

A pioneer squad needed help. Five were injured, two of them on litters. "What happened?"

"We got into it with some wasps." The squad leader had a thick Hanfelder brogue.

I knelt beside a litter. The man there groaned. His face and hands were covered with sting welts. He could not open his eyes. I worried that he might have been blinded.

The man on the other litter was almost as bad.

"Did you beat the nest with sticks?"

The squad leader grumbled, "That idiot Marker dropped it." He said no more. He had received a warning look. They had been up to something.

I asked, "Paper wasps or bald-face hornets? Do you know?" Both made nests that hung from branches. Both were common. Both had nasty stings and a hair trigger temper. Bald-face hornets, sometimes mistaken for bumblebees, were the worst. They were vindictive. They would hunt you down.

Unlike bees, both nasty bugs could sting you over and over.

"Paper wasps."

"You were lucky, then. Bald-faces probably would have killed you."

The Captain stood a few yards away, considering the casualties, glowering. He disapproved of people getting hurt in the field. Not only would a sword fall out of the line, another man might have to stand down to care for him.

I treated the fools. The poultice I used was a cousin to that used for treating the purple. No new cases of that had been reported.

One choice left. Keep these men here or send them back. I looked up, meaning to ask the Captain. He was gone. And still no sign of Goblin or Silent. Elmo was hard at it being an infantry platoon sergeant. There was no recreation going on. Men not on duty or asleep were fixing gear or sharpening weapons.

I went back to my wagons. The genius waspnappers were gone.

I finished my chores, wrapped up in my blanket, fell asleep to the joyful singing of feasting mosquitoes. I needed to recruit some apprentices. I needed somebody to bark at when I was in a bad mood.

Morning comes early in the field. Everyone was afoot, fed, packed, hitched, harnessed, and ready to roll by the time there was light enough to travel. I dealt with bruises and scrapes during the day. Nobody complained about dizziness or itching. Nobody fumbled a wasps' nest. We climbed a long hill covered by scruffy hardwoods. We descended the far slope, piled up at a rickety bridge for two hours while the engineers reinforced it. There was no point looking for a ford. The water was still high and in a hurry. The countryside, normally mostly brown this time of year, had turned exuberantly green.

We climbed a longer, less steep hill populated by small, scraggly groves and singleton oaks. This was grazing country. Several flocks were visible in the distance, along with other livestock. Initially, I supposed their herders were taking advantage of the new grass, but then realized that they were all headed toward the thicker woods.

Peasants were taking their wealth into hiding. And they were headed in our direction, away from their declared liberators. Interesting.

So. Cannon Shear was real. And he was ten days late for his appointment with destiny.

I had not been convinced before.

We make things up all the time and put them out so our enemies will worry.

The long far slope descended to a stream wider and deeper than the one we had crossed earlier. The pasture land boasted numerous limestone outcrops, brush-choked gullies and ravines, and small stands of scrub oaks not connected with denser woods out to left and right. Someone had tried to establish vineyards down slope but had given up. The view northward, beyond the river, was vast, a green plain featuring villages, satellite farming communes, and a lot more undulating pasture. In the extreme distance a dust cloud partially masked remote hills. It would take a large gang to create that.

Our officers knew what was expected. Men began digging in before I was done gawking. Clearly, need to know had not included the medical staff.

Candy came by with a map. He showed me where he wanted me to set up, behind a screen of trees to our left, on the ridgeline, not far from the road we would use if we had to run.

That map was finely detailed. It was not new. More proof that the medical staff was out of the loop.

Once my hospital was set up I went snooping.

The Captain had been way ahead of me. He had been ready for this. His chosen ground, with the trenches, pitfalls, tangle foot, sharpened stakes, and whatnot added, could not have been more favorable. The Rebel would have to start by coming at us across two bridges, one stone, the other rickety wood a half mile upstream.

The Old Man could not expect Cannon Shear to come straight at us, whatever his numerical advantage, could he?

I THINK WELL of my brain. I *am* smarter than most. It is embarrassing to have to admit that I charged into the wrong story at the beginning. While I obsessed about spin devils, common summer phenomena round Aloe, and worried incessantly about the purple, so easily treated, and about One-Eye, that clumsy bear we call the Captain lumbered down his own path, outthinking everybody.

The Company prides itself on using deception, distraction, trickery, or occasional assassination, to avoid combat or to make an enemy think wrong if we do have to fight. Mostly the wizards handle that, making people see things that are not there. They love to conjure specters to make the Company look bigger and badder.

Specters do not contribute much once the action begins.

Though given hints and told outright I never really understood that similar tools could be used against me. Gentle nudges at the outset fixed my thinking in a rut. I saw things that were not there as well as what was there in the wrong light.

I was still in that wrong space, trying to separate the imaginary from the real, as Cannon Shear's force moved toward the two bridges. I saw few obvious specters and fewer living and breathing men than ought to be the case on our side.

I refused to believe that the Rebels, less numerous than predicted, meant to force those bridges under concentrated missile fires. Something was off about all this, from both sides.

The oddness on my side irked me. I am the Annalist. I need to know.

—Ɑ—

WHILE WE SPLATTERED Cannon Shear, nearly damming that river with Rebel flesh, he kept us fixed, twenty-one miles out, while a second column hooked in on Aloe from farther east.

The key moments happened elsewhere. I witnessed nothing. There was a reason. Somebody smarter than me worked it out.

If you were the Limper, most badass of the Taken, had a hard-on for the Company, and wanted to keep tabs from afar, what individual would you target? What fool always has his nose into everything because he has to know so he can record it in his precious Annals? You are correct, sir! Right in one. Croaker. Involuntary traitor gifted with induced paranoia and ensorcelled quills that let our little persecutor know every character they scribbled, wherever he happened to be.

The Old Man distracted, mislead, and mislaid me all the way, though.

From now on I'll go into every encounter with him mumbling: "Don't judge this guy by what he lets you see."

For events at the compound I rely on the questionable testimony of a few frightened operators who observed by the light of a sliver of moon, plus my own exemplary imagination.

—Ɑ—

A BLACK RECTANGLE drifted in over the west wall, settled noiselessly into the deep shadow beside the Admin building. A short blob of darkness entered the wan moonlight and scuttled to the building door. It dragged one leg. It paused, listened, but only for a moment. It knew it was not expected and it had sent a sleep spell ahead to neutralize any stay behinds.

Inside, a word and gesture created a ball of ivory glow. It floated a foot above the Limper's head. It shed just enough light to let him avoid furniture moved since his previous visit.

He felt something. A pool of the power of sorcery, quiescent. One of the Company sorcerers, asleep, tempting him to murder. Why not? The Annalist would discover the loss of the critical evidence anyway, unless the Rebels killed him.

He did not count on those idiots to do their part, out there, in Aloe, or here at the Company compound. The current class were worse than amateur.

He could not treat himself to the pleasure of a kill. The sorcerers were critical to the execution of the plan. And they would not live long afterward, anyway.

These wicked Company men were clever. They would have copies of the rescript cached somewhere. The suborned wizards would deal with those, once the original was safe. He would spell them orders through the spider fangs, which would kill them soon enough. But he *had* to have that original document. There was no way it could be brushed off as a forgery. The damning insult to the Lady was scrawled in his own hand.

The spark ahead stirred as though sensing his presence. There it was. Under the Annalist's table. A barrel, on its side, rocking. Two more barrels stood close by, upright.

One-Eye, then. The key to it all. Why was he not at the battle site?

They had put their best wizard into a barrel instead? Why? That was insane. Maybe the answer was in the Annalist's notes. Or soon would be. Meantime, this had to be done fast. It was a long flight to his station. He had to get back before he was missed.

He shifted the nearest upright barrel. It was not empty but its contents did not weigh much. He could dump them, fill the barrel with the Annalist's papers, then sort everything out later. He could be headed west moments later.

Otto and Hagop, shielded against sleep spells, slipped up to the Limper's flying carpet. Otto lifted a corner. The frame was almost weightless. Hagop slipped under. By the light of a glow weaker than the moonlight he attached a round wooden container four inches in diameter and two feet long. He pulled a string on one end, then got out of there. Both men headed for town, trotting to join others who had not gone out to meet Cannon Shear.

The barrel under the table rocked. The man inside wanted to make it roll. It could go nowhere because two other barrels blocked it. Limper whispered, "I'll have you out in a minute." Not meaning a word. Tools for seating and unseating a barrelhead lay on the Annalist's table. "But first…"

Limper popped the head out of the nearest upright barrel. It was filled with gray paper maché globs. Those should dump easily.

A thud. A flash. A bang. The barrel hopped a foot off the floor, came down hard and fell over. Limper caught the slightest whiff of the initiating spell.

There was another one! There, in the dark! Overlooked because of the smell of the man in the barrel! Ambush!

The wasps and hornets came awake, freed from the sleep spell.

They tore him a new asshole, Silent signed. *Tore him a whole new set. Even bundled up the way he always is. But he kept on stuffing that barrel, screaming worse than the Howler ever did. The hornets stayed with him till he was a hundred feet up.*

There was a lot of laughter. The Captain had pulled a good one. He had begun laying the groundwork after the Limper's last visit, when he noticed the little shit messing with my quills and inks.

Still, not everything had gone the way he wanted.

He opened the barrel! I still cannot believe he did that. I thought the bugs would have to get at him through the fill hole, fighting each other all the way.

I looked across at One-Eye. He was not thrilled, not least because somebody had washed his clothes while he was confined, but also because he now stank of pickle instead of like an idiot a year overdue for a bath.

I went to get the Captain's story. "Why so glum, sir?"

"I miscalculated. Understating it big-time. Whisper didn't do what I expected. I know she had to be in on it. I thought the Lieutenant would chase his Rebels right into the force she would try to sneak in behind us."

There had been no such force. The ambush of the second Rebel column did nothing but scatter panicky amateurs.

"She isn't stupid, Captain. She went down with the Limper once. Never again."

He shrugged. "Whatever, it was a good few days' work, whether I'm happy or not."

"Look on the bright side. There hasn't been a new case of the purple reported in three days."

To GET BACK to where he was supposed to be the Limper had to over-fly the deadly strangeness of the Plain of Fear. As always, giant flying things rose to contest the passage of an outsider. Limper ducked, darted, and maneuvered. Getting through was not difficult for one of the Taken. They could fall back on their sorcery if their situation got too tight.

All that motion caused the contents of the tube beneath Limper's carpet to slosh and mix. One especially violent jig finally shook loose a jammed trigger.

The explosion destroyed the fore half of the carpet. The Limper was making a shrieking climb at the time, twenty-three hundred feet above ground. He arced one way. A barrel followed a similar trajectory. Bits of carpet and frame, aflame and otherwise, began to flutter down.

The situation was tight enough for the Taken to call on his sorcery. He cursed all the way to the ground.

The damned Black Company had done him wrong again.

He might not be able to cover this up. He was going to be way late for work.

$\mathscr{T}$HE DAPPLED THING |

William Browning Spencer

$)$ WHEN *HER GLORY of Empire* rolled out of the jungle and stopped at the edge of the black river, two dozen green and yellow parrots exploded from the trees. Sir Bertram Rudge, unsealing the topside hatch, emerged in time to see the birds blow across the river like gaudy silks, but the sight stirred no aesthetic shivers within his stout frame. He and his team were heading into the wild heart of the jungle, and he had no time for beauty's wiles. This savage land had swallowed Wallister's party, which included Lord Addison's granddaughter, Lavinia, a girl of twelve when Rudge had last seen her and now, by all accounts, a willful and beautiful young woman who had shocked high society and sundered a dozen foppish hearts when she left London to cross the Atlantic on the *Cloud King*, a chartered zeppelin, in the company of Henry Wallister, famous explorer, member of the Royal Geographical Society, and, according to Lord Addison, a thorough scoundrel.

"Lavinia's a good girl," Lord Addison had declared. "Spirited, not utterly without brains, but a fool for a rogue like Wallister." His Lordship, face red, eyes maddened by the hearth's fire, fixed Rudge with a wild stare. "Bring her back to me, Bertie. By force, if you must."

WITH THE OPENING of the hatch, a railing of gleaming steel pipes rose up from the silvery surface of the great sphere and snapped into place with a hydraulic exhalation. Rudge gripped the railing and leaned out to study the river below. Here was a test he didn't relish.

"Hot down there!"

Rudge turned at the voice and saw that Tommy Strand, the expedition's naturalist, had come up from below and was wiping his face with a cloth. A hank of his blond hair fell forward and, in profile, he looked like an addled cockatoo. The day was dying, and a large bird swooped low over the river. This inspired Strand, who spread his arms wide, something a cockatoo might do in preparation for flight, but this flight, alas, was merely verbal. He recited:

"I wandered lonely as a clown
Whose heart of red is filled with rue,
When all at once I saw an owl,
A bird of nighttime, nocturnal,
Up in the sky and all a-hooting,
A lovely balm for my heart's soothing."

Why, Rudge wondered, were supposedly educated young men so often inclined to declaim in meter? Rudge recognized the quoted poet, the insufferable Wadsworth, one of the fashionable Lake Poets (although where, one might ask, were the corresponding numbers of River Poets, Pond Poets, Bog Poets?).

Strand continued to bellow out Wadsworth, and Rudge unfurled the rope ladder he'd brought from below, secured it to two of the steel posts, tested his knots with a yank, and methodically descended the ladder. He was huffing a bit by the time his boots met the mud, but still—and the thought pleased him—steady on his legs, hale and hearty (by God!) in a world where so many of his old comrades were content to drowse in armchairs, poor old sweats muttering about some bloody wog, some worthless *apke wasti*.

On the ground, where a fishy smell contended with the green odor of rotting vegetation, Rudge walked to the very edge of the water and looked down. He saw no piranhas, no fer-de-lance, no giant anaconda, no cunning crocodile. The only animate life he observed was the vile cloud of black flies and mosquitoes that rose up from the mud to greet him. He tried to ignore them, as he had done in a younger life in another jungle, but the years of his retirement had drained some of his stoicism. He swatted and cursed the mindless buggers, then turned to regard the rescue vehicle.

Her Glory of Empire was a vast silver sphere, easily big enough to contain several row houses, and it burned in the twilight, pink and gold, with an authority that reduced the surrounding elements (the clutter of greenery, the outlandish verdancy of the jungle) to a shadowy backdrop. The machine was presently feeding, a strange business that Rudge found endlessly fascinating. Great mechanical tentacles, armored like the carapace of a millipede, stretched to the tree tops, clutched branches, and broke them with its segmented strength or severed them with small spinning blades. The thin, tapered end of a tentacle would wrap itself around a leafy bundle and carry it to an open hatch that glowed with ruddy light. The furnace within could devour any sort of vegetation by subjecting the green and unpromising material to a series of processing containers—rather like the multiple stomachs of a cow—before turning the altered material into a blazing motive force.

Her Glory of Empire was the fevered brained-child of the eccentric and fabulously wealthy Hugh Edmonds, whom Rudge had met only once, briefly, when Lord Addison had driven Rudge to Edmonds's estate. There they had found the estate's master in avid conversation with one of his gardeners.

Since Edmonds was a notorious recluse, Rudge's friends would ask what the man was like, and, in the privacy of his club, Rudge would respond by saying that the man was well-spoken, erudite, somewhat small and frail with an unusually large penis, a description that gave some people pause. One had to understand that Hugh Edmonds was a devout Christian who believed that hiding one's nakedness was "giving in to the serpent." He never wore clothes while at home.

Edmonds was a self-taught scientist, a not uncommon condition among English madmen of independent means, and had been the architect of this immense traveling rotundity, discovering new principles for the science that informed it, and offering detailed instructions for its manufacture.

The machine had not been designed expressly to rescue Lord Addison's granddaughter, but Providence had nicely timed its completion to correspond with that task, and this was its maiden voyage.

Rudge watched as the furnace hatch closed. The several tentacles retreated into the body of the sphere, and iris-like portals closed behind them. Rudge turned his back on the vehicle and regarded the sunset. *I'm too old for this*, he thought.

—⌐—

WHEN RUDGE CLIMBED back down into the bowels of the vehicle, he found Mallory already strapped into the pilot's chair, checking the various gauges and wrestling his arms into the appendage lacings. A red-faced, whiskered man, Mallory was always slightly damp and became quickly soaked with perspiration when exerting himself. He wore—and apparently slept in—a dirty linen outfit that looked to be of some unknown military lineage, with mud-spattered puttees wrapping his calves and even his forearms, as though he had planned to mummify himself but had been distracted by other, more pressing matters.

It was hot in the enclosed space, and only two of the duct fans were running. Rudge could hear the furnace rumble and the hiss of pipes as valves obeyed the engineer's commands.

This circular floor space, with its bolted chairs and equipment, comfortably accommodated its five travelers. Had the expedition contained twice that number, it would have been crowded indeed. Returning with Wallister's group might prove difficult, Rudge thought—if, of course, Wallister and his party were still alive. Rudge was not a pessimist, but he'd lived long enough to know that hope had to be kept on a short leash.

Six weeks ago a column of smoke had drawn the attention of the denizens of a nearby mission, and after a day's trek into the forest, the mission's priest and his companions had come upon a clearing and the fire-ravaged remains of a zeppelin. Since the skeletal frame was still intact, the priest concluded that the conflagration was not the result of a crash. No charred corpses were discovered amid the airship's remains. Various scorched artifacts revealed its identity as that of the luxury cruiser *Cloud King*. All of the passengers were missing, their whereabouts a source of much conjecture. Perhaps Wallister's group had found refuge with one of the tribes to the north of the Negro, although the priest thought it more likely they had been captured or killed by hostile, deep-forest denizens he referred to as the Yami. "Crazy peoples," the priest had said. "Eat you up. Of your head, they make a jar."

Rudge had heard stories of the Yami or a similar tribe inhabiting the same region. These natives of the deep rain forest filed their teeth to points, fought constantly with neighboring tribes and with members of their own tribe, and taught their children violence—a young boy who beat his sister was praised. They ate the dead.

—*a*—

"ALL RIGHT, THEN," Mallory said, his voice returning Rudge to the moment. "Here we go."

The machine began to rumble and shiver as Rudge took his seat and strapped himself in. From his position behind the engineer, Rudge could see the panel of instruments and the glass portal that offered a view of weeds and mud and the river beyond.

The outer shell, the hull, began to move and the rat-scrambling sound of the steel brushes that generated a weak Faraday Effect as they spun between the inner and outer shells set Rudge's teeth on edge. Now the view portal flickered, no longer a direct view of the landscape beyond but an ever-changing image retrieved by mirrors from ports that opened and closed as the behemoth rolled forward.

The floor swayed some, like the deck of a ship in open sea, but it was marvelously steady considering that portions—and sometimes the entirety—of the outer hull was moving, a gleaming, rolling monstrosity that thundered down the muddy bank and into the rushing black water. Directly, water spit and hissed from the two open fan ducts, and Jon Bans, the fifth member of the crew, slapped the portals closed with a curse, his tall, seaman's frame contorted over the walking cage that allowed him to move easily across the floor. Rudge felt his lungs contract in the visceral certainty that the meager bubble of air that now sustained them beneath the river would be breached by black torrents.

The weak radiance created by the Faraday Effect made blocky shadows of the men within. The view portal was useless now, and they would have to depend on the compass and the questing touch of mechanical tentacles to guide them to the other side.

"I'm sending some air tubes up," Mallory said. He pulled several levers and a hollow clattering announced the rise of the tubes. He studied the dials, then nodded. "That should do her." He turned his head and shouted to Jon Bans. "Open four, five and six above and the furnace feeds."

The fans spit briefly and then the cool air above the river blew through the cabin, and Rudge felt the tightness go out of his chest.

Now they moved without the rolling hull, dragged forward by grapples and propelled by bundles of uneven, jointed pipes that sprouted from the base of the vehicle to produce a slow, lumbering motion, a falling forward, then catching, then falling again that translated to the ship's floor as a lazy, rocking-horse gallop.

In the blackness, time congealed. Rudge became convinced that they were making no progress at all, that they were stuck in mud, rocking back and forth, like some poor idiot who has lost his way in the night and seeks to console himself by hugging his knees and aping a pendulum or the clapper in a bell.

Something exploded, echoing in his skull. Booming, scratching, rending sounds sent Rudge's heart racing as he imagined some monstrous water beast attempting to rip open this hard-shelled egg and lap up the life within.

"It's all right!" Mallory shouted. "It's a submerged tree."

Stolid Mallory, sweat beading on his forehead, moved his arms as though fondling a ghost, and external tentacles obeyed his pantomime. The vessel clambered against the current, and the sunken branches grasped for them with a scorned lover's desperation. Rudge tried to picture it: a drowned tree wrestling with a mechanical squid whose belly was full of people (soft flesh over breakable bones) and all in black murk, an invisible battle raging, meaningless and unimaginable to some beast or savage gazing at the river's roiling surface.

So Sir Bertram Rudge contemplated the unutterable strangeness of his situation, and this acknowledgment of his insignificance and vulnerability calmed him, as it always did at such times.

THEY LUNGED AND grappled, fought to escape, were hopelessly mired, and then, in an instant, as though the struggle had been a game, a tug-of-war with a giant who had abruptly lost interest and abandoned his end of the rope, they were free and rising into shallower water, and aground again.

There was little light in the sky by then, but they traveled on, not wishing to camp too close to the river. That night, all but Mallory pitched their tents outside the vehicle and slept swaddled in mosquito netting, weapons by their sides. They might have been safer within *Her Glory of Empire*'s armored orb, where no wild beasts could find them, but, for the moment, their hearts were done with dank, enclosed enterprises, and they preferred to take their chances on the ground.

Snug in his tent, Rudge reached out to douse the kerosene lamp and a small round object bounced twice as though dropped from the ceiling. Rudge jerked his hand back, wary of spiders and other stinging, biting vermin. Leaning forward, he saw a tiny pale frog. He moved his hand slowly over it—with no thought except to test his reflexes—and snatched it. He slowly uncurled his fingers and looked at the pop-eyed creature. It was walnut-sized, its skin transparent so that you could see the organs within. Turning the creature toward the light, Rudge could see its tiny beating heart, the twist of its intestines (like a water-drowned worm), and its fragile green bones. Rudge leaned forward, stretched his arm out and under the tent flap, and opened his hand. The creature leapt away, and Rudge pulled his empty hand back inside the tent and lay down again. *You are far from green England's cozy hearth*, he thought.

IT WAS THE dry season, a relative term, and Rudge cursed a so-called *dry* season that could grow mold on a man's skin and generated a pale mist in which monsters seemed to lurk.

Their progress through this world was loud and violent. *Her Glory of Empire* was not designed for stealth. It moved by thrashing and saw-ing its way through the jungle, pulling trees down or climbing them like an ungainly spider until they bent beneath its weight. Sometimes monkeys would scream from the trees, following the vehicle for days, hooting with outrage or, perhaps, a kind of carnival glee, delighting in destruction, as Rudge had seen men do in the frenzy of war.

He was fascinated with *Her Glory of Empire*, but there was some-thing about the machine that he distrusted. It was, Rudge thought, against Nature, by which he did not mean that it was some kind of Devil's work, but that, being fashioned by immutable physical laws, and, consequently, itself a creature of Nature, its destruction of the natural world seemed a perversity, a subverting of those laws God had stamped on His Creation. Rudge could not have explained this to anyone, and if, somehow, he *had* managed to voice his reservations, no one would have taken him seriously. They would have been amused, would have seen him as some foolish old codger at odds with inevitable change.

Well, he was old and set in his ways. Maybe that was all there was to it.

On the eleventh day of travel beyond the site of the burned zeppelin, they had a bit of good luck. They came upon a small village of round huts, a village they might have passed if the cacophony of their passage hadn't attracted the natives, who were friendly and showed some acquaintance with civilization, even to the point of wearing clothing and emulating Jesus by pushing thorns into the palms of their hands. Rudge's manservant, Jacobs, had a gift with languages, or, more precisely, communication itself. A small, swarthy man, Jacobs possessed a gray explosive mustache that suggested belligerence, but he was, in fact, as calm as a cat, and capable of getting the meaning from any human being with vocal chords.

After talking at length to the village elder, Jacobs was able to relate the good news. Wallister's party had passed this way heading north. "He says he warned them about the Yami, but they seemed unperturbed on that score," Jacobs said. He added, "The old fella says he thought they might have been earth or water spirits because they didn't know things that even a child knows."

Rudge asked what that would be.

"He said they didn't know that they could die."

THE NEXT DAY, they ate lunch in a small clearing with a bright stream running through it. The stream was bordered by thin pale-green trees and lush black-green ferns. When Rudge went off to relieve his bladder by the edge of the forest, tiny blue butterflies fluttered around the stream of his urine and settled on the wet grass as though he were spilling a rare elixir. When he returned, Rudge found Tommy Strand sitting by the brook. Strand started declaiming immediately, as though Rudge's presence required it. It was another poem:

"Glory be to God for dappled things,
For skies of couple-color as a brinded cow,
For rose-moles all in stipple upon trout that swim;
Fresh-firecoal chestnut-falls, finches's wings;
Landscape plotted and pieced, fold, fallow and plough…"

It went on like that for a while. Rudge thought the verse was apt enough: a jungle was definitely dappled, light tumbling through the leaves, water, always moving, the light within it alive, mottled and animate. But it was a stretch to compare the sky to a cow. Poets often did that: started out well enough but then let go of the reins, let language get the best of them in their zeal.

Strand said the poem was by a fellow named Manly Hopkins. Rudge didn't think of poets as being all that manly, except for that Kipling fellow who had some grit in his lines and knew how to tell a story.

ANOTHER NINE DAYS of travel were consumed in slow progress northward. The jungle was crisscrossed with a hundred nameless tributaries, none deep enough to require harrowing underwater descents but the sum of them creating a daunting maze that made *Her Glory of Empire's* steady compass-guided route seem arbitrary and futile. Morale was suffering, and the spongy, sodden ground—dry season, indeed!—required that Rudge and his men spend their nights within the vehicle. In this forced, uncomfortable proximity, it was no surprise that Jon Bans and Tommy Strand got in a scuffle, nor was it any surprise that the older, hard-muscled sailor won. The manifestations of Strand's defeat were minor (a bloody nose, a black eye, a swollen lip) but Rudge couldn't let the fight pass unremarked. He tried to sort out the altercation's cause.

Apparently Strand had objected to the way Bans had referred to a woman, calling her, among other things, a "doxy." Bans, in his defense, said that the woman he was referring to was his own wife. He loved his wife but felt that he was better acquainted with her than some young dandy stuffed full of fairy dust whose sole knowledge of women came from reading love poetry (which, everyone knew, was designed to seduce women not to portray them accurately) and who had no business, in any event, instructing a man on the proper way to describe his own wife.

When the two cooled off, Rudge sat them down and addressed them solemnly. "I will not tolerate fighting," he said. "We are on a rescue mission, and personal differences must be put aside." He added, wistfully, "There was a time when I could have had the both of you shot." There: he was getting nostalgic again, an old man's affliction.

As more days passed, the sun began to send long shafts of light down through the trees, yellow light like celestial grain pouring from some angelic silo, and Rudge felt that God was surely in His Heaven and looking out for those denizens of His most cherished island, dear emerald England.

God does not, however, wish anyone to lie too easy in his hammock, complacency being a sin that can easily escalate into pride. The next day, around noon, just after he'd finished his lunch and was folding his tarp, Rudge looked up to see a man, naked except for a black patch above his groin, poised between two trees not ten yards away and staring at Rudge over the sharp stone point of an arrow.

Civilization had dulled Rudge's survival instinct, and, instead of taking immediate evasive action, he shouted, "I say!" and might have added something equally inane like "That won't do!" The arrow snatched the folded tarp from his hands and pinned it to a tree.

The old warrior within him was roused by the attack. Rudge knew better than to turn and flee and take an arrow in the back. He charged the man and slapped soundly into him before the savage had another arrow notched. Down they both went. Rudge was roaring now: "Bloody bastard!"

The savage was not a big man, but he was strong and feral-fast and hissed like a snake and his body was slick with sweat or animal oils, and Rudge couldn't pin him. Rudge had knocked the man down, and they both rolled on the ground, thrashing amid the wet leaves and mud, and doing this for an inordinately long time, exchanging blows, making pig noises and grunts of menace, and then the savage was on top of him, his knees slamming into Rudge's chest and Rudge couldn't catch his breath, and he saw that the hand raised above him held a sharp killing-stone, and Rudge raised his forearm to block the blow.

THE MAN LEANED back slightly. Rudge could see the swollen scars that marked the man's cheeks and the way his eyes suddenly widened, and Rudge felt his own lungs gasp for air as the weight of his attacker seemed to lift.

The savage uttered a sharp cry, bird-like and quick, and he floated away, rising up into the trees, squeezed magically small by perspective, twisting and kicking and howling now, and Rudge saw the thick, gleaming coil that encircled the man's chest and fell away like a burnished silver vine, and he swung his head to follow the arc of the silver cord, his eye still sorting details while the logic of what he saw lagged behind. The great sun-struck curve of the shining mirrored orb showed his own reflection, and he saw where the tentacle protruded from the vessel, and his eye traced it back again and up to where the man squirmed high and small in the canopy of trees.

In an instant, Rudge understood what had happened. Mallory had witnessed the attack from within the vessel and had acted quickly, sending a segmented tentacle stretching to the edge of the clearing to snatch Rudge's assailant and haul him skyward.

As Rudge sorted this out, he was surprised by a hand on his shoulder. It was Jacobs. "Are you all right, Sir Bertram?"

"Yes," Rudge said, getting to his feet and brushing muck from his thighs. "Bit out of breath, but—"

He was interrupted by the body that came crashing and tumbling down from the trees to land on its back with a wet smack on the forest floor. Mallory had either released the man or the man had wriggled out of the tentacle's grasp without reflecting on the consequences of that maneuver.

The man's eyes were open as was his mouth. He was dead and wore a dumbfounded expression, as though the other side was not at all what he expected.

"Sir!" Jacobs said, and Rudge looked up to see more naked men, armed with spears and bows and arrows, moving out of the trees and into the sunlight.

"Over here," another voice shouted, and Rudge looked over his shoulder and saw Jon Bans and Tommy Strand. Jon Bans was aiming an ancient Enfield Musketoon at one of the natives, but Rudge felt that the odds of Bans killing anyone other than himself were slim. Rudge had examined the moldering gun weeks ago and pronounced it worthless. Tommy Strand was holding Rudge's own Lee-Metford, a fine bolt-action rifle that Rudge trusted with his life. He did not, however, trust the abilities of the feckless naturalist who was presently holding it. Rudge wondered how many savages Mallory could wring the life out of with his mechanical tentacles.

But the savages seemed uninterested in Rudge or any of his comrades. They surrounded the dead man and began talking and grunting and slapping each other on the back. One of the men threw his feet up in the air, threw his arms wide, and sprawled on his back to the accompaniment of loud hoots and grunts which Rudge identified as expressions of mirth.

"These boys have a hell of a sense of humor, don't they?" The man who had just walked out of the forest and uttered this remark was dressed as though for tennis, or, perhaps, croquet. He was smoking a cheroot with an insouciant air, and a black-rimmed monocle was screwed into his left eye.

"Wallister!" Rudge blurted. He'd never met the man, but his likeness was famously familiar.

"I am," the man said. "I don't know who you are, but I bet you are looking for Lavinia. There's always someone chasing after her."

THE YAMI VILLAGE was less than a mile away, and Rudge and his men accompanied Wallister on foot. Mallory followed behind in *Her Glory*, maintaining a distance of several hundred yards so that the falling trees and flying branches that were an inevitable byproduct of the vehicle's progress wouldn't maim anyone. The natives walked ahead of Rudge and Wallister.

"Didn't know that fellow was going to try to shoot an arrow through you," Wallister said, as they pressed on through the jungle. "I wouldn't have stood still for that if I'd seen it coming. Sorry though. I should have been paying more attention." He shot a glance at Rudge. "Although you know how to look out for yourself. I can see that. That was quite a trick with that machine of yours. Never seen anything like that."

They were silent for a while, and then Wallister said, "Lord Addison sent you, didn't he?" and Rudge nodded and said that Lavinia's grandfather had been concerned for her welfare, and that Rudge had volunteered to find her and report on her safety. He'd become, of course, much more worried when he and his men came upon the burned out shell of the zeppelin.

Wallister was surprised to learn that the zeppelin had burned— "wasn't burning when we set off," he said—but he didn't seem particularly upset. He had a cavalier manner that suited his heavy-lidded eyes and too-full lips, and the slightly vexed expression of a man often misunderstood by his inferiors. He moved through the jungle with a twisting of hips and shoulders that suggested a man wending his way through a party crowd with the bar as his destination. Rudge better understood Lord Addison's antipathy for Wallister and, consequently, felt less ambivalent about getting Lavinia back to England and her grandfather by whatever means necessary.

Their arrival at the village was heralded by a dozen or so small children, who ran down the path to meet them, silent, swift, pale creatures, weaving and darting and ogling the new intruders and then running on down the path to where *Her Glory of Empire* was shaking the jungle and throwing up debris. They would flee it, then stop, turn, and run toward it, stand wiggling and flapping their arms and uttering rude noises, then flee again.

When Rudge and his companions arrived at the village, they found every man, woman and child who had not set out to greet them, the lot standing in a fleshy mass of expectancy, and, as Rudge entered the clearing, the crowd parted to reveal a hut from which a young woman emerged, a strikingly beautiful girl with raven hair that fell loosely from under a pith helmet decorated with pink and purple orchids.

She seemed dazed by the sunlight; she brought a hand to her throat, and her eyes widened, blue eyes that pierced old Rudge's memory and brought her name to his lips, reflexively. Could this vision be the precocious twelve-year he had known so long ago?

But before her name could pass his lips, a voice shouted in his ear: "Vinia!" And he saw Lavinia's eyes grow yet wider, impossibly large, and she began to run toward him, and he felt something like pain—perhaps acute embarrassment at an old man's fancy—when he realized she was not running toward him but toward the man who had just raced by Rudge to close the distance in mere seconds, take Lavinia in his arms and spin her in the air while she laughed with that merriment that only the young have access to.

Tommy Strand and Lavinia Addison hugged and kissed, sobbed and laughed, aware perhaps of their audience—as the young so often are—and portraying two besotted lovers with a skill well beyond that of the most accomplished thespians.

It was the evening of the next day. The sun was still in the sky, but, in less than an hour, it would slide precipitously into the water. Rudge stood at the end of a ramshackle pier, which, he suspected, had not fallen into disrepair but been born in that state. A sizeable lake spread out in front of him, its mirrored surface full of the cloudy sky, not a dimple on its surface (curious, that). There was no sign of life at all, and a strange, dank odor filled the air. Nonetheless, Rudge was delighted to have evaded, if only briefly, the chatter of the Yami, their idiotic bluster and pomp. Primitive peoples did not inspire Rudge, who saw in them the worst aspects of human nature, reminding him that superstition, ignorance, violence, and cruelty were inherent human traits, first impulses, and that civilization was a cheap coat of paint over a rotten edifice.

He was not, he decided, angered by Tommy Strand's subterfuge. The young man was not a naturalist, a fact which should have been apparent from the beginning; he was, in truth, the feckless son of Arthur Strand, a powerful industrialist who had prevailed upon Lord Addison to take his son on board for this rescue mission. Neither Arthur Strand nor Lord Addison had any idea that young Tommy and Lavinia were enamored of each other—or had been until an unfortunate misunderstanding had led to a heated argument which had prompted Lavinia, obeying an impulse not uncommon in young people, to put an entire ocean between herself and her unhappy suitor.

She had quickly come to regret this. Wallister proved an unpleasant man, a "brute," (although he had not, according to Lavinia, indulged in any sexual impropriety beyond a certain sly familiarity and presumption). The jungle had failed to improve her disposition, and the insufferable Yami were the last straw, a noisy, foul-smelling lot who wore no clothes except—how stupid was this?—a small black patch to cover the navel, a kind of spiritual precaution, since demons tended to enter a person via this umbilical entrance. You were just asking for trouble if you didn't hide your navel under a mollusk shell or bit of sloth hide.

In any event, the lovers were reunited, and it looked like a happy—

The sky seemed to die and fall upon him. A cold fist squeezed his heart. He fell to his knees. Suddenly it was as though his body were fashioned from clay; surely this numbness heralded his death, and yet this mortal fear was nothing compared to an overwhelming sense of desolation. If he had been told that everyone he knew and cared for had died, hideously, that might have engendered such despair; a palpable evil, a malevolent spirit, had settled in his mind with the authority of truth, bringing with it a suffocating terror, a need to run, to flee, but robbing him of volition.

Somehow he managed to stagger to his feet and gaze down into the water from which this malign psychic force seemed to emanate. The water was clear, and he saw the lake's bottom, which rippled with shadows, black blotches that shifted and danced, as though cast by broad leaves shivering in a strong wind. He had thought the lake deeper, even here at the end of the pier, and this shift in perception created a kind of panicky vertigo. What did it matter how deep—? Then he understood. He was not looking at the lake's bottom; he was gazing down upon the back of some unknowable beast. It was gliding under the water, a vast, translucent creature, shapeless, or shifting in shape, a kind of ovoid whale-sized jellyfish. The mottled, black shapes within it pulsated and moved, and these black undulating inkblots were not organs beating to some animal pulse—how Rudge knew this he could not say; but know it he did—they were mouths opening and closing to reveal a terrible hunger, more ancient and ravenous than any jungle beast or mythical monster.

Rudge did not know if he walked or ran or crawled back down the pier and over the ground and back to the hut. He had some memory of falling upon his blankets and being seized by a deep and unrelenting lethargy, which a scientist of the mind might have identified as a strategy of the subconscious designed to defend the self from a horror it found untenable.

In the morning, when Jacobs brought him his tea, Rudge came awake, groggy but in full possession of the previous night's horror.

THE OLD MAN could speak English, having spent four years in a mission before deciding that one god was not enough for a jungle life, and now, having heard Rudge out, he nodded.

"This in-the-lake thing big. Very big, very bad. It not live here. It from some other. It splash into this world and very angry, and it kill-kill everything thing and eat up everything. Mostly, it stay in the night, wait for the night when the sun is shy. We Yami, we try to kill it. It eat up Yami. Ha ha!" The old shaman laughed and slapped his thigh. "We stick him with spear. We stick him with arrow. He eat up spear and arrow and Yami!" The old man glowered, as though suddenly struck with the seriousness of this Yami-eating business.

"It make slave of some Yami. It catch Yami and make him fetch food and trick other Yami to lake, but it take Yami soul to make of him slave, and we see that. We say, 'That man, he have no soul,' and we kill him."

The Yami were not fools. They had discovered several things about the beast. It could not travel on land, and its substance, its flesh, was, consequently, trapped within the lake. It needed to eat, to feed, and it had done that until there was nothing left for it to eat. No birds, no fish, no frogs, no turtles, nothing. It would die in its dead lake.

"We kill it with nothing," he said, his smile revealing half a dozen ragged black teeth.

Rudge was about to ask something about the Yami slaves when a series of high-pitched screams made him leap to his feet and run outside.

The screams were coming from the lake, and as soon as Rudge rounded a gnarled clump of trees, he understood what was happening. So much for the shaman's assertion that the creature shunned the daylight. It was, no doubt, growing desperate.

Wallister and Lavinia were both kneeling on the end of the pier, clutching the weather-battered logs and desiccated vines that comprised it. The pier had been ripped from the shore and was moving out into the lake, riding the back of the beast, a raft surrounded by white turbulence and leaving a wild, frothing wake.

Rudge saw Tommy Strand running toward the lake. He stood on the edge, preparing to dive in and swim valiantly after his beloved, but a shout stopped him, and Rudge turned too, and spied Mallory, standing atop *Her Glory of Empire* and urging Strand to hurry.

Mallory disappeared before Strand reached the vehicle, and a silver tentacle reached out and lifted the young man up to the hatch. Rudge marveled at Mallory's skill. He was an artist with old Edmonds's invention.

Her Glory rolled into the lake and water rollicked all over the banks and then, amid several flying tentacles and the ball-ended air tubes, it disappeared beneath the surface. The steady progress of the bobbing tubes was all that marked its journey. Those air tubes gained on the floundering pier, and suddenly a tentacle reached out of the water and encircled Lavinia's waist. The girl screamed, no doubt thinking the beast had her, and continued to scream until, suddenly, she fell from the tentacle's clasp. The tentacle sank beneath the waves, and so did Lavinia. On the bank, Rudge shouted, appalled, crazy in his helplessness. Then Lavinia's head and shoulders broke the surface, and Tommy Strand could be seen behind her. Lavinia's eyes were closed, but Tommy had his arm around her and was in no danger of losing her. With strong, purposeful strokes he drew her to the shore.

Rudge turned back to where the pier now lay motionless in the middle of the lake. Wallister was nowhere to be seen, and *Her Glory of Empire* had failed to resurface.

Time passed. The crowd of naked men, women, and children, silent at first and keeping a cautious distance from the shore, began to talk excitedly and gesture among themselves.

Rudge spied Tommy and Lavinia on the shore to his right. Tommy had an arm around her shoulders and she was sitting up, coughing. Rudge was about to set off in their direction when a great funnel of water erupted and *Her Glory of Empire* rose up, all twelve of its tentacles thrashing, shimmering in the blazing sun, seeming to dance upon the water. It was up and on the shore in an instant, and then it was among the Yami who screamed and fled in all directions. The machine snatched them up, each tentacle moving of its own accord, independent of all others. Mallory's skill was nothing like this. Men, women, and children were tossed in the air, slammed against tree trunks, torn to bits by tentacles that sliced them with gleaming blades. An old warrior's head bounced at Rudge's feet. He jumped back as it rolled past, blood splattering his boots.

And then this great machine stood tall on six tentacles, in defiance of all engineering principles, and Rudge saw the slumped form of Wallister, sodden and surely lifeless, bound by several coils of a single tentacle, and the machine, moving with an unholy ease that suggested a watchful intelligence, darted into the jungle, parting trees and brush in a welter of sound and fury—and was gone. In less than five minutes, its progress could no longer be marked by the noise that accompanied it, although Rudge could still discern the cloud of dust and twigs and leaves that rose above it.

As he walked to meet Tommy and Lavinia, Rudge saw, on the lake's bank, a litter of pipes and seals and broken gauges, the mechanical guts of *Her Glory*, instruments of no interest to the creature that now wore the vehicle like a suit of armor.

ALL'S WELL THAT ends well. That's what Rudge told himself on his return to England. And certainly Lord Addison was pleased to have his granddaughter safely home.

But what is the end? When, six weeks after his disappearance, Wallister walked out of the jungle, miraculously whole, was that the end? When the great explorer abandoned his travels and devoted his fortune to industry, was that the end? When a factory in Sheffield began producing great hollow steel orbs that dwarfed the men who made them, and when the public learned that these were the prototypes of a new and glorious engine based on Hugh Edmonds's invention, what was one to make of that?

People said that Wallister had changed, was serious, almost solemn, and the flamboyance that had delighted the public and annoyed his fellows was gone for good. Was there anyone in England who could discern the absence of a soul?

Rudge would have liked to know if these manufactured steel casings awaited cunning furnaces and engines and navigational devices. Or did they await creatures in need of external skeletons? If these empty spheres were waiting upon the latter then that, Rudge thought, might well be the end.

Not Last Night But The Night Before | *Steven R. Boyett*

Michael's death showed up one rainy Sunday afternoon when the windows were misty and the barometer was high and Michael himself was in bed with a hangover so bad he could hear his hair growing. At the crack of noon Michael finally exhumed himself to slap together a pot of kona, and as he bumped toward the kitchen he glanced at his frumpy sleeper couch and saw his death sitting there, quietly reading the Sunday paper he'd thoughtfully brought in from the front porch. He was wearing Michael's oatmeal-colored Turkish bathrobe, Michael's only memento of Jillian. The robe was really too small for Michael but his death was fairly swaddled in it.

In the kitchen Michael put six shaky tablespoons of beans into the grinder and leaned on the button and winced as the grinder's whine sawed through his head. He held on like a trooper until the beans were uniformly ground for the Italian coffeemaker Aimy had given him.

Unbleached No. 4 filter into gold mesh basket, ground beans into filter, water into reservoir, lids on all around, press ON. While the machine's odd respiratory distress got underway Michael leaned out to peek into the livingroom. His death still sat there on the couch, reading Doonesbury without expression. Michael stared. Even over the coffeemaker's monster movie gargle the rustle of the comics pages turning seemed loud.

Michael stumbled into his afterthought of a bathroom and stared down at the toilet and tried to decide if he was going to throw up. A few minutes later and slightly more pale he went into the living room carefully bearing two steaming mugs of coffee. He set one on the coffee table and sipped from the other one and stood looking down at his uninvited visitor.

Michael's death folded down a corner of the comics section and stared long and mute at Edie's old Bugs Bunny coffee mug before him. He looked up at Michael and back down at the mug and made no move to pick it up.

Michael frowned. Finally he picked up the Bugs Bunny mug and padded back into the kitchen to add some half and half.

On Monday Michael's death came with him to work. He sat on the gray carpet near Michael's desk and read a Dan Brown novel like some solemn child accustomed to being left alone to entertain itself. Michael tried to ignore him but it wasn't easy. Having his death so close at hand made it hard to get any real work done.

One of the attorneys brought a deposition summary to be transcribed and grew irritated as Michael's gaze kept straying to an empty corner of his cube while the details were being explained to him. The attorney asked Do you understand the assignment and Michael nodded but still didn't look at him. The attorney scowled and stalked away. Michael's death never even looked up from his book.

The new assignment took top priority but Michael only stared at the triaged stack in his IN box. How could you concentrate with your own death staring you right in the face. How were you supposed to pretend your work meant anything while death hovered over your shoulder.

But his death wasn't staring him in the face or hovering over his shoulder at all. He remained absorbed in his book, occasionally wetting a finger to turn a page with odd earnestness. He didn't seem to read very quickly.

Michael often ate lunch in the park at the downtown library because it was one of the few patches of green within walking distance of Bunker Hill. The girlwatching was topnotch too.

Today people were enjoying the clear air and odd uplift that follow a good unseasonal Southern California rainstorm. Michael did not share their enjoyment, probably because his death sat right beside him on the side of the wooden bench most encrusted with pigeonshit.

Along the winding pathway came a tall redhead. Black business dress and low heels and black nylon laptop tote. The whole world turning on her hips. Michael's gaze followed her until it included his death sitting there beside him and Michael felt his face go tight. Is it asking too much to look at pretty girls during my lunch hour without my own death breathing down my neck.

But his death wasn't breathing down his neck. Oblivious to Michael's poison glare he was staring at a bag lady rooting through a garbage can as he kicked harmlessly at fat insipid pigeons that waddled too close to his skinny legs. Offended pigeons twitched their tails and scattered.

Michael set aside his unfinished McDonald's lunch and rubbed his temples and then glanced at the pocket watch Corinne had given him some birthday ago that remained a pleasant and impractical affectation. Twelve fiftyfive. He pushed off from the bench and jammed his hands into his front pockets and stalked away and kept his gaze on the sidewalk. People who noticed him thought Now there's an angry young man on such a pretty day. They couldn't see Michael's death of course but still. A pretty day's a pretty day.

Behind him Michael's death retrieved the pack of french fries from the McDonald's bag and took some for himself and left the rest for the bag lady and then hurried after Michael.

Driving home that evening Michael saw somebody else's death for the first time. He was tracksurfing through his iPod, trying to find a song he liked, but they all sounded like mush and he ended up just turning it off. He glanced in the rearview at his death who sat with thin legs primly crossed as he blankly studied drivers creeping along in traffic. The Honda held but just themselves.

One lane over tires screeched and Michael's death craned forward in sudden brighteyed interest as a Nissan braked to avoid a black BMW that cut in front of it. No contact was made and Michael's death leaned back in the seat and resumed his inscrutable survey.

Michael glimpsed an adult sized figure in the backseat of the Nissan, which was odd because the passenger seat was empty. The figure seemed oddly familiar. Then it leaned forward to stare at his own death passing by and Michael realized why. He half expected it to lift a hand and wave indifferently but no.

It was hard to concentrate on driving with his own death sitting right behind him. You couldn't drive a mile in this city without some kind of close call it seemed, and every time there was one Michael wondered Is this it, is this why he's here.

But after each close call he'd glance in the rearview and see his death simply looking out the window like a tourist in a city he hadn't planned to visit. Which perhaps he was.

WHEN MICHAEL LEFT for work the next morning his death stayed behind, sitting on the sleeper couch in the living room and staring at the wall. Michael should have felt relieved but he didn't. Instead he kept imagining glimpses of his death throughout the day. It made him edgy and irritable and his lack of sleep only made it worse. His coworkers and some of the attorneys noticed but Michael didn't notice that they did.

At lunch all the benches were taken in the little park outside the library and he said hell with it and sat on the grass. It didn't make him feel footloose and fancy free. His pants got damp and his lunch tasted phony. He kept looking at his pastrami sandwich and trying to connect it with any creature that had ever breathed upon the earth. Something that had walked alive beneath the sky was here in his hand between two slices of rye wrapped in paper. How does that happen.

He started to throw the sandwich away but remembered the way his death would always leave unfinished food for others and so left the bag perched on a garbage can. No point in staying out here really. He headed back up the Bunker Hill steps unsatisfied and scowling. His death now a presence in its absence.

At home that evening he found no evidence of his death at all except for the day's mail neatly sorted on the coffee table. Bills on top and junkmail on the bottom. Still when he made dinner he set two places. He chewed and swallowed and tasted nothing and watched teevee. He'd taken to watching all kinds of reality shows about people's working lives. Cops and fishermen and mechanics. Around midnight he jerked awake and looked from the flatscreen to see his death beside him on the couch, the remains of dinner on the plate on the coffee table.

Michael watched the teevee light moving on his death's flat doll eyes. He sighed theatrically but of course his death said nothing. He didn't even look away from the show that engrossed him. Michael leaned back on the couch and tried to watch but it was all just moving pictures on a wall now. He caught himself nodding off and dragged himself to bed but left the teevee on. His death still watching blankeyed in the strobing light with the universal remote near one thin hand. Voices and music and explosions and power tools sang Michael to a fitful sleep.

Mornings Michael would slap the snooze button and stare at the ceiling and dread getting out of bed. Why get up when you know your death is waiting out there somewhere.

Because you have to pay your rent, he'd say out loud. Like some mantra. And bearlike he'd get out of bed and sure as shit his death would be there on the couch working a crossword puzzle, or in the kitchen making a botch of obscenely expensive kona coffee, and Michael would dress with little of his former attention to appearance and stumble unshaven into the gray morning blinking like some disgorged thing. Some planecrash survivor stunned and not yet comprehending his terrible good fortune. In traffic he no longer even got upset at the mercenary competition among the rush hour drivers. The passers in the breakdown lane, single drivers in the diamond lane, lefthand turns from righthand lanes. It all just washed right off him now. He drove as if he were part of his own car. He parked and paid and took the Angel's

Flight funicular and gave his ticket and a noncommittal wave to Henry the ticket man and he'd show up at the office often late and dreading the vast unpopulated plain of his working day.

—*Q*—

Two weeks after Michael's death arrived he went out on a date.

Andrea was a paralegal from the Atlanta office. For months the firm had been shuttling her to the west coast to lock her up like Rapunzel in the auxiliary office on the eleventh floor so she could conduct a dreary document review. She surfaced intermittently. Whenever their paths would cross she and Michael would blush and look at the floor and stammer out hellos. If there was any one place in his life Michael felt selfassured it was when approaching women, but somehow Andrea wobbled his foundation. Which itself was enough to keep him interested.

Only a few days before that first time he'd awakened to find his death in the livingroom Michael had found an excuse to visit the eleventh floor. A lawsuit by a former secretary with carpal tunnel syndrome had caused the firm to buy new ergonomic keyboard trays and Michael offered to take the old ones to the Morgue, which was what they called the storage closet on eleven stacked with daisywheel printers and IBM PS-2 computers and tiny monochrome monitors like some jumbled museum of office computing.

Andrea had done a doubletake when Michael walked by her paper laden desk, which flattered him but cost him some composure. He thought Andrea noticed it but was willing to work with him so he asked her about visiting Los Angeles, did she hate the long flight, did she ever get out to see any of the city, would she like to one night soon.

It turned out she was heading back to Atlanta next morning but would be happy to go out tonight. She'd always wanted to see a movie at Graumann's Chinese Theater on Hollywood Boulevard, so about three minutes after agreeing to a time to pick her up Michael had bought a pair of tickets on his cell phone. Some big loud action movie. But even a bad movie is better at the Chinese, which Michael realized he had not been to in ages.

Outside the theater Andrea matched her shoes against Betty Grable's concrete shoeprints. She saw Michael grinning at her and asked in her sleepy Georgia accent What's so funny. Michael said, "I've been to this theater, I don't know, dozens of times, and I've never done this."

"Well why should you. Betty Grable's feet are much smaller than yours."

He easily covered John Wayne's shoeprint with his own. "I mean this. The whole touristy thing."

She wiped grit from Betty Grable's handprint off her palms. "Sometimes it's good for you to be a tourist in your own town." She clasped his arm as they went through the red doors of the entrance.

After the movie he'd taken her to the revolving restaurant high atop the Bonaventure Hotel precisely because it was touristy and tacky with its Vegas casino carpets and decorative ceramic drink mugs and baksheesh for a window seat. Andrea drank something in a hideous decorative ceramic mug complete with paper parasol and took in the creeping gyre of constellated city. Recent rain had rarefied the air to give an unencumbered vista of the city spread below them. Andrea had been staying in a hotel not a thousand yards from here with no idea this place existed. Or this view.

Michael felt she had been showing him as good a time as he had been trying to show her, but he also sensed some part of her reluctant to relax. He asked her why she wanted to be a lawyer.

She sipped her drink and set it in its ring of wet and watched the pilgrim lights in slow march from the right. One for every soul, he wondered. "Corporate law's exciting. The stakes are crazy. The negotiations are so tense. Like countries trying not to go to war but also kind of wanting to because they're both sure they can wipe the floor with the other one and wouldn't mind proving it. Ever watch the attorneys when they come out of those meetings? They're high as a kite."

"I figured it was relief. They're all laughing a little too loud. Shaking hands, patting backs."

"Sure, it's that too. But mostly they're riding that big adrenaline rush. Especially when they know they won."

"And the ones who lose still get to bill four fifty an hour."

She shrugged. "Those are the rules."

"You don't seem like a competitive person. Aggressive, I mean."

She turned away from the turning city and picked up her drink and looked at him over the toothpick ribs of the umbrella and said Oh but I am. And toasted him and drank.

Michael laughed. A little too loud.

Back at her hotel he had saved her the worry of having to politely fend him off by walking her across the lobby and giving her a goodnight kiss on the cheek at the elevator. When the doors slid opened he leaned back instead of in. She smiled at that. Perhaps she found it quaint. Perhaps he'd killed his chances by not being competitive and aggressive. Perhaps he thought too goddamned much. But she told him she'd be back again in two weeks and they made another date. Michael had driven home feeling pretty damned good for the first time in who knew how long and feeling corny as hell about it, and feeling good that it felt corny as hell. Then his death had shown up on the living room couch with the Sunday Times and Michael forgot all about his next date with Andrea.

UNTIL SHE LEANED against his cube and said Knock knock. He looked up at her and made an absurd little eek and jerked back in his chair. The headphone cord went taut and the transcription headset yanked off his head.

She smiled and blushed and apologized for startling him and asked Are we still on for tonight.

"Tonight, sure, of course. Sorry, you startled me. Tonight. Definitely." The more he went on the more skeptical she looked. "Pick you up at ... seven?"

"It's a date."

MICHAEL'S DEATH WAS nowhere in evidence when he got home that evening. Still it was all he could think about as he got ready for his date.

It had gotten pretty bad. Now Michael regularly saw other people's deaths as well as his own. Strangers eating lunch beside each other on park benches, their deaths playing checkers on the grass nearby. Like solemn children or feckless nannies, riding beside them when they drove, struggling along on rollerblades near the beach, watching teevee next to them on the couch, shuffling forward in theater lines, warily looking both ways before stepping out at crosswalks flashing DONT WALK. Mostly their deaths seemed little affected by their surroundings, showing interest only when brakes squealed, when cigarettes were lit, when food went down the wrong way, rickety ladders were climbed, redlights run, or any of the other myriad and largely unrecognized mortal encounters of daily life.

Clearly other people couldn't see their deaths and this really pissed Michael off. He wanted to shout at them. Hey! Your death is right in front of you! It's on you like a suit! Wake up and smell the formaldehyde! How can you not see it. How can you live like this.

He put on a clean solid colored tee shirt and put a collared shirt over it and buttoned it most of the way up and squinted at himself in the mirror of his tiny and utilitarian bathroom. Why am I doing this. Where will we go. What could we possibly talk about. Laws? Cities? Food? I'm supposed to talk about crabcakes with my death staring me in the face? The omens for a good date were not auspicious.

MICHAEL'S DEATH WAS waiting for him in the lobby of Andrea's hotel. He sat on a couch that looked more decorative than comfortable, absorbed in a news magazine six weeks out of date. When Michael saw his death he scowled and stalked past him to the elevator.

Michael was nervous as he knocked on Andrea's door. If he was going to avoid making a fool of himself tonight he would have to practice ignoring his death looming nearby. Though right now his death wasn't looming nearby but was down the hall lifting the cover off a room service tray to pilfer half a roast beef sandwich.

Andrea answered the door with her hair wet and said I'm so sorry, they had me at the office till sixthirty and I'm running behind, I'll be just a minute, I'm so sorry. She opened the door wider and stepped back.

"Some people have no consideration," Michael said as he walked in. Andrea looked startled. "The firm, I mean. Um. Is my face as red as it feels.

"How red does it feel."

"I'd go with sundried tomato."

"Getting there." She hesitated and then nodded and went into the bathroom. "Have a seat. I'll just be a minute."

"No hurry. They won't cook our dinner till we get there. This joint's all classy like that." He glanced around as he walked in from the foyer. "Hey, these rooms are pretty—" He looked at the couch and his nervous sweat turned cold.

From the bathroom Andrea said They're not that pretty.

"Um, pretty big."

On the couch, channel surfing with the remote, sat Andrea's death.

—♀—

The four of them went to Traxx, a restaurant in Union Station with seating on the main concourse. Michael and Andrea watched dazed and weary travelers amble around the concourse and looked up at the distant Mission style wooden ceiling and listened to a constant hollow booming echo like Mass in some train cathedral.

"This has been right by my hotel this whole time?"

"Naw, I had them build it the other day. The paint's still wet in places." He drank water.

"You'd think there'd be more people here."

"People who live here don't even know about it. Or if they do they're way too cool to come here."

She looked around. "Is this because of what I said last time."

"Being a tourist in your own home town? It definitely got me thinking."

"It wasn't meant to be a challenge."

"But I had fun last time. Exactly because it was something nobody here does because everyone else does it. This city's full of stuff like that. The bar at the Biltmore. High tea at the Huntington. You go there and it's amazing and all you can think is that there's like twelve million people here and maybe eight of them are in this amazing place, and how can that be."

"Well, I'm. I don't know." She looked at her plate. "Flattered."

Michael glanced inside the restaurant where his and Andrea's deaths sat discreetly at a corner table. They looked at each other unblinkingly and not at Michael or Andrea, and Michael realized that for three whole minutes he hadn't given a single thought to his death.

He looked back to see Andrea curious about his distraction. "Where would we go if we were back in Atlanta."

She looked around the station again as if comparing. "I'm partial to Dante's in Buckhead."

"Buckhead? Seriously?"

She shrugged. "It's a fondue restaurant that looks like it belongs in Disneyland."

"Obvious or nonobvious place to go?"

"It's usually crowded so I'd have to say so obvious that you wouldn't think to go there."

"Nobody goes there anymore. It's too crowded."

She grinned and nodded.

There was more food than they could eat and they had the waiter box the leftovers. Michael asked Andrea if she had been to the beach yet and she said no. He said That's just criminal and suggested Point Dume, which was not close but worth the drive. Andrea was game and he got two coffees to go and glanced inside the restaurant again as they got up to leave. His death saw them leaving and hurriedly put down his glass of milk and tapped Andrea's death on the shoulder and helped her on with her shawl. As they rose to follow them Andrea's death handed Michael's death a napkin to wipe away his milk moustache.

A vagrant hit them up for change while they waited for the valet to bring Michael's car around. Michael shook his head and said Sorry. Their deaths caught up to them just as Michael closed Andrea's door and went around to the driver's side. Michael's death dropped some change into the bum's cup and Andrea's death gave the bum the boxed dinner leftovers that Michael and Andrea had forgotten at their table.

Michael frowned and tipped the valet and sped away, aware of the valet's puzzlement and Andrea's surprised look beside him. But hurrying hadn't made any difference. In the rearview he saw their deaths sitting in the back seat. Straightbacked and unblinking. Seatbelts securely fastened.

—*C*—

CLUMSY SILENCE PREVAILED for the first half of the drive toward Malibu. Michael thought about drowning it with music but instead just sipped his coffee and let the silence play. Tires loud on pavement as the car swerved on the westering road. He felt Andrea's puzzlement at the date going sour but had no idea how to address it.

Finally they turned off of Pacific Coast Highway and parked off the road in an affluent neighborhood. "They won't let you park near the Point," said Michael. "I guess it weeds out the riffraff."

More accustomed to sultry Georgia summer nights than L.A. desert Andrea had not brought a coat, so Michael grabbed a blanket from the trunk and wrapped it round her shoulders. They walked the quiet moonlit street. Their deaths walked quietly behind them looking up at the bright moon.

"There's a beach around here?" Andrea said.

Michael nodded. "Over that way, where the land runs out."

"Funny how that works."

"You gotta watch that water stuff. It sneaks up on land every chance it gets."

"So is this obvious or nonobvious."

"Definitely non. It takes some work to get here, which means—"

"Most people don't bother."

"Exactly."

"So now you're saying nobody comes here—"

"Because it isn't crowded. Yeah." He laughed and then realized it was his first unaffected laugh in weeks. "So don't tell anyone about it, okay. In fact tell them how much you hate this town. The traffic. The smog. The shallow people. If everyone who hated it would move away it'd be a nice little town. I can't tell you how many people I've met who hate Los Angeles and then you find out they've never been here but they hate it anyway. It's like I hate your furniture and I've never been to your house." He felt himself on the slippery slope of runon monologue. Nervous babbling to fill a silence that otherwise would be occupied by his death, her death, their own deaths shadowing them, gaping at the glowing moon or counting stars or listening for surf or doing whatever the hell someone's death does when it's biding its time.

"Michael."

He stopped talking and looked back. She had stopped walking. He started to ask What's wrong and was stopped by her moonlit face. Her swaddled shoulders. Their deaths behind them shadowless and still.

"I like the furniture," she said. "I do."

Something woke him in the middle of the night and he lay still a moment listening. Slow and even breathing beside him. The unaccustomed feel of her. That was what it was.

He eased out of bed. In the bathroom, he ran the tap until the water warmed and then he splashed his face and pressed a towel hard against it. Liking the plush, the feel of getting dry.

What was different. What had changed. He couldn't place it. Or couldn't find a word for it if he could. Some hidden pivot on which the night had turned.

He glanced around the small bright unadorned bathroom and his fingers drummed his naked thigh. Something gnawed at him. Mental car keys he'd forgotten somewhere.

Back in the bedroom he noticed pale blue coruscating television light ghostly in the living room. He went to turn the teevee off and just before he saw them there together on the couch it all came back to him. His death, her death. They sat close together on the couch working the PlayStation controls to shoot computer generated zombies. Michael watched their somber play for a few minutes. A heavy and invisible cloak settling back down around him. They didn't look at him but he knew they knew that he was there.

ANDREA SLEEPING. SETTLED into bottom sediment unaware of tides or eddies or distant light above her. Face smooth and brow untroubled. Breathing steady. What vessels sailed there went by wakeless.

—❦—

HE AWOKE AGAIN surprised he'd slept. Alone in bed. Her voice low from the living room. He listened but could make out no words. She kept her voice down and continued some conversation.

He sat up.

—❦—

"I'M SORRY, I don't know the address. I'll have to go outside and see what street—" She glanced up from her phone when he came into the living room.

"I'll take you back. You don't have to do that."

"I don't mind—no, hold on a moment please." She lowered the phone. "I don't mind. I didn't mean to wake you."

"I'll take you back. I'm going that way anyway, remember."

"It's okay really." Dressed in last night's clothes and ready to go.

"A cab will cost a ton."

"That's okay." Raising the phone again. "What's your address here."

—❦—

THEY HAD NO awkward encounter later on at work because she was kept locked up all day in her tower on eleven. He could feel her there. Rapunzel immersed in her document review.

His death sat in his customary corner playing games on Michael's phone. For once Michael found it easy to ignore him. Though he wondered if her death were up there with her and what it might be doing. Playing Pong on old computers maybe.

Michael kept his earphones in and let his hands type words he did not hear. However many times and ways he replayed the date last night the only speedbump he could find was his sullenness on leaving the restaurant and driving toward Point Dume. But he'd snapped out of it before they had arrived, had been charming and thoughtful and funny and his old smooth witty self as they had trudged the long way down the wooden steps and then walked barefoot on the moonlit halfmoon beach. Had that been enough to make her regret staying over. Had staying over been enough. She was ambitious and driven and focused on her career. Partner material someday. Very bad form to sleep with one of the firm's glorified typists.

Maybe he was just supposed to have been some distraction from her slog through dreary documents and an anonymous hotel room but she'd realized that she liked him more than she'd realized and so felt compelled to cut it off because they could hardly have a relationship twentytwo hundred miles apart. Maybe he was lousy in bed. Maybe he had stinky breath. Maybe bats flew out of his ass while he slept.

He realized he was staring at his death sitting on the floor against the wall playing Tetris on his phone. He said The hell with this and turned off the transcriber and pulled off the earphones and got out of the thousand dollar ergonomic chair he hated with a passion and stalked toward the elevator. His death hurried to catch up.

SHE DIDN'T BAT an eye when he darkened her desk and said Good morning.

"Morning. Can I take you to lunch today."

She waved at the stacks of folders imprisoning her. "No lunch for Andrea today."

"I'd like talk with you if I can. When you can." He shrugged. "Let me know, okay." He started away.

"Now's good."

"Now?"

"Sure. Why not. No one here but us chickens."

That's what you think, he didn't say. "Okay. Um. Well." He frowned past her. "I mean, what woke me up this morning was the sound of you chewing your leg off to escape."

She studied him. Summation time. "I had a good time last night. I did. You're really smart. You have good manners. You're very attractive. Funny."

"I sense the word But in my future."

"But there's something dark about you. Not cultivated dark like Ooh I'm a sensitive poet. I mean really dark. Like turning on a light won't make it go away. And I think it's kind of your default mode and all the smart attractive funny stuff is piled on top of it. But when you get down to cases, well. I mean there's great sex and then there's I don't know. Raising demons." She lifted a hand palm up and set it back down.

Fuck it. "I see people's deaths."

"Excuse me."

"I see people's deaths."

"Like how they're going to die?"

"Like their death who comes to get them. It's different for everyone I guess."

"Well I'd imagine."

"You don't have to humor me, okay. I mean maybe I'm crazy but that doesn't mean it isn't true. I don't want to see this. I don't want to tell you something crazy like this."

"Well what am I supposed to say. It does sort of alter the landscape."

"Sure it does. Five seconds ago I had a dark side that made you think that you ought to keep your distance. Now I have a dark side because I'm wacked as cherry flavored Thorazine."

"What am I supposed to say."

"I suppose it's a good sign you haven't asked me to leave or called security or something."

"Actually."

Oh. "Actually you want me to go."

"I think that would be best."

Michael nodded. He could see it all. The sense it made from where she stood.

"Okay. I don't blame you really. I think it's crazy too. I'm sorry and I won't bother you again."

She was already opening a folder. Michael looked past her at her death who was staring back at Michael's own death. She raised her hand which looked like a child's drawing of a hand and his death did the same and that was it really. Michael left.

—*♪*—

THE ORDINARY MAY be defined as the expected repetition of the miraculous. Thirty thousand sunsets in a lifetime. Commuter flights. Bootprints on the moon.

Andrea finished her document review and went back to Atlanta. Michael came to work and typed and ate lunch at the library park or at the Water Court and accepted the fact that his death would tag along and feed the pigeons. That half the teevee shows on his DVR were not ones he had programmed. That he now spent twice as much on decent coffee. That he lived alone but wasn't by himself or really living either. As the weeks went by what he accepted was the fact that he had in fact accepted. It wasn't liberating or enlightening. It felt like surrender.

At first he entertained notions of quitting his job, cashing out his 401K, traveling somewhere and staying there and staying so drunk he wouldn't give a fat rat's ass if his death was slamming margaritas right beside him with a cokewhore on each skinny elbow. But what nailed those notions to the door was that Michael couldn't picture getting so drunk he wouldn't give a shit if his own death were getting hammered right beside him. Who could.

So running away was out. And in the meantime there was rent and car payments and utilities and dental appointments, and being able to see his death or the death of every person in Los Angeles and his dog didn't do one goddamn thing to alleviate those daily truths.

A friend of Michael's—when he'd had friends, when he'd returned phonecalls—had once confided that he had prescient dreams. "They're not like regular dreams. I have those too but these feel different. And when I have them I know which ones they are. And they come true, I swear to god. But the thing is, they're always totally trivial. Like I'll dream that I'm getting my card back from an ATM machine I've never been to, and six months later I'll be out of town and getting cash from a machine and it'll be that machine. I mean big deal, right. Some reality show I'd make, huh."

Michael had admitted that as psychic powers go it did seem kind of useless but it would still be a fun ability to possess. The little charge you'd get when you realized you were acting out your dream however inconsequential.

His own unique talent seemed much more weighty but really it was just as useless. Seeing his own death, other people's deaths, didn't tell him a thing about the person or how the person was going to die or where or when. There was no information beyond the observation itself that Michael could impart to anyone. And imparting the observation kind of altered the landscape. As Andrea had succinctly put it. And it sure as shit wasn't fun. In fact his amazing and totally unique ability wasn't good for much besides fucking up his life.

Then he saw somebody die.

IT HAPPENED ON the morning commute. The righthand feeder lane was creeping toward the merge at its usual fifteen miles an hour and a silver Mercedes darted from it into a break in the slow lane. Slow lane traffic was still going at least fifty and the driver of a little Kia stood on his brakes when the Mercedes pulled in front of him going a lot slower. Michael was behind the Kia and saw the whole thing. The Kia's brakelights flashed and the little car slowed quickly, but then the brakelights went off and the car slewed left into the next lane and wedged between the front and rear wheels of a semi and was dragged fifty feet. Michael saw the driver through the little car's rear windshield. The brakelights flashed again and the little car stopped dragging and the semi scraped along it and then drove right over it.

Michael hit his brakes when the Kia veered into the truck and then stood on them when the semi humped over the little white car and then stopped. Surrounding traffic halted and people stared in disbelief, half of them already pressing cell phones to their cheeks. The Mercedes that began this ballet mechanique had never even slowed. It had fitted into morning traffic and driven out of sight.

Michael was the first one out of his car. He looked back for oncoming traffic but the freeway was already at a standstill. He got to the crushed white car as the driver's death emerged from the passenger side and walked around to the driver's side and stood looking at the buckled roof and pebbled windshield glass. Michael couldn't see the driver. The semi smelled of diesel and hot oil. The truck driver coming around now. His look of wonder almost comical.

Michael's death came up beside him. Michael looked at him a moment but his death was looking at the Kia driver's death staring at the mangled car as if waiting for something. The startling quiet. Other people were getting out of their cars now. Disbelief and wonder. Silent deaths beside them looking at the Kia driver's death with what Michael sensed was apprehension.

"I didn't even know he was there," the truck driver was saying. "How did he get there."

Michael looked at him. He leaned toward the crumpled Kia. Could a person even fit into that compressed space. "Can you hear me." he said. There was no reply. "Paramedics will be here soon. Can you—"

Something shot out from the fractured windshield. Small and glinting gold and darting like a firefly it hovered for a moment and a deep black hole opened in the air beside it and a starveling gray bald birdlike thing leapt from the hole with knobteethed jaws stretched wide to snatch it from the mortal world. The Kia driver's death moved startling fast and grabbed the firefly from the very mouth of what dread beast had come to claim it and the dark wide mouth clacked shut on empty air. The same leap that had carried the thing into the world now carried it as suddenly away, an orca leaping briefly through the airfilled world and gone.

The Kia driver's death stood firm and staring at its own tightshut fist. As if stunned by what it had just done. What it now held.

All the other deaths around it bowed their heads. Michael looked at his own death standing quiet with its large ungainly head inclined.

Holding its catch hard to its bony chest the Kia driver's death turned in a circle to take in the respectful and relieved acknowledgement of its own grave kind. Free hand covering its knobby fist as if expressing heartache. If heart it had at all. And bearing gift or burden it walked away from the crushed vessel now unoccupied and passed among its counterparts. Unhurried pace but purposeful. The branchlike hands of those it passed pressed branchlike to their chests. Passed among them now and past and bound for where?

Unaccountably Michael found himself fighting not to cry.

People gathered round the crushed car now. The truck driver explaining to anyone who would listen that he hadn't even known the car was there, how had it got there.

I'll need to give a statement, Michael thought. Remember what I can about the car that drove away. Mercedes. Silver. Fourdoor. Late model. Passenger? Plate? I have to call work and tell them I'll be late because I saw an accident. A fatal accident. Someone died.

The gold flicker, the hole in the air, the streaking creature, the swift catch. Sudden cold in his gut. Nausea and joy. We have souls. We are souls.

He walked back to his car to get his cell phone and stopped with his door half open.

Between stopped cars she stood straight and quiet with the upright posture and detached manner he had come to know so well. Head bowed and hand against her breast. The hand not sticklike and remote but fleshed and manicured. Paleblue scrubs and white tennis shoes. A ponytail of ash blonde hair.

The hand lowered and the head raised and she saw Michael looking at her. Not flat doll eyes but close set blue. Michael brought his own hand to his chest and looked at the wrecked car and looked back at her. He made a grabbing motion as if catching a fly. She looked surprised and then she nodded. Yes I see them. I can see them too.

HE'D BEEN AT work not half an hour when Marilyn called and asked him to come into her office. He hung up and wondered if he would even protest what was about to happen. He shut off the transcriber and glanced around at his cube and at his death and then he got up. His death following. At her office he knocked on her doorframe and she looked up from a folder and beckoned him in and said Close the door please.

Everything fit into a medium sized cardboard box. The measure of his vestment in the place after three and a half years. Not even a goodbye to anyone. No one to say goodbye to. Carrying his box through the lobby, the security guard opening a door for him, Have a great day now. Too late but thanks anyway. A final nod to Henry the Angel's Flight ticket taker. The short ride down the hill toward Grand, the slanted railcar clacking and swerving. Already calculating savings, unemployment, how far could he stretch it all before he'd have to find another job. His death unaccountable on the rear bench seat, looking up and out at the towers of Bunker Hill.

At home he set the box on the coffee table and just stood in the living-room feeling empty but not feeling bad. About the job at least. He hadn't argued, objected, defended himself. He'd nodded and said okay and that was pretty much it. Knowing that if Marilyn hadn't called him in today she would have one day soon. He'd been headed that way ever since his death had shown up at his door.

His death. On the couch already with thin fingers interlaced on his thin lap and staring at the darkgray teevee screen as if it were on. Some inexplicable inherited pet I am beholden to.

That catch. That impossible World Series gamesaver. The ensuing silent acquiescence and acknowledgement and relief. Souls. Is that really why you're here. Why all of you are here.

His death looked at Michael's effects in the cardboard box on the coffee table and then briefly at Michael and then back to the blank teevee.

From his pocket Michael pulled the torn and folded strip of legal pad she'd given him. Her name and number written there in blue pen. Hayley. "After six, okay?" she'd said as she handed it to him. "I'm coming off shift and I really need to sleep."

He looked at the clock. It was going to be a long five hours.

Michael ordered a decaf grande drip and then sat fidgeting. He tried to read the paper but he couldn't focus long enough to make the words make sense. He glanced at the door whenever someone entered but none of them were her. Then he saw her getting out of her car, the same car she'd been driving a thousand years ago this morning at the accident that had led to Michael waiting for her here. Still in her scrubs. Or more likely new ones.

Her death followed her and Hayley held the door open and her death went in ahead of her as if accustomed to this. Hayley kept the door open for a couple and their deaths who were leaving and she nodded cheerfully to them even though they didn't acknowledge her. She saw Michael and came to his table and set down her little backpack and pulled out a nylon Hello Kitty billfold and smiled and said You okay?

"To be honest I don't know."

She nodded but said she'd meant his coffee.

"Oh. Um. I'm okay. Yes. Thanks."

"Okay. I need serious caffeine. I'm running on fumes."

"I thought you went home to sleep."

"That's how it's supposed to work. The rest of the world isn't on my schedule though." She started away and then stopped and looked at him. "Hard day, huh."

He shrugged. "I saw someone else have worse."

She set a hand on his shoulder. "Be right back."

She went to join the line and he looked at the shoulder she had squeezed. Her death had joined his at a corner table and was pulling out a rubberbanded deck of playing cards. Michael watched her shuffle clumsily and then deal thirteen cards apiece and turn one card faceup on the discard pile.

Hayley came back with some kind of godawful confection masquerading as a coffee drink. Whipped topping pressing up against a plastic dome. "So you got fired?"

"Cause I was late."

"That seems a bit heartless. You told them about the accident?"

He shook his head. "It wasn't the first time."

"It wasn't a surprise either I take it."

"I think I'm actually grateful." And realized as he said it that he was.

"Ah. Work stopped being fun after our little friends showed up, did it."

"Friends. Yeah." He sipped coffee. "Work's the least of what stopped being fun since my buddy there moved in. I've, you know. Been kind of alone with it. Can't really tell anyone. Well, one person. That didn't go so great."

"Did she walk backward to the nearest exit."

"I think she left skidmarks."

She grinned. "It's good you can still laugh."

"I'm crying on the inside."

She sipped her drink and set it down. "Good god what's in these. So what are you going to do now."

"I think that depends on you."

She raised an eyebrow.

"Seeing our little friends doesn't seem to be making you crazy."

"Maybe I've had longer to get used to it."

"You work in an ER. What happened this morning, you must see that every day."

"Cardiac intensive care unit. Yeah. Four or five times a week I guess."

"So why aren't you crazy."

"How do you know I'm not. How do I know I'm not."

"Well maybe you are. Maybe we're both crazy the same way. Maybe that's why we're the only ones who can see our little friends."

"How do you know we are." Her smile so disquieting.

He hesitated. "Well okay, sure. There have to be more of us, you're right. Maybe we should put an ad on craigslist. Have a barbecue, trade My Little Friend stories."

"I think more people'd show up than you realize."

"You think a lot of people see this?"

She picked up her drink again. "I think almost everybody does."

SHE HAD TO go to work and couldn't talk much longer. She held up her hands to stem his tide of questions. What it all meant. What they'd seen this morning. Why they could see people's deaths. How almost everyone could see them as she claimed without anyone admitting it. "I think you should think about this stuff a while without me saying anything. Come up with your own answers."

"But I want to hear yours."

"But mine aren't answers. I haven't been able to compare them to anything. To anyone else's experience. They're just theories. Opinions."

"Well then I'd like to hear your theories and opinions."

"It will mean a lot more to both of us if you come up with your own explanations and we compare them and they turn out to be similar."

"You want to be scientific."

"If it ain't science it ain't shit." She finished her drink and stood and picked up her backpack. "Okay?"

Michael nodded. What else could he do. "Okay."

"All right." Her hand on his shoulder again. "It'll be a great adventure." And off to face her day.

Michael's great adventure continued without his little friend around as much. Entire evenings sometimes without his death in sight. Even into the morning a few times. Michael would shove something in the microwave and watch teevee or read a book or just take an aimless drive and his death would not be with him. He saw other people's though. The ability hadn't left him. And then mornings his death would be there on the couch or at the little dining table. One night he got up late to take a piss and saw the television light from the living room and went in to check and there was his death watching Discovery Channel. "Been out with your little friends?" he said. But of course his death said nothing.

Michael spent his days reading or doing minor repairs or useless rearrangements of things in his apartment. He did not job hunt and did not feel a need to. He applied for unemployment and he toyed with resurrecting any number of projects waylaid through the years, consigned to bullet lists and rough sketches in spiral notebooks but never manifested beyond the wondering on paper.

As Hayley had suggested he thought a lot about what he'd seen that day on the freeway. As if he had a choice. He also thought a lot about his meeting with Hayley. The example of her even briefly encountered loomed before him often. He considered calling her but could not bring himself to. What she must think of him. She saw her death, she saw other people's deaths, and yet she seemed engaged with her own life. She worked in a cardiac intensive care unit for christ sake. Out there fighting in the trenches while you type deposition summaries and pleadings for corporate litigation firms and whine about the imminence of your own mortality. Well boo fucking hoo you pussy.

He went on like this, variously numbed or debating or self flagellating, for two weeks after getting fired. Then one night Hayley called and said I think we should talk.

—————

She watched him gulp his coffee down and asked how he was doing. He set the cup on the little table and wiped his mouth and asked if her interest was professional. When she didn't say anything he looked down and shook his head and said Sorry.

She accepted with a nod. "It gets to me sometimes too."

"In the ER? Sorry, the ICU?"

Their deaths were combing through the newspaper bin for something to read.

"Sure. Nurses aren't robots you know."

"How do you deal with it."

"Is your interest professional." She grinned. "Sorry. The first couple of times I didn't deal with all that great. Now." She shrugged. "You see some pretty awful things on the ward anyway. You develop coping mechanisms."

"Like a robot."

"Are you mad because I wouldn't tell you what I think it means."

"No." He thought about it. "Yes. But not mad at you."

"Tell me what you think first. About what you saw that day on the freeway. Show me yours and I'll show you mine."

"I haven't played doctor in a long time."

"I do it for a living. Sort of."

"You win." He drummed his fingers, glanced at their deaths reading the comics and metro sections. "I thought about it of course. Replayed it over and over, looked at it from every angle I could."

"And."

"And I'll be honest, I have absolutely no idea what I saw."

She narrowed her eyes. "Don't wimp out on me."

"I really don't know."

"You'd have to have no imagination whatsoever to have no idea. What do you think the tinkerbell is."

"The tinkerbell. The firefly?"

She nodded. "The gold fairy light that flitters around."

"I." He felt himself turn red. "Okay." He looked down at his cup. "I think it's a soul. The soul."

"I do too. See, we're making progress."

"Scientific."

"Two people in the fog have a better chance of getting through it if they call out to each other."

"You just make that up?"

"Yeah, I'm all poetic like that. How about the dog."

"The dog?"

"The thing that jumps out of nowhere and tries to eat the tinkerbell."

"It looked like a bird to me."

"Really."

"Well that's what I saw. Thought I saw. It was pretty goddamn fast."

"What do you think it was."

"No idea." He stopped at the look on her face. Deep breath. "Okay. I think it was a monster. A demon. A devil. An alien taking samples. An embodiment of guilt. Agent of justice. Karma. Retribution." He spread his hands. "Something from somewhere else that came to get the firefly."

She leaned toward him. "And why do you think our little friends catch them." Softly.

He couldn't have said why he felt afraid. "Do they."

"You saw it didn't you."

"I mean is that what happens every time."

"Oh." She stirred her drink and then nodded. "Yes. Yes it is." Memories of just such happenings ghosting her eyes.

"This is what happens when people die."

"Not always."

"What else."

"Sometimes they don't make the catch."

He stared. "Then what happens."

"Then the bird dog gets it."

He thought about that.

"So why do you think our little friends do it," she asked again.

"Make the catch? Or try to anyway."

She nodded.

"I don't know." He held up his hands. "Really. I can't come up with anything. I mean, angels, delivery boys, bounty hunters, I don't know. Maybe they're the bad guys and the bird dogs are on our side."

"And you said you have no idea." She drank her sugar drink. "Bounty hunters. That's good."

"Maybe they work on commission. I don't know. I've only seen this once. You see it every day before lunch. So what do you think it means."

"Mine's a lot weirder than yours."

"I'm in no position to poke fun."

"Okay." She turned to look at their deaths while she spoke and he had to crane forward to hear her. "I think we do have souls. I think that when we die they leave our bodies. I think when they do they're disoriented. Like they're in shock or traumatized. Maybe only at first. I don't know. But they're vulnerable. Like baby birds. A scared little baby chicken running around making all kinds of noise. Generating all kinds of attention. And I think there are hawks out there. Things that prey on frightened little chickens."

He nodded at their deaths trading newspaper sections across the room. "And they're what. Scarecrows?"

"Not the word I'd use. They don't really scare them away, do they."

"What word would you use."

"I don't know. I don't know if there is one."

"And they're there to keep the hawks from getting us."

She nodded.

"How good are they at this. I mean what's the, the success rate."

"Pretty good. I'd say ninety percent."

"Ninety percent. Nine out of ten. Nine hundred out of a thousand." He glanced around the coffee shop and then back to her. "Do you mind if I tell you that this idea scares the living shit out of me."

She laughed but sniffled afterward and he realized she was trying not to cry. "Well. Misery loves company. It scares me too."

"No no. You can't cry. You can't be scared. You're Miss Tough Chick. You're the hardened veteran. You answer codes and crack chests and push meds. You're the living proof that someone can know about this and figure out some way to lead their goddamn life."

She laughed and then blew her nose into a napkin that she wadded and stuffed into her mostly empty cup. "Sorry to disappoint you."

THE NEIGHBORHOOD WAS unfamiliar to both of them but the day was bright and warm and it was better to walk and talk about this than try to have this discussion in a fucking Starbucks. Their deaths kept close behind them. Michael thought he should hold Hayley's hand and then wondered why he thought that.

"So this is the big answer?" he said. "The end of the great adventure? Every human being who ever lived ends up popping out of his body when he dies like something at a batting cage, and one time in ten he gets eaten by a dog from hell."

"I didn't design this Monopoly game. I'm just a little metal car on the board."

"No one said you did. But—well, I mean. Fuck. Shit."

"That about sums it up."

He shook his head. "I always liked the top hat."

She snorted. "So listen. I think they're supposed to stay with us all the time. Twentyfour seven, rain or shine."

"For richer or poorer, in sickness and in health."

"Something like that." They were walking on a block that seemed to be holding some informal remodeling contest. Half the houses were built out to within feet of the lot borders with not enough space between to run a pushmower.

"But mine isn't always around. At first it was but then there were times it left me alone. And lately it's been gone a lot. Since I met you in fact."

"Yeah. That's why I called you. I think there's something wrong with yours."

"Like what."

She craned to look behind them. "Where do you think it's been going off to since you met me."

Michael stopped. On the sidewalk there before a small tract house enribbed by the hope of a second floor. Stopped and turned to Hayley and Hayley nodded and he turned to look behind them. At their deaths standing on the sidewalk holding hands.

MICHAEL CONVINCED HAYLEY to take some time off work while they tried to sort this out and then felt guilty when he saw how many calls she had to make to trade shifts, owe favors, juggle hours, and play with accrued PTO. But she agreed it was important and didn't complain.

At first they met at coffee shops and restaurants, until Michael admitted that his savings wouldn't let him keep this up for long. Unsaid was the fact that his death's absence now upset him even more than his death's presence ever had. What if he got hit by a bus. Nine out of ten was a hell of a lot better odds than none out of ten.

For her part Hayley was not freaked out by her death's absence but she seemed to understand that Michael was. She suggested they take turns visiting each other at their respective apartments.

It was awkward but manageable. Hayley's apartment was much larger and nicer than his and much less worn. It had a lot of white-curtained windows and was painted in pale yellows and sea greens and got a lot of sun. It felt like her. Not very decorated though because she had so little time. His own place suffered in comparison. Battened down against the world and dark. He had made of it a tawdry museum filled with remnants from the vanished civilizations of relationships fallen to conquest, to apathy, attrition, climate change. Their timeworn relics the source of much puzzlement and speculation.

Their deaths did not leave them while they remained together.

They talked about what to do about the situation but arrived at nothing. They watched teevee and went out for coffee and read novels. They talked about favorite movies and their lives and what had led them here. She had dated doctors mostly and was fiercely dedicated to her work. He was surprised to learn that what attracted her to both had more to do with science than with people. She seemed as knowledgeable and authoritative as most doctors and in fact resented nurses who contented themselves with being little more than glorified maids and counted few of these among her friends. She was not lonely but she feared becoming some kind of crazy cat lady, alone with what she saw and what she knew and separated from friendship, from love, from life.

But you, she told Michael after they had finished chinese takeout on her couch, "are more crazy cat lady than I could imagine ever being.

"I don't own any cats," he said. "I hate cats."

In the kitchen their deaths struggled with the leftovers, dropping most of the food from the chopsticks.

Hayley took her sneakers off and flexed her toes in her white socks and turned on the couch and set her feet on Michael's lap and said You know what I mean.

He began to rub her foot through her sock. "Why don't you tell me what you mean and I'll see if it matches what I think you mean. Scientific."

"Scientific. All right." She closed her eyes and arched her back to slide her feet closer to him. "I think you're so afraid of dying that you've given up on life."

He bent her toes back with one hand and knuckled the ball of her foot with the other. "Do you."

"You asked."

"I did." He peeled the sock off. Her toenails painted india red. "Maybe I'm just mad about it."

She waved it away. "Mad, afraid. Giving up is giving up."

"What am I supposed to do, hold a party."

"But that is what people do. They hold parties. They hold them instead of giving up. And the thing is, I think you were like this before you started seeing all this. It makes me angry."

"Angry?"

She jerked her foot back at his surprised laugh. "Yes angry. You can't deal with knowing something everybody else already knows even if they can't see what you can, so you've given up and let it win ahead of time. I see it every day. People quit and they stay quit. What's the point and Why bother and None of it means anything. They're done. Their lives stop happening to them and from that point on they're only waiting. Whether it's another week or fifty years. And if it is a week or fifty years it doesn't matter because they aren't leading any kind of life during it. I mean, how much more wasteful can you get. Afraid to live your life because one day it'll be gone. It doesn't make any sense to me at all."

He beckoned to her socked foot and she extended it and he took off the sock and began to rub the arch. "All right then. What does make sense."

She pulled her shirttail from the waistband of her pants. "You go. That's all. You go until you stop."

He moved her free foot atop the zipper of his jeans and resumed rubbing the other one. "I'm not a quitter," he said. "I don't want to stop. I want to keep going. I'm trying to find a reason to."

She sat up. Hair disheveled. Pupils wide. Takeout wrappers on the table. Her foot in his hand. Their quick breathing in the pale yellow livingroom. She took her feet off his lap and moved forward to her knees and put a hand on his shoulder and pulled his face close to hers and said Well look harder, Michael.

Everyone attending agreed that even though the wedding had been very nice, the reception that followed was one of the best parties they had ever been to. The booze was good, the food was great, the DJ was a lightning rod, you'd have to be made of stone not to get half smashed and get your ass out there on the floor and shake it up and flirt and make a happy idiot of yourself and then realize somewhere in the joyous mess of sweating bodies that this was someone's wedding reception. In fact the only odd detail in an otherwise picture perfect celebration, a detail that the happy couple cheerfully refused to comment on at all, was the presence of four figures on the weddingcake instead of two.

HYDRAGUROS | *Caitlín R. Kiernan*

01.

THE VERY FIRST time I see silver, it's five minutes past noon on a Monday and I'm crammed into a seat on the Bridge Line, racing over the slate-gray Delaware River. Philly is crouched at my back, and a one o'clock with the Czech and a couple of his meatheads is waiting for me on the Jersey side of the Ben Franklin. I've been popping since I woke up half an hour late, the lucky greens Eli scores from his chemist somewhere in Devil's Pocket, so my head's buzzing almost bright and cold as the sun pouring down through the late January clouds. My gums are tingling, and my fucking fingertips, too, and I'm sitting there, wishing I was just about anywhere else but on my way to Camden, payday at journey's end or no payday at journey's end. I'm trying to look at nothing that isn't *out there*, on the opposite side of the window, because faces always make me jumpy when I'm using the stuff Eli assures me is mostly only methylphenidate with a little Phenotropil by way of his chemists' Russian connections. I'm in my seat, trying to concentrate on the shadow of the span and the Speedline on the water below, on the silhouettes of buildings to the south, on a goddamn flock of birds, anything out there to keep me focused, keep me jake. But then my ears pop, and there's a second or two of dizziness before I smell ozone and ammonia and something with the carbon stink of burning sugar.

We're almost across the bridge by then, and I tell myself not to look, not to dare fucking look, just mind my own business and watch the window, my sickly, pale reflection *in* the window, and the dingy winter scene the window's holding at bay. But I look anyhow.

There's a very pretty woman sitting across the aisle from me, her skin as dark as freshly ground coffee, her hair dreadlocked and pulled back away from her face. Her skin is dark, but her eyes are a brilliant, bottomless green. For a seemingly elastic moment, I am unable to look away from those incongruent, unexpected eyes. They manage to be both merciful and fierce, like the painted eyes of Catholic saints rendered in plaster of Paris. And I'm thinking it's no big, and I'll be able to look back out the window; who gives a shit what that smell might have been. It's already starting to fade. But then the pretty woman turns her head to the left, towards the front of the car, and quicksilver trickles from her left nostril and spatters her jeans. If she felt it—if she's in any way aware of this strange excrescence—she shows no sign that she felt it. She doesn't wipe her nose, or look down at her pants. If anyone else saw what I saw, they're busy pretending like they didn't. I call it quicksilver, though I know that's not what I'm seeing. Even this first time, I know it's only something that *looks* like mercury, because I have no frame of reference to think of it any other way.

The woman turns back towards me, and she smiles. It's a nervous, slightly embarrassed sort of smile, and I suppose I must have been sitting there gawking at her. I want to apologize. Instead, I force myself to go back to the window, and curse that Irish cunt that's been selling Eli fuck knows what. I curse myself for being such a lazy asshole and popping whatever's at hand when I have access to good clean junk. And then the train is across that filthy, poisoned river and rolling past Campbell Field and Pearl Street. My heart's going a mile a minute, and I'm sweating like it's August. I grip the handle of the shiny aluminum briefcase I'm supposed to hand over to the Czech, assuming he has the cash, and do my best to push back everything but my trepidation of things I know I'm not imagining. You don't go into a face-to-face with one of El Diamante's bastards with a shake on, not if you want to keep the red stuff on the inside where it fucking belongs.

I don't look at the pretty black woman again.

02.

THE VERY FIRST thing you learn about the Czech is that he's not from the Czech Republic or the dear departed Czech Socialist Republic or, for that matter, Slovakia. He's not even European. He's just some Canuck motherfucker who used to haunt Montreal, selling cloned phones and heroin and whores. A genuine Renaissance crook, the Czech. I have no idea where or when or why he picked up the nickname, but it stuck like shit on the wall of a gorilla's cage. The second thing you learn about the Czech is not to ask about the scars. If you're lucky, you've learned both these things before you have the misfortune of making his acquaintance up close and personal.

Anyway, he has a car waiting for me when the train dumps me out at Broadway Station, but I make the driver wait while I pay too much for bottled water at Starbucks. The lucky greens have me in such a fizz I'm almost seeing double, and there are rare occasions when a little H_2O seems to help bring me down again. I don't actually expect *this* will be one of those times, but I'm still a bit weirded out by what I think I saw on the Speedline, and I'm a lot pissed that the Czech's dragged me all the way over to Jersey at this indecent hour on a Monday. So, let the driver wait for five while I buy a lukewarm bottle of Dasani that I know is just twelve ounces of Philly tap water with a fancy blue label slapped on it.

"Czech, he don't like to be kept waiting," says the skinny Mexican kid behind the wheel when I climb into the backseat. I show him my middle finger, and he shrugs and pulls away from the curb. I set the briefcase on the seat beside me, just wanting to be free of the package and on my way back to Eli and our cozy dump of an apartment in Chinatown. As the jet-black Lincoln MKS turns off Broadway on Mickle Boulevard, heading west, carrying me back towards the river, I'm thinking how I'm going to have a chat with Eli about finding a better pusher. My gums feel like I've been chewing foil, and there are wasps darting about behind my eyes. At least the wasps are keeping their stingers to themselves.

"Just how late are we?" I ask the driver.

"Ten minutes," he replies.

"Blame the train."

"You blame the train, Mister. I don't talk to the Czech unless he talks to me, and he never talks to me."

"Lucky you," I say and take another swallow of Dasani. It tastes more like the polyethylene terephthalate bottle than water, and I try not to think about toxicity and esters of phthalic acid, endocrine disruption and antimony trioxide, because that just puts me right back on the Bridge Line watching a pretty woman's silver nosebleed.

We stop at a red light, then turn left onto South Third Street, paralleling the waterfront, and I realize the drop's going to be the warehouse on Spruce. I want to close my eyes, but all those lucky green wasps won't let me. The sun is so bright it seems to be flashing off even the most nonreflective of surfaces. Vast seas of asphalt might as well be goddamn mirrors. I drum my fingers on the lid of the aluminum briefcase, wishing the driver had the radio on or a DVD playing, anything to distract me from the buzz in my skull and the noise the tires make against the pavement. Another three or four long minutes and we're bumping off the road into a parking lot that might have last been paved when Obama was in the White House. And the Mexican kid pulls up at the loading bay, and I open the door and step out into the cold, sunny day. The Lincoln has stirred up a shroud of red-gray dust, but all that sunlight doesn't give a shit. It shines straight on through the haze and almost lays me open, head to fucking toe. I cough a few times on my way from the car to the bald-headed goon in Ray-Bans waiting to usher me to my rendezvous with the Czech. However, the wasps do not take my cough as an opportunity to vacate my cranium, so maybe they're here to stay. The goon pats me down and then double checks with a security wand. When he's sure I'm not packing anything more menacing than my Blackberry, he leads me out of the flaying day and into merciful shadows and muted pools of halogen light.

"You're late," the Czech says, just in case I haven't noticed, and he points at a clock on the wall. "You're almost twelve minutes late."

I glance over my shoulder at the clock, because it seems rude not to look after he's gone to the trouble to point. Actually, I'm almost eleven minutes late.

"You got some more important place to be, Czech?" I ask, deciding it's as good a day as any to push my luck a few extra inches.

"Maybe I do at that, you sick homo fuck. Maybe your ass is sitting at the very bottom of my to-do list this fine day. So, how about you zip it and let's get this over with."

I turn away from the clock and back to the fold-out card table where the Czech's sitting in a fold-out chair. He's smoking a Parliament and in front of him there's a half-eaten corned beef sandwich cradled in white butcher's paper. I try not to stare at the scars, but you might as well try to make your heart stop beating for a minute or two. Way I heard it, the stupid son of a bitch got drunk and went bear-hunting in some Alaskan national park or another, only he tried to make do with a bottle of vodka and a .22 caliber pocket pistol instead of a rifle. No, that's probably not the truth of it, but his face does look like something a grizzly's been gnawing at.

"You got the goods?" he asks, and I have the impression I'm watching Quasimodo quoting old Jimmy Cagney gangster films. I hold up the briefcase and he nods and puffs his cigarette.

"But I am curious as hell why you went and switched the drop date," I say, wondering if it's really me talking this trash to the Czech, or if maybe the lucky greens have highjacked the speech centers of my brain and are determined to get me shot in the face. "I might have had plans, you know. And El Diamante usually sticks to the script."

"What El Diamante does, that ain't none of your business, and that ain't my business, neither. Now, didn't I say zip it?" And then he jabs a thumb at a second metal folding chair, a few feet in front of the card table, and he tells me to give him the case and sit the fuck down. Which is what I do. Maybe the greens have decided to give me a break, after all. Or maybe they just want to draw this out as long as possible. The Czech dials the three-digit combination and opens the aluminum briefcase. He has a long look inside. Then he grunts and shuts it again. And that's when I notice something shimmering on the toe of his left shoe. It looks a lot like a few drops of spilled mercury. This is the second time I see silver.

03.

THIS IS HOURS later, and I'm back in Philly, trying to forget all about the woman on the train and the Czech's shoes and whatever might have been in the briefcase I delivered. The sun's been down for hours.

The city is dark and cold, and there's supposed to be snow before the sun comes up again. I'm lying in the bed I share with Eli, just lying there on my right side watching him read. There are things I want to tell him, but I know full fucking well that I won't. I won't because some of those things might get him killed if a deal ever goes wrong somewhere down the line (and it's only a matter of time) or if I should fall from grace with Her Majesty Madam Adrianne and all the powers that be and keep the axles upon which the world spins greased up and relatively friction free. And other things I will not tell him because maybe it was only the pills, or maybe it's stress, or maybe I'm losing my goddamn mind, and if it's the latter, I'd rather keep that morsel to myself as long as possible, pretty please and thank you.

Eli turns a page and shifts slightly, to better take advantage of the reading lamp on the little table beside the bed. I scan the spine of the hardback, the words printed on the dust jacket, like I don't already know it by heart. Eli reads books, and I read their dust jackets. Catch me in just the right mood, I might read the cover and flap copy.

"I thought you were asleep," Eli says without bothering to look at me.

"Maybe later, *chica*," I reply, and Eli nods the way he does when he's far more interested in whatever he's reading than in talking to me. So, I read the spine again, aloud this time, purposefully mispronouncing the Korean author's name. Which is enough to get Eli to glance my way. Eli's eyes are emeralds, crossed with some less precious stone. Agate maybe. Eli's eyes are emerald and agate, cut and polished to precision, flawed in ways that only make them more perfect.

"Go to sleep," he tells me, pretending to frown. "You look exhausted. You look exhausted and back again."

"Yeah, sure, but I got this fucking hard on like you wouldn't believe."

"Last time I checked, you also had two good hands and a more than adequate knowledge of how they work."

"That's cold," I say. "That is some cold shit to say to someone who had to go spend the day in Jersey."

Eli snorts, and his emerald and agate eyes, which might pass for only hazel-green if you haven't lived with them as long as I have lived with them, drift back to the printed page.

"The lube warms up just fine," he says, "you hold it a minute or so first." He doesn't laugh, but I do, and then I roll over to stare at the wall instead of watching Eli read. The wall is flat and dull, and sometimes it makes me sleepy. I'd take something, but after the lucky greens, it's probably best if I forego the cocktail of pot and prescription benzodiazepines I usually rely on to beat my insomnia into submission. I don't masturbate, because, boner from hell or not, I'm not in the right frame of mind to give myself a hand job. So, I lie and stare at the wall and listen to the soft sounds of Eli reading his biography of South Korean astronaut Yi So-Yeon, who I do recall, and without having to read the book, was the first Korean in space. She might also have been the second Asian woman to slip the surly fucking bonds of Earth and dance the skies or what the hell ever.

"Why don't you take something if you can't sleep," Eli says after maybe half an hour of me lying there.

"I don't think so, chica. My brain's still rocking and rolling from the breath mints you been buying off that mick cocksucker you call a dealer. Me, I think he's using drain cleaner again."

"No way," Eli says, and I can tell from the tone of his voice he's only half interested, at best, in whether or not the mad chemist holed up in Devil's Pocket is using Drano to cut his shit. "Donncha's merchandise is clean."

"Maybe *Mr.* Clean," I reply, and Eli smacks me lightly on the back of the head with his book. He tells me to jack off and go to sleep. I tell him to blow me. We spar with the age-old poetry of true love's tin-eared wit. Then he goes back to reading, and I go back to staring at the bedroom wall.

Eli is the only guy I've been with more than a month, and here we are going on two years. I found him waiting tables in a noodle and sushi joint over on Race Street. Most of the waiters in the place were either drag queens or trannies, dressed up like geisha whores from some sort of post-apocalyptic Yakuza flick. He was wearing so much makeup, and I was so drunk on Sapporo Black Label and saki, I didn't even realize he was every bit *gai-ko* as me. That first night, back at Eli's old apartment not far from the noodle shop, we screwed liked goddamn bunnies on crank. I must have walked funny for a week.

I started eating in that place every night, and almost every night, we'd wind up in bed together, and that's probably the happiest I've ever been or ever will be. Sure, the sex was absolute supremo, stand-out—state of the fucking *art* of fucking—but it never would have been enough to keep things going after a few weeks. I don't care how sweet the cock, sooner or later, if that's all there is interest wanes and I start to drift. I used to think maybe my libido had ADD or something, or I'd convinced myself that commitment meant I might miss out on something better. What matters, though, there was more, and four months later Eli packed up his shit and moved in with me. He never asked what I do to pay the rent, and I've never felt compelled to volunteer that piece of intel.

"You're still awake," Eli says, and I hear him toss his book onto the table beside the bed. I hear him reach for a pill bottle.

"Yeah, I'm still awake."

"Good, 'cause there's something I meant to tell you earlier, and I almost forgot."

"And what is that, pray tell?" I ask, listening as he rattles a few milligrams of this or that out into his palm.

"This woman in the restaurant. It was the weirdest thing. I mean, I'd think maybe I was hallucinating or imagining crap, only Jules saw it, too. Think it scared her, to tell you the truth."

Jules is the noodle shop's tranny hostess, who sometimes comes over to play, when Eli and I find ourselves inclined for takeout of that particular variety. It happens. But, point is, Eli says these words, words that ought to be nothing more than a passing fleck of conversation peering in on the edge of my not getting to sleep, and I get goddamn goose bumps and my stomach does some sort of roll like it just discovered the pommel horse. Because I know what he's going to say. Not exactly, no, but close enough that I want to tell him to please shut the fuck up and turn off the light and never mind what it is he *thinks* he saw.

But I don't, and he says, "This woman came in alone and so Jules sat her at the bar, right? Total dyke, but she had this whole butch-glam demeanor working for her, like Nicole Kidman with a buzz cut."

"You're right," I mutter at the wall, as if it's not too late for intervention. "That's pretty goddamn weird."

"No, you ass. That's not the weird part. The weird part was when I brought her order out, and I noticed there was this shiny silver stuff dripping out of her left ear. At first, I thought it was only a piercing or something, and I just wasn't seeing it right. But then…well, I looked again, and it had run down her neck and was soaking into the collar of her dress. Jules saw it, too. Freaky, yeah?"

"Yeah," I say, but I don't say much more, and a few minutes later, Eli finally switches off the lamp, and I can stare at the wall without actually having to see it.

04.

It's two days later, as the crow flies, and I'm waiting on a call from one of Her Majesty's lieutenants. I'm holed up in the backroom of a meat market in Bella Vista, on a side street just off Washington, me and Joey the Kike. We're bored and second-guessing our daily marching orders from the pampered, privileged pit bulls those of us so much nearer the bottom of this miscreant food chain refer to as carrion dispatch. Not very clever, sure, but all too fucking often, it hits the nail on the proverbial head. I might not like having to ride the Speedline out to Camden for a handoff with the Czech, but it beats waiting, and it sure as hell beats scraping up someone else's road kill and seeing to its discrete and final disposition. Which is where I have a feeling today is bound. Joey keeps trying to lure me into a game of whiskey poker, even though he knows I don't play cards or dice or dominoes or anything else that might lighten my wallet. You work for Madam Adrianne, you already got enough debt stacked up without gambling, even if it's only penny-ante foolishness to make the time go faster.

Joey the Kike isn't the absolute last person I'd pick to spend a morning with, but he's just next door. Back in the Ohs, when he was still just a kid, Joey did a stint in Afganistan and lost three fingers off his left hand and more than a few of his marbles. He still checks his shoes for scorpions. And most of us, we trust that whatever you hear coming out of his mouth is pure and unadulterated baloney. It's not that he lies, or even exaggerates to make something more interesting. It's more like he's a bottomless well of bullshit, and every conversation with Joey is another tour through the byways of his shattered psyche. For years, we've been waiting for the bastard to get yanked off the street and sent away to his own padded rumpus room at Norristown, where he can while away the days trading his crapola with other guys stuck on that same ever-tilting mental plane of existence. Still, I'll be the first to admit he's ace on the job, and nobody ever has to clean up after Joey the Kike.

He lights a cigarette and takes off his left shoe, and his sock, too, because you never can tell where a scorpion might turn up.

"You didn't open the case?" he asks, banging the heel of his shoe against the edge of a shipping crate.

"Hell no, I didn't open the case. You think we'd be having this delightful conversation today if I'd delivered a violated parcel to the Czech. Or anybody else, for that matter. For pity's sake, Joey."

"You ain't sleeping," he says, not a question, just a statement of the obvious.

"I'm getting very good at lying awake," I reply. "Anyway, what's that got to do with anything?"

"Sleep deprivation makes people paranoid," he says, and bangs his loafer against the crate two or three more times. But if he manages to dislodge any scorpions, they're the invisible brand. "Makes you prone to erratic behavior."

"Joey, please put your damn shoe back on."

"Hey, dude, you want to hear about the Trenton drop or not?" he asks, turning his sock wrong-side out for the second time. Ash falls from the cigarette dangling at the corner of his mouth.

I don't answer the question. Instead, I pick up my phone and stare at the screen, like I can will the thing to ring. All I really want right now is to get on with whatever inconvenience and unpleasantness the day holds in store, because Joey's a lot easier to take when confined spaces and the odor of raw pork fat aren't involved.

Not that he needs my permission to keep going. Not that my saying no, I don't want to hear about the Trenton drop is going to put an end to it.

"Well," he says, lowering his voice like he's about to spill a state secret, "what we saw when Tony Palamara opened that briefcase—and keep in mind, it was me *and* Jack on that job, so I've got backup if you need that sort of thing—what we saw was five or six of these silver vials. I'm not sure Tony realized we got a look inside or not, and, actually, it wasn't much more than a peek. It's not like either of us was *trying* to see inside. But, yeah, that's what we saw, these silver vials lined up neat as houses, each one maybe sixty or seventy milliliters, and they all had a piece of yellow tape or a yellow sticker on them. Jack, he thinks it was some sort of high-tech, next-gen explosive, maybe something you have to mix with something else to get the big bang, right?"

And I stare at him for a few seconds, and he stares back at me, that one green-and-black argyle sock drooping from his hand like some giant's idea of a novelty prophylactic. Whatever he sees in my face, it can't be good, not if his expression is any indication. He takes the cigarette out of his mouth and balances it on the edge of the shipping crate

"Joey, were the tubes silver, or was the silver what was inside of the tubes?"

And I can tell right away it hasn't occurred to him to wonder which. Why the hell would it? He asks me what difference it makes, sounding confused and suspicious and wary all at the same time.

"So you couldn't tell?"

"Like I said, it wasn't much more than a peek. Then Tony Palamara shut the case again. But if I had to speculate, if this was a wager and there was money on the line, I'd probably say the silver stuff was inside the tubes."

"If you had to speculate?" I ask him, and Joey the Kike bobs his head and turns his sock right-side out again.

"What difference does it make?" he wants to know. "I haven't even gotten around to the interesting part of the story yet."

And then, before I can ask him what the interesting part might be, my phone rings, and it's dispatch, and I stand there and listen while the dog barks. Straightforward janitorial work, because some asshole decided to use a shotgun when a 9mm would have sufficed. Nothing I haven't had to deal with a dozen times or more. I tell the dog we're on our way, and then I tell Joey it's his balls on the cutting board if we're late because he can't keep his shoes and socks on his goddamn feet.

05.

SOME NIGHTS, MOSTLY in the summer, Eli and me, we climb the rickety fire escape onto the roof to try to see the stars. There are a couple of injection-molded plastic lawn chairs up there, left behind by a former tenant, someone who moved out years before I moved into the building. We sit in those chairs that have come all the way from some East Asian factory shithole in Hong Kong or Taiwan, and we drink beer and smoke weed and stare up at the night spread out above Philly, trying to see anything at all. Mostly, it's a white-orange sky-glow haze, the opaque murk of photopollution, and I suspect we imagine far more stars than we actually see. I tell him that some night or another we'll drive way the hell out to the middle of nowhere, someplace where the sky is still mostly dark. He humors me, but Eli is a city kid, born and bred, and I think his idea of a pastoral landscape is Marconi Plaza. We might sit there and wax poetic about planets and nebulas and shit, but I have a feeling that if he ever found himself standing beneath the real deal, with all those twinkling pinpricks scattered overhead and maybe a full moon to boot, it'd probably freak him right the fuck on out.

One night he said to me, "Maybe this is preferable," and I had to ask what he meant.

"I just mean, maybe it's better this way, not being able to see the sky. Maybe, all this light, it's sort of like camouflage."

I squinted back at Eli through a cloud of fresh pot smoke, and when he reached for the pipe I passed it to him.

"I have no idea what you're talking about," I told him, and Eli shrugged and took a big hit of the 990 Master Kush I get from a grower who's well aware how much time I've spent in Amsterdam, so she knows better than to sell me dirt grass. Eli exhaled and passed the pipe back to me.

"Maybe I don't mean anything at all," he said and gave me half a smile. "Maybe I'm just stoned and tired and talking out my ass."

I think that was the same night we might have seen a falling star, though Eli was of the opinion it wasn't anything but a pile of space junk burning up as it tumbled back to earth.

06.

I'VE BEEN HANDLING the consequences of other people's half-assed *mokroye delo* since I was sixteen going on forty-five. So, yeah, takes an awfully bad scene to get me to so much as flinch, which is not to say I *enjoy* the shit. Truth of it, nothing pisses me off worse or quicker than some bastard spinning off the rails, running around with that first-person shooter mentality that, more often than not, turns a simple, straight-up hit into a bloodbath. And that is precisely the brand of unnecessary crimson pageantry that me and Joey the Kike have just spent the last three hours mopping up. What's left of the recently deceased, along with a bin of bloody rags and sponges and the latex gloves and coveralls we wore, is stowed snuggly in the trunk of the car. Another ten minutes, it won't be our problem anymore, soon as we make the scheduled meet and greet with one of Madam Adrianne's garbage men.

So, it's hardly business as usual that Joey's behind the wheel because my hands won't stop shaking enough that I can drive. They won't stop shaking long enough for me to even light a cigarette.

"You really aren't gonna tell me what it was happened back there?" he asks for, I don't know, the hundredth time in the last thirty or forty minutes. I glance at my watch, then to the speedometer, making sure we're not late and he's not speeding. At least I have that much presence of mind left to me.

"Never yet known you to be the squeamish type with wet work," he says and stops for a red light.

Most of the snow from Tuesday night has melted, but there are still plenty of off-white scabs hiding in the shadows, and there's also the filthy mix of ice and sand and schmutz heaped at either side of the street. There are people out there shivering at a bus stop, people rushing along the icy sidewalk, a homeless guy huddled in the doorway of abandoned office building. Every last bit of that tableau is as ordinary as it gets, the humdrum day-to-day of the ineptly named City of Brotherly Love, and that ought to help, but it doesn't. All of it comes across as window dressing, meticulously crafted misdirection meant to keep me from getting a good look at what's really going down.

"Dude, seriously, you're starting to give me the heebie-jeebies," Joey says.

"Why don't you just concentrate on getting us where we're going," I tell him. "See if you can do that, all right? Cause it's about the only thing in the world you have to worry about right now."

"We're not gonna be late," says Joey the Kike. "At this rate, we might be fucking early, but we sure as hell ain't gonna be late."

I keep my mouth shut. Out there, a thin woman with a toy Doberman on a pink rhinestone leash walks past. She's wearing galoshes and a pink wool coat that only comes down to her knees. At the bus stop, tucked safe inside that translucent half-shell, a man lays down a newspaper and answers his phone. The homeless guy scratches at his beard and talks to himself. Then the traffic light turns green, and we're moving again.

This is the day that I saw silver for the third time. But no way in hell I'm going to tell Joey that.

Just like the first time, sitting on the train as it barreled towards Camden and my tryst with the Czech, I felt my ears pop, and then there was the same brief dizziness, followed by the commingled reek of ammonia, ozone, and burnt sugar. Me and Joey, we'd just found the room with the body, some poor son of a bitch who'd taken both barrels of a Remington in the face. Who knows what he'd done, or if he'd done anything at all. Could have been over money or dope or maybe someone just wanted him out of the way. I don't let myself think too much about that sort of thing. Better not to even think of the body as *someone*. Better to treat it the way a stock boy handles a messy cleanup on aisle five after someone's shopping cart has careened into a towering display of spaghetti sauce.

"Sometimes," said Joey, "I wish I'd gone to college. What about you, man? Ever long for another line of work? Something that *don't* involve scraping brains off the linoleum after a throw-down."

But me, I was too busy simply trying to breathe to remind him that I *had* gone to college, too busy trying not to gag to partake in witty repartee. The dizziness had come and gone, but that acrid stench was forcing its way past my nostrils, scalding my sinuses and the back of my throat. And I knew that Joey didn't smell it, not so much as a whiff, and that his ears hadn't popped, and that he'd not shared that fleeting moment of vertigo. He stood there, glaring at me, his expression equal parts confusion and annoyance. Finally, he shook his head and stepped over the dead guy's legs.

"Jesus and Mary, we've both seen way worse than this," he said, and right then, that's when I caught the dull sparkle on the floor. The lower jaw was still in one piece, mostly, so for half a second or so I pretended I was only seeing the glint of fluorescent lighting off a filling or a crown. But then the silvery puddle, no larger than a dime, moved. It stood out very starkly against all that blood, against the soup of brain and muscle tissue punctuated by countless shards of human skull. It flowed a few inches before encountering a jellied lump of cerebellum, and then I watched as it slowly extended…what? What the fuck would you call what I saw? A *pseudopod*? Yeah, sure. I watched as it extended a pseudopod and began crawling *over* the obstacle in its path. That's when I turned away, and when I looked back, it wasn't there anymore.

Joey curses and honks the horn. I don't know why. I don't ask him. I don't care. I'm still staring out the passenger-side window at this brilliant winter day that wants or needs me to believe it's all nothing more or less than another round of the same old same old. I'm thinking about the woman on the Speedline and about the scuffed toe of the Czech's shoe, about whatever Eli saw at the noodle shop and the silver tubes Joey and Jack got a peep at when Tony Palamara opened the case they'd delivered to him. I'm drawing lines and making correlations, parsing best I can, dot-to-fucking-dot, right? Nothing it takes a genius to see, even if I've no idea whatsoever what it all adds up to in the end. I blink, and the sun sparks brutally off distant blue-black towers of mirrored glass. Joey hits the horn again, broadcasting his displeasure for all Girard Avenue to hear, and I shut my eyes.

07.

AND IT'S A night or two later that I have the dream for the first time.

I've never given much thought to nightmares. Sure, I rack up more than my fair share. I wake up sweating and the sheets soaked,

Eli awake, too, and asking if I'm okay. But what would you fucking expect? That's how it goes when your life is a never ending game of Stepin Fetchit and "Mistress may I have another," when you exist in the everlasting umbrage of Madam Adrianne's Grand Guignol of vice and crime and profit. No one lives this life and expects to sleep well—leastways, no one with walking-around sense. That's why white-coated bastards in pharmaceutical labs had to go and invent zolpidem and so many other merciful soporifics, so the bad guys could get a little more shut eye every now and again.

This is not my recollection of that first time. Hell, this is not my recollection of *any* single instance of the dream. It has a hundred subtle and not-so-subtle permutations, but always it stays the same. It wears a hundred gaudy masks to half conceal an immutable underlying face. So, take this as the amalgam or composite that it is. Take this as a rough approximation. Be smart, and take this with a goddamn grain of salt.

Let's say it starts with me and Eli in our plastic lawn chairs, sitting on the roof, gazing heavenward, like either one of us has half a snowball's chance at salvation. Sure. This is as good a place to begin as any other. There we sit, holding hands, scrounging mean comfort in one another's company—only, this time, some human agency or force of nature has intervened and swept back all that orange sky glow. The stars are spread out overhead like an astronomer's banquet, and neither of us can look away. You see pictures like that online, sure, but you don't look up and expect to behold the dazzling entrails of the Milky Way draped above your head. You don't live your whole life in the over-illuminated filth of cities and ever expect to glimpse all those stars arching pretty as you please across the celestial hemisphere.

We sit there, content and amazed, and I want to tell Eli those aren't stars. It's only fireworks on the Fourth of July or the moment the clock strikes the New Year. But he's too busy naming constellations to hear me. How Eli would know a constellation from throbbing gristle is beyond me. But there he sits, reciting them for my edification.

"That's Sagittarius," he says. "Right there, between Ophiuchus and Capricornus. The centaur, between the serpent in the west and the goat in the east." And he tells me that more extrasolar planets have been discovered in Sagittarius than in any other constellation. "*That's* why we should keep a close watch on it."

And I realize then, whiz-bang, presto, abracadabra, that the stars are wheeling overhead, exchanging positions in some crazy cosmic square dance, and Eli sees it too, and he laughs. I've never heard Eli laugh like this before, not while I was awake. It's the laughter of a child. It's a laughter filled with delight. There's innocence in a laugh like this.

And maybe, after that, I'm not on the roof anymore. Maybe, after that, I'm sitting in a crowded bar down on Locust Street. I know the place, but I can never remember its name, not in the dream. Nothing to write home about, one way or the other. Neither classy enough nor sleazy enough to be especially memorable. Just fags and dykes wall to fucking wall and lousy disco blaring through unseen speakers. There's a pint bottle of Wild Turkey sitting on the bar in front of me, and an empty shot glass. Someone's holding a gun to the back of my head. And, yeah, I *know* the feeling of having a gun to my head, because it happened this one time on a run to Atlantic City that went bad as bad can be. I also know that it's Joey the Kike holding the pistol, seeing as how there's a dead scorpion the color of pus lying right there on the bar beside the bottle of bourbon.

"This ain't the way it ought to be," he says, and I'm surprised I can hear his voice over the shitty music and all those queers trying to talk *over* the shitty music.

"Then how about we find some other way to work it out," I say, sounding lame as any asshole ever tried to talk his way out of a slug to the brain. "How about you sit down here next to me and we have a drink and make sure there are no more bugs in your shoes."

"I shouldn't be seen in a place like this," he says, and I hear him pull the hammer back. "People talk, they see you hanging round a place like this."

"People do fucking talk," I agree. With my left index finger, I flick the dead scorpion off the bar. No one seems to notice. For that matter, no one seems to notice he's got a gun to my head. I say, "Maybe you should skedaddle before some hardnosed bastard takes a notion to make you his bitch, yeah? You ever taken it up the ass, Joey?"

"You're such a smart guy," Joey replies, "you're still gonna be passing woof tickets when you're six-feet under, ain't you? Expect you'll manage to smack talk your way out of Hell, given half a chance."

"Well, you know me, Joey. Never let 'em see you sweat. *Vini, vedi, vici* and all that *hùnzhàng.*"

And I'm sitting there waiting to die, when the music stops, and all eyes turn towards the rear of the bar. I look, too, though Joey's still got his 9mm parked on my scalp. A baby spot with a green gel is playing across a tiny stage, and there's Eli with a microphone. I'd think he was fish if I didn't know better, that's how good Eli looks in a black evening gown and pumps and a wig that makes me think of Isabella Rossellini playing Dorothy Vallens in *Blue Velvet.* The din of voices is only a murmur now, only a gentle whisper of expectation as we all wait to see which way the wind's about to blow.

"Damn, she's hot," Joey says.

"Fuckin' A, she's hot," I tell him. "You should be so goddamn lucky to get a piece of ass like that one day."

He tells me to keep quiet, zip it and toss the key, that he wants to hear, but it's not *me* he wants to hear. So I make like a good boy and oblige. After all, I want to hear this nightingale, too. And then Eli begins to sing, a cappella and in Spanish, and everyone goes hushed as midnight after Judgment Day. His voice is his voice, not some dream impersonation, and I wonder why I never knew Eli could sing.

Bueno, ahora, pagar la atención
Sólo en caso de que no había oído...

And I'm still right there in the bar, but I'm somewhere else, as well. I'm walking in a desert somewhere, like something out of an old Western flick, and the sun beats down on me from a sky so blue it's almost white. There are mountains far, far away, a jagged silhouette on the horizon, and I wonder if that's where I'm trying to go. If there's something in the mountains that I need to see. The playa stretches out all around me, a lifeless plain of alkali flats and desiccation cracks. Maybe this was a lake or inland sea, long, long ago. Maybe the water still comes back, from time to time. Sweat runs into my eyes, and I squint against the sting.

On the little stage, Eli sings in Spanish, and I sit on my barstool with the barrel of Joey's gun prodding my skull. I wish the shot glass weren't empty, cause the baking desert sun has me thirsty as a mother-fucker. I keep my eyes on Eli, and I hear the parching salt wind whipping across the flats, and I hear that song in a language that I can only half understand.

Basta con mirar hacia el cielo
Y gracias al Gobierno por la nieve
Y cantar la baja hacia abajo…

"What's she sayin'?" Joey the Kike wants to know, and I ask him which part of me looks Mexican.

In the desert, I stop walking and peer up at the sun. High above me, there are contrails. And I know that's what Eli's singing about—those vaporous wakes—even if I have no idea why.

"It's a dream," I tell Joey the Kike, growing impatient with the gun. "Specifically, it's *my* dream. I come here all the time, and I don't remember ever inviting you."

The playa crunches loudly beneath my feet.

Tony Palamara opens a briefcase, and I see half a dozen silver vials marked with red tape.

A woman on a train wipes at her nose, and my ears pop.

Eli is no longer singing in Spanish, though I don't recall the transition. No one says a word. They're all much too busy watching him make love to the resonant phallus of his microphone.

Trying to make it rain.
So when you're out there in that blizzard,
Shivering in the cold,
Just look up to the sky…

I kneel on that plain and dig my fingers into the scorched saline crust. I crush the sandy dirt in my hand, and the wind sweeps it away. And that's when I notice what looks like a kid's spinning top—only big around as a tractor-trailer's wheel—lying on the ground maybe twenty yards ahead of me. What looks like a tattered drogue parachute is attached to the enormous top by a tangled skein of nylon kernmantle cord. The wind ruffles wildly through the drogue chute, and I notice the skid marks leading from the spinning top that isn't a spinning top, leading away into the distance.

And sing the low-down experimental cloud-seeding

Who-needs-'em-baby? Silver-iodide blues...

I stand, and look back the way I've come. In the dream, I guess I've come from the south, walking north. So, looking south, the desert seems to run on forever, with no unobtainable mountainous El Dorado to upset the monotony. There's only the sky above, crisscrossed with contrails, and the yellow-brown playa below, the line drawn between them sharp as a paper cut. There's not even the mirage shimmer of heat I'd have expected, but, of course, this desert is only required to obey the dictates of my unconscious mind, not any laws of physical science. I stand staring at the horizon for a moment, and then resume my northwards march. I know now I'm not trying to reach the mountains. No one reaches those mountains, not no way, not no how, right? I'm only trying to go as far as the top that's not a top and its rippling nylon parachute. I understand that now, and I tell Joey to either pull the trigger or put his piece away. I don't have time for reindeer games tonight. And if I did, I still wouldn't be looking for action from the likes of him.

I glance at the bar, and the pus-colored scorpion's returned. This time, I don't bother to make it go away. I do wonder if dead scorpions can still kill a guy.

All those people in the bar have begun applauding, and Eli takes a bow and sets his mike back into its stand.

"What you saw," Joey sneers, "I got as much right to know as you. We were both slopping about in that stiff's innards, and if something was wrong with him, I deserve to know. You got no place keeping it from me."

"I didn't see anything," I tell him, wishing it were the truth. "Now, are you going to shoot me or put away the roscoe and make nice?"

"Making you nervous?" asks Joey.

"Not really, but it pisses me off righteously."

I reach the top that's not a top, and now I'm almost certain it's actually some sort of return capsule from a space probe. One side is scorched black, so I suppose that must be the heat shield. I stand three or four feet back, and I never, in any version of the dream, have touched the thing. It's maybe five feet in diameter, maybe a little less. I'm wondering how long it's been out here, and where it might have traveled before hurtling back to earth, and why no retrieval team's come along to fetch it. I wonder if it's even a NASA probe, or maybe a chunk of foreign hardware that strayed from its target area. Either way, no one leaves shit like this lying around in the goddamn desert. I know *that* much.

"Yeah, you know it all," Joey says, and jabs me a little harder with the muzzle of his gun. "You must be the original Doctor Einstein, and me, I'm just some schmuck can't be trusted with the time of day."

Catch a falling star an' put it in your pocket...

And on the rooftop, Eli tells me, "The star at the centaur's knee is Alpha Sagittarii, or Rukbat, which means 'knee' in Arabic. Rukbat is a blue class B star, 118 light years away. It's twice as hot as the sun and forty times brighter."

"You been holding out on me, *chica*. Here I thought you were nothing but good looks and grace, and then you get all Wikipedia on me."

Eli laughs, and the crowded, noisy bar on Locust Street dissolves like fog, and the desert fades to half a memory. Joey the Kike and his pea-shooter, the dead scorpion and the bottle of Wild Turkey, every bit of it merely the echo of an echo now. I'm standing at the doorway of our bathroom, the tiny bathroom in mine and Eli's place in Chinatown. Regardless which variation of the dream we're talking about, sooner or later they *all* end here. I'm standing in the open door of the bathroom, and Eli's in the old claw-foot tub. The air is thick with steam, and condensation drips in crystal beads from the mirror on the medicine cabinet. Even the floor, that mosaic of white hexagonal tiles, is slick. I'm barefoot, and the ceramic tiles feel slick beneath my feet. I ask Eli if he thinks he got the water hot enough, and he asks me about the briefcase I delivered to the Czech. It doesn't even occur to me to ask how the hell he knows about the delivery.

"What about we don't talk shop just this once," I say, as though it's something we make a habit of doing. "And how about we most especially don't linger on the subject of the fucking Czech?"

"Hey, *you* brought it up, lover, not me," Eli says, returning the soap to the scallop-shaped soap dish. His hand leaves behind a smear of silver on the sudsy bar. I stare at it, trying hard to recall something important that's teetering right there on the tip end of my tongue.

For love may come an' tap you on the shoulder,
some starless night...

"Make yourself useful and hand me a towel," he says, "long as you're standing there, I mean."

I reach into the linen closet for a bath towel, and when I turn back to pass it to Eli, he's standing, the water lapping about his lower calves. Only it's not water anymore. It's something that looks like mercury, and it flows quickly up his legs, his hips, his ass, and drips like cum from the end of his dick. Eli either isn't aware of what's going on, or he doesn't care. I hand him the towel as the silver reaches his smooth, hairless chest and begins to makes its way down both his arms.

"Anyway," he says, "we can talk about it or we can not talk about it. Either way's fine by me. So long as you don't start fooling yourself into thinking *your* hands are clean. I don't want to hear about how you were only following orders, you know?"

It's easy to forget them without tryin', with just a pocketful of starlight.

My ears haven't popped, and there's been no dizziness, but, all the same, the bathroom is redolent with those caustic triplets, ammonia and ozone, and, more subtly, sugar boiling away to a black carbon scum. The silver has reached Eli's throat, and rushes up over his chin, finding its way into his mouth and nostrils. A moment more, and he stands staring back at me with eyes like polished ball bearings.

"You and your gangster buddies, you get it in your heads you're only blameless errand boys," Eli says, and his voice has become smooth and shiny as what the silver has made of his flesh. "You think ignorance is some kind of virtue, and none of the evil shit you do for your taskmasters is ever coming back to haunt you."

I don't argue with him, no matter whether Eli (or the sterling apparition standing where Eli stood a few moments before) is right or wrong or someplace in between. I could, sure, but I don't. I'm reasonably fucking confident it no longer makes any difference. The towel falls to the floor, fluttering like a parachute in a desert gale, and Eli steps out of the tub, spreading silver in his wake.

$\mathcal{T}$HE PARTHENOPEAN SCALPEL |

Bruce Sterling

$\big)$ THE THOUSAND INTRIGUES of the Minister we had borne as best
we could. But when he poisoned the mind of the Holy Father
against our National Cause, we vowed revenge.

Lots were chosen among our Cenacle. To my satisfaction, this signal honor fell to me. The usurper would die at my own hand. He
would perish on the very steps of his Chancellery, stabbed in the midst
of his Swiss Guards, dead in broad daylight. As the wretch breathed
his last, he would know—(thanks to the shouted slogans that I had
rehearsed)—that we had avenged an exasperated People.

Having no doubt of my ability to carry out this deed, I accepted
my destiny with calm resolution.

Some days passed. It then chagrined me to learn—from my
Cenacle—that I would have an accomplice in the task.

Unfortunately, we were not the only Cenacle of the Carbonari
inside Rome. For safety against many spies, our conspiracy was divided
into many cells. One of our colleague Cenacles—as righteously indig-
nant as ourselves—had also chosen an assassin to kill the Minister.

I met this rival of mine in a torchlit cellar at midnight. My under-
study was a bug-eyed, epileptic fanatic. I disliked him at once. Still, his
task was similar to mine. Should I (by some strange mishap) fail to slay
the Minister, then the Minister's guards would surely hurry him toward
the safety of his carriage. Waiting on the street near that carriage, this
pallid boy, disguised as a priest, would deploy an infernal device.

The Minister and his bodyguards would all be blown to fragments.

At first, I considered this an affront to my honor. A dagger is
the noble weapon of Brutus. Everyone understands that tyrants fall
to daggers. A bomb is a sordid modern device with many complex

working parts. Only engineers understand bombs.

However, on mature consideration, I grasped the wisdom in the plan. Let us be frank and objective. A political assassination is a form of public theater. How would a wise director, a mastermind, arrange such a matter?

Suppose that I succeeded in my debut—in my role as a hero to History. Well and good! What harm could there be, in my rival's idly standing by with some bomb? And if I failed? But I would not fail.

Reasoning in this manner, I forgave the affront. I devoted myself to rehearsals.

The Cenacle had offered me some rough-and-ready advice. "Place your thumb on the flat of your blade, and strike upward." Time-tested folk wisdom, to be sure! But where was the modern science behind this "rule of thumb"?

I conducted research in the morgue of my medical college. Human ribs form a "rib-cage." It is necessary to slide the blade through that cage, piercing the gristle that unites the solid rib-bones. If the blade is narrow and supple (as is logical), then a further sharp twist is needed to lacerate the vital organs.

Our medical school had cadavers a-plenty. Nameless paupers ceaselessly breathed their last on the grimy streets of Rome—dead from phthisis, dead from quartan fever, mostly dead from hunger. On their unresisting bodies, I methodically tested my favorite stiletto. It consoled me to know that even the dead could avenge my country's misery.

I carefully burned my many notebooks. I bade a farewell to my mistress—she wept, for returning to her husband's cold embraces was a dire matter for her. Then I wrote tender farewell letters to the last addresses I held for my scattered family: in Providence, Charleston, Nice, Geneva, and Buenos Aires.

Once, my dear family had been a distinguished house in the Parthenopean Republic. We were noble in sentiment, full of ambition and purpose. But our personal attachment to Murat had brought the insensate resentment of the Bourbon dynasty against us.

That unworthy envy had shattered our house. It had scattered my loved ones to the four winds. Yet one wasp among us had spurned to flee and was keen to sting!

The appointed day arrived for the retribution. I rose at dawn, I ate a hearty meal, I dressed in my finest apparel, and I dismissed my trusted valet forever.

I then proceeded to a last appointed rendez-vous with my fellow conspirators.

There I met yet another group of comrades—from a third Roman Cenacle. These men were strangers to the other two cells. In the haste and confusion that so often accompanies great deeds, they had given the boy a dagger, and saved the iron bomb for me.

The bomb was under my priestly skirts when screams rang out across the Roman piazza. The boy had simply and clumsily cut the Minister's throat.

THE BOY WAS arrested, and of course he told everything he knew. The police do have their methods. So do we. All the boy knew about me was that I was called "the Parthenopean." The boy was known to me only as "the Calabrian." Together, we had met "the Hussar," "the Scorpion," "the Illuminatus," and "the Englishman," a very clever fellow who was certainly not English. So the boy could babble whatever he thought that he knew. To the police, it was one vast labyrinth of mirrors.

The chairman of my Cenacle was known to our cell as "the Chairman." After giving me a fresh nom-de-guerre (I would henceforth be known as "the Scalpel") he arranged for my escape.

I lacked the papers needed to cross the borders of the Papal States. So, with the sacrifice of my beard (a clever idea in itself) and with the addition of a bonnet, a mantelet, kid gloves, and a good stiff set of petticoats, I became the "wife" of a Carbonari comrade. This man was a respectable bourgeois who travelled in trade. As his wife, I required no more papers than his horses did.

"The Chairman" confided to me that he had been taught this trick by the great Mazzini himself. Giuseppe Mazzini—philosopher, humanitarian, and tireless writer—was our movement's spiritual leader. Mazzini was known throughout the Concert of Europe as "the Prince of Assassins."

Safely across the border, and restored to my masculine attire, I was lent a horse by new friends. These men were certainly not Carbonari. They were democratically elected politicians from the "Liberal Party" of the Grand Duchy of Tuscany.

These useful idiots said nothing of the deeds convulsing Rome. They were full of their petty Tuscan intrigues. I made no complaint about their oversight, however.

We rode north for three days, our little party of politicians much refreshed by cigars and fine Tuscan wines. The sun shone upon us, the little birds chirped their love-songs, and the very sky seemed born anew and full of wonderment to me.

Blazing with an occult passion, I had sought to embrace historical necessity. Yet that dark union had gone unconsummated. My trip to that altar would have to wait.

The Parthenopean Scalpel yet lived!

MY NEW HOST, my new master in conspiracy, was the Count of R———. His home was a picturesque, crumbling castle on a rambling Tuscan estate. The Count's noble family was very ancient, related by blood to the Visconti and the House of Hapsburg-Lorraine. It followed that much of his home was in ruin.

No ruins within pretty Tuscany could compare to the monstrous urban ruins of Rome. Besides, the patriotic Count was manfully reviving the fortunes of his tenants. The Count's many fields were freshly manured, contour-plowed and sown in clover—clear evidence of his advanced agronomical thinking. The Count's stony manor was, yes, rather tumbledown and much heaped in thorns and ivy, and yet, many parts of it were visibly progressing. An entire new guest-wing was under construction, built to the exacting tastes of British and German millionaire tourists.

Servants in green livery showed me to my quarters, in the castle's freshest section. Fitted in the finest modern papier-mâché, my room lacked for nothing: razors, pomade, combs, gleaming full-length mirrors, a wardrobe rustling with fresh linens, a private fireplace, my own bell-pull and speaking-tube. I searched in vain for the chamber-pot, until I found water-closets!

A household tailor measured me, so that I could meet his excellency in proper attire. I spent the next three days happily devouring excellent meals, and a host of up-to-date newspapers.

Not only was I not fallen in combat, not locked in some dank Roman dungeon—I was free to witness how rapidly our times progressed! The Grand Duchy of Tuscany had liberalized its censorship of printed matter. In Rome, we Carbonari doggedly smuggled a few pamphlets past the priests, but the Count had modern magazines in lavish heaps. Books at every hand as well, terrific books fit to shake the very earth: the works of Balbo, Gioberti, d'Azeglio, and the entire bound proceedings of the "Congresso degli Scienziata."

At once I began taking notes.

I should explain why I took this foolish risk, for it was strictly against Carbonari practice to write anything. Any scrap of written knowledge about our activities could be seized by the police. To take notes was to court the grim fate of Silvio Pellico, a Carbonari intellectual who spent ten years in Austrian prisons, mostly taking notes there about his prison life, for a later confessional masterpiece, "My Prisons."

My strong need to narrate my own deeds to myself was entirely my personal failing. The truth there was rather sad and simple: I was cursed with a very poor memory. Few people had noticed this unhappy fact about me, for my memory for slights and resentments was extremely keen. I could recite every misfortune the people of Italy had suffered since the invasion of Alaric in the year 401. However, my memory was like a Roman ruin: a noble structure, full of gaps, absences and lacunae.

Somehow, my merely personal activities had always seemed to me unworthy of my own regard. My dead mother's face was lost to me. My dead father's many words of counsel, I could never recall.

I did have my virtues, let me assure you: I was bold, self-sacrificing, patient under toil, noble in my sentiments, devoted to people and country, and sensitive to the sufferings of the less fortunate. I had struggled hard to become a doctor, but the practice of medicine was beyond me. I could not learn medical Latin—or, having learnt the Latin, I could never remember the grammar.

A doctor requires a ready memory for the cavalcade of ills that assault the human body. I could never mentally catalog that endless host of symptoms. I loved medical textbooks—I could read them for hours on end—but the details there slipped through my fingers.

I believe the fault was in my blood. There was a legend in my family that my grandmother had once been the mistress of Murat, Napoleon's greatest general and the famous "First Horseman of Europe." There was a bitterness among us about this story, for Murat had charged on horseback to the throne of Naples. The adventurous Murat, so fearless, so headlong, had become a king among the Crowned Heads of Europe, and we had once prospered through him. Yet his over-bold gallantry had made him a poor ruler. His fall had cost Murat his own life, and also cost us our too-brief prosperity.

I do not want to idly claim that I am the grandson of a King. I have no objective proof to offer on that subject. But surely a man cannot help his own blood. Isn't every Italian descended from some King or some Emperor? We are a very old people.

If my craft of public murder was in some sense theatrical, it followed that my personal life was, in some sense, literary. Prepared to immolate myself for the causes of Freedom and Unity, I had burned a hundred diaries. I had expected no further use for those volumes, of course. Now I had to hastily scribble everything I could recall.

Naturally, I did not want my confessions to be found by anyone. Writing in cipher, or right-to-left like Leonardo da Vinci, merely attracts attention from spies. However, I knew a brilliant method to finesse this.

From the teeming shelves of the Count's library, I picked a volume of the pious Catholic verses of Alessandro Manzoni. Since the great Manzoni is so much respected, this volume is in every literate Italian home. Yet, it is never opened or read by anyone. Those rich vellum pages and the spacious typography made my new notebook a pleasure to use.

Once I was properly dressed by the tailor of his household, I was granted my first personal audience by the Count of R——.

The Count of R—— was a philosopher. He was a courteous man, but he did not simply put me at my ease within his presence. In mere moments, the Count could make the most difficult, tangled matters seem clear.

The Count was lucid, he was educated, he was ambitious, and he wanted the very best from futurity. I do not want to be ungallant about the Count. Personal failings among the great are often better glossed-over. However, I am compelled to reveal at this point that the Count of R—— was a hunchback.

The Count had certain other detriments as well, notably the lantern jaw and the poorly-spaced teeth of the Hapsburgs, but that hunchback was impossible to overlook. The great man's spine was bent like the letter "S" and his head rose only to my sternum.

Due to this sad handicap, the Count had never cut any great figure in the tumultuous events of our period. The Count was physically unable to mount a horse. So, although he had noble blood, he could never take command of an army, or even lead a common street rebellion. I pitied him this misfortune. Our Italian nobility was much like the rest of European nobility, only older. Their endless marriage-politics could not refresh their bloodlines. They were older than Charlemagne.

I cannot recount exactly what the Count told me at that first meeting, because I was not taking notes. Also, at first, the Count's refined and literary Tuscan dialect was rather difficult for me. Mostly, we discussed our nation's politics. In that subject, we were equally impassioned.

I would not claim that we were equals. I understood him as a modern Count, and he understood me as a modern assassin. That was sufficient to the purpose.

My new patron, the Count, was a covert master of the Carbonari. This dark secret was known only to a handful. He was also a public member of the Congress of Science, the well-known body of scholars from all over Italy. The Count was also a founding member of the newly-formed National Society. This new group, I had known nothing about. The National Society was mostly restricted to the enlightened regions of Piedmont, Milan, Venice and Tuscany. It had not yet spread its tentacles of progressive subversion into the south of the Peninsula.

The Count set forth to clarify the situation. I was a wanted fugitive, so I could never return to Rome. I certainly understood this. I was originally from Naples, and I took care never to return to Naples.

The Count offered me a formal choice. I could flee to South America, where our national movement tended to store its heroes. Or, I could aspire once more to immortal glory on the soil of Italy. I pretended to give this matter some thought (for I admired the suave way he had pretended to offer it to me). Then I placed my blade at his service.

The arrangement was settled. Weeks passed. A pleasant spring blessed the blossoming Tuscan countryside. Like many who have suffered since birth, the Count was a very patient man. He never raised his voice, he never acted in haste, and he never showed any surprise.

I was disguised as a doctor, a new household retainer for the Count. I methodically changed my attire, my accent—any other quirks that might betray me. I was granted the run of the Count's estates. I came to know the grounds, the servants, and much of the local food.

I was introduced to another of the count's secret retainers: an engineer. I never learned this old man's real name, but he was a long-trusted comrade. He created infernal devices. This was his calling.

The maestro had been making bombs since the days of Napoleon, maybe since the French Revolution. His eyes had lost their keenness, and his hands had lost three fingers, but he still had both his thumbs.

The maestro and I met regularly in a castle workshop near the library, where he set to work to pass on his craft heritage to me. The maestro had a method of building bombs which was entirely oral. Nothing was ever to be written about building bombs, because the guilty possession of any bomb-making texts meant a swift trip to the galleys, the gallows or the guillotine.

The maestro further insisted that I should build the bombs with my left hand alone. Why? Firstly, because bombs were infernal, and Satan was infernal, and the left hand was the sinister, Satanic hand. Secondly, because the use of my left hand would force me to concentrate precisely. Working left-handed, I would not become careless, habitual, or hasty. Thirdly and lastly, because any premature detonations of the black powder or the mercury fulminate would only tear my left hand.

While the old man's failing eyes left me, I wrote down all his instructions. I transformed his whispered folklore into simple recipes. The complexity of infernal devices is much exaggerated. Anyone who can bake a cake can build a bomb. A woman could do it.

The Count's extensive estates allowed us to test our bombs discreetly. My maiden efforts were as clumsy as most maiden efforts. Still, the task aroused me, so I soon gave satisfaction.

There then followed the Milanese incident, which I will narrate briefly. The situation within that city was exceedingly turbulent. One member of our brotherhood was suspected of being an Austrian police informant. This man had once been trusted by the Count, so his missteps were troublesome.

I went to Milan. I followed the man for five days. He was a financier, fat, myopic, and clumsy; he never grasped that I had become his shadow. The Austrian secret police who infested Milan had rewarded him for his double game; not in a clumsy way, but in a way that seemed like business.

Since he considered himself a businessman, he was not afraid.

This wretch was pursuing two lives within a single existence. His perfidy disgusted me. I confronted him at night outside a brothel, which he owned. I stabbed him. I painted the cobblestones with the word VENGEANCE, in his blood. I retrieved some documents from the dead man's wallet. I left his money scattered in the street, for patriots scorn to be thieves.

The Count showed no surprise when I gave him this written proof of my success. He did not reward me, or praise me at any length; but he did take me deeper into his confidence.

The Count's castle had certain areas closed to me; not through anything so crass as locks and keys, but through a manly courtesy. I had heard, from the servants' whispers, that the Count had a 'sister.' I had assumed that she was not his 'sister' but, as the French deftly put it, his 'petite amie.' Perhaps his 'little friend' was a midget, a woman even smaller than himself? Or she might be his normal-sized mistress; women care much less for a man's body than men imagine they do. Besides, the Count had great wealth, and normal women rarely overlook that.

But no, the Count of R—— indeed had a sister. Why his parents had again assayed the marriage bed after his unfortunate birth…but why should I speculate? A man and woman who love each other will do whatever they must.

The Count's parents had given the world a second issue from their union. She, or they, were even more remarkable than the Count himself.

The first head was christened "Vittoria," while the second head was named "Clemenza." As a united woman, the twins, or the girl, was known as "Ida." One could not very well say, "Vittoria, come here," when Clemenza was bound to come along anyway. So, among her very small circle of intimates, both Clemenza and Vittoria were mostly called "Ida."

No one within the castle had ever been able to overcome the severe grammatical problems associated with Ida. Sometimes she was "she," sometimes they were "they." There were further problems with the singular form, the plural form, the feminine plural possessives, the feminine singular and plural pronoun declensions, and so forth.

Even when I came to know Ida, Clemenza, Vittoria, particularly well, so much so that I used affectionate diminutives for her, and the intimate familiar form rather than any formal honorifics, I used to stumble over the simplest Italian sentences: "You" (singular) come embrace me," or "You (plural) please give me a kiss."

There was simply no help for that.

Ida was not a hunchback, like her unfortunate brother. Her medical case was both simpler and more complex. Her spine had split between the shoulder blades, and she had grown two heads. Vittoria, the left head, had hair of glossy black. She was the more assertive of the two. Clemenza, blonder and finer of features, was the more thoughtful.

To further complicate matters, Vittoria owned the body's right hand, while Clemenza commanded the left. Their legs they owned in common. Anything below the waist was, simply, the body of a woman. A very charming woman who happened to possess two heads.

Ida was remarkably intelligent, certainly twice as intelligent as most women, but she had led, for inevitable reasons, a sheltered life. All of her gowns, bodices, chemisettes, anything with dual collars, were all made for her by her servants. She had the most delicate of appetites, for she never ate in public. A true aristocrat, she had never been exposed to the cruel gaze of the common herd. She had been privately educated by some of Italy's best tutors. She passed most of her days in literary endeavour.

To spare her noble family embarrassment, she wrote entirely under pen-names. I do not claim that my mistress was a major poet. She never won any fame for her verses, nor did she desire that. However, she carried out an extensive correspondence with leading lights of European poesy. She wrote at especial length, in classical Greek, to Miss Elizabeth Barrett of London, a fellow bluestocking with a deep, sympathetic interest in Italian affairs.

Lady readers will take a natural interest in the details of our romance. Our intercourse took place mostly at the bench of the piano-forte. Although she dearly loved music, Ida could never properly play the piano. Clemenza controlled the left hand, and Vittoria the right. So although they could confer at length about their keyboard, they were hard-put to coordinate.

I therefore offered to play the piano for her. My proposal was accepted. As long as music was playing, her elderly duenna would leave the two of us alone together.

We therefore got up to delicious mischief at that pianoforte. Certain Latin terms known to medical men describe these activities.

Let the priests say whatever they please; a woman who has never known love is simply not a woman. If I made them a woman, they repaid me doubly, by making me the servant-cavalier of two noble sisters.

Of course we could never unite in marriage. That is not the romantic custom in these Italian understandings, and in any case, that would be bigamy on my part, and a mesalliance for her. Furthermore, I was a doomed man, sworn to throw my own life away on any turn of the cards in the Congress of Europe. Our love was sincere, but those were our harsh truths. Who can blame the two or three of us for our stolen moments of bliss?

There has been so much fine work written on this all-consuming subject: Goethe's "Elective Affinities," Rousseau's "Nouvelle Heloise," and Madame de Stael's immortal "Corinne," a tender romance set in Italy and of particular interest to them, or rather to her. I have seen the two of her discuss "Corinne" for hours. We also gleefully revived much useful ancient learning from the unexpurgated Ovid, Juvenal, Martial and Catullus. The Venetian Casanova, for his part, was an overrated braggart. Yet, Casanova showed wisdom when he wrote that a man in bed with two sisters will find that they surpass one another in daring.

A gentleman will not belabor the point here. The scientist will. Is it not this secret side of life, this fertile intercourse in darkness, which grants us life itself? Is this not the netherworld from which each of us—men, women, and two-headed monsters—all emerge? Can we deny the medical facts in this matter? Some day—I do not say tomorrow—a light will shine on all this.

There then passed the titanic events of the Five Days of Milan. These five days, in all their nobility and drama, will never be forgotten by a wondering mankind. The Hope of Italy hung on the very scales.

Like every thinking couple in Italy, Vittoria, Clemenza and I were convulsed. One might suppose that this intense political turmoil would distract us from our dalliance. No, not at all: the Revolution fed our subterranean flames. As the Count's couriers came and went, bearing heaps of badly-printed broadsheets from the Milanese barricades: the bold defiance of Conservatism, the last words of our martyrs—our romance rose to a mania.

I loved her so. I loved her as a man can only love two women. Yet I could not loll in every comfort while Italians fell to the imperial bayonets of an alien power. And not just us Italians: democratic Poles, exiled from their stricken country, were shedding their blood on our soil. The Hungarians of Kossuth as well—men from a very prison-house of European nations were seeking freedom in Italy. Young Europe was there in the flesh, fearless, bold, progressive, scientific, careless of death, on the bloody streets of Venice, Rome and Milan, with guns in their hands. And I—"the Parthenopean Scalpel"—was I to stand idly by?

Ida shed four hot streams of tears; but I went to the Count to demand my release.

The Count denied me this favor. "We are going to lose," the Count told me. "Our war of independence will fail, and you and I, conspirators, will never walk in honest daylight in our lives." They were very bitter words, so I can remember those words as clearly as I remember anything.

The Count was working on a set of geometrical papers, for mathematics was the Queen of Sciences to him. "I shall demonstrate the sources of our inevitable defeat," he told me. He had inscribed them all on paper, in a pattern of wondrous intricacy.

There was, he said to me, a superb unproven theory called "the Italian people." But Italy was, as yet, merely a geographical expression. This was not the mere physical problem, already known to everyone, of somehow uniting Venice, Milan, Piedmont-Sardinia, Parma, Tuscany, the Papal States, and the Two Sicilies.

No: there was a deeper meaning to all of this. This fragmentation of Italy, he told me, was useful to the Concert of Europe, for it had broken a European nation into convenient pocket change for the Great Powers.

Where else were the Great Powers to hide their sore embarrassments, such as the widow of the Emperor Napoleon? Let her conceal herself in that bloody tumult of Italian obscurities. Let the failed Empress of Europe retreat to Europe's dark closet. Let her rule over little Parma.

The further weakness lurked within the body of the People. The great majority of the People were the peasants of the countryside, poor, hungry, dulled with superstition, and glumly opposed to Progress. The poor within the cities were the urban Mob, brave, turbulent, ever ready to struggle and bleed, but unable to govern anyone—least of all themselves.

The bourgeoisie, our class of modern industry, were few in number, split among many tiny markets, scheming, competitive, jealous. They were too busy mastering steam to master any statesmanship.

The aristocrats of Italy were the oldest and highest class, but they too were split between their ancient gentry, fettered to their ancestral lands, and the new industrial barons, keen to profit, yet devoid of any sense of service.

The Church was in every last village of Italy. Yet the Roman Church was Universal, and therefore bitterly opposed to Italian nationhood.

"Now I must inform you," the Count concluded, "that we are at the bottom of that long list. We, the Italian conspirators. We too, are a body which is fatally split. Most Italian conspirators are simple, thick-headed mafia. They much outnumber us patriots. These ageless bandits will survive to flourish when we are dust.

"But you, my dear friend,"—(it was the first time he had called me that)—"you are a terrorist. Men like you are in critically short supply, for you can bring upon this world the 'vast commotions' prophesied by our visionaries. So I cannot release you to die in the streets of the Roman Republic with the scum of Europe. No. Men like ourselves are sternly bound to a higher purpose!"

I was moved to weep, for it was the first time the great hunchback had spoken to me, so directly and frankly, as a man like himself.

"There is a matter I must confess to you, sir," I began.

"Yes," he sighed, "it's about my sisters. I already know that."

I thought it wisest to say nothing more.

"My friend," he said, toying with a jeweled letter-opener, "I am an aristocrat. My class is very antiquated, and we are doomed to pass from the scene. Breeding ourselves like our own race-horses, we are tethered to our farms. That is sad, but we do have one saving grace. It is this: we do not care one stinking fig for any common, sordid, petit-bourgeois, marital fidelity."

"Nobly said," I told him.

The Count nodded somberly. An ormolu clock ticked on the mantelpiece. We were both having a certain difficulty discussing the matter. Commonly, when a man corrupts another man's sister, they are required to come to blows. Yet this was the last thing on our minds. We were the progressives of a truly European freedom.

"You must have a favorite among them," he said at last.

"No, Your Excellency. I love both her and them. I have come to understand that she is what they are. A woman accepts a man, expecting that he will change. A man takes a woman, expecting that she will never change. They are both disappointed. Yet within this very disappointment is the primal source of all new men and all new women."

"You do study the human heart. You might make a good father," said the Count.

"Sir, I am not an agent of birth. I am an agent of death."

And then, without being dismissed, I left the Count's study. I had wanted to raise a further delicate issue with him, for there were many between us, but having delivered such a profound exit line, I had to leave those things unaddressed.

I had no evidence to refute my master's dark suppositions about the tragic fate of our nation. I had only my own patience, my will to endure the unendurable. The unendurable indeed arrived. The Count's suspicions were proven entirely correct.

The hope of Italy was swiftly, comprehensively crushed. The hope was crushed, primarily, by Marshal Radetzky. I was keen to murder Radetzky—a man born within the melancholy, captive nation of the Czechs—and yet in loyal service to the blood-drinking Austrian Empire! What satanic hypocrisy could motivate such a man? The troops of Austria called this fiend "Father Radetzky." Radetzky was alarmingly old and yet he never seemed to die.

This Czech vampire was impervious to us. He was also the father of four Italian children, by his mistress, the Milanese washerwoman. The triumph of the Concert of Europe was total. We were dismembered at the hands of our oppressors. Bleeding Italy, stricken Italy, a nation whose very being was a fantasy. Italy had not been free of foreign occupation for one thousand years.

Italy was like the olive tree, that most Italian of trees. For the passerby who sees its pretty leaves, a sweet expanse of lively green. From beneath that olive tree—prostrate, in the dust—a dusky, rustling foliage of unbroken gray.

A certain coldness arose between Ida and myself. A woman with a servant cavalier desires a gallant cavalier. Does she want a man reduced to moral rags, a knight who has tumbled from his horse?

Of course she sympathizes—at first. In the poetry of Sir Walter Scott—that little-known colleague of Manzoni—there is a beautiful line about Woman as the ministering angel to the fevered brow of Man.

But when the Man cannot recover his vigor, when his overthrow is complete and his darkness overwhelming, the Woman becomes practical.

For all the Count's wisdom—and it was a great wisdom, it was impersonal, it was detached, it was telescopic, it was astronomical—the Count himself was not immune from our nation's general ruin. From his covert harbor in Tuscany, the Count had thoroughly busied himself in the failed revolt of Austrian Milan.

The diplomats of Austria had a motto, to go with their scheming banks, their marching armies, their steaming fleets, their steaming railroads. *"Nemo me impune lacessit."* If you know Latin, "Good!" you may well say to that. But if you know Italian—a language two millennia more modern than Latin—that is a bitter motto. Where is justice found, when the stern avenger is himself avenged upon by his oppressor?

My enemy came to Tuscany—and he came across the border with men-at-arms. It would tire me to tell you how this wicked intriguer thrust himself into innocent Tuscany. Suffice it to say that empires are large, while duchies are small.

He came in a way that was diplomatic, conservative, and entirely legitimate. He came against us with the law at his back.

This man...I cannot bear to give you his name. He had a long name, with many imperial titles. Let us agree to call him simply "the Transylvanian."

The Transylvanian wore a splendid military uniform. I did not. The Transylvanian carried legal passports. I did not. The Transylvanian had four stout fortresses dominating northern Italy. I did not. The Transylvanian had a sword and I had my newspapers.

Or rather, I had once had my newspapers. In captive Milan all the presses were silenced.

This imperialist came to visit the Count, and he came in sympathy. That was the deepest, the direst, the deadliest of his many insults to us: his sympathy. He sympathized with the Count for the terrible rumors whispered about the Count. Said against the Count by the people of decency. The people of stability. The people of law and order.

The Count kissed the hand and bowed the knee. That was tactically necessary. Machiavelli would certainly have approved. Machiavelli was an Italian philosopher, diplomat, politician, and writer of plays; Machiavelli was the founder of modern political science. Machiavelli was exiled, he was tortured, and he died in disgrace. His grave is unknown.

So, the Count behaved as Machiavelli had taught us. Comprehensively defeated on the martial battlefield, he had to choose some subtler field of play.

The Count therefore turned his beautiful sister over to the Transylvanian. The Count freely admitted that many dark rumors circulated about the doings in his castle. But, he said, those rumors had nothing to do with any political conspiracy, with subversion, with murder.

Instead, the issue was entirely personal. This was another matter, a treasure he had always sought to protect and conceal from a hostile and cynical world. A woman of learning and poetry, a delicate, harmless creature.

And then he let the filthy Transylvanian touch their hand.

The vilest part was that she perfectly understood all of this. She understood her own part to the very letter. She had her role to play in the great drama of our defeat, and she undertook it like a diva. She was full of fluency, vivacity and charm.

One might even say that she overplayed that role. I wanted to kill her for that. However, to kill one of her was not possible, and to kill both of her was excessive, even for a jealous man.

The Transylvanian was entirely delighted. The whole situation beguiled and intrigued him. He was enraptured by this exotic, unexpected discovery. Italy was so sunny, tender, bedecked with flowers; so elegant and precious.

My heart died within me. This made me his equal. A struggle over a woman always makes men equals.

I confronted the Transylvanian. I slapped his smiling face. I challenged him.

We met at dawn. Everything was perfect: matched weapons, matched witnesses. We heard the pleasant piping of the same awakening birds.

We lunged, we parried. The Transylvanian was old and cynical. His face never moved as we fought together. He was like an oil portrait.

I stabbed him. Dust burst from his medalled coat. Yet he did not fall. He merely pressed his attack against me, which cost me a scar. I stabbed him again. This time the blade burst clear from the back of his coat. Yet still he stood upright, and his riposte cost me half of my ear. I stabbed him through the very guts, so that my sword-hilt lodged in his belly. In return, he slashed my right arm to ribbons. He slashed it to the bone, so that I could never grip a blade again. Then, at last, I fell.

The Transylvanian walked away, with a weapon rusting in his belly. Honor was satisfied. He did not press the issue any further.

I did not die from my many ugly wounds. I persisted and I recovered. But, for the rest of my life, I was not to be the lover of two women. Because I had become half a man. I had given my good right arm to the lost cause of unity. That sacrifice had proved useless. Yet I still had my left arm.

I had my left arm, and the skill within it, and I found a cellar in London. London, that city of fog, that city of ten thousand exiles. London, Europe's indomitable city: the city that shall never, never be a slave.

May ten thousand bombs depart from foggy London, for the scorching liberation of a drowsing Europe.

ℐ Pulp Called Joe | *David Prill*

They didn't begin using human blood at the Long Rapids Paper Mill until the mid-1940s. This was during the ramping up of American industry during World War II and so there were many shortages, including certain dyes used in the paper-making process, the most prominent example of which was the critical dye #33-R. Yeah, I know. Things were that bad. The bloodletting wasn't scary, it wasn't horror, it was done in broad daylight and everybody felt good about it. Line up and get drained. Spill for the Mill. It was just something that had to be done to keep the biggest employer in town in business. It was a patriotic duty to donate a pint of juice to the Mill. Folks were already giving blood to the Red Cross, so why not a little more for the good of the town? It was like a blood-stained Victory Garden. Our sons were spilling their vital essence overseas, so it was only fair that we did the same on the home front. The red was right there in the red, white and blue of Old Glory. Nobody complained. Complainers were traitors. This was one fight we had to win.

The Mill had been around long before the war, though. It was built by Franklin Blonde on Pokegama Falls, about as close to the source of the Mississippi as you can get, back around the turn of the century. He owned a pair of newspapers down in the Cities, and it was vital to have a reliable, inexpensive way to keep up with the demands of his publishing business. Although the Mill was the lifeblood of the town, the relationship hadn't always been so intimate. It was a big part of people's lives, but at the end of the day it was still just a job.

Once the blood flowed, though, the relationship changed. People began to think about the Mill differently. The town and the mill became like blood brothers. You could always smell the wood pulp fumes that billowed out of the trio of tall smokestacks rising from the center of the long building. If the wind was right, the fumes covered the whole town. It was worse if you worked there, especially if you were a paper production operative like myself. It got into your eyes, into your lungs. Into your body. Part of you became wood, the processed pulp, the paper. As you were in the paper, so the paper was in you. An off-trail biological process that was as curious as it was quick, not surprising as these were cartwheeling-into-the-future times, the go-go years of postwar America. The changes were passed down from one generation to the next. Our skin took on a stiff, mottled look. Some tanning occurred. Bugs were a problem. Chipping and flaking replaced halitosis and B.O. on the hit parade of everyday worries. There was some alarm, but Doc Billingsley said he didn't see any reason to worry, the human body was amazing in its adaptability. Doc had shepherded the town through epidemics and panics, including the Great German Measles Outbreak of '51, so we trusted him and went on with our lives.

But many folks didn't like their new look, and sought treatment. At least the ones who could afford it. Not removing the paper fiber itself—it was too ingrained—but upgrading it. Folks in town lived and breathed paper, it was in their blood. They could work wonders with it. A cottage industry was born. From the tackiness of pulp and com-modity paper to the tony glories of antique and lace paper in a matter of days, with just a handful of simple though expensive treatments. The pulpy look by definition made you part of the lower class. Those untrimmed edges, egads!

That's where we come to me, a pulp called Joe, and the girl of my dreams, Penelope Vellum.

Oh, and Jack Dankworth. Who wasn't paper at all. Pure flesh and blood, that Dankworth. Pure flesh and blood.

It began on a Saturday morning about a month ago at Peavy's Drug Store. A bunch of us fellas from the plant hung out there on Saturdays, pounding coffee, nose in the *Gazette*, shooting the breeze, badgering Peavy.

"Say Joe," Billy Willesden, certified wood chipper, piped up, "did ya hear Jack Dankworth is coming back to town?"

"No, I hadn't heard that."

"Yeah, he's comin' in Friday night on the noon train."

Things moved at a slower pace in small towns like ours.

"I thought he gave up on Long Rapids for good."

"From what I heard," said Charlie Bogus, our stock prep engineer, "he just got a job as a sales rep for a drug company, maybe hoping to drum up some business with his old friends. Peavy, is Jack Dankworth coming to see you this weekend?"

"He certainly is," said Peavy in his usual narcoleptic drawl, as he washed a tall soda glass.

Dankworth and I used to be classmates if not exactly best friends, back when I had less baggage around my waist. He was president of the class at Long Rapids High School, football hero, prom king, a charmed life he led. I wasn't in his league in any of those departments. He had been going seriously steady with Penelope, but they had a fight and broke up right before graduation. He moved out of town to go to school, while she stayed here in Long Rapids. This was years ago, and I hadn't seen him since.

"You'd better look out," said Billy. "He'll steal your girl."

"She's not my girl," I said too quickly.

Billy laughed.

"Well, she isn't." It was true, sort of anyway. Even though we lived in two different worlds, Penelope and I had gotten friendly lately. I'm not even sure how it started. Nothing serious, just a warm hello when we ran into each other around town. Some casual conversation. We walked together a couple of times, when we happened to be going in the same direction. I suspected she was just being friendly. After all, what could she see in a pulp called Joe? But my heart was in deep.

Penelope was beautiful. She was vellum. Not literally so—originally vellum was made out of animal skin and was used for medieval manuscripts and in the art world for drawings and watercolors. Later it was made from plasticized cotton, a translucent form of paper commonly used in architectural drawings. Vellum in the Penelope sense just meant she was made of a high quality paper. Her skin was cream-colored, and had apparently been treated, because there was no yellowing at all. No rough edges, that goes without saying. On some people the paper/skin combination looked strange, almost like the paper had been pasted on. But on Penelope it was seamless. Her skin seemed to glow. She was out of my league and I knew it.

But out in the pulps we do dream. Sometimes, especially thinking about how shabby our little world is compared to the neighborhoods where the paper is fine, it seems like dreams are all we have.

I was worried about Dankworth, and my worry turned worse when I saw in the *Long Rapids Gazette* that there was a big dance at the Country Club Saturday night. My thoughts skipped ahead. Dankworth comes into town on Friday and on Saturday night he's on the dance floor, doing the Continental with Penelope Vellum. And from the Continental to something much cozier. Back when we were in high school the Dankworths were members of the Long Rapids Country Club. I caddied there for a summer, and hadn't been back for an encore. Didn't really fit into that scene.

"She's really got your head in a spin," said Billy, donut poised above his coffee cup.

"Oh, go flake away," I told him, pushing away from the counter and heading for the peace and quiet of the magazine rack.

Although the rack displayed all types of magazines made of all types of paper, I gravitated to the pulp section. Train Stories, Sports, Westerns, Detectives, Science Fiction, Horror and so on.

I picked up a magazine without thinking. It was the latest issue of *My Romantic Adventures*, featuring, according to the cover, "Chained to a Dream," "Fools in Love," "Roving Eyes" and "Jilted." The cover scene depicted a woman with a Lois Lane hairstyle, a hand to her head and a dreamy look in her big blue eyes. She sort of looked like Penelope, in an idealized, one hundred percent flesh-and-blood kind of way. Maybe that's what prompted me to pluck her from the rack. In the background, a man in a brown suit was walking down the sidewalk, away from her, his face hidden. Who was he? What had he done to her to produce such a blissful look in her eyes? What was his secret?

Suddenly, I became self-conscious. I glanced back at the soda fountain counter, then quickly returned *My Romantic Adventures* to its place on the shelf, picking up a copy of a different magazine instead. So when the wise guys asked what I was reading…

"*Fight Stories*," I replied coolly. "*Fight Stories*."

—*C*—

LATER THAT MORNING, as I slipped back into my protective sleeve and left Peavy's, I saw Penelope Vellum walking on the other side of the street, heading toward HPL Hardware. I didn't want it to look like I was pursuing her, but my guard was down, my heart laid bare. She didn't seem like she was in a hurry, so I crossed myself and then the street. She saw me before I reached the center line, right as a fully loaded logging truck rumbled past; she waved, smiled and stopped.

So did my heart.

Her skin was stunning in the sunlight. She looked like a supple limited edition, flawless vellum with printed silk panels. I blushed when my eyes drifted down to her peach endpapers. She was like new, not even a hint of foxing. I felt fair to poor in her presence, but at least I was in her orbit.

"Hello, Penelope," I said, trying not to flake on her shoes.

"Hi, Joe. Good to see you again."

"Where are you headed?"

"Just down to the Francie's Fineries. I need to pick up a new dress for a dance this weekend. Walk with me?"

"That's the dance at the Country Club?"

"Yes, the Swinging to the Moon Dance. It's okay, but it's sort of stuffy. But I'll go, always do…say Joe, do you want to go to the dance, too?"

"Well, I don't know…I'm not a member…"

"You can come as my guest. It'll be nice to have someone normal to talk to."

I hesitated, looking at my chipping arms beneath the plastic and said, "I'm not sure I'd fit in over there."

"You're not like the other fellows from the plant," she said. "You speak better, you have better manners."

"But my edges are so rough, so untrimmed."

"You're fine, Joe. You'd fit in anywhere. You'll have fun. Come to the dance."

I couldn't believe it. I heard myself say yes. Yes, yes, yes.

We arrived at the dress shop. Penelope smiled warmly at me. "The dance starts at eight. It's not formal, just a sport coat is fine. I'll make sure they have your name at the door." She touched my hand. "See you then!"

I went on home in a happy daze. Everything looked beautiful on the other side of the tracks. The tiny bits of paper that habitually hung in the air were like a gentle snowfall. The yellowing paper houses appeared to be illuminated from within by an ethereal light. The only thing that put a damper on my spirits was the coughing fit that hit me as soon as I crossed over into the pulp side of town. Reluctantly, I donned my dust mask and headed down the street to my house. The neighborhood was tranquil, a few folks doing yard work, vacuuming their front lawns, repairing the plastic sheeting that covered their flimsy houses. A new house was going up at the end of the block. The carpenters were chewing on a pile of timber and regurgitating the grayish moistened pulp onto the frame. Local builders really went to school on the techniques of the Vespula vulgaris, aka the common wasp. Today's block fire attendant, Al Drinkman, gave me a nod as I walked by.

"Any action today?" I asked.

"Some kids fooling around with a magnifying glass started a small conflagration over at Bob Wheelhouse's place. Otherwise, pretty quiet."

"Good to hear, Al. Catch you later."

"See ya, Joe."

When I got home I went right to the bathroom and looked at myself in the mirror under the harsh light of the vanity.

Brother, I had nothing to be vain about. I needed a trip to the barber, although there was only so much one man and a scissors could do. The thought of going to a high-gloss shindig looking like I did made my skin curl. I couldn't back out now, though. I didn't want to back out. This was the chance I had been waiting for. I would have preferred a more intimate setting, someplace where I wouldn't stick out like a tawdry pocket book on a shelf of morocco-bound masterpieces, but I had to grab this opportunity while I had it in hand.

Clothes were another issue. I would have to leave my protective sleeve at home, regardless of the potential for deterioration. Mylar wouldn't cut it if I was trying to make time with Penelope. The folks on her side of town only used Mylar at bedtime. I couldn't afford to be so casual about it. If I let down my guard for even a day, I'd be flaking all over creation.

I did need a trim, though, so the morning before the dance I headed over to Lloyd's Barber Shop.

"What'll it be, Joe?" Lloyd asked as I grabbed a copy of the mill's in-house magazine, *The Broke Pile*, and dropped down onto the chair. A lot of the fellas from the plant got their locks sheared here, so he kept copies around. The broke pile was the name for a pile of waste paper trimmings that were dumped back into the tub to be reused.

"Make me look like a new man."

"What's wrong with the old one?" Lloyd asked as he hooked the red-striped barber cloth around my neck and I settled in.

"Nothing, but he's not good enough for the Country Club."

"You're goin' to that big dance?"

"Not if I look like this."

"I'll do what I can."

"Trim my edges first, and we'll go from there."

I opened *The Broke Pile*. Interesting columns as always: "Rrrrumbles from the Wrapper," "Fumes From the Lab," "Finishing Room Wrinkles," "Wood Tics." It was a good way to keep up on marriages, births, bowling results, meat raffle winners and so forth.

As I read, Lloyd trimmed, buffed, lacquered. He cleaned the mildew from behind my ears. He applied glue where needed. He hung a bag of cloves around my neck to keep the bugs away.

When he was done, Lloyd twirled the cloth off me and spun the chair around so that I could see myself in the room-length mirror. I don't know why I was hopeful. What did I expect to happen? There are no miracles to be found in a barber chair. I looked better than when I sat down, but I looked at myself in the mirror every day. It wouldn't count for anything at the Country Club. You can pretty up pulp, but at the end of the day it's still a low-grade type of paper, gives even bogus paper a good name.

"You look like a million bucks."

"Thanks, Lloyd," I said, getting up and reaching for my wallet. I gave him a nice tip and left, trying to convince myself that I was looking fine. As I took one last glance at myself as I left the shop, I wondered if maybe he was right. Maybe his skill had made a difference, and when I went to the Country Club I would fit right in. If I carried myself like just another pulp, then that's how people would treat me. If I held my head high and wasn't self-conscious, then nobody would notice, I would have a great time and get the girl, too.

It was Saturday morning, which meant the fellas were assembled at Peavy's Drug Store for our weekly meeting. I didn't want to join them, not today. The drug store was three doors down. I was going to cross the street so they wouldn't see me pass by, but then I stopped, turned and went down to Peavy's anyway.

"You look like a vision!" Billy said the moment I walked into the drug store.

"Yeah, a real dreamboat," Charlie chimed in.

"Very funny. I have a question for you comedians. Got a social engagement on the other side of town tonight. Problem is my vehicle is going to look like a wreck compared to the other cars there. Anybody got some decent wheels I can borrow?"

"No better than yours."

"My heap has been in the shop for a week."

I was about to give up and walk to the Country Club when Peavy spoke up.

"I might be able to help you, Joe."

"You, Peavy?"

"I may have a car that would be to your liking."

"I thought you drove a rusty Duster."

"That's just my everyday car. I also have restored '51 Hudson. Hardly ever take it out of the garage. I like to work on it, modify it. Sort of a hobby of mine."

"Peavy, you're a treasure. When can I come pick it up?"

"Well...how about if I pick you up?"

The fellas hooted at that one.

"I don't know, Peavy? How would that look?"

Peavy didn't say anything. He neatened up the straws in the silver holder.

"Peavy..."

Then I realized it was perfect.

"A chauffeur. Peavy, you'll be my chauffeur."

"Call it what you will. Where the car goes, so go I."

"Perfect, Peavy. Perfect. I bet I'll be the only one at that clambake with a chauffeur." I grinned. "It's going to be a great night, fellas. A great night."

—·*o*—

I DRESSED EARLY, right after dinner, not wanting to be late for the ball. Pale yellow sport coat, white shirt and a black tie with canary yellow stripes, brown slacks, white loafers. Stuck a red paper carnation in my vest pocket. Felt good about myself. I finally relaxed, looked outside myself and began to ponder Penelope. How many dances would we have together? Maybe a stroll by ourselves under the summer moon? A pause by a secluded stream where we would hold hands?

I was waiting on the curb when Peavy pulled up. His pale blue Hudson looked fantastic, but already had a thin coating of dust on the hood. Peavy lived midway between the pulp side of town and the more exclusive areas, so he was used to the residue. I climbed in the back seat and away we went.

"Thanks again, Peavy," I said.

"Glad I could help. Good to get the car on the road occasionally."

I coughed some.

"I sell a very nice cough suppressant," said Peavy. "Tastes like fresh-picked cherries. Many customers have remarked on how effective it is."

"I'll just shut my window." The car was stirring up some of the dust in the street.

We were in the downtown area now, the paper plant occupying multiple blocks on the south side of the main drag. White smoke billowed from the triple stacks. The second shift was hard at work. The plant never slept. It was a living thing. A three-headed creature that demanded to be fed. The staff of life were the trees from the Big Woods that surrounded Long Rapids.

As we left the downtown area and headed north on Pokegama Avenue, the air seemed to clear. I opened my window and breathed deeply. It was strange to see the world with such clarity. The sun, heading toward the horizon, was actually yellow, not the red bleeding ball that we said goodnight to on my side of town. The streets were clean;

even now, on a weekend evening, water trucks rolled down the avenue, strong jets sweeping the dust down into the sewer drain.

"Wouldn't mind living here myself," said Peavy.

"Oh, I don't know, it's not so great. How could you relax with those water trucks roaring down the street at all hours?"

"I do like my rest," Peavy concurred.

"That sun is blinding."

"It is bright, isn't it?"

The car began to make an odd noise as we rounded a curve by Lake Howell. Coughing like I had been. Peavy frowned, leaning forward to listen more closely. The coughing became a wheeze. The car slowed down. As it began to shake, Peavy maneuvered it to the side of the road. One final, heavy hack, and the car stopped dead.

Peavy didn't look alarmed or even concerned. We both got out of the car and I watched as Peavy popped the hood. He inspected the engine, then said mildly, "I thought keeping the car in the garage all the time would protect it from the dust."

"Can't you brush it off and get it started?"

"Afraid not. No, I believe my car may require some service."

"How am I supposed to get to the dance?"

"The Country Club isn't far from here. Maybe a mile, mile and a quarter."

"Peavy, can't you at least try?"

"I'm afraid, Joe, that it's a bit more than I can handle. Might have to wait until the morning to get it towed."

"Why wait until morning?"

"Jim Beedley, he's the tow truck driver I patronize, well he was in the store this week and happened to mention that he's going to a birthday party for his cousin Erma tonight. Wouldn't want to make him miss that. They're serving angel food cake with pureed cling peaches: he can tow me in the morning."

I shook my head. "I'm going to be late."

"Won't take you long," said Peavy, lowering the hood. "Twenty minutes, at a steady pace."

I checked my growing anxiety, took a major breath. "You're right, Peavy. It'll be fine. Twenty minutes either way isn't going to make much difference. Are you going to be okay? It's a long walk back."

"Nice evening for a stroll. I'll stop by the store and call the missus, let her know I'll be late."

We parted, then, leaving the car behind. My pace was far from steady, it was manic, like a horse straining at the reins. The walk felt far longer than twenty minutes. Every step was punctuated by a voice in my head that said late, late, late. I began sweating. I worried about bugs. I fought back against the negative. I held my head high, and soon saw the white clubhouse in the distance. I eased back. Relaxed. Walked steady. Nobody would even know I had hiked to the dance.

The parking lot was full, the cars all looking like they had come direct from the dealer's lot. Polished to a glare. No rust or dust in sight. Steady. Heads up. You're going to see Penelope. She invited you. She wants to see you, and who knows what might follow from that fond request.

As I passed through the flowered portico and approached the glass arched entrance to the Country Club, I could hear music playing. A nimble, swingy melody, perfect for dancing. I pulled open the door and went inside.

Just past the entryway was a table, manned by a pair of young men, blond twins, wearing matching navy blue jackets. Their eyes tracked as one up and down my person, and identical looks of disapproval arose on their acid-free faces.

I smiled nervously and said, "Good evening. My name's Joe Gravure. I'm a guest of Penelope Vellum."

They appeared to be skeptical, but the twin on my left ran his finger down a list that was on the table. He did it twice, then jabbed at the paper and showed it to the other. They exchanged a look, shrugged, then twin number one dug into a small box, pulled out a name tag and handed it to me.

"Thank you," I said with a nod, and proceeded inside.

The dance was being held out back, in the large patio and lawn area behind the clubhouse. When I was a caddy, that area was off limits. As I came to the glass doors that led outside, I stopped. My hands felt cold. It was like the scene from a movie, a social setting beyond the world I knew. The band was playing off to the left, licorice sticks and tenor saxes bouncing to the beat. Couples were dancing, steps I could only follow in my mind, because my feet were cemented to the floor. The folks who weren't dancing were huddled around the buffet tables.

I had never seen such a collection of high-quality paper in my life.

Antique!

Art!

Laid!

Rag!

Lace!

Vellum…

I saw Penelope.

She was dancing.

With Jack Dankworth.

My heart cried. I couldn't believe it. How did they get together so fast?

Maybe I wasn't too late. After all, one innocent dance didn't mean anything. They hadn't seen each other for years. Of course they would share a dance. I shouldn't have been surprised at that.

I swallowed hard and went through the doors.

The music amplified, the chatter filling in the spaces where there were rests. I didn't know what to do. I looked for familiar faces, but who was I expecting to see?

There, someone I knew, although not someone I particularly wanted to see. It was my boss down at the plant, Mr. Bagasse (the second 'A' was long, as he frequently reminded us). We didn't get along all that well, although he knew I did good work. He was standing next to a potted plant, arms crossed, foot tapping to the music. He was stout and had slicked-back gray hair. He was wearing a sports jacket that was almost identical to mine. Twins.

"Evenin,' Mr. Bagasse," I said jauntily, coming over to him.

His face showed more than mild surprise, then he recovered. "Gravure, get me another cocktail, pronto."

"Mr. Bagasse, I'm a guest just like you," I said.

"A guest? I don't believe it. Who invited you?"

"What difference does it make?"

"Because if I find out who let you in, I'll see that their club membership is revoked!"

Our mild confrontation had attracted some attention. Some of other guests were watching us, shaking their heads in disapproval. I could feel the love. What was a pulp like me doing in their very fine domain. Lloyd wasn't able to work miracles after all. I stuck out like a sore thumb at a hitchhiking contest.

I had to get away. I retreated, lost myself in the gaggle, ended up at the punch bowl. I didn't know what happened to Penelope, but at that very moment Jack Dankworth came sauntering over in my direction.

I searched for something to say, and he didn't seem to notice me at first as he wielded the ladle.

What surprised, even shocked me about him was his skin. It was clear. Showed no sign of paper. Flesh and blood all the way. I hadn't been out of town for awhile, so it was jarring to see.

Then he turned to me, looked at me with a blank stare, brightened and said, "Joe Gravure!"

"Hello, Jack. Heard you were coming back to town, in the pharmaceutical business I understand. How have you been?"

"Can't complain. And if I do have a complaint, one of our products will fix me up good as new!"

"How long are you in town then?"

"A few days. I'm having a good time. Great to see old friends. High school seems like yesterday. Good times."

"Yeah, good times."

"Super to see Penelope again. She hasn't changed a bit. Beautiful as ever."

Her name coming from his mouth was like a buzz-saw chewing up my heart.

"Well, I think we've all changed since high school. Hope so anyways."

"Yeah, I guess that's true," he agreed. "You know, Penelope and I talked about our break-up, and it's funny but we can't even remember why we split. There was an argument, but that's all we can remember. So I guess we have grown up. Funny how that goes."

"Yeah." I hesitated, then said, "Your skin…"

Stroking his chin, Dankworth said, "Isn't that something? The paper is gone. Once I left town, it left me, and I became a man of flesh and blood. Seemed pretty strange at first, but I got used to it."

"Penelope is paper."

"Looks good on *her*. She'd look good no matter what, flesh, paper, skin and bones." Filling up glasses with punch he said, "Well, I'd better get back to her before some other guy steals her." He grinned. "Talk to you later!"

I didn't reply, just watched as Dankworth wove his way back through it all, disappearing amid a sea of hoofers. As the crowd parted, I got my first serious gander at Penelope. She was a vision in vellum. I waved, wanting to get her attention before Dankworth reached her, but she didn't see me and the crowd closed ranks around her.

I circled the gathering, a solo dance, slipping behind the buffet table, taking a narrow grassy path that tracked between the patio and an evergreen hedge. I got glimpses of Penelope, short scenes from the night I wished I was having, another song firing up and now she and Jack were twirling together on the far side of the patio, right near the spot I had just vacated.

Someone else was on the path, too, angling in my direction. A trio of young men, dressed in black sport coats with their shirttails wagging. They were walking rapidly, with purpose, and they appeared to have a target in mind.

I turned as they approached, kept turning as they surrounded me.

"What are you doing here, pulp?"

"You don't belong here. You and your low-grade paper."

"Stay on your own side of town, pulp."

One of them shoved me. I kept my cool.

"I'm a guest, whether you like it or not," I said. "So knock it off or I'll have you guys tossed out of here."

"A guest, huh," one of them said.

"That's right."

"If anybody's going to be doing the tossing, it's us."

"We'll strip that pulp right offa you, man."

"We'll burn you, pulp."

Another shove.

I shoved back. I worked on the floor at the mill, not in the front office. The shovee went sprawling.

As he slowly got to his feet, he looked at me for a long moment, then smirked and said, "Come on, guys, let's find some booze. We'll see you later, pulp. You can count on it."

They made time back down the path. My heart was in time with the big bass drum. I was more angry than afraid. It wasn't fair. Jack should be treated as the outsider, not me. He's not paper at all. I have more in common with those punks than he does.

I stepped off the path, edging between a pair of fake palms, and rejoined the party.

I searched for Penelope, but couldn't pick her out in the mob. I cut across the patio, to where I had last seen them, thinking maybe they had decided to sit this one out.

Mr. Bagasse was keeping the potted plant company.

"You still here, Gravure?"

"Yeah. Have you seen Jack Dankworth?"

"Dankworth? Sure. He was here a minute ago. I think he left with Penelope Vellum."

My heart bled. "Which way did they go? I…I have to talk to him about something."

Mr. Bagasse waggled his thumb, pointing at the way I came in. "They went thataway."

I wasn't thinking straight, so I pursued them. What did I think I could accomplish now? I didn't know, I didn't care. I headed back through the clubhouse at a trot, through the lobby and past the twins, who looked relieved as I exited the premises.

Out in the parking lot, I saw a white convertible speed away. Jack was driving, Penelope beside him in the passenger seat. They were both laughing as they split. Where were they going?

I ran a couple of steps, then stopped, suddenly realizing how pathetic I was acting.

"There he is!"

I whirled. My fan club had arrived, wanting to make sure I had a bad time at the party. They had brought their friends this time.

I didn't want to think about them. I didn't want to think about Penelope. I didn't want to think about anything. I just wanted to get out of this place, leave these clean, well-watered avenues and get back to the familiar dust of home.

They were younger than me, and although I had a pretty fair head start, they intercepted me before I reached the street.

They circled, silent, feinting rushes at me. I kept turning, trying not to give them an easy target.

Then they stopped. The punk I had knocked down held a silver lighter in his hand. He flipped it open, creating a flame.

Reflexively, I shrunk backwards. Fire, a pulp's biggest fear. Those who could afford to upgrade the quality of their paper could also afford a flame-resistant coating. But out in the pulps, we were vulnerable. We were combustible.

"Gonna burn you, pulp," the ringleader said with a soulless smile.

I didn't respond. Instinct kicked in. I tried to escape, but his friends pinned my arms and held me tight.

"Strip off his jacket and shirt," commanded the ringleader.

They did, fists raining on my head when I struggled.

The flame came closer.

I choked out a protest.

He jabbed the lighter at my chest, held it there for a moment, pulled it back.

I smelled myself burning. I tried to put it out, but my arms were locked down.

My eyes teared as the smoke rose up my body.

They forced me to the pavement.

I felt heat on my biceps, smelled the burning pulp.

I was in shock, unable to move or speak.

Then, strangely, I saw a bright light. I wondered if I was dying.

A bright light.

And the roar of an engine.

"He's comin' right for us!"

"Let's get out of here!"

I didn't move.

I still felt the heat.

The light came closer, brakes wailed, the roar quieted.

I heard a car door open.

Then Peavy was kneeling beside me, tamping out the flames with his shirt.

"You still with us, Joe?"

"I...I think I'm okay, Peavy...just a little singed...help me up."

"Let's get your clothes back on you."

I looked at my arms, my chest. Black streaks, a stinging pain, but nothing serious.

I put an arm around his shoulder and he got me into the Hudson.

"Peavy, you're a life-saver," I said as he swung around and headed out of the Country Club parking lot. "I don't know how far they were planning to take it, glad I didn't have to find out."

"Those boys are troublemakers. They come into my store and act tough. Never buy anything, though." Peavy glanced over at me. "You going to press charges?"

"You know how that goes."

He nodded.

"But Peavy, the Hudson...how did you get it started?"

"Well, that's a good question," Peavy said. "After I got back to the store and called the missus, I got to thinking that maybe I didn't like the idea of her, and by her I mean the car, sitting out there all night. You never know, kids, water trucks and so forth. So I came back. Just needed some cleaning up. The air filter was completely clogged. Didn't like the idea of you having to walk home, either."

After two or three blocks, Peavy said quietly, "Seems a little early for a dance to be over."

"Didn't go well, Peavy."

"No?"

"Jack Dankworth was dancing with her when I got there, and left with her before I had a chance to even say hello. They drove off together. So I decided to go home."

"I thought I saw them drive by. Nice car that Skyliner, a real classic."

"I'm not sure what I was expecting. Maybe I was expecting too much."

"She should have at least said hello to you."

"I know. But she got caught up in things, she was excited to see Jack again. Can't blame her, they were quite the couple back in the day. I would have done the same in her position. But Peavy, get this: Jack's skin was clear. All flesh. No paper. Not even a fiber."

"Well, that's different."

"Maybe a little too different."

"You think perhaps this feature had some appeal for the young lady?"

"I think it's very likely, Peavy."

"Not much we can do about that."

"No, there isn't."

"You know, Joe, I take a lot of pride in this car. I work hard to keep it looking nice, give her a lot of attention. But then she breaks down and leaves me stranded. I don't like it, but there's nothing I can do about it. What do I do about it? Get mad? Try to hurt the car in some way? Sell the car and get a new one? No, I become patient, give her more attention, try to understand what happened. And eventually, with some luck, maybe she'll come around...and here we are, driving home just like always."

"I don't know, Peavy. She was never really mine. Maybe in my head. I don't know what she thinks of me. Or maybe now I do."

"You never told her how you felt about her?"

"No."

"Why not?"

"Because I'm pulp, and she's vellum."

"You feel you don't measure up?"

"In so many words, yes."

"Think she was feeling sorry for you?"

"I don't know about that. I don't know what she was thinking."

"If you hold onto your anger, you're never going to know."

"Maybe I don't want to know."

"You walked a mile, mile and a quarter to see her."

"I'll handle it, Peavy. Thanks for the advice."

"As you wish. I'll drop you off at home or is there somewhere else you'd like to go?"

"Home is perfect. Home is where I belong."

—*C*—

THE NEXT TIME I saw Penelope she was walking past Long Rapids State Bank, the Bank That Likes to Say Yes, while I was coming out of Cake Kingdom, where I had just purchased a bag of day-old kolackys.

She waved. She called my name. I pretended not to hear her. I kept my head down. Kept walking, right around the corner and out of sight. I should have listened to Peavy, I thought, slowing my pace. But it wasn't anger that made me duck away from her, it was fear. Fear of rejection. Fear of not being good enough to be in her company. I saw myself in the butcher shop window, all pulp and despair, and remembered how fine Jack looked. Flesh and blood, that Dankworth. Pure flesh and blood.

─*C*─

MUCH LATER, ON a blustery October morning, I stopped by the drug store for the usual Saturday fellowship. Before I could remove my scarf Billy Willesden asked me if I had heard the news.

"What news?" I asked.

"Penelope Vellum is leaving town."

"No kidding," I said, dying for real on the inside.

"She gettin' hitched to Jack Dankworth."

My face started twitching. Somehow I made it stop.

"It's like one of those storybook things, them getting back together after so many years," Billy said.

"Yeah, a real fairy tale," added Charlie.

From behind the soda fountain, Peavy said, "Joe, come on over and have a hot cocoa. On the house."

"Thanks, Peavy, some other time," I said, and hurried out into the biting wind. Snow or mill dust, or maybe both, was snaking down the street. Why did it still hurt? I wondered. It's not supposed to hurt after so long. It's not supposed to hurt after I made sure I wouldn't get hurt, after I kept my head down, and avoided her gaze, avoided her in every way I could conjure up.

Penelope was gone, lost in a tangle of cold feet, blown opportunities, bad luck. When she was here, even though we weren't a couple, I used to imagine what might be coming in the future, how we might go from being casual friends to something more. A whole world of possibilities in store for me. Now the future was here, at my feet. It had taken root in my present, roped off my dreams, cut a hole in my heart.

When the wedding announcement appeared in the *Gazette*, there was no photo, just the black and white words that had been haunting my head for so long. I could imagine what the couple looked like, I could imagine the changes that Penelope had been going through since she left town. Her lovely vellum, so textured, so supple, would have begun to melt away by now. She had become flesh and blood, too, just like Dankworth. And when I realized that, my heart stopped hurting. The bond between us was gone. Gone.

COLDER NOW, WINTER on the doorsteps of Long Rapids, a gale from the north sweeping me down Main Street. Stack bogus paper up against the side of the house and pray for April. It was getting toward five o'clock, and the sun was already most of the way down. Businesses were flipping their signs over to "Sorry, We're Closed," dinner and dog waiting at home.

I passed by the drug store, went inside. I wanted to talk to Peavy. I wanted him to understand.

The only customer was at the counter, paying for a purchase. I headed over to the magazine rack to wait until he was out the door. Glancing back at the counter, I absently picked up a magazine. The rough edge felt good in my hands. It felt familiar.

I looked at the cover. It was the December issue of *My Romantic Adventures*.

The cover…

It was the same character as before, the one with the Lois Lane hairstyle, the one who looked like Penelope surely did now. She was wearing a white fur hood, her cheeks red from the cold, her blue eyes downcast. She was standing on a street corner, nearby trees heavy with snow. She was alone, no mysterious suitor in the background. The title of the feature story was "The Man Who Betrayed My Heart!"

Maybe it was my fault after all.

This time, I didn't put her back.

The bell over the door jingled as the other customer left.

I took the magazine over to the counter.

Peavy didn't bat an eye. He rang it up and said, "That'll be fifty cents, Joe."

I handed him the money.

"Would you like that in a bag? We've got some nice new bags, better than Mylar, they'll keep a magazine pristine pretty much forever, at least according to the sales rep."

I was about to say yes, then decisively shook my head. "That won't be necessary."

"Have a good evening, then."

"So long, Peavy."

I hurried home with the magazine, cradling it under my jacket. I set it down on an end table in the living room, right next to my easy chair.

She was perfect, the girl on the cover of *My Romantic Adventures*. For now.

Soon, she would start flaking away, along the edges first, then every part of her, disintegrating, leaving little pieces of herself on my fingers, at my feet. Like witnessing the cycle of life and death itself; in that way, and perhaps many others, pulp spoke truth more than any other type of paper. Together we would watch our decline, our lost fragments mixing together where they fell, dust to dust, until we became indistinguishable, until we became one.

𝒱ampire Lake | *Norman Partridge*

PART ONE: RUMSON'S SALOON

They heard the bounty killer an hour before they saw him. Out there in the desert night. Playing that harmonica of his, though the sounds that came out of it weren't anything you'd call music. But he kept at it, and the racket carved the desert sands like Lucifer trenching a brimstone field with his pitchfork. A man who could raise that kind of hell with a harmonica was a man who could unsettle a room full of other men.

And that's why the customers sitting in Rumson's saloon did the things they did. Some slapped coin to the bar and made their exits. Others ordered up and drank more deeply, which pleased the barkeep. Still others unbuckled their gunbelts as the man with the harmonica drew nearer. They rolled leather studded with sheathed bullets around holstered Colts, and they stowed those weapons far from reluctant hands.

Outside, the harmonica had grown silent. The creak of saddle-leather put a crease in the night. Then footsteps sounded across plank boards, and the bounty killer came through the batwings of Rumson's place.

He wore a patched coat the color of the desert, and he was dragging a man on a chain. One yank and the bounty killer bellied up to the bar. The gunman set his harmonica on the nicked pine surface. No one noticed the blood on the tarnished instrument, not with the poor skinny bastard trussed up in chains and padlocks crouching at the killer's feet. As far as the occupants of Rumson's saloon were concerned, that was the hunk of misery worth looking at, not a bloodstained Hohner that blew sour even on days that were sweet.

The bartender asked the bounty killer where he'd captured the man, and the gunman shook his head. Said the raw-boned Mex was a dynamite man who'd been locked up for years, and just tonight the bounty killer had broken him out of Yuma Territorial. "His name is Indio. If he put his mind to it, he could blow the gates off hell with a pissed-on fuse and a quarter-stick sweating nitro."

"The hell you say," Rumson said.

"The hell I do," said the bounty killer.

The bartender shrugged. "What can I get you?"

"Salt. Tequila. A guide."

"A guide? Where to?"

"Vampire Lake."

The bartender raised an eyebrow. "Most folks say there ain't no place like that in the world. It's just a legend, like the cave that's supposed to hold it. Of course, other folks say differently."

"That's what I hear. Same way I hear there's a kid in this town who's paid hell's own tab for a visit to that brimstone pit. Same way I hear there's a saloon-keeper who keeps that kid locked up in a cage and charges folks a double eagle to hear his story."

"Sounds to me like you're talking about a man who's got a piece of property and a piece of business. And that business would be the kid talking, not getting on a horse and riding to hell and gone out of here. A piece of business like you're talking about would be worth a good deal more than the freight you'd pay to hear an evening's worth of words."

"Let me talk to the boy about that."

"Let me see the color of your money."

"I think you've seen plenty enough money out of this deal already. My business is with the boy, not the half-shingled bastard who keeps him locked up like a circus chimp."

At the sound of those words, the bartender jerked in his boots. The two men stared at each other across the bar, nothing between them but dim quiet. Both of them watching and waiting for the thing that would happen next.

It was the dynamite man who broke the silence. "Amigo. If you're so soft on men in cages, what about me? I've been in a cage up in Yuma for three damn years. Why don't you crank a key in these locks and let me go, and we can call it square?"

"Shut up," the bounty killer said. "You're doing time for armed robbery and murder. Three years ago, you blew out a bank wall in

Tucamcari and killed four men. I caught up to you in a whorehouse, stuck a pistol in your face, and the Territory of Arizona locked you in the poke. But I'm the one who put you in there, so I figure that gives me the right to take you out if I have the need. Once I'm done with you, maybe I'll take you back."

"You can get started on that little trip right now," Rumson said. "Get the hell out of my bar, and take that Mexican trash with you."

"Uh-uh. I don't move until you bring me that boy."

"You'll move. And directly—"

Rumson reached under the bar for a sawed-off shotgun. Before his hands could make the trip the barkeep lost the equipment to say anything. The stranger's pistol saw to that. It came out of its holster rattler-quick and sprayed Rumson's head across the barroom wall. In the brief moment after the bullet did its work, what was left of Rumson's skull looked like a diseased egg dropped by one sick chicken. By the time that bloody hunk of gristle hit the floor, the bounty killer's black rattler of a pistol was back in its holster.

Rumson's corpse followed his head, thudding against the bar, toppling bottles on its way to the floor. After that, the only sound was the barkeep's blood dripping off the wall and ceiling, making scarlet divots in a patch of sawdust behind the bar. Leastways, that was the only sound until the real commotion started. Chair legs scraped hardwood as men scrambled for the batwing doors, but it was the click of pistol hammers in the hands of fools with more guts than brains that brought the bounty killer's gun out of its holster again. When that happened there was more terror and tumult in Rumson's Saloon than there were shadows, and the gleam of that black Colt springing through the darkness sent a stampede scrambling for the doorway as the first shots were fired. As the crowd scrambled more men filled their hands with pistols of their own, but none of those pistols would put a man in mind of a snake.

The bounty killer's black rattler did its work. And when it was empty he ducked behind the bar and came up with Rumson's shotgun. And when that was empty, it was all over.

Or more properly: It had just begun.

—◊—

FOUR MEN REMAINED alive in the bar. The bounty killer. The dynamite man on a chain. A dark-eyed blacksmith roughly the size of a barn door. And a calculating preacher who kept a running ledger on the flyleaf pages of the prayer book tucked inside a pocket of his clawhammer coat.

"Where's the boy?" the gunman asked.

"Probably out back eating a live chicken, feathers and all," the preacher said. "That child is crazy, mister. Apaches captured him in the desert. God knows what lies he told those red bastards, but it put them in a temper. A few days later some scalphunters found the boy tied to a wagon wheel, his head cooking over a Mescalaro fire along with a couple of scrawny prairie hens. The birds had gone to cinders, but the kid had it worse. Half his face was burned off, and his brain was boiling in his skull like a Christmas pudding. Just because that misery scorched some nightmares in his head don't make them true."

"You talk but you don't tell me anything I need to know." The killer reloaded his pistol, slapped the cylinder closed, and gave it a spin for emphasis. "I asked one question. That question was: Where?"

"You don't need gun for answer." The blacksmith's voice was heavy with an accent born in a German forest he'd never see again. "Boy is out back—in cage in barn, behind horse stalls. No rivets in cage; all welds. Three locks on it. Hasps as strong as bars. Double-thick, like plates."

"How do you know all that?"

The blacksmith blinked. Words jumped from one tongue to another in his head, then made the trip through his lips. "I forge bars. I build locks and hasps. I make cage."

The bounty killer cocked his black rattler.

"Let's take a look," he said.

—◊—

THE BARN DOORS swung open. Boots whispered over the dirty hay that covered the barn floor. A lantern swung on a creaky handle in the preacher's hand. It was close to midnight now, and the place was so dark it seemed the night had heaved in a dozen extra buckets of shadow.

The darkness lay heaviest in a patch transfixed by iron bars near the back corner of the barn. "Give me that lantern," the bounty killer said. Light played across the black bars as he took it from the preacher, and light painted the occupant along with the contents of the cage—a scuffed plate that didn't get used much and a few tattered books that did: *Idylls of the King, The Thousand and One Nights*, and a dime novel about Billy the Kid.

"Look at that damned animal," the preacher said. "Face like a scorched biscuit. The brain of a kicked chicken. Stinks like an Arizona outhouse in August."

Everyone squinted in the lantern's glow. Only the blacksmith knew better than to look. He stared down at his mule-eared boots. But the dynamite man didn't know better. He took a good long look. Then he turned his head and retched up his supper.

The bounty killer stared through the bars without saying a word. He fished the dead bartender's key ring from his pocket. A moment later he went to work with three of the keys, slipping padlocks from hasps, opening the door.

PART TWO: THE TOWN

"COME OUT OF there," the bounty killer said.

"Yes, sir," I said.

I picked up my chicken. Henrietta flapped some, shedding a few of the feathers I hadn't plucked. I petted her and told her to hush, but she flapped her naked wings and squawked up a storm.

"Looks like we interrupted his supper," the preacher said.

I glared at him and didn't say a word, though there were plenty inside me I could have put to work. Instead I held Henrietta close, stretched myself in the lantern glow, and watched my shadow cast a path that led straight to the door.

WE STOOD OUTSIDE around an empty barrel, the lantern set on top of it. The bounty killer pulled a bank book from his pocket. "You get me to Vampire Lake, what's in this book is yours. It amounts to twenty years of killing and twenty years of bounties. The four of you get back alive, you can split it four ways." With that, he slapped the book on the barrelhead next to the lantern so we could get a look at it.

The blacksmith was confused. "This is book. Just paper."

"These days money is just paper, too, amigo," Indio said. "Banks are full of it, and one page from a book like this can bring many dollars. What our friend here collected for me and my gang alone would keep us in whores for a year."

"But I am blacksmith. Not killer."

"I take care of that job," the bounty killer said. "But there are other jobs that need doing. The kid here, he's our guide. He'll take us through the desert, find that cave, lead us down to the underground lake where those dead things roost. And Indio will take care of any trouble we run into along the way that can be handled with dynamite."

The big man said it again: "But I am blacksmith."

"Yeah. That's what you've got inside you, but it's bundled up in one hell of a package. Where we're going, I need a man who tops a couple hundred pounds and doesn't mind the scorch of hot coals. You're elected."

"Those three I understand." The preacher picked up the bank book and stared hard at the balance. "You need yourself a birddog, you've got a biscuit-faced geek uglier than Satan's own bitch. You think you're going to dynamite the gates of hell, you want the Mex along. The other one is a freight train on legs and too stupid to think for himself. But what about me? Why do you want a preacher along?"

"That's a lot of hard tongue for a man who carries a Bible," the bounty killer said.

"Fair enough…but right now I'm not behind a pulpit, friend. I'm doing business, and business calls for straight tongue. So what is it? What do you want from me? Is there something down in that devil's shithole that you want prayed to death?"

The gunslinger didn't blink.

"It's simple. I want words said over anything I kill tonight. The way I see it, you may not be the best man for the job, but you're the only one around."

The preacher bit off a hard laugh. "Sometimes finding work is just a matter of being in the right place at the right time. And as far as words go, no one said a single damn one over those poor bastards you slaughtered back in the saloon."

"We're going to fix that right now."

"Well, we can talk about it. You killed a lot of men back there. Generally my fees for funeral services are one per customer. And since this piece of business doesn't have anything to do with going down in a cave, it's got to be a separate deal—"

"I already told you the deal." The bounty killer snatched the bank book out of the preacher's hand and grabbed him by the collar. The fuss the preacher put up did not last long, not after a couple hard slaps put the button to his lip.

We went back to the bar. Except for the dead men, it was empty. Even the whores were gone. God knows where the ladies had hustled off to, but they'd made themselves scarce after the gunfight.

The blacksmith and the bounty killer took a few doors off their hinges in the whores' rooms upstairs. They placed the doors flat, each one resting between a couple of chairs, and they laid the dead men on top of them. They crossed the corpses' arms over their chests—the ones who had two arms, anyway. One of the men who'd been sprayed with Rumson's sawed-off street howitzer was missing a wing. He lay there just as still as the others, the stiffening fingers of his remaining hand embracing the ruined socket just north of his heart. Rumson's headless corpse lay next to him; the leavings of his skull were in a canvas bag at his feet.

Once the dead were settled, the preacher said his piece. It was a short piece, and bereft of flowers. That was just fine with me. I was not much on flowers. As it turned out, the preacher was not much on words...especially when payday was a ways off.

When the praying was over, he sidled past the dynamite man.

A little blood trickled from the preacher's lip, and he wiped it away.

"He's one dirty bastard we're working for," he said. "But that was money in the bank."

THE BLACKSMITH DID most of the grunt work. He harnessed a team of swaybacks to a wagon while Indio and the preacher looted the general store for supplies. I tipped a dude's beaver-skinned bowler out of a hatbox and nestled Henrietta inside it, then helped myself to a new set of clothes. It had been a while since I'd had one. I was almost seventeen, and had been wearing the set I had on for something like two years. They were tight and stiff with the sweat of misery. The preacher watched me as I stripped out of them.

"Jesus, you're ugly. You look worse than that half-plucked chicken."

"I don't have to speak to you," I said.

"Tell the truth. When we found you in that cage, you were ready to eat that chicken raw. You're probably still going to eat it as soon as you get a chance. Why else would you pluck the damn bird, anyway?"

"I keep Henrietta's wings plucked so she won't get away. She's not half-grown, even. She needs me to keep her warm. And that man with the gun is right. You don't talk like a preacher."

The man in black laughed. "Hell, I talk the way I please when there's not a collection plate around. And as for pets, you want one, get a dog. You want victuals, get a chicken. That's what god intended, son...unless you're a damn heathen Apache that'll eat both and follow the meal with a little skin jerky baked off a white boy's face for dessert."

I ignored him. After I had dressed, I helped myself to a wide-brimmed hat to shadow my scars. That was when I heard the others chattering over the events in Rumson's saloon. I closed my eyes and listened, saw everything happen in my head. It was just the way I pictured things when I read a book. When the men finished the story, the blacksmith and I loaded up the supplies in the wagon.

While I worked, I added pieces of the story to the things I'd already learned about the men. And I'll admit it. I thought about money while I did that. I thought about freedom, too. A place where I could be by myself, except for Henrietta and maybe some old tomcat. It'd be a place where I wouldn't have to tell that story about the cave, or have anyone look at me at all if I didn't want them to. Maybe it'd be a place where I could tell other stories, write them down and send them off to folks who would print them between hard covers. They'd send me money, and I'd write more when I wanted to. It seemed like that would be a square deal, and a lot better than the one I'd had at Rumson's place.

I thought about it long and hard.

Pretty soon I'd made a decision.

A smart person might risk just about anything for a setup like the one I'd imagined.

Even a return trip to hell.

Soon the wagon was loaded, and that put the end to my thoughts. It was time to move on. The preacher and Indio went off somewhere and came back with a crate of dynamite. After the murders in Rumson's saloon, it was easy pickings in town tonight. We left the general store with the door wide open. It didn't matter. Sheriff Needham was nowhere in sight. I didn't know where the hard-eyed little lawdog and his deputy had got to, but whether they had made the trip out of luck or fear I figured they were smart to be clear of things this night.

We returned to the bar to get the bounty killer. He'd remained with the dead men, knowing there was no worry about any of us running off now that the numbers from his bank book were dancing in our heads. The desert night was cold, wind blowing down from the mountain. Dust devils swirled around us, erasing the footsteps of the men who lay dead in Rumson's bar. It was like the night wanted to clear off the last trace of them. The moon was full up by then, and it hung low in the sky, and light spilled from it like an Apache buck's knife had slit it straight across and turned all that bleeding white loose.

I sat in the wagon with the reins in my hands. Henrietta was asleep in the hatbox at my side. The other men were on horseback. We heard the bounty killer coughing inside Rumson's place as he walked from dead man to dead man, not getting too close to any of them, staring down at each one. Between coughs, he tried to work words through his lips. The batwings creaked in the wind, swinging in and out, and the gunman seemed to be strangling on those words, and through the gap

I saw him go down on his knees as quick as if someone had clubbed him with an ax-handle.

He started to retch, and we heard a thick splatter slap the floorboards.

"The bastard gunned down those men like dogs," the preacher said. "You'd think he'd have the nerve to face them dead."

"Nerve ain't his problem," Indio said. "He's got plenty of nerve."

I wondered about that as I watched the bounty killer there in the shadows. His guts bucked him something awful. The sound was horrible, like something alive trying to eat its way out of him. We all looked away.

I closed my eyes. The night was black, but the only color in my head was red. It painted the barroom floor and the bounty killer's lips and the things I saw. They were things that had happened in the night, some that I'd seen and some that I hadn't, but all of them were broiling in my thoughts nonetheless. The bloodstained harmonica on the bar. The murders in the barroom. Rumson's head toppling off his shoulders, kicking up a sawdust cloud as it hit the floor. I saw all that like the blood on King Arthur's sword in the tales I read, and Aladdin's scimitar flashing through Arabian shadows, and Billy the Kid blasting a man's guts to ribbons with a shotgun. Everything I saw played to the sound of a harmonica scrabbling over the ribs of the night, and gunshots from a black rattler of a pistol, and whispered voices in a general store at midnight. All of it was red, and it went down my spine like a bucket of ice, and it made me sit up straight on that wagon box with my breath trapped in my throat.

And that was a long time ago. The night it happened, I mean. But I knew even then that there was power in those stories, in seeing them slide up against one another like cards in a poker hand you know will win the pot. That was like having a headful of magic, and a brain that could cast a thousand-league spell, and I let it spin awhile.

I didn't open my eyes until I heard the stiff creak of batwing doors. The bounty killer stepped out of Rumson's saloon. His pistol was in its holster, and his harmonica was in his hand.

He coughed a few times, then spit a mouthful of blood in the dirt. "Let's ride," was all he said.

PART THREE: THE DESERT

THE MORNING WASN'T bright. Not right off, anyway. It churned up out of the night slow and gray, like a dull reflection in an old mirror. I rode in the wagon behind the men. All I saw of them that morning was their backs and the dust raised by their horses. The gray light washed over them and the dust churned at their stirruped heels just as sure as the gray light, and when the light married up with the dirt it was like heaven and earth were stitching shrouds for the four men who'd walked out of Rumson's saloon alive the night before.

That was not an image born of fancy. I stared hard and saw straight through the men to things that lay ahead of them. Doing that was like reading a book, and seeing a scene bloom in my head before I so much as turned the page and sent my eyes across the black lines that told the same tale I'd imagined.

Some folks say that's a kind of witchcraft. They call it second sight. I say it's just paying attention. That's why I understood about Rumson and the rest of them in that town before they showed their true colors. I watched them and paid attention. In my mind's eye, I saw them do the things they'd do before they so much as thought about doing them. I understood which way they'd jump when push came to shove. I knew it the way I knew what Rumson did with his whores when the bar was closed and I was locked up tight in my cage, the same way I knew what he'd do if anyone ever challenged him the way the bounty killer did.

And I saw these men the same way. Bits of the night came back to me, that reverie in red glimpsed just hours before. Words blew at me through the wind, and the fisted nubs of my scorched ears caught them. They built the story that waited ahead of us. It sang in my head the way my memories sang, and with it came the crackle of fires that had warmed me and maimed me, and the red glow of the fire we'd build in the night that waited ahead. And in that night were other deeds and stories, some I saw clear and some I only felt like an October wind that promises the stark cold of November.

But everywhere I looked, the men were there. The preacher, with his ledger book Bible. The blacksmith, a man who found it easier to do what others told him than the things he might want to do for himself. And Indio, the dynamite man, whose mind was set on a life without shackles.

Those three were easy to know. But some men aren't so easy. You can't tell what they'll do until they do it. That's the way it was with the bounty killer. Men like that come straight at you, but you can't shear them of surprises. They have faces that show you nothing, and hearts that hold secrets maybe even they don't understand.

Of course, it took me a lifetime to learn that. I had good teachers. I learned the lesson from dead men with hearts built from shadows, who came out of a grave hole in the desert and took me down to hell. I learned it from Apaches who tied me to a wagon wheel and roasted my face while their faces wore no expressions at all. I learned that lesson, and I learned it as well as the story I told in Rumson's saloon. Red or white, living or dead, sooner or later most men show you what they have inside…even if you can't see it coming.

I figured that's the way it would be with the bounty killer.

I figured it was only a matter of time.

Towards dusk, we camped in the middle of nothing. Just a playa of cracked earth that powdered an inch deep with every step so that it was like walking on pie crust. The preacher wrung the necks of a couple of hens he'd stolen from a coop behind the general store, and Indio cleaned them and set those birds on a spit over the fire. The blacksmith rigged a little crank on the end of the spit, turning it with a hand which had long ago befriended the lick of flame. The wind came at us and churned the white earth as I told my story, and the campfire kicked up spark and cinder that snapped at those dead birds like a hungry dog.

"We were part of a wagon train," I said, holding Henrietta close. "My family and me. One night we camped in a place like this. Big open space. White everywhere, too much white for the night to blanket. Just a little sliver of a moon above, but it lit up the whole place just as sure as that full moon is doing tonight. And I don't know—maybe this was the very same place where we camped. It could be, I guess. It seems just like.it."

"Ain't that always the way it is." The preacher snorted a laugh. "Watch out, boys—there might be a booger-man behind you."

"Button it," the bounty killer said.

I went on with the story. "They came for us in the night. They didn't look like men. Looked more like shadows. Just patches of black moving with the wind, sliding over that desert with faces as white as smoke. They rose up out of a hole in the ground no bigger than a dug grave and did their business. Snatched blankets off folks so quick it was like they were tearing up the night, and they tossed those blankets to the wind and ripped folks open with clawed hands. Did it so fast it was like they'd popped the stitches on a goatskin canteen and spilled a fiesta's worth of Mexican wine.

"They gathered around drinking their fill before the earth soaked it up. There must have been fifty of those things, and they killed most everyone before we even knew what was happening. I woke up in a puddle of my older sister's blood with a leather strap tied around my ankles. I guess by then those bloodsuckers had chugged down their fill of blood, same way cowhands get their fill of whiskey when they're on a spree. But they weren't so full that they didn't want to rustle a bottle from behind the bar to see them through the next day and the night beyond.

"One yank of that strap and I dropped from the wagon bed. Another and I skidded across the sand. The dead man dragging me had no more trouble than if he was pulling a canteen behind him. He was just a shadow, but he was strong, with hands and arms like vined midnight. He turned that face built of smoke in my direction and smiled a butcher-shop smile. I screamed my head off, but there was no one to help me—every one of us who was still sucking wind was in the same fix. But those shadows didn't care. They just dragged us along, through the dirt and the patches of blood spilled by our kinfolks. And we set up a chorus of screams that sounded sure enough like a parade of souls headed straight for Satan's pit."

The wind rose just then, and the fire kicked up a crackle. The Mex crossed himself, and so did the blacksmith. Their eyes were trained on the campfire and the white smoke that rose from it, which swirled and twisted like it was trying to knot the darkness.

"Jesus, Mary, and Joseph," the blacksmith said.

Indio nodded. "*Madre de dios.*"

"What a load of horseshit," the preacher said.

"I told you once to shut up," the bounty killer warned. And to me: "Go on."

"They dragged us into that coffin hole one by one, then through a burrow no wider than one a wolf would dig. That burrow widened into a tunnel, and then a cave. It was nothing but dark in there. Still, I heard things and nailed them up in my memory. The scrape of a key in a lock. A creaking iron door. Wind through a wall of bars. Then that door swinging shut on rusty hinges, and a key finding its notch. One turn and that door locked. The vampires put us on our feet on the other side of the gate and cut our bonds. Then they marched us down black tunnels, deep into the earth. A mole would have been lost in that darkness. Miles and miles we went, lower and deeper, with no sound but our footsteps, and folks crying, and walls that talked. Those walls told us, 'Welcome to hell, pilgrims,' laughing at us as we passed by. And if you reached out a hand in the darkness to steady yourself, you'd bring it back bit and bloody, because those walls were hungry for a taste of what the vampires had gorged on that night.

"The deeper we went, the lighter it got. Not any kind of light you'd find in the sky above you, but a kind that was just bright enough so you could keep your bearings. Mushrooms grew in patches on the wall, glowing the way fireflies do. So did smears of fungus that lay like a carpet at our feet. Air blew up the tunnel like it couldn't wait to escape through that grave hole up above in the piecrust earth, and the bite of that wind was as sharp as the bite of those things that lived in the walls behind us.

"And with that wind came the smell of Vampire Lake. It was waiting below. One whiff and I knew the water would be black. Suddenly I could see the shore in my mind's eye, the sand as white as bones. I knew there'd be dead men sitting there on coffin boxes. Waiting, just waiting, for us."

"I think you ate yourself a bellyful of those mushrooms down there in that hole," the preacher said. "And a couple of bushels of loco weed, too."

I ignored him. "They kept me locked up down there for weeks. Months, maybe. I was never sure how much time had passed. We were corralled in a barred cave near a bridge that stretched out across the black water. The bridge was narrow, made of old planks that had nearly rotted through with time. It led to a small island in the middle of the lake. One of the guards told us that was where the vampire queen roosted, as solitary as a black widow spider. At least once a day the guards would come and get a prisoner. More often two. They'd march those folks across that bridge, and it was like watching someone mount the steps to a gallows. The shadow-faced guards marched them forward, and those old planks creaked under their trod, and that black water churned beneath them with every step. Something was down there, beneath the surface, waiting. Something just as hungry as those dead men and that wicked queen—"

"Save that part for later," the bounty killer said. "Tell us about that queen. What was her story?"

"I never saw her. Leastways, not face to face. That guard, he said she'd been down there since the days of the conquistadors. Made a trip into that cave with a captain and his men looking for Indian gold, found a lake that bubbled up out of hell. Of course, they didn't know that then. They camped down there in the dark while they searched for treasure. Drank from that lake. Swam in its waters. And one day those soldiers weren't men any more, and that señorita wasn't a woman. After that, they say she drank down a thousand men, and still she was always thirsty. Skinny as a rake she was, out there alone on that island with only a Navajo slave girl for company. She used that girl for a footstool. Made her sit still for hours, her cold bony feet on that girl's back, toenails digging in like tiny shovels. She'd sit there on a throne of bones with her feet up on that Navajo girl, her eyes so black they looked like giant ticks burrowed into her sockets. Staring across that dark water, never blinking, always watching. Waiting for a full belly she could never have no matter how many souls she drank down."

"And what made you so special?" the preacher asked, staring at the coals. "Why didn't that queen bee suck on you? You weren't as ugly then as you are now."

"She might have done the job…had I waited around. One night I managed to sneak out of there. The guards dragged off a couple of the younger girls. There was a big shivaree around the coffin boxes near the shore as the dead men took them down, and while that was going on I worked some rocks loose and made a gap near the end bar along the edge of the cave mouth. Soon enough, I wriggled my way out. I found a tunnel and followed those glowing mushrooms, and when the mushrooms started to thin out and the light began to dim I smeared myself all over with that fungus from the floor, made the rest of the trip glowing like a funeral candle with a short wick. I could hardly see at all, but I saw enough, and the things I saw set me running. I don't even remember what I did when I came to the gate at the end of the tunnel, but I figure I was so skinny and greased with sweat that I must have squeezed my way between the bars. I crawled out of that grave hole into another pocket of darkness. It was night, and the air was so fresh it seemed like ice poured straight into my lungs. I saw the stars above and they set me running again. I ran for miles, stumbling into the middle of an Apache camp. They grabbed me, and—"

"And you was out of the frying pan and into the fire." The preacher laughed heartily. "Then those red bastards took one look at you, thought you was some kind of devil, and cinched you to a wagon wheel. Cooked you up just like these here hens."

"I'm not going to tell you a third time," the bounty killer said.

"Yeah," said Indio. "Let the kid be."

The preacher cussed a blue streak. "You men are as weepy as a church choir. Let's all take up a collection plate for poor little biscuit-face, why don't we?" He turned to me, grinning. "Boy, I've got to say that bartender taught you one hell of a story to feed the rubes. Did he give you a live chicken to chew on when you finally learned to tell it right? I mean, I know telling whoppers is the only way a geek like you could make a living, but it's hell's own price for us to have to stare at the leavings of your face while you do the work."

With the sound of those words, Indio and the bounty killer started to move. The blacksmith was faster. He snatched the preacher by the scruff of the neck, lifted him off his feet like he was a sack of sugar.

Then he spilled him across one knee as he crouched, and held his face just short of the fire.

"You like to talk. Maybe we fix your face now, and then you tell us story."

"Jesus!" the preacher shouted. "Get this bastard off me!"

Disgusted, the blacksmith chucked him backwards. The preacher flew a few feet, landing on his ass. A puff of desert playa rose up around him, and he scrambled around on all fours like a spider popping on a hot griddle before he gained his feet.

"I'll get even with you, you goddamn square-headed Heinie bastard," the preacher said. "And then you'll be a quarter-mile past sorry."

The blacksmith thought about that for a long moment.

"No," he said finally. "You can put bullet in me. You can put knife in me. You can open Bible and bring Jehovah down on white horse and have him twist me to a leper. You can do what you want. But I won't be sorry."

IT WAS QUIET after that. I stared at the fire. At the spit. I watched as the blacksmith turned his little homemade crank, and I watched the chickens go 'round and 'round. One was bigger than the other. The skin on that one started to crack and drip juice, while the little one's skin crisped up like a shell. Watching that, I started to sweat a little bit, and the scars on my face began to itch.

Finally, the bounty killer said, "Tell the rest of it, boy."

"No. I've said enough. Right now, you either believe me or you don't. Tomorrow, you can see for yourselves."

No one said anything for a while. The bounty killer tore a loaf of brown bread into four sections and gave one to everybody but the preacher. Soon, the first chicken was ready. Indio took a knife and carved up the scrawny bird. He passed hunks around on tin plates. He didn't give one to the preacher. By the time the Mexican was done with that knife, all that was left was the gizzard, and one black wing, and a knotted little lump of a head. The preacher helped himself to all that, swearing a little bit, and moved off from the fire to a spot behind the blacksmith.

Soon the other bird was done, but by then the men had eaten their fill...except the blacksmith, of course. The big German ate a couple of legs and half a breast, then left the rest of the chicken on his plate. I could tell that the preacher was eyeing the meal, but he didn't come into the blacksmith's range. Despite his hard tongue, he didn't dare.

But a little while later, the man in black passed me by. He bent low at my ear and shook that blackened chicken head like it was some big medicine.

Inside, the bird's dry brain rattled around like a pea in a whistle, and the preacher laughed. "That's all most folks have inside their skulls. You and me know that, don't we, boy?"

THE OTHER MEN rolled up in their blankets. All but the preacher and me. He sat ten feet distant, just short of the fire's glow, toting numbers in the back of his Bible. I stared into the fire's dying flames while Henrietta skirted the withering coals, her naked wings flapping against her fat little body. 'Round and 'round the fire she went, but in a different way than those birds we'd cooked. And all the while she pecked at the piecrust playa, her little beak burying itself in the white dirt time and time again. There was nothing much to eat there, but she kept at it. That's the way she was.

I guess I was, too. My brain kept pecking at the story churning in my head. The old and familiar parts had slipped over my tongue just an hour before, but it was the new parts that were on the boil and wouldn't let go of me. They tumbled around in my head along with the heartbeat of the day—the desert heat that had put all of us on edge, those pole-ax blows the preacher had landed with his tongue and not his fists, the greasy chicken I could barely choke down. I thought long and hard about all that, and the tale I'd told, and the way my heart had thundered when the blacksmith held the preacher's face to the fire.

And I remembered the way the men's eyes had flashed while they heard the different parts my story, the way some of them had looked away and some of them had tried to look deep inside me as the tale hit its peaks and valleys. But most of all I remember the one question the bounty killer had asked—that question about the vampire queen.

The bounty killer's voice was there in my head, and so was his question, and so was the sound of his bloodstained harmonica. Suddenly my gaze seemed to burrow into that dying fire circled with chicken tracks, and down through those glowing coals, and I found myself standing at the edge of Vampire Lake. The sandy shoreline gleamed like powdered bone, and the waves beyond were a dark whisper. Dead men sat on their coffin boxes, their faces bloody from a whipping they'd never expected. Funeral clothes hung in tatters from their cleaved skin. Others were history, dead straight through this time, their black blood spilled by blades and bullets coated with silver.

Beyond the carnage, that narrow bridge stretched across black water. In my vision I traveled across it like a bat on the wing, following an empty mile of hanging planks. I plunged headlong through a burrow of shadow, dropping to roost before the vampire queen.

She waited on a throne of bones, her tick eyes unblinking. She did not seem to notice me. Her black lace dress was tightly gathered around her narrow waist and the layered architecture of her collar bones and ribs. Her naked white feet rested hard on the bent back of the Navajo slave girl who served as her footstool. Now and then, the queen curled her toes and her sharp nails sliced into the girl's back, deep enough to raise a tiny scream. And even so the vampire did not smile. For she was waiting, staring across the water with no expression on her face, waiting with a cigarillo between her cold lips. Tobacco smoke traveled from her dead lungs through tight nostrils, whispering into the air on lifeless breaths.

And I turned away and saw why the vampire queen stared and didn't blink. I saw why she waited. The bounty killer was walking across the bridge, coming toward her. Black water gleamed through gaps in the rotten boards, churning beneath his every step. Albino alligators snapped against the water. Their great armored tails thrashed, casting guillotine ripples in waves that couldn't hold a shadow. Tired of a diet of dead carcasses discarded by the queen and her minions, the reptiles gnashed their teeth for a taste of something vital and alive. The bounty killer's scent drove them wild; it was as if they scented the dead men's shadows that dragged at his heels and thundered in his heart.

And that was something I felt in my gut as much as my head, for nothing in the bounty killer's expression conjured so much as a single word. He was a stone, and the expression he wore made the one on the face of the vampire queen seem as expressive as a Mexican carnival mask.

And then the vision was over, and just that fast. I blinked and I was back on the playa. Henrietta still circled the fire, pecking at the dirt. Shivering, I drew closer to the coals. The cold shadow of midnight had descended, so I wrapped up Henrietta in a Mexican sash one of Rumson's whores had given me and tucked her inside my coat. I put a little more wood on the fire. Suddenly I was hungry, and I slipped the leavings of the second chicken off the blacksmith's plate. I skewered the half-picked carcass and hung it over the fire to warm. Soon enough, the bird sizzled against the flame.

Just as before, the sound brought back memories. When memories came for you, you had to sit with them. I knew that much. If you were the kind who carried them with you, there was no way around it.

I was that kind, but that didn't mean I had to let those memories have their way with me.

I listened to the chicken crackle on the spit.

But I ate it all the same.

For now I was hungry, and the chicken tasted good.

I woke in the middle of the night and rose from my blankets. The moon still hung above, fat and full, and I moved easily beneath its light. I put the wagon between myself and the campfire, following a straight line behind my shadow for a couple hundred feet. Then I undid my drawers and waited for nature to make its call.

"Hey pretty," the preacher said.

He was behind me, and I jerked as if slapped. Quickly, I buttoned my pants and turned to face him. There he was, maybe fifteen feet away. Laughing a little bit. Walking my way. His shadow spilling before him against the moonlight, that Bible in his hands. He held it up and gave it a tap. And then he started talking.

narrow grave of a mouth above. Thanks to Indio's dynamite, the iron gate that corralled the vampires' corner of the world was now a twisted mess. That gate had once been a hell of a sight, scored with chains the blacksmith could never have cut, and spikes set with dead men's skulls and tattered human hides that flapped like scarecrow warnings in the subterranean breeze. But now the whole thing was so much scrap— just something to get on through, and get on past.

And that's what we did. The bounty killer hurried through the shorn hunk of darkness where the barred door had stood, past broken skulls and those tattered sheets of jerky flesh. Flames from his coal-oil torch licked the cold stone ceiling as we continued our descent. We followed, our torches blazing orange streaks where the bounty killer had passed.

The gunman had parceled out supplies before we entered the cave. He had come prepared and then some, and we all had our own stock. There were the torches, of course, and other things that gleamed in their light—and most everything that gleamed did the job with silver. The bounty killer had his black rattler tied down low, plus a pair of bandoleers crisscrossing his chest that held four other pistols charged with silver bullets. Indio carried a rucksack packed with dynamite, fuses, and a couple boxes of Lucifers, plus a Bowie knife with a silver-dipped blade sheathed on his hip in a rig not unlike the holster that held the gunman's black rattler. A steel can filled with coal oil was strapped to the blacksmith's back. He carried a branding iron in his big right hand, the brand-piece a silver cross cinched in place with a hard twist of barbed-wire. Me, I had Rumson's sawed-off shotgun and the pictures in my head. And the preacher didn't have anything but his Bible, which he held as if he wished it was a gun, or a knife, or a silver-plated pole-ax.

But as fast as we were moving, there was no watching any of the men too closely. The air rippled against the flames from our torches, and the sound was like oars cutting water as we traveled lower. Our lungs pumped like bellows as we advanced down that black gullet, moving fast, and lower...and lower...and lower still. The bounty killer pulled ahead of us, his desert-colored coat like a hunk of the surface world misplaced in its belly. I was glad I'd left Henrietta on the surface, one leg tied to a wagon wheel. If she were here with me, wrapped up in that Mexican sash, she would have been wriggling as if she'd been sucked down and swallowed whole by the hungry earth itself.

But it was only the four of us who'd suffered that fate. Deeper we went, and lower, and deeper still. The tunnel grew narrower. Our torches began to flicker, flames licking low. We stopped to charge them—we had to stop. My heart thundered drumbeats, and the pulse filled my ears, and I could barely hear the talk that went back and forth in the darkness. The bounty killer tossed orders, telling the blacksmith to unstopper his coal-oil can and get busy charging those torches, and mind that oil around the flame because nary a one of us was bacon ready for the skillet and neither were those dynamite sticks Indio carried in his rucksack.

The blacksmith set about his work, slipping that steel tank off his back. Dying blue fire rippled over the torch heads. As darkness closed in, the patchy fungus carpet at our feet began to glow. Then the light from the torches grew dimmer still, and fat round blotches shimmered into view on the cave walls—those glowing mushrooms I remembered.

The preacher's torch went out. Suddenly the mushrooms glowed bigger...fuller...brighter. They put a filter to the rising wall of eternal night that loomed ahead of us, but it was light you couldn't trust, one that was only fit for ghosts. The walls seemed alive with it, rippling and pulsing in the growing darkness, and—

"Torches," the blacksmith said. "Put heads together."

And we did. Knotted lengths of oak gripped tightly in our hands, thick torch heads meeting between us. Dying flames danced as they joined, and the blacksmith poured coal oil over the top. Blue fire surged, then rose to a sunflower yellow, and soon the torch heads glowed between us like the fat moon that had hung in the desert sky the night before. Light swelled around us, finding the cave walls. The mushrooms seemed to turn their heads to it, and then some of them started moving—

A wind rose deep in the cavern. Just that fast, light filled the cave like whiskey brimming in a full bottle. It found the things that lived between those mushrooms, things that had been trapped alone in the darkness on my last trip to the cave. Since then a fresh crop of mushrooms had filled this corridor—growing along its walls, pillowing its ceiling as they spread—and now the unseen things that had once cursed a wagon party on their way to hell were wedged between them.

Splashes of whiskey light washed those creatures, and every one of them screamed with Satan's own fury. I saw them clearly now, nestling between thriving fungus on guano-caked walls. Some had faces like sick babies, and others looked like wretched old men with walnut skulls that begged to be cracked. I had no idea who they were or what they were. Maybe they were the lost souls of the vampires' victims, and they'd been trapped after death as they tried to make their journey to the surface and the heavens above. They sure enough screamed like creatures worthy of such a horror.

One other thing was sure—the tunnel was full of them. They roiled in their mushroom nests like maggots feeding on a rotting carcass, and their curses put the freeze to my bones and sent the preacher to his knees. He wasn't moving. I wasn't moving. Neither were Indio and the blacksmith. At first I thought the bounty killer was frozen, too. And maybe part of him was…but the part that pulled the black rattler wasn't.

The pistol fired six times. Mushrooms flew apart like dropped cakes, sending glowing spatters raining to the floor. Walnut skulls exploded, and dark blood slapped against stone. And then the gunman yanked another pistol from his bandoleer and put it to work. And another. And soon the bounty killer yelled: "Torches! Now!"

And in an instant we were all moving, raking our torches across the walls of the tunnel. Those mushrooms caught fire, caps burning as quickly as crumpled parchment. The screaming heads burrowed between them had no place to go. Fire licked the walls, and the mushrooms flaked to lumped coal and cindered off to smoke. And that smoke swirled around us and snaked deep into our lungs like a crawling thing, and I nearly hit the ground at the stink of it, and it busted off the cinches on everything I saw.

The bounty killer's pistol hissed past me in the haze. There were fangs set in its barrel, and reptile scales on the gunman's hand, and his eyes were yellow with black-pupil slits. The preacher screamed in one corner of the cavern, begging for mercy while walnut-faced devils roped him to a wagon wheel and set it turning over a brimstone spit. Then Indio carved through the smoke wearing armor like King Arthur of old, swinging his silver Bowie knife like Excalibur. And with him came Billy the Kid, loaded for bear, and Aladdin, and forty thieves ready to lay siege to hell.

And then the bounty killer grabbed me and shook me loose from my reverie. He pulled me out of there, into another tunnel. The subterranean wind whipped at me as the gunman sent me stumbling, and I caught that other scent on its breath…the scent of Vampire Lake.

We kept moving.

The mushroom smoke worked through me.

Pretty soon it was a bad memory, and we charged into an enormous cavern.

That's when all hell really broke loose.

PART FIVE: THE LAKE

I'D SEEN APACHES do their worst. I'd seen white men match them sin for sin and then go them one better. But I never saw anything like the horror I saw at Vampire Lake.

Indio and the blacksmith worked as a team, moving from coffin to coffin along the shore. One threw open the lid, and the other set to business. The Mexican slashing away like a wild butcher with that silver-bladed Bowie knife, carving until the throbbing pound of flesh in the vampire's chest came a cropper. The blacksmith roasting dead men's flesh with his silver branding-iron cross, planting his big hand over each squirming bloodsucker's heart while the poor devil bucked against the pain of unforgiving metal. And I did my part, too, taking care of any vampires who rushed Indio or the blacksmith. They came at any of us, they got a taste of Rumson's sawed-off shotgun.

I worked steady, blasting dead men with loads of silver and buckshot. I blew the fangs through the backs of their heads and reloaded as quickly as I could. But stack me up against the bounty killer and I was a full bucket of nothing at all. He was a clockwork reaping machine, working that black rattler and those four other pistols he kept holstered in his bandoleers, trading one for the other as the legion of shadowmen rushed him.

You can't truly believe something like that unless you've seen it. For the next few minutes, the shore of that lake was a flurry of black whispers and bloody fireworks. The bounty killer moved forward, dead men rushing him from all directions. Across the sand he went, and through the shadows, slaughtering the dead queen's minions as they tried to slow his progress toward that bridge.

He moved forward without a pause, pistols blazing, leaving nothing but gunsmoke where darkness had reigned. And the bridge was closer now. Behind the bounty killer lay a trail of paintbrush splatters and corpses that had hit the ground without so much as the rattle of a medicine man's spirit pouch. His narrowed lids squinted tight across cat-green eyes, as if the gunman were watching the whole blazing hell-riot from behind an iron mask. And when the killing was over you'd have thought he might have smiled, but he didn't have it in him. Instead he went down on his knees at the foot of the bridge, a litter of dead men behind him, surrounded by nothing except the pistols he dropped in the sand.

He started heaving again, and now it was his own blood that paintbrushed the shore. It was an awful sight—just as it had been back at the saloon. The bounty killer tried to get up, drove his fists down against the sand and pushed for all he was worth, but such was his misery he couldn't make the trip.

"Preacher," he said. "I'm out of steam. Say the words."

I looked around, because I'd lost track of the man in black. He was hiding behind a clutch of rocks further down the shore, crouching like a crab dreading a boiling pot.

"Preacher!" the gunman yelled. "Time to earn your money! Get over here now!"

The preacher hurried toward us, clutching his Bible, his face whiter than the faces of the devils we'd killed. His hands were shaking so badly he could barely open the book, but soon he managed to find the verse he was looking for, and he began to read.

"Louder!" the bounty killer said. "Make those damn words count!"

And the preacher tried. I really think he gave it his all, and maybe for the first time ever. His voice rang out over the bodies of men who'd died, and lived, and died again. It rang across the water. And it filled up the cavern, but at its heart it was a hollow echo. Soon enough, another sound eclipsed it.

It was the bounty killer. He was back on his knees, retching blood again. Red rushed from his mouth in a torrent. I'd never seen that much blood spill out of anything living in my life. It was as if the gullet that traveled from his mouth to his belly was his very own grave hole of a cave, and men and monsters were doing battle in a cavern beneath his ribs, ripping him up from deep inside, filling every hollow space with blood.

This was the one time the preacher didn't twitch. In spite of the horror, he knelt at the bounty killer's side and kept on reading. His words charged harder now, and he spoke of Lazarus, and Jonah and the whale, and Noah and the flood. He put one hand on the gunman's shoulder and the words spilled out of his mouth as he begged for deliverance. But the bounty killer only cried out, his body bucking hard against the misery convulsing inside him. It looked like the devil had hold of his tongue, and was going to yank him inside-out.

With one hand, the gunman pushed the preacher away.

He hawked another mouthful of blood on the ground.

"Damn," he said. "Damn."

Then he got to his feet. I saw it happen, but I still can't believe it. I don't know how the bounty man did it, but I do know it didn't have anything to do with any of the words the preacher had said. No. The gunman made the trip on his own, the same way a man climbs a gallows stairway. He made the journey deliberately, as if every inch of movement cost him more than he had inside, and once he was up he had the look of a man who wasn't going down again unless it was his own idea.

Spatters of blood were thick on his shirt and face. The preacher took one look at him and backed away. Other words rushed from the spindly man's mouth, and they were about money, and the deal he'd made with the bounty killer, and how there might be another bit of business he could try if the gunman cut him in for a bigger piece of the pie—

"I can't believe I spent a night and a day listening to you jabber like a damn parrot in a cage," the bounty killer said. "You're useless. It's time your feathers flew."

The black rattler filled the gunman's hand. None of us had even seen the bounty killer snatch it from the sand. One finger did all the work. Three quick tugs and three bullets hit the preacher square, and the man in black crumpled among the dead vampires.

Bank notes spilled from the preacher's prayer book as he hit the ground.

That low subterranean wind caught them.

Some of the money blew into the black water.

Some clung to patches of spilled blood on the shore.

But there wasn't one of us wanted to touch any of it.

We left that money alone, and we did the same with the preacher.

THE BOUNTY KILLER went down to the water and washed his face in the lapping waves. I gathered up his pistols and walked to his side.

"Need any help?" I asked.

He smiled at me, red lines of blood filling the creased spaces between his teeth. "I've killed a lot of men," he said. "They're still inside me. That's why I'm here. I'm full up with dead men, and there ain't nothing that can turn them loose."

"That isn't so bad," I said. "I've got nothing but *alone* inside me. Sometimes I think it would be nice to have some company."

The bounty killer laughed at that, and then he stifled a cough. "You know, it's funny how life sets you on a trail. I first heard about you in a bar down in Tombstone. Brought in a dead horse-thief and collected the bounty from the marshal. After he handed over my bankroll, Virgil Earp told me your story over a beer. The marshal said he heard the tale from a prisoner who'd visited Rumson's place. That was the first I heard of Vampire Lake. First I'd heard of the vampire queen, too.

"Earp said she was a devil woman who could never drink her fill of blood. By then I'd been heaving red for three months, and the dead men trapped inside me were never far from my thoughts. They haunted me night and day. I knew I had to get shed of them. I figured that queen was the only woman who could see me clear of the hell I was living. I figured I'd track her down and let her drink her fill, and maybe if I managed to walk away I'd be a different man. That's when I busted Indio out of jail and came looking for you…and that's what brought us down in this hole tonight."

"But if you let her do that… If that queen sinks her fangs into you—"

"I let her do it. And I see where that trail takes me."

"But—"

The bounty killer held up a hand. "There's different kinds of death, boy. Different kinds of life, too. I don't want one spent down on my knees, strangling on my own blood. I don't want one that sidles up alongside me when my back is turned, wearing the face of some tin-horn who wants to prove he can gun down hell's worst. No. I want one I can stare square in the eye. One that'll stare right back and not blink so much as an eyelash. That queen sounds like the ticket to me."

"But what if she drinks you dry?"

"That's a chance I'll take. Whatever hand I draw out there on that island is the hand I'll play. A man can't do more than that."

The bounty killer splashed water on his face and wiped it clean with the back of his sleeve. He stood up. I stared at his face, but there was nothing else there. Not a single sign that could put the measure to his words. Just those cat-green eyes, slitted in his skin. He didn't even blink as he unbuckled his gunbelt and handed his sheathed black rattler over to me.

"You keep this for me," he said. "If you never see me again, you can call it yours."

"But what about you?"

The gunman patted the bandoleers crisscrossing his chest. "I still have four pistols here. Whatever's coming, they should see me through."

The bounty killer turned away from me then. Just that fast. Like he was done.

He motioned at the blacksmith. "You. Come here."

The big man came over, still sweating from exertion. The bounty killer pulled out his bank book. He asked us for our names, wrote them on the flyleaf, then scrawled a note and signed it.

"Ain't none of us lawyers, but this'll seal our bargain." He pressed the book into the German's hands. "I'm giving this to you, because I'm sure as hell not giving it to Indio. You'll see this job through for me, won't you?"

The blacksmith nodded. None of us knew what else to say. We stood there a moment, and it seemed it was as quiet as it had ever been in the world. And then the bounty killer turned toward the lake, and he took out his harmonica. He started playing, his eyes trained on that island, and the uneasy music that had raked over the desert two nights before seemed right at home down here in the earth's own belly.

Out there in the darkness, the bridge started to creak and sway as the Navajo slave girl started across it. She was just a slip of a thing, and the bounty killer watched her as she drew nearer.

He slipped his harmonica into his pocket. She walked up to him, barely making a sound.

The girl said a few words in Spanish, and that was it.

The bounty killer turned to Indio.

"What'd she say?" he asked.

"That dead queen wants you," Indio said. "She wants you now."

THERE WAS NO reason for us to stay down there in the cavern after that, but we did. Even the Navajo slave girl stuck close to the shore. We watched the bounty killer walk over the half-planked bridge, heard the old wood moan beneath his tread. Those albino gators thrashed in the water beneath him, driven wild by the scent of the dead men's tide rushing through his veins.

Once the bounty killer hit the shore of the island, that queen didn't parley long. She rose from her throne of bones, tossed her cigarillo into the water. Next came a couple minutes of jaw, and one long stare between them that said more than any words could. Maybe that was the thing that did the trick. Whatever it was, a second later she attacked the bounty killer like a ravenous spider.

That was what he wanted, after all. Her skinny arms scrabbled over his big shoulders. That black dress hiked up around the shanks of her white legs as she wrapped herself around his hips like a harlot flying the eagle. But it was those teeth of hers that did the work no words could.

Her fangs trenched the bounty killer's neck, digging in like coffin nails. We heard him grunt even though we were far across the water, and we watched blood geyser from his wounds. The red shower caught the shadows and matched their darkness inch for inch, and it flowed over the shrouded island and seeped into the ebony water beyond.

They say that queen had drank down a thousand men, but it was a fact she'd never met one like the bounty killer. He was a gusher, filled up with life and filled up with death, and too much of both had spent years stoppered up inside him. He was more than that queen could handle. The wet sound of her feasting sent a horrible echo rippling through the cavern, and soon she began to swell like some monstrous babe that had nursed too long at the devil's own teat. The back of her dress ripped apart, black lace shredding like cobwebs. Still, the queen didn't cut loose of the gunman's pumping artery. She hung on and burrowed in deeper, and still she drank.

Another vein let loose, spewing blood from the bounty killer's neck. Red mist sprayed across the island, and dead men rose in its wake. We'd had no hint that the queen had companions out there, but there must have been one last pack of shadowmen that served as bodyguards. They hurried to her side, fanged maws spreading for bad business, teeth latching onto the bounty killer as if he were a lone steer turned loose in an empty butcher shop.

But he did not fall, and he did not go to his knees. The killer stood there with those things roiling over him. Every bite was like another hole burrowed into a dam. The bounty man's blood was everywhere now. It was a red mist driven by underground winds, spreading over the water. It ran in thick rivulets over his shirt and down his boots and across the island shore, sending scarlet veins rushing into the lapping tide. That was when the gators went crazy. They swam toward the island, thick tails cutting steely wakes, thrashing in the blood-charged water as if the lake itself were on the boil.

And soon that lake wasn't black anymore. It was as red as everything else. On the island, a few of the vampires burst like ticks. Others drank furiously. Still others tried to stopper the bounty killer's wounds with clawed hands, but there was no plugging the dike. Everything on the island was the color of blood, and the red lake was rising all around it.

At last, the queen and her shadowmen broke away from that wild gusher of a man. They started across the bridge, coming our way. The queen was sow-fat now, her tattered lace dress a rag on the shore. She ran naked and white and round like the moon, the bridge swaying under her weight. It was her and her followers above the lake, and those rotten planks between, and a riptide of white gators below. And the whole pack of them were coming our way, with nothing behind them but the bounty killer, dancing alone on that island like a man trapped in a scarlet hurricane.

And the lake was rising higher, blood lapping the bone-colored beach at our feet. The gators and vampires were closer now. One of the albino reptiles charged between a couple rocks and latched onto the blacksmith. The big German went over like a falling redwood, and two more gators hit him like bait on a hook. I saw the bounty killer's bank book tumble from his shorn pocket, watched it disappear into a gator's mouth. Then the blacksmith screamed as the same beast came after him, and he caught a pair of snapping jawbones between his big hands.

I yanked the bounty killer's black rattler, but by the time I got it out of the holster the blacksmith's head was already gone. I fired at the gator anyway. The bullets drilled it straight through. Three of the other beasts set on the dead monster and slaked their hunger. By the time I reloaded the bounty killer's Colt, Indio had shoved me backward. He had his rucksack open, and dynamite sticks filled his hand.

He scratched a Lucifer alive and put those sticks to work.

The bridge exploded in a million toothpicks.

The queen and her men did just about the same.

Blood was everywhere, but the gators didn't mind.

They were hungry.

They ate.

PART SIX: RUMSON'S SALOON

WE CAME UP out of that empty grave hole in the desert. Indio and I did, plus the Navajo girl. Double-quick, we grabbed that crate of dynamite out of the wagon and took it into the cave. Indio set a couple charges near the twisted iron gate, set another couple farther down the tunnel, then ran fuses through the burrow that led to the surface. He put a match to them and we slapped leather for safety, Indio on horseback and me with the Navajo girl in the wagon.

Henrietta was with us, too. In the ruckus I almost forgot to untie the rawhide cord that held her to the wagon wheel, but I remembered at the last moment. We were less than a mile away when thunder exploded in the earth's belly. A huge cloud coughed out of the ground like the wave of blood that had risen from the lake. Only this wave caught us, then overtook us, then set us riding even faster with bandanas wrapped around our faces. Me in the wagon slapping the ribbons while Henrietta squawked from her hatbox nest beneath the seat, and the Navajo girl holding on for dear life at my side, and Indio in front of us giving his horse plenty of spur.

In other words, we didn't look back. What was behind us had been blown to hell and gone, and we knew it. The deal was finished, and in more ways than one. Without the bounty killer's bank book there was nothing between Indio and me at all anymore. That book was in some dead gator's belly down there in hell, and we'd never touch it in this lifetime. So there was nothing to fight over, and nothing to celebrate. We parted ways without much more than a handshake, and Indio headed south for Mexico.

The Navajo girl and I camped in the desert that night. When I awoke the next morning, she was gone. So I came back to town. There really wasn't anywhere else to go. After a few weeks I discovered Rumson had written a will, leaving his saloon to the whores. They decided to go into another business—or the same business, but minus the beds upstairs—and they hired me. So here I am, standing behind the bar where Rumson used to stand.

Still minus half a face, of course.

But plus another story.

Besides the whiskey, that's what we sell around here. I tend this bar night after night and tell it, and then I sleep the wee hours through and get up in the morning and do it all over again.

And some nights, even as the words spill out of my mouth, I think about the bounty killer. A man like that, you want to imagine there was something else in him. Something that could excuse the killing, and his hard ways, and the things that brought him to the point where he'd ride into a town and do the horrible things he did, then go down in a hole in the ground and do worse. And maybe there was something, and maybe there wasn't. Maybe there was only a kind of desire. The kind you can't really know until death starts to push the door closed behind you. The kind that pushes at you when you put the spurs to a horse and ride it hard toward a place you've never been.

Some nights I think it was one way, and some nights I think it might have been another. And maybe that's what keeps me here, night after night, telling the story. The wondering, I mean. Maybe that's why I do what I do. I don't rightly know. I can't rightly say.

But that's my story, stranger. You can believe it or not. If you want to know more, come back tomorrow morning. We've got a little museum out back. You can see the bounty killer's black rattler of a pistol. You can look at Rumson's sawed-off shotgun, too. There's a glass case with Indio's shackles, and a letter from the warden up at Yuma which testifies to the fact that they're real. In one corner there's the hatbox I took from the general store on the night Rumson died, and most afternoons you'll find Henrietta sleeping in it. She's old now, doesn't get around much. You can even buy a book I wrote where I set down the story straight. It's illustrated by a fellow from Philadelphia who does drawings for all the Eastern magazines. I'll even sign it for you if you want.

But the story you heard tonight, that one's cash on the barrelhead.

Now pay up and hit the trail, amigo.

We're closed for the night.

A Room with a View | *K. J. Parker*

THE DOOR WASN'T locked. "Is he in?" I asked.

She looked at me. "Depends."

I nodded. "I'll go on up," I said.

I hate border towns. They have that insubstantial something-and-nothing quality, to be expected in a settlement that exists precisely because it's neither one thing nor the other. Aperesia Apoina was my seventeenth posting; twelve out of seventeen, border towns. I have mentioned my feelings on this issue, but I don't think anybody cares much.

The stairs were pine, chipped white paint, shows the dirt. His door was shut. I knocked, not that it mattered. No reply, so I thumbed the latch and let myself in.

Nobody behind the desk. It was a small room, mostly full of biscuit-boxes crammed with paper. There was a low, broken chair for visitors. I fixed it with *choris anthropou*, which I'm not particularly good at, and sat down. It creaked, but held.

A form, even something as mundane as *choris anthropou*, would put him on notice, as effectively as the ringing of a bell. I settled down to wait. It was only boredom that made me pick up a letter from the desk.

"You put that down," he said, materialising in the chair and scowling at me. "Restricted."

I grinned at him. He's three grades my senior but I was a year ahead of him in school. "Balls," I said. "It's the office copy of last month's charcoal requisition." I glanced at it again. "What a lot of charcoal you get through in this small building," I said. "I'm surprised. It's quite chilly in here."

He glared at me. He can't resist small, pointless scams and fiddles. He was pulling the charcoal dodge back when he was a junior prefect, in sixth year. "That's still restricted," he said, snapping the paper out of my hand and stuffing it in a box on his desk. "Hence the red seal in the corner, which you can't have failed to notice. What do you want?"

"You sent for me."

"Did I? Why would I do that?"

I shrugged. "How's things, anyway?"

"Dismal." Yes, but they always are. If he dies and goes straight to the Court of the Sun, he'll complain about the cold. And probably put in a spurious charcoal requisition. "Studium's on my back about the Clearwater case, I'm two men short and nobody ever *does* anything around here except me. Did I really send for you?"

"Yes."

"Then I must've had a damn good reason." He opened the big book on his desk and made a show of examining it closely. All theatre, of course, to put me in my place. I made a better show of yawning. I'd have put my feet up on the desk, only I didn't trust the chair.

"Oh, right," he said, and closed the book with a thump. "What's your view of compliance work?"

"I hate it," I said. "I'd rather cut turf."

He nodded. "How about mentoring?"

"Worse."

"Thought so." He was writing something on a scrap of paper, a corner he'd torn off some old letter. "Got a job for you. Compliance *and* mentoring. As soon as it came in, I immediately thought of you."

I'm what you might call something of an under-achiever. I was recognised when I was six years old, immediately admitted to the Temple under-school, won an open scholarship to the main school, straight on to the Studium after that, came fifth in my year out of a class of forty-six. Everybody said I had a remarkable natural talent, that I'd sail through my induction year, qualify before I was thirty and get a research post by forty. It didn't turn out that way. I struggled through induction, failed, retook twice, scraped through, interviewed badly for all my chosen postings, got one rubbishy job after another and ended up here, a freelance on the reserve list. When people ask me what someone like me is doing in a place like this, I must confess I find it hard to explain. Usually I hint at a scandal or a disastrous error of judgement; it's easier than telling the truth, and people are so ready to believe it. Fact is, I do have a remarkable natural talent and on my day I'm as good as any adept in the College. But my days don't come round as often as I'd like, and the rest of the time, I flounder. Silly little mistakes, inattention to detail, failure of concentration, that sort of thing. People tell me it's because my heart isn't in it, and when I've finished slandering them under my breath I have to admit they've got a point. I just don't care much for the work. I'd rather not have the gift and do something else. Not an option, of course. Anyway, I'm too old now to start on a new profession, so it's this or unskilled manual labour.

"Sweet of you," I said. "So, what's it involve?"

He grinned at me. "Here's the address," he said. "They'll explain when you get there."

THERE IS NO such thing, they tell you on your first day in school, as magic. Instead, there's natural philosophy, science; logical, provable facts and predictable, repeatable reactions and effects. What the ignorant and uninformed call magic is simply the area of natural philosophy where we've recorded and codified a certain number of causes and effects, but as yet can't wholly explain how or why they work. Research is, of course, ongoing, and in due course it'll all seem as simple and straightforward and ordinary as the miracles of procreation, metallurgy or fermentation. Until then, foolish country people insist on calling it magic and calling us wizards. Meanwhile, since we can do all this useful stuff and they can't, we get to charge them large sums of money for exercising our strictly controlled and regulated powers. The cynic in me wonders whether the research that will finally strip away the curtain, explain it all and make it so that anyone can do it would be a bit further along if we didn't hold such a profitable monopoly.

I say 'we.' I have no profitable monopolies. I don't even have a job. I have jobs, from time to time, and that's another thing entirely.

Compliance is bread-and-butter stuff to failures and no-hopers like me; I guess I just don't like bread and butter terribly much, or at least not for every meal. It's boring, it's repetitive and the pay's garbage. Mentoring, though, is worse. Mentoring is taking some pushy young kid under your wing for a fortnight, knowing that once the ordeal's over, he's going on somewhere better and you're stuck here. That makes it so much worse, somehow. Besides, I don't like young people. I didn't like them when I was one, and I like them even less now I've grown out of it.

YOU CAN'T REALLY comment on how close laughter is to tears without sounding trite, so I won't bother. By a supreme effort of mental strength and discipline I managed to avoid both. And they say there's no such thing as magic.

"That's it?" I asked.

He looked at me. "That's it. You want the job or not?"

Want, no. Need, yes. "When do I start?"

"Now."

And that's how I came to be there, at that time, in that place. Fundamentally, I believe, comedy and tragedy are the same thing, right up to the end. At the end, in comedy they get out of the mess they're in and live happily ever after. In tragedy, they all die. But there's a tipping point, a moment when it's so evenly balanced it could go either way.

Dogs; that's what the job was. Our wonderful empire is blessed with many old and distinguished noble families, who among other things love to hunt. The best hunting dogs come from Razo, on the other side of the border from Aperesia Apoina. Razo's one of those mountain towns; desperately poor, can't grow anything, can't keep any useful livestock apart from goats, and nobody ever got rich, or even comfortable, raising goats. Can't be done. They graze so close that they wreck the pasture. Result: either you severely limit the size of your herd (so no expansion, no surplus, no wealth) or you overgraze and end up stripping your ground down to bare rock. Luckily for the Razoans, they have the dogs, for which our gilded nobility are prepared to pay silly money. Every Razoan is therefore a full or part-time dog breeder, and twice a month they bring a convoy of the stupid animals over the mountain passes to Apoina, where dealers buy them for a fraction of what the end users will eventually pay. My part in all this? It's a legal requirement (I'm not making this up) that every dog coming into the country from abroad is examined by a Studium-qualified practitioner for signs of demonic possession.

I know. I agree. But it started a long time ago, back when serious people seriously believed in all that stuff. Apparently, four hundred years ago or thereabouts, Apoina and the neighbouring countryside was afflicted by an outbreak of the dancing plague. There hasn't been a case in I don't know how long, but it's a recognised disease, properly documented. The symptoms are uncontrollable shaking, groaning, thrashing about, inability to keep still, eventually leading to a rather horrible death from mental and physical exhaustion. The Apoina outbreak finally burnt itself out, but not before close on a hundred people had died. The city fathers ordered an enquiry, and the examiners came to the conclusion that the plague had been caused by a demon or malign spirit, who'd entered the country from Razo inside the body or mind of a hunting dog. Hence the requirement (city statute D&K47, 106(ii)) which is still very much in force, even though the plague's never been back and not one demonically possessed dog has been impounded in all that time. Of course, the Apoinans say the plague's never returned precisely because of the inspections, and the evil spirits don't even try to sneak in that way because they know they'll be detected and cast out. They're a quaint, old-fashioned lot in Apoina, and their national dish is pigs' feet on a bed of pickled cabbage.

Now perhaps you can see the true evil of the pit that had been dug for me. Under normal circumstances, I'd have spent my two weeks' secondment daydreaming, surreptitiously reading or writing a paper for one of the learned journals. No chance, because I'd also be mentoring. Pitiful though it may seem, I was actually going to have to see into the tiny minds of thousands of dogs, so that my temporary apprentice could watch me and learn how it's done. In other words, I was going to have to take this awful job seriously, or else risk being informed on by a credit-hungry student.

The shed was huge, about fifty yards long, and bitterly cold. Outside dog season it was where they penned up sheep waiting to be sold at market. The whole of the back end was divided up with hurdles, against which the dogs jumped and pawed and scrabbled, barking all the damn time; I tried *ouden menei* to lay down an invisible barrier in the hope it'd keep the sound out, but it didn't work so I gave up. Meanwhile, the owners led their wares past me, one at a time, while I executed the pointless, demeaning but really rather difficult form that allows you to climb inside the mind of another living creature.

It's really just *epoiesen noon* scaled down and differently keyed, without a verbal access-point. You need to climb in though the third Room, but if you're doing hundreds of subjects in a single day, obviously you can't move from there to here and back again every single time, you'd boil your brain trying. So you have to do it in Separation, which in theory is less demanding, but I find that more than an hour in Separation gives me the most appalling headache. Of course, most practitioners who do these forms are working with humans, dangerously ill, in comas. They go in, find the problem, fix it and lead the patient out; five minutes perceived time, practically instantaneous in real time, and then a lie-down being crooned over and abjectly thanked by a grateful family, until you're feeling strong enough to write a receipt for your four-figure fee. Actually, I think dogs are harder than people. True, all you do is poke your head round the door, so to speak, to make sure nobody's home who shouldn't be. But the dog mind is so wretchedly *small*. It's like crawling into a house up the coal-shute rather than walking in through the front door.

I was on my own for the first day, which was a relief; the young hopeful hadn't shown up (they muttered something about bad roads and flooding) so at least I was able to flounder about getting the hang of it unobserved. Just as well. It had been a long time since I'd done anything even remotely similar, and needless to say I made a lot of stupid mistakes before I managed to figure out a reliable and efficient way of doing the job. Even then it was a hell of a strain. I was so determined not to show myself up in front of the kid the next day that I actually did a proper examination on every single dog, and there were hundreds. When they eventually let me go, I crawled off to the quarters they'd prepared for me (three sacks stuffed with straw and a horse-blanket in a mostly-swept-out feed store) and collapsed, my head full of dog, too tired to face the stale bread and crumbly cheese they'd so thoughtfully provided for my evening meal. I seem to remember turning round three times before finally settling down to sleep.

I WOKE UP with a growl and found myself looking at a pair of shoes.

Let me tell you something about them. If I close my eyes, I can picture them still. For a start, they were red, sort of half-way between blood and a good apple. They shone; not like gold or burnished steel, it was a warmer, deeper glow, such as comes from the application of wax and a great deal of work. The toes were quite savagely pointed, and they arched, like a cat stretching, on account of the three-inch heels. They were quite small, and they did up on one side with a row of tiny silver buttons.

"Excuse me," said a voice, "but are you Master Chrysodorus Alexicacus, from the Studium?"

Hadn't been called that in a long time. These days it's Manuo, which is what my father called me, usually coupled with an unflatteringly apt epithet. The use of my academic name, together with the shoes, made me wonder if I was still asleep and dreaming.

"Mm," I said, rubbing my eyes. "Who are you?"

"My name's Comitissa Aureliana," the voice said. "I think you're supposed to be mentoring me."

Well, it's not unheard of. Every now and then, you get a female with the talent. In my time, I may have come across half a dozen— and very competent practitioners they were too, though limited in the range of their abilities, as most of us are. Five of them were exclusively healers, and the sixth was the best water-diviner I've ever worked with. Women can do the job, no question about that, if they happen to have the gift. It's just that very few of them do; the same way that not many women have genuine moustaches. Also, in women it tends to surface much later, usually around puberty. Compared to men, that's very late, which means that by the time a woman's finished her training, even assuming she hasn't had to repeat a year or do retakes, she's likely to be in her late twenties or early thirties, by which time her male contemporaries should (unless they're no-hopers like me) be three or even four grades up the ladder. By and large, the few women we do have in the profession have a pretty rough time of it, though I can't say I've lost too much sleep because of it over the years.

Comitissa Aureliana, though; that was a hell of a name. I looked up.

You know what students tend to look like. There's a general rule-of-thumb formula, quite reliable in my experience, which states that if you add together the age of the student and the age of his coat, you get exactly one hundred. The Lady Aureliana was definitely an exception. An awful lot of time, money and wool had gone into making her coat, and I have to say, there were worse things you could have done with all three. As well as the coat, there was a hat and a skirt, both constructed on the same principles. Holding the components of all this splendour together was a thin-faced woman, about thirty-five, of the kind that my mother used to describe as being prettier than she looks. Not, of course, that stuff like that had any relevance to me, given the nature and requirements of my calling. But you can't help noticing.

"You're it?" I asked.

She nodded. "Afraid so," she replied. "I'm in my second year at the Lusso academy. We have to do a two months' practical before we take our diploma."

Once the surprise had worn off a bit, I came to the conclusion that it could have been a lot worse. I'd been expecting a seventeen-year-old with roughly equal numbers of hairs on his chin and spots on his face. A grown-up was a much more appealing proposition. You can talk to grown-ups, for one thing. Female and a member of the aristocracy weren't aspects I'd have chosen myself, but I'm not exactly opposed on principle to either. Live and let live, I always say.

I hauled myself to my feet, making a nominal effort to brush bits of hay off my coat. "You just got here," I said.

"That's right," she replied. "My coach got stuck trying to cross the river at Ferabrune. Flooding."

I nodded. *"Andra moi ennepe,"* I said. "To modulate and reduce a flow of water. Or haven't you done that yet?"

"Elemental and environmental is next year," she replied. "I have actually read it up in the book, but I didn't want to try it before I'd covered it in class, in case it went wrong."

I couldn't help grinning. I tried to put out a house fire in my second year, using *proelthe*. Put the fire out, flattened half the street. "Very sensible," I said. "Come on, we'd better make a move."

"What exactly is it that we'll be doing?"

They hadn't told her. Well, why should they? Nobody ever told me anything when I was a student; expected me to find out for myself, or know by light of nature. Which was entirely appropriate for seventeen-year-olds who, as everybody knows, thrive on humiliation the way roses grow in horseshit. But a grown-up deserves more respect, surely.

How to phrase it, though. "Do you like dogs?"

"Yes."

"You're going to have a ball," I said. "This way."

SOME PEOPLE ARE born teachers. I'm not one of them. I get impatient if I have to tell someone something more than once. I tend to forget how many times I had to do various simple procedures before I got the hang of them. When I'm teaching someone and they don't get it right first time, I assume they're stupid, or being dense on purpose, or not listening to me, or else for some reason they don't believe me when I tell them something.

But the Lady Comitissa would have tried the patience of the most skilled and dedicated teacher—like the ones who taught me, for instance. She had the ability, she wasn't stupid and she wanted to learn, but things just didn't sink in. She shrugged off new knowledge the way oilskin repels water. I could tell she was no happier about this than I was, and she did her best to keep her temper, remember what we were there for and that we were both on the same side, etcetera. But after the first hour it was obvious to me that she'd been brought up in a world where she was never wrong, simply because of who her father and grandfather had been, and it took her an exceptional amount of effort and application to get past that. The aristocracy are like that. They're comfortable with the idea that it's easier and more fitting to change the world rather than change themselves. Of course, that very quality stands them in good stead in our profession; but only once they've learned the basics and qualified. Not the most helpful mind-set for a trainee. Of course, if she'd been a man, she'd have done all this stuff in her teens, when the mind (even the aristocratic version) is so much more pliable. At her time of life, trying to teach her was like trying to file hardened steel.

And meanwhile, there were dogs. They came along every few minutes, on the ends of ropes, with grim-looking Razoans holding the other end and scowling at me as though it was all my fault. If you think I'm making a fuss about nothing, you try it: a Third room examination of an animal, in Separation, in under three minutes real time, while simultaneously trying to explain what you're doing to an increasingly short-tempered noblewoman who just can't seem to get it. Now I look back on it, I reckon it must've been one of the best days' work I've ever put in, and all for next to nothing.

Finally, just when I knew I couldn't take any more, the flow of dogs dried up. We sat there for a while, me just absorbed in the sheer golden joy of having stopped, until the foreman came by and asked us to leave so his men could start clearing up the mess.

Aperesia Apoina has many places where you can buy strong drink. I marched her to the nearest one, ordered a quart jug of whatever was cheapest, and ordered her to shut up, sit still and listen. I think the only reason I'm still alive is that she was too frazzled to argue.

"I don't see what your problem is," I said. Whatever-was-cheapest tasted horrible and didn't do anything to cure my headache, but after a long pull at the stuff I really didn't care. "All you've got to do is cross into the Third room—"

I stopped short. She was looking at me. "I've got a confession to make," she said. "I can't do rooms."

It was a bit like walking into a wall you hadn't noticed was there. "But you're in second year," I said. "Surely—"

"I can't do rooms," she repeated. "I just can't. Luckily I'm really good at forms, so my marks sort of balance out. Next year, of course, it's all bloody rooms, and they'll realise I can't do them and throw me out. And that'll be two years of my life completely wasted."

Can't do rooms... Like someone admitting to you that they've lived for thirty-odd years and never managed to learn how to breathe. "But they're easy," I said. "And if you can do forms—"

She sighed. It came from deep down. "That's what everybody keeps telling me," she said. "But—" She shook her head. "It's all a bit ridiculous, really. When we first did them I didn't understand, not a word of it, but everybody else did, and I didn't want to stick my hand up and confess, because I didn't want to look totally stupid. Doesn't help that I'm old enough to be my classmates' mother. Anyway, it snowballed from there. Everything in the course is predicated on understanding the basics, and I didn't. The longer I left it, the worse it got, till I reached the point where I gave up. Guess I thought I'd be able to get by on my forms work. Stupid."

I took a while to get a grip. Stunned is putting it mildly. Rooms are *easy*. But then I thought: correction, *I* find rooms easy. She doesn't. I took a deep breath, and tried to imagine what I'd do in this situation if I was an ordinary decent, compassionate human being.

"It's like this," I said. "Imagine the universe is an old, neglected house. The family's fallen on hard times, so they only use one of the rooms. The rest are all boarded up and dust-sheeted. With me so far?"

She actually smiled. "I've got cousins like that."

"Fine. Imagine your cousins, in their one room. That room is the world that anybody can see: people without the gift, normal people. Now imagine they've been living in that one room so long that their kids and grandkids have grown up there, and don't even realise there are any other rooms. That's how it is for the untalented."

She pulled a face. "And me."

"Not anymore," I said firmly. "Now, obviously, what you need to get from one room to another is a door. Untalenteds only ever see two doors, birth and death, and generally speaking they have no control over when they encounter them or go through. We're different. We can *make* doors, any time we choose."

Little scowl. "Speak for yourself."

"No, listen," I said. "It's so simple. Provided you've got the gift, of course, otherwise you can't do it at all. But you can. If you can do forms—"

"Forms are completely different."

I let her have a moment before I contradicted her. "My old teacher used to say, forms are just tools we bring back from other rooms. If you can do forms, *trust me*, you can do rooms. Come on," I added, as she shot me that I-don't-think-so look. "It's like swimming. For ages and ages you're convinced you'll never be able to, and then suddenly something clicks into place and suddenly you're doing it. Rooms are like that. You just need to—"

"I can't swim, either," she said.

I'm really proud of the way I didn't hit her at that point. "Fine," I said. "You can't swim. But you can do rooms. No, really," I added, as she opened her mouth. "You can. You're going to do it right now. Understood?"

The best time for anything, according to my old and much-loved copy of *The Art of War*, is when the enemy is tired. "All right," she snapped at me. "So, what do I do?"

I gave her a big, warm smile I hadn't realised I had. "Just look at that wall over there," I said, "and imagine a door."

"Yes, but—"

"Try it."

She decided to humour me, presumably as her best shot at getting me to shut up and leave her alone. She turned her head, held it for a second or so and closed her eyes. And then it happened.

UNTALENTEDS SAY THINGS like, "I saw him flicker" or "there was a flash of light." Sometimes they hear noises, or feel a slipstream. Pure imagination. There's nothing to see, hear or feel because nothing's happened. Someone who was there a millionth of a second ago is still there. Big deal.

She looked at me. Her eyes were huge. "There was a door," she said.

"Yes," I replied.

"Really. It was *there*. You do believe me, don't you?"

I restrained myself, and just rolled my eyes instead. "So," I said, "what did you do?"

She frowned. "Well, I suppose I must've opened it, but I don't remember standing up or walking across the room—"

"Don't worry about it," I said quickly. "You were by the door. You opened it. Did you go through?"

She nodded. "The door swung open, so I went in."

"What did you see?"

"It was just—" She looked helpless for a moment. "Well, just a room, really."

"Hence the name," I said. "Did you recognise it?"

"No, of course not. It was just—well, a room. Empty. Plain floorboards, no furniture. I don't remember seeing any windows—"

"You wouldn't have," I assured her. "They come later. Advanced level. So, what did you do?"

"I turned round and came back."

I smiled. I was feeling really rather pleased with myself. "There you are, you see," I said. "You did it. You can swim."

"Yes, but how did I—?"

"Don't ask," I cut her off. "No, really, don't ask. Don't even think about it, not till you've got used to it. Just tell yourself, I can do this, because I've already done it once. That's all."

She grabbed her cup and drank some of the disgusting strong liquor, which she hadn't touched before. "All right," she said quietly. "But *what* did I do?"

"You went into the First room," I said.

"What does that mean?"

Curiously, I didn't feel quite so tired. "The First room is pretty straightforward," I said. "We use it for simple things, like moving from place to place instantaneously, disappearing, moving objects. As you saw for yourself, it's empty, you only find what you've brought yourself. It's worth bothering with because when you're in the First room, you can open a door back to anywhere you like; where you just came from, or somewhere completely different. So, if I wanted to nip back to the Studium to look something up, I'd just go into the First room, then open a door back into Long Cloister, and I'd be looking straight at the Library gates."

Her mouth had dropped open. "That's—"

"A piece of cake," I said. "In actual fact there's slightly more to it than that. There are restrictions and limitations, which you'll need to know eventually. But don't even think about them now, or you'll lose confidence. For the time being, just assume you can go anywhere you like. And that's just the First room," I couldn't resist adding. "Really, the First's only important because it leads to the others."

Well. I said it because that's what my teacher said to me, when I was a kid; an unusually talented and promising kid, who had the misfortune to grow up to be me. All my teachers had to do was engage my enthusiasm.

The trouble with me is, when I get interested, I get impatient. "Come on," I said, "I'll come with you this time."

"You want me to go there again?"

"Sure. It won't hurt, I promise."

Imagine you were born and brought up on Temple Street, or in a cottage on the slopes of Mons Tonans. To you, it's familiar, it's just home, no big deal. To the people who sail across the sea and walk a hundred miles just to see it, it's the most amazing thing ever. But you never even bother to look. I guess that's me and the rooms. By the time I was seven years old I'd already made it to the Third room; I used to go exploring, and not tell anybody. And somehow, I always knew exactly what I had to do. I'm prepared to bet that if room time was real time, I've spent more of my life in rooms than I have here.

It's easy to forget that other people aren't like you.

Before she could start arguing, I opened a door. I left it open behind me. A moment later, she followed me in.

"Is this how it looked the first time?" I asked.

She nodded. "Maybe not quite so filthy," she said.

I looked down. There was dust on the floor. I tried to remember if that was normal, but I couldn't. I tend not to look at floors much. "This is how it should look," I said. "Remember, nothing but what you bring with you."

She looked round. "Is this is?"

Blasé already. "It's a transit point," I said. "Like I told you. We can use it for getting where we want to go in our room, or we can move on." I smiled at her, trying to be reassuring. She just looked mildly disappointed. "Which would you prefer?"

"Whichever's easiest."

Sensible attitude. But I'm not exactly famous for being sensible. "Just for that," I said—I was so full of myself I was dripping out of my own ear—"we'll move on. Door," I said (though of course it's not necessary. I just wanted to impress) and a door appeared in the opposite wall. "Second room," I said. "Come on."

You know, there's a reason why adepts in our profession are required to be celibate. I've given the matter a degree of thought over the years, and I don't believe it's to preserve us from the distractions of worldly affection or bodily pleasure. It's because when we're around women, we can't help showing off. Whether that's cause or effect I can't rightly say, but in any event it makes us a danger to ourselves and others.

I opened the door and asked, "What do you see?"

"A staircase," she replied.

"Yes?"

"Just a staircase. All right," she went on, after I'd frowned at her. "It's painted white, the paint's a bit chipped in places. It could do with a good washing-down."

Something nagged at the back of my mind, but I was too busy showing off to care. "Very good," I said. "Up the stairs to the Second room. Would you like me to go first?"

"All right," she said. "But don't get too far ahead of me."

I ran up the stairs two at a time. I can do that, in the Second room, and not arrive at the top gasping for breath. I waited for her to join me. She took her time.

"Ready?" I asked.

"I suppose so."

The Second room isn't like the others. It's above and to the side; in other words, you can't get directly back to normality from it, you need to go back to the First or on into the Third. Researchers and academics spend a certain amount of time there. The whole of one wall is covered with bookshelves, and the shelves are crammed with books. Men have gone mad trying to figure out how to read them. There are long, polished tables lined with fascinating instruments, with dials and pointers and scales; they measure something, or record changes, or register variations or fluctuations. There are things that look and work like clocks, and things with lenses and eyepieces; there are miniature furnaces, and wheels that spin round when you touch them, with compartments for the placing of samples. There's a rack of small, fine tools, but no one has any idea what they're for. Also, if you try tossing a coin in the Second room, it always comes down tails. Sometimes there's a big glass tank full of water, with small, brightly-coloured birds flying in it. We assume that's an experiment being conducted by scientists from somewhere else. We've never met them, of course. The best thing you can do in the Second room is pass through it as quickly as you can.

I looked at her. She seemed fine. I was surprised, and impressed. The length of time (subjective time, naturally) you can stay in the Second room is directly connected to the strength of your ability. You can learn how to extend that time, a bit, in the same way you can train yourself to hold your breath. I can manage an hour, on my day. Novices are usually gasping for breath in a couple of minutes. Some quite experienced and talented adepts have to get through the Second room at a run.

She was standing there looking about, like a country woman in the Museum.

"Like it?" I asked.

"What on earth is all this *junk*?" she asked.

For some reason, I felt like I should take that personally. But I remembered; I was the guide, not the proprietor. "Your guess is as good as mine," I said. "How are you feeling?"

"What? Oh, fine." She touched one of the instruments, a brass thing with four spring-loaded arms and a dial. The needle quivered and moved a few degrees on the scale. "Shouldn't I be?"

"Would you like to go on to the Third room?"

She shook her head. "I want to go back," she said. "This is all a bit—"

I nodded. "Fine," I said. "You've done really well for a—"

She wasn't listening. She was staring at something over my shoulder. Ah, I thought. "It's all right," I said, and turned round.

I've seen worse. It had a human body (the arms were unnaturally long) with a pig's head; very long, curled-over fingernails, like the sad people you see sleeping in doorways. "Don't worry," I said. It opened its mouth; rows of teeth, like bent needles. *Elthe chelidon* sorted it out in two seconds flat. All that was left was a little fine ash.

She was frozen. I had to make an effort not to laugh. But the first time, it can be really scary.

"Nothing to worry about," I told her. "They aren't even alive. It's just a bit of—well, something, we brought in with us."

She looked at me as if I was mad. "Something?"

I shrugged. "Anything," I said. "It can be a stray thought, a memory, a little rush of emotion, even toothache. In the rooms, they sort of gather matter. *Elthe chelidon* is all you need, like you just saw. Really, I should've let you do it, and then you'd know it's no big deal."

She was looking at the place where it had been. "You're sure about that?"

I laughed. "Absolutely," I said. "Anything weird or strange-looking you meet in the rooms is nothing to worry about, so long as it's moving, acting like it's alive. In fact, the weirder they are, the better. It's only the ones who look exactly like ordinary people you need to worry about."

"Oh, right," she said. "What if I meet one of them?"

"Run," I said. "But you won't. They're incredibly rare. And if you do, chances are it'll have six fingers on one hand or a stub of a tail, in which case it's nothing. Better not to stick around and find out, though."

She gave me a nasty look. "I really want to go back now," she said.

WE REPEATED THE exercise the next morning, just before I was due to start work. I was really pleased with how quickly she'd taken to it; she was quietly ecstatic, I could tell. "I really do appreciate this," she told me, when we'd come back. "You've no idea how ashamed of myself I was. I mean, everyone else in my year can do it, and they're just *kids*."

"My pleasure," I replied, truthfully. After all, for years I reckoned I was a hopeless teacher. I think I was as relieved as she was. For one thing, there's steady work in teaching. "Anyhow," I went on, "I don't think you'll have any problems now. In fact, you're doing really well. Most people—"

"You're very kind," she said. "I expect I'm pretty hopeless really. But I do feel much better about it."

I didn't labour the point in case it made her over-confident, which would have been doing her no favours. "At least there'll be some purpose to this exercise," I said. "Now at least you'll be able to watch what I'm doing. You might even learn something."

Admiration is a wonderful thing. I like it in the same way I like hundred-year-old brandy, and both of them come my way about as frequently. The other similarity is the way it goes to my head.

"It's amazing," she said. "I don't know how you can do that."

God help me, I simpered. "It's not like it's difficult or anything," I told her. "Just a lot of work."

Which it is, of course. Every time they confronted me with a new dog, I had to open a door, go through the First room, up the stairs, through the Second room (*elthe chelidon*-ing any nasties that might happen to pop out at me; and of course, the more tired and hacked off I got as the day progressed, the more nasties there inevitably were) and into the Third, from which I could use a projection to take a quick glance inside the mutt's head to make sure there wasn't anything in there that shouldn't be. Then all the way back again, to nod to the dog-handlers so they could take it away. You don't get tired running up and down the stairs in rooms, of course, but although your brain knows that, your body doesn't. It thinks it ought to be tired, so that's how you feel. And all in Separation, remember, which really doesn't help. Even so; it's hard work, but it's simple and straightforward, the kind of work the sort of person who just scrapes a pass in Finals can be relied on to handle. For a talented chronic under-achiever like myself, a piece of cake.

She started to say something, then decided against it. "What?" I said.

"Nothing."

"Please," I said. "Don't go all female on me. What is it?"

She laughed. "I was going to ask you if I thought I could have a go. But obviously I can't."

We'd been working for five hours. Three hundred dogs. Six hundred traverses of the staircase. "I don't see why not," I said.

"But I haven't even been in the Third room yet. And I don't know how to do a projection—"

"Easy," I told her. "You just look. Visualise. The door between rooms is a projection. Think of it as opening a window into the dog's head."

"And I wouldn't know what I was looking for, anyway," she said.

"Oh, that's not a problem," I replied. "If there's something nasty in there, you'll know it when you see it. Trust me on that."

She looked doubtful. So did the two men with a dog, who were waiting for us to stop chattering. Just as well they couldn't have had a clue what we were talking about. "I don't know," she said. I could tell she was wavering. "What's the Third room like, anyhow?"

"Come with me," I said. "I'll show you."

On the stairs up to the Second room, I said; "Third room's not scary or anything, but you do need to take care." Just then, a nasty reared up right in front of her. She blew it apart without a moment's hesitation, like she'd been doing it for years. "You can run into—well, awkward stuff."

"Awkward?"

I nodded. "It's like—well, you know when you're walking after it's been raining, and sometimes you glimpse your reflection in puddles?"

We were at the top of the stairs. I had to wait for her. "Yes?"

"Well," I said. "The Third room is principally used for looking inside people's minds. In a place like that, a mirror can be a real nuisance."

She got the point. "Are there mirrors in there?"

"Define mirrors," I replied, pushing open the door. A nasty tried to stop me; I dealt with it. "A mirror in the real world is a shiny thing that reflects light. In the Third room, there are various objects that reflect thought."

"I see what you mean," she said. "How do I—?"

"Just concentrate on what you're there for," I said. "You'll be fine. And it's not dangerous, even if you do bump into a mirror. It can just be—well, uncomfortable, all right? So be careful."

Second room was dark, lit by a long row of candles on the table. It's like that sometimes. Nobody knows why.

"What do I do?" she asked. "Just open a door, same as usual?"

For a moment, I felt really proud of her. Open a door, same as usual. This from the woman who'd sworn blind she'd never be able to do it, less than twenty-four hours earlier. "Go ahead," I replied.

"Um, which wall?"

I laughed. Valid point. All the walls in Second room are covered in stuff—bookshelves, paintings (did I mention them? Really strange, some of them), tapestries, ornamental trophies of weapons. "Just go ahead," I said. "The stuff gets out of the way."

I've known people to have real difficulty with that; but she opened a door right in the middle of a shelf of books, no trouble at all. "That's amazing," she said, as the door swung open. "I just—"

"Go on in," I said.

This is going to sound completely stupid, but never mind. I'd never been in the Third room with anyone before. Accordingly, I wasn't prepared.

I followed her through the open door, and stopped dead. Stunned, confused. I'd been in there just a moment ago, and hundreds of times before that, since breakfast. But it was all different.

Well, of course it was. Everybody's Third room is different; and because she went in ahead of me, what I walked into was her version of it. Took me a minute to figure that out, of course.

My Third room is basically a study; the sort of study I always thought I'd have one day, when I'm Regent professor at a high-class provincial academy somewhere. In my Third room, there are two chairs. There's mine, a beautiful old carved number that belonged to all my predecessors back through five hundred years (it creaks when you sit on it, but it's really comfortable, and you can put your feet up on the crossbar under the desk), and there's another plain, old, rosewood, straight-backed, for the few select students I condescend to teach when I'm not engrossed in my research. The walls are all book-lined—there's a long shelf, just above my head where I sit, that's all the books I've written; it stretches from wall to wall. There's piles of books on the floor, too, with five or six bookmarks in each one, and a small round table with crystal decanters. It has a drawer in its side, into which over the years all the commendations and medals of honour I've been awarded have been stuffed any old how, because of course that sort of thing doesn't really matter to me. And there's a window, looking down into the main quad, except when it's pointed into somebody's, or some dog's, head.

Spot the difference. Her Third room was—

Empty. Nothing. I had to look quite hard before I could see floor-boards on the floor, instead of a light brown blur. Three bare walls and ceiling. The fourth wall was a frameless window. I peered over her shoulder at it, and was marginally reassured. That was a dog's mind, all right.

"What should I be looking for?" she said.

"It'll be in colour," I replied.

(Well, obvious. Dogs don't see colours like we do, just an infinite variety of shades of grey. Any stowaways show up coloured, you can spot them at a glance.)

"I'm colour-blind," she said.

Oh. "Doesn't matter," I replied. "Anything not moving."

Images streamed past in the window, intermittent. I saw my own face, huge, as I moved my head slightly. When I held still, I vanished. I saw one of the dog-handlers scratching his chin. Fine. Nothing here. "That's all there is to it," I said. "We'd better go back."

"How do you get to the Fourth room?" she said.

I'd already turned my back on her. "Same basic idea," I said, not looking round. "So I understand. Never been there myself."

"You just open a door. By imagining it."

"Yes," I said. "But you don't want to go trying it. Come on, we've got dogs to molest."

We went back. I worked. She was quiet and I was busy. Up and down those bloody stairs, in and out of my study—it looked different, though I didn't stop to look closely. But I got the impression that some of the books had been moved, and my father's portrait was by the window instead of the door. The Fourth room. I really didn't want to think about that. My fault, for letting her get over-confident.

"Can I have a go?" she said, at some point. "On my own?"

Sure, I thought, why not? "Later," I said. "Let's just get through the rush, and then we'll see."

—⚬—

THERE ARE PEOPLE—LOADS of them—who really like dogs. I don't object to them, most of the time. By mid afternoon, however, I'd had enough. The Razoan hunting dog isn't, in any case, a thing of beauty. Its head is too big for its body, and all its ribs stick out, and it drools. It's about the size of a large goat, and it only eats raw meat. The smell, accordingly, can be a bit intense.

This one was nothing out of the ordinary; it was a silver-point roan (that means brown; they're all brown) bitch with an underslung jaw—that's a fault, apparently, means it's worth less money, I have no idea why. Its owners were two sad old men in coats way too big for them, so that the sleeves came down to the quicks of their fingernails. I was beginning to ask myself, quite forcefully, why I was bothering. After all, nobody would know if I just sat there, rapt mystic expression on face, then nodded and said "Next." Nobody would care. Nobody.

I hadn't let her have a go on her own yet. She hadn't asked again. She looked bored.

I opened a door. Second room, stairs, Third room. On my way through, I helped myself to a stiff drink from one of the crystal decanters. One of the great disappointments about rooms is that anything you drink there tastes of cold tea and doesn't *do* anything. I checked the silver label on the decanter. *Hundred-year-old brandy*. Cold tea.

I turned to the window. Everything normal, everything grey. Might as well not have bothered.

Something moved in the room.

You know how, in really good portraits, they play tricks on you. The eyes follow you around the room, or the feet are always pointed at you, no matter where you stand. I understand that artists train for years to learn how to do that. You can't do it with a form, by the way. I've tried.

If you were to ask me why I put a portrait of my father in my dream study, I couldn't tell you. I don't actually remember putting it there. It just turned up one day, and I accepted it. It's a very over-stuffed room. By the same token, I can't remember calling into existence each of the thousand or so books on the shelves; but if you look closely, each one's got a title, and if you pull one down at random and open it, there are words on the pages and everything. Most of them are books I've read at some time; others, I can only assume, are books I will read one day but haven't read yet. None of them are any good. I've always believed that the room pulled them out of my mind, so to speak, to fill gaps on the shelves; the same, presumably, with the portrait.

But it's not a good portrait. In fact, it's pretty ghastly. In that respect, I'd always given the room due credit. Catch me paying fancy money for a portrait of my father. It's just a daub, makes him look like a lobster in a fake beard. And it shows him in profile, so the eyes most definitely don't follow you around.

He was looking at me.

I did the only thing I could. I looked back.

A NECESSARY DIGRESSION.

Not all practitioners are as celibate as they ought to be. My father, for example. He entered the Academy at Oudeis Oudemia when he was five—child prodigy—and was formally inducted at thirteen. I imagine he was insufferable at that age. He went on to be senior lecturer at Oudeis for forty years, and ended his career as vice-chancellor of the Studium. No under-achiever. Not like his son.

I still don't know exactly how he came by me. He never said, I never asked. I take it that an opportunity arose, and he made full use of it. Rules were things he made; they didn't apply to him. Anyway, I was one of the many rare and curious objects cluttering up his lodgings for fourteen years, and then I was packed off to the Studium. Other kids went home for the holidays. I took advantage of the empty library. Didn't occur to me to find it strange.

I saw him once, after I left home. That's the memory of him that found its way into the portrait. I came back to my lodgings after my induction ceremony, and he was there waiting. He'd brought me a present, the only one he ever gave me: a copy of Sthenelaus' *Reflections and Maxims*. I sold it two years ago, and was surprised at how much it was worth. He handed me the book, scowled at me down his ridiculously long nose (that and Sthenelaus are all I ever got from him) and said, "Don't disappoint me." Then he walked out.

—*Ø*—

"BUT YOU HAVE," he said.

I wasn't having any of that. I looked him straight in his painted eye, and said: "You aren't real. You're a room artefact. Presumably you're my inner guilt, reminding me I'm a failure. It's just because I'm pissed off after two days with the dogs."

He looked at me. I felt the need to break the silence. I said; "Probably the mentoring's got something to do with it. I'm upset that she's done so well, it's reminded me that I've got all this talent and I'm here mind-reading dogs, while she's on the brink of a splendid career. Stop looking at me like that or I'll turn you to the wall."

He didn't blink. "You disappointed me," he said.

"So what?" I turned back to the window, and saw the inside of a closed shutter.

"You're a fool," he said.

He used to say that a lot: when I got a homework question wrong—he always went over my homework after I'd done it, made me do it again, then tore up what I'd written and dictated an answer. The teachers knew, but he was their boss. "Quite probably," I said. "But this is my room. Get out."

He laughed; and he was standing in front of me, towering, much taller than he'd ever been (but he was that much taller than me when I was fourteen). "Work it out," he said. "Do it again."

"That proves my point," I answered, stepping back until my heel collided with the desk. "You're just pulling phrases out of my memory. You aren't real."

He pushed past me, went behind the desk and sat down, in my chair. I had no option. I sat down in the student's chair. "You're guilty of a false premise," he said.

I thought about it. "I don't think so," I replied. "This is my room. Therefore, if you're in it, I must have created you."

"That's the false premise," he said.

Oh, I thought.

Do it again. How do things arrive in the Third room? They come in with you, or from outside. If he hadn't—

"Come in with you," he said, "therefore I must have come in from outside. What's outside?"

I nodded, couldn't help it. "The dog's mind," I said.

"Correct." He tapped the desktop with his fingertip, his way of awarding me a single, begrudged mark.

"So what are you?" I said. "Are you a—?"

"Demon." He shook his head. "An unquiet inhabitant of a far, dark room, determined to creep through into the light. Is that what you believe?"

I didn't answer.

"In which case," he went on, "you must believe that I have infiltrated your memory and pulled out the most intimidating identity I found there, with the aim of dominating you and taking possession of your physical body." He scowled. "Is that really how you think of me? Your worst nightmare?"

I didn't say anything.

"You're guilty of limited thinking," he said. "Do it again."

I took my time. One thing I'll say for him, he was always patient with me, in a brutal sort of a way. I said, "The rooms are where we come from, and where we go to. Even the untalenteds have access to two of them."

He nodded. "Birth and death."

"The Third room—"

"You're forgetting," he said. "How did I come in here?"

I frowned. "In the dog's head," I said.

"False premise."

I could feel my hands clenching into fists. "All right," I said. "I admit it, I'm too stupid to figure it out for myself. So just tell me, all right?"

He shook his head sadly. I'd disappointed him again. "Very well."

"What are you?"

"I am what I look like," he said.

I thought about that. "You died nine years ago," I said.

"I went into another room," he replied. "But I confess I didn't find it much to my taste. That disappointed me. I'd always hoped that the far room would be beguiling, fascinating, a place of answers, a room I'd never been able to reach. Instead—" He shrugged his broad, thin shoulders. "The windows all face the courtyard and all the books are ones I'd read before. The rules say I have to stay there. But the rules—"

I think it was that that clinched it for me. It was him all right. "What do you want?" I asked.

"To come back, of course," he replied. "I find the far room intolerable. Recently I have once again become aware of the passage of time. They assure me that that is not possible, that there is no time in the far room. I fear that that is yet another rule that doesn't apply to me." He closed his eyes for a moment, then went on; "There are days in my death: hours, minutes. They pass very slowly. My mind is every bit as active as it ever was. I need to come back. There is so much I want to do. I can discover new things. I can be useful. You, on the other hand—"

He didn't need to be explicit. Fair point, after all. I'm a chronic under-achiever, and who would miss me? "Is that possible?" I said.

"It can be done," he replied. Then he leaned forward, unusually animated. I'd only ever seen him this passionate once or twice before. "Be logical," he said. "There are two of us, and only one body. Which of us should have it? Which of us will make the better use of it? It's an old ethical question, you could never get it right: where there are needs and resources, who has the better right to them? I say there can only be one correct answer. Look at yourself. What have you ever done to justify your existence?"

The Third room can be full of mirrors sometimes. This was one of those times.

We looked in the mirror together. I saw my entire life. I had to admit, he had a point.

"I asked you," he said, "not to disappoint me. I knew that one day I must pass into the far room. I had high hopes of it, but I was deceived. I trusted you to fulfill those promises I had made but would not live to keep: research, discovery, the amazing things I could have done had I lived. I gave you intelligence, a prodigious talent. You failed me. Accordingly, I have the right."

I thought about it. "You can't come back," I said.

"The rules don't apply to me."

"Maybe not," I said. "But this is my room. Get out."

He stood up, looming over me. He reached out, and his hands closed around my throat. "You will go into the far room," he said. "It resembles the life you've made for yourself so closely that I dare say you won't notice the difference. I, on the other hand, am simply taking back what's mine."

I could feel his fingers tightening. I put my hand on the desk and fumbled for something to use as a weapon. I found a knife. I stuck it in him.

He looked at me. His face was so close to mine that I could feel his breath. A demon, of course, wouldn't breathe.

"Go back," I said.

His eyes were fading. "Please," he said. I didn't reply. I wasn't there when he died, the first time. I made up for that.

He faded, bit by bit. When he was completely gone, I looked for his portrait on the wall. Not there any more.

Then I looked at the knife.

— ❦ —

I WENT BACK and did the rest of the dogs. Nothing; everything was grey, like it's supposed to be. I looked for the portrait, but I couldn't find it. Ever since then, I have difficulty remembering what he looked like. Ah well, no great loss.

When the last dog had been led away, I said; "Let's go and have a drink. I need one."

We sat on opposite sides of a wobbly table. I swilled down a jug of the local poison before she said anything.

"You didn't let me have a go on my own," she said.

"No." I drained the last drop into my cup and swallowed it. No effect, like the booze in the Third room. I wondered if my punishment was a life of unbreakable sobriety. "Just as well I didn't, really. Don't you think?"

She looked at me. "You know," she said.

I nodded wearily. "Yes," I said. "Took me long enough to figure it out, but I did, eventually. Had to be told," I added. "Couldn't see it for myself."

She didn't say anything. Apparently, it was up to me.

"Things can only get into the Third room," I said, "if someone brings them there. Earlier today, I found a knife, just when I needed one. I didn't bring it there. You did."

She just looked at me.

"Thank you," I said.

"You're welcome," she replied.

"But that's not all you left there," I went on. "Was it?"

She shrugged. "What's a girl to do?" she said.

I almost felt sorry for her. But it hadn't been her hands on my throat. I could have forgiven that. It was his.

"You don't belong here," I said. "And you didn't come here in the head of some dog."

"I just want to go home," she said. "What's so terrible about that?"

"But you can't," I replied. "It's against the rules."

"Some rules don't apply to some people."

I laughed. "How much time did you spend with him?" I asked.

"Longer than you did." She smiled bleakly. "Actually, it really was all his fault. He conjured me, from the room where I lived. I didn't want to go, but he was very strong. I was his familiar for fifty years."

I nodded. "And when he died—"

"I was stuck here. I didn't even have a body, not for a long time, not till he died and I was able to wriggle free. This was the only body I could get." She grinned. "Not what I'd have chosen."

"Because the talent is so rare among women." I nodded. "And the late onset, too."

"Nine years," she said. "When he died. It fitted rather nicely. Don't blame yourself for not suspecting."

"I should have," I replied. "You got out of breath on the stairs, which should've told me you were at home there, not an intruder. You saw the stairs as the staircase up to the appointments office, when I got this job; you took that from my mind. You couldn't do rooms; then, as soon as I teach you, you're a natural at them. You played on my vanity. I hadn't realised I still had one."

She laughed at that. "Of course you do," she said. "You think you're amazingly brilliant, but your life's been ruined by your father. Which is largely true," she added. "That's something we have in common."

"You took him in there," I said, "when we went there together. You left him there to wait for me. I should've known when you said you're colour-blind."

"Silly of me," she said. "Maybe I wanted you to guess, so I gave you a great big hint."

I looked in my cup but it was still empty. "Was that the deal?" I said. "You'd take him back, and in return he'd let you through? After he'd murdered me?"

She looked down at her hands. "If that was the deal," she said, "why did I leave you the knife?"

I took a deep breath. "I think that question is the reason we're having this conversation," I said. "Otherwise I'd have blown you away with *philon hetor* the moment I got back."

She looked at me, again. "I must have changed my mind," she said.

"I suppose you must," I said. "How did you find me?"

"Wasn't easy," she said. "You disappeared into obscurity, it took me most of the nine years just to track you down. I wanted to use someone else, but he insisted. He said he didn't have a right to take anybody else's life. Just yours."

"He always was a very ethical man," I said. "And a great one for rules."

"Well?" she said. "Will you? You owe me, for the knife."

I thought about it. "I'm not sure I know how."

"He did. He told me. I can tell you." She grinned. "It's not too difficult, actually. Even you should be able to manage it."

I thought: about him, my life, under-achievement generally. I thought: I am my father's son, and he left unfinished business. And the rules: the rules don't apply to me.

—✺—

THE DOOR WASN'T locked. He was in his office.

"Had a good time in the sticks?" he said, not looking up from his paperwork.

"A bit boring," I replied. "But thanks anyway."

He looked up. "You're welcome," he said. "How were the dogs?"

"Very much as you'd expect," I said. "I think I might get myself one, for the company."

He nodded slowly. "And the mentoring," he said. "How did that work out?"

I shrugged. "She wasn't suited," I said. "She's given up. Gone home."

"Ah well." He shook his head. "Probably just as well. There isn't really a place for women in the profession." He uncorked the bottle on his desk, poured himself one, offered me one. I refused. "Really," he said, "there ought to be a rule about it."

"Quite," I said. "Well, thanks again. Please bear me in mind when something else turns up."

I left, down the stairs, out into the street. My two weeks' work had earned me forty shillings. I spent one of them on a bottle of hundred-and-fifty proof. Sadly, like the rules, I found it didn't apply to me.

THE INSPIRED WORD

THE INSPIRED WORD

Scripture in the Light of Language and Literature

LUIS ALONSO SCHÖKEL, S.J.

Translated by
Francis Martin, O.C.S.O.

HERDER AND HERDER

1965
HERDER AND HERDER NEW YORK
232 Madison Avenue, New York 10016

This translation made from the original manuscript,
La Palabra Inspirada,
published by Editorial Herder S.A., Barcelona, 1966.

Nihil obstat: Rt. Rev. Msgr. William J. Collins, S.T.L.
Censor Librorum

Imprimatur: ✠ Ernest J. Primeau
Bishop of Manchester
July 23, 1965

The *Nihil obstat* and *Imprimatur* are official declarations that a book or pamphlet is free of doctrinal or moral error. No implication is contained therein that those who have granted the *Nihil obstat* and *Imprimatur* agree with the contents, opinions, or statements expressed.

General Table of Contents

ABBREVIATIONS

AAS	*Acta Apostolicae Sedis*
Ang	*Angelicum*
Bib	*Biblica*
BJRylL	*Bulletin of the John Rylands Library*
CB	*Cultura Bíblica*
CBQ	*Catholic Biblical Quarterly*
CCL	*Corpus Christianorum*, Series Latina
Const.	*Constitution on the Sacred Liturgy*, Latin and English Texts, Liturgical Press, 1964
CTSA	Papers read at the annual meeting of the Catholic Theological Society of America
DBS	*Dictionnaire de la Bible, Supplement*, ed. by L. Pirot, A. Robert, H. Cazelles, Paris, 1928–
D-S	*Enchiridion Symbolorum Definitionum et Declarationum*, last edited by Schönmetzer (22nd ed.), Herder and Herder, 1963
DivTh	*Divus Thomas*
EB	*Enchiridion Biblicum*
EstBíb	*Estudios Bíblicos*
EstEc	*Estudios Eclesiásticos*
ETL	*Ephemerides Theologicae Lovanienses*
GCS	*Griechische christliche Schriftsteller*, ed. by the Kirchenväter-Kommission der Preussischen Akademie, Berlin
Gnom	*Gnomon*
IPQ	*International Philosophical Quarterly*
JTS	*Journal of Theological Studies*
LumVi	*Lumière et Vie*

9

Mansi	Mansi, *Sacrorum Conciliorum*
NRT	*Nouvelle Revue Théologique*
Pesch	Christian Pesch, *De Inspiratione Sacrae Scripturae*, Freiburg, 1905
PG	Migne, *Patrologia Graeca*
PL	Migne, *Patrologia Latina*
PT	*Philosophy Today*
RB	*Revue Biblique*
RevScPhTh	*Revue des Sciences Philosophiques et Théologiques*
RSS	*Rome and the Study of Scripture*, 6th ed., Grail, 1958
Schol	*Scholastik*
SZ	*Stimmen der Zeit*
TD	*Theology Digest*
TLZ	*Theologische Literaturzeitung*
TRu	*Theologische Rundschau*
TS	*Theological Studies*
VD	*Verbum Domini*
VT	*Vetus Testamentum*
ZAW	*Zeitschrift für die Alttestamentliche Wissenschaft*
ZKT	*Zeitschrift für Katholische Theologie*

Acknowledgments

The translations of the Old Testament, when they are not original, are taken from the Confraternity of Christian Doctrine version. The New Testament translations, when they are not original, are taken from the New English Bible. Spellings of biblical names and places, however, are those of the King James version. Numbering of the psalms is likewise that used in the King James version. Whenever patristic and other texts are not my own translation, credit is given in the footnotes. Thanks are here expressed to the following publishers for permission to reprint: New Directions, for the two selections from "Requiem for Wolf Graf von Kalckreuth," in *Rainer Maria Rilke. Selected Works*, volume 2, translated by J. B. Leishman, 1960, p. 209; to the same publisher for the selection from *The Literary Essays of Ezra Pound*, edited by T. S. Eliot, 1960, p. 25; and to Penquin Books for the selection from *Poems of St. John of the Cross*, translated by Roy Campbell, 1951, pp. 42–43.

Preface

This book is not meant to be a treatise on inspiration, as can be seen from its theme, the categories in which it moves, and its manner of exposition.

Rather than inspiration, its theme is the word. That is, it centers on that article of faith which declares that God "spoke through the prophets." In my consideration of a mystery which is broad and unfathomable, I have attempted to approach it from a precisely determined viewpoint. Christian Pesch introduced me to the centuries-old tradition of the Church in regard to this mystery, and beginning from that position, I have attempted to bring to it the categories and acquisitions of the philosophy of language and literary analysis. These represent a limited aspect, but one that embraces many more particular aspects in a unifying synthesis.

This approach determines the general lines of our essay. The radical human capacity to speak is realized in various languages and actualized in the individual speech act. This individual act may be given form in a literary work which is then actualized by being re-presented and repeated, and then finally consummated in the act by which it is received. God also descends to speak to us, taking hold of the human capacity to speak (Logos, condescension) which is realized in two languages concretely (election in history, language in society). These chosen languages are given literary form by means of a divine impulse given to certain men (inspiration, psychology of literary creation), and this results in a series of works which go to make up one work (the inspired work, the Scriptures) which is in turn actualized by being proclaimed and read in the Church wherein it is received and given its consummation. Thus, God speaks to man, and man listens and responds.

This book is not a strictly scientific study: there is no vast accumulation of erudition or profound and exclusive penetration into one problem. It is rather the result of frequent reflection on the mystery of the word of God in the Church.

I have sought in these reflections to achieve breadth rather than depth. And, in a certain sense, this book is more or less a review of these reflections, ordering them and examining them so as to prepare the way for future reflection. I hope to profit from the criticism and interest of others, for in these matters monologue is less fruitful than dialogue.

I have preferred the expositive tone of an essay in order to be more conversational and accessible, and thus I have put the more technical matters in footnotes. The essay form has allowed me to express my reflections in terms that are imaginative and symbolic, without always bringing them to the last stage of conceptual refinement.

As I was writing this book, I kept in mind the educated Christian public who have become aware of the modern biblical movement. The study which follows seeks to preserve contact with those who were already actively present as it was being written.

Jerusalem, Easter 1964
Rome, All Saints Day 1964

I
THE WORD
HUMAN AND DIVINE

I

THE WORD
HUMAN AND DIVINE

Locutus Est per Prophetas

1. An Article of Faith

During Mass on Sunday, the people stand and, led by the priest, make profession of their faith. In this solemn liturgical act, the community is assembled and arrayed in readiness—not for war, but to declare its belief. The people stand firm and united, showing forth the strength of the Spirit which inspires them and the unanimity of their convictions. Yet they stand humbly, for an act of faith is an act of humility and a gift of grace. At this moment in the liturgy, a flood tide of grace levels all other differences by raising those present to the level of the priest-mediator, to the level of the supernatural. The community is activated by a force more than human, because within it there flows the power of grace.

Do all understand what they profess? Yes, at least in a rudimentary fashion; for to believe is already to understand, in the sense that faith means an opening out of oneself and a surrendering to an insight. Do all understand in the same way? Do all believe with the same awareness, depth, clarity, and fullness? No, for these perfections of faith vary and can increase with meditation and study. Intellectual effort which has as its object a reality of faith enables us to grow in knowledge. This is what we mean by theology; it is faith seeking to understand.

This increase in understanding the faith we profess can take place in the liturgy itself. The structure of the liturgical office for a feast day, its various components: Scripture readings, prayers, hymns, and actions, are designed to shed light on the mystery being commemorated. Then, too, during the service, a preacher may explain the meaning of the feast and its mystery and thereby increase our understanding. This growth in understanding which is effected by the liturgy tends to be living and spontaneous rather

19

than reflexive or systematic. Thus, the Christian inspired by the liturgy may continue his search for understanding outside of it in a science which is called theology.

Our profession of faith as expressed in the Creed is divided into articles. In the third section, which treats of the Holy Spirit, we declare of Him that He "spoke through the prophets" . . . "qui locutus est per prophetas." These words express the substance of our faith regarding sacred Scripture, our inspired books. Does everyone grasp the meaning of what they are professing to believe? Again, yes—they do. It is quite easy to understand what it means to speak, and not too difficult to have some notion of what a prophet is, while we all know in general what it means to speak through another. It is precisely this rudimentary understanding of the activity of the Holy Spirit and of the word of God which can be enriched by theological study. We can reflect on the movement of the Holy Spirit which we call inspiration, or on the historical context of the inspired authors. We can consider the presence of the inspired books within the Church, and see the consequences implied by such a reality for our own lives as Christians. These are some of the directions in which we can turn our gaze in order to enlarge our view and understanding of what it means when we say "Who spoke through the prophets."

THE SPIRIT

Before descending to particulars, let us first examine the context in which we are going to move—the context of the Spirit.[1] The Spirit is a "divine wind" (Gn 1), an elemental force. The Spirit hovered over the abyss at the beginning of creation; the Spirit swooped down on the warrior Samson and drove him on to great exploits for the salvation of his people. The same Spirit gathered from the four winds gave life to dry bones, while Ezekiel the prophet looked on; just as it was this Spirit which God breathed into Adam to give him life. The Spirit was a soft breeze relieving the anguish of Elijah, and a fourfold docile wind, resting on the shoot of Jesse. The Spirit is a hurricane and tongues of Pentecostal fire, the secret prompter of our cry to God as "Father," prodigal of His gifts and graces in the early Church and throughout all time.

[1] We will treat of the context of the Trinity later on: cf. chs. 14 and 15.

It is thus that we should think of the Spirit; mighty, sovereignly free, restless and many-sided, present and yet unseen. It is within this context of vitality and freedom that we must consider the inspiration of the sacred books. We search for neat precision, but the Spirit eludes the pigeonholes of our thinking. We attempt to focus our concepts, but the Wind will not be contained; we make airtight distinctions, yet the Spirit renders them porous. The Spirit breathes where He will; we hear His voice but we know not whence He comes or where He goes. This is the context in which to situate the charism of inspiration. It finds actual and living existence only in intimate connection with the many other charisms conferred on Israel and the Church.

With such suppleness of mind, sensitive to these dynamic realities, and humble enough to see ourselves baffled, we approach the study of the inspired authors and their inspired books. We are undertaking an investigation of what is radically a mystery of faith. May the Spirit Himself give us the gift of understanding that we may penetrate a little into this mystery of His action.

When we call inspiration a charism, we are describing one of the characteristics of the Church. The sacred books pertain to the institution of the Church, to her structure. They are something institutional and constitutive. Yet, in the Church, what is institutional remains open to charismatic activity, since without charisms, the Church could not endure. All of her institutions, the papacy, episcapacy, priesthood, dogmatic definitions, and the rest, are permeated with the charismatic, that is to say, they are activated by the presence of the Spirit Who guarantees to the Church the possession of supernatural realities such as infallibility and holiness. But even these recognized and established institutions must leave room for charismatic activity which is unforeseen and irresistible. The Spirit Who acts within the Church will not be bound.

When we say, then, that inspiration is a charism, there are important consequences. The presence of the Scriptures within the Church is a presence of the Spirit, and that means the presence of activity. The Bible is one of the institutional channels for the working of the Holy Spirit, and at the same time it lies open and ready at hand for any new and unexpected activity on His part. The very reading and interpreting of the sacred text pertain to the realm of the charismatic. There is an infallible and authoritative interpretation as well as one that is inspired and free. And at the service of both of these is the more modest, human effort of the scholar, who may also receive the Spirit's touch.[2]

By designating inspiration as a charism, we are not led to think of it as something apart from the other charisms which give life to the Church: the charisms of sanctity, of inspiration, of miracles and healing, of wisdom, counsel, and preaching, are as so many interwoven threads forming the design of a unique and beautiful tapestry.

Pierre Benoit [3] has attempted to extend the range covered by the term "inspiration," distinguishing and organizing its application by means of "analogies." Thus, he speaks of a "cognitive inspiration," conferring knowledge; an "oratorical inspiration," which can be subdivided into "prophetic" and "apostolic"; a "hagiographical inspiration," conferring the power to write; and a "dramatic inspiration," conferring the power to act. This last can be operative either within the people of God as a whole or conferred on specially chosen individuals, and is realized today in ecclesiastical inspiration or in the assistance given to the magisterium.

This schema of Benoit, by indicating the mutual relations and common source in the Spirit of the various charisms, restores to the inspiration of sacred Scripture a context which is full, more complex, and "analogous." One could cite in its favor the etymology of the word "in-spiration" itself (breathe into), as well as the free use made of the word by early writers who applied the term "inspired" to councils and to some ecclesiastical authors.

However, all things considered, we cannot accept Benoit's terminology. Nowadays, usage has consecrated the term "inspiration" and given it a specific significance. To use it now, and ignore this specification, could easily cause us to slide from analogy to ambiguity. A much more traditional and less risky procedure would be to use the term "charism" to indicate this common context and intimate interconnection, keeping "inspiration" as a technical term. This would not prevent us from distinguishing within the over-all process of inspiration itself various stages or aspects. In such a line

[2] During the third session of Vatican II (October 5th, 1964), Bishop Edelby gave a very forceful presentation of this theme of the Spirit in Scriptures.

[3] P. Benoit, "Les Analogies de l'inspiration," in *Sacra Pagina*, Gembloux, 1959, vol. 1, pp. 86–99.

of investigation, the studies of Benoit can be seen to have contributed greatly to the speculative clarification of the mystery.

St. Thomas has taught us to situate the gift of "prophecy" (not, strictly speaking, inspiration) among the charisms, or *gratiae gratis datae*.[4] With his predilection for the sapiential ordering of things he divides the charisms into three groups. There are gifts pertaining to knowledge, namely prophecy and ecstasy; gifts pertaining to speech, namely the gift of tongues, and of eloquence; and gifts pertaining to action, that is, the gift of miracles. Rigid adherence to this division has brought with it unnecessary problems in the neo-scholastic tracts *"de inspiratione sacrae Scripturae."* Later, we shall have occasion to return to this idea. For the present, without entering into "disputed questions," we simply assert the fact that inspiration is a charism pertaining to language— "Who spoke through the prophets."

The Word

In the charism of inspiration, the activity of the Spirit is characterized by language. There is assertion, communication, and knowledge. Now all of these pertain to the realm of Logos which means precisely knowledge and its communication in words, and they constitute the elements of revelation which involves thinking, speaking, communication, and understanding.

Let us take the word "revelation" in a very wide sense; then we shall be able to begin our consideration on the level of strictly human experience. For example, we say that the image made by light on a sensitive film is "revealed" during the developing process. Or we say that the atom or heredity "reveal" their secrets to a mathematical or experimental investigation. Then there is a higher, or deeper, meaning to the term. I might say that a landscape, tempest, or a tropical sky at night has been a revelation to me because it led me to see something behind or beyond it. Is it that things reveal themselves, or is it that something which is not a mere object, is discovered in them?

But we need not go so far or so deep. The most insignificant thing in the world lies open, manifesting itself to man. Its being is a presence, a manifestation; its being is knowable, and yet we

[4] *Summa Theol.* II–II, 171–178.

would not say of it that it lays aside its veil or reveals itself. When a man takes possession of such a manifestation and contemplates a being which manifests itself to his understanding, he names it in an act of his spirit; he gives to it a power to be manifest, and confers on it a new kind of presence and openness; he reveals it to himself and to others.

Already we can see the radical connection which binds "revelation" and "language" together. If we wish to proceed, cautious in our terminology, we might reserve the term "revelation" to a more exalted sphere. But since everyday language knows no such scruples, we think it better to begin at this level, so rich in suggestive possibilities, which comes before any strict terminological precisions. The child is the great explorer of a "new world" because all the world is new to him. Everything is for him a revelation, and to bestow names on objects and use them is for a child sheer delight.

Actually, the word "revelation" is more often used in connection with persons, or subjects. Two characteristics serve to describe a person: intellectual self-possession, or consciousness; and volitional self-possession, or liberty. A dog also has knowledge in a sensory way, but it does not know that it is knowing; it possesses tendencies, but not freely. I, on the contrary, when I know an object, am aware of myself as a knower in the act of knowing. I can store up knowledge and bring it to bear on new situations, aware of it as past and as mine. I possess my knowledge, and, in it, myself. In a way still more radical, I possess my will. For I make decisions, and suspend them or revoke them. I direct my activity to a goal I have determined; I reflect and ponder before deciding, and after having acted, I know that I am master of these acts and responsible for them. This possession is something interior to itself, it is enclosed on itself. Thus, I can keep this activity as my own exclusive possession; I can veil it from other eyes, or again, I may reveal it. Because I possess myself, I am able to hide myself and cut myself off, no matter what pressure or violence is brought to bear. Because I possess myself, I am able to open myself in communication with another person, revealing myself in a gift freely given. Here, in acts which are fully personal, do we find completely justified the use of the term "revelation."

It is true, of course, that even without wishing it, we reveal ourselves by our actions and spontaneous reactions. There are sciences and methods which interpret such symptoms. But in a full and free self-revelation, one which is desired and realized, there is no need to interpret symptoms; there is a mutual knowledge and penetration. This personal revelation, both conscious and free, can be expressed through some deliberate action such as the giving of a bouquet of flowers ("say it with flowers"), or by a handshake, or it can be expressed in words. By personal revelation, we make another person a sharer in our own intimate possession, and he in his turn makes us a sharer in his.

Once again our analysis has brought us to language as the ideal medium for personal revelation. What is more, our theme of mutual revelation, consummated in dialogue, has been struck. This theme will recur again. For the moment, however, let us be content only with having enunciated it.

And what about God? Is He a Person? May He, too, veil Himself or reveal Himself? Here faith comes to our aid, and tells us that God subsists in three Persons; indeed, this faith itself already implies a revelation. The Augustinian speculations on the Trinity, which rely on data taken from the Scriptures, will be our guide here.

No one possesses himself by knowledge and liberty as God does. The plenitude of God can be possessed only by God. The Father possesses the fullness of God, which means He possesses Himself; but He does not keep this possession for Himself. Rather, in a Word, mysterious and all-embracing, He communicates the divine plenitude to the Person of the Son in such a way that the Son possesses the whole of divinity just as the Father does. He is the Son, the Image, the Word of the Father. This fullness of divinity, which the Father and the Son possess as shared, is communicated by them to the Holy Spirit, again in such a way that He, too, possesses the whole of divinity. If we stretch the term "revelation" to its limits, we could say that within God there is a sort of revelation. Or better, we might say that the divine life is an interior revelation of the Father to the Son, of the Father in the Son. But this is to speculate on a truth which must remain a mystery.

We have not yet left the interior of the divinity; rather, we have followed the bold speculations of St. Augustine into the very center of the divine life. If, however, we limit the term "revelation" to a narrower sense, then the inner life of God does not meet its requirements. We have need of some action on the part of God, by which He would open Himself, "externalize" Himself in actions or words. But is such a revelation compatible with the nature of God? Again, relying on the authority of St. Augustine, who is, in turn, basing his writings on Scripture, we can say that it is precisely because there is within God a Word Who is the adequate expression of the divinity, that there can be some act external to God which is a partial, many-sided reflection of what He is. The reason why St. John and St. Paul say that all things were made by the Word and in the Word is that any external manifestation of God is rooted in this inner manifestation, in the Son, the Image, the Word. All revelation of God outside Himself is an imitation of the mysterious manifestation within.

If we know anything or are able to say anything about the inner life of God, it is because this life has been given external expression in a revelation, and has provided us with a means of entering dimly into the very source of its mystery.

THE THREE MEDIA OF REVELATION

The Epistle to the Hebrews opens with a solemn, closely worded introduction: "When in former times God spoke to our forefathers, he spoke in fragmentary and varied fashion through the prophets. But in this, the final age, he has spoken to us in the Son, Whom he has made heir to the whole universe, and through whom he created all orders of existence: the Son who is the effulgence of God's splendour and the stamp of God's very Being, and sustains the universe by his word of power. When he had brought about the purgation of sins, he took his seat at the right hand of majesty on high, raised as far above the angels, as the title he has inherited is superior to theirs." [5]

In the above theological synthesis, all that is lacking for completeness is some reference to God's revelation in history. This we find in Chapter 11, and even here in Chapter 1 it is implied in the verbal forms which are used. Christ is referred to as the effulgence of God's splendor and the stamp of God's very Being. Strictly speaking, these words refer to the Incarnate Christ. But since, in

[5] Heb 1:1–4.

the Incarnation, the substantial image of the divinity enters into the world, these words may be referred also to the intimate life of the Trinity. We learn further that the world, the first revelation of God outside Himself, was created through Christ, the Word. Prior to His historical coming, and by way of preparation for this final stage of salvation history, there was a "fragmentary and varied" revelation made through the prophets. We have the final and definitive revelation in Christ, Who in His Person is the splendor and the Image of the Father, Who in His acts has "brought about the purgation of sins," and Who in His words has pronounced the message of the Father. The creation, the Scriptures, and redemption in Christ are all intimately related to one another and constitute for us the revelation of God.

REVELATION IN CREATION

Expressions such as "nature," "universe," and "cosmos," are poor substitutes for the word "creation." For the true substance of all nature is found in the fact that it is a creature and as such it is a revelation, or, if we wish to be more precise, a manifestation of God. Everything that God works outside Himself makes Him known and is a sort of language. "The heavens declare the glory of God" by their very existence and motion. When men's eyes are not closed to it, they understand this language of nature which speaks as a creature of its Creator. Indeed, it is a literary commonplace to speak of "the book of creation."

> Everything in this creation
> is to us a book or painting
> or, indeed, a looking glass.[6]

Or, as St. Bonaventure observes in his *Breviloquium*,[7] "The world is like some book in which there appears . . . the Trinity, its Maker."

[6] "*Omnis mundi creatura*
Quasi liber, et pictura
Nobis est, et speculum." Alan of Lille, "Poem," PL 210, 579.

[7] "*Creatura mundi est quasi quidam liber in quo relucet . . . Trinitas fabricatrix.*" Brevil. II, 12.

E. R. Curtius dedicates a chapter to this theme in his study of European literature, *European Literature and the Latin Middle Ages*, New York, 1963, ch. 16, "The Book as a Symbol." There he traces the idea from Greek litera-

St. Paul tells us that "all that may be known of God by men lies plain before their eyes; indeed, God Himself has disclosed it to them. His invisible attributes, that is to say, His everlasting power and deity, have been visible ever since the world began, to the eye of reason, in the things He has made." [8] In other words, for a mind that knows how to reflect, things visible are a revelation of God. St. Paul does not specify exactly what he means by this process of reflection, though he does employ a technical philosophical term, "*nooúmena*," which ought to be translated more or less as "thought out." One form of reflection would be by means of syllogisms, which, based on the principle of causality, rise step by step to God and His attributes and perfection. The different "ways" or methods proving the existence of God are more or less various realizations of the principle of sufficient reason. For the Greeks of St. Paul's time and for the men of an age of science, the "ways" of syllogistic thought lie always accessible, and all such roads terminate in God. And fundamentally, given the fact that rationality is of the essence of man, the capacity to reason, as this is actuated by man, can lead him to God. We speak here of possibility in the sense in which the notion is used by Vatican I.[9]

For primitive people of a pre-philosophical culture, there seems to be another "way," and this is usually called the way of symbolic thought. I do not mean to imply that we have here another "demonstration." To demonstrate something is to proceed by precise philosophical method, whereas symbolic thought leads us to God without this strict use of syllogisms. There is, for example, the feeling of some transcendent power within a storm. The storm is somehow greater than itself. It bears the revelation of something transcendent and majestic, something sacred and divine; and this is communicated not through any reasoning process, but in a deep emotional experience. The same can be said about a jet-black sky, all covered with stars; the roar of a volcano; the vast silence of the sea; or the imperious stillness of a forest. Such a "way" is open to

---

ture to Shakespeare, and clearly shows the constant recurrence of the theme. This is of particular interest in the study of Scripture, especially in view of the medieval notion of the three "books" of nature, the soul, and the Scriptures (cf. H. de Lubac, *Exégèse Médièvale*, Paris, 1959–1961, vol. 1, pp. 121–125).

[8] Rom 1:19–20.

[9] D-S 3004. Cf. R. Latourelle, *Théologie de la Révélation*, Bruges, 1963, p. 356.

innumerable vagaries, as the study of comparative religion can well attest. Nevertheless, this same study demonstrates quite clearly that such an approach is deeply religious, and that for many peoples it is a sincere expression of religion. Granted that this be the way of the imagination, one freighted with emotion, still, this does not exclude its fundamentally intellectual character. All symbolic perception has an intellectual content, and is rooted in the subconscious structures of the soul. Afterward, this same perception is transmitted in myths and in powerful poetic images which are of great value both for their intelligible content and their communicative efficacy.[10]

If among the Psalms we find one which is taken and adapted from the cult of Canaan, this only serves as proof that the sacred author saw in this poem an authentic religious experience, expressed correctly enough to be taken over bodily and inserted into a Yahwistic context. This is, in fact, the case with Psalm 29, which honors God present in a storm. It is authentic poetry, intuitive, and free of any trace of a strict reasoning process. A surging, commanding event in nature is contemplated and becomes the object of a symbolic reflection—*nooúmena*—in which thunder becomes the voice of God. In a similar way, the Hebrew religious poets never hesitated to borrow the classical images of Canaanite poetry in order to express some aspect of God. Thus, the restless ocean appears as a rebellion or confusion on which God victoriously imposes His rule:

> The floods lift up, O Lord
> the floods lift up their voice;
> the floods lift up their tumult.
> More powerful than the roar of many waters,
> more powerful than the breakers of the sea—
> powerful on high is the Lord.[11]

We should not think of the images, symbols, and myths of these Oriental religions as though they were so many illusions or errors, suddenly become holy and true by being incorporated in the Israelite religion. The transmutation process at work within the biblical tradition is not of this order. It would be even more ridiculous to

---

[10] Cf. R. Guardini, *Religion und Offenbarung*, Würzburg, 1958, ch. 1.
[11] Ps 93.

imagine the biblical authors as men who, though they themselves thought syllogistically, still couched their thought in images because of the rude culture of their people. Poetry is not the art of dressing up syllogisms.

In these and many other biblical examples which could be cited, there is an obvious point of contact with the religions of the ancient Near East. This means that, at least with regard to these points of contact, better still these interchanges of contact, the extra-biblical religions bear witness to an authentic experience of God, even though this may have become contaminated and twisted by other elements.

This is the view commonly held today, and admitted by those who still persist in thinking of myths in categories drawn from rationalism or the Enlightenment. Scholars may discuss the advantages of these ways of approaching God. Here we are only concerned with the fact, creation shows forth God.

Is this manifestation of God a sort of divine language, or must there be some addition made by human language to the data provided by nature? It would seem that the word *nooúmena* in the Epistle to the Romans implies some kind of interior speech; such activity seems to involve a symbolic synthesis or process of reasoning by which propositions are linked together. While it is certainly true that in these processes there is always some sort of rudimentary interior language, for the present we would prefer not to speak of such intellectual activity as an act of language in the formal sense. We have yet to clarify and become familiar with the various shades of meaning in the term "language."

In the Logos, the Father expresses Himself to Himself and communicates to His Son the whole of the divinity. The nature of this vital expressive act itself entitles us to call it analogically a Word—"Logos." The Word is unique and all-sufficient. It is simple, not divided or composed; it is a natural subsisting image, rather than one which is conventional and passing. But when God begins to act outside Himself through the Son, the case is different. God cannot exhaust the infinite virtualities of His image in just one creature. He must now divide and spell out, as it were, this unique image in a well-ordered series of images. These, indeed, make up a sort of language, for they are an ordered system of substitute forms. God cannot communicate to anything outside Himself His own subsisting Being, but only gives to it an existence which is contingent. The necessary loss of a subsistent mode of being is one more factor which makes a creature resemble a language. Every being, though it be on a lesser scale of existence and deprived of the subsistent Being of that for which it stands, represents some interior perfection within God. It is like some immense vocabulary of meaningful words. Created things, by their mutual relationship to one another within a certain order, show forth something of the unity and the relations in God, and go to make up well-formed sentences: while the whole of creation is an ordered system, like some perfect literary masterpiece. As we have seen, this image of the book of creation is not a new one. Fray Luis of Granada, ranging himself in this tradition, speaks of the creatures of this world as so many letters—"beautiful in their consummate perfection, resembling illuminated initial letters which bespeak the handicraft and wisdom of their Fashioner," while Dante compares the world to sheaves of paper *elegantly* bound:

> Within its depths I saw assembled,
> bound by love in one great volume,
> the scattered sheaves of all the world.[12]

The Old Testament employs the idea of language in describing the very moment of creation. The author draws a fine distinction in relating these first creative acts of God. There is first a command, then its execution, and then a naming. This is seen clearly when the call into existence is distinct from the imposition of the name: "Let there be light, and there was light . . . and God called the light Day." We can speak of a "vocation" to exist; and then afterward a "nomination" of a thing in its being. The call to existence is a "saying" on the part of God: "And God said . . ."— and it presents itself as a great and invincible act of language, couched in the form of an imperative, and followed by a series of nouns: light, water, land. As the name of each successive thing is called out by God, its individual reality, its intelligible presence, is established. Things are named at the beginning and remain forever capable of receiving a name. In the creative acts which follow, the

[12] *"Nel suo profundo vidi che s'interna,*
legato con amore in un volume,
ciò che per l'universo si squaderna." Paradiso 33, 83.

author maintains his sublime economy of description, and renounces any attempt to convey the world's objective multiplicity. Thus, on the fourth day God called the "lights" into existence and distinguished between the two more important lights. One is for the day and the other for the night, and they are named respectively "sun" and "moon." But it would be quite foreign to the simple hieratic style of our author to continue his enumeration by naming all the stars. He says simply: ". . . and the stars." Yet, we read in Psalm 147 that God calls all the stars by name, implying at least that at the beginning He had conferred names on them in the same way as He had named the sun and the moon. Something similar happens in the creative acts which follow. The author insists that everything was made "according to its kind" and given powers "according to its kind," but he never stops to tell us what name God gave to each of these many creatures.

In the Bible as we have it, where Chapter 2 seems to continue the story of Chapter 1, it appears that God ceded to Adam the right of naming all the animals. But since man is the image and likeness of God, his naming of things in no way excludes a prior constitutive naming by God. The redactor who joined these first two chapters did not broach every theological problem. We may consider the "saying" of God as the cause of a thing's existence, and the "naming" by God as the reason why it can receive a name. For to name things means to differentiate them and place them in order. We may recall in this connection that the first attempts at science on the part of the Sumerians and Babylonians consisted in drawing up lists of things, grouped according to some similarity, plants, animals, atmospheric phenomena, etc. Indeed, this practice continues into our own time, in the classifying work done by Linnaeus or Mendeleev, as well as in the textbooks of descriptive anatomy, and linguistic dictionaries.[13]

God creates with His Word, placing things outside Himself which share in His wisdom and power. This action of His can be considered a manifestation made through an articulated language which in its turn is able to divide and order. The result of this activity is a well-ordered system of things which may be compared

[13] For a treatment of this *"Listenwissenschaft,"* cf. G. von Rad, *Old Testament Theology*, New York, 1962, p. 425, and the bibliographical material in n. 23.

to a language system in that it contains a differentiated yet ordered body of reality, capable of being named, and which, in fact, is named and becomes formally language with the advent of man.

This may seem to some people to be a vicious circle. We started from our common experience of language in order to explain by analogy the creative activity of God. Then we saw a similarity to language in this activity itself as described in the Scriptures and by theology. However, the constant practice of the Bible in describing creation as an act of language, the theological formulas of St. John and their subsequent use by the Fathers, assure us of the validity of our explanation. If we are able to take our experience of language as the analogical basis for explaining the divine activity, it is because in a real sense our language imitates this activity. Later, we will see how this is so.

Thus, the first manifestation of God, which is revelation in the broad sense, is accomplished by the works of creation, by creatures themselves. We see in these an image and an analogy of formal language in which revelation in the strict sense will be found.

REVELATION IN HISTORY

Nature is but the stage for history. Absolutely speaking, only man can possess a history, a continual process of irreversible events. Evolutionist thought, even in its acceptable version, tends to transpose this historical dimension of man to the order of a process of nature. Man's history is a revelation of man. Is it also a revelation of God? One hastens to answer in the affirmative, since history makes manifest the providence of God. But in many respects, human history is more a scandal than a manifestation of God, and it is no easy accomplishment to see always and in every event of our lives, whether adverse, humiliating, senseless, or boring, the providence of God.

Psalm 136 is an admirable synthesis of nature and history. It chooses from among creatures a stage-setting of three levels: heaven, the abode of God; earth, the dwelling place of man; and the waters under the earth, which house dark and contrary forces. Then there is mention of the two "lights" which rule the day and night. Even if this veiled reference to time and history is not fully intended, it still remains a fortunate intuition. Nature tends to-

33

ward history, and shares already in the dimension of the historical.

Leaving aside for the moment the discussion of providence which could seem too remote and general for our consideration, we wish to ask another question more immediate and concrete. Can God take a personal role in history and reveal Himself in this activity?

A scholar who would wish to write a genuine history of a town called Lourdes would have to take into account a person who often plays a leading role in the life of that town. That person is God. Of course, in order to explain correctly these historical facts, a special light would be needed, namely faith. An agnostic would be inclined to list a series of enigmatic happenings which have undoubtedly affected the history of the town. He would finally confront this series of facts with a negative conclusion that they are "at present inexplicable." A believer would have the same facts, but he could give them their true interpretation. But in order to convey this deep meaning which lies revealed, yet hidden, he would have to use narrative techniques which, according to Bernheim, are not allowed in modern historiography. Again, only readers who were also believers would be able to understand the true history of Lourdes.

What we say of Lourdes can be applied also to other times and places in which the presence and power of the Church demand an explanation exceeding that of mere history. But even further afield, we are confronted with a people whose name and deeds are recorded by the chroniclers of this world, but whose history is only explicable when God is seen to be its protagonist. Their history, recounted by those who made it, does not conform to the norms of our modern critical historical writing. This is due not only to their cultural and temporal distance from us, but also to the particular type of history they wish to tell. For they wish to present a true picture of the events they are recounting, one whose depths can only be sounded by faith, and this history is a story whose hero is God.

When God comes down from His transcendence in order to intervene in human history, He manifests His presence and His action. If these interventions are repeated often enough to form a continuity of action, then the individual manifestations, which are as so many points, join to form a line, and this line begins to trace a pattern. This pattern is one of constancy and faithfulness. God's activity reveals His "constants," and man comes to know Him as a loving friend seeking a response, all-seeing, all-powerful, and concerned. God reveals Himself in history.

History is to a people what biography is to an individual. For an individual is also able to reflect on his own life and see there a series of special divine interventions, which make up a line and finally a pattern which reveals God. This revelation is of the same nature as that discussed above, though, of course, it remains private. But even as private, we must not forget that this revelation can be communicated to others and shared with them, and can become a center from which radiates the light of God to many persons, and these individuals make up a people.

Theoretically, the action of God, by its power and uniqueness, can suffice of itself to make itself known. Thus, when the third plague fell upon Egypt, the magicians exclaimed: "The finger of God is here." But ordinarily, we require that words be joined to actions, in order that the real meaning of these latter be understood.

In the movie "The End of the Affair" (adapted from the novel by Graham Greene), the director Dmytryk has us look upon a scene in which no word is spoken. The house of Maurice Bendrix is bombed during the London Blitz, and we see the terror of it: actions, gestures, the roar and the din, yet not a word. The story continues, but Sarah, the heroine, begins to act in a strange, incoherent way which neither Bendrix nor the audience is able to understand. Then, at one point, Bendrix begins to read Sarah's diary out loud, and he (and the audience) begins to understand. As he reads, his voice conjures up the scene once again, and we see the same incidents and images which now become intelligible because of the spoken word.

This example, borrowed from the cinema, suggests to us a question. "Isn't God's action in history a sort of language?" Insofar as it is an expression outside Himself, one which is characterized by differentiation and order, we may say that it is a language. It pertains to that type of language which, if we accept the term, may be called "cinematographic." Eisenstein among the creators of this language, and Renato among its analysts, may have discussed its qualities and described its formal elements and their semantic and expressive functions, as well as questions of syntax and style. The analogy is quite sound and not at all fanciful, and it helps us to a real understanding of this new medium.[14] Though sound is important, a movie substantially consists of images. These images succeed one another, uniting and dividing, to present a story. They portray a series of actions which sketch some intelligible pattern by which persons and their histories are made known. We have only to think of the unforgettable achievements of the silent movies: "The Battleship Potemkin" of Eisenstein, "Mother" by Pudovkin, "The Passion of Joan of Arc" by Dreyer, and we will see how true it is that action is a language—provided, of course, that its "vocabulary" be carefully chosen and artistically handled.

It is in this sense that we are entitled to call God's activity in history a sort of language, made up of actions chosen and arranged by Himself in such a way that they "speak" to us. Then, too, God uses language itself as a means of acting in history. The prophet not only foresees what is to happen and predicts it, his very words help to bring it about.[15] The people of God began to exist when they were called together by God. They were assembled as the people of God and began to exist as such when they were called "My people," "the Lord's people," by the imposition of a name which not only defined them, but also established them in their existence. The people received a divine ordinance of a religious and ethical nature which was framed in a series of commandments, called "the ten words."

The story of any love can only be told by introducing elements of dialogue. A child becomes aware of his own personal existence because of the actions and dialogue of his father, just as the people of God achieved self-consciousness because of a relationship with God, in which He both acted in their behalf and spoke with them. We cannot separate, except logically, God's revelation in history and His revelation in words.

We should note in passing that God acts in history using nature as His instrument. That is what characterizes the theophanies, the

14 Cf. S. Eisenstein, *Film Form. Film Sense*, New York, 1957; and R. May, *L'avventura del film; immagini, suono, colore*, Rome, 1952, and *Civiltà della immagini; la TV e il cinema*, Rome, 1957.

15 Von Rad, *op. cit.* (n. 13), treats of the power of the prophetic word in ch. C. Cf. esp. pp. 340ff.

action of God on the "day of the Lord," and the presence of the cosmos as a witness to the justice of God's judgments.

And now we return to the example of a film, in order to draw some conclusions. History usually needs to be explained by word in order to achieve full intelligibility and to make its meaning known. In a film, events, be they real or fictional, are transformed into a series of well-organized images, and in this process they both receive and transmit an interpretation. Mediocre indeed is the director who has to provide, either by a narrator or through one of his characters, a commentary on the scenes he has created. God acts in history, creating and directing it, and then sends His word to "cast the scenes," and convey its deepest meaning. This is the task of the prophet, of the inspired author; they give a meaning to history in the way that they tell it. It is not as though they first related the facts, like some voice off stage, and then interpreted them. No, it is in their very manner of relating the facts that they give to them an interpretation. Their selection and arrangement of events convey in the telling their true interpretation, and give evidence of the deep significance of these events, revealing God as the protagonist. Of course, the sacred author maintains his right to use other facets of language in order to interpret events: speeches placed in the mouth of the principal actors, introductions to his stories, reflections on them, and the rest. By means of the message of Moses and the prophets, the people of God are led to an understanding of the history which they are living. This understanding has been bequeathed to us in writings which might be called "the memoirs of God." St. Paul says that "all these things happened to them by way of symbol, and were written down for our instruction." [16] Events become the narrated word, and thus receive their authentic interpretation through this word which raises them to the level of formal revelation.

Again we see in this second form of revelation, which is through history, that it has its own specific character, and yet it, too, is intimately linked to language and inseparable from word, both acting and interpreting.

[16] 1 Cor 10:11.

REVELATION THROUGH THE WORD

God also has especially chosen this way of communicating Himself, of revealing Himself to us.

Let us take any intense human experience—love, pain, beauty, discovery. Its vitality is something total and all-engaging, and it appears to us that the "I" sails on, swept along by the force of the current, and that we behold all this, completely surrounded by the waves, unable to speak, hardly able to understand. Then we are free from the rush of the waters and we retreat some quiet distance, to confront ourselves reflectively with our new experience. First, we divide the continuous whole into various segments. Then we form these segments into some meaningful unity, some structured totality. Thus, our experience becomes language.[17]

> My chest, my chest, —the pain!
> The house of my heart, inside my heart is surging,
> I cannot be still!
>
> My soul hears the trumpet, the cry of war—
> Ruin calls upon ruin, the whole land is asunder.
> Suddenly my tents, quickly my coverings are torn open.
> How long must I see that banner, must I hear that trumpet?
>
> How stupid my people, they know me not.
> Degenerate children, unable to think,
> Wise enough for evil, to do good they know not.
>
> I look at the earth, behold
> waste and emptiness,
> at the heavens—
> there is no light.
> I look at the mountains, behold
> they are shaking,
> at the hills—
> and they quake.
> I look, behold
> there is no one,

---

[17] For a good treatment of these aspects of poetic language, see Amado Alonso, *Materia y forma en poesía*, Madrid, 1955, esp. the first chapter, "Sentimiento e intuición en la lírica," pp. 11–20.

the birds of the heavens have flown away.
I look, behold
the garden is desert,
all the cities are ravaged and charred
before Yahweh,
before his scowling flame.[18]

Once I have given form to my experience, I dominate it and possess it. Later, I can make it live again with freshness and communicate it. I have described the movement by which we divide the continuum of our experience into elements, which we then order by language. The natural unit of this movement of articulation is the sentence. There are two other movements also possible within language; the first of these complements the one just described, while the other tends in just the opposite direction. The complementary movement occurs when, in place of an intense emotional experience, I am faced with a great multiplicity or a whole series of impressions which seem about to overwhelm me with their abundance. Such realities may be likened to the totality and indivisibility of a vivid experience; and then again language comes to my aid to divide, order, articulate, and compose.

But more important than that activity which is complementary to the movement of articulation is that movement which goes in the opposite direction. It begins with an act of naming. A being actually and concretely existing, manifests itself in its intelligible presence, and is grasped by the mind which gives a name to this presence. It is an elemental and spiritual act in which, by naming a thing, possession is gained both of it and of the self. The name designates the actually existing thing in a total way, without further precisions or distinctions. Distinction pertains to the movement of articulation. The name is co-extensive with the thing for which it stands, since its whole nature is to signify, though in a global and concrete manner. From the act of naming, we pass to the sentence. This is an act by which two names, designations, or significations are joined because of some perceived relation and mutual influence. This relation and influence once understood are possessed by the sentence, which on the one hand renders more precise the global significance of the two names it uses, and on the other raises these designations to a new level of meaning. Once

[18] Jer 4:19–26.

again, this meaning is co-extensive with the sentence, and is also global and concrete. However, the sentence can receive a further significance from its context within life, or action, or thought. Thus, in forming a sentence, man takes possession in a greater measure both of things and of himself in a spiritual act which rises to a unity amid diversity.

This third ascending movement has the same structural character as the two which we have discussed previously. There is differentiation and order, the capacity for division and composition, and both possession and communicability are involved.

But why do I name things and form sentences at all? Is it for my own benefit, my own possession of reality and of myself? Or does my need to communicate with others impel me to articulate my experience, to name and to enunciate in order to share my possession with someone else in a desire for mutual and personal exchange? Man was created social. "Male and female He created them," and this has reference not only to that first and fundamental community of two persons, but also envisages these two as the origin of all society: "increase and multiply." Man lives socially, reaches his perfection in society, and in society achieves his vocation as ruler of the earth. Now, the natural means of establishing a social existence is language, or, if one prefers, dialogue. It seems, then, that the question of deciding whether or not language is primarily a personal or social act is not only difficult, but somewhat pointless. Given the social environment in which I grew up, it is possible either that I conform my expressions of experience to my environment, or that I name things for my own benefit, though even this is consequent on a social situation.[19] Within a diversified community, there will always be these two types, the communicative and the reserved, but this does not lessen the social nature of language and its natural expression in dialogue.

The world becomes human by entering into our life; we change it, conferring on it a new order in which we reveal ourselves. Language is a creation of man, made in his image and likeness. It is manifold and systematic, abundant and ordered. But language, even in the greatest works of literature, never has the subsistent

----

[19] The monological functions of language are usually considered to be consequent on its dialogical functions; cf. Fr. Kainz, *Psychologie der Sprache*, Stuttgart, 1954, vol. 1, part 3, A. 1, 2.

quality of a human person. Man reveals himself by breaking down what is within himself as he places it outside himself, where it lacks something of his own subsistence. In the act of language, man is true to his role as the image and likeness of God. He, too, must create an order of reality in which to reveal himself.

Language embodies the apex of human revelation, and therefore God has chosen this means of communicating and revealing Himself to men, overcoming the anonymity of nature and history. This is, in the strict sense, formal revelation.

All supernatural revelation is immediate in comparison with the natural revelation of God. For in natural revelation, God makes and governs creatures which man can use as a means of knowing God by analogy. That is, God manifests Himself as an *object*, knowable but mediately. In supernatural revelation, however, God reveals His interior, the way one *person* communicates his thoughts to another person, in speech properly so called. This personal and subjective manifestation is of its nature more direct and immediate than the purely objective manifestation of a cause in its effect. Therefore, we may say that *in the Scriptures God speaks to us immediately* because Scripture is the word of God in a formal and proper sense.[20]

We have thus established the context of our act of faith. God's speaking pertains to the realm of Logos, of revelation. And this in the formal sense and in the concrete means that God has spoken, using words. God opens Himself out and reveals Himself to us as one person to another, using the personal, or interpersonal, means of communicating. It is interesting to observe that in the text of the letter to the Hebrews, the verb "to speak" takes no direct object; only the speakers are mentioned. "Of old God spoke to our fathers. . . . now . . . He has spoken to us."

We must now proceed to render this context more precise, following the lead of the article of faith in which we say: "Who spoke

[20] *Omnis revelatio supernaturalis est immediata, prout opponitur revelationi Dei naturali. Nam in revelatione naturali Deus producit et gubernat creaturas, quibus homo uti possit ut mediis ad Deum secundum earum analogiam cognoscendum, seu Deus se exhibet ut* OBJECTUM *mediate cognoscibile. In revelatione vero supernaturali Deus mentem suam manifestat eo modo, quo* PERSONA *cum persona communicat cogitationes suas, seu locutione proprie dicta. Haec personalis et subiectiva manifestatio ex genere suo est magis immediata quam manifestatio pure obiectiva causae per effectum, Eatenus igitur* DEUS NOBIS IN SCRIPTURA IMMEDIATE LOQUITUR, *quia Scriptura est verbum Dei formale et proprie dictum.* Pesch, no. 411.

through the prophets." God spoke to us in human language and through human beings. It is here that this mystery of faith begins to reveal its hiddenness.

HUMAN WORDS

But does God really speak to us in human words? Well, if He wishes to address us as men, He must. Words can only be a vehicle of interpersonal communication when both persons share their meaning; the two beings who wish to communicate must have a common medium.

But there still remains the question whether God could ever have a language in common with men. Suppose a missionary attempted to translate our elaborate theological science, or some part of it, into a primitive language. Between a sophisticated occidental language and this hypothetical primitive language there will be a considerable difference in the linguistic material available, especially in the area of intellectual concepts and relations. In order to remedy this difference, the missionary will take some elements of his teaching and suit them to the capacity of a less well-wrought language. If he continues, his effort to adapt and translate will inevitably result in raising the level of the primitive language. Even here in the West, such interchanges of adaptation and translation have served to level off, in the good sense of the term, many of our languages. But in all these examples there is a common basis, since all languages result from the common human capacity for articulate communication, and have an essential common likeness.

But this cannot apply to the language of God, for here the differences are infinite. The divine transcendence must be taken seriously. It can only be by some special act of self-abasement, of condescension, that God could direct His speech to us in human words. It is necessarily a completely free and gratuitous act by which God opens Himself to us, and does so in a language truly human. It may be that this divine abasement has left our language touched by the Godhead, raising it to a new level, giving it a new capacity for meaning. Still, it will always be a human language. When we speak of the language of God, it is an analogous predication.

This act by which God lowered Himself to our level was called by the Greek Fathers *"Sunkatabasis,"* which the Latin rendered as *"condescendentia."* [21] St. John Chrysostom invokes this principle when he comes on some biblical passage that cannot be taken too literally, as for example the statement that "God walked in the garden in the cool of day." He says in this connection:

We should not take these words too lightly, but neither should we interpret them as they stand. We ought rather to reflect that such simple speech is used because of our weakness, and in order that our salvation be brought about in a manner worthy of God. For if we wish to take words just as they are, and not explain them in a way which befits God, will not the result be utter absurdity? [22]

We should note in the above passage the twofold theme of our weakness and the divine dignity. It is for our salvation that God uses human words, and it is in this sense that they are to be interpreted. The principle of our weakness, and of a salvation worthy of God, is operative throughout all Scripture, and, indeed, certain passages demand its intelligent application. Thus, with regard to the creation of Adam, Chrysostom says:

Do not take these words too humanly, but attribute their style to our weakness. For unless such words were used, how could we ever understand ineffable mysteries? We ought not, therefore, to adhere to the words alone, but should rather understand all things in a way worthy of God.[23]

Here, in addition to the themes mentioned above, we have the notion of a mystery which is to be revealed, but which cannot be revealed except through poor, human language. This principle is also valid throughout all Scripture.

St. Thomas enunciates the same principle in his commentary on

21 Cf. F. Fabbi, "La condiscendenza divina nell'ispirazione biblica secondo S. Giovanni Crisostomo," *Bib* 14, 1933, pp. 330–347.

22 Μὴ ἁπλῶς παραδράμωμεν, ἀγαπητοί, τὰ εἰρημένα παρὰ τῆς Θείας Γραφῆς, μῆδε ταῖς λέξεσιν ἐναπομείνωμεν, ἀλλ'ἐννοῶμεν, ὅτι διὰ τὴν ἀσθένειαν τὴν ἡμετέραν ἡ ταπεινότης τῶν λέξεων ἔγκειται, καὶ θεοπρεπῶς ἅπαντα γίγνεται διὰ τὴν σωτηρίαν τὴν ἡμετέραν. Εἰπὲ γάρ μοι, εἰ βουληθείημεν τῇ προφορᾷ τῶν ῥημάτων κατακολου-θῆσαι, καὶ μὴ θεοπρεπῶς ἐκλαβεῖν τὰ λεγόμενα, πῶς οὐ πολλὰ ἔψεται τὰ ἄτοπα. St. John Chrys., "Homily 17 on Gn 3," *PG* 53, 135.

23 Μὴ ἀνθρωπίνως δέχου τὰ λεγόμενα, ἀλλὰ παχύτητα τῶν λέξεων τῇ ἀσθενείᾳ λογίζου τῇ ἀνθρωπίνῃ. Εἰ γὰρ μὴ τούτοις τοῖς ῥήμασιν ἐχρήσατο, πῶς ἂν μαθεῖν ἐδυνήθημεν ταῦτα τὰ ἀπόρρετα μυστήρια; μὴ τοῖς ῥήμασιν οὖν μόνοις ἐναπομίνωμεν, ἀλλὰ θεοπρεπῶς ἅπαντα νοῶμεν ὡς ἐπὶ Θεοῦ. St. John Chrys., "Homily 15 on Gn 2," *PG* 53, 121.

the Epistle to the Hebrews, when he says: "In the Scriptures, divine things are communicated to us in the way usually employed among men." [24]

THE WORDS OF MEN

If God were to cause the air to vibrate according to certain frequencies, He could form a sentence, and the man who heard this sentence would hear human words. But they would not be spoken through men. In a similar way, God could have an angel speak, or He could act directly on the nervous system to produce an effect equivalent to speech, or He could form images in the imagination. All this might be called human language, but it would not have been spoken by men. Some seem to think that this would be the ideal manner for God to communicate Himself; it should be through angels, or through some interior word. But such an opinion has little appreciation for the mystery of the Incarnation.

God has wished to speak to us in words which are fully human, and which are spoken by men—"through the prophets." And this means that He has selected a determined language, either Hebrew or Greek, and has chosen certain men: Jeremiah or Paul. In these words, in Hebrew or Greek, written by these authors, God is speaking to me.

But how is that possible? Jeremiah speaks, pouring out his soul, and it is God Who is speaking. St. Paul speaks with all his vibrant emotion, and it is God Who is speaking. Something mysterious must happen within St. Paul or Jeremiah, so that when they speak, God speaks. In reality, what happens is that a mysterious force is at work, one well-described in the Second Epistle of Peter:

But first note this: no one can interpret any prophecy of Scripture by himself. For it was not through any human whim that men prophesied of old; men they were, but, impelled by the Holy Spirit, they spoke the words of God.[25]

Like some ship, impelled by the wind which marks out the wake of its passage, so the biblical writers spoke in the name of God,

---

[24] *In scriptura autem divina traduntur nobis per modum quo homines solent uti.* "Comm. on Heb, ch. 1, L. 4" (Marietti ed., no. 64).
[25] 2 Pt. 1:20–21.

under the action of the Spirit. We call this action "inspiration." It is a work of the Spirit in the realm of language. The effect of this action is described in the Second Epistle to Timothy: "All Scripture is divinely inspired and useful . . ." [26] Scripture comes about by the Breath of God, by the action of the Spirit.

The two passages quoted above, the one from Second Peter and the other from the Second Epistle to Timothy, are the classical statements on the fact of biblical inspiration. With them, we have come full circle, and have fitted the context of the Logos with that of the Spirit or Pneuma. God reveals Himself; He does so in words, and these words are human words, spoken by men. Yet, it is the Spirit Who moves these men to speak and directs them. It is He Whom we profess to have spoken through the prophets.

We have thus completed the circle of our inquiry, and now another, perhaps still more challenging, opens out before us. How exactly does the Spirit act? We wish to penetrate more deeply into the *manner* in which inspiration takes place, in order to appreciate more fully the mystery, though we are aware that our question brings us face to face with problems that are, ultimately, insoluble.

Bibliography for Chapter 1

The Context of the Spirit. For a study of the charismatic gifts, in addition to the commentaries on Romans and First Corinthians (Allo is especially good here), one may consult the theologies of the New Testament: J. Bonsirven, *Theology of the New Testament*, Westminster, 1963; M. Meinertz, *Theologie des Neuen Testaments*, Bonn, 1950. Also the articles in the various theological and biblical dictionaries: *Encyclopedic Dictionary of the Bible* (EDB), a translation and adaptation of *Bijbels Woordenboek*, 2nd ed., by Louis Hartman, New York, 1963; *Dictionary of the Bible*, rev. ed., ed. by J. Hastings, New York, 1963, under "Spiritual Gifts"; *The Interpreter's Dictionary of the Bible*, Nashville, 1962, under "Spiritual Gifts"; and, of course,

[26] 2 Tim 3:16. For a discussion of these texts, cf. A. Bea, *De inspiratione et inerrantia Sacrae Scripturae. Notae historicae et dogmaticae*, Rome, 1947, pp. 2–6.

G. Kittel's *Theologisches Wörterbuch zum Neuen Testament*, Stuttgart, 1933–/, *Theological Dictionary of the Bible*, Grand Rapids 1964–/, ed. by G. W. Bromiley: the first two volumes are available. The finest monograph is that by Karl Rahner, *The Dynamic Element in the Church*, New York, 1964. There are also some good pages in F. Prat, *The Theology of St. Paul*, New York, 1952.

The Context of the Word. Karl Rahner begins his first essay in "Toward a Theology of the Word" (in *The Word*, "Readings in Theology" series, ed. by the Canisianum, New York, 1964) with the remark: "To the poet is entrusted the word. Alas that there is no theology of the word! Why has no one yet begun, like an Ezekiel, to collect the limbs strewn about upon the fields of philosophy and theology, and then to speak the word of the spirit over them so that they rise up a living body?" (p. 3). The renewal of interest can also be seen in the excellent study by R. Latourelle, *Théologie de la Révélation*, Bruges, 1963. In his historical section, he presents us with a clear and concise résumé of the opinions and controversies. The speculative part begins with three chapters entitled "Revelation as Word, Witness and Encounter," "Revelation and Creation," and "History and Revelation." Each is treated briefly and there is not much development of the interrelation of these realities (cf. the review by A. Dulles in *TS* 25, 1964, pp. 43–58). In addition to the bibliography at the end of the book, each chapter is provided with a special bibliography at the beginning of each chapter.

Hans Urs von Balthasar now has *Word and Revelation. Essays in Theology 1*, New York, 1964, and *Word and Redemption. Essays in Theology 2*, New York, 1965; and there is still the excellent study of R. Guardini, *Religion und Offenbarung*, Würzburg, 1958: this latter is less scholastic than Latourelle and approaches the problem more phenomenologically. The first section describes the fact or the phenomenon of religious experience. The second section discusses certain concrete patterns of this experience, while the third section treats of the articulation and formulation of the experience in concepts and images. The work of H. Fries, *Glauben-Wissen. Wege zu einer Lösung des Problems*, Berlin, 1960, is marked by great clarity and is especially valuable for the discussion of faith as directed to a person and faith directed toward propositions. Just recently J. L. McKenzie has collected some of his essays under the title *Myths and Realities*, Milwaukee, 1964; chapter 3, "The Word of God in the Old Testament" (*TS* 21, 1960, pp. 183–206), is very valuable, as is *The Old Testament as Word of God* by S. Mowinckel, New York, 1959. More bibliographical information on this aspect will be given in Chapter 13.

Creation. In addition to the chapter in Latourelle's book, we should mention here the problem of myth and mythopoeic thought. The bibliographical material is immense, much of it is assembled by J. L. McKenzie in his article, "Myth and the Old Testament" (above and *CBQ* 21, 1959, pp. 265–82). The most important single investigator in this field is undoubtedly Mircea Eliade; the works most relevant to our theme are: *Patterns in Comparative Religion*, New York, 1963; *Images and Symbols. Studies in Religious Symbolism*, New York, 1961; *Cosmos and History*, New York, 1959. A more philosophical approach can be found in the works of Ernst Cassirer; cf. esp. *The Philosophy of Symbolic Forms*, vol. 2, *Mythical Thought*, New Haven, 1955; *Language and Myth*, New York, 1946. There are some valuable intuitions in G. van der Leeuw, *Religion. Its Essence and Manifestation*, New York, 1963. A form-critical approach to the problem of myth in the Old Testament can be found in Brevard Childs' *Myth and Reality in the Old Testament*, Studies in Biblical Theology, no. 27, Naperville, 1960. This problem also brings us into the question of the "demythologizing" of the New Testament; the *Elenchus Bibliographicus* compiled by Father Nober in *Biblica* is obliged to accord this question a special section. Some preliminary discussion of the problem can be found in M. Bourke's "Rudolf Bultmann's Demythologizing of the New Testament," *CTSA* 12, 1957, pp. 103–33. A good introduction to Bultmann's thought can be found in L. Malevez, *The Christian Message and Myth. The Theology of Rudolph Bultmann*, Westminster, 1960. Cf. also H. Noack, *Sprache und Offenbarung*, Gütersloh, 1960 (though the language is hard to follow), and J. Pépin, *Mythe et Allégorie*, Paris, 1958 (but only the first chapter: his explanation of Christian allegory is equivocal, as H. de Lubac points out in his *Exégèse Médiévale*).

History. The theme of God's revelation in history is very prominent today. A bibliography relating to the techniques of history writing will be found in Chapter 3. In relation to the Old Testament, there is a fine summary of present thought on the question (though with some misunderstanding of the role of systematic theology) in G. E. Wright, *God Who Acts*, Studies in Biblical Theology no. 8, Naperville, 1952. There is some excellent material in R. A. F. MacKenzie, *Faith and History*, Minneapolis, 1963. W. Pannenberg dedicates a book to the theme of revelation and history (*Offenbarung als Geschichte*, Göttingen, 1961) and returns to the idea in *Essays in Old Testament Hermeneutics*, ed. by C. Westermann, Richmond, 1963; (cf. "Redemption Event and History"). G. von Rad's two-volume *Theologie des Alten Testaments* is extremely helpful (though controversial because of the

47

epistemological views inherent in his view of history); both volumes are available in German, Munich, 1961; the first volume is available in English, *Old Testament Theology*, New York, 1962. The English edition of W. Eichrodt's first volume of his *Theologie des Alten Testaments*, Stuttgart, 1933–1939, Philadelphia, 1961, contains an appendix in which the author vigorously discusses von Rad's historical minimalism. A popular treatment of some of these aspects can be found in J. L. McKenzie, *The Two-Edged Sword*, Milwaukee, 1955. The transposition of historical revelation to the realm of the Christ fact is often mentioned but seldom treated specifically. Studies dealing with the mysteries of the life of Christ are rare. St. Thomas includes thirty-three questions in the third part of the Summa (27–59), and there is a helpful commentary by I. M. Voste, *Commentarius in Summam Theologicam S. Thomae. De Mysteriis Vitae Christi*, Rome, 1940. The continuing revelation in history effected through the sacraments can be studied with the aid of the books by Rahner and Schillebeeckx mentioned in Chapter 15.

2. The Word Divine and Human

THE ACTION OF THE SPIRIT

Once Jesus Christ was describing for an intellectual of His time the mystery of the Spirit—"It blows where it will; you hear its sound, but you know not whence it comes or where it goes."

The Spirit is like that. Is it not then rash to try to seek out His paths? Will He not turn and confound our human speculations, as God once did to Job? Then, too, sometimes His voice is but the whispering of a breeze, and there are times when not even the one inspired hears the noise of the wind astir within him, which moves him.

And so, once again, we are called on to believe in the suppleness and power of the Spirit, able to work in many ways and to traverse untrammeled both the heavens and the earth, able to move men, without forcing their freedom, their personality, or their style.

How ought we to think of this action of the Spirit, so soft that at times no man is aware of it, yet so effective that to Him is attributed whatever is achieved? The activity of the Spirit by which the word of men is also the word of God is quite simply a mystery. In His presence, we ought first to make an act of faith and to confess ourselves too ignorant and weak to understand it. Then we must go on, with humility, to seek understanding.

INSPIRATION AND THE INCARNATION

We are seeking some understanding of a mystery. Well, then, the first thing we must do with any mystery of our redemption is to refer it to the central mystery of this redemption, the Incarnation. This is not an attempt to explain the obscure by what is more obscure. For, given the unity of the work of our salvation and the unity of revelation, to refer a mystery to this center is already to shed light on it and make it more intelligible. It is especially true of the mystery of inspiration, that in making such a reference there is no artificiality. The movement is already well established by Scripture and tradition, and the famous passage in the letter to the Hebrews has given it classical expression.

". . . God spoke to our forefathers in fragmentary and varied fashion through the prophets. But in this the final age he has spoken to us in the Son. . . ."

The "fragmentary and varied" utterances of the prophets all culminate in God's message delivered "in the Son." We find often in the early Fathers of the Church the notion that Christ was speaking in the Old Testament, preparing for His coming, and foretelling it Himself. I do not refer to that theory which attributes to the Word, or Logos, as the Second Person of the Blessed Trinity, all the words of Scripture; I refer rather to Christ as incarnate. But, actually, it is not easy to distinguish these two aspects in the writings of the Fathers, especially since for some of them "Word" is practically equivalent to "Word Incarnate." Here are some examples of their way of speaking:

St. Hippolytus wrote an essay refuting the errors of a certain Noetus, who held that the Father and the Son were identical. When speaking of the prophets, St. Hippolytus said:

The Word dwelt in these men and spoke of Himself. He was His own herald, pointing out that the Word would appear among men. . . .

By the Word of the Lord the heavens were made: and this is the Word which has been openly made manifest. Thus we behold the Word made flesh and we know the Father through Him. . . .

Only the Word of God is visible, man's word is audible.[1]

St. Ambrose implies the same comparison, putting it in a Eucharistic context:

---

[1] Ἐν τούτοις τοίνυν πολιτευόμενος ὁ Λόγος ἐφθέγγετο περὶ ἑαυτοῦ. Ἤδη γὰρ αὐτὸς ἑαυτοῦ κῆρυξ ἐγένετο, δεικνύων μέλλοντα Λόγον φαίνεσθαι ἐν ἀνθρώποις. . . . τῷ λόγῳ Κυρίου οἱ οὐρανοὶ ἐστερεώθησαν ἄρα οὗτός ἐστιν ὁ λόγος ὁ καὶ ἐμφανὴς δεικνύμενος. Οὐκοῦν ἔνσαρκον λόγον θεοροῦμεν, Πατέρα δ᾽αὐτοῦ νοοῦμεν. . . . Λόγος δὲ Θεοῦ μόνος ὁρατὸς, ἀνθρώπον δε ἀκουστός. St. Hippolytus, "Against Noetus, ch. 12," PG 10, 820.

Drink of Christ that you may drink His words. His word is the Old Testament, His word is the New Testament. The divine Scriptures are taken as drink and consumed as food when the sweetness of the eternal Word sinks into the very marrow and powers of the soul.[2]

St. Cyril of Jerusalem, stressing the unity of the two testaments, the work of one Spirit, concludes with this Trinitarian formula borrowed from St. Paul:

One God, the Father, the Lord of the Old Testament and the New; One Lord, Jesus Christ, Who was foretold in the Old Testament and came in the New; and One Holy Spirit, Who through the prophets preached concerning Christ, and when Christ had come descended on Him and made Him known.[3]

The comparison between the Word Incarnate and the word of the Scriptures was dear to many medieval theologians, whose reflections on the *"verbum dei abbreviatum"* gave rise to many passages of real beauty. Rupert of Deutz, for instance, in his treatise on the Holy Spirit says:

What do we believe the Scriptures to be if not the Word of God? . . . The whole of the Scriptures is but the One Word of God. . . . Therefore, when we read the holy Scriptures, we are dealing with the Word of God, we behold the Son of God through a mirror, darkly.[4]

When Moses and the prophets composed the Scriptures, which are the word of God, what did they do but conceive Christ spiritually in their hearts by the spirit of prophecy, and bring Him to birth with their mouth?[5]

---

[2] *"Bibe Christum, ut bibas sermones eius; sermo eius Testamentum est Vetus, sermo eius Testamentum est Novum. Bibitur Scriptura divina et devoratur Scriptura divina, cum in venas mentis ac vires animae succus Verbi descendat aeterni."* St. Ambrose, "Comm. on Ps 1:33," PL 14, 984.

[3] Εἰς Θεὸς, ὁ Πατὴρ, παλαιᾶς και Καινῆς Διαθήκης Δεσπότης; κὰι (εἰς) Κύριος Ἰησοῦς Χριστὸς, ὁ ἐν Παλαιᾳ προφητευθεὶς κὰι ἐν Καινῇ παραγενόμενος; κὰι ἕν Πνεῦμα ἅγιον, διὰ προφητῶν μὲν περὶ τοῦ Χριστοῦ κηρύξαν, ἐλθόντος δὲ τοῦ Χριστοῦ καταβὰν, κάι ἐπιδεῖξαν αὐτόν. St. Cyril of Jer., "Catech. 16, On the Holy Spirit," PG 33, 920.

[4] *"Quid autem Scripturam sanctam nisi verbum Dei esse credimus? —sed unum est Dei Verbum universitas Scripturarum. Cum igitur Scripturam sanctam legimus, Verbum Dei tractamus Filium Dei per speculum et in aenigmate prae oculis habemus."* "On the Works of the Holy Spirit," PL 167, 1575.

[5] *"Quid, inquam, fuit Moysi et prophetis sanctam Scripturam quae verbum*

51

Thus the Scriptures, the law, and the prophets were in existence before God concentrated the whole of the Scriptures, His Word, in the womb of the virgin. This virgin conceived first in her mind and then in her flesh; first prophesying with her tongue before bringing to birth from her womb. Therefore, it is false to say that Christ did not exist before Mary was. Since, before His flesh was born, Sion, the Blessed, had brought forth the self-same Christ, the self-same Word.[6]

Then Garnier has the following words in one of his Christmas sermons:

Of old, God wrote a book by which in many words one Word was uttered; today He has opened a book for us in which by One Word many words are said. . . . This is the book which has for its pages the flesh of man and for writing the Word of the Father. . . . The greatest of all books is the Incarnate Son, because just as through writing words are joined to a page, so by assuming a human nature the Word of God is joined to flesh.[7]

Finally, Pius XII applied this traditional comparison to the domain of inspiration and hermeneutics:

For as the substantial Word of God became like to men in all things "except sin," so the words of God expressed in human language are made like to human speech in every respect, except error.[8]

Dei est, contexere, nisi Christum et corde per spiritum propheticum concipere et ore parere?" "Comm. on the Book of Kings," PL 167, 1175.

[6] *"Sic omnis Scriptura legalis et prophetica condita est, antequam omnis Scripturae universitatem, omne Verbum suum Deus in utero Virginis coadunaret. Ipsa Virgo prius mente quam carne concepit, prius ore prophetando quam ventre parturiendo. Igitur falsum est ante Mariam non exstitisse Christum. Nam antequam carnem ejus parturiret, peperit ore prophetarum, beata Sion unum eumdemque Christum, unum idemque Dei Verbum."* "Comm. on Isaiah," PL 167, 1362.

[7] *"Olim librum scripsit nobis Deus, in quo sub multis verbis unum comprehendit: hodie librum nobis aperuit, in quo multa sub uno verbo conclusit . . . Ipse enim liber est, qui pro pelle carnem habuit, et pro scriptura Verbum Patris . . . Liber maximus est Filius incarnatus, quia per scripturam verbum unitur pelli, ita per assumpsionem hominis Verbum Patris unitum est carni."* "Sixth Sermon for Christmas," PL 205, 609–610.

[8] *"Sicut enim substantiale Dei Verbum hominibus simile factum est quoad omnia 'absque peccato,' ita etiam Dei verba, humanis linguis expressa, quoad omnia humano sermoni assimilia facta sunt, excepto errore. . . ."* EB 559; RSS, p. 98.

For a discussion on the patristic use of this analogy, see J. H. Crehan, "The Analogy between *Verbum Dei Incarnatum* and *Verbum Dei scriptum*

The texts adduced above both enable and entitle us to conclude that the inspiration of sacred Scripture is ordered to the mystery of the Incarnation; it prepares for it, prolongs it, and explains it. It follows that the resemblance between these two mysteries establishes a basis, in virtue of which they mutually shed light on one another. Most important of all, we see now clearly the twofold nature of the inspired word. It, too, is both divine and human. Just as the Christological heresies veer from one extreme to the other, so in this mystery, too, there are analogous exaggerations. There can be a sort of Docetism or Monophysitism which denies or diminishes the human quality of the inspired word; there can be a Nestorianism which denies its divine character.

Another result of this confrontation between the two mysteries is that we constantly look to the mystery of the Incarnation when particular questions arise, and profit from the light shed thereby on our investigation. We will be following this method throughout these pages.

Finally, we should remember that just as the Incarnation is a transcendent mystery to be adored in grateful silence, so, too, inspiration pertains to the realm of this same mystery. Thus, when we inquire into the fundamental problem in the mystery of inspiration and ask: "How can words be at once both divine and human?", the answer is spontaneous: in a way similar to that by which Christ is both man and God. Beginning with this basic insight, we will go on to investigate a few other aspects, both negative and positive.

FIRST NEGATIVE ASPECT

The First Vatican Council, in its decree on revelation, eliminated two explanations which were then currently being given of the dignity of the sacred Scriptures:

---

in the Fathers," *JTS* 6, 1955, pp. 87–90; and P. Bellet, "El sentido de la analogia 'Verbum Dei Incarnatum—Verbum Dei Scriptum,' " *EstBib* 14, 1955, pp. 415–428. The first author begins by citing modern authors who are in favor or opposed to the analogy, and then goes on to invoke the authority of the Fathers. The second author replies by showing that the analogy, as used by the Fathers, was inspired by the desire to interpret the Old Testament allegorically and to draw out the full meaning of the New Testament.

The Church regards the books of the Old and New Testaments as sacred and canonical, not because, after having been composed by purely human effort, they were then approved by her authority, nor because they contain revelation without error. . . .[9]

Let us suppose, for example, that the Church were to give official approval of some spiritual book, say *The Imitation of Christ* or *The Spiritual Exercises* of St. Ignatius. Such approbation would not make these books the word of God. The Church cannot change mere human words into words that are divine, nor can the Holy Spirit wait until a human work is completed, and then take possession of it. This is not how He makes it a work of His own. In the same way, Jesus Christ is not God because of an apotheosis which took place within the bosom of the early Church, nor because of some great divine action which took hold of a man already complete in his own right. There was never a moment in the life of Jesus when He was not True God. The action of the Holy Spirit took place at the moment of conception—"The Holy Spirit will come upon you, and the Power of the Most High will overshadow you; and for that reason the Holy Child to be born will be called 'Son of God.' "

But in denying that a completed reality was subsequently assumed by God in the case either of the Incarnation or the inspiration of the Scriptures, we are not denying the presence of pre-existing material. The Holy Spirit did not create the matter for the body of Jesus out of nothing, but used the sanctified body and life processes of a virgin. So, too, the biblical authors overshadowed by the Spirit utilized preëxisting material: language, literary themes, stylistic devices, citations, etc., and it is not necessary that this material be also the direct result of the Spirit's activity. There is one important difference in our comparison, however. In the realm of literature, a piece can be transposed bodily into a new context and receive thereby an entirely new literary existence. Such an act would be a true literary creation, and we cannot, *a priori*, exclude such procedures from the Bible.[10]

---

[9] "*Eos vero Ecclesia pro sacris et canonicis habet, non ideo, quod sola humana industria concinnati, sua deinde auctoritate sint approbati; nec ideo dumtaxat, quod revelationem sine errore contineant; . . .*" D–S 3006.

[10] That is, if we take inspiration in the strict sense as we are doing here. It is not impossible that the Holy Spirit was active in the composition of

SECOND NEGATIVE ASPECT

". . . nor because they contain revelation without error." Theoretically, we could imagine some book, composed by purely human effort, which would collect and formulate revelation.[11] It is possible that such a book would contain no errors, but, in the strict sense, it would not be inspired or the word of God. The matter would be from God, as would be the theme and the facts. But the activity which conferred on such matter a literary existence would still be human, not divine. In the same way, a book which collected all the infallible pronouncements of the Church would contain and correctly formulate revelation, but it would not, for all that, be the word of God.

The statement of Vatican I implies a distinction which is very important for our consideration. It is that between revelation and inspiration. Oversimplifying for the moment, we could say that revelation affects the materials out of which the literary work is formed, while inspiration affects rather the literary process which brings the work into existence. But have we not already agreed that inspiration pertains to the realm of revelation? Yes, but recall that we said this while considering the mystery of human speech. We should make a distinction here between a revelation which precedes the act of literary composition, and one which follows it. Thus the sacred author, while being moved by the Spirit, could be busily engaged in drawing up court documents or in composing a song in imitation of some model, and not receive any revelation from God either before or during his work. In this case, there would be inspiration without any revelation preceding. But so long as our author has written under the motion of the Spirit, his words are the words of God, and the words of God reveal Him. These words would constitute a revelation in our regard, and would constitute what may be termed "subsequent revelation." The whole Bible is revelation for us, because it is the word of God; but not all the Bible was composed as a result of some previous revelation made to its authors.

---

some material before the moment when it was transposed to an inspired work within the life of the Chosen People.

11 N. Lohfink calls this a "hagiographical act." Cf. Über die Irrtumslosigkeit und Einheit der Schrift," SZ 84, 1964, pp. 161–181.

The distinction between revelation and inspiration has already been elaborated on by St. Thomas[12] as well as his distinction between the act by which reality is received into the mind and that by which it is judged. We dare say that this distinction constitutes one of the keys to an understanding of the whole treatise on inspiration. It will appear often in these pages. Yet, there is danger of an oversimplification. We must not consider revelation which precedes literary composition too exclusively in terms derived from the notion of a fully formed proposition, meant only to be handed on.

We would like to add another negative aspect to the two given by Vatican I. In order that human words be also the words of God, there must be more than moral activity, such as a counsel or command from God. For such an activity would make God the moral source of the work, but it would leave intact its totally human character. The action of the Spirit must be physical; it must reach the author in his act of eliciting language. This motion is not moral, but physical; it pertains to the supernatural order; we call it, using our terms strictly now, the charism of inspiration.

There are other negative aspects of this mystery, but most of them will become apparent in our study of the analogies used in a positive elucidation.

Four Analogies

In order to arrive at some understanding of the mystery of words which are at once divine and human, the Church's theologians have from the earliest times made use of various analogies. These are instruments leading us to knowledge; they are illustrations, valid though limited, pointing to a reality which is transcendent. We should note, however, that there is no question here of some purely abstract intellectual process, which then looks for apt images in which to convey its thought. Most often, an analogy is the result of an intuition which precedes conceptual elaboration. This is what is meant by a "theology in symbols." It is a type of thinking which historically preceded a more conceptualized theology, and which must complement this latter under pain of sterility at every stage of its development. The Fathers spoke of St. John as "the Theologian," and St. John's theology is often in symbols.

[12] II–II, 173.

It is certainly true that when we speak of "the Word of God" or of the "verbal" nature of the world, we are using metaphors. But these are more than pretty comparisons; they are metaphors of weighty metaphysical import. We speak in images, but not figuratively. Or better, we speak using imagery, but it is proper. A theologian or a philosopher begins to be such, when first he sees what is metaphysical in metaphors, and the metaphors in metaphysics. There is a metaphysics of the schools which is oblivious of metaphor and which renounces thereby that without which no great and original metaphysics has ever been formed. Metaphysics does not spell the end of metaphor. Thus, such expressions as "the Word of God," "the Word of the Creator," and "the Word in God" are for the human mind metaphors. But they are not purely imaginative language. They are rather analogous expressions, not purely metaphorical analogies, but essential predications in the order of being and operation.[13]

Thus does Söhngen, the theologian and philosopher, express himself. Theology cannot dispense with symbols or images, since all creation is image of God, and man himself is created in God's image and likeness. Analogy is not the exclusive possession of abstract reasoning; it belongs also to the realm of the concrete and sensory, and this is the secret of all great literary metaphors.

We see, then, that language is something deeply human. We have already borrowed its images, in order to ascend by means of analogy to the mystery of divine words in human language. It is in this spirit of serious inquiry that we now approach the more classical images of traditional theology, even adding to their number a contribution of our own.

13 "Gewiss reden wir, wenn wir vom Worten Gottes und vom Gewortet-sein der Welt reden, in Metaphern, aber nicht in bloss schönen Vergleichen, sondern in Metaphern von metaphysischen Schwergewicht; wir reden bildlich, aber nicht uneigentlich, oder vielmehr wir reden bildhaft, und gerade so auch eigentlich. Theologe und Philosoph sind es beide doch erst, wenn sie das Metaphysische im Metaphorischen und das Metaphorische im Metaphysischen zusammenschauend sehen. Es mag Schulmetaphysik geben, die auf die Metaphern vergisst (verzichtet), ohne die keine grosse, ursprüngliche Metaphysik gestaltet ist. Metaphysik besagt also nicht den Ausschluss der Metaphorik. So sind für den Menschenverstand "Wort Gottes" und "Wort des Schöpfers" und "das Wort in Gott" Metaphern; es sind aber keine bloss bildlichen, sondern analoge Ausdrücke, und zwar eben keine bloss metaphorischen Analogien, sondern überwesentliche Aussagen in der Wesens- und Tätigkeitsordnung." G. Söhngen, Analogie und Metaphern. Kleine Philosophie und Theologie der Sprache, Munich, 1962, p. 104.

Instrument

Without doubt, the image which has met with the greatest success in this field is that of an instrument. In some scholastic treatises, it is the only one employed.[14] There was a time when scholars discussed whether the tract should take as its foundation the concept (not the image) of instrument or that of author. This discussion is no longer relevant. A single image is able to provide us with more light than a whole sheaf of them bound together.

Neither nature nor human devising can enable men to know things so great and so divine. This is accomplished by the gift which came down from above on holy men who had no need of the craft of words, or of speaking anything contentiously, or with a love of argument. Rather, they offered themselves up pure to the energy of the divine Spirit, so that the divine Plectrum itself, coming down from heaven and using just men as some instrument, such as a harp or lyre, might reveal to us a knowledge of things divine and heavenly.[15]

For having begun by expounding minutely the principle that the inspired writer, in composing the sacred book, is the living and reasonable instrument of the Holy Spirit, they rightly observe that, impelled by the divine motion, he so uses his faculties and powers, that from the book composed by him all may easily infer "the special character of each one and, as it were, his personal traits." [16]

Seventeen centuries elapsed between the two statements given above, yet they evince a remarkable continuity of thought. Chris-

[14] Grelot is quite frankly optimistic about the value of this notion in its philosophical conceptualization: *"Bref, la notion philosophique d'instrument est assez souple pour pouvoir épouser tous les contours d'une réalité complexe òu la nature est assumée par le surnaturel."* "L'inspiration scripturaire," RSR 51, 1963, p. 368.

[15] Οὔτε γὰρ φύσει οὔτε ἀνφρωπίνη ἐννοίᾳ οὕτω μεγάλα καὶ Θεῖα γινώσκειν ἀνφρώποις δυνατὸν, ἀλλὰ τῇ ἄνωθεν ἐπὶ τοὺς ἁγίους ἄνδρας τηνκαῦτα κατελθούσῃ δωρεᾷ, οἷς οὐ λόγων ἐδέησε τέχνης, οὐδὲ τοῦ ἐριστικῶς τι καὶ φιλονείκως εἰπεῖν, ἀλλὰ καθαροὺς ἑαυτοὺς τῇ τοῦ Ϩείου Πνεύματος παρασχεῖν ἐνεργείᾳ, ἵν' αὐτὸ τὸ Ϩεῖον ἐξ οὐρανοῦ κατιὸν πλῆκτρον, ὥσπερ ὀργάνῳ κιθάρας τινὸς ἤ λύρας, τοῖς δικαίοις ἀνδράσι χρώμενον, τὴν τῶν Ϩείων ἡμῖν καὶ οὐρανίων ἀποκαλύψῃ γνῶσιν. "Exhortation to the Greeks" (second or third century), PG 6, 256.

[16] *"Ex eo enim edisserendo profecti, quod hagiographus in sacro conficiendo libro est Spiritus Sancti* ORGANON *seu instrumentum, idque vivum ac ratione praeditum, recte animadvertunt illum, divina motione actum, ita suis uti facultatibus et viribus, 'ut propriam uniuscuiusque indolem et veluti singulares notas ac lineamenta.'"* EB 556; RSS, p. 96.

tian Pesch[17] has collected twenty-four different theological texts representing all ages, which employ the image of instrument in their study of this mystery of inspiration. It is worth a little trouble to read some of these texts and appreciate for ourselves their consistency and variations.

St. Athenagoras:

For those things which we know and believe, we have the prophets as witnesses. Those men who, possessed by the Spirit, spoke out concerning God and the things of God . . . The Holy Spirit Who moved the mouths of the prophets like some instrument . . . The Spirit used them as a flute player blows through his flute.[18]

St. Hippolytus:

These Fathers were endowed with a prophetic spirit, and were worthily honored by the Word Himself. Just like musical instruments, they had the Word with them as a plectrum, so that when they were touched by Him, these prophets announced the things that God had willed.[19]

Theophilus of Antioch:

Moses, . . . or rather the Word of God, through Moses as an instrument, said: "In the beginning God created heaven and earth." [20]

St. Jerome (on the verse, "my tongue is quick like the pen of a scribe"—Ps 45:2):

I ought therefore to prepare my tongue as a quill or pen, so that by means of it the Holy Spirit can write in the heart and hearing of my audience. My role is to offer my tongue as an instrument, His to make it sound with His composition. . . . If the law which came through a

---

[17] *De Inspiratione Sacrae Scripturae*, Freiburg, 1906.

[18] Ἡμεῖς δὲ ὧν νοοῦμεν καὶ πεπιστεύκαμεν, ἔχομεν προφήτας μάρτυρας, οἳ Πνεύματι ἐνθέῳ ἐκπεφωνήκασι καὶ περὶ τοῦ Θεοῦ καὶ των τοῦ Θεου. Εἴποιτε δ'ἂν καὶ ὑμεῖς, συνέσι καὶ τῇ περὶ ὄντως θεῖον εὐσεβίᾳ τοὺς ἄλλος προύχοντες, ὡς ἔστιν ἄλογον, παραλιπόντας πιστεύειν τῷ παρὰ τοῦ Θεοῦ Πνεύματι, ὡς ὄργανα κεκινηκότι τὰ προφητῶν στόματα, προσέχειν δόξαις ἀνθρωπίναις. . . . συγχρησαμένου τοῦ Πνεύματος, ὡσει καὶ αὐλητὴς αὐλὸν ἐμπνεῦσαι. St. Athenagoras, "Supplication for the Christians, 7 and 9," PG 6, 904, 908.

[19] Οὗτοι γὰρ πνεύματι προφητικῷ οἱ πατέρες κατηρτισμένοι, καὶ ὑπ' αὐτοῦ τοῦ Λόγου ἀξίως τετιμημένοι, ὀργάνων δίκην ἑαυτοῖς ἀεὶ τὸν Λόγον ὡς πλῆκτρον. δι' οὗ κινούμενοι ἀπήγελλον ταῦτα, ἅπερ ἤθελεν ὁ Θεός, οἱ προφῆται. St. Hippolytus, "On the Antichrist, 1," PG 10, 728–729.

[20] Μωυσῆς δὲ ὁ καὶ Σολομῶνος πρὸ πολλῶν ἐτῶν γενόμενος, μᾶλλον δὲ ὁ Λόγος ὁ τοῦ Θεοῦ ὡς δι' ὀργάνου δι' αὐτοῦ φησίν. Ἐν ἀρχῇ ἐποίσεν ὁ Θεὸς τὸν οὐρανὸν κὰι τὴν γῆν. Theophilus of Antioch, "To Autolycus, bk. 2, 10," PG 6, 1065.

mediator was written by the finger of God, if what was abolished was so glorified, then the good news, which abides, is written by the Holy Spirit through means of my tongue.[21]

St. Gregory the Great (while discussing the problem as to who the writer of the Book of Job might be, he declares it to be a useless question):

Suppose we were to receive a letter from some eminent man, and after having read it, were to inquire as to what pen actually wrote the letter; it would be ridiculous, along with our knowledge of the author and our understanding of his meaning, were we to insist on knowing just which pen made the marks on the paper. So, when we possess the message and know that the Holy Spirit is its author, and then go on to try to find out who the writer is, what are we doing but reading a letter and wondering about the pen? [22]

St. Augustine:

He is the Head of all His disciples, who are as members of His body through that human nature which He has assumed. Thus, when they write what He has taught and said, it should not be asserted that He did not write it, since the members only put down what they had come to know at the dictation of the Head. Therefore, whatever He wanted us to read concerning His words and deeds, He commanded the disciples, His hands, to write. Whoever understands this shared unity and the convergence in divine functions of many members under one Head, cannot but receive what he reads in the Gospels, though written by the disciples, as though it were written by the very hand of the Lord Himself.[23]

21 "*Debeo ergo et linguam meam quasi stilum et calamum praeparare ut per illam in corde et auribus audientium scribat Sanctus Spiritus. Meum enim est organum praebere linguam: illius quasi per organum sonare quae sunt. . . . Si enim Lex per manum Mediatoris digito scripta est, et quod destructum est, glorificatum est: quanto magis Evangelium; quod mansurum est, per meam linguam scribetur a Spiritu Sancto.*" "Letter 65," PL 22, 627.
Note that St. Jerome puts these words on the lips of the Psalmist, whom he considers to be an evangelist because he foretold Christ.
22 "*Si magnicujusdam viri susceptis epistolis legeremus verba, sed quo calamo fuissent scripta quaereremus, ridiculum profecto esset epistolarum auctorem scire sensumque cognoscere, sed quali calamo earum verba impressa fuerint indagare. Cum ergo rem cognoscimus ejusque rei Spiritum Sanctum auctorem tenemus, quia scriptorem quaerimus, quid aliud agimus nisi legentes literas, de calamo percontamur?*" "Moralia on Job, Preface," PL 75, 517.
23 "*Omnibus autem discipulis suis per hominem quem assumpsit, tanquam membris sui corporis caput est. Itaque cum illi scripserunt quae ille ostendit*

We have here three series of texts, which show interesting variations. The first and oldest group employs the image of a musical instrument, the second does not specify any particular instrument or refers to a pen, etc., while St. Augustine speaks of the organs of the body.

Instrument pertains to fundamental human experience. Man, either as *homo faber* or as *homo ludens*, either as a workman or at play, is prone to avail himself of instruments in order to realize his activity. Chapter 4 of Genesis describing the origins of culture tells us of Jubal, who was the ancestor of all those who "play the lyre and the flute," and of Tubal-Cain, "the forger of bronze and iron utensils." [24] The description is of a semi-nomadic culture which followed the neolithic era. The making of tools is the sign of *homo faber*. From the stone axes of paleolithic man to our immense mechanized factories there runs a deep underlying continuity. Of course, the experience of primitive man with his plow or spear was deeper, more intimate, and more vivid. He was conscious of his instrument as some part of himself, as an extension, needed and docile, of his own activity. An instrument depends on man, and man on his instrument. Early man's experience was a complex awareness of the mysterious union between a man and his tool, a union in which, by an intimate interchange, man's activity was given new dimensions. The mass production of tools has helped to diminish the intensity of such experiences, and we would need to relive the feeling of being without tools in order to appreciate once again our dependence on them.

Let us take the example of a musical instrument. Man has sung with no instrument; but he has invented the art of accompaniment, and has made for himself instruments distinct from his voice which he calls "musical instruments." The musician dominates his instrument and at the same time is subject to it. Factors, such as

---

et dixit, nequaquam dicendum est quod ipse non scripserit; quandoquidem membra ejus id operata sunt, quod dictante capite cognoverunt. Quidquid enim ille de suis factis et dictis nos legere voluit, hoc scribendum illis tanquam suis manibus imperavit. Hoc unitatis consortium et in diversis officiis concordium membrorum sub uno capite ministerium quisquis intellexerit, non aliter accipiet quod narrantibus discipulis Christi in Evangelio legerit, quam si ipsam manum Domini, quam in proprio corpore gestabat, scribentem conspexerit." "De Consensu Evangelistarum," PL 34, 1070.

[24] Gn 4:21–22.

timber, range, and expression, are conditioned by the instrument which thus vitally influences the total musical effect. When a harpsichord is well tempered, it can render a harmonious system; when it is sensitive to touch, it yields new possibilities of expression, and if it were fitted with a series of quartertone strings, it would acquire still further dimensions of musical expression. Electronic instruments, theoretically at least, could broaden the range of possibilities. Think, for instance, of the regard a soloist has for his instrument. There are pianists who take their own piano with them when they tour. Think of the care a flutist gives to the reed which receives his breath and the touch of his fingers. Or take some personal experience: what a difference between an instrument which is out of tune or broken and one that is of real quality! Now we see what an instrument means to man at play, to *homo ludens*.

The Spirit has a similar relationship to the human instruments which He has taken up in order to produce His work in language. He breathes into them, and each human author has his unique timber and key, language and style. The melody results from them both. There is but one song, perfectly human, yet somehow divine.

The comparison with a pen is much less suggestive and also less frequent in the early documents, even though it fits in the context of Scripture so very well. In the final analysis, the writing down of language is a much more artificial and extrinsic type of operation, and the role of the instrument is scarcely noticed, except, of course, when it is a question of expert calligraphy.[25]

The third example has reference to the organs of the body. It is difficult to determine whether or not primitive man ever experienced the quasi-instrumentality of bodily limbs. It is a fact that the Greek word for instrument is *"organon,"* which has developed semantically in two different directions in our language; we give the name "organ" to a musical instrument, and we also speak of bodily organs, the organs of public opinion, etc. If, by a certain reflection on myself, I consider the difference between my intention and the

---

[25] Theodore of Mopsuestia utilizes this image in a curious way, dividing it into three elements: writer, ink, and pen; and by transposition these become: the Holy Spirit, revelation, and the sacred writer. There is another transposition effected with regard to speech, since the text commented on has, "my tongue is the pen of a scribe." Cf. R. Devreesse, *Essai sur Théodore de Mopsueste*, Studi e Testi, no. 141, Rome, 1948.

hand which carries it out, or between my thought and the tongue which gives it expression, I experience the fact of instrumentality under its most vital and intimate aspect. The work done is mine, and it belongs to my hand; the words spoken pertain to me and to the tongue which uttered them; they are both material and spiritual. An impulse goes from the brain through the nervous system to the hand or tongue, which execute the order. We could picture to ourselves the relationship between the Holy Spirit and the sacred authors in much the same way. St. Augustine applies it rather to Christ and the disciples. We could perhaps introduce a new factor into his speculations. The impulse given by Christ, the Head, is in fact the Holy Spirit.

There is another interesting facet to St. Augustine's example. By invoking the image of the Mystical Body, he highlights the social and ecclesiastical roles played by the hagiographers of the New Testament, who wrote as organs of a great mystical body, which is the Church. In the Old Testament, the prophet often called himself "the mouth of God." In Isaiah 30:2, God charges His people: ". . . you did not consult My mouth"; in Jeremiah He promises: "If you repent, so that I restore you, in My presence you shall stand; if you bring forth the precious without the vile, you shall be My mouth" (15:19). Frequent also is the expression that God carries out something *"beyad,"* "by the hand," of his prophet. Etymologically, *"beyad"* signifies "in" or "by the hand of," but semantically it became an ordinary expression with the meaning "by," "by means of," etc. Thus, we find such phrases as "the precept of the Lord [delivered] by means of Moses" (Nm 36:13); "the Word of the Lord through the prophet Haggai" (Hag 1:1; 1:3; 2:2); "the words which the Lord proclaimed through the prophets of old" (Za 7:7, 12).

Thus we find two images: one generic, referring to some indetermined relationship of instrumentality, the other more specific and employing the notion of bodily organ. By a similar thought process, the enemy ruler is often pictured as an instrument of chastisement in the hand of Yahweh, a rod, a hammer, etc.

The scholastics took up the image of instrument, and gave it a conceptual elaboration according to the Aristotelian system of the four causes: efficient, material, formal, and final. An efficient cause can be either principal or instrumental.[26] An instrumental cause, which is in the order of efficient cause, has a secondary and subordinate role and is elevated by the principal cause to produce an effect which exceeds its own power. The result is brought about by both causes, and bears a resemblance to each. Thus, for example, the pen is raised by the human hand to produce a series of marks on paper, which have a spiritual significance; or a flute produces sound which, because of the artist, is music. The sacred writer receives from the Spirit, Who is the principal cause, an impulse, in virtue of which the human instrument is raised above itself to produce effects exceeding its innate capacities, either of knowledge or of communication. There is a difference, however; in our examples, the instrument is an inert object, while the sacred writer is a person, living, intelligent, and free.

Benoit observes that St. Thomas is very sparing in his use of the term "instrument" when explaining the charism of prophecy. He speaks rather of a "quasi-instrument," of an instrument in the wide sense of the term, or else he avoids the term altogether.[27]

In our neo-scholastic theology manuals, the notion of instrumental cause and its application to the mystery of inspiration plays a preponderant role. Tromp, for example, has this to say:

Inspiration is that act by which God becomes the primary Author of a sacred book and man its secondary author. In this activity, God, in his writing of a sacred book, uses man as an instrumental cause which has been raised by a supernatural power.[28]

Tromp goes on to divide instrument according to whether or not it can move itself and whether its action is one of receiving or of performing; then he describes instruments as either adequate or inadequate, separate or joined, inanimate or animate; and finally, he notes that the activity of an instrument can be considered either

---

[26] Grelot has distinguished well between the pre-philosophical use of this notion by the Fathers and the philosophical elaboration of the scholastics; he prefers the latter. *Art. cit.*, n.14.

[27] Cf. P. Synave and P. Benoit, *Prophecy and Inspiration*, New York, 1961, esp. pp. 40, 77–83.

[28] "*Inspiratio, qua Deus est vere auctor principalis libri sacri, homo autem vere auctor secundarius, in eo est, quod Deus in ordine ad librum sacrum conficiendum homine utitur tamquam causa instrumentali, supernaturali virtute elevata.*" *De Sacrae Scripturae Inspiratione*, 3rd ed., Rome, 1936.

as proper to it or as pertaining to its nature as instrument. He then applies these distinctions to biblical inspiration.

In the index of Pesch's book, under the entry *"Instrumentum,"* we are referred to *"causa instrumentalis."* In his text itself, we read: "In these and other sayings, the holy Fathers clearly teach that the sacred writers are the instrumental causes, and that God is the principal cause." [29]

Pesch thus attributes to the Fathers a metaphysical elaboration of the doctrine more proper to scholasticism. For if we compare the conceptual formulations of the mystery given by medieval and modern authors with the symbolic expressions of the ancients, we see that we have gained in precision, but that we have lost something of the vitality and rich intuitive power of those early theological symbols. The encyclical *Divino afflante Spiritu* simply uses the term "instrument" in Greek or in Latin, and refers to a "divine motion" without making any explicit mention of the metaphysical doctrine of the four causes.[30]

The notion of instrument, both as a symbol on the anthropological level, and as a concept on the metaphysical level of instrumental cause, has helped us somewhat to understand the twofold nature of the sacred writings. We say "somewhat," because the analogy, though positive and enlightening, demands that we remain always conscious of its limits. The danger of forgetting these limits tragically illustrated in the crisis of Montanism.[31]

Montanus, who lived in the middle of the second century, availed himself of the image of a plectrum and a lyre, in order to conclude that a man who was inspired was possessed by the power of God. Such a person acted without consciousness, being moved completely by the Holy Spirit while in an ecstasy or *"mania,"* as the Greeks called it. This theory, which leans heavily on some Platonic doctrines, tries to eliminate any specifically human activity and ends up in a sort of Monophysite heresy in regard to the Scriptures. The Church quickly saw the danger, and Montanus was vig-

---

[29] No. 403.

[30] EB 556. On the question of instrumental cause, cf. G. Mortari, *La nozione di causa istrumentale e le sue applicazione alla questione dell'inspirazione verbale,* Verona, 1928.

[31] Cf. P. de Labriolle, *La crise montaniste,* Paris, 1913.

orously attacked by the theologians of the age, among whom St. Epiphanius was prominent.

Montanism had carried the analogy beyond its limits, and the final result was that its adherents proclaimed a new age of revelation inaugurated by the Holy Spirit through two "prophetesses" of the sect—Prisca and Maximilla.

Since a man is a person endowed with freedom, he can be moved by moral influence, command, persuasion, or threats. If a man is moved by physical violence or by drugs, his action is not human. Thus, if he were forced to sign a document or to fire a pistol, he would not be held responsible for the results of the action. Now, the influence of the Holy Spirit cannot be classified as physical violence, in which He would use a man as though he were some machine; but then, moral causality would not suffice to make the Holy Spirit the author of a book written by a man. We must try to conceive of some physical action which does no violence and which is effective but not mechanical. Such is the nature of the mysterious movement of the Spirit Who breathes where He will.

The scholastics were also aware that their conceptual equipment had its limitations. These were made explicit by Pius XII in his use of two qualifying adjectives. ". . . the inspired writer . . . is the living and reasonable instrument of the Holy Spirit." [32]

Dictation

Among the Latin Fathers, we find the term *"dictare"* also used to describe that action of the Spirit present in the writing of the Scriptures. Thus, St. Jerome could say:

The whole of the Epistle to the Romans requires an interpretation, and is so fraught with difficulties that in order to understand it, we need the grace of the Holy Spirit Who dictated all this through the apostle. [33]

[32] Text quoted above, n. 16. St. Thomas also elaborates the doctrine of the humanity of Christ as an instrument of the Divinity (of the Divine Nature) in the work of salvation. The humanity, full of grace dynamically, was an instrument during the whole of Christ's life here on earth, and is so now in His active presence in the Church. Cf. T. Tschipke, *Die Menschheit Christi als Heilsorgan der Gottheit, unter besonderer Berücksichtigung der Lehre des hl. Thomas von Aquin*, Freiburger Theologische Studien, no. 55, Freiburg, 1940.

[33] "Omnis quidem ad Romanos Epistula interpretatione indigit, et tantis obscuritatibus involuta est, ut ad intelligendam eam, Spiritus Sancti indigeamus auxilio, qui per Apostolum haec ipsa dictavit." "Letter 120," PL 22, 997.

And we have seen already that phrase of St. Augustine in which he says:

The members put down what they know at the dictation of the Head.[34]

St. Gregory the Great says simply:

He wrote these things, Who dictated what was to be written.[35]

And the Council of Trent uses the formula:

At the dictation of the Holy Spirit . . .[36]

to describe tradition.

The words "dictate" and "dictation" are familiar in our culture, and it would seem that an analogy based on them would be easy for us to understand. But there is a danger of misunderstanding precisely because of this familiarity. Today, as a result of dictaphones and tape recorders, we have achieved a scientific exactitude in dictating which even shorthand (a method known also to the ancients) must emulate. When we hear the word "dictation," we think immediately of some executive with his secretary, or of some prompter in his box below stage, or even, as the Egyptian statutes picture it, a bird perched on the shoulder of a man whispering to him what to write. But this image is false. The Holy Spirit does not come down as a dove on the shoulder of the sacred author and act as some sort of prompter, dictating His lines to him. In the traditional context, the word has another meaning.

If we look back, for instance, at the patristic texts just cited, we will see that St. Jerome does not say that the Holy Spirit dictated to the apostles, but that he dictated *through* them. St. Augustine says that the members put down what they *knew* at the dictation of the Head. The phrase of St. Gregory and St. Isidore is even more explicit: "He *wrote* these things, Who dictated to his prophets what was to be written."

Since the Council of Trent, the way was opened for a concept of the term "dictation" in our modern sense, one which reduced the sacred writer to the role of a junior secretary. For such a role, one

---

[34] Text quoted above, n. 23.
[35] "*Ipse igitur haec scripsit, qui scribenda dictavit.*" "Moralia on Job, Preface," PL 75, 517.
[36] "Spiritu Sancto dictante . . ." D-S 1501.

need only understand the words materially and be able to write them correctly, nothing more. But is this the proper understanding of the Council of Trent? Some theologians seem to have thought so.

In 1584, Dominic Bañez published at Rome his *Scholastic Commentary on the first Part of the Summa of the Angelic Doctor, St. Thomas, as far as Question 64.* There we read:

The second conclusion. The Holy Spirit not only inspired the matter contained in the Scriptures, but also dictated and suggested every word in which it was written. . . . To dictate means to determine every word.

The third conclusion (which is not of faith, but is the safer opinion). Since God disposes all things sweetly, He enlightens the mind of each individual sacred author and dictates to him words which well befit his state and condition.[37]

In the middle of the eighteenth century, C. R. Billuart published his *Summa Theologica*, which has had a very great influence. Speaking of the norms of faith, he says:

I presuppose that all the phrases of Scripture are inspired and dictated by the Holy Spirit. . . . It seems more probable that the nature of sacred Scripture would require that not only the general sense and the phrases of Scripture be dictated by the Holy Spirit, but even every single word. It is the more common opinion . . . that the Holy Spirit accommodated Himself to the way of thinking, the style, and the temperament of each of the sacred writers, and concurred with them as He dictated every word, just as though the author had written from his own resources.[38]

---

[37] "*Spiritus Sanctus non solum res in Scriptura contentas inspiravit, sed etiam singula verba, quibus scriberentur, dictavit atque suggessit. . . . Dictare autem verba ipsa determinare significat. . . . Cum Deus omnia suaviter disponat, ita uniuscuiusque scriptoris sacri mentem illuminabat eidemque verba dictabat quae maxime illorum statum et condicionem decebant.*" As cited by Pesch, no. 278.

[38] "*Suppono omnes Scripturae sententias esse a Spiritu Sancto inspiratas. . . . Probabilius videtur ad rationem Scripturae Sacrae requiri, quod non solum sensus et sententiae, sed etiam singula verba sint a Spiritu Sancto dictata. Est communior . . . Spiritus Sanctus se accomodavit genio, stilo et affectionibus cuiusque scriptoris sacri sicque concurrit dictando singula, ac ipse scriptor de suo scripsisset.*" Cited by Pesch, no. 280.

The "orthodox" Protestants proceeded in much the same manner. In the profession of faith known as the *Formula Consensus Helvetica*, we read that the text of the Old Testament is inspired "with regard both to the consonants and to the vowel points, both the punctuation and its equivalent." Among the classical Protestant authors, we find Johann Gerhard (*Loci communes theologici*, 1610–1622) holding as a theological conclusion that God inspired the Hebrew text, including its vowel points and punctuation, just as we have it today. Quenstedt, in his *Theologia Didactica-Polemica* (1657), calls the sacred writers the "amanuenses" and notaries of the Holy Spirit, who are only authors in the improper sense of the term. The Holy Spirit "supplied, inspired, and dictated every single word and phrase to each of the sacred writers." The differences in style are explained by the fact that the Holy Spirit accommodated Himself to the temperament of each author, dictating those words which the author would have used, had he been drawing on his own resources.

These parallel positions, adopted by both Catholics and Protestants, smack of a certain Monophysitism and provoked a variety of reactions. Among the Protestants, there arose a rationalism which went to the other extreme and denied to God any activity in the composition of the Scriptures, while among Catholics there arose the famous controversy over "verbal inspiration."

The statement of the problem among Catholics went something like this: Inspiration cannot be dictation, since dictation eliminates any properly human activity. Therefore, in order to understand the formula, "God is the author of Scripture, and man is the author of Scripture," we have to make a distinction. The distinction is not difficult. God provides the matter or the content, and man provides the form; God gives the ideas, and man elaborates the style. In the last century, the great champion of this position was Cardinal Franzelin, who was simply developing the ideas of some theologians who came immediately after the Council of Trent, such as Lessius, Suarez, Cornelius à Lapide, and others. Pesch wrote his book while under the burden of this controversy, and he often has the Fathers of the Church employing his distinction.[39]

39 Obviously, the "form" had some influence on the "matter" or the choice of words, and this was admitted by all. The theme which God willed to be treated already restricted the area of language, and the exposition of

At the present moment, we have gone beyond such a statement of the problem. Not only is it no longer solved by the distinction, "God—the ideas, man—the words," but the whole view of literature which thinks in terms of "either the ideas or the words" has been abandoned. Such a distinction has no basis in reality; it is a product of the laboratory, suffering from an intellectualism which values only "ideas." As a matter of fact, such an approach was vitiated by the way it first posed the problem: "Either God dictated the words, or the words are solely from the sacred writer." There is a third possibility, namely that of a divine motion permeating every phase of the literary production, making it a work of God, and all the while enshrining and elevating man's freedom and creativity. Today, most theologians accept the literary work in the concrete as inspired, without distinguishing content and form. A piece of literature is an organized complex of words whose meaning is inseparable from its medium. The term "dictate" is still applicable, but not in its modern connotation.

A related problem is that discussed by the Council Fathers during Vatican I: "Is sacred Scripture the word of God, or does it contain the word of God?" The distinction was prompted by the phrases often found in the prophets, which seemed to set apart certain divine oracles as they introduced them: "Thus does God speak," "an oracle of Yahweh," "the Word of the Lord." [40] Tradition has always considered all the Scripture as the word of God. St. John Chrysostom has this to say about one of St. Paul's phrases in his first letter to the Thessalonians: "Paul said all these things by the Spirit, but what he says now, he heard literally from God." [41]

A third problem, one which is much discussed today, concerns the "ipsissima verba" of the prophets or of Our Lord. We hear such questions as: "Does the prophet give us the very words of

---

the theme demanded apt formulation. According to this theory, God moved the author immediately in regard to the ideas, and mediately in regard to their formulation. In the words of Tromp: "*Rerum conceptio est simpliciter ex illustratione divina; verba sunt etiam ex illustratione divina, attamen non necessario quatenus sunt haec verba simpliciter, sed quatenus sunt haec verba apta.*" *Op. cit.*, no. 28, p. 91.

[40] For a discussion of this question at the First Vatican Council, cf. N. I. Weyns, "De notione inspirationis biblicae iuxta Concilium Vaticanum," *Ang* 30, 1953, pp. 315–336.

[41] Ἐκεῖνα μὲν οὖν πνεύματι πάντα ἐφθέγγετο, τοῦτο δὲ, ὁ λέγει νῦν,καὶ ῥητῶς ἤκουσε παρὰ τοῦ Θεοῦ. "On 1 Th 4:15," PG 62, 439.

THE WORD DIVINE AND HUMAN

God, or does he elaborate the message?"; "Can we discern in a prophetic oracle one part which is the direct message of God, and another which is the explanation given by the prophet?" [42] In regard to the New Testament, the question takes the form: "Did the evangelists give us the very words which Christ spoke, or is their message only the word of Christ, in the sense that it comes from the Spirit of Christ?" Later on, we will come back to this question; for the moment, however, we must continue our analysis of the term "dictate."

The semantic evolution of the Latin word *"dictare"* is extremely interesting. On the one hand, it has given rise to such words as the German *"dichten"* ("compose as an author or poet"), *"Gedicht"* ("poem"), etc., while on the other hand we have such words as "dictation" and even "dictator." The first line of thought appears in medieval treatises on the "art of composition" (*"ars dictaminis"*). These were simply manuals which taught the art of writing and composing poetically. *"Dictare"* in the medieval world implied real intellectual and even poetic activity. We see its origin in the administrative bureaus of the government or Church, where men were employed who could draw up, in the appropriate style, the decrees and correspondence of the ruler. They called their profession the "art of dictation." The term was then transferred from the realm of prose and rhetoric to that of poetic composition, and finally gave rise to the maxim, "Whoever wishes to be a poet [*dictator*] must study the art of composing well [*ars dictaminis*]." Dante even calls the poets the *"dictatores illustres."* The second line of development refers more to the realm of volition, and is concerned with command, legislation, etc. In this sense, we speak of the will of the ruler dictating norms of conduct for the nation, and also of the "dictate" of our conscience.

The twofold possibility of the word should make us cautious in our attempt to understand this second traditional analogy. In a modern context, we should think of a good secretary who knows how to take the notes jotted down by the executive, and expand them into a letter; or we should think of a manner in which some of our modern heads of government use speech writers. In these cases, there is a close collaboration, a union of mind and will, in

[42] Cf. H. Wildberger, *Jahwewort und prophetische Rede bei Jeremia,* Zurich, 1942.

71

order to produce the end result. The executive gives the general theme, sketches its development and some of its leading ideas, and perhaps proposes one or two good phrases which ought to be incorporated. The secretary draws up the document, which is then corrected and written once again in its final form. To whom do we attribute authorship? In one sense, both are authors; in another sense, there is a principal author and a secondary author, since both worked together intelligently. In the case of a speech of the president, for example, the juridical effects of what he says are due to his authorship, while their literary form is due mostly to his secretary who knows the *"ars dictaminis."*

It does not seem that a modern ghost writer or the editor of a magazine is a good example of this type of joint authorship, since the original "author" merely provides the material and is not a true literary author.

Understood in the sense described above, the analogy based on the notion of dictation can help us to penetrate more deeply into the mystery. But while we appreciate its light, we must not forget its limitations. Even in the example we just gave, of an executive and his secretary, we can apportion to each his share in the final result. We know when one worked on the document, and at what stage the other made his contribution, and on this basis we can distinguish what part was played by each. Again, we suppose that the contribution of the secretary was more in the order of literary composition, while that of the executive was more in the realm of creative thought. To one we attribute the knowledge, to the other the style. But this type of "division of labor" is inapplicable to a work produced by the Holy Spirit through the inspired writer.

In Christ, there are two wills and two principles of operation which are neither confused nor opposed, since the will of Christ is completely submissive to the divine. So also in the mystery of inspiration there is a human literary effort which is submissive and in no way opposed to the operation of the Holy Spirit. To diminish the human reality of this effort, and to make of it the mere activity of an amanuensis, does nothing to increase the glory of God's causality.[43]

[43] Cf. D-S 550–559.

A Messenger

The image of a man bearing a message from another is one whose echoes are found throughout the Bible. The prophets are the envoys of God, the messengers and heralds of Yahweh—just as the apostles are later to be called the envoys and heralds of Christ. In a culture without telegraph, telephone, or airplane, the messenger played an important role. Sometimes, all that was required of him was that he deliver written documents and carry back written replies; then it sufficed if he could ride a horse. However, since writing was not as common as it is today, he was often obliged to memorize a message and then carry back an oral reply, in which case he needed also to have mastered the techniques then in use for the memorization of long passages. There were also messengers who, after having received the general tenor of the instructions, were empowered to deliver and explain them according to circumstances. These latter were much like our modern special envoys or ambassadors. They had very precise instructions, but were expected to adapt them to the exigencies of the moment. The duty of such people is to make known the will of those who sent them, but we would not say that their words are the words of the president or king.

The prophets presented themselves as envoys from God, and used the words and formulas which characterized the messenger's style of the age: "Thus says Yahweh to . . . N"). They overcame the distance between God and man by means of their word.

As can be seen, this third analogy adds very little to the second. In one case, the messenger need not even speak, in another he memorized and delivered the message as dictated. In the third case, he is the "secondary author" of what he says, and in a certain sense through his own activity he allows the one who sent him to speak.

An Author and the Characters He Creates

We find this analogy, taken from the world of literary creation, very attractive. Admittedly, it lacks noble lineage and a long history, at least in the tract on inspiration. St. Justin, who seems to be one of the few ancients ever to have made this comparison (other aspects of the passage are more difficult to understand), has noted:

When you hear the words of the prophets, spoken as it were in their own person, do not consider that they were uttered by these inspired people, but rather by the divine Word who moves them. For sometimes he declares things that are yet to happen, as one foretelling the future; sometimes he speaks as if in the role of the Lord of all, God the Father; sometimes as Christ; sometimes as if in the role of the people, answering to the Lord or to his Father. You find a similar thing among your own writers: one man writes the whole work introducing the roles of the various people who speak.[44]

A second-rate novelist cannot create real people in his work. He takes up puppets and has them perform in the interest of some preconceived theory or plot. Nothing must interfere, everything must conspire to the achievement of the end foreseen. The characters in the novel speak and act as they cross the pages, yet their words and actions do not ring true. Our author provides them with words which seem unfelt or unsuited.

Great writers, however, can truly create people whose action determines the plot, and whose words well up from some depth within themselves. We need only think, for instance, of Don Quixote, Hamlet, the Brothers Karamazov, or Anna Karenina. If we hear the words of these personalities read out loud, we have little trouble in determining who is speaking. No one can confuse Ivan with Aloysha, Don Quixote with his Squire. But then, suppose we push the question further, and ask: "Whose words are these?" "Do they belong to Aloysha or Dostoevski?" "Are they from Sancho or Cervantes; from Laertes or Shakespeare?" The question makes us think.

These people in a novel are the creation of their authors; they depend on him for their existence, life, and movement, yet he depends on them, too, and must respect them.

Some writers tell us how they hear within themselves the conversation of their characters, as though they themselves were specta-

---

44 "Ὅταν δὲ τὰς λέξεις τῶν προφητῶν λεγομένας ὡς ἀπὸ προσώπου ἀκούητε, μὴ ἀπ᾽ αὐτῶν τῶν ἐμπεπνευσμένων λέγεσθαι νομίσητε, ἀλλ᾽ ἀπὸ τοῦ κινοῦντος αὐτοὺς θείου λόγου. Ποτὲ μὲν γὰρ ὡς προαγγελτικῶς τὰ μέλλοντα γενήσεσθαι λέγει, ποτὲ δ᾽ ὡς ἀπὸ προσώπου τοῦ Δεσπότου πάντων καὶ Πατρὸς Θεοῦ φθέγγεται, ποτὲ δὲ ὡς ἀπὸ προσώπου τοῦ Χριστοῦ, ποτὲ δὲ ὡς ἀπὸ προσώπου λαῶν ἀποκρινομένων τῷ Κυρίῳ, ἢ τῷ Πατρὶ αὐτοῦ. ὁποῖον καὶ ἐπὶ τῶν παρ᾽ ὑμῖν συγγραφέων ἰδεῖν ἔστιν, ἕνα μὲν τὸν τὰ πάντα συγγράφοντα ὄντα, πρόσωπα δὲ τὰ διαλεγόμενα παραφέροντα. "First Apology for the Christians, ch. 36," PG 6, 385,

tors rather than authors, though, paradoxically, they more than we hear only a figment of the imagination. A novelist once admitted to me that he was forced to make one of his characters die, because this person was becoming so strong that he threatened to absorb the whole novel. Trollope tells us how he lived with his characters, how he knew the tone of their voice and what each would say in a given situation; he tried to introduce his readers to these people. But no one has equaled Pirandello in his description of the process by which life is conferred on these literary personalities within the mind of their author. It is not the author who seeks out his characters, but rather there are *Six Characters in Search of an Author*, in order to live and act and speak.

It is interesting to see how some of these "people" acquire an independent existence and solidity. We need only think of the life of Sherlock Holmes (with the subsequent discussion as to whether he studied at Oxford or Cambridge), or the *Vida de Don Quijote y Sancho* by Unamuno, or the *Memoirs of Maigret* by Simenon. Anthropology and psychology alike study such great figures as Don Juan, Hamlet, and Richard III.

All this indicates the power of these personalities of fancy, and the respect they claim for the words they have uttered. None of us can forget the soliloquies of Hamlet or Henry IV, the anguish of Ivan Karamazov, the bitter reveries of Segismund.

Yet we have only said half the truth. The words of these characters belong to them and come somehow from within them, yet, and this is the other half of the truth, they are also the words of the author. There is no doubt that Calderón is reflecting on life's dream as Segismund speaks, or that Ivan gives voice to the fullness of suffering experienced by Dostoevski, and we hear Shakespeare musing in the monologue of Henry IV. Shakespeare, Cervantes, or Dostoevski can lay claim to every word spoken by the characters they have created. Even when these people confront one another and are diametrically opposed, Cervantes speaks in Don Quixote and Sancho, as does Shakespeare in Othello and Iago, or Dostoevski in Ivan and Smeryakov.

Guy de Maupassant, contrasting the "objective" novel with one based on psychological analysis, defends the latter on the ground that it provides the subjectivity of the author diverse facets of self-expression by enabling him to assume different personalities. "How should I act if I were a king, an assassin, a thief, a prostitute, a nun, a young boy, or a street vendor?" It is only by this means that the author is able to "transfer his own view of the world, his knowledge of it, and his ideas about life." This reminds us of the famous remark of Flaubert: *"Madame Bovary, c'est moi."*

A novelist speaks in his works, not only when he recounts his autobiography or when he relates facts, but also when his characters express their ideas; and a dramatist is on the stage speaking in the personalities he has created. But then a special problem arises when an author creates two characters who are opposed to one another. In which of these is the author really speaking? It depends somewhat on the author and on the situation he has created. It may be that the thought of the writer arises within him in a dialectical movement that demands such opposition, or perhaps one of the antagonists is subtly condemned by the context in which he speaks. Then, too, there are cases in which an author creates someone whom he hates, even though he speaks through him. Care must be taken in such a case, however, since dislike for a character can easily give rise to a lack of authenticity. One novelist recommended to her colleagues "a love which is universal like that of Christ."

It is hard for us to understand this manifold unfolding, this union in word between an author and the character he creates. It is only made possible by the depth and richness of the human experience granted to the geniuses of literature. This is captured and expressed by his intuitive penetration which extends to the smallest detail, appreciating its every shade of meaning and able to enlarge and adapt it to a variety of contexts. But, above all, there is within a great writer a capacity to live with his characters, to enter into them and incarnate himself in them.

We have just used the term "incarnate"; it is a sort of metaphor in reverse, taking its concept and terminology from a mystery, and then extending itself to the world of men. We say that God has become incarnate in man or in human words, just as an artist incarnates himself in his literary creation. This is the point of our analogy.

As an analogy, this image shares with its predecessors the fact of limitation. A literary character is not a real person with a body and soul, rights and duties. Even the richest and most complete of these personalities, those which E. M. Forster calls "round characters," are at best stylized simplifications. As Somerset Maugham puts it: "The writer does not copy his originals; he takes what he wants from them, a few traits that have caught his attention, a turn of mind that has fired his imagination, and therefrom constructs his characters." To speak of the existence, liberty, and responsibility of a literary character is ultimately only figurative language. In a real human being, the personality exists and acts continually, and his speech gives expression to this subsistence. A literary personality, on the other hand, only exists when he speaks, when he is on the stage, or when someone else speaks of him. To move and live within an assumed character who is made of language is a very different thing from moving a real person within his own liberty and literary activity.

This is the obvious limitation of our analogy. Nevertheless, we would presume to close our discussion of it with these words of St. Augustine: "If He is the head, then we are the body; one man is speaking. Whether the head speaks or the members speak, it is the One Christ Who speaks." [45]

GOD THE AUTHOR OF SCRIPTURE

The use of this term "author" to describe the activity of God gives rise to many questions. First of all, do we mean it to be but one more illustrative image? If so, why not include it along with the others in the section above? Or do we consider that we have here a concept which needs further scientific precision, in order to be applicable to God? The discussion ought to begin with the observation that this term already forms part of a definition of faith. The Council of Florence declared in 1442:

[The Roman Church] professes that one and the same God is the author of both the Old and New Testaments, that is, the law, the prophets, and the Gospel, since the holy men of both testaments have spoken under the inspiration of the same Holy Spirit.[46]

---

45 "*Si ergo ille caput, nos corpus, unus homo loquitur; sive caput loquatur, sive membra, unus Christus loquitur.*" "Comm. on Ps 140," CCL 40, 2027.

46 "*Unum atque eundem Deum Veteris et Novi Testamenti, hoc est, Legis et Prophetarum atque Evangelii profitetur auctorem: quoniam eodem Spiritu Sancto inspirante utriusque Testamenti Sancti locuti sunt.*" D-S 1334.

About one hundred years later, the Council of Trent, describing its acceptance and veneration of Scripture and tradition, said:

[The Council] follows the example of the orthodox Fathers . . . accepts and venerates the books of both the Old and New Testaments since one God is the author of both. . . .[47]

The Vatican Council (1870) said:

The Church holds the books [of both the Old and New Testaments] to be sacred and canonical . . . because, written under the inspiration of the Holy Spirit, they have God for their author.[48]

In the first two formulas, the accent falls on the word "one." The intention of these definitions is to assert first and foremost the unity of the two testaments or economies of salvation against the errors once proposed by Marcion and the Manichaeans, who attributed the Old Testament to some evil spirit or some other god. The One True God is the author of both testaments. This is the reason why they are so closely bound in unity. Intimately linked with this declaration is the assertion of the indisputable fact that God is the author of sacred Scripture.

The formula of Vatican I goes further and enters into a discussion of the nature of inspiration. It first considers two negative aspects, as we have seen. It then goes on to describe the mystery positively in a sentence which syntactically links "inspired" with "author," and whose principle verb is in the phrase, "have God for their author."

We cannot draw from the simple fact that the definition was made any clear indication of the sense in which we ought to understand its key word. Should we consider that the Council is using the word "author" as an image, somewhat like the symbolic terms "ascended" and "heavens" of other formulas describing the glorious Christ, or should we give it its modern conceptual content? In

---

[47] ". . . orthodoxorum Patrum exempla secuta, omnes libros tam Veteris quam Novi Testamenti, cum utriusque unus Deus sit auctor, nec non traditiones ipsas, tum ad fidem, tum ad mores pertinentes, tamquam vel oretenus a Christo, vel Spiritu Sancto dictatas et continua successione in Ecclesia catholica conservatas, pari pietatis affectu ac reverentia suscipit et veneratur." D-S 1501.

[48] "Eos vero Ecclesia pro sacris et canonicis habet . . . propterea quod Spiritu Sancto inspirante conscripti Deum habent auctorem, atque ut tales ipsi Ecclesiae traditi sunt." D-S 3006.

our culture, the meaning attached to the word "author" derives principally from the world of literature, and its concept is quite precise. When a history of literature speaks of authors, there is no doubt as to what is intended, and such expressions as "authors' club," "author's copyright," etc., refer to well-defined aspects of our culture. But is this the meaning of the term as applied to the Scriptures?

We should remember first of all that, in ancient times, and especially in the biblical world, an author was something very different from what we conceive of him as today. Works were very often anonymous or pseudonymous, and nearly everything literary underwent a process of collaboration, reëlaboration, corruption, borrowing, and addition simply unknown in our world of the printed book. However, our discussion at the moment has to do with the authorship of God. Can we take the term "author" and apply it in exactly the same sense to God and to some human writer? Once again, this question places us in the world of literary creation, and the meaning we give to the term "author" is one which is specifically literary. This is the context familiar to the passage we read of St. Gregory the Great, in which he speaks of the recipient of a letter who makes inquiries about the pen which wrote it. He compares such inquiries to the action of someone who would seek to know the human author of sacred Scripture when he knows that the author is God. Here, obviously, we have an analogous use of the term, and it this use which introduces us to the *fifth* analogy in our consideration.

But we should ask first of all whether or not the strict literary interpretation of the word "author" is actually demanded by the conciliar use of *"auctor."* Is it a *dogma* that God is the literary author of the Scriptures? Could the word "author" have no other sense in the early ecclesiastical documents?

The Greek language makes a distinction between *sungrapheus* and *archegos*, or *aitios*, which corresponds rather closely with our "writer" and "originator" ("author" has both meanings), and the German *"Verfasser"* and *"Urheber."* For example, some prominent man may ask a writer to compose the biography of one of his family, the general of a religious order may commission one of his subjects to write the life of the order's founder, or a government may appoint some professor to publish a history of the country during the early nineteenth century. In all these cases, the literary author of the work is the man who is enlisted to do the work and does it, be he paid, commanded, or appointed, while the cause or originator of the book is the one who commissioned him. The celebrity, the general of an order, or the appointing government official would not be called the "author" of the work in a literary context.

Now, we have said that the action of God in inspiration does not pertain merely to the order of moral cause, but rather that God's action is real or physical. The question then arises: "Does this activity of God make Him the writer or simply the originator of the Scriptures?" "Should we say that He is the literary author, or that He is the cause in a more general sense?" This distinction brings us face to face with two differing schools of opinion. We are in the presence here of an open and "disputed question."

N. I. Weyns,[49] after an analysis of the conciliar acts of Vatican I, proceeds to a study of the meaning of the definition given by this Council on the sacred Scriptures. We have just seen the principal phrases of this definition on a preceding page. In the profession of faith, proposed to Michael VIII Palaeologus (1274), God is called "author" ("*auctor*") of both the Old and New Testaments. The Greek text has at this point not "*sungrapheus*" ("writer or literary author"), but "*archegos*" ("originator"). It is interesting to note that in the formulas from the Councils of Florence and Trent, which we have seen, the term "*auctor*" does not receive any further specification and is used in connection with the words "Old and New Testaments" (or "dispositions"). In the schema proposed at Vatican I in December, 1869, the word "author" was clearly defined by the phrase, "they have God for their author and thus contain in a true and proper sense the word of God." The explanation of these words was as follows:

God is the author of the books, that is, the author of the writing, in such a way that the actual committing of things to paper [*consignatio*] or writing ought to be attributed principally to the divine operation acting in and through man.

A new schema corrected the phrase, "contain the word of God," to read: "are the word of God." Finally, after discussion, the

[49] *Op. cit.*, n. 40.

Council decided to omit this last phrase altogether. It thus defined nothing new in this regard, and left open the discussion as to the manner and extension of inspiration. Weyns concludes his study by interpreting the decree to mean: "... the Scriptures were written under some positive influence of the Holy Spirit, they have a divine origin." [50]

Karl Rahner also prefers the term "originator" ("*Urheber*") to "writer" or "literary author" ("*Verfasser*"). God is the originator or source of the Scriptures, because He "pre-defined" that the Church in the act of constituting herself should express herself to herself. The literary authors of that expression are men. God and man are both causes of the same effect, namely the Scriptures, under different formalities. The formality under which God is the cause, is that act by which the Church confers on herself her act of self-expression. The formality under which man is the cause, is that by which a man gives this expression literary existence. According to Rahner, it is not exact to say that God wrote a letter to Philemon. Therefore, we do not think that he would accept this phrase of St. John Chrysostom:

When Paul writes, or better, not Paul but the Holy Spirit dictates a letter to a whole city or to such a people and through them to the whole world . . .[51]

The other line of thought is best represented by the writings of Augustin Cardinal Bea. While recognizing that the question is open, he prefers to take the word "author" in its more usual ac-

---

[50] *Ibid.*: " . . . *sub influxu quodam positivo Spiritus Sancti conscripti sunt, divinam habent originem.*" Desroches implicitly accepts this opinion when he writes: "*On sera étonné, sans doute, de nous voir revenir à la notion d'auteur, pour éclairer la phénomène surnaturel de l'inspiration. Il semblerait que le Père Lagrange ait fait justice de cette méthode surannée, comme nous l'avons souligné dans la première partie de ce travail. Nous admettons sans difficultés après lui et son éminent disciple, le Père Benoit, que la formule Dieu-auteur ne puisse servir de point de départ a notre explication. Mais avec eux encore, il nous faut affirmer avec autant de force que cette formule doit se rencontrer au point d'arrivée.*" A. Desroches, *Jugement pratique et Jugement spéculatif chez l'Ecrivain inspiré,* Ottawa, 1958, p. 107. (However, the formula which Desroches avoids is found in the Vatican definition.)

[51] Παύλου δὲ γράφοντος, μᾶλλον δὲ οὐ τοῦ Παύλου, ἀλλὰ τῆς τοῦ Πνεύματος χάριτος τὴν ἐπιστολὴν ὑπαγορευούσης ὁλοκλήρῳ πόλει καὶ δήμῳ τοσούτῳ καὶ δι' ἐκείνων τῇ οἰκουμένῃ πάσῃ. . . . "Homily on Rom 16:3," PG 51, 187.

ceptance, as the ancients did.[52] The formula, *"Deus Auctor,"* appears for the first time in the so-called "Ancient Statutes of the Church" (*Statuta Ecclesiae Antiqua*), in which it is laid down that before a man be consecrated a bishop, it should be determined if he believe ". . . that there be one and the same author of the Old and New Testaments, that is, the law, the prophets, and the apostles." [53] This text was already known at the beginning of the sixth century, and its intention is clearly anti-Manichaean. St. Augustine, in his controversy with the Manichaeans, cites Faustus to the effect that the Manichaean Church "finds distasteful the gifts of the Old Testament and of its author. A most jealous guardian of its own prestige, it receives letters only if they are from its Spouse." [54] However, neither of these two texts which we have just seen are absolutely clear, and neither relates the word "author" to any body of writings. In fact, the text of St. Augustine is of a decidedly metaphorical character. However, in other anti-Manichaean writers, the application of the term "author" is clearly made to the written documents, and not only to the covenants or dispositions of God. The "Acts of Archelaus" describes the Manichaean doctrine as maintaining that "what is written in the law and the prophets should be attributed to Satan . . . who willed to write some truths, so that moved by these, people would accept the errors also." And Serapion of Thmuis presents the Manichaeans with this argument: "If the evil one, who possesses no splendor but is all darkness, wrote the law, how did he know about the coming of the Son?" Bea thus concludes his historical investigation by interpreting the word "author" in its strict sense of "literary author."

These, then, are the two lines of thought in this disputed question. It would seem that the formula in the Credo, "Who spoke through the prophets," as well as frequent patristic allusions to this aspect of the mystery favor the opinion that the term "author"

[52] Cf. A. Bea, "Deus Auctor Sacrae Scripturae: Herkunft und Bedeutung der Formel," Ang 20, 1943, pp. 16–31.

[53] *"Quaerendum etiam ab eo, si novi et veteris testamenti, id est, legis et prophetarum, et apostolorum unum eundumque credat auctorem et Deum."* EB 30.

[54] *". . . sordent ei Testamenti Veteris et ejus auctoris munera, famaeque suae custos diligentissima, nisi sponsi sui non accipit litteras."* "Contra Faustum," PL 42, 303.

should be interpreted as literary author, and be used in this sense in constructing an analogy. Though, of course, the Fathers did not consider explicitly the problem with which we are faced today, still their spontaneous recourse to such words as "pronounced," "spoke," "wrote," etc., seem to fit best in this context of "literary author."

Eusebius:

They either do not believe that the divine writings were pronounced by the Holy Spirit, in which case they are heretics, or . . .[55]

St. Irenaeus:

. . . the Scriptures are perfect, because they were uttered by the Word of God and His Spirit.[56]

St. Clement of Alexandria:

The Lord speaks in person through Isaiah, through Elijah, through the mouth of the prophets.[57]

Origen:

The Holy Spirit relates this.[58]

St. Cyril of Alexandria:

All of Scripture is but one book, uttered by the One Holy Spirit.[59]

St. Cyril of Jerusalem:

Who else knows the deep things of God, but the Holy Spirit alone Who has spoken the divine writings? . . . Why are you so preoccu-

[55] "Ἡ γὰρ ὃν πιστεύουσιν ἁγίῳ Πνεύματι λελέχϑαι τὰς Θείας Γραφὰς, κὰι εἰσὶν ἄπιστοι, ἤ ἑαυτοὺς ἡγοῦνται σοφωτέρους τοῦ ἁγίου Πνεύματος ὑμάρχειν. Eusebius, "Ecclesiastical History, 5," PG 20, 517.

[56] "Scripturae quidem perfectae sunt, quippe a Verbo Dei et Spiritu ejus dictae." "Adversus Haereses, 5," PG 7, 805.

[57] Αὐτὸς ἐν Ἡσαΐᾳ ὁ Κύριος λαλῶν, αὐτὸς ἐν Ἠλίᾳ, ἐν στόματι προφητῶν αὐτός. "Exhortation to the Gentiles, 1," PG 8, 64.

[58] "Qui haec gesta narrat quae legimus, neque puer est, qualem supra descripsimus, neque vir talis aliquis, neque senior, nec omnino aliquis homo est: et ut amplius aliquid dicam, nec angelorum aliquis, aut virtutum coelestium est, sed sicut traditio majorum tenet, Spiritus sanctus haec narrat." "Homily 26 on the Book of Numbers," PG 12, 774.

[59] Ἐν γὰρ ἡ πᾶσα ἐστι κὰι λελάληται δι᾽ἑνὸς τοῦ ἁγίου Πνεύματος. "On Is 29:12," PG 70, 656.

pied about things which even the Holy Spirit did not write in the Scriptures? [60]

The Holy Spirit Himself pronounced the Scriptures. . . . Let those things be said which He has said, and what He has not said neither let us dare to say.[61]

The above list could be extended without great difficulty, but this sampling of patristic texts is sufficient to give us an idea of their orientation. They all seem to favor a conception of God's activity in inspiration which is better described as "literary author" than as "origin." We will conclude with this passage from St. Isidore, which synthesizes both aspects:

These are the writers of the sacred books. . . . But the author of these same Scriptures is believed to be the Holy Spirit. For He Himself wrote those things which He dictated to the prophets to be written.[62]

Once we have decided to take the term "author" in the sense of "literary author," we are, of course, in the realm of analogy, since the authorship of the Holy Spirit is necessarily unique. He is an author who writes by means of others who are also truly authors. This analogy, then, also has its limitations.

CONCLUSION

In our effort to shed some light on the mystery of inspiration, we have considered some of the images used to describe it. The image latent in the term itself, *"in-spirare"* ("breathe into") evokes the picture of an all-pervading wind or breath. Drawn from this most elemental experience of the cosmos, it accentuates the notion of vitality and dynamism, and since it is an analogy whose origin is completely biblical, its privileged position is assured. Its conceptual

---

[60] Τί ἐστιν ἕτερον γινῶσκον τὰ βάθη τοῦ Θεοῦ, εἰ μὴ μόνον τὸ Πνεῦμα τὸ ἅγιον, τὸ λαλῆσαν τὰς θείας Γραφάς; . . . Τί τοίνυν πολυπραγμονεῖς, ἃ μηδὲ τὸ Πνεῦμα τὸ ἅγιον ἔγραψεν ἐν ταῖς Γραφαῖς; . . . "Catech. 12, On the Only Begotten," PG 33, 705.

[61] Αὐτὸ τὸ Πνεῦμα τὸ ἅγιον ἐλάλησε τὰς Γραφάς. . . . Λεγέσθω οὖν ἃ εἴρηκεν. ὅσα γὰρ οὐκ εἴρηκεν, ἡμεῖς οὐ τολμῶμεν. "Catech. 16, On the Holy Spirit," PG 33, 920.

[62] "Hi sunt scriptorum librorum. . . . Auctor autem earumdem Scripturarum Spiritus Sanctus esse creditur. Ipse enim scripsit, qui prophetas suos scribenda dictavit." "De Eccl. Officiis," PL 83, 750.

elaboration in theology, however, has tended to empty it of any imaginative content.

The image of instrument comes from the world of man and human culture, from work and music. It rests on the two qualities of man—*homo faber* and *homo ludens*. Though scanty biblical support can be found for the image, its symbolic value is unchallenged, and it has lent itself readily to a metaphysical transposition. Even today, its possibilities as a symbol are quite rich, while its use in metaphysics has not dulled its human resources.

The image evoked by the word "dictation" comes from the world of chancelleries and curiae and is at home in the realm of literature. It has a firm biblical basis in some of the phrases used by the prophets, but its subsequent conceptual elaboration has often tended to a rigidity which obliges us to be cautious in its application. At the same time, the progress made in overcoming the dangers in such conceptualization is a good indication of the advancement made in our understanding of the doctrine.

The image of a messenger derives also from the world of the court and the curia. It is a well-established biblical frame of reference, but has received hardly any conceptual refinement. Perhaps this is because it adds but little to the two preceding images.

The image of an author and the literary personalities he fashions, proceeds directly from the world of literary creation. It has no biblical roots, since formerly men gave little reflective consideration to the nature of literary activity. In its application to the Scriptures, there has not been as yet any process of conceptual analysis.

If the term "author" is used as an image when it is predicated of God's activity in regard to the Scriptures, then it clearly derives from the world of literature and can be shown to have its roots in the Bible itself. Its use in the tract on inspiration has occasioned many discussions, but as yet there is no commonly accepted view as to its area of meaning.

Everyone of these analogies can offer us some positive understanding of the fact of inspiration. By making the contribution in the full consciousness of their limitations, they enlighten us while yet affirming the transcendence of the mystery.

We should note however, that if we are to place this whole study in its proper context, we must distinguish clearly between two different ways of considering and comparing realities in their relation to the Incarnation. They are called, respectively, "communication of idiom" and "analogy."

Because of the Incarnation it is possible to speak of Christ, using a communication of idiom or interchange of predicate in the following way: with Christ as the subject of the sentence, I may say that God died for us, or that this man is omnipotent. However, I cannot interchange predicates when speaking of the separate natures as such, because they exist "without commingling or confusion."

When I consider Christ as a concrete totality, I am obliged to refer to many human factors in order to understand and describe Him. But if I want to know what God is in Himself, or what the Word is as a Divine Person, then I cannot avail myself of the human factors in Christ except by way of analogy. I am able to say and to know something of God by taking man as my starting point because man is the image of God, and not solely because God has become man. Thus in the case of Christ, when it is a question of an analogy, we must be conscious of its limits and be aware of the nature of these limits. In order to know and say something about the Trinity, I use the analogy of human filiation while remaining aware of its limitations: generation in the Trinity is a true generation but it is not like human generation which involves the union of a man and woman, a body, succession in time, etc. On the other hand, the human generation of Christ is unlike other human generations in that it was virginal. If in my effort to understand something of the Trinity, I take as the basis for my analogy the mental conception of a word, I must also remember the limitations imposed by the fact of the infinity of God, the fact that the "Word" in the Trinity is a Person, etc.

Nevertheless, in this matter of analogy, since Christ is truly man, truly the son of Mary, his human nature is an especially privileged analogue by which God, the Trinity, can be known analogically.

As we pass now to a consideration of the inspired word, we should bear the foregoing considerations in mind. There is here also, a sort of "communication of idiom" when we consider the Bible in the concrete: an oracle, a story, a psalm, etc. We may say that we hear the word of God which bears the power of God. Then if I wish to describe this concrete divine-human reality, I am obliged to employ a whole series of human qualities which are present because it is truly human language, and literature.

86

But if I wish to understand the divine aspect of this concrete reality, its divine quality as such, then I no longer use a "communication of idiom" but analogy, aware of course of its limitations. I can arrive at a partial understanding of this word of God outside Himself by making an analogy with human speech. Since it is an analogy, there will not be correspondence at every point, and I must recognize this if I am not to slip into equivocation. Nevertheless, the inspired language, the biblical word, occupies a privileged position in our attempt to understand the divine Word.

We could put it this way: If we wish to understand or say anything with regard to the divine aspect of the inspired word, which is the divine word addressed to man, then we cannot use a communication of idiom, but analogy. We must consider human language in general, then more particularly, and finally the language of the Bible as an especially valuable analogue. If we wish to know or say anything about the divine-human word, then we must use the way of interchange of predicates as applied to the concrete fact of language; and we must describe the human reality assumed by God.

The first consideration, that of the divine aspect of the inspired word, was treated briefly in Chapter 1, using the analogy of human language in general and employing as common point of reference the notion of "manifestation." In this chapter we have reflected upon the mystery of the union of the divine and the human. As our study progresses, we will speak of the concrete reality giving to it the name, "the inspired word" and concentrating especially on the fact of its being a human word and human literature.

If we wish to avoid the danger of equivocation, we must bear these distinctions in mind. Whatever of revelation and grace is contained in the inspired word, accrues to it because it has been assumed by the divine word to man become incarnate in a word truly human. If we concentrate our attention here on describing the wealth of meaning and power contained in the human word, that is only because it is the verbal body in which divine revelation and grace has become incarnate. That is why we have entitled our study *The Inspired Word*, putting the accent on the concrete fact of the Bible as a reality both divine and human.

Bibliography for Chapter 2

The Action of the Spirit. The question of word and its relation to human thought and divine revelation has not received sufficient study. We have already given a bibliography for the biblical background of the concept, and there will be a bibliography in Chapter 4 in regard to the linguistic aspects. Here it will suffice to mention the short article by H. Krings, "Wort," in *Handbuch Theologischer Grundbegriffe*, ed. by H. Volk and H. Fries, Munich, 1963, also the articles in the biblical dictionaries mentioned in Chapter 1. There are two studies of the concept of the word in Origen: von Balthasar, *Parole et Mystère chez Origene*, Paris, 1957; R. Gögler, *Zur Theologie des Biblischen Wortes bei Origenes*, Düsseldorf, 1963.

Inspiration and the Incarnation. For a discussion of the comparison incarnate Word—inspired word, the fundamental study is that by H. de Lubac in his *Exégèse Médiévale*, vol. 2, pp. 181–197, "Verbum Abbreviatum." There is an article in *JTS* 6, 1955, pp. 87–90, by J. Crehan entitled "The Analogy between *Verbum Dei Incarnatum* and *Verbum scriptum* in the Fathers" (cf. the discussion concerning this work in Chapter 2, n. 8). Origen's views have exerted a great influence in Christian thought in this regard, as the works by von Balthasar and Gögler mentioned above witness. There is an interesting article by H. Schelkle, "Sacred Scripture and Word of God," in *Dogmatic vs. Biblical Theology*, ed. by H. Vorgrimler, Baltimore, 1964; and the work by Mowinckel, *The Old Testament as the Word of God*, mentioned in Chapter 1, is also helpful. A good résumé of present thought on this question may be found in C. Charlier, "Le Christ, Parole de Dieu," in *La Parole de Dieu en Jésus Christ*, Cahiers de l'actualité religieuse, no. 15, Paris, 1961, while a profound analysis of the philosophical basis for our analogous predication of the term "word" of the Son of God may be found in B. Lonergan's articles in *TS* 7, 1964, pp. 349–392; 8, 1947, pp. 35–79, 404–444; 10, 1949, pp. 3–40, 359–393; and also *De Deo Trino*, vol. 2, *Pars Systematica*, Rome, 1964.

Negative Aspects. The best treatment is that of C. Pesch (cf. Appendix).

Four Analogies. For a discussion of the cognitive function of symbol there is, in addition to the work of Söhngen cited in the text (*Analogie und Metaphern*), the work of W. Stählin, *Symbolon. Vom gleichnishaften Denken,* Stuttgart, 1958. A more general work, but in English, is that by E. Cassirer mentioned in Chapter 1 (*The Philosophy of Symbolic Forms,* esp. vol. 1). The function of symbols in religion is studied by A. Brunner in *Die Religion. Eine Philosophische Untersuchung auf geschichtlicher Grundlage,* Freiburg, 1956 (cf. the remarks of G. McCool in *IPQ* 1, 1961, pp. 671–81). There have been some interesting articles on the question of symbol, analogy, and religious language in recent philosophical periodicals. Since there is little work in English in book form, some of the more important articles will be listed here: M. J. Charlesworth, "Linguistic Analysis and Language About God," *IPQ* 1, 1961, pp. 193–167, and J. Ross, in the same volume of *IPQ* (pp. 633–662), where there is an interesting discussion of R. McInerny's *The Logic of Analogy,* The Hague, 1961, carried on by D. Burrell and J. Ross; another aspect can be seen in the same volume of *IPQ* (pp. 191–218) in the article by P. Ricoeur, "The Hermeneutics of Symbols and Philosophical Reflection," which is extremely helpful; earlier ideas of the same author can be seen in the translation of his article (*Espirit,* 1959) found in *PT* 4, 1960, pp. 192–207, "The Symbol, Food for Thought." Finally, there are some very enlightening (though difficult) pages in B. Lonergan's *Insight,* 2nd ed., New York, 1958 (consult the index under "Symbol" and "Analogy," as well as Chapter 20, "Special Transcendent Knowledge."

Instrument. Since these concepts are more familiar, there is less need for bibliographical material in this book. The fundamental work for the division of the tract on inspiration into an analysis of the analogies is A. Bea, *De Inspiratione et Inerrantia Sacrae Scripturae,* Rome, 1947; the analogies that he uses are: *theopneustos,* instrument, dictation, and author. There is a select bibliography up until 1946. On the notion of instrument, cf. R. Krumholtz, "Instrumentality and the *Sensus Plenior,*" *CBQ* 20, 1958, pp. 200–205. In Chapter 2, we insisted more on the image aspect of these analogies, putting the emphasis on their concrete, cultural realizations.

Dictation. A. Bea, "Libri sacri Deo dictante conscripti," *EstEc* 34, 1960, pp. 329–337, and in the book of E. R. Curtius, *European Literature in the Latin Middle Ages,* New York, 1963, p. 75ff., "Ars dictaminis."

A Messenger. There is a good historical résumé and bibliography in the article by James Ross, "The Prophet as Yahweh's Messenger," in *Israel's Prophetic Heritage,* Essays in Honor of James Muilenburg, ed. by B. W. Anderson and W. Harrelson, New York, 1962, pp. 98–107. Ross briefly discusses the work of C. Westermann, *Grundformen prophetischer Rede,* Munich, 1962, which is very thorough in its historical analysis of the history of this idea in biblical research and some-what unique in its conclusions.

An Author and the Characters He Creates. Generally, works which deal with the art of writing fiction touch on this aspect in one way or another. The fundamental work from the aspect of literary criticism is that by R. Wellek and A. Warren, *Theory of Literature,* New York, 1956; the bibliographical material there is quite complete. There is a selection of statements by authors themselves in *Writers on Writing,* ed. by W. Allen, New York, 1948, Chapter 13 "Characters," and F. Fergusson has some very penetrating remarks in his *The Human Image in Dramatic Literature,* New York, 1957. There is a wealth of insight to be gained by reading E. Auerbach, *Mimesis,* New York, 1953, even though his line of investigation is slightly different.

God the Author of Scripture. The two fundamental articles are A. Bea, "Deus Auctor Scripturae: Herkunft und Bedeutung der Formel," *Ang* 20, 1943, pp. 16-31, and N. I. Weyns, "De notione inspirationis biblicae iuxta Concilium Vaticanum," *Ang* 30, 1953, pp. 315–336. There is a further discussion of this analogy and reference to the work of K. Rahner in Chapter 8.

3. The Witness of the Scriptures

We are about to embark on a new journey, through the realm of the Scriptures, in order to enrich our idea of the meaning of inspiration. We will begin this trip by repeating once again the words of the Creed, 'Who spoke through the prophets," and then we will visit the sacred text itself, not with the idea of finding proofs and arguments, but simply to allow what we meet there to form in us a more realistic idea of the mystery. We will base ourselves on the facts as they are available to us. It would be hazardous, indeed, to 'try to form some clear, precise idea of inspiration without ever consulting the inspired text. We would be running the risk of finding ourselves forced to leave out of our brilliantly constructed system some information or even some books of the Bible. Our idea of inspiration must be spacious enough to allow room for all its concrete expressions and all the varieties of the inspired books. It is not up to us to set boundaries for the Spirit.

THE OLD TESTAMENT

The Prophets

The Creed itself invites us to begin our study with a consideration of the prophets. St. Thomas never wrote a tract on inspiration. Rather, what he has to say on the subject is to be found in his tract on "prophecy," and it is from there that many modern authors have drawn much of what they have to say on inspiration. The prophets were not the only men who had the gift of inspiration, but in them we are able to see this reality in its most dynamic form, and to derive therefrom a clearer idea of the action of the

91

Spirit. The prophets are the "prime analogates" of our study, and so it will be well to begin with them.

Vocation. Three of the prophets have left us a rather detailed description of their vocation. Once, when Isaiah[1] was in the Temple, he beheld Yahweh on His throne, "and the train of his garment filled the Temple." He heard the song of the Seraphim, "and the threshold of the entrance shook, and the whole place was filled with smoke." He cried out, "Woe is me, I am doomed! For I am a man of unclean lips, living among a people of unclean lips." The first reaction of the future prophet was the painful awareness, not of any incapacity or inelegance in his speech, but of the fact that his language, that of his whole people, was profane and utterly unequal to the holiness which he experienced so overwhelmingly. A sacred fire borne by one of the seraphim touched and sanctified his lips. He spoke the same language, and had acquired no new style or talent for expression, but now his lips had been made holy and consecrated; somehow, they had been transferred to the realm of the divine holiness or transcendence. He then received his mission. He heard the voice of Yahweh saying, " 'Whom shall I send? Who will go for us?' 'Here I am,' I said; 'send me!' And He replied, 'Go and say to this people . . .' " His whole mission consisted in speaking in behalf of God to the people of God. If we were to express this mission in our well-defined modern categories, we would say that the prophet had received a commission and corresponding charism in the order of speech or language. Nothing is said about committing anything to writing. Many other particular commissions were to be given to Isaiah, specifying this initial calling, yet these, too, were always in the realm of speech and proclamation.

The Book of Jeremiah[2] begins with an account of his vocation. Even before he was born, God had chosen him, sanctified or set him apart, and made him a prophet. Jeremiah well understood the role that God was giving him, and he objected: "Ah, Lord God, I know not how to speak, I am too young." Many commentators have wanted to see in these words an attempt, inspired by fear, to

[1] Cf. Is 6.

[2] Jer 1. Von Reventlow, in an extreme reaction against the psychological preoccupations of a former generation, has tried to reduce everything to a set of prophetic formulas. Cf. H. von Reventlow, *Das Amt des Propheten bei Amos,* Göttingen, 1962.

avoid the inevitable consequences of the prophetic vocation. But, in fact, the objection makes its plea by pointing to an incapacity in the realm of language. Obviously, Jeremiah knew how to speak; he had just framed his objection to God. His reluctance is based on his inability to speak as a prophet; perhaps he felt a lack of literary training. God responds by asserting the efficacy of the mission on which He has determined to send Jeremiah: "Wherever I send you, you will go; and whatever I command you, you will declare." The commission is then sealed by a ritual, sacramental gesture. "Then the Lord extended His hand and touched my mouth saying, "See, I place My words in your mouth! This day I set you over nations and over kingdoms, to root up and to tear down, to destroy and to demolish, to build and to plant." Jeremiah's mission was to speak; he was to declare the message of God in words of power. This is what characterizes his vocation; no mention is made here of any obligation to write. God had conferred on him the charism of speech, in order to make known and effect His will.

Ezekiel, though he tells his story with less restraint and clarity, conveys the same fundamental notions. He is commissioned: "I send you to them" (2:4). He receives the word of the Lord: ". . . Open your mouth and eat what I shall give you. It was then I saw a hand stretched out to me, in which was a written scroll which He unrolled before me. It was covered with writing, front and back, and written on it there were words of lamentation, mourning, and woe. He said to me: Son of man, eat what is before you; eat this scroll, then go, speak to the house of Israel. So I opened my mouth and He gave me the scroll to eat. Son of man, He then said to me, feed your belly and fill your stomach with this scroll I am giving you. I ate it, and it was as sweet as honey in my mouth. He said: Son of man, go now to the house of Israel and speak My words to them" (2:8—3:4). The predominant theme here is also one of speaking. The scroll already contained writing; the prophet was able to make out the various literary types that were written there. But his task was not to take the scroll in his hands and, unrolling it, read out its burden to the people. He was obliged, rather, to eat the scroll, assimilate what it held, and then from this interior fullness utter his message. There is nothing mechanistic about the prophetic activity; it is vital, dynamic, and interior. In the same section as that which we quoted above, we read that God said to Ezekiel: "Son of man, . . . take into your heart all My words that I speak to you; hear them well. Now go to the exiles, to your countrymen and say to them . . ." The phrase "take into your heart" could also be translated "take by heart," or "memorize," but if this is the correct interpretation, it is a unique realization of the messenger aspect of the prophetic role.

The elements of prophetic vocation are thus seen to be three: mission, consecration, and speech. There is no hint here of dictaphones or school-boy repetition, but of a living and deeply personal activity. The lips of Isaiah were consecrated; Jeremiah received the word of God in his mouth, while Ezekiel had it penetrate his entrails.

Autobiography. The objective accounts of vocation which we have just seen, can be completed with some intimate autobiographical passages found in the prophets. Jeremiah's comments are the most explicit, and his work is particularly rich in these "modern" self-reflections. The task that God had laid on Jeremiah was not only difficult, but positively dangerous. Men either laughed at him or tried to kill him, and it finally occurred to Jeremiah that his only chance of avoiding persecution was to keep silent. He has left us an account of his subsequent prayer:

> You led me on, O Yahweh,
> and I let myself be led.
> You forced me, and you won.
> And I? —a laughingstock all day,
> sport for every passer-by.

> Whenever I speak, I shout Violence!
> Plunder is my cry.

> For Yahweh's word to me—
> scorn and derision all the day long.
> I said:
> I will not remember it,
> No more will I speak in his name.
> Then in my heart it turned to fire
> burning, imprisoned in my bones.
> I am weary holding it in,
> I can no longer.[3]

[3] Jer 20:7-9.

94

The prophet feels the word of God within his soul. It is like fire, burning in his very bones, or like molten lava, ready to erupt and spill out along the path of least resistance. This is a description which has much in common with that experience of creative compulsion attested to by many geniuses. But in Jeremiah's case, the deep source of the drive is the word of Yahweh. It does not take away liberty—Jeremiah had decided to keep silent, yet it is a force within him which demands realization. Ezekiel saw the problem of his liberty as a "case of conscience." He was a sentinel whose duty it was to cry "Danger!" If he shouted his warning, then he was not answerable for the lives of those who refused to take refuge; but if he kept silent, the guilt was his own.[4]

Prophetic Formulas. It is interesting to note that the phrases used in the prophetic messages all have reference to speech:

"The word of the Lord came to me."
"The word which was received by . . ."
"Listen to the word of the Lord."
"Thus says Yahweh."
"An oracle of Yahweh."

This word of the Lord is not distinct from the word of the prophet:

The House of Israel will refuse to listen to you, since they will not listen to Me (Ez 3:7).

I have sent them my servants, the prophets, morning and night, night and morning, yet they have not listened to Me or paid heed (Jer 7:25).

Confronted with such texts, it seems that the efforts of some moderns to separate within the oracles words that are God's from words that are the prophet's, are simply futile. There is a "communication of idiom" in these messages which recalls the relation established between an author and the characters he has created (the words of Hamlet and the words of Shakespeare). The prophet is the man of God (1 K 2:27), the man of the Spirit (Hos 9:7), the very mouth of God (Jer 15:19).

Literary Effort. Such descriptions of the prophet and the insistence on the identity of his message with that of God, might lead one to conclude that his role is that of a secretary or messenger, commissioned to record the dictation or memorize the message to

[4] Ez 33:1–9.

95

be delivered. But a close analysis of the actual writings of the prophets leads us to a very different conclusion. It is true that not every prophet has a fully developed personal style. Still, anyone can recognize the characteristics of a classical writter such as Isaiah and distinguish them from the romanticism of Jeremiah or the baroque of Ezekiel. If we approach these texts with the tools of literary criticism, we begin to appreciate how well some of these men both knew and practiced the writer's craft. We see them searching for onomatopoeia, assembling assonance, laying out a chiastic phrase of six or more members, subtly changing a rhythmic formula, constructing an oracle piece by piece, exploiting the possibility of a topical image or formula, sometimes changing it and sometimes consciously modelling themselves on a predecessor. We come to know these men in their toil, and we can almost reach out and wipe the sweat from their brow as their poem or oracle takes shape, chiselled from the quarry of language. When our analysis has allowed us to share and appreciate this effort, we are prepared to offer the prophet a medal for his honest and capable craftsmanship. But he pushes it away: "It is the word of God." Strange dictation which costs its literary fashioner so dearly. The fact of the matter is that it is not dictation at all.

If we wish to reconcile these two facts, that of the obvious literary effort of the prophet, and his repeated phrase, "the word of the Lord," we will have to follow another path than that indicated by the term "dictation." The Spirit's action is not one of dictating a message word by word, it is not something mechanical at all. It is found deep within the wellsprings of the act of language, and more precisely at the sources of literary effort.

This much we can learn from the prophets, our "prime analogates." If anyone would be expected to have received his words immediately from God, if anyone should merely receive and repeat the divine message, it is the prophet. Yet precisely here, in the obvious tension between the conscious toil of the literary craft and the oft-repeated "word of the Lord," we begin to appreciate the dimensions of the mystery of inspiration. It is something that transpires deep inside one; it is marvellous yet hidden.

The divine and the human are both present; the divine elevates the human, it does not suppress it. God's call elevates the personality of the prophet rather than destroys it; literary sensibilities are polarized, creativity is delivered not chained. A prophet belongs to his society, pertains to a certain school of prophecy or literary tradition, and may have a function within some religious institution. The prophets are the most forceful personalities of the Old Testament. For the Spirit knows how to awaken and sustain the forces of true greatness. A writer of any stature does not reveal his talent in creating literary puppets; his greatness does not make his characters puny, but just the contrary. So, too, the action of the Spirit reveals its power in raising up great men, endowed with literary gifts of a high order. But there are also lesser lights in the literary world of the Bible, craftsmen of a more modest achievement, "minor prophets" according to the standards of literary excellence.

Sapiential Literature

The conclusions of the preceding analysis can be strengthened by studying another group of men who have contributed to the composition of the Scriptures. By way of example, we will choose out one of these writers, a fascinating personality who calls himself "the Preacher." He is a confirmed non-conformist who turns his disenchantment into challenge and makes his attack by way of suggestion. Let us take a few of the phrases he uses to introduce his observations, and compare them with the formulas of the prophets:

I applied my mind to search and investigate in wisdom all things that are done under the sun (Eccl 1:13).

And I said to myself . . . (1:16) ("Thus says the Lord").

. . . yet when I applied my mind to know wisdom and knowledge . . . (1:17).

I said to myself (2:1) ("Listen to the word of the Lord").

I have considered the task which God has appointed for men (3:10).

I turned and looked at all the oppression that take place under the sun (4:1) ("The word of the Lord came to me").

I have seen all manner of things in my vain days . . . (7:15).

97

I turned my thoughts toward knowledge; I sought and pursued wisdom and reason (7:25).

All this I took to heart . . . (9:1).

I said: "Better wisdom than power . . ." (9:16) ("What I have heard from the Lord, I pass on to you").

And so it goes throughout his work. Never once does he say that he received the word of the Lord; never is there any pretension to a divine oracle. On the contrary, we hear constantly of his observation, study, and reflection, all reported in the first person, yet in a way that never strikes us as heavy. We never get the impression of pedantic self-sufficiency, but rather of disillusionment and resignation.[5]

But though our author tells us quite frankly of his efforts and their results, the Church tells us that his work is part of the sacred Scripture, the word of God. The writer felt no fire or breeze of the Spirit, yet the Church says that his book is inspired.

Certainly, in this case we cannot think of inspiration as some process of dictation. Inspiration did not eliminate the man's personality, but rather enshrined it. If these words, so pathetically human, are also the words of God, it is because somewhere deep within the act which gave them existence, there was the action of the Holy Spirit, mysterious yet effective. This motion from God must have something in common with the motion we discerned in the prophets, if we are able to use the same term, "inspiration," of both of them. Yet the great difference between these two extreme instances of the same divine action seems to recommend the suggestion of Benoit, that we take the term "inspiration" as representing an analogous concept.

There is another author in the sapiential tradition who has left us a somewhat different account of his literary activity. This man, Jesus Ben Sirach, the last in the series of Hebrew wisdom writers, is fully aware of and quite content with his literary talents and effort.

[5] O. Loretz interprets the use of the first person as a literary device of the author. This does not invalidate what we have said, but only highlights the literary self-consciousness of the author, who certainly then is making no pretensions at passing on a revelation received. Nevertheless, we do not think that the "I" is a literary device (cf. O. Loretz, "Zur Darbietungsform 'ich-Erzählung' im Buche Qohelet," CBQ 25, 1963, pp. 46–59).

He tells us that his travels have taught him much (34:9–12), and he often appeals to his experience. In his view, "when an intelligent man hears words of wisdom, he approves them and adds to them" (21:14), and he hints modestly that he knows more than he is saying (34:11). The prophet called out: "Hear the word of the Lord"; Ben Sirach says: "Listen to me, O princes."

In Chapter 39 of his work, Ben Sirach gives us a sketch of the ideal wise man. It is a poem of four strophes in which the first speaks of his studies, the second of his activities at court, his journeys and his prayer, the third of wisdom as the fruit of study and prayer, and the fourth of the glory accruing to a man of these attainments:

> How different the man who devotes himself
> to the study of the Law of the Most High:
> He explores the wisdom of the men of old
> and occupies himself with the prophecies;
> He treasures the discourses of famous men,
> and goes to the heart of involved sayings;
> He studies obscure parables,
> and is busied with the hidden meanings of the sages.
>
> He is in attendance on the great
> and has entrance to the ruler.
> He travels among the peoples of foreign lands
> to learn what is good and evil among men.
> His care is to seek the Lord, his Maker,
> to petition the Most High,
> To open his lips in prayer,
> to ask pardon for his sins.
>
> Then, if it pleases the Lord Almighty,
> he will be filled with the spirit of understanding;
> He will pour forth his words of wisdom
> and in prayer give thanks to the Lord,
> Who will direct his knowledge and his counsel,
> as he meditates upon his mysteries.
> He will show the wisdom of what he has learned
> and glory in the Law of the Lord's covenant.
>
> Many will praise his understanding;
> his fame can never be effaced;

Unfading will be his memory,
through all generations his name will live;
Peoples will speak of his wisdom,
and in assembly sing his praises.
While he lives he is one out of a thousand,
and when he dies his renown will not cease.[6]

The wise man has recourse to God in prayer, and receives from Him the spirit of wisdom, not that of prophecy; he goes to the Scriptures and meditates on the prophecies and the sayings of famous men. But even this act is a purely human effort.

Once again, we see the same two aspects of the mystery. The fruit of this human reflection and literary effort is the word of God; the man who has applied himself so earnestly has received the gift of inspiration. Our idea of inspiration, then, must be supple enough to adapt itself to these undeniable facts presented by the Scriptures. There is a passage in Ben Sirach which, in fleeting glance, seems to give evidence that our professional wise man himself had some inkling of the mystery at work within him. At any rate, his comparison is interesting, especially in the light of his obvious regard for the inspired books which he knew so well: "I pour out instruction like prophecy and bestow it on generations to come" (24:31).

It is significant to observe in this connection that the prophetic formula "the word of God" has its exact equivalent in the description given of the sayings of the ancient scholars, "the words of the wise men." [7] This wisdom is a human achievement, an international possession characterized by a free exchange of ideas whose basic theme is man—which is not to say that it is irreligious—and whose methods consist in the thoroughly human procedure of observation and experimentation.[8] A comparison of this literature with that of the prophets indicates to us how deep and subtle the action of the Spirit can sometimes be. These scholars and well-travelled men of letters have written and published works which we receive as the word of God.

This, we feel, is what Theodore of Mopsuestia intended to say in

[6] Sir 39:1–11.
[7] Cf. Prv 22:17; 24:23.
[8] Cf. W. Zimmerli, "Zur Struktur der alttestamentlichen Weisheit," ZAW 51, 1933, pp. 177-204.

one of those passages which have unjustly earned him the reputation for a certain biblical rationalism and a desire to restrict the extent of inspiration:

Among works written for human instruction are to be counted the writings of Solomon, that is, the Book of Proverbs and Ecclesiastes. These he composed on his own initiative as a service to others. He did not receive the grace of prophecy but that of prudence, which is a different gift, as Paul has indicated.[9]

Theodore does not use the term "inspiration," but he does accord to Solomon a charism which we would call part of the charism of prophecy. His purpose is not to deny or limit the gift of inspiration, but to point out an objective difference between the sapiential writings and those of the prophets. Ben Sirach claimed for himself a "spirit of wisdom," not prophecy. A man such as Theodore, writing at the beginning of the fifth century, does not view the question of inspiration exactly as we do.[10]

Other Writers

The greater part of the writings of the Old Testament lie somewhere between the two extremes we have just considered. Many times it is very difficult to determine exactly to which group a certain work belongs, or which type of literature it approximates. Should we, for instance, classify the narrators of history, Genesis, Exodus, Josuah, Samuel, and Kings as prophets or wise men? Jewish tradition has always called the "historic" books outside of the Torah "nebi'im," or "prophets," while Moses, whose name is linked with the Torah, is called the greatest of the prophets.

The technical name for the Decalogue is "The words of Yahweh," and the term seems to have been extended to cover other legal presciptions. The narrators of history, insofar as they interpret events with the aid of a special light, share in the charism of

---

[9] "His quae pro doctrina hominum scripta sunt et Salomonis libri connumerandi sunt, id est Proverbia et Ecclesiastes, quae ipse ex sua persona ad aliorum utilitatem composuit, cum prophetiae quidem gratiam non accepisset, prudentiae vero gratiam quae evidenter altera est praeter illa secundum beati Pauli vocem." Mansi 9, 223.

[10] For an evaluation of the text we have just cited, and for a more complete study of acts of the Council of Constantinople where the text is cited, cf. R. Devreesse, Essai sur Théodore de Mopsueste, Studi e Testi, no. 141, Rome, 1948, esp. pp. 34–35, 243–258, 283–285.

prophecy, yet in their method of proceeding they bear a closer resemblance to the sapiential tradition. They collect material, consult court archives, and preserve and elaborate ancient poems. They make no appeal to a special revelation, and they never speak of their work as the "word of God." In some cases, the account of Paradise and the Fall for instance, we find clear traces of that type of intellectual reflection characteristic of the wise men.[11] The author of the Book of Deuteronomy poses theological questions to himself and seeks the explanation for certain facts of sacred history. His activity is a kind of "faith seeking understanding" which brings him close to the outlook of the wise men. For just as the author of Deuteronomy reflects on sacred history, so Ben Sirach reflects on the sacred text. In *apocalyptic literature*, the writer seeks the meaning of history, organizes the past according to a schema of periods, and transposes his reflections into a series of elaborate intellectual allegories. If he prefaces his work by appealing to a divine revelation, it is because such is the literary convention for this type of writing. Those who wrote the Psalms never think to call their poems the word of God, since they are the words in which the people are to make answer to God.

Then, to this list of authors, we must add an indeterminate number of those who contributed to the inspired text as we have it today. There were editors, compilers of anthologies, and men who inserted glosses or explanatory notes to bring the text "up to date." All of these shared in the gift of inspiration. They may have been prophets of a sort, pointing out the relevance of ancient texts, or, as was most often the case, scholars whose activity resembled that of the wise men.

We may sum up our considerations, then, by saying that the greater part of the Old Testament does not contain that type of literature which we call prophetic in the strict sense of the term, but represents rather a type of activity approximating that of the wisdom tradition. Nevertheless, we accept the whole of the Old Testament as the word of God. If the Letter to the Hebrews mentions only the prophets when it says, "God spoke to our fathers through the prophets," and if the Creed employs the same phrase, "Who spoke through the prophets," we know that all the Old Tes-

---

[11] Cf. L. Alonso Schökel, "Motivos sapienciales y de alianza en Gn 2–3, *Bib* 43, 1962, pp. 295–316.

tament is prophetic, because it looks forward to the New. We know, too, that all of sacred Scripture, Old and New Testament, is the word of God. The councils apply the term "inspiration" to the whole of the Bible. From this it follows that we cannot possibly conceive of inspiration as some kind of standardized mechanical dictation. It is an action of the Holy Spirit which moves a man mysteriously yet unfailingly from within the very wellspring of his free activity. Given the distance which separates the two extreme instances of inspiration, prophetic and sapiential, it seems quite reasonable to accept the term "inspiration" as analogous predication, and thereby to acknowledge the great range of the Spirit's power, moving men who were so different, who lived in social and political milieux so varied, and who wrote a literature so prolific in types, in order to reveal God to us in His word.

For the needs of the present investigation into the nature of inspiration, the division of Hebrew literature which we have already made is quite sufficient. It is possible to apply the norms of literary criticism to the contents of Scripture, and to differentiate the various modes of inspiration according to the work produced. But such a classification would occupy too much space, and would not perhaps be of very great use. The variety of literary types or genera employed by the authors of the Old Testament witnesses to the vibrant religious life and rich literary activity of the people of God. It testifies also to the virtuosity of the Spirit, Who awakened and sustained this many-sided activity in order to address us, using the whole range of human language. "God spoke to our forefathers in fragmentary and varied fashion." [12]

The scholastic theologians were quite appreciative of this rich variation, and they often discussed the various "modes" of sacred Scripture. They held that the science of theology was based on sacred Scripture, but that the text itself did not proceed by way of science. The mode of science includes *definition* (defining the terms), *division* (refining the concepts by distinguishing), and *argument* (deduction and syllogism), whereas the mode of Scripture

[12] A description and classification of the various literary genera can be found in most introductions to the Old Testament: A. Robert and A. Tricot, *Guide to the Bible*, 2 vols., New York, 1955–1960; A. Robert and A. Feuillet, *Introduction à la Bible*, Bruges, 1959, vol. 1; O. Eissfeldt, *Einleitung in das Alte Testament*, 3rd. ed., Tübingen, 1963; also the articles by L. Alonso Schökel on Hebrew poetry in *DBS* and the New Catholic Encyclopedia.

is characterized by "narration, commandment, prohibition, exhortation, instruction, commination, promise, supplication, and praise."
This variety is explained by the end which Scripture has in view;
it must reach all men, for to them is it directed.

For instance, were a man to remain unmoved by a command or a
prohibition, he might perhaps be moved by a concrete example; were
this to fail, he might be moved by the favors shown him; were this
again to fail, he might be moved by wise admonitions, trustworthy
promises, or terrifying threats, and thus be stirred, if not in one way,
then in another, to devotion and praise of God.[13]

Alexander of Hales enumerates five "modes" of sacred Scripture:

Command, as in the law and the Gospel; example, as in the historical
books; exhortation, as in the books of Solomon and the letters of the
Apostle; revelation in the prophecies; prayer in the Psalms.[14]

He goes on, in true scholastic style, to justify this multiplicity by
an analysis of the four causes of Scripture:

The modes of Scripture ought to be manifold, both by reason of their
efficient cause, as well as by reason of their final and material cause
. . . . The first is by reason of efficient cause, that is the Holy Spirit
Who is (according to Wis 7:22) a Spirit of understanding, manifold
and unique. Therefore, in order that the mode of its efficient cause
should be apparent, sacred science ought to be complex and many-
sided. The second is by reason of material cause, which is the manifold
wisdom of God. And therefore [sacred science] ought to be many-
sided in order to correspond to the mode of its material cause. The
third is by reason of final cause, which is instruction in those things
which pertain to salvation.[15]

---

[13] ". . . narrativus, praeceptorius, prohibitivus, comminatorius, prommis-
sivus, deprecatorius, et laudativus . . . ut si quis non movetur ad praecepta
et prohibita, saltem moveatur per exempla narrata; si quis non per haec
movetur, moveatur per beneficia sibi ostensa; si quis nec per haec movetur,
moveatur per monitiones sagaces, per promissiones veraces, per comminationes
terribiles, ut sic saltem excitetur ad devotionem et laudem Dei." St. Bonaventure, The Works of St. Bonaventure, vol. 2, The Breviloquium, tr. by José de
Vinck, Paterson, 1963.
[14] ". . . modus dicitur esse praeceptivus (in lege et evangelio), exempli-
ficativus (in historicis libris), exhortativus (in libris Salomonis et epistulis
apostolicis), revelativus (in prophetis), orativus (in psalmis), quia huiusmodi
affectui pietatis." Cited by Pesch, no. 157, Summa I, 1.
[15] "Sacrae Scripturae modum ratione efficientiae et ratione finis ac materiae

Not only were the medieval scholastics sensitive to these various literary types in the scriptures, but they applied themselves to finding a theological reason to explain them.[16]

Pesch allows that there were various degrees of intensity in the graces of inspiration given to the writers of the sacred text, but he will not concede that there are various degrees of inspiration in the books themselves, as though one book could be more inspired than another.[17] However, in the following article[18] he does add a very nuanced treatment, explaining how the various statements in the Bible are the word of God. His point of view is too cerebral and tends toward a certain atomism, but still, he opens up a very interesting line of approach.

Conclusion

Our trip through the Old Testament, rather than provide us with a precise, easily managed concept of inspiration, has imposed even greater flexibility and openness on our thinking. Our concept or idea might be less precise, but at least it corresponds to reality, and allows a place to all the facts. Later, we will have occasion to study more closely some aspects of the mystery which we have discovered in our investigation.[19]

THE INSPIRATION OF THE NEW TESTAMENT

In the New Testament, something new and definitive takes place. The various words have been spoken, now the Word resounds. It is a Word which can be heard and seen and touched;[20] a Word which

---

multiformem esse decuit. . . . Prima est ratio efficientis, id est Spiritus Sancti, qui est (ut dicitur Sap 7:22) Spiritus intellegentiae multiplex unicus. Propterea, ut in scientia sacra modus efficientis appareat, debet esse multiplex seu multiformis. Secunda est ratio materiae, quae est multiformis sapientia Dei. Propterea, ut materiae modus respondeat, debet esse multiformis. Tertia est ratio finis, qui est instructio in iis, quae pertinent ad salutem." Summa I, 3, Pesch, ibid.

[16] Curtius describes how this theory of the "modes" reached as far as the poetic theories of Dante. *European Literature and the Latin Middle Ages*, p. 222ff.

[17] No. 429.

[18] Nos. 436–450.

[19] Cf. ch. 7.

[20] 1 Jn 1:1.

justifies all that has gone before: their summation (*verbum abbre-viatum*) and explanation. This Word is complete and definitive, addressed to all men, because He is the true Light. In order to reach all men, this Word, Who is Jesus Christ, must continue to resound, to be present and alive to all generations. "For this deliverance was first announced through the lips of the Lord Himself; those who heard Him confirmed it to us . . ." [21]

In order that His word, He Himself as Word, might continue to resound, Christ sent His apostles and sends them still, and to them He gives His Spirit. The apostles, both by name (*apo-stello*) and by function are the "sent ones"; their mission is precisely their "mission" from Christ. It is with this theme that the Gospel closes —and yet remains open. [22]

The Apostles and Prophets

The fact that the vocation of the apostles is to be sent, established a relationship between them and the prophets of the Old Testament who were also sent to proclaim the word of God. St. Augustine has said it briefly:

He, Who before He descended to us sent the prophets, is the same Who sent the apostles after His ascension. [23]

He repeats the same thing elsewhere:

God spoke first by the prophets, then by Himself, and then by the apostles, what He judged sufficient . . . [24]

The comparison between the apostles and the prophets is frequent in the New Testament. The passage in the Epistle to the Ephesians which describes the Church as "built on the foundation of the apostles and prophets, with Christ Jesus Himself as the cornerstone" (2:20), seems to intend a reference to the prophets of the New Testament as other passages in the same letter indicate (3:5; 4:11). However, it would be difficult to exclude completely any reference to the prophets of the Old Testament.

[21] Heb 2:3.
[22] Cf. Mt 28:18–20; Mk 16:15–16; Lk 24:47–49; Jn 20:21.
[23] *Proinde qui Prophetas ante descensionem suam praemisit, ipse et Apostolos post ascensionem suam misit."* "De Consensu Evangelistarum," *PL* 34, 1070.
[24] "*Hic prius per Prophetas, deinde per seipsum, postea per Apostolos, quantum satis esse judicavit. . . ."* "City of God, bk. 11," *PL* 41, 318.

In this same line of thought, we find a very significant statement in the First Epistle of Peter (1:10–12)

This salvation was the theme which the prophets pondered and explored, those who prophesied about the grace of God awaiting you. They tried to find out what was the time, and what the circumstances, to which the spirit of Christ in them pointed, foretelling the sufferings in store for Christ and the splendours to follow; and it was disclosed to them that the matter they treated of was not for their time, but for yours. And now it has been openly announced to you through preachers who brought you the Gospel in the power of the Holy Spirit sent from heaven. These are things that angels long to see into.

This somewhat difficult text compresses in a few lines the whole synthesis of what we have been saying. At the core of the mystery of inspiration lies the mystery of Christ, which is a mystery of "salvation" and "grace," and whose very life-center is found in His "sufferings" and "splendors to follow." This mystery was glimpsed and announced by the prophets, who had "the Spirit of Christ in them." Here we see the inspiration of the prophets described as an interior possession of a Spirit Who is the Spirit of Christ, enlightening them as to the mystery yet leaving them ignorant of the "time and circumstances" of its realization. "Now," that is, in this definitive era of salvation, the "preachers" have received the "Holy Spirit sent from heaven," from the glorified Christ. Their inspiration consists in possessing this Spirit, and in virtue of His power announcing the Gospel, the good news of salvation in Christ.

That which the apostles announced is the "word of God," and they do not hesitate to use the same prophetic formula:

This is why we thank God continually, because when we handed on God's message, you received it, not as the word of men, but as what it truly is, the very word of God at work in you who hold the faith.[25]

There are other formulas which indicate a very interesting transition in which the activity of God is predicated of Christ:

. . . When I come this time, I will show no leniency. Then you will have the proof you seek of the Christ who speaks through me, the Christ who, far from being weak with you, makes his power felt among you.[26]

[25] 1 Th 2:13–14.
[26] 2 Cor 13:3.

It is interesting to observe that the words translated as "speaks through me" are literally "speaks *in* me." The Greek construction here is identical with that in the Epistle to the Hebrews: "God has spoken to us *in* the Son" (Heb 1:2). Christ speaks *in* St. Paul (2 Cor 13:3). The Greek preposition *"en"* establishes an intimate and immediate relationships whose theological importance is stressed elsewhere in the text: "as the Father sent me, so I send you" (Jn 20:21). There is another text in the same Second Epistle to the Corinthians (2:17) which echoes this same theme: "We are not like many others, peddlers of God's word; rather, commissioned by God and in God's presence, we speak in Christ." This second formula, "in Christ," recalls the prophetic "in the Spirit" (inspiration). This phrase is also represented in the New Testament:

Our Gospel came to you not in words alone, but in power and *in the Holy Spirit*" (1 Th 1:5).

[The mystery of Christ] was not made known to the men of former generations, but now it has been revealed to His holy apostles and prophets, *in the Spirit*" (Eph 3:5).

The same words are applied in St. Matthew's Gospel to a writer of the Old Testament:

Then how does David *in the Spirit* call Him Lord?" (22:43).

Distinctions and Unity

Can we divide the New Testament according to literary types as we did in the Old Testament? There would certainly seem to be some basis for division in the fact that there are Gospels, Acts, Epistles, and an Apocalypse. The divisions are not as clearly marked as in the Old Testament, but the same types seem to be represented.

But before distinguishing, we must appreciate the unity. The New Testament is one in Christ in a way that could never be said of the manifold variety found in the writings of the Old Testament. St. Paul, in his epistles, refers to his "Gospel," and considers that his activity either of preaching or writing is one of "evangelization."

When Paul writes: "according to my Gospel," we can use these words to show that all of the New Testament is Gospel, for among the writings of Paul there is none which is usually called a Gospel. What he preached and said was Gospel. However, he wrote those things which he preached and said, and therefore his writings are Gospel. If, then, the writings of Paul are Gospel, it follows that the same can be said of Peter, and, more generally, of those writings which treat of Christ's sojourn among us, or prepare for His Parousia, or which produce it in the souls of those who desire to receive Him Who stands at the door knocking and wishing to come into them: the Word of God.[27]

We might answer that, before the visit of Christ, the law and the prophets, since He Who was to make plain their mysteries had not yet come, did not contain the message according to the terms of the Gospel. But when the Savior came and gave body to the Gospel, by means of the Gospel He made of all these a sort of Gospel too.[28]

The reason for this profound inner unity lies in the fact that no one can add anything to the word of Christ. Christ as the Word, the expression and revelation of the Father, is infinitely complete. No one can add to the Father's self-expression. This is not to say that nothing can be added to the words that Christ spoke. These were limited in number, and many things that St. Paul says, Our Lord had not pronounced before him. But Christ did not only speak words; He is a Word, an expression, in His very being and in His acts and speech. Therefore, since Christ is the ultimate revelation of God, any new knowledge of God must consist in penetrating ever deeper into the fullness which dwells in Him. All of the New Testament is one, since it derives from and speaks of this mystery.

But is it not the role of the Spirit to teach us many things? Yes,

---

27 "Εστι δὲ προσαχϑῆναι ἀπὸ τῶν ὑπὸ Παύλου λεγομένων περὶ τοῦ πᾶσαν τὴν καινὴν εἶναι εὐαγγέλια, ὅταν γράφῃ Κατὰ τὸ εὐαγγέλιόν μου. Ἐν γράμματι ὑπὸ Παύλου οὐκ ἔχομεν βιβλίον εὐαγγέλιον συνήϑως καλούμενον. Ἀλλὰ πᾶν ὃ ἐκήρυσσε καὶ ἔλεγε τὸ εὐαγγέλιον ἦν. ἃ καὶ ἐκήρυσσε καὶ ἔλεγε, ταῦτα καὶ ἔγραφε. καὶ ἃ ἔγραφε ἄρα εὐαγγέλιον ἦν. Εἰ δὲ τὰ Παύλου εὐαγγέλιον ἦν, ἀκόλουϑον λέγειν ὅτι καὶ τὰ Πέτρου εὐαγγέλιον ἦν, καὶ ἁπαξαπλῶς τὰ συνιστάντα τοῦ Χριστοῦ ἐπιδημίαν, καὶ κατασκευάζοντα τὴν παρουσίαν αὐτοῦ, ἐμποιοῦντά τε αὐτὴν ταῖς ψυχαῖς τῶν βουλομένων παραδέξεσϑαι τὸν ἑστῶτα ἐπὶ τὴν ϑύραν, καὶ κρούοντα, καὶ εἰσελϑεῖν βουλόμενον εἰς τὰς ψυχὰς λόγον Θεοῦ. Origen, "Comm. on Jn 1:6," PG 14, 32.

28 Ἀεχϑείη δ᾽ ἂν πρὸς τοῦτο ὅτι πρὸ τῆς Χριστοῦ ἐπιδημίας ὁ νόμος καὶ οἱ προφῆται, ἄτε μηδέπω ἐληλυϑότος τοῦ τὰ ἐν αὐτοῖς μυστήρια σαφηνίζοντος, οὐκ εἶχον τὸ ἐπάγγελμα τοῦ περὶ τοῦ εὐαγγελίου ὅρου. Ὁ δὲ Σωτὴρ ἐπιδημήσας καὶ τὸ εὐαγγέλιον σωματοποιηϑῆναι ποιήσας, τῷ εὐαγγελίῳ πάντα ὡσεὶ εὐαγγέλιον πεποίηκεν. Ibid., "Jn 1:8," PG 14, 33.

but whatever He teaches, and whatever He taught the apostles, is contained in the mystery of Christ: "He will glorify me, for everything that he makes known to you he will draw from what is mine" (Jn 16:15). The Spirit adds nothing to the Word which is Christ and which stands revealed in His actions and speech. "All that the Father has is mine, and that is why I said, 'Everything that he makes known to you he will draw from what is mine'" (Jn 16:16). The letters and preaching of St. Paul are Gospel, and the same can be said of the other letters; the Book of Acts is specifically called part two of St. Luke's Gospel, and the Apocalypse is described as "the revelation of Jesus Christ, which God has given to Him to make known to His servants . . ." From this it follows that when we read the epistles of St. Paul, we are reading the word of Christ, even though these words were never pronounced by Christ.

With this unity firmly in mind, we can now go on to consider the variety present in the New Testament. St. Paul said in his letter to the Thessalonians (1 Th 4:15): "This I say on the word of the Lord." St. John Chrysostom comments: "Everything that Paul says is inspired, but what he says here he heard literally from God." [29] Interestingly enough, modern commentators prefer to see in the phrase "the word of the Lord" an instance of early tradition rather than a direct revelation. Nevertheless, the distinction indicated by St. John Chrysostom does represent a real difference in the way St. Paul acquired his knowledge about Christ. St. Paul had undoubtedly received many special revelations from God, and he knew many words of Christ from the oral tradition, but to these he added a profound and enlightened theological reflection which we might compare to the activity of the Hebrew wise men. St. Paul's way of using the Old Testament stems from the same tradition which gave us Ben Sirach, while on at least one occasion he expressly says that the doctrine he is giving is his own: "To the married I give this ruling, which is not mine but the Lord's . . . To the rest I say this, as my own word, not the Lord's . . . About virgins I have no ordinance of the Lord, but I give my judgment as one who by God's mercy is fit to be trusted" (1 Cor 7:10, 12, 25). At other times, we can trace the development of St. Paul's thought, as it grows in depth and clarity, as can be seen, for instance, in a com-

[29] "On 1 Th." Cf. ch. 2, n. 41.

parison of the Epistle to the Galatians with the more mature treatment of the same themes in the Epistle to the Romans. Inspiration did not mean for St. Paul the simple recording of what the Holy Spirit dictated or what he received as the words and statements of Christ. His charism did not dispense him from serious work, both theological and literary. There is a great difference between the theological treatise to the Romans and the "postcard" recommending Onesimus to Philemon; yet both these extremes and the whole New Testament range of literature which lies between them are the inspired word of God.[30]

The Gospels

The Word of God resounds in a unique way in the Gospels, which represent for us the words and deeds of Jesus, and this accounts for the special reverence and recognition which has always been accorded to them. But when we say that they hand on to us the words of Christ, what meaning does this phrase have?

Suppose that Christ decided to transmit His words in the most authentic way possible to all generations of men, and that He asked our advice on how best to do this. What would we answer? Probably our first suggestion would be a tape recorder. The preservation would be uniquely faithful, even down to the original tone of voice, and we would hear Jesus just as now we can listen to the address John XXIII gave at the opening of Vatican II. What better remembrance could we have? Why, we would even want to study Aramaic in order to understand for ourselves just what Our Lord had said. The fact that there were no electric means of preserving sound back in those days is not really an objection. God could have arranged things so that these machines would have

---

30 "*Qui nolunt inter epistulas Pauli eam recipere, quae ad Philemonem scribitur, aiunt non apostolum nec omnia Christo in se loquente dixisse, quia nec humana imbecillitas unum tenorem Spiritus Sancti ferre potuisset nec huius corpusculi necessitates sub praesentia Domini semper complerentur, velut disponere prandium, cibum capere. . . . His et ceteris eiusmodi volunt aut epistulam non esse Pauli, quae ad Philemonem scribitur, aut etiam, si Pauli sit, nihil habere quod aedificare possit, et a plerisque veteribus repudiatam, dum commendandi tantum scribatur officio, non docendi. . . . Sed mihi videtur, dum epistulam simplicitatis arguunt, suam imperitiam prodere, non intelligentes, quid in singulis sermonibus virtutis ac sapientiae lateat.*" St. Jerome, "Prologue to Phil," PL 26, 637–638.

been in existence when Christ came. It would have sufficed to turn the clock ahead a few centuries and everything would have been in readiness.

But God did not choose this method. We are often surprised when we think over the plans of God and imagine ways of improving them. We think that we could have done things a little more efficiently and simply. But God smiles at our childish pretensions. "Who is this that obscures divine plans with words of ignorance?" (Jb 38:2). A roll of tape is lifeless and mechanical, whereas God has chosen the path of the Incarnation, making use of living men.

Well, then, we have another solution, not as safe as the first, of course, but sufficiently reliable. Choose out the man with the best memory in the world. Someone who can retain and repeat exactly whole paragraphs and speeches after he has heard them only once. Or better, hire four of them or even a dozen and have them listen to everything that is said. Then, if one of them makes a mistake, the others will be able to act as a control. Now we have a system that is not mechanical, but human, consisting of a select group of collaborators. This will be more in keeping with the plan of the Incarnation.

Again, God only shakes His head at our brilliant scheme. "Who has directed the Spirit of the Lord, or has instructed Him as his counselor? Whom did he consult to gain knowledge? Who taught him the path of judgment, or showed him the way of understanding?" (Is 40:13–14). God did not seek out professional memory men, completely passive and quasi-automatic. It is not through such that the word of God will resound in authentic tones throughout the ages.

Christ chose a way which was more subtle and unexpected. And, let us have the humility to admit it, He has shown that His grasp of what was needed far exceeds our own. He ascended into heaven and from there He sent his Spirit with the task of teaching the apostles about the mystery of Christ. He brought to their minds whatever Jesus had said to them, and guided them in their mission of spreading and preserving Christ's message. Between His own words and the ever attentive ears of the Church, Christ has placed the mystery of inspiration. The New Testament, and in particular the four Gospels, are the word of Christ, not because they mechanically reproduce everything that Christ has said, but because they are written under the impulse of the Spirit Whom Christ has sent.

I have told you all this while I am still here with you; that your Advocate, the Holy Spirit Whom the Father will send in My name, will teach you everything, and will call to mind all that I have told you.[31]

But when your Advocate has come, Whom I will send you from the Father—the Spirit of Truth that issues from the Father—he will bear witness to me. And you also are my witnesses, because you have been with me from the first.[32]

However, when he comes Who is the Spirit of truth, he will guide you into all truth; for he will not speak on his own authority, but will tell only what he hears; and he will make known to you the things that are coming.[33]

Faced with such realities, some people feel a sort of disillusionment, as though someone had just proved that their favorite relic was a fake. "You mean to say, then, that the evangelists do not repeat word for word what Jesus said?" It is quite certain that many times they do not. They wrote in Greek, while Our Lord spoke Aramaic, and even the Greek words of one evangelist do not correspond to those of another, for example in the Our Father, or the words of consecration. "Well, then, the words really don't matter; all that counts is the sense." Absolutely false! These words are important because they are inspired, because they are written by God, and because they come to us still redolent of the words which Christ originally spoke.

Our expressions of disillusionment are just another way of trying to teach God how He should have arranged His plan of salvation. Such protestations might pass for the apex of piety, but at bottom they are not far from rebellion. There is in them no joyous acceptance of God's plan, and no admiring gratitude for His wisdom. Such people insist on treating the words of Scripture as though they were relics, precious but inert. But God's word is living, and the inspired text is meant to come alive for us and awaken in us the

[31] Jn 14:25–26.
[32] Jn 15:26–27.
[33] Jn 16:13–14.

same life that it awakened in its authors. Let us repeat again our conviction that the best plan is that of the Incarnation. And in the realm of the Scriptures, this means that by the inspiration of the Holy Spirit the words of Christ, and Christ as Word, take flesh in the human speech of the evangelists.

The gift of inspiration in the New Testament implies not only that the evangelists remembered well or were reminded of what they should write, but also that they thought about the words of Christ and listened anew to their message

After his resurrection, his disciples recalled what he had said, and they believed the Scripture and the words that Jesus had spoken.[34]

At the time, his disciples did not understand this, but after Jesus had been glorified they remembered that this had been written about him, and that this had happened to him.[35]

You do not understand now what I am doing, but one day you will.[36]

The glorification of Christ, which includes the mission of the Spirit Who was sent specifically to "glorify" Christ (Jn 16:14), enabled the apostles to recall and understand things that they never understood before. The Spirit stirred their memories and enlightened their minds, and they transmitted the revelation they had received in Christ.

But it was not only their memories and minds that were affected. Every step in the whole process of literary activity, composing, redacting, and organizing, was governed by the motion of the Spirit. St. Ambrose in his commentary on St. Luke's gospel remarks on the words of the prologue which mention that "many writers have attempted to draw up an account . . .":

Therefore, there were many who began but did not finish. We have sufficient testimony in Luke who says that "many have attempted." Whoever strives to set something in order strives to do so by his work, but he does not finish. However, the gifts and grace of God are without this striving. For wherever the grace of God is poured out, it flows so abundantly that the talents of the writer are not needed and are, in fact, superfluous. Matthew did not strive, Mark did not strive, John did

[34] Jn 2:22.
[35] Jn 12:16.
[36] Jn 13:7.

not strive; rather, with the Spirit providing them with an abundance of words and all of the deeds, they brought their work to completion without effort.[37]

The explanation of St. Ambrose is not exactly correct. In the first place, "attempt" does not necessarily mean "fail," and in the second place St. Luke himself, rather than appeal to some motion of the Holy Spirit which dispensed him from effort, takes care to mention his diligent investigations and labor. The grace of God does not dispense from human effort; it raises it, directs it, and even makes it possible. Anyone who has studied the techniques of redaction employed by the evangelists can appreciate the conscious resolve and meticulous care exercised by these writers. These men worked in the sweat of their brow and by the breath of the Spirit.

St. Augustine showed a much greater capacity to reflect on the nature of literary activity. He was very interested in the problem of how the evangelists remembered all the things that they recorded about Christ, and this is how he explains the discrepancies in their accounts:

Of what great importance is it to notice where an evangelist places an incident, whether he puts an event in its proper order, or whether he inserts something he forgot, or inverses the order of events, so long as he does not contradict another evangelist who relates this same incident or some other, nor indeed contradict himself. No one has it in his power, no matter how well he knows the events, to remember exactly the order in which they occurred. (For the fact that one event comes to our mind before or after another does not depend on our will, but simply happens so.) Most probably, each evangelist wrote down the events in that order which he felt to be the best, and which God willed to recall to his mind in regard to those things whose order one way or the other does not lessen the truth of the Gospel. The Holy Spirit Who gives to each as He wills, for the sake of those books which were to be given such a preëminence, directed and controlled the minds of

---

[37] "*Ergo multos coepisse, nec implevisse, etiam Sanctus Lucas testimonio locupletiore testatur, dicens plurimos esse conatos. Qui enim conatus est ordinare, suo labore conatus est, nec implevit. Sine conatu sunt enim donationes et gratia Dei, quae ubi se infuderit, rigare consuevit, ut non egeat, sed redundet scriptoris ingenium. Non conatus est Matthaeus, non conatus est Marcus, non conatus est Joannes, non conatus est Lucas, sed divino Spiritu ubertatem dictorum rerumque omnium ministrante, sine ullo molinine coepta complerunt.*" "Comm. on St. Luke, bk. 1," PL 15, 1613; CCL 14, 7–8.

the saints as He recalled to them that which they ought to write, allowing each one to dispose the events in his narration, one man this way, another that, as it was given to each to view things with the aid of the divine light.[38]

St. Augustine takes into account the techniques of composition and narration used by the evangelists, the action of the Spirit recalling things to their memory and directing their intelligence, the will of God, the end of the Scriptures which is to teach the truth, and their corresponding authority. He was preoccupied with the problem of the different order of events in each of the Gospels, but his solution and the principles he invokes are equally valid when applied to the whole of the literary activity of the evangelists. As a matter of fact, modern research has shown both the relevance and the solidity of this approach.

Conclusion

Our analysis of the New Testament has revealed to us its striking variety. The writers are dependent on a well established oral tradition; at times they utilize preëxisting documents, or repeat formulas from the liturgy and Christian preaching, all the while deftly weaving into their narrative words and texts from the Old Testament. There are other writings which seem to have been composed as the occasion presented itself, in order to answer some concrete need in the Church. Each of these writers had a personal style, evinced preferences for certain literary devices, and viewed his message in the context of a distinctive theological outlook.[39]

[38] "*Quid autem interest quis quo loco ponat, sive quod ex ordine inserit, sive quod omissum recolit, sive quod postea factum ante praeoccupat; dum tamen non adversetur eadem vel alia narranti, nec sibi, nec alteri? Quia enim nullius in potestate est, quamvis optime fideliterque res cognatas, quo quisque ordine recordetur (quid enim prius posteriusve homini veniat in mentem, non est ut volumus, sed ut datur); satis probabile est quod unusquisque Evangelistarum eo se ordine credidit debuisse narrare, quo voluisset Deus ea ipsa quae narrabat ejus recordationi suggere, in eis duntaxat rebus, quarum ordo, sive ille, sive ille sit, nihil minuit auctoritati veritatique evangelicae.*

"*Cur autem Spiritus sanctus dividens propria unicuique prout vult* (1 Cor 12:11), *et ideo mentes quoque sanctorum propter Libros in tanto auctoritatis culmine collocandos, in recolando quae scriberent sine dubio gubernans et regens, alium sic, alium vero sic narrationem suam ordinare permiserit, quisquis pia diligentia quaesiverit, divinitus adjutus poterit invenire.*" "De Consensu Evangelistarum," *PL* 34, 1102.

[39] Consult any introduction to the New Testament: A. Wikenhauser,

This great variety bears its own witness to the human nature of the divinely inspired writings, as well as to the vitality of the Church. We may apply to the New Testament the "modes" of the medieval scholastics, or, in this regard, the concept of analogy proposed by Benoit. For though we stopped to investigate some of the aspects peculiar to the New Testament, the differences in literary characteristics are of the same type within both the Old Testament and the New Testament.

Bibliography for Chapter 3

The Prophets. J. Lindblom, *Prophecy in Ancient Israel*, New York, 1962, is an excellent general study of this question (cf. the review by P. Beauchamp in *Bib* 45, 1964, pp. 433–438), as is the older work of A. Neher, *L'Essence de Prophétisme*, Paris, 1955. A complete résumé of the work done during the last ten years in this area can be found in *TRu* 28, 1962, pp. 1–75, 235–297, 301–415.

In regard to the prophetic formulas, the work of Cl. Westermann mentioned in Chapter 2 is the best single source of information (*Grundformen prophetischer Rede*).

The most complete work on the literary analysis of the Bible is L. Alonso Schökel, *Estudios de Poética Hebrea*, Barcelona, 1963, with an ample bibliography; among works in English, there is still the pioneering work of Robert Lowth, *The Sacred Poetry of the Hebrews*, in Latin, London, 1753, in English, London, 1754; R. Moulton, *The Literary Study of the Bible*, New York, 1899, and G. B. Gray, *The Forms of Hebrew Poetry*, Hodder New York, 1915. For an appreciation of some of the literary qualities of Job, cf. R. Sewall, *The Vision of Tragedy*, New Haven, 1959.

Sapiential Literature. There is a clear presentation combined with a sense of literature in A. M. Dubarle, *Les Sages d'Israel*, Lectio Divina, No. 1, Paris, 1946. The article of W. Baumgartner, "The Wisdom Literature," in *The Old Testament and Modern Study*, New York, 1956,

New Testament Introduction, New York, 1958; A. Robert and A. Feuillet, Introduction à la Bible, vol. 2, Bruges, 1959; E. C. Hoskyns and F. N. Davey, The Riddle of the New Testament, Naperville, 1957.

as well as his "Die israelitische Weisheitsliteratur," *TRu* 5, 1933, pp. 259–288, are very valuable though more technical than the work of Dubarle. There are some very helpful articles in *VT*, Suppl. III, 1955, "Wisdom in Israel and in the Ancient Near East." In a more popular vein, there is the excellent work of R. Murphy, *Seven Books of Wisdom*, Milwaukee, 1960. Volume one of von Rad's *Old Testament Theology* (pp. 418–459) treats of the wisdom tradition in Israel.

Other Writers. For an excellent study of Hebrew methods of history writing, cf. the article by C. R. North on "History" in *The Interpreter's Dictionary of the Bible*, ed. by G. A. Buttrick, 4 vols., Nashville, 1962, with the bibliography that he gives there. There is also the work edited by R. Denton, *The Idea of History in the Ancient Near East*, New Haven, 1955. The article by M. Noth, "History and the Word of God in the Old Testament," *BJrylL* 32, 1949–1950, pp. 194–206, is helpful, as well as Chapter 7, "The Deuteronomistic Theology of History in the Books of Kings," in G. von Rad's *Studies in Deuteronomy*, Studies in Biblical Theology, no. 9, Naperville, 1956. Cf. also Alan Richardson's *History, Sacred and Profane*, Westminster, 1964, as well as G. Hölscher, *Die Anfänge der hebräischen Geschichtsschreibung*, Heidelberg, 1942, and O. Eissfeldt, *Geschichtsschreibung im Alten Testament*, Berlin, 1948. For a wider approach to the question of history writing, cf. J. Shotwell, *The Story of Ancient History*, New York, 1961 (the early chapters are uneven).

Distinctions and Unity. The second part of Gögler's study on Origen, mentioned in Chapter 1, unifies revelation around the concept of word. The same can be said of the contributions to *La Parole de Dieu en Jésus-Christ*, mentioned in Chapter 2. None of the extant theologies of the New Testament attempts an explicit unifying perspective as does Eichrodt's *Theology of the Old Testament*.

The problem of the relationship between the Old and New Testaments is hotly discussed today. Different approaches can be found in J. Guillet, *Themes of the Bible*, Notre Dame, 1960, and C. Larcher, *L'actualité chrétienne de l'Ancien Testament d'après le Nouveau Testament*, Lectio Divina, no. 34, Paris, 1962. Cf. also P. Grelot, *Sens Chrétien de L'Ancien Testament*, Paris, 1962, and *The Old Testament and Christian Faith*, ed. by B. W. Anderson, New York, 1963.

II
THE INSPIRED WORD

ΠΟΛΥΜΕΡΩΣ ΚΑΙ ΠΟΛΥΤΡΟΠΩΣ
Ο ΘΕΟΣ ΛΑΛΗΣΑΣ

4. Inspiration and Language

In the Context of Language

The article of the Creed which we have been considering states that God *spoke* through the prophets, and the Fathers of the Church never tired of dwelling on this mystery, saying often that God has talked to us or that He has written to us. The Bible, as we have seen, is called the word of God. The conclusion of all this, to say it once again, is that inspiration pertains to the realm of language. This means that if we can acquire a deeper understanding of what language is, we shall by that very fact be better prepared to penetrate into the mystery of inspiration.

The Bible is the word of God, God speaks to us. But what is a word? And what does it really mean to speak? There is a danger that we will so accentuate the qualifying "of God" that we will obliterate the force of the analogy contained in the noun "word." We are tempted to think that God could not possibly allow Himself to be associated with our poor, earth-bound words, or at least that He would choose some special little part of them less unworthy of His majesty. It is indeed laudable to insist on the divine transcendence, but we do not make God greater by our minimal respect for what is human. Let us listen again to the words of Pope Pius XII: "For as the substantial Word of God became like to men in all things, 'except sin,' so the words of God, expressed in human language, are made like to human speech in every respect, except error." [1] The reference here to the Incarnation is of the

---

[1] "Sicut enim substantiale Dei Verbum hominibus simile factum est quoad omnia 'absque peccato,' ita etiam Dei verba, humanis linguis expressa, quoad omnia humani sermoni assimilia facta sunt, excepto errore." EB 559, RSS, p. 98.

greatest importance. God did not choose some elements of human nature, those most worthy of Him, and join Himself to these only. The mystery of the Incarnation lies precisely in the fact that God assumed a true and whole human nature. The Docetists thought that they were doing honor to God by denying that His body was real, and they were condemned as heretics. Christ's body was material and mortal, and our refusal to accept this fact gives Him no glory.

We may apply these same criteria to the Scriptures. God does not assume only ideas as the "soul" of language and disdain their human dimensions. "Pure ideas" are not language at all, and in the world of men ideas themselves can hardly exist without some form of language. We cannot restrict inspiration to the assertion of formulas completely purified of all images and emotions. Such restrictions have nothing in common with the patristic outlook or the statements of the encyclicals, and they savor somewhat of a certain Docetism or Monophysitism. God assumed human language as it is, in its total reality, in order to speak to us. "God speaks through a man, in a human way, because in thus speaking he is looking for us." [2] We are confronted with a mystery of divine condescension inspired by love. God's lowering of Himself to human language shares in the kenosis or "self-emptying" of the Incarnation.[3] But by this we do not mean to imply that God adopted a poor style, as some of the Fathers mistakenly thought, but simply that God has deigned to use human language in all its dimensions and limitations.

These are the principles that should govern our approach to an understanding of inspiration. We ought not to begin by trying so to purify and spiritualize human language that it resembles the speech of angels. Nor should we start by accentuating the distance between the human and the divine and arming ourselves with a catalogue of negations. We can make a better beginning, one freer of prejudice and more adequate to the truth, if we set out simply and humbly, taking our language as it is and expanding our study

[2] "Sed per hominem more hominum loquitur; quia et sic loquendo nos quaerit." St. Augustine, "The City of God, bk. 17," PL 41, 537.
[3] Cf. R. Gögler, Zur Theologie des biblischen Wortes bei Origenes, Düsseldorf, 1963, part 2, ch. 6, pp. 307ff.

of it to include all the rich multiplicity of the thing as it actually exists. To understand what it means when we say that God has spoken to us, we need only accept the reality of the human language He has used, error alone excepted, just as we believe that Christ was like us in all things, but without sin.

Such will be the spirit of the study we are beginning now. It is traditional in that it attempts to arrive at understanding by the positive use of analogy, though there are some original contributions. Its newness lies in its orientation: The way the data are formally organized and reflected on.

But why has this type of approach never been used before? We believe that there are two principal reasons:

First, St. Thomas located the prophetic charism in the category of knowledge, and this has influenced theologians of a later age who undertook to treat explicitly of inspiration, which is closely related to prophecy.

Secondly, philosophical reflection on the nature of language is a fairly modern discipline. Plato discusses language in "Cratylus," it is true, and there were subsequent discussions concerning language as natural or conventional. Aristotle studied some aspects of literary language, but the scholastics added little to our knowledge of this branch of the human sciences.[4] It is with Wilhelm von Humboldt that our present philosophy of language assumed the form and importance which it has today. However, since modern treatises on inspiration pertain rather to the neo-scholastic movement, it is not surprising that they embody nothing of this aspect of the study of man. If here or there we find a slight exception to this rule, the procedure reveals an ingenuous realism or complete ignorance of the depths of the problem of language.[5]

In recent years, there has been a considerable movement toward re-thinking this question, and attempts have been made to integrate modern acquisitions with the thousand-year-old theological tradition of the West. Many of these efforts begin from a reëxami-

---

[4] R. Latourelle in *Théologie de la Révélation*, Bruges, 1963, credits de Lugo with having been the first among the scholastics to study this question at any length (cf. pp. 195–197).

[5] A selected bibliography can be found in our article, "Hermeneutics in the Light of Language and Literature," CBQ 25, 1963, pp. 371ff.

nation of the role of language in the economy of salvation, and it is in this line that we wish to place our study of inspiration and its relation to the language.[6]

The obvious lacunae in the neo-scholastic treatment of inspiration, and the renewed theological interest in revelation as word, explain the orientation of this present study, which is offered as a complement to the traditional approach, not as a supplement.

THE SCRIPTURES AS WORD

In the Old Testament, we find persons, events, and words, both of God and of men. We meet real human persons and God as a Person, we come to know real human events and see God as their protagonist, we hear real human words and we hear the word of God echoing throughout all history. All of these come to us as language, in the strict ontological sense of the term. For the events do not happen again, nor do men live again to speak and reënact their original existence. These men and their actions have passed, and they only reach us as language. This is, of course, not true of God, Who transcends time: but of the human actors in the drama of salvation we may repeat the words of St. Paul: "These things . . . happened to them . . . and were written for our instruction" (1 Cor 10:11); "Let these be written for generations to come" (Ps 102:19).

These same reflections are valid for the New Testament also. We meet many people, including the Person of Christ; and we possess many facts and words, again including the words and deeds of Christ. These men were mortal, they have passed from this life and what they said and did here comes to us only in language. Christ as glorified transcends this law of limitation, yet even He does not make the past present again precisely in its dimension as past.

Now, it is precisely this language with its mission of bringing to

[6] Indication of this interest can be found in a collection of articles published in the "Readings in Theology" series entitled *The Word*, New York, 1964. Contributions are taken from books and reviews, dating from 1939 (H. Rahner, S.J., *Eine Theologie der Verkündigung*) up to 1963 (L. Claussen, *Theologisches Jahrbuch*). Among the authors are A. Deissler, L. M. Dewailly, J. Giblet, D. Grasso, R. Latourelle, A. Léonard, K. Rahner, J. Ratzinger, E. Schillebeeckx, O. Semmelroth, Y. B. Trémel.

us the words and deeds in which our salvation was wrought, which is the word of God. As Tertullian expresses it:

> In order that we might have access to God more fully and more swiftly, in His determinations and designs He has added the means of literature to aid those who might wish to seek God, to find Him Whom they seek, and once found, believe in Him, and believing serve Him. . . . The words [of the prophets] and the miracles which they performed in order to lead men to faith in the divinity, are now kept in the treasury of literature where they are available to us even now.[7]

The written text preserves the words and activities of the past, keeping them alive for each generation; it is a means helping us to draw nearer to God.[8] And if we want to understand the nature of this means, it seems logical to begin with a study of the nature of language. Thus, the themes of this study are clear enough; they would include the inspired word, the inspired authors, and their inspired books.

The Fourfold Meaning of the Word "Language"

We have spoken a great deal about language and about its mystery. Before proceeding further with the study of language, we should discuss the four areas of meaning which are covered by the term.

(1) Language signifies, in the first place, the radical human capacity for self-expression. It includes the twofold movement of naming and joining, of articulating and differentiating. This capacity is the basis of social, interpersonal communication. It is the capacity to "humanize" the world, creating a new world in the image and likeness of man, and in which man reveals himself. We spoke of this aspect of language in the first chapter, when we considered inspiration in the context of Logos. This is the proper field for the philosophy of language.

---

[7] "*Sed quo plenius et impressius tam ipsum quam dispositiones ejus et voluntates adiremus, instrumentum adjecit litteraturae, si qui velit de Deo inquirere, et inquisito invenire, et invento credere, et credito deservire. . . . Voces eorum itemque virtutes, quas ad fidem divinitatis edebant, in thesauris litterarum manent, nec ista nunc latent.*" Tertullian, "Apologeticum, 18," CCL 1, 118; PL 1, 434–435.

[8] Some ecclesiastical writers call Scripture simply "*instrumentum,*" perhaps deriving its meaning from the legal and juridical usage. Cf. Tertullian, "Apol. 18, 19, 21," CCL 1.

(2) Secondly, when we say "language," we can be referring to any one of the various linguistic systems in which men actually do express themselves. In this sense, the word exists only in the plural. That is not to say that such was always the case, but simply that it is the fact with which we start. Humboldt began at this point as is clear from the title of his work, *The Heterogeneity of Language and its Influence on the Intellectual Development of Mankind.*[9]

There are two consequences following from the plurality of language. First, the simple fact of variety in which the identical language capacity of man is realized differently; and second, the reality of each language as a social unit. The first consequence is obvious and should cause no surprise. The multiplicity of language has given rise to many speculations, one of the earliest of which is to be found in Chapter 11 of the Book of Genesis.

Each language exists as a social reality, belonging to a group of related systems which is called a linguistic "family." As such, every language is the product of a society in its historical continuity. Generations have contributed to its richness and peculiar character as they met in spiritual interchange; and this was reflectively elevated and enriched by those who developed its literature, either oral or written. The reality is found already existing by the individual to whom it presents itself as a necessity and enrichment, and a condition. By means of it, the individual enters the realm of interpersonal communication, and the communal life of the group. Within its framework his personality unfolds.

As a social reality, language is more than a conglomeration of grammatical rules—with their exceptions—and a range of vocabulary. Many other elements, idioms, turns of phrase, literary formulas, cultural clichés, must be included in any consideration of language as a social fact. These are all preëxisting material offering a set of possibilities to be actualized in the vitality of the language and employed by him who would use it freely.[10]

---

[9] W. von Humboldt, *Über die Verschiedenheit des menschlichen Sprachbaues und ihren Einfluss auf die geistige Entwicklung des Menschengeschlects,* Berlin, 1830–1835.

[10] In relation to the liberty involved in the usage of language, cf. Ph. Lersch, *Sprache als Freiheit und Verhängnis,* Munich, 1947. For a more philosophic viewpoint, cf. H. G. Gadamer, *Wahrheit und Methode,* Tübingen, 1960, esp. pp. 419–420. H. Urs von Balthasar, in "God Speaks as Man," in *Word and Revelation,* treats especially of the first characteristic.

As a social reality which is learned and assimilated by the individual, language exercises a certain influence on intellectual formation. It is true, of course, that a genuine intellectual formation is conveyed not so much by the mere teaching of language, but rather by assimilating the works that are written in the language. Nevertheless, a language system conditions a man's way of thinking, his way of looking at the world and expressing himself. This is realized in a decided degree in someone of quite average attainments, who assimilates rather than creates his language. Such a person usually accepts the common meaning given to words with their overtones, their precision or lack of it, their clarity, or their power of suggestion. At the same time, he accepts the complex of categories and divisions inherent in the language as a means of shaping his own thought, and this thought itself is colored by the logical connections established by syntax. In this way, language collaborates in the education of a man's power of appreciation and thought. Though its role is subordinate to the principal factors of education —statements, theories and doctrines—nevertheless, the collaboration is real and the effect is unmistakable.

Now let us apply this notion to inspiration. The word of God in order to be incarnate must assume a concrete, specific language. The human capacity of self-expression exists only as a diversified series of concretely existing languages. A specific language, of a specific group, is the point at which the Transcendent enters time, and through which the divine message reaches human ears. The choice depends on the free decision of God, Who, as we know, has assumed for this purpose the languages of Hebrew and Greek, and to a lesser extent Aramaic.

In the case of Hebrew, as it received successive formulation by generations of inspired writers, it exercised in its turn a far-reaching influence on the formation of the language system. The speech of Israel and the land of Palestine are both criss-crossed by the footprints of God. The beginning was simple, the language already existed; it was a variety of Canaanite. But this speech was to develop, influenced by the preaching of the prophets, the prayer of the Psalms, and the sacred story of Israel's adventures. This process enriched, refined, and elevated the language, exploiting all its possibilities without destroying its nature. Of course, we should note that all the ancient Hebrew we possess is in the Bible; we have no examples of the everyday or at least the non-sacral language of Israel. Our judgment, then, must remain but partial since it is based on an acquaintance with Hebrew derived almost exclusively from a language already raised to the level of revelation.

The matter stands quite differently when we come to discuss Greek. In this case, the language which offered itself to the inspired writers was already quite sophisticated and habituated to its role as the medium for a rich literary and philosophical tradition. Its subsequent use by the Holy Spirit developed this language in the sphere of religion, initiating semantic evolutions, and appropriating common words to serve as technical terms. Hebrew, too, exercised its influence on the Greek language, obliging it to serve as the vehicle for Semitic ideas when the Old Testament was translated at Alexandria. It suffices to compare the Greek of the Book of Wisdom with that of some parts of the Old Testament as translated in the Septuagint to appreciate the nature of this influence.

The actual multiplicity of human languages imposes on the word of God the necessity of translation with all its concomitant problems, both theoretical and practical. We will discuss this problem more explicitly later on.[11]

The people of God when acting as such—and the people of God today is the Church in its Christ-life—also has a language which constitutes for it a social reality. This language was prepared by the action of the Holy Spirit, and it presents itself as a well-ordered system capable of forming both the individual and the community in a mentality open to God. The Hebrew child, and now the Christian child, are introduced to their relationship with God by the language peculiar to God's people; and this language is inspired. In order to learn this language, they have recourse to the treasures of literature which it contains, and then reciprocally, as they grow in a knowledge of these treasures, they acquire a mastery of the language. We cannot afford to take lightly this question of the language which the Christian learns to use in his relations with God—the language of the books about God that he hears, and in which he prays. Religious language collaborates in the development of a man's powers of appreciation and thought at the deepest level of his existence. We have only to think of the sentimentalism, the cloudy thinking, the loss of the true sense of mystery that oc-

[11] Cf. ch. 11.

curs whenever good formation in a religious language is lacking. The remedy is a return to the language of the Scriptures, and the most effective way of securing this return is the liturgy. "To bring once again the word of God to the people of God," is a watchword embodying an ideal of the greatest consequence. Of course, by far the greater part of the people of God will effect this return to the word of God through translations. Christ, when He became incarnate, entered into one race and became a citizen of one nation. Yet, because He is Lord, He has transcended the limits and obstacles inherent in such a situation in order to reach out to all peoples and races. So, too, the word of God of necessity assumed one language, but through the very fact of this incarnation it can now burst through the limits of that language, and by means of translation identify itself and express itself in all languages.

The various languages, in their social dimension, can constitute the object of a sociological investigation. Insofar as they are languages though, they are matter for linguistic disciplines: structural linguistics, comparative linguistics, or historical linguistics, and the allied branches of phonetics, syntax, semantics, etc.[12] This is the reason why the eruption of the word of God into human language has enlisted the service of all these linguistic sciences. Their positive method demands disciplined and even arid work, but when applied to the Bible, the results of such studies can be the means of securing great insight into the revealed message.[13] The protests raised against these investigations are simply not legitimate. No one claims that they are the principal or ultimate concern of exegetes, but refusal to approach the word of God with the tools by which we study human speech is tantamount to denying the very essence of the mystery of the divine condescension.

(3) We also use the term "language" in a third sense to indicate the use an individual actually makes of the social reality we have just described. Scholars are accustomed to call this individual use "speech." Language, as a system of significant forms providing possibilities for expression, exists only in the individual speech act. The whole process involved in this act is studied by the psychology

---

[12] Cf. F. Kainz, *Psychologie der Sprache*, vol. 1., part 1, A 6, "Die Sprachpsychologie im System der gesammten Sprachwissenschaft." Also, W. Porzig's book, *Das Wunder der Sprache*, Berne, 1950.
[13] Cf. *EB* 561.

of language. Normally, language is actualized in a series of reciprocal acts in which what is spoken is heard, and to which reply is made in kind. This is what we call dialogue.

As a means of communication, language has a whole range of functions, some of which are primary and others secondary. What is said may be recorded in a series of written signs which are then reinterpreted by the process we call "reading." This activity of reading and writing is also the field of the psychology of language.

An individual's use of language may acquire certain characteristics, certain constants of expression or preferences in phraseology, which in time constitute a personal style. These facets of language, especially as they are present in the great writers, form the object of a study known as "descriptive stylistics." [14] The methods of this discipline are not restricted only to the study of individual works, but can be extended to the classification and analysis of the stylistic procedures of an author, a period, or a school.

Then, too, an individual in his use of language may belong to one of three categories. There are those who take their language as they find it, using it and submitting to it without much reflection. Then there are those who dominate their language, and use it with great reflective awareness of its structure and possibilities. And finally, there are those whose genius makes them creators within the realm of the language at their disposal.[15]

Many of these aspects of language will occupy our attention in the chapters to follow. It suffices to note here that inspiration must move within the process of the individual actualization of language as a social reality. It should be possible to study a typical occurrence of this process and then go on from there to speculate on the nature of the Spirit's activity, taking into account, of course, the individual differences which will modify the realization of this activity.

Hermeneutics for its part cannot remain content with a grammatical analysis of the text before it, but must also institute a stylis-

---

[14] For an idea of the orientation and methods of stylistic analysis, see the adequate bibliography of H. Hatzfeld, *Bibliografía crítica de la Nueva Estilística*, Madrid, 1955. Also see various chapters of M. Wehrli's informative work, *Allgemeine Literaturwissenschaft*, Zurich, 1951. We have applied this method to the Old Testament in our book *Estudios de Poética Hebrea*, Barcelona, 1963, with complete bibliography.

[15] Cf. J. L. Weisgerber, *Das Gesetz der Sprache*, Heidelberg, 1951, pp. 137–147.

tic analysis of the individual work in order truly to interpret the message of the author.[16]

(4) In the fourth place, the term "language" can be used to designate the works themselves which embody the individual use of language. These include literary texts in the strict sense of the term, as well as all classes of written language. Such texts make up concrete intelligible systems composed of words, fixed by an oral tradition and often enough also by other written documents.

These literary realities, the texts and literary works of the language, form the object of philology which is the science or art of determining exactly the meaning of a given text. And since our human culture exists for the most part in written texts—except for that part of it which is actually being formed and lived at the moment—it has been justly said that philology is to the sciences of the mind what mathematics is to the natural sciences.[17]

The science of literature, or of literary criticism, also has for its object the actual text in which literature is contained, though some seem to have thought that its proper sphere was the personality or even the private life of the authors.[18]

The word "Bible" comes from the Greek "*biblia*," and indicates a plurality of books. This fact already informs us as to its nature. It is a collection of literary works, of linguistic expressions which are fixed once for all by the fact that they are written. The distinctions we have made before will have a great deal of relevance when we come to pose the question as to where we should place inspiration: in the author or in his work? These considerations are also quite relevant to the science of hermeneutics, which must avail itself of the precision instruments of philology, and of the instruments, less precise but often more apt, of literary criticism. Then, too, it is possible to apply phenomenological methods to the study of a work of literature in order to explain what meaning the work has within

[16] See the new series, "New Frontiers in Theology" esp. vol. 2, *The New Hermeneutic*, ed. by J. M. Robinson and J. B. Cobb, Jr., New York, 1964.

[17] ". . . I had to use the scientific technique which is the foundation of all historical investigation: philology. For the intellectual sciences it has the same significance as mathematics has for the natural sciences. . . . The accidental truths of fact can only be established by philology. Philology is the handmaid of the historical disciplines. . . . Geometry demonstrates with figures, philology with texts." Curtius, *op. cit.* p. x (cf. ch. 1, n. 7).

[18] The fundamental work in this regard is that by R. Wellek and A. Warren, *Theory of Literature*, New York, 1956.

the society in which it lives. In our case, this society is the Church.

Finally, the concrete realization of language in a work of literature highlights the problem of translation, since this is the ordinary means by which such a work is diffused and made accessible to a great number. This is especially true in our case, since the mastery of the original languages of the text is, for the greater part of the people of God, an extraordinary means of approach.

CONCLUSION

These four meanings given to the term "language" are progressively more and more concrete. There is first the radical human capacity for speech, which is actually realized in a whole series of diverse languages, each forming a social reality, which then becomes existing in the individual actualization of self-expression; and this in turn, as it is forged by constant use on the part of the community and individuals, can become fixed by assuming the new dimension of a written work.

The four aspects thus considered provide a broad avenue of approach in studying the mystery of the inspired word. Many facets of the problem have, of course, been studied before, but the full systematic investigation of what is contained in our outline is yet to be written. The pages which follow can only aspire to be an initial attempt in that direction.

Bibliography for Chapter 4

The Context of Language. There are three collections of essays which treat of biblical revelation in the context of language: the papers given at the Third National Congress of the Centre de Pastorale Liturgique, Strasbourg, 1958, *The Liturgy and the Word of God,* Collegeville, 1959, especially the paper by Hans Urs von Balthasar, "God Has Spoken in Human Language," center around this theme. The volume, *La Parole de Dieu en Jésus-Christ,* Paris, 1961, which we have mentioned before, concentrates more exclusively on the word as found

in the Bible. There is an introduction by A. Léonard, "Vers une théologie de la Parole de Dieu"; an article by J. Giblet, "La théologie
du Logos selon l'évangile de Jean"; another by E. Verdonc, "Phé-
noménologie de la parole" (more or less dependent on Merleau-
Ponty); articles by Dupont, Holstein, von Balthasar, etc. and a conclusion by A. Léonard, "La Parole de Dieu, mystère et événement,
vérité et présence." The Protestant viewpoint is well represented by
Das Problem der Sprache in Theologie und Kirche, ed. by W. Schnee-
melcher, Berlin, 1959, and also *Worship in Scripture and Tradition*,
ed. by Massey H. Shepherd, Jr., New York, 1963.

The Fourfold Meaning of the Word "Language." The basic study
is that by F. Kainz, *Psychologie der Sprache*, Stuttgart, 1954, esp. vol. 1,
A 5, "Die verschiedenen Seiten der Sprache." Humboldt's book,
*Über die Verschiedenheit des menschlichen Sprachbaues und ihren
Einfluss auf die geistige Entwicklung des Menschengeschlechts*, Berlin,
1830–1835, is still basic (though for some reason not yet translated into
English). J. L. Weisgerber, *Das Gesetz der Sprache*, Heidelberg, 1951,
follows in the line of Humboldt not without exaggerating some of his
positions. A manageable one-volume work which is clear is W. Porzig,
Das Wunder der Sprache, Berne, 1950. There is little in English
which treats of language from this point of view. The articles mentioned in relation to symbol and analogy in Chapter 2 are useful here,
and there is an excellent introduction to the whole field of semantics
in *General Semantics and Contemporary Thomism*, by Mother Mar-
garet Gorman, R.S.C.J., Lincoln, 1962. Also helpful but a bit too
positivistic is the work by Samuel I. Hayakawa, *Language in Action*,
New York, 1941; a nice summary of the field can be found in David
Crystal's *Linguistics, Language and Religion*, Twentieth Century Encyclopedia, no. 126, New York, 1965.

5. The Three Functions of Language

LANGUAGE'S THREE FUNCTIONS

According to the classical work of Karl Bühler,[1] language can be considered as an instrument or *"organon,"* and is to be designated according to its three principal functions: "statement" (*Darstellung*), "expression" (*Kundgabe*), and "address" (*Auslösung*), (Actually, this earlier work uses the terms *"Ausdruck"* and *"Appell,"* which were later changed to *"Kundgabe"* and *"Auslösung."*)

We make statements about facts, things, and events with a certain preference for the third person and the indicative mood. This function of language is objective; it regards the outside world and is the proper medium for history and didactic literature.

We also express our interior state, our emotions and feelings, our participation in the reality of things and events. For this purpose, we prefer language in the first person; it is a subjective function of language, one which regards the individual, and it is the proper medium for memoirs, confessions, and lyric.

We address an interlocutor, attempting to stir him to action by way of response. We want to influence him and impress upon him our sentiments, preferring for this purpose the second person and the imperative mood. This function of language is intersubjective; it has regard to society and is the proper medium for oratory.

It must be admitted that this schema, so clear and intelligible, is a product of the laboratory, not because these three functions of language do not exist, but rather because the schema tries to categorize them too neatly, and also because the "statement" in its quality of being a representation tends to dominate and polarize the other two factors. Rarely do we find in language as it actually

[1] *Sprachtheorie. Die Darstellungsfunktion der Sprache*, Jena, 1934.

exists any of these three functions in a pure state: Language is not the juxtaposition of clinical statements, pure interjections, and simple commands. In reality, these functions are operative conjointly, mutually affecting one another. If we wish to distinguish various aspects of language as it actually exists, we must speak of language as *symbolizing* (embodying statements and re-presentation) as *expressing* (indicating an interior state) and *beckoning* (addressing or calling another).

A statement is mine because I make it, and yours because you hear it. Already we are in the realm of the subjective and intersubjective. In a statement or act of declaring, I express myself and make an impression on you. You are "impressed" precisely because I have expressed myself; and your impression derives its nature and depth from the contents of my statement and my manner of enunciating it. And since the statement in which I express myself evokes a reaction in you, you answer me, thus initiating a reversal of the process which goes on, exploiting the possibilities and heightening the tension of language. It is a dialogue. In a dialogue, there are mutual statements, mutual expressions, and a mutual influence, all unfolding within the fullness of a single act of interpersonal communication. Statement or representation may continue to dominate and polarize, yet by itself it is unequal to the fullness of communication. The threefold actualization of language's functions gives to them a well-rounded richness, and restores to them their fundamental primacy.[2]

INSPIRED LANGUAGE

Which of these functions of language has God assumed in the sacred Scriptures?[3] Those who are accustomed to distinguish between words and ideas would be inclined to say that God only uses human language in its function as statement.

[2] That is, as a formal dynamic unity, it cannot be reduced to the mere sum of its parts or to the simple fact of their juxtaposition. The respect for the inner dynamism of an organic reality can be demonstrated by the "Gestalt Psychology" school of thought in another field, or by the phenomenological approach to the study of comparative religion.

[3] Cf. L. Alonso Schökel, "Preguntas nuevas de la inspiración," XVI Semana Bíblica Española, 1956; R. Latourelle, "La révélation comme parole, témoignage et rencontre" in *op. cit.* (ch. 1, n. 9); E. H. Schillebeeckx, "Parole et Sacrement dans l'Eglise," *LumVi* 9, 46, 1960, pp. 25–43.

The same conclusion is reached by those who view revelation as a collection of objective propositions. God proposes a series of revealed truths in which the expressive or evocative functions of language are accessory and peripheral, being merely the contribution of the human author.[4]

Faith, too, if it is considered a purely objective statement of "revealed truths," must prescind from all but the informative functions of language. Again, we must leave the expressive and evocative functions aside and restrict ourselves to language which is informative. If we wish the other aspects of language to play a role in faith, we must raise their content to the level of proposition and not care too much if in the process the immediacy of their original function is lost.

Now, it is certainly true that faith is an act of the mind, that its content can be formulated in proposition. Faith is by no means a vague sentiment completely devoid of intelligible content. It is a supernatural virtue by which "we believe that those things which God has revealed are true." However, this definition of faith given by Vatican I is an assertion, not an exclusion. In the same paragraph, we read that "we must offer to God, by faith, the full homage of our intellect and will." Faith includes an intellectual factor, but it cannot be reduced to this alone. It is a free act, "the beginning of our salvation," an act which engages the whole personality. Revelation can be defined as "a declaration made and attested by God"[5] (*locutio Dei attestans*), but again, while this definition is correct in what it asserts, it is not all inclusive. Revelation in its highest act is the manifestation of God as someone, as a person whose self-expression should evoke a response. We read in the Gospel of St. John: "This is eternal life: to know You, the unique and true God, and Him Whom You have sent, Jesus Christ" (17:3). Notice how this formula concentrates entirely on *persons*: "To know You, to know Jesus Christ." No mention is

---

[4] Cf. Latourelle, *op. cit.*, pp. 336–337.

[5] "*Cum homo a Deo tamquam creatore et Domino suo totus dependeat et ratio creata increatae Veritati penitus subiecta sit, plenum revelanti Deo intellectus et voluntatis obsequium fide praestare tenemur. Hanc vero fidem quae, 'humanae satutis initium est,' Ecclesia catholica profitetur, virtutem esse supernaturalem, qua, Dei aspirante et adiuvante gratia, ab eo revelata vera esse credimus, non propter intrinsecam rerum veritatem naturali rationis lumine perspectam, sed propter auctoritatem ipsius Dei revelantis, qui nec falli nec fallere potest.*" D-S 3008.

made of propositions, but of a deeper knowledge, one that is personal, or better, interpersonal. (Recall, for instance, the mystical theology of St. Bernard, or the method by which St. Ignatius in his Exercises concentrates all the disciples' attention on the acts of knowing and loving Jesus Christ.)

True, a person refracts his inner unity in a series of "multicolored" statements, and it is by means of these statements that we are able to get an insight into the personality of the other who has revealed himself to us. Yet, this is not accomplished by some process in which we add up his statements or convert them into syllogisms. A person does not only use formal propositions in his self revelation; his medium is the totality of language.[6]

PRELIMINARY CONCLUSIONS

If God, in a personal exchange, wishes to reveal Himself to us as a Person, then He must use the medium of language in all of its functions. Or to look at it the other way, the very fact that God has chosen all of language as His medium of communication proves that He desires to make a personal revelation; ". . . the words of God, expressed in human language, are made like to human speech in every respect, except error."

The consequences of such a view, both for the reading and understanding of sacred Scripture, are quite extensive. Once such an outlook is adopted, it is no longer legitimate to approach the Bible with the object of dismantling it piece by piece in order to construct a few thousand propositions each one of which would contain an article of faith. It is no longer legitimate to suppress those facets of Scripture's language which fulfill the functions of expression or address. Scripture must be read as an integral literary work embodying all the functions of language and in which God speaks to me.

Let each one consider that through the tongue of the prophets, we hear God speaking to us.[7]

---

[6] There is a very clear exposition of these aspects of the problem in H. Fries, *Glauben und Wissen. Wege zu einer Lösung des Problems*, Berlin, 1960.

[7] ἀλλ'ἐννοῶν τῆς πνευματικῆς ταύτης συνόδου τὸ ἀξίωμα καὶ ὅτι διὰ τῆς προϑητῶν γλώττης τοῦ Θεοῦ πρὸς ἡμᾶς διαλεγομένου ἀκούομεν. St. John Chrys., "Homily 15 on Gn," *PG* 53, 119.

In order that I might know You, You have, I believe, composed the sacred writings by means of Your servants Moses and the prophets.[8]

This treasure house in which all the treasures of wisdom and knowledge are hidden, is the Word of God, or the sacred Scriptures in which resides the knowledge of the Savior.[9]

To be ignorant of the Scriptures, is to know not Christ.[10]

SOME EXAMPLES

Suppose that we were to come upon a thesis in some theology manual which ran like this: "God loves His people." First, we would have the definitions: what "love" means, what "people" means, the meaning of the term "His people," etc. Then there would be the divisions: carnal love, emotional, spiritual; the people of Israel, the Church . . . Then we would have the proof from Scripture fortified with the text: "God so loved the world . . ." "God is love," etc. We do not know if there would be any proof from the councils. In the Index of Denzinger-Schönmetzer under "Love" and "Charity," we find only references pertaining to that virtue by which we love God. This would all conclude with a scholion: "consequences for the spiritual life." (In the theology manual that we studied, there was a thesis on the omnipresence of God, on His knowledge—including the distinction between His knowledge of possibles and His knowledge of futures—but there was no thesis on the love of God.)

Now let us compare this imaginary thesis composed of propositions of well-defined concepts, with a page from Hosea in which God speaks in the first person. We ask the reader to pause a moment and put himself in a different frame of mind in order to hear the word of God.

---

[8] "Ad cognitionem me tui sacris, ut arbitror, per servos tuos Moysen et prophetas voluminibus erudisti." St. Hilary, "On the Trinity, bk. 6," PL 10, 171.

[9] "Thesaurus iste in quo sunt omnes thesauri sapientiae et scientiae absconditi, aut Dei Verbum est, qui in carne Christi videtur absconditus, aut Sanctae Scripturae, in quibus reposita est notitia Salvatoris." St. Jerome, "Comm. on Mt," PL 26, 97.

[10] "Ignoratio Scripturarum ignoratio Christi est." St. Jerome, "Prol. to Comm. on Is," PL 24, 17.

When Israel was a child, I loved him;
Out of Egypt I called my son.

I call to them,
But they only walk away from me;
to the Baals they sacrifice
to idols they burn their incense.

Yet it was I who taught Ephraim to walk.
I took him up in my arms,
and they did not know
that I cared for them.
With human ties I tugged at them,
with cords of love.
I was to them
like one raising a suckling child
up close to his cheek.
I stooped to them
and fed them.

Now to Egypt he shall return;
Assur will be his king

Because they refused to return
to me.
The sword will whirl through their cities
and destroy their fields
and consume their plots completely.
My people hang back from returning
to God the Exalted; they call out together
but he will not raise them up.

How could I give you up O Ephraim—
give you away O Israel?
Can I give you up like Adamah—
or treat you like Zeboim?
My own heart turns against me—
within me, my pity is aflame;
I will not give rein to my anger,
I will not return to ruin Ephraim.
For I am God
not man;

In the midst of you
the Holy One;
I do not come to destroy.[11]

Now that we have read the text, let us reflect a bit. Is there any comparison between the well-constructed thesis and this vibrant passage? Which one is more "revealing"? The words of Hosea, which include a series of statements whose predominant function is informative, actuate the other two elemental functions of language. God expresses Himself and I am deeply impressed. After having read the propositions of the thesis, I can still remain cold or indifferent. If the passage from Hosea leaves me cold or indifferent, it is simply because I have never really read it.

Granted that the language of Hosea is symbolic and even anthropomorphic; still, it is an analogy which confers real understanding. As St. Gregory the Great says, "Come to know the heart of God in the words of God." [12]

We purposely selected an outstanding example in order to make our point with greater clarity. Our procedure may give rise to a whole series of objections all of which say in effect: "Not all of Scripture is like that." Our first answer would be that one instance suffices to prove our point that not all of Scripture can be reduced to propositions whose sole function is to simply state a truth.

Let us take another example in which not God but man speaks. St. Paul, in Chapter 7 of his Epistle to the Romans, movingly describes the internal conflict in the heart of man. His description moves in a series of powerful crescendos beset with repetitions and culminating in the climax of the concluding phrase.[13] In the Latin Vulgate, this concluding phrase has a syntax somewhat different from the original Greek. In order that we may have the experience of this difference for ourselves, we should read carefully first one text and then the other. We will first give a translation of the Latin, and then, after an interruption, we will present a translation of the Greek text. First, the Vulgate:

[11] Hos 11:1–9. For an excellent treatment of this passage and on the whole of Hosea, cf. H. W. Wolff, *Dodekapropheton 1. Hosea*, Neukirchen, 1961.

[12] *"Disce cor Dei in verbis Dei."* "Letter to Theodore," PL 77, 706.

[13] For an analysis of this passage (Rom 7:14–25), cf. M.-J. Lagrange, *Epitre aux Romains*, Paris, 1950 (written 1915), pp. 172ff.

We know that the Law is spiritual, but I am carnal, sold into the power of sin.

I do not understand what I do. For the good that I will, I do not do; but the evil that I hate, that I do.

If I do what I do not will, then I admit that the Law is good.

Now it is longer I who do it, but sin which dwells in me.

I know that good does not dwell in me, that is in my flesh: for to will is present to me, but to perform the good, that I do not find.

The good that I will, I do not, but the evil that I will not, that I do.

If what I do not will, I do, then it is not I who carry it out, but sin which dwells in me.

Therefore, I find that this is a law for me who want to do good: that evil is at hand.

I delight in the Law of God according to the inner man:

But I see another law in my members fighting against the law of my mind, and holding me captive in the law of sin, which is in my members.

Unhappy man am I. Who will free me from this body of death?

The grace of God, through Jesus Christ Our Lord.

Someone reading this text notices immediately a break between the last two lines. The crescendo that has been building up terminates in a dramatic question; and the answer is given in an exact proposition. This is not what we were expecting, and we feel that the result is somewhat jagged stylistically. Now let us see how the Greek text sounds (without skipping anything):

Yes, we know that the Law is spiritual; but I am carnal, sold in slavery to sin.

For the things that I accomplish, I do not understand: It is not what I want that I do, but what I hate, that I do.

If, then, what I do not want is what I do, I acknowledge that the Law is good.

Now it is no longer I who accomplish these things, but sin which dwells in me.

I know that good does not dwell in me, that is, in my flesh.

To want is close at hand, but to accomplish the good—no.

Not the good that I want to do, but the evil that I do not want, that I do.

If, then, what I do not want, I do, it is no longer I but sin that dwells in me that accomplishes it.

And so I, wanting to do good, find this the law: that evil is at hand.

Deep within myself I delight in the Law of God; but I see another law

in my members making war on the law of my mind and imprisoning
me in the law of sin which is in my members.
Wretched man that I am! Who will set me free from this deadly body?
Thanks to God through Jesus Christ Our Lord!

In the Greek text, the pathetic, nearly desperate question is answered by a shout of liberation. St. Paul debates with himself, recording in divergent movements the battle in which he is at once
onlooker, aggressor, and defender. He is simultaneously the battle-
ground, the disputed territory, and the two contenders. He calls, he
questions, he shouts; in his language, all three functions are intensely operative.

But where is the revelation of God in such a page? The answer is
that the Scriptures not only reveal God to us as He acts in regard to
men, but also reveals man's reaction when confronted with God.
In this passage from St. Paul, we recognize ourselves before God,
in our encounter with Him, and the description of our reactions
reveals God to us through the medium of His action within us. It is
always the word of God, and reveals God speaking to us and enlightening us.

Just as our eyes see the external world and do not see themselves unless
they fall on some hard and polished object in which they see themselves
reflected, . . . so our soul, which sees all things, in order to see itself
must behold itself reflected in the sacred Scriptures. The light which
they give forth is reflected and enables us to see ourselves.[14]

Here the analogy of an author and his literary creations can be very
useful. We wanted to use this example of St. Paul since it is a good
illustration of the functions of inspired language, and because we
have here a passage in which God, the author, does not speak in
the first person.

We could investigate many other ways in which God speaks and
communicates Himself, but for the moment it will suffice to have
appreciated the fundamental fact that inspired language utilizes all
three of language's functions. These three functions can be related

---

[14] Ὥσπερ γὰρ οἱ ὀφθαλμοὶ ἡμῶν τὰ ἔξω βλέποντες, ἑαυτοὺς οὐχ ὁρῶσιν, ἐάν
μή που λείου τινὸς ἄψωνται στερεοῦ, κἀκεῖθεν ἀνακλασθεῖσα ἡ ὄψις, ὥσπερ ἀπὸ
παλιρροίας, ὁρᾶν αὐτοὺς ποιήσῃ τὰ ἑαυτῶν κατόπιν. οὕτω καὶ ὁ νοῦς ὁ ἡμέτερος,
ἄλλα ὁρῶν, ἄλλως ἑαυτὸν οὐ βλέπει, ἐάν μὴ ταῖς Γραφαῖς ἐγκύψῃ. τὸ γὰρ ἐνταῦθα
φῶς, ανακλώμενον, τοῦ καθορᾶσθαι ἕκαστον αἴτιον ἡμῶν γίνεται. "On the Structure
of Man" (wrongly attributed to St. Basil), ". . . ," PG 30, 12.

to the three fundamental aspects of divine revelation. For revelation is objective, personal, and dynamic. This means that from now on we must always regard the inspired text under these three aspects: It is objective, in that it reveals facts and events; it is personal, in that it shows us God as personal in the act of revealing himself; and it is dynamic, calling forth and making possible a response on the part of man. The consequences of this three-dimensional view of the Scriptures will be continually unfolding in the pages which follow.

Language and Monologue

The three functions we have just described are called "dialogue functions," since they all have reference to an interlocutor and are meant for communication. There are three other functions, modeled on these which are called "monologue functions." Language serves an informative function even within me since I use it to help myself think. I can express my feelings to myself and listen to myself as to another, and I can also address myself and stir myself to action. It is difficult to see how Scripture could fulfill these three functions, since as the word of God it is directed to others. Yet, the notion may prove useful in our analysis of two hypotheses.

At some point in a biblical text, there may occur a moment of monologue, caught up, as it were, in the movement of a dialogue. It is as though some strictly private papers were to be published along with the work, now that the author is dead. It might be that the Book of Ecclesiastes contains some passages of monologue, unless, of course, the "I" is merely a stylistic device of the author. It would be difficult to think of Qoheleth writing this book just for himself, but it is not impossible that here and there he has set down sections which are predominantly monologue. Similarly, it is quite possible that St. Paul has included in his letters some moments of soliloquy, some intimate reflections in which he poured out his soul. But in every case, as we have said, the predominant current is dialogue, and whenever monologue is present it is borne along on its movement; and all of the work, as we have it today, is addressed to the reader. In the canticle of Moses, there are certain lines in which by a literary fiction God is portrayed in interior monologue.

I said: I will scatter them,
I will blot out their memory among men;
except that I feared the scorn of the enemy,
lest their adversaries judge it amiss. . . .[15]

Even more important is the instance of prayer, more specifically, inspired prayer.[16] We have, for example, in Psalm 73 a monologue which is really a troubled, dissatisfied reflection on the traditional doctrine concerning the retribution made to the good and evil. However, most of the Psalms are predominantly dialogue in form, praising God or making supplication to Him. Some have objected that this human praise of God has, after all, no effect on God, and is in reality but a pouring out of one's soul in monologue. It can have a certain function in society if the Psalms are recited together. Others have maintained that the sole function of the prayer of petition is to provide a personal stimulus on those occasions when we are moved to action, or to be a simple unburdening of our heart when we remain inactive.

Such ideas are untenable: The inspired prayer of the Bible can always initiate dialogue in the mystery of grace, and such prayer actually reaches God. God really hears our song of praise, and this is our greatest dignity; He lets Himself be really touched by our supplications, and this is our greatest hope. The most intimate of our interior reflections is a "pouring out of our heart before God." But this does not mean that prayer does not have its elements of monologue.

Pour out your heart before Him (Ps 62:9).

With a loud voice I cry out to the Lord;
with a loud voice I beseech the Lord.
My complaint I pour out before Him;
before Him I lay bare my distress. . . .
I cry out to You, O Lord:

[15] Dt 32:26–27. On the question of interior monologue in literature, cf. R. Humphrey, *Stream of Consciousness in the Modern Novel*, Berkeley, 1962, esp. ch. 2, "The Techniques: Interior Monologue."
[16] On the question of prayer from the point of view of comparative religion, cf. F. Heiler, *Prayer*, New York, 1958; for a theological view, cf. H. Fries, art. "Gebet," in *Handbuch Theologischer Grundbegriffe*, and Hans Urs von Balthasar, *Prayer*, New York, 1961.

I say, "You are my refuge. . . .
Attend to my cry" (Ps 142:2–4, 6, 7).

. . . the Lord has heard the sound of my weeping;
The Lord has heard my plea;
The Lord has accepted my prayer (Ps 6:9–10).

Our prayer, made up of inspired words, the Our Father or the Psalms, is a real dialogue. Such prayer is a response to God for the goodness He has shown; it is communion with God, a manifestation of ourselves to Him, and a power which enables us to move Him. This may be an anthropomorphic and analogous way of speaking, but it is not false. In inspired prayer, human language in its reality as dialogue reaches a transcendent fulfillment. It is a plenitude conferred on it by the very fact that it is inspired.

Prayer written under the motion of the Holy Spirit is the word of God teaching us to pray. Man utters this prayer. God cannot reveal Himself as a sinner or as in need, but He can reveal Himself as Savior, as accessible and concerned, the companion of our wanderings now and through life and forever.

We will conclude this section with an example from the Gospels. The Word made flesh was walking one day through Galilee and He came to a city gate. Just then a widow came out from the gate weeping and following the corpse of her only son. Jesus Christ "was deeply moved when He saw her." Jesus shared all that is human. This quality, related by St. Luke in his narrative statement, is also a characteristic of the Scriptures in the realm of language. Christ "approached and touched the bier—the bearers halted. Then He said: "Young man, I say to you, rise up!" This efficacious word of Christ, addressed in the imperative and expressing concern, is also a characteristic of the Scriptures. "And the dead man sat up and began to talk." This is the effect of our hearing the word of God: We take life and begin to speak, we establish a dialogue.

OTHER FUNCTIONS OF LANGUAGE

Scholars customarily add to the primary function of language in dialogue or monologue, other functions which they call secondary and which can be classified as the aesthetic and ethical functions of language. Among aesthetic factors, there are such things as the question of plasticity in narrative, the evocative quality of onomatopoeia, etc., while among ethical considerations there are the questions of lying, euphemism, etc.

G. Söhngen, in the book to which we have made reference before,[17] has lately constructed a well-balanced system coördinating language, philosophy, and theology, erected along the lines of the functions of language. His work is divided into three major sections, each of which contains four subdivisions. The sections are devoted to the study of: the logical functions of language, the aesthetic functions, and the dynamic-ethical functions. The four logical functions are considered in their vital orientation toward conceptual precision. They are: denomination, enunciation, syllogism, and finally term. The four aesthetic functions are: the imitation of things, personal expression, metaphor, and world conception, with the third of these functions (metaphor) playing a dominant role in the study as is indicated by the title of the book. The dynamic-ethical functions are also four in number: Efficacious action, witness and declaration, persuasion, formation of opinion through dialogue. The proportion which the author has established between these three groups of four sections, as well as their harmonious interrelation, is well-nigh ideal.[18]

The one hundred twenty pages of Söhngen's book provide suggestive, closely worded reading, and though we have not time here to investigate the book further, we recommend it to anyone who may wish to pursue this line of thought more thoroughly. The aesthetic functions of language will form the subject of study in the next chapter, while the dynamic or "energic" functions will be studied at the end of the book.

Before going on, however, we would like to note here how closely Söhngen's categories resemble the psychological classification of the three functions of language that we have been considering. What Söhngen calls "action and persuasion" can be reduced to the third function, "address," since they are directed to an audience or an interlocutor, while "declaration" or "profession" is actually a total form of "expression" by which a man commits himself in the presence of others to something in the realm of morality or religion, and which can demand an equivalent response from

[17] *Analogie und Metapher* (cf. ch. 2, n. 13).
[18] See the review by H. G. Fritzsche in *TLZ* 89, 1964, pp. 373–375.

others. Thus, in the Scriptures God declares Himself and requires in response our declaration of faith—it is a reciprocal or dialogue movement. Söhngen also contributes a nicely shaded distinction within the third elementary function of language ("address") with his categories of action and persuasion. The dynamism of the spoken word can have either of these as its effect when addressed to another. The last part of his book treats of the dialogical functions of language quite completely; he gives less attention to the monological functions, however.

Krings proposes another line of thought altogether.[19] Rather than distinguish the fundamental functions of language, he speaks of the basic forms of speech. There is first the discursive form, which is the successive and temporal division of the unity by means of logical relations which maintain and manifest the unity in dialectic. The second form of speech is that which "actualizes" reality by rendering it present in the very act of saying it: This is the language of poetry and cult. The third form is called "existential": It is at once the manifestation and full realization of a man in that act by which he engages himself. Krings' terminology is quite different from the preceding studies, and it reveals its close connection with some modern trends in philosophy. Of the forms he discusses, the second is most relevant to our purposes, since most of the inspired text is poetic and is actualized in the cult.

APPLICATION TO INSPIRED LANGUAGE

Let us see some of the consequences of our preceding reflections as they are applied to the inspired word. If God has assumed only the first function of language, the statement of doctrines and ideas on the one hand, and the presentation of facts on the other, then our task is to extract this "inspired" element, separating it from the dross of what is human and not inspired. We will then refine the part that we have extracted by means of formulas that are more and more precise, until the Scriptures will no longer be necessary since they will have been brought to their ultimate goal. (Recall how Söhngen's first function of language tends toward conceptual precision.) We will have in the formulas of dogmatic theology and the conceptualized propositions of speculative theology a purified

[19] The article "Wort" in *Handbuch Theologischer Grundbegriffe*.

form of the "inspired" doctrine, and the Bible will be superfluous. Such has been the practice—though neither openly proclaimed nor defended—of some schools of theology.

In regard to the events which the Bible relates, we could, with a "statement-centered" preoccupation, assume the polemic stance of the controversialist: St. Robert Bellarmine, for instance.[20] Bellarmine set out to prove that sacred Scripture was inferior to tradition and moreover unnecessary. One of the reasons he alleged for this is that Scripture relates many events, which have no connection with doctrine. These facts are not recounted in order that we might believe, rather we believe them because they are recounted. And since the events are only proposed for their informative value, and have no particular doctrinal relevance, it is not necessary to elaborate them conceptually; our only duty is to believe that they happened, and the only problem in their regard is historicity. We adduce this example here to show that such an attitude is not a chimera of our own inventing.

But if the informative or statement function of language is the only one that is inspired, and if this function finds its *raison d'être* in doctrine, why are there so many repetitions in the sacred text? Why so many past events which have no interest for us, why the dialectic of a Qoheleth or Job?

On the other hand, once we admit the plurality of functions in sacred language, we see more clearly why the early Fathers sought and found in Scripture not only Christian doctrine, but also Christian prayer and life. In this integral language of the Bible, there is no such distinction between dogma and life, between theory and practice, which weighs so heavily on us moderns and which we are attempting to correct precisely by a return to the Scriptures and the liturgy.

Liturgy is meant to actualize the language of the Bible in all three of its functions. The reading out of the text is a proclamation which presents the facts of salvation, which highlights God's self-expression, and which is addressed to us in order that we may respond. In liturgy, the Scriptures become once again the medium of dialogue.

[20] Cf. J. R. Geiselmann, *Die Heilige Schrift und die Tradition*, Quaestiones Disputate, no. 18, Freiburg, 1962, section 7.

And in private prayer, too, we do not ordinarily begin with doctrinal propositions and then turn them into a language which is more personal and vital; rather, we spontaneously adopt the language of the Scriptures in the integrity of all its dimensions.

There is yet another way of dissecting the sacred text: It is performed by a new existential interpretation.[21] The inspired (watch the metaphor) function of Scripture is that which calls me to an existential response; it is based on the nature of the existential declaration made by the author. However, in its active function of eliciting my response, this declaration can and indeed ought to be separated from the language in which the author first expressed it. The testimony of the author must be transposed completely into another language if it is to fulfill its function in me. Whatever there is of statement, of doctrine, or of events, can be left aside; and even the function of addressing or impressing me is better described as a meta-function of the biblical text. Thus, the designation "inspired" is a deceptive metaphor which must itself be transposed entirely into another formula in order to be meaningful, in which it means: "Having a power to speak directly to me."

In the theology manuals which treat of inspiration, there is usually a chapter entitled, "The Extent of Inspiration." This chapter has been occasioned by the efforts of some authors to trim down the Scriptures, leaving certain sections of the Bible outside the pale of inspiration. They wanted to omit casual remarks or passing phrases, which are not doctrinal and have no reference to faith or morals. Some have performed a dissection along the latitudinal lines of the text, omitting phrases, sentences, and verses, and combining the rest to obtain a book "purely inspired." Both the solution and this whole manner of posing the question are rejected today. Others made a deeper incision and distinguished, as we have already noted, between matter and form, content and style, ideas and words. This is, of course, the famous discussion on "verbal

[21] This whole question is very much in the forefront today. The "Elenchus Bibliographicus" in *Bib* 1963 lists fourteen titles referring to Bultmann. Cf. R. Brown, "After Bultmann, What? An Introduction to the Post-Bultmannians," CBQ 26, 1964, pp. 1–30, with the works referred to there, esp. L. Malevez, *The Christian Message and Myth. The Theology of Rudolf Bultmann*, New York, 1960; and *The Later Heidegger and Theology*, ed. J. M. Robinson and J. B. Cobb, Jr., "New Frontiers in Theology" series, New York, 1963.

inspiration" which Pesch attempts to refute within thirty well-compressed pages. Again, let us say that such limitations on the charism of inspiration find few supporters today.

Benoit divides his chapter on the extent of inspiration in the following way: "To all the faculties, to all those who concurred in the composition of the book and to the whole content." This frame of reference is more inclusive. In line with such a scholastic outlook, we would add that the charism of inspiration extends to all the functions of language. For we cannot limit the action of the Spirit to only this or that dimension of language.

Bibliography for Chapter 5

Language's Three Functions. The basic work is K. Bühler, *Sprachtheorie. Die darstellungsfunktion der Sprache*, Jena, 1934. A study of his work can be found in R. Ceñal, *La teoria del lenguaje de Carlos Bühler*, Madrid, 1941. Kainz accepts for the most part Bühler's position. Söhngen seems to be unaware of Bühler's work.

Language and Monologue. The best study is in Kainz's book, *Psychologie der Sprache*, vol. 1, part 3, A 2, "Die monologischen Sprachfunktionen"; in the same volume, part 3, B, Kainz speaks of the other functions of language. His classification is curious, but the list is interesting and can serve as a basis for further reflection. A more balanced categorization is found in Söhngen's book, *Analogie und Metapher, Kleine Philosophie und Theologie der Sprache*, Munich, 1962, which we discuss in this chapter.

Application to Inspired Language. The use that the liturgy and theology make of inspired language will be given in their bibliographies later on. In regard to the existential view of language, cf. M. Heidegger's essays, "Remembrance of the Poet" and "Hölderlin and the Essence of Poetry," found in *Existence and Being*, Chicago, 1949. Excellent discussions of this aspect can be found in the "New Frontiers in Theology" series, vol. 1, *The Later Heidegger and Theology*, ed. by J. M. Robinson and J. B. Cobb, Jr., New York, 1963, and vol. 2, *The New Hermeneutic*, same editors, New York, 1964.

6. The Three Levels of Language

Language is actualized on three fundamental levels with some intervening strata and many areas of interpenetration. The three fundamental levels are: common language, technical language, and literary language.

COMMON LANGUAGE

Common language is the ground for all the rest. It is the language of familiar intercourse—to which we return with the joy of a child; it is the language in which we share our love and our ideals. The great wealth of this language lies in the area of personal communication; its precision is only moderate. Common language spontaneously actualizes the three fundamental functions of language. Sometimes it answers our zest for knowing; then at other times, though its objective content is minimal, it offers us the joy of personal exchange with a friend; or, finally, it can give us the satisfaction of influencing others with our words.

This is the language of ordinary conversation, familiar and social, so dedicated to the reality which it communicates that the process of transforming experiences, objects, and events into a series of significant sounds, takes place unconsciously—we are annoyed by someone who "listens to himself talking"—and only mistakes or some striking phrase recall us to an awareness of the fact of language.[1]

Words such as these, produced spontaneously, do not result in phrases that are meant to perdure, but to reveal. Valéry says of

[1] For an analysis of this aspect of speech, cf. Kainz, *Psychologie der Sprache*, vol. 3.

such a phrase, *"elle se dissout dans la clarté."* It is meant to pass, and as it passes it communicates, as a moving river which joins both its sides, or even as a zipper which by passing interlocks the two pieces of cloth.

Common language can be reduced to little more than a utilitarian schema: such is the language when buying and selling and travelling (it includes especially numbers and also gestures which emphasize or supply); it is "German in two weeks" or "basic English." This is not the same as a limited knowledge of a foreign tongue; such a barrier can be overcome by great powers of communication (we remember how once in Rome a Spaniard who knew about ten words of Italian yet held an audience of Americans in suspense with the tale of his adventures). Even a language poorly mastered can be a means of communication; utilitarian language, on the other hand, is a means of preserving one's distance as though in an effort to avoid being soiled by contact.

Does such everyday conversational language exist in the Bible? St. Jerome, defending the inspiration of the Epistle to Philemon, says:

There are many things in the Epistle to the Romans and to the other churches, especially to the Corinthians, which are written in a simple and almost everyday style.[2]

We should note that St. Jerome's use of the word "simple" (*remissius*) is a technical term in rhetoric, designating a low and a simple style. Epistolary style is more easily given to using common language. Leo XIII, defending biblical inerrancy in those passages which describe nature, says of the authors of Scripture:

They did not seek to penetrate the secrets of nature, but rather described and dealt with things in more or less figurative language, or in terms which were commonly used at the time. . . .[3]

Pius XII, speaking about historical passages, gives a similar explanation:

[2] *"Inveniri plurima et ad Romanos, et ad ceteras Ecclesias maximeque ad Corinthios remissius et quotidiano pene sermone dictata. . . ."* "Comm. on Phil," PL 26, 637.

[3] *". . . quare eos, potius quam explorationem naturae recta persequantur, res ipsas aliquando describere et tractare aut quodam translationis modo, aut sicut communis sermo per ea ferebat tempora, hodieque de multis fert rebus in*

When some persons reproachfully charge the sacred writers with some historical error or inaccuracy in the recording of facts, on closer examination it turns out to be nothing else than those customary modes of expression and narration peculiar to the ancients, which used to be employed in the mutual dealings of social life and which, in fact, were sanctioned by common usage.[4]

However, neither St. Jerome nor the recent encyclicals answer our question with an unequivocal affirmative, since it is not the question they explicitly propose to themselves. Common language in its pure state does not exist in the Bible. But insofar as it is the ground of all language, from which proceed the other types and to which they return, common language cannot be totally absent from the sacred text.

In the religious language of a private prayer to God, speech may lose importance or consistency; the language act can become automatic and flow on uniting me to God. But this is not the language of the Bible or the liturgy. We have said that the other levels of language grow out of common language. In the case of inspired language, there was no preëxisting adequate religious language to be subsequently raised by the action of the Spirit. Rather, common language, ordinary and profane, provided the raw material from which inspired language drew its resources, except, of course, in those cases in which the inspired authors used and adapted the religious language of other peoples. However, since all language reverts back one way or another to common language, the inspired word can have an indirect influence on common religious language, and even on ordinary language. A striking witness to this fact is provided by the traces of biblical language to be found in Western literature.[5]

---

quotidiana vita, ipsos inter homines scientissimos." "Providentissimus," EB 121; RSS 22.

4 "Non raro enim . . . cum Sacros Auctores ab historiae fide aberasse, aut res minus accurate rettulisse obiurgando nonnulli iactant, nulla alia de re agi comperitur, nisi de suetis illis nativis antiquorum dicendi narrandique modis, qui in mutuo hominum inter se commercio passim adhiberi solebant, ac reapse licito communique more adhibebantur." Divino afflante Spiritu, EB 560; RSS 99.

5 Fritz Melzer follows up some of these traces within the German language in his book, Our Language in the Light of the Ancient Christian Revelation (Unsere Sprache im Lichte der Christus-Offenbarung, 2nd ed., Tübingen, 1962). In chs. 7 and 8, which are especially interesting in this regard, we find

TECHNICAL LANGUAGE

The second level which we must study is that of technical or scientific language.

A mother arrives at the doctor's. She is with her six-year-old boy, and she is very excited. She bursts into a series of explanations interspersed with words of compassion; she heaps up detail on detail amid a stream of tenderness; then she asks the help of the doctor. The doctor tries to calm the woman in order to sort out the facts which interest him from those which confuse him. He proposes a list of questions, in order to reduce the explanation to symptoms. He continues this until he arrives at a precise diagnosis, which he expresses in a language which the mother does not understand, but which she receives confidently; finally, he prescribes a remedy and gives her a prescription. The mother had used all the resources of her maternal language operating at full speed. However, the doctor did not allow himself to be "impressed" by these "expressions"; rather, he subjected them to a sifting process in order to arrive at his objective. The boy's ailments became "symptoms," the vague descriptive phrases became an exact, precise diagnosis. The language of the mother has been reduced to the language of the clinic. A policeman or a lawyer proceeds in the same way in order to transform an agitated, controversial story into a judicial or criminal brief.

When man as worker (*homo faber*) develops a specific technique, or when man as thinker (*homo sapiens*) evolves a science, he immediately elaborates a scientific or technical language. Even primitive people who had mastered certain techniques, fishing, hunting and so forth, likewise possessed in their language certain categories of precise terms. In our Western culture, the Greeks were the outstanding creators of scientific language.[6]

Technical language proceeds from common language by a proc-

---

the following subtitles: "The Death of Pagan Words"; "The New Life of Pagan-German Words"; "Words Derived from Latin"; "Derived translations." By way of proof, he selects a few Christian words which begin with the letter "D," following out their semantic evolution, their relations, and their derivatives. In ch. 10, we read the title, "How Prayer Has Influenced Language."

[6] For a treatment of the language of primitive peoples, cf. Kainz, *Psychologie der Sprache*, vol. 2, pp. 90–169.

ess of detachment, delimitation, and division. It detaches itself from what is personal and subjective, in order to reach a maximum of objectivity, or, to say the same thing in another way, it attempts to inhibit the expressive function of language and its function of address, in order to remove the contingent qualities of concrete language and produce a quasi-universal or at least easily translatable medium of communication. It uses abstract concepts which it continues to subdivide down to the smallest precision. Its sentences are short and simple, easily qualified by circumstantial descriptions.[7]

The ideal of technical language would be an absolute series of terms. As a matter of fact, such a utopian ideal has been pursued by logistics, but the result has been a series of mathematical formulas, not true language. However, this utopian extreme does serve at least as a concrete example of the goal to which technical language aspires. As Heisenberg[8] has shown, the most refined aspects of physics cannot prescind from some elements of common language, and at the same time they retain metaphors which they have more or less standardized.

In technical language, each word is important. Terms must remain fixed in their meanings and precise in their use; formulas must be exact, all their elements sacrosanct (a professor in an examination wants the "precise term"). The conceptual system of a science becomes in its turn an instrument of thought and further discovery, thus joining the two aspects of "the thing accomplished" (*ergon*), and the "power to accomplish" (*energeia*).

Do we find such language in Scripture? Or, to ask the question in another way, does inspiration ever assume a preëxisting technical language? Or, does a technical religious language ever develop under the action of the Holy Spirit? To these two latter questions the answer is yes.

We find in the legal sections of the Bible laws of a casuistic type, employing language which is quite technical and which has been borrowed from the more general culture of the Near East, mediated to Israel through Canaan. The ceremonial laws are also framed in technical language, which does not seem to have been

---

[7] Cf. H. G. Gadamer, *Wahrheit und Methode*, Tübingen, 1960, pp. 392–395.

[8] Cf. W. Heisenberg *et al.*, *Our Modern Physics*, New York, 1961.

the original creation of the biblical authors.[9] We must be careful, however, not to confuse technical language with the established formulas or the "*topoi*" which may characterize a type of literature or a literary school: Though these latter may be fixed, they are not used as technical terms.[10]

More important than this assumption of technical language is the process of "technicalization" by which common words assume a technical significance. Such a process was implied in the second question we asked above, concerning the development of a technical religious language under the influence of inspiration.

Let us study three examples in which this process is at various stages of development.

(1) The Book of Deuteronomy has a special vocabulary to designate the law and its precepts: *huqqim, mishpatim, miswot, debarim, 'edot, tora, dibre hattora.* This series of seven words, everyone of which has a technical shade of meaning, are consciously confused and combined by the author, in order to convey to us a sense of fullness and interpenetration.[11]

(2) We find in Chapter 7 of the Book of Joshua a very interesting literary procedure which exploits all the semantic possibilities of the Hebrew word "*herem.*" The word means fundamentally "dedicate" or "consecrate," but usually in the sense of making a sacrificial offering to God of one's enemy or booty in a holy war. From this sense are derived the ideas of the extermination of a people or of the warriors, and the dedication of precious objects to the cult.

The Israelites broke the law of consecration. . . . they sequestered some things from the consecration (1). . . . they took from the consecration (11). . . . they have become execrated themselves . . . unless you destroy the things that are consecrated (12). . . . there is desecration among you . . . until you remove the consecrated things (13). . . . he who is found desecrated (15).

---

[9] The basic study is still that of A. Alt, *Die Ursprünge des Israelitischen Rechts* (cf. *Kleine Schriften*, vol. 1, pp. 278–332, Munich, 1959).

[10] Some aspects of this question and a bibliography can be found in our "Hermeneutics in the Light of Language and Literature," *art. cit.*, p. 371; cf. ch. 4, n. 5.

[11] N. Lohfink, *Das Hauptgebot. Eine Untersuchung literarischer Einleitungsfragen zu Dt 5–11*, Rome, 1963, pp. 54–58.

This change of meaning, operating concretely within the same word, conjures up the image of some powerful reality, mysterious yet active. The author can create this impression by his use of a word; there is no need to describe or name this presence exactly.

(3) This is the way that St. Paul uses the Greek word "*amartía*," which is not so much a technical designation of an individual sin, as a deep and terrible reality: the world of sin actively manifesting itself.

It is not legitimate to approach such passages with the outlook of a technician, nor is it exegesis to reduce to a specific and technical meaning a word which an author has left imprecise in its resonances.

A word or a formula can acquire a certain fixity because of its constant use in a definite context; it begins to assume some of the qualities of a technical term. For example, the formula "a land flowing with milk and honey" is redolent of mythopoeic thought, and evokes the image of a land inhabited by the gods, abounding in luxuriant vegetation which requires no work to procure. The Israelites borrowed this phrase from Canaan, and applied it to the land which God had given them. They sang these words in their cultic credo and used them in their doctrine. Thus, the formula became relatively fixed and technical without, however, losing its mythic resonances which were sometimes latent and sometimes actualized. In much the same way, certain institutions or religious practices possessed a fixed vocabulary and phraseology which in time became quasi-technical.[12] We can see a similar process operative in pairs of words which are opposed or complementary. Thus, for example, the word "*mamlaka*," which ordinarily means "kingdom," takes on the sense of "king" in the contrast, "*goymamlakto*," "the people—their king." "*Am*" usually signifies simply "people"; however, when it is opposed to the word "*goyyim*," it takes on the meaning of "chosen people."

A similar phenomenon can be observed in the way in which a certain fact or name undergoes a process of spiritualization and

---

[12] That K. Baltzer follows this line of investigation is evident from the title of his book, *Das Bundesformular*, Neukirchen, 1960. Lohfink, in the work just cited (n. 11), also adopts this orientation, as does Richter in his *Traditionsgeschichtliche Untersuchungen zum Richterbuch*, Bonn, 1963.

abstraction. Speculation tends to deprive such realities of their concrete existence and they take on the nature of a symbol. Such, for instance, is the explanation of the various biblical descriptions of the "manna" in the desert.[13]

This process received a powerful impulse when the Hebrew Bible was translated into Greek. The Greek language itself, the more reflective mentality of the men of this later age, and the fact that long distant events and institutions had by now become a "book," all combined to produce this process of spiritualization. As it translated, the Septuagint tended to spiritualize many concrete formulas, and to convert simple designations into technical terms, at times eliminating the symbolic quality of the original, and at other times seriously reducing it. In this way, the process of "technicalization" was accelerated. At the same time, however, the tendency toward spiritualization resulted in a new series of symbols, since concrete reality took on a spiritual meaning, and acquired, in the process of receiving a new name, a new and deeper synthesis on a theological level. Thus, the Greek translators prepared a sort of intermediate language which became an invaluable instrument in the hands of the early Christian theologians who were attempting to formulate the mystery of the Christ-fact for their fellow Christians and their prospective converts. The Septuagint is a spiritual bridge, erected by divine Providence between the Old Testament and the New.[14]

Of course, when these words and phrases have once acquired a technical or quasi-technical meaning, they also assume a certain mediating capacity in their new role as formulas; it is important to find just the right word and use it consistently, especially when there is question of making a translation. Then, too, these terms and formulas can serve as the basis for a biblical theology, either by maintaining the terms at the technical level they have reached in the Scriptures, or by continuing the process with the aid of our modern thought categories.

There is a greater proportion of technical elements in the language of the New Testament, especially in the theological specula-

[13] Cf. G. von Rad, *Das formgeschichtliche Problem des Hexateuch*, Gessammelte Studien zum Alten Testament, Munich, 1961, pp. 9–86.

[14] Authoritative information regarding the Septuagint can be had by consulting *Mitteilungen des Septuaginta Unternehmens*, Göttingen. Among the authors, cf. esp. the works of J. Ziegler and I. L. Seeligman.

tion of St. Paul. For, while St. John remains intensely symbolic, St. Paul at times strives for a certain conceptual exactitude, though he, too, respects the frontiers of mystery.

A full analysis of the Bible's technical language is of special relevance in hermeneutics or the science of interpretation. In a study such as ours, it suffices merely to note the fact. Because of the unity of the Spirit and the continuity of His action, inspiring different authors of successive ages, this process of technicalization must be attributed to His activity. It is a progressive revelation, incarnating revelation in a continuity which is advancing. Inspired language is the medium for this dynamic process.

Apart from inspiration, a theology which would aspire to the level of science must develop a technical theological language as an instrument of thought and exposition. We shall have to return to this point later on.

LITERARY LANGUAGE

Literary language springs from the same soil, the same common language, as do the other types of speech. It does not arise from utilitarian language, yet neither is it merely anti-utilitarian. It does not arise from technical language as though it were a parallel specialization moving in the opposite direction. Ortega has defined abstract poetry as "a higher algebra of metaphors," yet this itself is a metaphor.

Literary language does not proceed from common language by means of detachment, purification, and specialization, as though it were some "pure poetry" desiring to exist in a state of complete and absolute purgation, hermetically sealed and containing its own quintessence. Rather, literary language proceeds from common language by raising it to a new power. Rarely does the language of conversation enable us to share all the wealth of an experience, or to communicate the richness of what we live within ourselves: Common language is unable to confer on such realities an adequate objectivity. Many factors can concur to offset this inadequacy: the context, previous acquaintance, a whole series of hyperlogical elements that can accompany dialogue. But often, as we leave a conversation, we feel the distance, the impotency of the words, which have been uttered, and which have only half-accomplished their task. There is a sudden spark, but we are obliged to dissipate it in the extended intricacies of our explanation; a vital intuition becomes too self-conscious or remains inert; the urgency of dialogue robs us of words; the very intensity of our feeling inhibits at times its best expression. These are the moments in which we complain: "I didn't know how to say it. . . . I couldn't find the words. . . ."

Literary language does not have to resign itself to this dilemma, but attempts to actualize experience and make it fully objective, exploiting all the functions of language by causing them to yield their maximum productivity. A literary man takes advantage of every expressive possibility in his language, even those possibilities which have never been actualized before. When he feels that his language is failing him, he does not acknowledge himself conquered, rather he reaches out and intensifies his effort; the very shortcomings and unyielding nature of his medium serve only to incite him, as marble challenges a sculptor.

To empower is not the same as to multiply, and in this instance it is certainly not the increase of multiplication. Literary language often delights in density and concentration. What a world, and how much soul there is in some poems of just a few verses:

> To see a world in a grain of sand
> and Heaven in a wild flower,
> hold Infinity in the palm of your hand,
> and eternity in an hour.
>
> BLAKE

By means of this force, and for the sake of it, literary language stylizes and simplifies, skipping over insignificant spaces.

In literary language, words have an absolute importance, and they are sought with the greatest care. They are not merely a way of saying something completely separable from what they say. Words are important for their sound quality, for their rhythm in a phrase, for their aura of associations, and for their resonances in the periphery of our consciousness. . . .

A certain painter once said to his friend Mallarmé: "I also am a poet; many thoughts come to me, however I cannot find the words." Mallarmé answered him: "Poetry is made with words." According to Valéry:

Meaning is not for the poet the essential nor, ultimately, the sole element of language; it is but one of its constituent factors. . . . Then, too, the simple notion of the meaning of words is not sufficient in poetry; I have already spoken of resonance. . . .[15]

For this reason, poetry always remains but partially translatable, and sometimes it cannot be translated at all.

Poetry delights in multiplicity, it accepts and even seeks ambiguity (Empson); it works with images and symbols, declining logic. Poetry fuses the objective with subjectivity; it creates a presence which is almost magic.

Finally, literary language which seeks to be permanent, ordinarily achieves this stability in the written work.

Do we find literary language in the sacred Scriptures? A greater part of the Old Testament and a good proportion of the New belong to this level of language. In a process much the same as that described above in relation to technical language, the sacred authors availed themselves of a preëxisting literary language, and, under the motion of the Holy Spirit, developed a literary medium of their own.

This fact, which is of some importance in a study of inspiration, has the greatest consequences in hermeneutics, for inspiration takes upon itself and actively exploits all the rich possibilities of literary language.

The Scriptures, then, are a reality of literary language. Their resources are abundant and their content full. They are an integrally human reality, and not simply a doctrinal textbook. They can contain all of revelation, but not in propositional form (Scripture and tradition).

Since the language of Scripture is literary, it demands a literary interpretation, and yet every interpretation still leaves the text unexhausted.

Such to us are the holy writings: they give birth to truth, yet they remain virgins, keeping closed the mysteries of the truth.[16]

---

[15] "Signification n'est donc pour le poète l'élement essentiel, et finalment le seul, du langage; il n'est que l'un des constituants. . . . De même la notion simple de sens des paroles ne suffit pas à la poésie; j'ai parlé de resonance. . . ." L'invention esthétique, Oeuvres ed. by J. Hytier, Paris, 1962, tome 1, pp. 1414ff.

[16] . . . τοιαῦται δ' ἡμῖν αἱ κυριακαὶ γραφαί, τὴν ἀλήθειαν ἀποτίκτουσαι καὶ

Such wealth of meaning can be viewed in different ways, all of which may be substantially correct. Since this language is literary, its content—and not only its meaning—can be manifold. Such multiplicity can be rationalized in successive interpretations, yet these must remain, individually and collectively, unequal to the original expression (R. Petsch).

Since this language is literary, it is not coarse or commonplace, nor can it be made commonplace in order to make it popular. Men must be lifted up and introduced to an understanding of the Scriptures so that they can appreciate its language and its message. The people of God must not be coarse.

Since this language is literary, it cannot be simply transposed to the level of technical language. It must retain its images, its symbols, and its concretization, which reveal and veil the mystery without rationalizing it (theology).

Since this language is literary and not merely intellectual, we are not entitled to go back to some supposed previous conceptual stage of its development which the author has subsequently "clothed" in literary form. This language comes before concepts, notions, and terms, and its meaning cannot be obtained by a systematic purification of its literary qualities (theology).

Since this language is literary, its interpretation cannot consist formally of a conceptual categorization and propositional presentation of its contents. We must proceed from the first, elementary understanding of the literary text to one that is deeper and more explicit, and thence to the content of the message.

Since this language is literary, it confers on words a substantial value; it subsists in them and lives by means of them; it is not a disembodied set of ideas which lives and moves independently of the words which incarnate it.

Since this language is literary, it obliges us to the greatest respect and discretion in applying the principle of "what the author wished to say." A literary man ordinarily says what he wishes to say. The principle is valid insofar as it disqualifies a superficial reading of the text, one that would be boorishly naïve, without feeling for the text, coarse, and "out of focus." But the principle is invalid

---

μένουσαι παρϑένοι μετὰ τῆς ἐπικρύψεως τῶν τῆς ἀληϑείας μυστηρίων. St. Clement of Alex., "Stromata 7, 16," PG 9, 529; GCS 3, 66.

if by it is meant that the author said what he did not wish to say, and failed to say what he wished, as though literature were some curse which descends on a literary man and clings to his bones. The principle is legitimate insofar as it does not allow us to treat the text simply as a text, but rather sharpens our appreciation of it as a medium in and by which a subjectively experienced reality receives its new objective existence.

In describing the demand placed upon an exegete by the literary nature of the text he studies, we have been forced to sketch an outline of the whole process of exegesis. Before going on, it may be worth while to discuss these ideas a little more completely. The following pages will therefore circle back, as it were, over the area we have just covered; there will be some reptitions and some new points of view.

A Comparison of the Various Levels

The above distinction had, necessarily, to be somewhat schematic. In reality, all three levels of language must be open to one another, even to the point of compenetration, if technical and literary language are to be truly rooted in the common ground of everyday speech. Our next step is to study these three levels in comparison with one another, pointing out where they are opposed and where they lie open to one another.

Common Language and Technical Language

Ordinary language exists before its technical development. It offers to technical language the words which become specialized in terms, and it places various radical forms at the disposition of technical language, so that the latter can evolve and distinguish its concepts (unless, of course, technical language borrows its terminology from an ancient or foreign language, as we often do with Greek). Also, the syntactical structure of common language provides the means by which sentences are constructed and demonstrations established. Syntax provides not only the framework, but also the "mortar" of the construction.

Technical language in its turn gives to everyday speech some of its formula and expressions. As these become popular, they lose their rigid precision and become capable of enriching common language (much to the annoyance of the scientists; for not only do people plunder their terms, they then go off and confuse them: "chain reaction," "antibiotic," "complex"). This lowering of technical language to the level of common speech is widespread in our modern culture due to the multiplication and effectiveness of the media of communication.

Sometimes science takes up an obvious and simple fact already expressed in common language. When such a simple thing is transposed into technical language, it provokes a reaction, first of surprise, and then of humor: "So that's what they wanted to say! They could have done it without all that fanfare!" At the present time, sociology is the prime example of such procedure. Though the danger of pedantry is obvious, the transposition is legitimate insofar as it renders all the concepts precise, and allows them to be handled exactly.

The Old Testament does not raise human experiences to the level of sociological science, but contents itself with a simply literary expression in proverb, character portrayal, etc.

Common Language and Literary Language

Ordinary language also precedes literary development, and is the raw material for literature. Literary language prefers to keep a certain distance from everyday speech. Usually, it begins in hieratic or stylized formulas, and gradually approaches realism. However, if it insists on maintaining its distance for too long a time and proceeding on a tangent from common speech, it can easily degenerate into isolationism or snobbishness. Then it must reëstablish ties with common language in order that its anemic poetry may be restored to vigor (T. S. Eliot).

Biblical language knows moments of great stylization—the first Book of Genesis, and of great refinement—the Book of Job, but it never becomes isolated or snobbish. And, insofar as we can judge today, it constantly drew its nourishment from the language of the people for whom it was destined. This is one way of understanding the phrase "*Sitz im Leben*": literature with its roots deeply embedded in the life of the people.

Literary language exerts a great influence on common language by modifying it, rendering it more flexible, and expanding it. Often, metaphors crystallize and become part of the ordinary vocabulary; many literary phrases have become standard expressions, clichés, or commonplaces. Leo Spitzer once said that grammar is style in the frozen state.[17]

Biblical language, through its numerous translations, has exerted an influence on the common language of all Christian lands (Melzer). These traces allow us to find our way back to their common source, and to revitalize expressions which have become profane. Such investigations can provide the language of preaching with valuable means of making its message relevant without becoming vulgar.

Literary Language and Technical Language

Technical language and literary language travel along different roads. Technical vocabulary can be very old, though, of course, no older than the technique which it embodies, while as a system literary language is always older than technical language. A study of their interrelations can be of help to us in understanding the Scriptures.

Earlier in this chapter, we cited two recent encyclicals. It will be useful to recall some of their teaching here:

. . . they did not seek to penetrate the secrets of nature, but rather described and dealt with things in more or less figurative language, or in terms which were commonly used at the time, and which in many instances are daily used at this day, even by the most eminent men of science.[18]

Those customary modes of expression and narration peculiar to the ancients, which used to be employed in the mutual dealings of social life, . . .[19]

Leo XIII speaks of ordinary language, of metaphor (which can be part of literary language), and of scientific language; he denies that the sacred authors were interested in the latter. Pius XII refers to ordinary language in a section which is concerned with literary forms; indirectly, he excludes scientific language. According to the

---

[17] In every nation with a cultural history, the study of one's native language includes the reading of its masterpieces (we usually start with Shakespeare in high school).

[18] *Supra*, n. 3.

[19] *Supra*, n. 4.

teaching of the popes, the Bible does not use the scientific language of astronomy or of the other natural sciences, nor the scientific language of our modern, critical history.

If we continue this line of thought a little further, we will discover that the biblical authors used a literary language in which elements from both common and technical language are still present, but transformed. The language of the first chapter of Genesis is not that of conversation. This solemn categorization of nature is based on the observations of the science of the period which, as we have seen, had already compiled lists of things according to groups. What is interesting to note is the fact that this "science" is completely transposed into a literary language of extraordinary density. There are no metaphors; this language derives from that dawn-age of naming which preceded metaphor. At the same time, there is a conscious distance, maintaining itself above all that is common and ordinary, while using the most common of words.

The story of the plagues in the Book of Exodus is told in a restrained literary language of epic proportions, which has more than a touch of irony, and yet never stoops to vulgarity. Many scenes from the lives of the patriarchs or in the stories of kings and prophets may appear at first glance to be quite ordinary and told in very common language, yet they are in reality extremely stylized compositions. A successful literary transposition of events consists largely in the skillful selection of crucial instants, and the skipping over of insignificant spaces. Dialogues with three or five exchanges, a bargaining process all done on a page—these are not the accomplishments of ordinary language.

When the medieval scholastics talked of the "modes" of the Scriptures, they had posed to themselves this same problem and they had resolved it correctly. Scripture does not employ the "modes" (which means the language) of science, consisting of definition, distinction, and argument; it uses the "modes" of literature.

So far, we have discussed in a general way the type of language found in the Bible, and we have seen that it is literature. At this point, it is possible to push the investigation further, comparing technical language and literary language and studying the relations that exist between them.

Technical language can take as its point of departure the literary descriptions given of a certain reality, which in this first stage depend completely on images and symbols. The beginning of philosophy among the pre-Socratics was intensely symbolic. The "water" of Thales is not our H_2O any more than the "fire" of Heraclitus is our "chemical reaction," or the "atoms" of Democritus our "constellation of protons and neutrons." These objects of early study were "elements," held fast in their quality as symbols, yet made already somewhat remote by the first stirrings of philosophical reflection. Whenever a new stage of philosophical reflection begins, it is not unusual to find once again a system of images and symbols prior to a conceptual development: Such is the case with Bergson and Teilhard de Chardin. But even writers as abstract as the scholastics speculated about the nature of the prophetic charism, invoking such realities as "the light of divine Truth" and the "mirror of eternity." Söhngen delights in filling three whole pages with images taken from the writings of no less a person than Kant! [20]

After this second stage of systematic conceptualization, technical language returns to literary language for the third stage in its own development, that of didactics or exposition. It uses images and symbols to clothe its conceptual functioning and conclusions. Now, we are entitled to pass from the words of the professor to "what he wishes to say" or "what he is trying to get across." The pity is that some professors of hermeneutics know only this third stage, and have attempted to enclose the biblical poets within its limits.[21]

Technical language can present literary language with some formulas or terms to be exploited by the poet's imagination. The transposition into literature of technical terminology is a relatively modern effort: Góngora tried it in poetry, and it is a common device in the modern essay.

Literary language can develop in the direction of technical language, as we have seen, by a process in which symbol is purified or rationalized ("instrument" becomes "instrumental cause"), or by

[20] Söhngen, *Analogie und Metapher*, pp. 65–68.
[21] The classification of the literature of the Old Testament which is current in our manuals can be misleading. They speak of the historical books, the prophetical books, and the didactic books, putting in this latter category the Book of Job, the Psalms, and the Canticle. Then, in addition, they usually reserve a consideration of Hebrew poetry for the introduction to the "didactic" books, in which they consider little more than parallelism and meter.

the constant repetition of a word in exactly the same sense, by the fixity of a certain formula in a given context, or finally by a process of spiritualization.

Literary language can be partially transposed into technical language by extracting the conceptual or propositional content and reformulating it. This results in a certain detached vision of the whole or in a conceptual paraphrase. The process of extraction ordinarily leads to an extract, and this, of course, is not equal to the original. There are some for whom such a procedure is the ideal of exegesis; however, this is not exegesis, but transposition. Some, whose background and outlook is conceptualist, may think that only conceptual formulation of a reality is intelligible, or at least that it is more intelligible. But this leaves aside the whole question of fidelity in interpreting a text which is not conceptual, or of fidelity in laying hold of a content which may be transcendent and pertain to the realm of mystery. Conceptual transposition of a text is not the same as exegesis: It is a distinct function, and one which is of the greatest importance.

On this map which we have traced, indicating the various frontiers, we have located one of the most vital questions of modern theology. There is charted here in outline form the problem of the relation between Scripture and tradition, and we have broadly indicated the problem of the relationship between sacred Scripture and theology, between biblical theology and dogmatic theology.

The effort at transposition is always operative in the preparation of a dogmatic definition. Scholars search for phrases which are more and more precise, in an attempt to frame statements and propositions which will formulate a truth contained in our faith. At one time, there will be the transposition of a biblical passage, at another, the formulation of a subtle link which binds together several passages. Even though a dogmatic formulation can never exhaust the Mystery or any individual mystery, it is nevertheless true that it is definitive and cannot be invalid. In its turn, such a definition does not exclude complementary formulas, nor other definitions which carry on the initial effort without rendering it obsolete.

Since dogmatic formulation continually strives for a precision which can only be achieved by concentrating more and more exclusively on a given area, it is easy to understand how Scripture will always contain more revelation than is formulated in dogmatic definitions. If the Scriptures had used a technical language, they would undoubtedly be more precise, but they would not be so rich.

Then, too, dogmatic formulas cannot prescind completely from symbols and images, since these have an essential function in the presentation of the mystery of salvation.

The biblical expression is superior to the dogmatic expression of a mystery, because it is formally the word of God. The dogmatic expression—after it has been distilled—is formally the word of the Church, and as such has specific functions which are not fulfilled by sacred Scripture. Thus it comes about that though the Scriptures contain all the revelation in a literary form, they are not completely self-sufficient. Often, what is called the "authentic interpretation" is, according to the terminology of these pages, an "authentic transposition" which encloses and defines a part of the total content. As an assertion it is true, but it does not exclude other, complementary, assertions. However, the attempt to ignore dogmatic definitions in the name of fidelity to the Scriptures is a failure to recognize the vitality of the word of God which demands and evokes these diverse forms of expression in order to give free range to its own inner dynamism.

A second transposition of biblical language is effected by scientific theology. Since it is a science, it has need of the instrumentality of technical language with its concepts and propositions. But where will theology get this instrument, and how will it perfect its serviceability in the cause of science? We can distinguish theoretically three sources: Theology either begins with dogmatic definitions, or adopts the conceptual equipment of some philosophy, or assumes the formulations found in the Scriptures.

The first line of approach is not direct, but reciprocal, since theological reflection is precisely the means by which dogmatic formulations are prepared. It is not only unhistorical, but positively ingenuous to imagine that the wording of the definitions was somehow esoterically whispered successively into the ears of the bishops and popes until the moment when they wished to make public the formulation. The experience and the reports of the deliberations during the sessions of Vatican II ought to have cured anyone who suffered from such naïveté, and to have inoculated him for the future. The other half of this reciprocal activity can be seen in those theological treatises which begin with the formula-

tions achieved thus far in her history by the magisterium of the
Church. This is a normal and necessary avenue of approach, but it
is important not to confuse the road with its destination.

Scientific theology also speculates with the aid of a philosophical
system external to revelation. For the scholastics, this instrument
was the philosophy of Aristotle. Roger Bacon describes the relation
between revelation and philosophy this way:

All wisdom is contained in sacred Scripture, but it must be made explicit by the use of law and philosophy; for just as that which is contained in the fist unfolds out into the palm, so all the wisdom useful
for man is contained in the sacred writings, but not explicitly—its unfolding pertains to Canon Law along with philosophy.[22]

No one can deny the validity and effectiveness of the Aristotelian instrument in the hands of the great scholastic theologians.
And by the same token, no one can insist that this system be the
principal or unique instrument of theology for all ages. A different
cultural context can, in principle, both demand and supply a different instrument for speculation.

There is one thing, however, that can never be lacking in the
science of theology without incurring the risk of irreparable harm:
There must be prolonged and studied contact with the expressions
used in Scripture. The language of the Bible must always have a
position, a privileged position, in scientific theology.

But this seems to contradict the entire preceding explanation. If
the language of the Scriptures is literary, and the language of theology is technical, how can theological language be scriptural?

Obviously, what is intended is not a restriction of all theological
language to just those terms found in the Bible. Theological language must begin from the Bible, and must maintain its contact
with biblical language, in order to widen its horizons and restore its
vitality.[23]

The best illustration of this fact is found in the terminology used

---

[22] ". . . tota sapientia concluditur in Sacra Scriptura, per ius tamen et
philosophiam explicanda, ut sicut in pugno colligitur, quod latius in palma
explicatur, sic tota sapientia utilis homini continetur in sacris litteris, licet non
totaliter explicatur, sed eius explicatio est ius canonicum cum philosophia."
Opus Maius, Pars II; cited by Pesch, no. 163.

[23] Cf. L. Alonso Schökel, "Biblische Theologie des Alten Testaments," SZ
172, 1963, pp. 34–51.

by the foremost students of biblical theology themselves. Gerhard von Rad, for instance, who is distinguished for his deep intuitive understanding of the Old Testament world, and for his gifts as a writer, does not restrict himself solely to the language of the Bible, but transposes many notions into a more conceptual frame of reference: "The dissolution of the patriarchal faith in the fertility cult of Canaan," "the intimation of a new salvific activity," "familiarity with the deeds of Yahweh in history." Phrases such as these are certainly not the language of the Bible.

In the New Testament, St. Paul has provided us with a rich theological vocabulary, yet here, too, the need has been felt to continue the process of conceptualization. The great theological dictionary founded by G. Kittel is not being written exclusively in biblical terms, but incorporates a whole tradition of German conceptual formulation. But then, if the professors of biblical theology cannot remain within the terminology of the Scriptures, why demand it of professors of systematic theology?

Analytical, speculative, and systematic theology can never consider themselves perfectly developed. There will always be biblical formulas and phrases awaiting transposition into the more conceptual language of theology. And by this process of returning to the language of Scripture in order to begin its journey anew, scientific theology keeps itself alive. In this sense, it is always legitimate to strive to make theology more biblical. The materials for such an effort are at hand: indirectly in the intermediate sources—biblical dictionaries, studies of biblical themes, monographs on biblical theology, and directly in the quiet, constant reading of the sacred text itself. A great part of the task left for theology is a work of language, in the deepest sense of that term.

Conclusion

We have cut a vertical cross-section into language in order to study its various levels. But this cross-section does not reveal an historical succession as do the various archeological strata of a "tell."

In a chronological schema, we would have to distinguish primitive language from cultured language. But such a distinction would be of little help in a study of the inspired word, since the language of the Bible is not a primitive language, but rather one which was

born and grew in an already existing culture. Though biblical Hebrew may be poor in adjectives, have a limited vocabulary, and
possess a very simple syntactical structure, it has in its favor an
extremely subtle conjugation, and when handled by its great poets,
it achieves sonorous force and elemental vigor.

It may be of interest to some to know that the language of the
Old Testament possesses power rather than refinement (though in
its handling of sound it can teach us some lessons), and both its
nouns and verbs have an almost solid quality in their concreteness.
These at least are the characteristics of the language which was
used by the biblical authors and which has come down to us; naturally, they cannot provide a complete description of all Hebrew.
On the other hand, Greek, as we all know, is one of the most
cultivated languages which ever existed. The New Testament is
content to exploit but few of its possibilities.

Bibliography for Chapter 6

Common Language. Most aspects of common language and its realization in the speech act are treated in discussions of the more general
aspects of language. There is a very interesting article by John Wild in
The Philosophical Review repeated in *PT* 2, 1958, pp. 150–161, "Is
there a World of Ordinary Language?" Since there is no other place in
which to mention Wittgenstein, the following articles are mentioned
here: there are three articles in *Philosophical Studies* (Maynooth):
H. A. Nielsen, "Wittgenstein on Language," 8, 1958, pp. 115–121;
C. B. Daly, "New Light on Wittgenstein" (part one), 10, 1960, pp.
5–49; (part 2) 11, 1961–1962, 28–62; cf. also M. J. Fairbanks,
"Language-Games and Sensationalism," *The Modern Schoolman* 40,
1963, pp. 275–280.

Technical Language. There is an interesting article by A. N. Whitehead, "The Organization of Thought," in *The Limits of Language*, ed.
by W. Gibson, New York, 1962.

Literary Language. A discussion of the way in which language is
actuated in literature can be found in "Language and Literature,"

ch. 11 of E. Sapir's *Language*, New York, 1921. Part four of the book, *Theory of Literature*, by Wellek and Warren is also very helpful. The best treatment of linguistics and literature is found in Leo Spitzer's *Linguistics and Literary History*, New York, 1962. Cf. also D. Alonso, *Poesía española*, Madrid, 1950.

III
THE INSPIRED AUTHORS

ΥΠΟ ΠΝΕΥΜΑΤΟΣ ΑΓΙΟΥ ΦΕΡΟΜΕΝΟΙ
ΕΛΑΛΗΣΑΝ ΑΠΟ ΘΕΟΥ ΑΝΘΡΩΠΟΙ

7. The Psychology of Inspiration

The charism of inspiration, considered formally as an action of the Holy Spirit, cannot be scrutinized by psychological investigations. However, the human literary activity which is moved and directed by the Holy Spirit can be subjected to speculative study and its result called "a proposed psychology of inspiration." A title for this chapter which would be more exact though less manageable would be something like, "The Psychology of the Inspired Human Literary Process."

Someone might ask if an analysis such as we propose is legitimate or even useful; perhaps it would be better to leave inspiration wrapped in its mystery. While, again, someone might object that the study of the human process of literary creation in an effort to understand the charism of inspiration is no more helpful than an analysis of the mathematical reasoning of a professor (who teaches in the state of grace and with a supernatural intention) to an understanding of the workings of grace.

But this objection overlooks an important distinction. Grace has no specific reference to mathematics, but inspiration is directed specifically to the act of language, and it is this which differentiates it from the other charisms. In undertaking a study of this question, we are but following in the footsteps of those who have written treatises on the subject of prophecy and inspiration.[1]

[1] If anyone still feels that such an analysis is not necessary, he is invited to go on to ch. 8.

THE LEONINE DESCRIPTION

Modern manuals usually base their treatment of the question on the following description of inspiration given by Leo XIII in his encyclical, *Providentissimus Deus:*

Hence, the fact that it was men whom the Holy Spirit took up as His instruments for writing does not mean that it was these inspired instruments—but not the primary author—who might have made an error. For by supernatural power He so moved and impelled them to write—He so assisted them when writing—that the things which He ordered, and those only, they, first, rightly understood, then willed faithfully to write down, and finally expressed in apt words and with infallible truth. Otherwise, it could not be said that He was the Author of the entire Scripture.[2]

We find this passage in that part of the encyclical in which Leo XIII is talking about inerrancy, and rejecting the false opinion of those who maintained that there were errors in the Bible but that these were due to the human authors, not to God. The Pope denies the validity of such a distinction and bases himself on the principle already defined: "God is the author of the entire Scripture," adding to this a speculative elaboration of what is meant by "author." The description of inspiration which is here given is thus not presented for its own sake, but is subordinated to and in the context of the question of inerrancy.

Any discussion of this Leonine description of inspiration should begin with an affirmation of its fundamental validity. A psychological schematization retains its validity so long as it is taken as such; it loses its validity the moment that it offers itself as the complete and adequate expression of the reality.

If we leave aside cases of completely mechanical writing or other instances of abnormal or pathological phenomena, we can schematically break any literary process down into the following stages: an intellectual stage in which there is knowledge of one kind or an-

---

[2] "*Quare nihil admodum refert, Spiritum Sanctum assumpsisse homines tamquam instrumenta ad scribendum, quasi, non quidem primario auctori, sed scriptoribus inspiratis quidpiam falsi elabi potuerit. Nam supernaturali ipse virtute ita eos ad scribendum excitavit et movit, ita scribentibus adstitit, ut ea omnia eaque sola, quae ipse iuberet, et recte mente conciperent, et fideliter conscribere vellent, et apte infallibili veritate exprimerent: secus, non ipse esset auctor Sacrae Scripturae universae.*" EB 125; RSS, p. 24.

other, a volitional stage in which there is a free decision to objectify knowledge in writing, and a stage of execution in which the intention is realized. In reality, these three stages intermingle, and as each unfolds it may adopt different forms, yet this does not invalidate the fundamental correctness of the schematization.)

In a study of the problems connected with the inspired literary process, it is quite helpful to adopt this schematization and then pursue the investigation by differentiating further within each stage of the schema. This is the method followed by most modern manuals; we wish first merely to reproduce and summarize their presentation.

The Description Given by the Theology Manuals

(1) The Intellectual Stage: The human author can receive his knowledge directly from God through a previous revelation, and this can come about in diverse ways: a vision, the ordering of phantasms in the imagination, or an intellectual perception. It is also possible that the human author arrive at his knowledge by his own efforts: his experience, his study, the consultation of sources etc. In this case, the inspired writer makes an interior judgment concerning his acquired knowledge and affirms, explicitly or implicitly, that "it is so." This judgment is made with the aid of divine light, "in the light of divine truth," and this illumination forms an integral part of the process of inspiration. Because the light is divine, the judgments made in virtue of this light are divine. Note that it is not the statement as such which is only the matter of the judgment that is inspired, but the affirmation of its truth—the formal element in the judgment. And since this formal element is of divine truth, it demands the assent of our faith to the reality revealed. It is not necessary or even usual that the hagiographer be conscious of the divine influence in his soul.

(2) The Volitional Stage: "No prophecy ever came about by the will of man." God moves the will of a man to write without destroying his freedom. This usually transpires without any conscious awareness of the movement on the part of the one inspired, though the divine action infallibly achieves its purpose. The movement must be interior and physical; it may at times also be moral, governing the circumstances which prompt the author to write. Under

this motion of God, a man's decision is divine: God is the author of the process by which the book comes about, and thus He is the author of the book.

(3) The Stage of Execution: This is the act of writing which the author accomplishes by himself or through others; it is the act of expressing the message in apt terms, without error. The process by which the work is realized is not under a special supernatural influence, but is carried out with the aid of a certain divine assistance which guarantees that the terms are apt and that there is no error. This assistance does not consist in a physical motion acting directly on the executive faculties.

We are sure that, as the reader studied the above description, he felt a veritable surge of questions and objections welling up within him—more even than he could express to himself: "The outline has become much too schematic. . . . The description is oversimplified. . . . It concentrates on the one example of a writer. . . . Is the creative imagination of a poet an executive faculty? . . . What about all those things in the Bible which are not formal judgments or doctrine? . . . The whole question of literary expression is treated as secondary. . . . There is no appreciation of the psychology of language. . . . The restriction of a prophetic insight to a charism of knowledge seems awkward. . . ."

We can remain calm, however, and proceed with our investigation. Others also have felt the inadequacy of the schematization, and have attempted in their theological speculations to render the description more realistic and more supple.

THE DESCRIPTION GIVEN BY BENOIT

We give Benoit's name to this description since he is responsible for its present and justifiable notoriety. Benoit himself tells us that the first person to propose the distinction was Nicolaus Serarius, an exegete of the sixteenth century. We find the following text in his *Prolegomena Biblica* (Mainz, 1612):

. . . Secondly, God illumines the mind of the writer with a certain light which is either entirely supernatural, or natural but supernaturally conferred or increased. This light is given in order to enable him to perceive what is dictated or to judge, or to do both. Thirdly, this judgment, which is made by the writer concerning what has been dictated, is either theoretical or practical. It is the former when the writer judges that what has been dictated, is true. It is the latter when he judges that he should write these things, in just these words, in this way, and at this time.[3]

The theoretical judgment has as its object, the true; the practical judgment has as its object, the good—an end to be achieved. The theoretical judgment is in the order of knowledge, the practical judgment has to do with activity. Both these two judgments exist and are diversely operative in the inspired authors.

In the case of the prophet, for instance, his announcement of the certainty of coming doom—"You are going into exile"—is the statement of a true proposition made in the name of God. The predominant factor in the oracle was the speculative judgment. However, when the prophet preaches a sermon to the people, his aim is to persuade and convert them, his intention is centered on the good end to be achieved. Here the practical judgment predominated, initiating and directing the literary activity, willing a certain goal and selecting the means toward it.

When the speculative judgment predominates, it elicits a practical judgment concerning the advisability and the means of communicating itself. When the practical judgment predominates, it utilizes various aspects of speculative judgments, ordering them to its own end. An evaluation of any text must first take into account which type of judgment predominates; if it is the theoretical judgment, we seek the truth of the statement and affirm its inerrancy; if, however, the practical judgment is predominant, we seek the practical truth, or the correspondence between what is intended and how and whether it is achieved.

Both procedures are inspired, each realizing the charism analogi-

---

[3] "Secundo. Intellectum scriptoris illuminat Deus luce quapiam vel omnino SUPERNATURALI, vel naturali quidem, sed SUPERNATURALITER DATA vel aucta. Et hoc vel ad PERCIPIENDUM tantum, quod dictatur; vel ad IUDICANDUM tantum, vel ad utrumque. Tertio. Hoc autem iudicium, quod a scriptoribus de dictatis fit, vel THEORETICUM est vel PRACTICUM. Illud est, quando scriptor iudicat ea quae dictantur, esse vera. Hoc autem practicum est, quando iudicat ea sibi scribenda, et his quidem verbis, isto modo, isto tempore." Both Desroches and Grelot cite Serarius. Most probably, the source for all these citations is the ample quotation from Serarius found in Institutiones Biblicae, put out by the Pontifical Biblical Institute, 6th ed., Rome, 1951 (the above text was taken from the 5th ed., Rome, 1937, vol. 1, p. 32—tr.).

cally according to its own nature, and each judgment gives rise to a process of execution in which the faculties engaged are operative with the aid of a special divine assistance.

Benoit has lately summed up his thought in three propositions:

1. The writing of the sacred Scriptures calls for speculative judgments as well as practical judgments.

2. These speculative judgments need not precede the practical judgments; they may accompany these latter or come after them.

3. Again, these speculative judgments may be modified under the influence of the practical judgments.[4]

Further on in the same article, enlisting the aid of another distinction proposed by A. Desroches,[5] Benoit enumerates three types of judgments, not merely two:

[1] An absolute speculative judgment, or one "purely speculative," which is made in regard to the truth considered in itself. . . . [2] A speculative judgment with regard to action, which considers the truth in relation to activity . . . the thing to be done is viewed as possible. . . . [3] A practical judgment which has as its proper object practical truth, that is, truth considered in its relation to a right desire . . . which tends unerringly to the goal of art—the work achieved.[6]

The distinction of Benoit is elaborated with an eye to the problem of inerrancy. It enables him to gradate the various degrees of commitment with which the authors make their affirmations down to and including those cases in which, while in the process of

---

[4] "1. La composition des livres saints exige des jugements spéculatifs surnaturels en plus des jugements pratiques. 2. Ces jugements spéculatifs ne sont pas forcément antérieurs aux jugements pratiques, mais peuvent leur être concomitants ou postérieurs. 3. Ces jugements spéculatifs peuvent être qualifiés par l'influence des jugements pratiques." RB 70, 1963, p. 358.

[5] Op. cit., "Jugement pratique et jugement spéculatif . . ." (cf. ch. 2, n. 50).

[6] "1. Le JUGEMENT SPÉCULATIF ABSOLU ou 'purement spéculatif,' qui porte sur la vérité considéré en elle-même, sans aucun rapport, même possible, à l'opération; 2. le JUGEMENT SPÉCULATIF D'ACTION, qui a pour objet 'la vérité dans son rapport à l'oeuvre,' mais ne la considère encore 'que comme objet de connaissance, comme mesure et norme appréciative des moyens'; 'l'opérable y est considéré comme possible.' On peut songer à l'appeler 'spéculativo-pratique,' encore que A. Desroches y répugne; 3. le JUGEMENT PRATIQUE, qui a proprement pour objet la vérité pratique, c'est-à-dire la vérité 'prise par rapport à l'appétit droit . . . qui tend d'une façon impeccable à la fin de l'art, qui est l'oeuvre.' " Art. cit., n. 5, pp. 361–362.

achieving a practical goal, they utilize statements without being completely committed to their speculative validity.

This same article includes an historical survey of recent discussion concerning the nature of the two judgments. We find there the opinions of Franzelin, Levesque, Crets, Clames, Pesch, Merkelbach, Lagrange, and Bea.

This line of thought, which we have named Benoit's, has undoubtedly made a great contribution, and has refined and nuanced the Leonine description considerably, bringing it closer to the psychological reality of literary creation. However, we still believe that the needs of the problem have not been entirely met, first, because the whole outlook gravitates too closely around the question of judgment, and secondly, because the operative or executive powers —so eminently creative in a poet—are assigned a negligible function. While recognizing, then, the value of these investigations, it seems that the time is ripe to essay another direction in the study of the problem, one that is more positive and more open to modern acquisitions in contiguous areas of research. That is to say, we would like to relate this problem to the study of literary creativity.

A Description Drawn from Literary Creation

We will proceed in this analysis first by elaborating a description of literary creation in general, basing ourselves on what writers themselves have said. Then we will attempt an application of this description to the biblical authors, again basing ourselves on what these authors have said and also on what their works can tell us.

Both stages in this investigation are liable to objection. In relation to the first stage, it might be pointed out that there is no "common doctrine" in this matter: There are only disparate testimonies whose selection and classification cannot result in a representative description. The second objection is more serious in that it denies that there is any parallel between an author in our culture and the men who wrote the Bible: The whole concept of "author" is so different that if the term is not equivocal, the analogy is too remote to be useful in an intellectual inquiry.

It is certainly true that the biblical authors are not romantic or modern poets. Their approach to literature is quite different.

Their composition often consists more in working with material already formed than in true creativity. The prophet is not concerned with his success as a literateur, but with announcing the message of God. And the biblical authors in general do not attempt to express their own personality or style in their work.)

Let these differences be granted. Still, we do not think we have the right to exaggerate them; an analogy is still possible. Sometimes we wonder whether those who so vigorously deny any resemblance between literature in general and the Bible are not really trying to pacify their own consciences in order to leave themselves free to approach the biblical authors with an utterly unique set of criteria and methods; other investigators give the impression of possessing little appreciation of literary values. Whoever would maintain that the Old Testament contains no literature and no poetry has a rather unique concept of these realities.

Think for a moment of the Canticle of Canticles—or the smaller units which compose it; think of the Book of Job—minus its additions; or of the introduction to Ecclesiastes; or of some Psalm or page from the prophets. If, while reading these, our artistic sense is awakened, then the literary world in which they move cannot be so alien to our own. And as we study each work in turn, the spiritual affinity which we discover is quite sufficient justification for the analysis we are about to undertake. Then, too, we need only reflect on the distance between works which we include within the ambit of our own culture: The differences between the *Ars Poetica* of Horace and that of Verlaine are great indeed, yet no one thinks them insuperable.

An Artist with Language

Let us begin with a pen-sketch of an artist in our own culture. Usually, he is a man possessing a capacity to experience many things intensely. These experiences need not be specifically poetic; much of what he lives is shared by the lot of men: disappointment in love, for example. He is capable of deeply personal experiences and at the same time, by reason of some mysterious sympathy with men and things, he can enter into the experiences of others and relive them. Life itself breaks in to make its impact and set up these intense vibrations, but then, so does literature: An artist usually has a unique grasp of poetry. In art, a man gives himself up to his experiences, admitting all their vividness and their pain.

> O ancient curse of poets!
> Being sorry for themselves instead of saying,
> forever passing judgment on their feeling
> instead of shaping it; forever thinking
> that what is sad or joyful in themselves
> is what they know and what in poems may fitly
> be mourned or celebrated. Invalids
> using a language full of woefulness
> to tell us where it hurts, instead of sternly
> transmuting into words those selves of theirs,
> as imperturbable cathedral carvers
> transposed themselves into the constant stone.

> That would have been salvation. Had you once
> perceived how fate may pass into a verse
> and not come back, how, once in, it turns image,
> nothing but image, but an ancestor,
> who sometimes, when you watch him in his frame,
> seems to be like you and again not like you:
> you would have persevered.[7]

[7] *"O alter Fluch der Dichter,*
die sich beklagen, wo sie sagen sollten,
die immer urteiln über ihr Gefühl
statt es zu bilden; die noch immer meinen,
was traurig ist in ihnen oder froh,
das wüssten sie und dürftens im Gedicht
bedauern oder rühmen. Wie die Kranken
gebrauchen sie die Sprache voller Wehleid,
um zu beschreiben, wo es ihnen wehtut,
statt hart sich in die Worte zu verwandeln,
wie sich der Steinmetzeiner Kathedrale
verbissen umsetzt in des Steines Gleichmut.

"Dies war die Rettung. Hättest du nur EIN *Mal*
gesehn, wie Schicksal in die Verse eingeht
und nicht zurückkommt, wie es drinnen Bild wird
und nichts als Bild, nicht anders als ein Ahnherr,
der dir im Rahmen, wenn du manchmal aufsiehst,
zu gleichen scheint und wieder nicht zu gleichen:
du hättest ausgeharrt."

Rilke, from "Requiem for Wolf Graf von Kalckreuth." German text, *Sämtliche Werke*, Insel-Verlag, 1955, vol. 1, p. 663. English translation by J. B. Leishman, *Rainer Maria Rilke. Selected Works*, vol. 2, New York, 1960, p. 209.

Recall, for instance, the complexity of Shakespeare, or Lope de Vega, the intensity of Antonio Machado or Donne, the self surrender of which Rilke speaks, or the sublime experience of St. John of the Cross, occasioned by a love poem. Though such people may seem to have something of the romantic about them, they are not all of this school of literature (none of the authors just mentioned is a romantic). Much of what is being written today, and many of the greatest classics, can lay claim to like intensity, complexity, sympathy, and self surrender—Petrarch or Fray Luis of Granada, for example—yet the same cannot be said of those exercises in imitation practiced by many notable writers, such as those responsible for the Petrarchism so prevalent in sixteenth century Europe.

Curiously enough, the artist, even as he abandons himself to the flood tide of his experience, remains somehow aloof from it, as though he had to divide himself in order to contemplate his own experience. To the entirety of the self-surrender there is opposed this distant vantage point from which the surrender is surveyed. The artist gives himself up to the intensity of love or pain as few men can, and yet he preserves a clear reflective consciousness of himself, observing himself in love or pain, and drawing from this quarry the stones for his trade. Rilke has magnificently described these aspects of an artist, and Thomas Mann has taken them as the theme for some of his stories: "Tonio Kröger" or "Tristan," for example. In some writers, this reflective distance is very great; it is a characteristic of the classical writers, but it can also be the sign of a self-scrutiny which is wholly modern. Then, again, as an artist views the experiences of others, he can keep too great a distance, replacing sincere sympathy with cold curiosity, and defensively erecting his vantage point into an unpitying egotistical security. However, a man must be somewhat detached from an experience, be it his own or another's, if he is to write of it.

A great artist begins with an intuition which forms the dominant life center and unifying principle of his work; such, for instance was the experience of a playwright such as Shakespeare or Calderón or the great Russian novelists. Poets, too, of lesser breadth, also begin with a dominating and unifying intuition: Keats, Juan Ramón, Valéry, etc.

Finally, the literary artist has the gift of language. Easily or painstakingly, he makes language serve him, harnessing it, or forging it to his task. The facility of Lope de Vega is in marked contrast with the struggles of Schiller; Tolstoy wrote *War and Peace* six times. If we wish now to convert these four characteristics of linguistic artistry into a process, we should maintain the same order: experience, reflective vision, intuition, and execution. For the moment, let this schema (one more schema) rest at that, and let us look now at the other extreme in literary creation; not now at the massive geniuses, but rather at the honest craftsman of language with his modest poetic grace and unspectacular insights, and even at the craftsman copier who has not received the gift of poetry at all. There are times when even the greatest artist finds himself alone with his craft as his only resource; and it is at such times that creativity can begin from craftsmanship. Valéry can be our witness:

The poet is awakened in a man by some unexpected happening, some event outside himself or within him: a tree, a face, a "subject," an emotion, a word. Sometimes it is the desire for expression which sets the thing in motion, a need to translate experience; but sometimes it is just the opposite, there is some fragment of style, some hint of expression which is searching for a cause, which seeks a meaning somewhere in my soul. . . . Note this possible duality: sometimes a thing wishes to be expressed, at other times a means of expression is looking for something to serve.[8]

SOME BIBLICAL EXAMPLES

With this preliminary information, let us undertake to explore the Promised Land of the Old Testament. We do not know if we will return with grape clusters the size of a man, or whether the complex terrain will overwhelm us. At any rate, it is worth the try.

[8] "*Le poète s'evéille dans l'homme par un événement inattendu, un incident extérieur ou intérieur: un arbre, un visage, un 'sujet,' une émotion, un mot. Et tantôt, c'est une volonté d'expression qui commence la partie, un besoin de traduire ce que l'on sent; mais tantôt c'est, au contraire, un élément de forme, une esquisse d'expression qui cherche sa cause, qui se cherche un sens dans l'espace de mon âme. . . . Observez bien cette dualité possible d'entrée en jeu: parfois quelque chose veut s'exprimer, parfois quelque moyen d'expression veut quelque chose a servir.*" Paul Valéry, *Oeuvres*, ed. by J. Hytier, Bibl. de la Pleiade, 1962, vol. 1, p. 1338.

A Great Poet

One of the most intense lyric pieces of the Old Testament is, undoubtedly, the poem of Hosea about his unfaithful wife.[9] Aside from some questions of detail, there is general agreement concerning the basic meaning of the poem, its substantial unity, and the power of its language. Everyone can appreciate, either immediately or on reflection, the powerful way in which marriage, the Promised Land, and the divine mystery are fused in the forge of his intuition.

One may question the possibility of reconstructing the creative process by which this poem came into being, but it will be worth the effort to try, availing ourselves of the narrative material in other chapters. Hosea appears to have been someone deeply in love with his wife; his love was strong, exclusive, and irrevocable, but his wife was unfaithful. He feels within him a deep, persistent pain which sinks down and lodges in his heart. Total love has become grief, and grief gives rise to anger, which, in turn, strives to turn into hate in order to dull the pain, but it cannot—this love refuses to be destroyed, it lives on memory and finally conquers. Now, up to this point in our reconstruction, Hosea is not yet a poet; he is only a husband who has been tragically deceived.

At some point, he succeeded in stepping back from himself, and looking at his pain. Perhaps he started to ask himself the reason for his grief, or perhaps he began to complain of a choice which he considers to have been made by God. In this atmosphere of heavy storm clouds, there is a sudden flash of blinding light and his experience is illumined from above; it becomes transparent and reveals in an instant its own deepest meaning. There now appears, not Hosea and his beloved, but God and His people, or, better, this very real experience of Hosea is seen to be a reflection and imitation of God's love for Israel. The prophet's experience had to be deep and painful if it was to convey any notion of the depth of the divine passion.

The insight was poetic: The prophet now feels the urge to transform his intuition into poetry so that in this form it will continue to have existence and reveal to others the love of God which he has discovered. So he sets himself to work, bringing to bear all his mas-

[9] Hos 1:2–3:5.

tery of language and his craftsman's patience: He listens to the sound of his words as he combines them; he measures the rhythm of his phrases; he elaborates his images with consistency; and he intensifies the dramatic movement of his piece, sustaining it up to the conclusion. As he works, he receives new insights which round out and support his original intuition, and as he manipulates words, his meaning becomes clearer, richer, and more delicately blended.

Hosea passes from the scene, but his poem remains. He knows that his poem is an oracle. He passes it on as the word of God, and it is as such that we receive it and read it.[10]

Accepting the above hypothesis as substantially correct, we can go on to ask the question: At what point did the motion of the Spirit begin to be operative? Pesch's remark that "Many times, poets are obliged to endure a cold sweat in their effort to clothe their thought fittingly," [11] does not adequately describe the process. This picture of a poet as a tailor seeking to outfit his ideas is a bit rationalistic. Poetry is not that kind of a sweatshop, or even a designer's salon.

What makes Hosea the author of his poem? The experience of life as such does not pertain to the creative process, except as preparatory for it; it provides the material for the poem. Literary activity has its true beginning in an intuition which provides the force and directive energy to the whole process in which it itself achieves objective existence. Thus, in our case we have to consider that the intuition of Hosea pertains to the realm of the charismatic: At this point, at least, the action of the Spirit must begin. The process which follows, in which intuition is given literary existence and solidity, transforming the preëxisting material into a poem, will then be dominated by this intuition under the influence of the charism.

The process of execution is a creative function: It is here that the powers of the poet in respect to language are acting in creative harmony:

---

[10] Even though it is not introduced by "Thus says the Lord," or something similar.

[11] ". . . ut exemplo sunt non soli poetae, qui saepe sudant et algent ad inveniendum vestitum aptum cogitationum suarum." No. 414.

. . . this state in which we are intimately affected, and in which all the properties of our language are indistinctly but harmoniously evoked.[12]

The error of many authors who treat of inspiration is found in the fact that they envisage the poem or the work to be written as already existing before it is given verbal form. This latter factor is considered quite secondary, and all that is demanded of it is that it be "apt." In poetry, and in literature more generally, the work only exists in its verbal expression; the central intuition becomes objective and communicable only in its literary realization, and the activity by which this existence is conferred characterizes a literary author or poet. (Let us recall here the words of Mallarmé: "Poetry is made with words.")

Obviously, then, we cannot place the specifically literary activity of the author outside the realm of inspiration. Neither can we decompose the process into a series of practical or speculative-practical judgments concerning the aptitude of a given literary formulation. We do not deny the existence of such judgments: Sometimes they are explicit and extend to the very last effort at expression; sometimes they are implicit, contained in the joy of a single, dazzling discovery. But we maintain that literary realization is greater than, and prior to, any such judgments. We cannot equate an intuition which contemplates its object with a speculative judgment which affirms explicitly or implicitly the truth of a proposition. The intuition may be accompanied by some tacit affirmation, "it is so"; but we find it difficult to reduce a poetic intuition to some form of speculative judgment.

The poetry of the Old Testament, at least a large portion of it, cannot be explained by the psychological description and its enumeration of various judgments; consequently, the charism in virtue of which it is inspired does not correspond to the schema proposed.

The example taken from Hosea has its limits as an hypothesis. For some centuries past, commentators, on account of a certain moral scrupulosity, have considered the matrimonial incident related by Hosea to be pure fiction—a species of allegory. Many

[12] *"Mais cet état de modification intime, dans lequel toutes les propriétés de notre langage sont indistinctement mais harmoniquement appelées, . . ."* Paul Valéry, *op. cit.*, n. 8, p. 1334.

modern commentators, however, accept the historicity of the fact, since it provides a psychological basis for the oracle. Others insist on what is called "symbolic action," which can be a real historical episode or merely pantomime. Even if we are inclined to see the action as symbolic, we believe that it is a genuine historical occurrence. Those who minimize the psychological factor do not hesitate to recognize the intensity of feeling present in the poem. This means that, though they deny the historical basis of Hosea's experience, they must by that very fact accord to him an extraordinary poetic capacity to enter into the experiences of others, and use them as the raw material for his own poetic creation.

A Simple Craftsman

Let us pass now from the great poet and prophet of love to an anonymous craftsman of a later date who had not a pennyworth of poetic temperament. He is a lover of the law, that law which is beginning to be an intermediary reality while at the same time maintaining its immediate link with God. It has occurred to our author to express his love and the glories of his beloved, the law, in verse. It will be a series of phrases which will convey the sense of totality and perfection. He has decided to use a stylistic artifice, an alphabetical acrostic which consists in beginning each verse with a letter of the alphabet. This technique had been used before in Hebrew literature: in a few Psalms, in the description of an "ideal wife," [13] and in the lamentations attributed to Jeremiah. In the lamentations, there are passages in which each strophe contains three verses, all beginning with the same letter. The author of our Psalm is going to surpass them all: In order to express the idea of plenitude, he will begin eight consecutive verses (seven plus one) with the same letter, which, multiplied by the twenty-two letters of the alphabet, gives to the "poem" a length of one hundred and seventy-six verses, each having six accents. Already the inspiration and proposal are not very poetic.

And so he sets to work: for the first strophe—the letter "aleph." This gives us two "happy's"; a conjunction, "but"; an adverb, "then"; a preposition, "to"; a pronoun, "you"; an interjection, "would that"; and a verb in the first person future, which in He-

[13] Prv 31:10ff.

brew begins with aleph. Naturally, the first word sets the tone for the rest of the verse or hemistich, with the result that from verse to verse there is no continuity—only succession.

The first strophe succeeded in avoiding a superabundance of "filler words." The second strophe, beginning with the letter "beth," repeats the preposition *"be"* (with, in) six times, and adds one "blessed": He has not sweated unduly over this. The third strophe—the letter "gimel"—reads nicely: "Ideal," "open," "stranger," "consumed," "rebuke," "take away," and then concludes with two "indeeds." The fourth strophe—the letter "daleth"—has to resort five times to the word "ways."

Our author arrives at the fifth strophe, which has to begin with the letter "he." (In our Hebrew dictionaries, the letter "h" takes up but a few pages.) He counts on using *"hinne"* (behold, lo), which he saves for the last verse. He searches painstakingly, and finally resorts to a colorless artifice. There is in Hebrew a conjugation which in the perfect tense has as preformative *"ha."* This conjugation is called *"hifil,"* and it expresses the notion of causation. We will translate the initial word of each verse, using our English "make" as an auxiliary: "make me understand," "make me appreciate," "make me walk," "make my heart incline," "make my eyes turn away," "make your words firm," "make shame pass from me," and then "behold I desire your precepts." We ought to say in defense of the author that perhaps he did not have our outsider's awareness of verbal roots and conjugations; in any case, his literary activity consisted at this point in a hunt for "h's." Where, then, is the poetic inspiration? There is none. However, the charismatic inspiration must be present.

If someone were to read this last strophe with a theological preoccupation, he would be positively enthusiastic; the author has voiced a profound truth. With all his love for the Law, and with all his expressions of the desire to keep it, he has enunciated here the most important fact about the Law: that its observance is more the work of God than of man. These causative verbs are the proof of it: "make my heart incline," "make my eyes turn away," "make me walk," "make me appreciate that I might keep your law." . . . God not only gives commandments, but also the power, the grace, to keep them. This is the great theological lesson contained in this rather prosaic prayer.

But if we turn our attention back to the literary efforts of the author, we see that his intention was not so much to teach theology as to find "h's." How should we interpret this craftsman's work in terms of inspiration? In general, we would say that the initial idea of the acrostic form multiplied by the number eight occurred under the influence of the Spirit; the patient pedestrian realization of the idea was also directed by the Spirit in such a way that, as the author strove to compose his work, he received new insights with which he could express and develop his love for the law. This love was the remote material for his verses, the point at which it took on the nature of inspiration is found in his craftsman's choice of a literary form.

Someone wishing to use the description of Benoit or Desroches, would say that the Psalm began with a practical judgment or a speculative judgment concerning action, and that this initial judgment gave rise to and modified subsequent speculative judgments. But he should not neglect to complete Benoit's description, acknowledging the decisive importance of verbal realization as a truly formative factor in the process by which the work is composed. This factor must also be accorded a place within the influence of the charismatic motion of the Spirit.

Joining now these examples of the two extremes, Hosea and Psalm 119, we can better appreciate the words of Valéry, which are worth repeating here:

The poet is awakened in a man by some unexpected happening, some event outside himself or within him: a tree, a face, a "subject," an emotion, a word. Sometimes it is the desire for expression which sets the thing in motion, a need to translate experience; but sometimes it is just the opposite, there is some fragment of style, some hint of expression which is searching for a cause, which seeks a meaning somewhere in my soul. . . . Note this possible duality: sometimes a thing wishes to be expressed, at other times a means of expression is looking for something to serve.

This is the place to defend the Leonine description against the inhibiting strictures it has had to endure in some theological manuals. The Pope speaks of the sacred authors as "conceiving correctly in their mind," but this term "concept" is quite broad. It can refer to concepts which are clearly defined, or to a very general idea, or it can even refer to the "conceiving" of a literary work.

Why must we interpret this term in the encyclical as referring exclusively to concepts and judgments? In our description of the creative process in Hosea, the first thing "conceived" was an intuition from which grew the general plan of the work. There then followed an intermediary stage characterized by a movement toward its realization, and finally the actual execution by which the intuition was given verbal existence. This same amplitude can be accorded the other Leonine phrase, "aptly express," which can refer to the authentic literary contours given to the initial conception (the phrase which follows, "with infallible truth," need not be identical with "apt"). If the Pontiff's words are thus understood, we can place emphasis on this third stage of composition, leaving for a later moment the question of "writing."

A *Tree*

Here is a very likely example of the same process of intuition. Valéry, in his list of things which can touch off poetry in a man, puts "a tree" at the head of the enumeration. One morning, just before Spring, a prophet was walking in the countryside and suddenly came upon a tree already in flower. The sight of it suggested its name, and the prophet said it aloud. As he pronounces the word, its obvious etymology comes into his mind: the almond tree has a name in Hebrew which is derived from the word "to watch," because it seems to be so anxiously on the watch for Spring and ready to flower early. As he hears himself say the name, there is a flash of association: "the watching tree"—"God on the watch" (*maqqel shaqed—Yahweh shoqed*). The name of the tree resounds with the echoes of a higher reality: God watching in history to make good His word. The spark of intuition contained a transcendent analogy.

Jeremiah recognized the insight as a message from God, and set to work to transform it into a communicable form. For this purpose, he enlisted the aid of a device already known since the time of Amos,[14] and perhaps even topical in prophetic utterances:

> The word of Yahweh came to me:
> What do you see Jeremiah?
> I said:
> I am looking at a branch of the vigilant tree.

[14] Am 7.

And Yahweh said to me:
Well seen!
For I am keeping vigil over my word
bringing it to completion.[15]

As we have constructed it, the inspired process begins with a flash of insight, is followed by a movement or impulse to write, and finally is completed by the exercise of the writer's craft. The last step could hardly be called creative in this instance, since it consisted in "re-filling" a used formula.

We like to compare this example from Jeremiah with a *poema Castellano* by Antonio Machado Ruiz. As the poet walked along, his eyes rested on an elm tree: A ray of light passed through its dormant branches and somehow caught the color of a few tiny leaves just appearing on the tip of one of its shoots. In this tree, just about to regain its verdure, the poet sees the mystery of life itself with its Spring and its hope: the gray melancholy of the branches intimate the secret. He decides to record this discovery before the tree be cut down and disappear.

. . . . .

Elm tree, let me record on this paper,
the favor of your vernal branches.

My heart is looking
also, toward the light and toward reliving,
another miracle of springtime.[16]

And though the medium is more complex, the same intuition resounds in these lines of Hopkins:

Not of áll my eyes see, wandering on the world,
Is anything a milk to the mind so, so sighs deep
Poetry tó it, as a tree whose boughs break in the sky.

---

[15] Jer 1:11–12.
[16] " . . . .
olmo, quiero anotar en mi cartera
la gracia de tu rama verdecida.

"Mi corazón espera
también, hacia la luz y hacia la vida,
otro milagro de la primavera."
Antonio Machado, "A Un Olmo Seco," *Poesías Completas*, Madrid, 1955, p. 169.

Say it is ásh-boughs: whether on a December day and furled
Fast ór they in clammyish lashtender combs creep
Apart wide and new-nestle at heaven most high.
They touch heaven, tabour on it; how their talons sweep
The smouldering enormous winter welkin! May
Mells blue and snow white through them, a fringe and fray
Of greenery: it is old earth's groping towards the steep
Heaven whom she childs us by.[17]

The poet of Castile and his English counterpart recognized in elms and ash boughs a human meaning in their cosmic mystery; the prophet from Anatoth, magnetized by his calling, saw divine meaning in an almond tree. The prophet couched his message in an accepted literary formulation of incisive brevity; the Spanish poet used the form of a "confession," revealing the state of his soul as it faced the vision of the elm tree; and the nineteenth-century English Jesuit adopted a sonnet form.

The Area of Probability

Our description of a walk in the countryside is a reconstruction. Perhaps the thought occurred while the poet looked out of the window. Some say that the flowering branch was really a staff made of almond wood (we don't know if the grain is that easily recognizable); even so, the role of the name "watching tree" remains, though its poetic resonances be somewhat diminished. Those who consider that the branch was seen in a vision or was only imagined, must still allow for the poetic role of its name. However, there is no need to have recourse to extraordinary visions when we know, for instance, that Jeremiah received an oracle while watching a potter at work (18:1ff.); and when there is the example of something as homespun as a boiling pot about to tip over (1:13ff.), we need not imagine a preternatural occurrence.

The example taken from Jeremiah provides us with a good illustration of the way in which the actual craft of poetry writing was profoundly influenced by tradition, and this may serve as a sample characteristic of most of the poetry of the Old Testament in which traditional forms and formulas played such a large role.

Jeremiah also tells us in his "confessions" of the interior impulse

[17] "Ash Boughs," *Poems of Gerard Manley Hopkins*, ed. W. H. Gardner, New York, 1959, p. 164.

he felt, which he could not restrain, driving him to give to the
words he heard within himself an objective literary existence:

> You led me on, O Yahweh,
> and I let myself be led.
> You forced me, and you won.
> And I? —a laughingstock all day,
> sport for every passer-by.
>
> Whenever I speak, I shout Violence!
> Plunder is my cry.
>
> For Yahweh's word to me—
> scorn and derision all the day long.
> I said:
> I will not remember it,
> no more will I speak in his name.
> Then in my heart it turned to fire
> burning, imprisoned in my bones.
> I am weary holding it in,
> I can no longer.[18]

This reminds us of the "spiritual compulsion" which Stephen
Spender avows in his article, "The Making of a Poem." [19]

In the poem of Jeremiah which we quoted above, he refers to his
oracle as consisting of the word "Violence!" According to von
Rad, this is the cry by which someone who is being oppressed demands protection or justice.[20] The role of the word in context can
be variously explained: (1) It could be a summary of Jeremiah's
message put here in this form for functional reasons. (2) It might
be a germinal word, capable of being articulated in a full oracle, as
for example in the oracle of the almond tree; a single cry becomes
the seed of a whole poem, setting its tone and providing its theme.
(3) It could be the oracle in its entirety; an elemental inspiration
suggests but one word and causes it to be pronounced. In such a
situation, intuitions and judgments in regard to literary realization
count for nothing. The unadorned cry acquires its concrete mean-

[18] Jer 20:7-9.
[19] Cf. R. W. Stallman, *Critics and Essays in Criticism. 1920–1948*, New
York, 1949.
[20] G. von Rad, *Genesis*, Philadelphia, 1961; cf. pp. 123, 187.

ing within the vital context of the people. We ought to note, of course, that such single-worded oracles were not left in their isolation in the collections of prophetic sayings as we have them, but this does not exclude the possibility of their existence in the prophetic preaching.

A Detail of Style

We are going to take a quick glance at the prophet Isaiah as he gives literary shape to a matrimonial litigation carried on between God and his people or his city. The exclamation "*ay*" could, in the instance we are studying, be said either, as "*ayka*" or "*ayk*" (which became in later pronunciation "*eka*" and "*ek*" respectively); Isaiah chooses the bisyllabic form. There are two words for city, "*ir*" and "*qirya*": here he chooses the latter. In order to see the reason behind these choices, it will suffice to read out loud the following alternatives:

> *'ayk hayetá lezoná 'ír ne' maná*
> *'ayká hayetá lezoná qiryá ne'maná.*[21]

The reality of the verse, and consequently of the poem, is changed because of the emphatic fivefold rhyme scheme found in the second of the two lines. Here, if we wish to speak of a judgment, we must place it in the choice between stylistic alternatives (Marouzeau—style consists in choice). The verse is not a simple statement or a judgment of truth; it is a cry and a complaint uttered by God. The intelligible content is dissolved in the expressive utterance. If the poet chooses to give to the divine complaint a form in which there are two more rhymes than need have been, then this choice is inspired, because the total message is more impressive and more revealing in this heightened literary form. Intensity is a dimension of the spirit (Bruno Snell) which plays an important role in interpersonal communication and in literary language. We have to realize that the technique and the style of Isaiah were elaborated under the influence of the Holy Spirit, and that the resulting literary work in all its dimensions is an inspired message. We may note in passing how aptly this verse illustrates the manner in which literary language assumes and exploits the possibilities inherent in common language.

[21] Is 1:21.

Imitation in a Psalm

We are going to prescind for a moment from the origin of Psalm 29. The activating force in the poem is the experience of a storm which, in itself, is but the material for the work. In an overpowering experience of the tempest, a man perceived the awesome yet fascinating presence of God. The storm is to his symbolic intuition a theophany—a manifestation of God in power. This perception of transcendence is the igniting point of the poem. In order to give his intuition an objective existence, the poet chooses the form of a liturgical hymn, and this selection of form dominates the whole tenor of the piece, which appears as a communal song of praise. As he shapes the poem, the author stylizes the storm in a series of seven thunder claps, nouns which can almost be felt, and which are dynamic subjects for his phrases. These factors came to light as he strove to execute his poem in an *élan* of genuine creativity.

So far, this example seems to be exactly the same as that of Hosea. But there is a new factor. This Psalm is in all probability of Canaanite origin, and has been adapted by an inspired biblical author. The probable provenience of the Psalm poses a new question: Who is inspired? At what point in the process did the action of the Spirit begin, and in what terms are we to describe this action? We will attempt an answer.

The Hebrew author experienced a storm in a way very similar to his Canaanite predecessor. There need be nothing unusual in this, considering the fact that a storm is a common enough occurrence, and taking into account the symbolic thought context in which both minds moved. Seeking to objectify his experience, the biblical author recalls or finds this Canaanite Psalm whose aptitude he easily recognizes and on which he works, retouching it and making additions and changes. It is almost the same process which we saw in the case of the question-and-answer formula employed by Jeremiah: more imitative than creative, but no less inspired.

Or there can be another explanation: An Israelite poet reads this Canaanite Psalm and is deeply and sympathetically affected. The power of the poetic word, re-creating the event and manifesting its content, causes in the reader the same experience as that first had by the author, except that this time the intuition vibrates within

the context of a faith in Yahweh. There is continuity and communion between the two experiences insofar as the Israelite relived
the previous emotion and intuition; and there is a real transposition insofar as the religious meaning of the poem has been specified in a new significant context. As the Hebrew reader strives to
give form to the experience touched off by the poem, he finds that
the best medium is the poem itself, and in this phase of literary
execution, he adapts it to a new context of faith making use of the
name of God, and God's relation with His people. His adaptation
was a creative process in that it substantially modified the meaning
of the poem. This is not a thing which can be established statisti-
cally by counting the number of words he changed, but must be
appreciated by observing the resonances set up by replacing the
preëxisting word figure in a new context, most probably with a
marked economy of artifices. In this second hypothesis, we can locate the action of the Spirit in that moment when there was a
relived experience in a new key, and then in the fundamental
choice to repeat the previous poem, as well as in the actual technique by which it was adapted to a new religious purpose. Observe,
however, that we admit a religious plane common to both experiences.

This is, as a matter of fact, that which would distinguish our
example from another, whose process of transposition we can control quite closely: We refer to the poem about the shepherd boy by
St. John of the Cross. We now possess the original love poem
which served as his model; it does not really excel other poems of
its type and era. The mystic, whose whole life force was polarized
by the Lord Jesus, read the poem and felt a living flame. Seeking to
confer existence and a communicability to the fire he felt within
him, he took the poem, retouched it here and there, and transposed it to a completely new image-context. The result is astound-
ing:

> A shepherd lad was mourning his distress,
> Far from all comfort, friendless and forlorn.
> He fixed his thought upon his shepherdess
> Because his breast by love was sorely torn.
>
> He did not weep that love had pierced him so,
> Nor with self-pity that the shaft was shot,

Though deep into his heart had sunk the blow,
It grieved him more that he had been forgot.

Only to think that he had been forgotten
By his sweet shepherdess, with travail sore,
He let his foes (in foreign lands begotten)
Gash the poor breast that love had gashed before.

"Alas! Alas! for him," the shepherd cries,
"Who tries from me my dearest love to part
So that she does not gaze into my eyes
Or see that I am wounded to the heart."

Then, after a long time, a tree he scaled,
Opened his strong arms bravely wide apart,
And clung upon that tree till death prevailed,
So sorely was he wounded in his heart.[22]

A critic with a positivist turn of mind, before the original was
discovered, suspected a similar process and sought to establish the

[22] "Un pastorcico solo está penado,
Ajeno de placer y de contento,
Y en su pastora puesto el pensamiento,
Y el pecho del amor muy lastimado.

"No llora por haberle amor llagado,
Que no le pena verse así afligido,
Aunque en el corazón está herido;
Mas llora por pensar que está olvidado.

"Que sólo de pensar que está olvidado
De su bella pastora, con gran pena
Se deja, maltratar en tierra ajena,
El pecho del amor muy lastimado,

"Y dice el Pastorcico¡ Ay, desdichado
De aquel que de mi amor ha hecho ausencia,
Y no quiere gozar la mi presencia,
Y el pecho por su amor muy lastimado!

"Y a cabo de un gran rato se ha encumbrado
Sobre un árbol do abrió sus brazos bellos,
Y muerto se ha quedado, asido de ellos,
El pecho del amor muy lastimado."

Text and translation taken from *The Poems of St. John of the Cross. The Spanish Text with a Translation by Roy Campbell*, New York, 1951, pp. 42-43.

lines of dependence for the verses of St. John of the Cross. Another critic, now that the model has been found, might see in it the complete explanation of the mystic's poem. He would go back to the "original," not bothering with the work of St. John since, for him, this is "a pure plagiarism with hardly an original detail." This critic, whom we have invented for the sake of illustration, has not entered into the poem: He has not understood it, and thus, of course, cannot explain it. He is forced to maintain that the work of St. John of the Cross has no interest for him. But genetic analysis and statistics are not the instruments by which poetry is detected. The example of St. John of the Cross illustrates a common literary procedure in Spain during "*el siglo del oro*" known as "*a lo divino*," by which profane works were taken as the inspiration for other works "with a divine intention." The originals were at times quite pedestrian as literature, though at other times they possessed a certain poetic charm.[23]

St. John of the Cross effected a transposition from a profane level to one intensely religious by the analogy of love. This process sheds light on similar transpositions made by the biblical authors: For example, the chant of field workers—a love song—made expressive of God's love for his people (the song of the vineyard—Is 5:1–7), or a sentinel's song (Is 21:11–12), and most probably the love poem which we call the Canticle of Canticles, are the result of this type of transposition.

We do not doubt that in the case of Psalm 29, it is possible to isolate speculative judgments directed toward activity—concerning the aptitude of a Canaanite Psalm for the Israelite liturgy; and practical judgments—concerned with the adaptation necessary to effect this transposition. If the first judgment is explicit, the others are concomitant with the exercise of the technique required to realize it, and are thus consequent on the effort and the choice. However, we are not sure that this type of analytic dissection is particularly useful here, whereas the moments of conception and execution mentioned in the Leonine description when they are broadly interpreted can provide real insight.

[23] Cf. Dámaso Alonso, *Poesía española. Ensayo de metodos y límites estilísticos*, Madrid, 1950, pp. 256–258.

A Narration

The story of the ten plagues in the Book of Exodus[24] is not a lyrical composition, nor does it burst forth from an intensely lived experience; it is a narrative of epic proportion, manifesting a calculated process of composition. No one can reasonably doubt that the author of the story as we now have it utilized preëxisting narrative material, some of which was contained in the Yahwistic account, while other elements pertained to the Priestly tradition. Some of the plagues were duplicated in these two compositions, others varied in their telling, and still others were simply diverse. The role of the personages involved, the tenor of the refrains used, as well as some other fixed formulas, were also different in the "J" and "P" traditions. But this does not matter: Our author took the two versions as the basis and source for his own composition. He chooses the number ten, because it is a simple figure on which to structure a story, and because of its capacity to signify seven plus three. The first and second plagues finish ambiguously; the third is decisive—"The finger of God is here." The fourth plague begins a mounting wave of affliction which subsides at the sixth plague, in order to prepare for the solemn entrance of the seventh: a theophany, which is announced in sonorous tones and culminates in the confession, "I have sinned." The eighth plague is preceded by a new prologue, announcing God's intentions and initiating a fresh series of calamities and concessions which culminate in the slaying of the first-born. We will not stop here to point out other ways in which the differences in the two preëxisting accounts are smoothed out or covered over (not always successfully). The final result is an epic narration of dynamic composition which, as such, is the work of the last author. (We presume, of course, that no one will equate "epic" with "pure fiction.")

In this instance, the most creative activity of the author lay in his work of composition, since the material and the formulas were already given. The execution was subordinated to a predetermined structure, and the whole was permeated by an epic tone which was intended to reveal the grandeur of the divine activity. We must, then, situate the impulse of charismatic inspiration within the whole process of composition from the very first choice of a struc-

[24] Ex 7–12.

ture until the whole work was realized. It is not difficult to describe this case in terms of speculative and practical judgments, or, indeed, in terms of conception and execution.

SUCCESSIVE INSPIRATION

The last example which we have just considered is of special importance, because many parts of the Old Testament as it has come down to us were composed in much the same way. The explanation of these passages forces on us a question which could be phrased like this: Are the preëxisting formulas and materials inspired, or is only the last stage of composition, the canonical text, inspired?

This is the question of "successive inspiration." Back in the time when Pesch and others were writing their manuals, it was possible to envisage the process of composition as having taken place in a way similar to our modern experience. Moses wrote his Pentateuch, Isaiah wrote his book, etc. But such thinking is untenable today. Many books of the Bible were composed in successive stages of literary creation: There were the traditions of local cult shrines, the composition of the Yahwist, the Elohistic variant on the same theme, the Priestly account with its cultic and legal interest, the various redactions and combinations of the above and other traditions; there were "chansons de geste," both secular and religious, collected in larger groups, unified on the basis of a religious theme, and rounded out by some passages of theological reflection (the Book of Judges); there were additions made to bring a text "up to date" (the last lines of Psalm 51); the insertion of the name "Judah" in oracles first addressed only to Israel is a commonplace. We find such procedures as the collection in a new dynamic unity of three oracles which were at first separate and of slightly different intent (as in Is 8); and so forth.

Must we imagine the Holy Spirit standing by with arms folded watching the whole process and then, just at the very last minute, stepping in to "inspire" the final stage of composition? Are we obliged to consider only the collector, or editor, or corrector as inspired? Ought we then to think that "inspiration" was only operative in the later period of Jewish history, between the Exile and the time of Esdras?

Such questions, obviously, answer themselves. A theory of inspiration so meager that it shuts out the Holy Spirit during the most creative moments in the composition of a work and then opens the door when there is practically nothing left to do, seems to us quite unacceptable. We are obliged to allow for some form or other of "successive inspiration" in order to explain the facts and apply the principles correctly. Wherever there is a real literary and religious contribution, there the Spirit acted. At the level of profane composition of non-Israelite origin, it is not necessary to invoke the charism of inspiration, and the same is true of a level of simple collection with no literary contribution. The books of the Bible grew along with the life of the people, and the Holy Spirit, far from looking on indifferently, was active in this process of growth and concomitant literary activity, breathing into it mysteriously yet powerfully.

Grelot treats this question by distinguishing three types of charisms which are related: (1) the prophetic charism in the Old Testament and the apostolic charism in the New Testament for the proclamation of the word of God; (2) the functional charism of language, by which the proclaimed word is preserved, elaborated, and developed; (3) the literary charism of language, by which the results of the former are fixed in written form. These three charisms all have relation to the word, that is, to language, but in varying degrees; the last mentioned is the least intense, but nonetheless essential in the constituting of the "Sacred Book." [25]

The Tone of a Work [26]

The example we gave above of the story of the plagues in Egypt suggests some other considerations. We spoke there of an "epic tone," which in the poet was an attitude of soul in the presence of his theme, and in the work was its unifying structure. We can attribute to this "tone," as a subjective attitude of the author, a creative function, because of its influence over the whole of the execution of the work in its structure and unity. If this attitude is not to be identified with the initial intuition, it certainly flows easily from

[25] Cf. the article of P. Grelot referred to above (ch. 2, n. 14).
[26] On the question of literary "tone," cf. W. Kayser, *Das sprachliche Kunstwerk*, Berne, 1948, esp. the last part of the book.

it, and as such must be considered to be under the influence of the Spirit.

The author of the Book of Judith envisaged his protagonist in an "heroic tone," while the tone of gentle irony pervades the characterization of Jonah. Joel (1:17–18) hears the bellows of the starving cattle with a compassion that is almost lyric. The tone of drama is felt in Nahum's contemplation of Nineveh's fall (2), or in the Book of Daniel's description of the scene in Belshazzar's dining hall where an empire changed hands (5).

The attitude or "tone" of soul on the part of the author determines the way in which the work is concretized as it receives its objective existence; in turn, the work determines the "tone" which the sympathetic reader will derive from it. For this reason, the tone of a biblical work assumes an important function as revelation, one which is at times as important as the thing being told. We find it very difficult to reduce this attitude or tone to any kind of "judgment," yet we cannot imagine that such an important factor could lie outside the influence of the charism of inspiration.

THE NEW TESTAMENT

The New Testament presents us with less variety. The Gospels began to acquire their consistency in a stage of oral tradition which was nevertheless Gospel. It was at this stage that they received many of their literary forms: There were larger units of composition such as the Passion narrative, and smaller unities which can be discerned because of the similarity of their structure: miracle stories, conflict stories, parables, etc. All of this provided the preëxisting material for the evangelists in their original work of literary composition.[27]

The literary efforts of the evangelists were profoundly personal contributions, and that is why each of them offers us a picture of Christ which is different yet complementary. They retain many of the forms and phrases which were found in the material that lay

[27] In regard to the formation of the Gospels, cf. X. Léon-Dufour, *Les Évangiles et l'Histoire de Jésus*, Paris, 1963; V. Taylor, *The Formation of the Gospel Tradition*, New York, 1957; C. Dodd, *The Apostolic Preaching and its Development*, 1st ed., London, 1936; J. R. Scheifler, *Así nacieron los Evangelios*, Bilbao, 1964. The bibliography and notes in this latter work are especially valuable.

before them, imposing on it a higher unity deriving from an over-all narrative schema and theological interpretation. Without a doubt, the literary work of the evangelists was inspired from the moment of the original intuition or intention which grew out of a personal understanding of Christ, until the last patient touches of redaction. It is not as certain that the previous stages of composition were inspired, but considering the extent of the influence that this stage had on the later literary Gospels, it seems reasonable to suppose that the successive elaborations of the material which later became the Gospels was inspired also.

The letters are in large measure doctrinal with parenetic material interspersed. Often, they give literary stability to formulas which were part of the apostolic preaching, thus posing for us the problem of where to place the emphasis in an analysis of their compositions: Is it in their writing or in their speaking? (we will treat of this problem in Chapter 9). The first Epistle of St. Peter is presented as a collaborative undertaking: "I write you this brief appeal through Silvanus, our trusty brother" (5:12). It appears as though the work of Silvanus was more than secretarial, and that he played a real role in the framing of the inspired message, which means, of course, that he was also inspired. The Epistle to the Hebrews seems to be a homily approved and recommended by St. Paul; but we cannot imagine that inspiration began with his "subsequent approval." The letters, especially of St. Peter and St. Paul, incorporate material found in the ancient liturgy. They refer to "spiritual canticles" (Eph 5:19; Col 3:16), and even quote from early hymns (Phil 2:5–11), or professions of faith (1 Cor 15:3ff.).

The New Testament has effected an immense work of transposition in which the Old Testament is placed within the new context of the Christ-fact. There is more here than the simple application of a few explicit prophecies, or the attempt to elucidate others that are more obscure; nor is it merely a question of the homiletical, theological, or pastoral use of a few passages from the ancient writings. The whole of the Old Testament is seen in the light of the glory shining on the face of Christ Jesus that transforms and elevates it by conferring on it a fullness of meaning which crowns its insights and tendential aspirations with a perfect but unsuspected plentitude. The new context is charged with transforming power. The original sense of the text is not denied but is rather transposed by its new context, being caught up in a dynamic movement and sharing a higher life. Thus, the Old Testament, to use Origen's favorite theme, becomes Gospel.

Once the Logos had touched them, they raised their eyes and saw only Jesus, no one else. Moses, the law, and Elijah, prophecy, had become one thing; they had become one with Jesus who is the Gospel. And so things are not as they were before; there are no longer three, for these three have become one Being.[28]

This transposition was effected by Christ, first of all by the very fact of His Incarnation, and then by His words which conveyed His own mystery and explained it. We see Him at Nazareth proclaiming: "Today in your hearing, this text has come true" (Lk 4:21); we hear Him explain, "but let the Scriptures be fulfilled" (Mk 14:49), and in a special way after the Resurrection, when "He began with Moses and all the prophets and explained to them the passages which referred to Himself in every part of the Scriptures" (Lk 24:27). It is not quite exact to say that the Church received the Bible directly from the Synagogue. The Bible was given to the Church by Christ, and all the apostles, fathers, doctors, and saints of the Church have understood and followed this example.

This transposition of meaning, this filling with meaning, is a true literary activity, one which Lohfink calls the "hagiographical act." [29] It is an activity by which literary form is given to a new and mysterious reality that completes the meaning of the older texts by joining them in a transcedent unity toward which they tended, but which they could never attain or demand. If this view is cor-

---

[28] Ἀγγὰ μετὰ ἀφὴν τοῦ λογοῦ, τοὺς ὀφθαλμοὺς ἐπαράντες εἶδον Ἰησοῦν μόνον, καὶ οὐδένα ἄλλον. Ἐν μόνον γέγονε Μωϋσῆς ὁ νόμος καὶ Ἡλίας ἡ προφητεία Ἰησοῦ τῷ Εὐαγγελίῳ. καὶ οὐχ ὥσπερ ἦσαν πρότερον τρεῖς οὕτω μεμενήκασιν, ἀλλὰ γεγόνασιν οἱ τρεῖς εἰς τὸ ἕν. "On Matthew, t. 12, 43," PG 13, 1084.

The same thought is expressed in a slightly different way in his sixth homily on Leviticus:

"Doceat te Evangelium, quia cum transformatus esset in gloriam Jesus, etiam Moyses et Elias simul cum ipso apparuerunt in gloria, ut scias quia lex et prophetae, et Evangelium in unum semper conveniunt, et in una gloria permanent. Denique et Petrus cum vellet eis tria facere tabernacula, imperitiae notatur, tanquam qui nesciret quid diceret. Legi enim, et prophetis, et Evangelio non tria, sed unum est tabernaculum, quae est Ecclesia Dei." "Hom 6 in Lev," PG 12, 468.

[29] In art. cit. (cf. ch. 6, n. 11).

rect, then the activity by which the fullness of meaning is conveyed was performed under the action of the Holy Spirit, and the necessity for a "spiritual understanding" of the Old Testament follows ineluctably.

SYNTHESIS

Now that we have seen the variety existing in the ways and results of literary activity, we would like to propose another schema, intended as complementary to those which we have already seen. It has three levels: the material, the intuition, and the execution.

(1) *The Material of a Literary Work.*
The stuff of which literature is made is living experience—one's own or another's—which has been appropriated. It may be a single vivid occurrence, or a series of events which accumulate in the consciousness with the rhythm: experience—reflection. The material that a novelist uses can be the experience of his own life, or it can be the life around him which he considers or discovers; it can come directly from life, or through the medium of something which is read. This material can be theoretical knowledge, or a series of facts, or some preëxisting literary elaboration.

Strictly speaking, the material does not pertain to the creative process, and has interest only because of its relation to the future literary work, insofar as it is transformed by the productive activity of the writer. It is in this light that we should view the biblical events, the court records, the preëxisting profane literature, etc. These things may exist as the result of a special action of God; they may be instances of a divine intervention in history, but they are not yet the object of the charism of inspiration.

(2) *The Intuition.*
At times, the light of understanding comes only after a long and painful period of gestation, and then in a flash, the formless mass of our experiences takes shape, and we see the results of our searching. At other times, the intuition comes suddenly, without any awareness of a period of preparation, and our soul is held, as it were, in suspense. We experience the insight as something unsuspected, imperative, or serene, which fills us with a sense of light

and the joy of discovery. It may be that we have caught the message of a symbol, or perhaps some analogy reveals a new dimension of reality.

This intuition becomes the life center, activating and illuminating the whole process to follow. It is what Stephen Spender calls the initial idea, it is masculine or germinal. Proust has pointed out how intuition precedes the work of the intellect, and Virginia Woolf has stressed its unifying power; it is itself simple. Pirandello, in a memorable passage, describes how, as he was at grips with some personalities which had presented themselves to his imagination, there came to him an intuition which shed light on the whole complex and was the seed of his *Six Characters in Search of an Author*. Writers are all in accord in assigning intuition as the true starting point for a work, and as the catalytic energy which fuses preëxisting material.

If the biblical authors have this in common with their literary counterparts, then we must maintain that this intuition in them takes place under the influence of inspiration, and that it manifests a reality, though not in propositional form. There must, of course, be some latitude allowed for variation in the intensity and extent of these germinal intuitions. The Bible is not a collection of nothing but masterpieces.

(3) *Execution.*

Consequent on the intuition, there may occur an impulse, felt as an inner necessity, to write or to compose. Goethe speaks of some poems which occurred to him all of a sudden, and demanded to be composed without delay with such insistence that he felt an instinctive or hypnotic force impelling him to write immediately.

This interior urge sets the whole process of execution in motion. It is directed toward an activity which the writer performs in regard to language; that is to say, the whole process by which the "poetic idea," or seed, or intuition is made objective, is ordered from the very moment of its inception toward language.

We ought not to consider language as some lifeless stone; it is a medium possessing a certain capacity to work along with the artist. By language we mean, as we said before, not merely the dictionary and the grammatical dimension of words, but the whole complex of possibilities and resonances assembled in a given linguistic entity.

But language can also present to the writer an aspect of resistance. Anyone can appreciate this quality of language who has tried to translate poetry, while maintaining the force and shades of the original. But even when we compose in our own language, we can encounter this resistance which will give rise either to a sense of challenge or to a "lapidary style," in which language is treated like a stone. When certain poets complain that their poem does not correspond to their interior vision, it is possible that, apart from the exaggerations of the romantics, they are referring to this resistance of language which has not been overcome by their intuition and technique. This is true not only of poetry or literature, but even didactic treatises can experience the intractability of words, thwarting the attempt of a teacher to hit upon the right formulation. Pesch speaks of this common experience in his discussion on the psychology of inspiration:

Someone can have the intention to write, and know what he wants to write, and still hesitate and labor in order to find the right expression of what he wants to say. This is true not only of poets who sweat and shiver in order to find apt clothing for their thought, but also of other writers who, after having removed all doubt as to what they want to say, still often cannot find the right way to say it, except after a long series of attempts, and then not infrequently in later editions they say the same thing in different words.[30]

Pesch does not sufficiently consider the act of expression as a creative element in composition. But to a large extent, the talent of a writer is found precisely in the art of expression. We do not readily accept the excuses of a bad writer who makes appeal to his profound and genial intuitions.

Actually what a writer does, is to transform his material, the world and his experience, into an organic significant system com-

[30] "*Potest aliquis velle scribere et scire, quid scribere velit, et interim anxius haerere et laborare de elocutione rerum scribendarum, ut exemplo sunt non soli poetae, qui saepe sudant et algent ad inveniendum vestitum aptum cogitationum suarum, sed etiam alii scriptores, qui saepe omni dubitatione iam remota de rebus, quae dicendae sint, modum dicendi convenientem non inveniunt nisi post multa tentamina, et in posterioribus editionibus easdem res non raro aliis verbis exprimunt.*" No. 414.

posed of words. This takes place by an act of language in which all the possibilities and resonances of language collaborate.

In the process of giving expression, new intuitions occur and are subordinated, and other, lesser insights are gained; but sometimes a greater intuition arises, dethroning and enlisting the former, and the work takes a new direction.

This collaboration of language in the act of realizing a work stands out clearly in writers who have a great sensitivity for language. Such men—trained perhaps in philology—have a feeling for the roots of words, and are often able to pass from a verbal analogy to one that is ontological.

At the end of the process, which may have been easy or painful, direct or intricate, the finished work emerges. It contains the preëxisting material in a different mode of being. It confers on the intuition an objective existence, though not enunciating it by way of proposition, and the work of execution, either manifest or hidden, receives stability.

An attentive analysis of the biblical writings sometimes reveals to us the work of execution. We do not know if it came easily to the writers, or if it cost them something, but the fact is there. These men labored over a language they had received and allowed it to come to their aid. Sometimes they capitalized on the sound of its words; sometimes they employed the alternating rhythm of parallelism to convey a sense of balance; sometimes they quickened the rhythm in order to concentrate their message.[31] All of this labor must be seen as having taken place under the motion of the Holy Spirit, for it is mainly here that we find the charism. The role of the sacred writers consisted in transforming into a significant word-system the history of the people, their own personal experiences, the insights they received from God, the meaning of history, the works of salvation, the response of the people of God. / . . . Inspiration is a charism of language, and language is forged at this stage of literary production. There is no problem in imagining two expressions of the same thing, both inspired, and one better than the other; they can even be from the same author, and indeed often are.

Before this stage of activity, the word does not exist, there is no word of God. It is in this process of expression that the word is

[31] We have treated this aspect, with many illustrative analyses, in *Estudios de Poética Hebrea*, Barcelona, 1963.

realized, and if the Bible is the word of God, it is because He has directed this process. The being of the words is their signification or meaning, and the being of the work is in the system of significant words. In the word of the Bible, revelation is present and available—it is the meaning of the words. We have avoided here using the expression "revelation is contained" in the words. Such terminology tends to make one think that there is some real distinction between the word as receptacle and the meaning as its content. But this is false; the meaning is realized in the word, and the being of the word is its meaning. Otherwise, it is nothing but fruitless sound.

The motion of the Spirit hovers over the language act of the sacred writer, and makes of it an act of revelation. The context of the Spirit and the context of the Logos—these two, which are united ontologically, meet here again at the term of our analysis.

Postscript

There are some who would not wish to see this chapter conclude without a more detailed discussion of the operation of the faculties which collaborate in the process of execution. But such a discussion would be interminable. There would have to be some treament of the sense of rhythm which plays such a large part in some passages, and which can register the most delicate shade of emotions; then there is the question of phonetics—the role of sound and tone in literary expression; we would have to enter into the question of imagination as creative and imitative, for this is essential in poetry. There should also be some consideration for the discernment of various shades and resonances of meaning, as well as an attempt to assess the various semi-conscious factors which find expression in a literary work.

It will be sufficient and briefer to invoke the principle of Benoit with regard to the analogous nature of inspiration: The charismatic influence extends to all the faculties according to their specific function in literary activity. To complete this statement, we will only add that this functioning is not parallel, but organically interrelated, and thus the charismatic influence should be conceived as central and all-pervasive.

Bibliography for Chapter 7

The Psychology of Inspiration

The Description Given by Benoit. It is probably best to begin with Benoit's most recent article, "Révélation et Inspiration," *RB* 70, 1963, pp. 321–370. (See *Aspects of Biblical Inspiration* translated by J. Murphy-O'Connor and S. K. Ashe, Chicago, 1965.) His other works are referred to there and the positions they set forth modified and clarified. The first part of the article, "Revelation and Inspiration According to St. Thomas" is dedicated to giving a more ample and flexible view of the Angelic Doctor's thought. The second part, "Revelation and Inspiration in the Bible," is also marked by a suppleness of treatment in regard to the sacred text. The third part, "Criticism and Suggestions in regard to the Modern Discussions," terminates the work and attempts to interpret the data in the light of the categories of speculative and practical judgment. The work of A. Desroches, *Jugement pratique et jugement spéculatif chez l'Ecrivain inspiré*, Ottawa, 1958, is a thesis of one hundred and forty pages. Its orientation is descriptive, its documentation meager. There is also the very competent thesis of Denis Farkasfalvy, *L'inspiration de l'Ecriture Sainte dans la théologie de Saint Bernard*, Studia Anselmiana, no. 53, Rome, 1964.

An Artist with Language. Since this aspect of the psychology of inspiration is seldom treated at length in manuals, the bibliography will be somewhat ample in order to familiarize readers with the names and opinions most current in this field. Monographs on inspiration have sometimes attempted to describe the psychology of inspiration: H. Lusseau in his *Essai sur l'inspiration scripturaire*, Paris, 1930 (a thesis defended in 1928), dedicates a chapter to this topic before discussing the description of *Providentissimus Deus*; it consists of thirteen pages. Among the authors cited, one finds Pesch, Billot, Schiffini, and St. Thomas; there is a citation from Boileau, and Pascal is also represented, along with some nineteenth-century French orators. A. Desroches in his work also dedicates a chapter to the psychology of the literary author (pp. 107–123). His authorities are Cajetan, St. Thomas, John of St. Thomas, and Aristotle. There is one quote from Chateaubriand, one from Maritain, and two from Longhaye. Such a method is simply insufficient. In order to discuss this question properly, we must begin from a wider experience of literature and techniques of composition. It would be impossible to cite all the authors who have exercised some influence on the ideas which we propose in the "Description Drawn from Literary Creation." The purpose of the enumeration which follows is, as we have said, to provide a point of departure for those who wish to study this aspect of the problem more fully.

From a philosophical point of view, the question of creativity has been studied only recently. The essays of Heidegger, mentioned in the bibliography of Chapter 5, are an interesting beginning. There is a good article by Carl Hausman, "Spontaneity: Its Rationality and Its Reality," in *IPQ* 4, 1964, pp. 20–47, in which there is a review of the opinions of Whitehead, Husserl, Hartmann, etc.; the bibliographical material in the footnotes is also valuable. J. Maritain in *Creative Intuition in Art and Poetry*, New York, 1953, treats of this theme in Thomistic categories (on Thomism's effort to account for the fact of poetry, cf. Curtius, *European Literature and the Latin Middle Ages*, p. 227). Maritain writes from his own experience as an author, and with a real sympathy and familiarity with poetry. The most important chapter for the topic which interests us here is ch. 4, "Creative Intuition and Poetic Knowledge." In the same tradition, but harder to follow, is the little study by T. Gilby, *Poetic Experience* (Essays in Order, no. 13), New York, 1934; ch. 9, "Presence," is especially good.

It is very important in a study of artistic creation to consult the statements of artists themselves, and in this regard we are fortunate to have good material in English. Brewster Ghiselin in *The Creative Process*, New York, 1955, collects the testimony of mathematicians (Poincaré, Einstein), musicians (Mozart), painters (van Gogh, Picasso), sculptors (Moore), and various literary authors. Charles Norman in *Poets on Poetry*, New York, 1962, presents the views of sixteen different English-speaking poets on their art; not all of these speak of the creative process, but all make interesting reading; the same can be said of the collection of essays in *The Limits of Language*, compiled by W. Gibson, New York, 1962, which includes in part 2, "Consequences of the Problem, Testimony from Artists and Writers"—articles written by Sartre, Virginia Woolf, Wallace Stevens, etc. There are four other excellent studies of the same type: H. Block and H. Salinger, *The Creative Vision. Modern European Writers on their Art*, New York, 1960; W. Allen, *Writers on Writing*, New York, 1948 (the essays here are all good and they are organized with great perception. We have used this book a great deal). M. Cowley, *Writers at Work*, New York, 1959 (a series of interviews, treats of the techniques of composition); and John W. Aldridge, *Critiques and Essays on Modern*

Fiction. 1920–1951, New York, 1952, which contains a wealth of valuable material, and a good bibliography: under part 2, ch. 2, "Writers on their Craft," there are fifty-six titles listed, and under part 3, ch. 3, "The Artist and the Creative Process," there are eighty-nine books and articles listed.

There are some good works that treat of creativity by an analysis of the works and the artists who produce them: A. Maurois, *The Art of Writing*, New York, 1960; Wallace Fowlie, *Jacob's Night*, New York, 1947. P. Valéry discusses both aspects in the series of essays which make up *The Art of Poetry*, New York, 1961; cf. especially "Problems of Poetry."

8. The Author and the Community:
The Sociology of Inspiration

We have often spoken of "the inspired author," presupposing that the inspired writers were individual authors. But is this not a modern idea of literary production, one that is inapplicable to the period and mentality of the biblical authors? According to some, we ought to speak of an inspired people rather than inspired authors. Inspiration would be a charism commonly held, a great wind which sweeps and whirls through the land of Palestine. To speak of inspired authors is to dole out the Spirit with a medicine dropper; the Spirit animates the whole of the Chosen People, all of the body of the Church. This is how we must view the Bible; it is the work of a whole people.

This idea, though still quite imprecise, is current in some circles today, and this invites us to treat of it explicitly under the somewhat simplified heading, "The Sociology of Inspiration."

The precursor of this theory seems to have been Friedrich Schleiermacher. The father of semi-rationalism also has some things to say about the Holy Spirit. According to him, the Holy Spirit is the spirit of the community: this is a thoroughly romantic concept, one enshrined in the magic word "*Geist*." It suffices to recall with what enthusiasm the romantics listened to the "spirit" of a people; Herder (a pre-romantic) studied the "spirit" of Hebrew poetry; Humboldt sought out the "spirit" of various languages. The Holy Spirit of the Church is the religious spirit which it has received from Christ, which is an arational impulse. Christ has "in-spirited" into the Church the true religious spirit, and in this sense has inspired all its activity, including the writings of its holy books. The historical writings are inspired in that the community recognizes itself and its deeds in them, and directs the conservation of its records. This is said of the New Testament: as for the Old Testament, only some fragments are inspired, because the Spirit is somehow there, even though it had not yet become fully defined as the common spirit of the Church.

We should note these two points: the spirit of the community activates, inspires literary activity; and the spirit of the community recognizes and expresses itself in narratives. So far, we have seen only the social dimension of the problem.

Schleiermacher goes on to coördinate the social factor with the personal factor: the Spirit of Christ was received by the apostles, and they are the ones who form the spirit of the community. All the activity of the apostles as individuals was inspired, and this includes their literary activity. Thus, the two factors, social and personal, are coördinated.[1]

In criticizing Schleiermacher, we should note first of all that we cannot conclude that an idea is automatically ridiculous or false, because derived from a romantic origin or context. Schleiermacher tried to find a compromise between the rationalism prevalent in his time and the Christian world outlook; thus, some of his ideas can be purified from error and transposed to a Catholic key, as has already been recognized by the theologians of the school of Tübingen.[2] For we, too, believe that the Holy Spirit animates the Church as a body; however, we do not go on to identify the Person of the Holy Spirit with communal feeling.

FORM CRITICISM

At the beginning of the century, the sociological outlook began to penetrate into the exegesis of the Old Testament. Pedersen wrote a

[1] But, of course, his refusal to admit that the Holy Spirit is a Person of the Trinity is unacceptable. We can not admit his explanation of the Spirit as something merely human and social, which is participated in by the individual. It is this humanism of Schleiermacher which irritates Karl Barth so much.

[2] Cf. P. Dausch, *Die Schriftinspiration. Eine biblisch-geschichtliche Studie,* Freiburg, 1891, esp. [tr.] "The Catholic School at Tübingen," pp. 186–192.

book on the social life of Israel, *Israel. Its Life and Culture*,[3] which rescued the Old Testament from intellectual rarefaction and placed it within the life of the people. Hermann Gunkel with his famous formula, "*Sitz im Leben*," sought and found the social situations which acted as origin and medium of transmission for many literary types, the cultic context of many of the psalms, for example. Neither Pedersen nor Gunkel gave any formal consideration to the problem of inspiration. In fact, Gunkel rejected the idea explicitly: "The pretty myth of inspiration has already vanished." Nevertheless, the social dimension of the Bible had been firmly established.

From Gunkel, the burden of the labor passed to the New Testament, due to the work of four pioneers: Dibelius, Bultmann, K. L. Schmidt, and Bertram. According to them, the synoptic Gospels are not the work of the evangelists—secondary redactors of minor importance, but of the whole Christian community, stimulated by the challenge of its various activities and needs.[4]

The words and deeds of Jesus, or those attributed to Him, are collected in stereotyped formulas which originated in and were transmitted by various specific "life-situations" (*Sitz im Leben*), which determined the form or pattern which the pericope or saying would take (form criticism). The community is creative and literarily active, and thus it is pointless to seek out the author of each literary unit: many have collaborated, and there are many authors. The most that can be done is to distinguish the Palestinian community from the Hellenistic community. The community in its cult effected the apotheosis of Christ, and thus from the cult, later on, there was derived the dogma of the divinity of Jesus (Bertram); the community in its missionary activity recounted or invented miracles in order to strike back at the propaganda used by the Hellenistic cults; the community placed on the lips of Jesus the solutions to problems it was experiencing.

This is not the place for an extensive criticism of such a theory, which has its origins in the writings of Durkheim, except to men-

[3] Foto reprint with additions, New York, 1959.
[4] A particularly clear exposition of this question can be found in Ed. Schick, *Formgeschichte und Synoptikerexegese. Eine kritische Untersuchung über die Möglichkeit und die Grenzen der formgeschichtlichen Methode*, Neutestamentliche Abhandlungen, no. 18, Münster, 1940. Other works are listed below in the bibliography.

tion that the theories of the French philosopher entered late into the study of the New Testament, long after they had been discredited in other areas of thought.

There is, however, in the theory an element of truth which is accepted and adopted in Catholic study of the New Testament, namely, the fact that the material worked on by the synoptic authors has its roots within the life, thought, and worship of the early community, and that it came to them, at least in some instances, already possessing a literary form. But the community here envisaged was organized and not a formless mass; it was governed by responsible leaders, and still possessed some early witnesses to the things which were being recorded. Lately, there has been a tendency to reëvaluate the intense and conscious work of the evangelists; this line of thought is being developed by a method known as "redaction criticism" (*Redaktionsgeschichte*).

The authors cited above do not consider the problem of inspiration, but the Catholic version of this theory must ask the question: Who is inspired? It seems logical to consider that the literary material, before reaching the hands of the gospel authors, had already experienced the influence of the charism of inspiration. This material had already been formulated and fashioned to some degree, and thus it is not a question of preëxisting material, but of material which is specifically literary.

KARL RAHNER

Karl Rahner takes another approach to the problem.[5] His effort is directed to penetrating and concretizing the meaning of a formula already venerable in the study of this question. What does it mean to say that God is the author of sacred Scripture?

The Church knew an initial stage of formation or "crystallization" at the time of her foundation which was not merely a moment of time, but extended throughout the apostolic age, that is, roughly, the first generation of eyewitnesses. Now, one of the constituent factors in this process of self-formation was the activity by which the Church declared and expressed herself in formulas which are permanent, definitive, and binding on future generations. This activity, which is an essential component in the

[5] *Inspiration in the Bible.* Cf. bibliography.

Church's structure, is that by which the Church's self-awareness achieves literary objectivity. God in His historic and salvific action founded a Church as an historical and eschatological reality, and caused it to crystallize in a structure which included all its essential components. This means, then, that God caused that activity by which the Church achieved literary self-expression, since this is one of her essential component factors; He determined this by an infallible and formal pre-definition. In this way, God is the author of Scripture. Thus, for example, God and St. Paul are both authors of the note to Philemon: Paul is the author of the note as such, and God is the author of the action by which the Church, through this note, gives expression to her charity—a constituent factor of her being. There is one common effect of the two activities, but there are two diverse formalities. In a similar way, the Old Testament is the expression of the community of the covenant people which prepared for the definitive fact of the Church.

We should note here that, according to Rahner, this activity of self-expression is accomplished in the Church by individual persons responding to specific occasions within her life, and under the impulse of the unifying direction of the Spirit. Those who accuse Rahner of denying the fact of personal inspiration either have not read or have not understood him. It is simply that he does not enter into the question as to how God actuated this formal pre-definition in each human author.

Rahner perfectly coördinated the personal and social aspects of inspiration, aptly stressing the ecclesial context of both the inspired authors and the works they produce. This is his greatest contribution to the discussion of the problem (and we seem to hear in it a distant echo of Schleiermacher).

Pierre Benoit touches on the question rather hastily. He speaks in his article on the analogies of inspiration[6] of a "dramatic inspiration": It is the motion of the Spirit directing the people in their historical activity, and providing the theme and the material for the inspired books. Considered from the point of view of its origin —the Spirit, and of its ultimate place in the sacred writings, this common activity partakes of the context of scriptural inspiration. As we mentioned before, we find this terminology unsatisfactory, and we would prefer to use the word "charism" to indicate the

[6] "Les analogies de l'inspiration," in Sacra Pagina, op. cit.

common denominator of these gifts, and then go on to distinguish various differences and relations.

D. J. McCarthy has undertaken a study of this question in a recent article, "Personality, Society, and Inspiration."[7] His opening remark that "the Bible was formed in, by, and for a society" is nicely balanced by some judicious reflections on the personal factor within tradition which sustains the society. The sacred author, writing for the community, knew that his work would be actively received and used by the community; the community took up his work, used it, and elaborated on it. We may not speak of some "impersonal" source of these works, but at most of anonymous authors.

John L. McKenzie

The theme of the social character of inspiration has been proposed with particular emphasis by J. L. McKenzie in a brief article which acknowledges its dependence on the works of Rahner and Benoit.[8]

The article treats of a series of problems, formulated quite forcibly, which derive from the critical study of biblical literature. It is dated April, 1962, and we note that, independently, it coincides with some of our own preoccupations in this area, such as the question of successive authors[9] and that of the relation between speech and writing. In regard to many basic points, we agree with McKenzie, for example, on the fact that the biblical authors functioned as members of a community. All that we wish to note here are a few positions which we think are exaggerated.

It seems to us that he exaggerates the picture somewhat when he attempts to break it down into its individual components:

We know, or we think we know, that in the ancient world the manuscript was treated with great freedom; it was subject to the revision and expansion of each successive owner, and it is this constant process which has created our critical problems. In oral tradition, the material is flexible to the extreme, and it can be said without exaggeration that each successive bard or balladist was the creator of the story anew.[10]

[7] Cf. bibliography.
[8] Cf. bibliography.
[9] Cf. "XVII Semana Bíblica Española," 1956, published in 1958.
[10] Art. cit. (bibliography), p. 117.

To say that the last statement is not an exaggeration seems to us to be equally an exaggeration. It is a fact that in the Bible we have vestiges of ancient written tradition. In any oral literary culture, there is a body of trained "reciters" who claim fidelity to an accepted version of what they relate; in Israel as among other peoples, there was the preservative and conservative factor of the cult, in which such texts were handed on.

It seems to us that there is another exaggeration, due to a lack of shading, in the neat opposition established between a modern author who wishes to express his individuality and the biblical author desirous of concealing his individuality in order to be the voice of the community. Many authors of our culture have been the authentic voices of their society and wished to be so, while some biblical authors express themselves in the first person—the prophets and wise men, for example. It is, however, certainly true that the degree of reflective self-consciousness has increased in man because of the self-awareness of the Renaissance, the cultivated self-reflection of the romantics, and liberal individualism. It is also true that a modern author wants to be known and recognized, whereas the fact that the name of an ancient writer was preserved was often due to the devotion of his disciples; but ancient times knew pseudonymous as well as anonymous authors.[11] In this regard, McCarthy's article, referred to above, is more to the point.

There is a third consideration: here and there, McKenzie refers to the biblical authors as the spokesmen of their society. In a general sense, this is quite true, but this generic meaning can be further specified, as we will see later on.

When McKenzie speaks of the experience which the prophets received from God, and of their efforts to articulate it,[12] he introduces once again the personal element which complements the social aspect of inspiration.

Once the exaggerations have been reduced, McKenzie's theory

[11] The fundamental study on this point is by J. A. Sint, *Pseudonymität im Altertum. Ihre Formen und Gründe*, Innsbruck, 1960. He was criticized by M. Forderer (*Gnom* 33, 1961, pp. 440–445) and answered in ZKT 83, 1961, pp. 493ff. For a later period, cf. K. Aland, "The Problem of Anonymity and Pseudonymity in Christian Literature of the First Two Centuries," *JTS* 12, 1961, pp. 39–49.

[12] *Art. cit.*, p. 121.

does not force the personalities of the authors into an amorphous mass, but rather gives them their roots in a society. In this sense, inspiration can be considered a communal charism which does not dispense with, but rather demands, the voice of its spokesman.

Israel expressed her faith and recited her traditions through her priests, prophets, kings, poets, sages, and even through her bards and balladists who created and transmitted oral traditions.[13]

There is another interesting point touched on in this article, namely, the fact that biblical criticism has given us a new awareness of man's social dimension, which fits in nicely with our renewed sense of the Church. This aspect, not explicitly formulated by the author, gives a special importance to the article.

EVALUATION

What should we think of such theories? We should first of all reject any notion of an amorphous community which is somehow creative; there is no such thing as a literary work produced by "everybody," and there is no need to revive the romantic theory which dissolved a work of art back into the masses. We reject this latter idea, not because it is romantic, but because it is wrong; there were many intuitions in that school of thought which will have to be rethought one day. But this aspect of the "Volksgeist" view of literature is certainly not one of them.

At first sight, it may seem as though the process which we have referred to as "successive inspiration" differs little from the romantic view. However, it is one thing to place a work indiscriminately within the masses, and quite another to discern in a text the combination of various sources, traditions, and redactors as in the Pentateuch, or to distinguish between an author and an editor as in the Book of Isaiah.

We would like now to adopt another point of view in order to appreciate the social dimension of the inspired books and their authors: let us look at this mystery from the angle of language and literature.

[13] Art. cit., p. 120.

LANGUAGE

We should recall here what was said about language as a social reality, and the limits of this dimension which we sketched in that discussion. Someone learns a language with its stock of words already formed, its power to develop new words by analogy, its outlook and expressions, its delicately shaded areas of meaning, and all the treasures of appreciation and description which have been deposited within it over the centuries. He consciously develops the power and the manner of communicating himself to another, of thinking and of being influenced; and in this sense, a person remains forever modified by the social dimension of the language he has learned.

Such modification is, however, only the remote preparation for the charism of inspiration: When Jeremiah complained that he did not know how to speak, he was alluding to his lack of literary competence; and Isaiah received the consecration of the power of speech which he already possessed. We are considering here a certain *energeia* or power of language which collaborates in the execution of a literary work, and which thus provides a means by which the society of the inspired author influences his work. And since language is not a purely inert factor in the literary process, we can envisage society present and active by means of language, during the whole of the author's effort. But we should not exaggerate this influence; many others, equally indebted to society for their language, use it without thereby becoming inspired.

When someone uses a language, it is possible for him to surrender himself to it simply and accept it as it is, adopting its formulas, idioms, and clichés; or he can submit to the inherent power of the language with a certain ingenuous realism, perhaps employing its sound patterns without fully grasping their meaning. And even if he does not go to this extreme, he can still accept language without any discussion, when he should have maintained a certain considered distance.

In many ways and in varying degrees, however, each individual usually adapts a language to his own needs and temperament, thus asserting his liberty in relation to the possibilities of the language: in this lies the greatness of language as a medium by which human liberty receives expression and realization. This liberty with language is in direct proportion to one's mastery of it; thus we see the balance between the personal and social factors in language: The personal is expressed in a social medium, manifesting and realizing itself in relation with other persons by means of a common possession. In this instance, the social dimension of language enters into the question of inspiration, which is a personal charism of communication, actuated and expressed in a social context and through a social medium.

The possibilities of a language are in some degree limited. We do not refer here to all the remote possibilities which, if accumulated, would actually change the language. There are some who maintain that everything can be said with language, everything can be translated. This is true, but only partially.

Let us consider a language in the concrete:[14] It has a limited number of words which express reality in a certain way, and whose contiguous areas of meaning or "*Sprachfeld*" serve to limit the meanings possible to each (Good morning—Good day; yellow—orange—red, etc.). There are words in other languages which express shades of thought intermediate to those which we possess. When we wish to translate these intermediate shades, we must have recourse to circumlocution or paraphrase. Perhaps the original and the translation will say the same thing at least in regard to the informative content, but the total content of one will not equal the other. And even if we are able to give full expression to the original so that its overtones are understood, we do it by a multiplicity of words, and we still lack conformity to the literary tone of the original. An incisive expression is never adequated by a paraphrase. We may perhaps seek to overcome the gaps in the language we are using, by having recourse to technical terms, but this means that we have left the domain and level of language.

The possibilities and limitations of translation are well expressed by Ezra Pound in his essay on "How to Read":[15]

If we chuck out the classifications which apply to the outer shape of the work, or to its occasion, and if we look at what actually happens,

[14] An excellent work on these aspects of language is that by J. Trier, *Der deutsche Wortschatz im Sinnbezirk des Verstandes; die Geschichte eines sprachlichen Feldes*, Heidelberg, 1931.

[15] *Literary Essays of Ezra Pound*, ed. by T. S. Eliot, New York, 1960, p. 25.

in, let us say, poetry, we will find that the language is charged or energized in various manners.

That is to say, there are three "kinds of poetry":

Melopoeia, wherein the words are charged, over and above their plain meaning, with some musical property, which directs the bearing or trend of that meaning.

Phanopoeia, which is a casting of images upon the visual imagination.

Logopoeia, "the dance of the intellect among words," that is to say, it employs words not only for their direct meaning, but it takes count in a special way of habits of usage, of the context we expect to find with the word, its usual concomitants, of its known acceptances, and of ironical play. It holds the aesthetic content which is peculiarly the domain of verbal manifestation, and cannot possibly be contained in plastic or in music. It is the latest come, and perhaps most tricky and undependable mode.

The melopoeia can be appreciated by a foreigner with a sensitive ear, even though he be ignorant of the language in which the poem is written. It is practically impossible to transfer or translate it from one language to another, save perhaps by divine accident, and for half a line at a time.

Phanopoeia can, on the other hand, be translated almost, or wholly, intact. When it is good enough, it is practically impossible for the translator to destroy it save by very crass bungling, and the neglect of perfectly well-known and formulative rules.

Logopoeia does not translate; though the attitude of mind it expresses may pass through a paraphrase. Or one might say, you can not translate it "locally," but having determined the original author's state of mind, you may or may not be able to find a derivative or an equivalent.

It is often in these areas of limitation that a great artist scores his triumphs, finding new solutions which then enlarge the area of possibilities in a language. This may occur in the ordering of words or in their combination; think of Góngora, Péguy, or cummings. A writer, by the way he uses language, has an indirect influence on the community which shares his medium.

We can envisage an activity of this type within the context of inspiration: Not only does society influence the writer by means of language, but, reciprocally, the writer can exercise an influence on those who read him. This type of activity on the part of the sacred writers has conferred on us many new possibilities of thought and expression in the sphere of religion.

There is also another factor to be considered: Just as a society develops its language in virtue of a common sentiment and outlook, so, after the language has been established, it acts as a cohesive force within the group. In a certain sense, language is a constitutive factor in a society. And this is true of the society of man in general, or of the smaller divisions within the human family. If we Christians are a people "called together," it is because we have all responded in faith to a call, to a word. And one of the cohesive forces of our community is the religious language which we share. This common language is inspired, not precisely as Hebrew or Greek or English, but as biblical. There is another important social dimension to the charism of inspiration. Few Christians are called to play a creative role in the development of religious language; this was the vocation of the inspired writers, and, as is the case with all charisms, it was conferred "for the good of the Church." We should not fear the liturgical reforms which have been and are now being introduced. We will be joined together as the people of God far more effectively by a shared understanding of biblical language as it reaches us through translations, than by a common incapacity to understand its Latin expression. The language of the Bible will continue through the centuries to sink deeper roots in the Church, to expand its own social dimension while acting as a factor of unity.

To sum up, then: (1) Man receives from language a certain general modifying influence; (2) he receives through language the influence of others, as they use speech concretely; (3) he works with language, expressing his liberty by his exercise and mastery over its possibilities; (4) by means of his speech, he influences others. The first two factors are prior to inspiration; the last two may enter into the inspired language process. Thus, through language in itself, inspiration acquires a social dimension.

LITERATURE

Usually, a future writer or author begins by learning, that is, by reading, listening to, and assimilating the literary works which have preceded him. He enters into a tradition—a prerequisite for any life—adopting its outlook and literary forms, and thus allows himself to be prepared traditionally and socially for his future activity. In the Bible, this preparation precedes the inspired process.[16]

The next step is taken when a literary man, without abandoning his capacity to learn, begins to create, utilizing that which he has received from the community. In his literary activity, he can have any one of a number of varying degrees of social integration, which we will classify under three general headings:

(1) The first possibility is that he will speak or write in the name of the people: *vox populi*. When the people hear him, they will recognize themselves and take him to themselves as *their* poet. He gives expression to the mind of the community in such a way that the community considers itself the author of his sentiments and thoughts, while yet recognizing and honoring the privilege and prestige of *its* spokesman. It may happen that because of distance in space or time, the community does not know the author, even though it accepts his works.

This is popular poetry in the best sense of the term, which is far from being the degeneration of true poetry to the level of vulgarization. It may easily come about that people will begin to sing the poetry, making it its own, and forgetting the author completely. This is an instance when "popular" would be equivalent to "anonymous." The song is not the product of an amorphous community; it is, rather, that the name of the author has disappeared because he has so identified himself with his people. No one has expressed this truth better than Manuel Machado, who himself composed so many *"soléas"* which are popular in this best sense of the word:

> Until the people sing them
> verses are really not verses;
> and when the people sing them
> no one remembers their author.
>
> Such is the glory, my friend,
> of those who write songs of the people;
> to hear it said quite simply
> that they were written by no one.

[16] For counsels on the formation of a writer, cf. A. Maurois, *The Art of Writing*, New York, 1962, esp. ch. 1, "The Writer's Craft."

Strive, then, to have your verses
go out to the people and finish
by ceasing to be your own,
that they may belong to others.

He who can fuse his heart
with the life-soul of his people,
will find that he loses his name
and gains eternity.[17]

In this sense, many of the liturgical pieces in the Old Testament are popular and social; and this is true also of some of the narrative material, as well as of the Proverbs—these latter were once well defined as "the wisdom of many and the wit of one" (Lord John Russell).

(2) The second way in which a man can be related to his society is by exercising his activity on it: directing it, reacting against it, leading the way for it as a precursor. In the case of opposition, the poet is social in the sense that he is stimulated and sustained in his purpose by the resistance of the community. The whole reason why he speaks or writes is his people, his community; he does not go off from them in desperation, or retreat in fear; he confronts them.

[17] *"Hasta que el pueblo las canta,*
las coplas, coplas no son;
y cuando las canta el pueblo,
ya nadie sabe el autor.

"Tal es la gloria, Guillén
de los que escriben cantares:
oir decir a la gente
que no los ha escrito nadie.

"Procura tú que tus coplas
vayan al pueblo a parar,
aunque dejen de ser tuyas
para ser de los demás.

"Que al fundir el corazón
con el alma popular,
lo que se pierde de nombre,
se gana de eternidad."
"Cualquiera Canta un Cantar," Manuel y Antonio Machado, *Obras Completas*, Madrid, 1947.

The greater part of prophetic literature pertains to this type in its social dimension. Jeremiah is a good example. God made him "a fortified city, a pillar of iron, a wall of brass" against his own people. And when his words produced, not conversion, but mockery, the prophet tried to escape, but God sent him back to the battle.

Unamuno is not a popular writer, but his works have a great power of communication. Let us listen to some of his principles: "The first thing necessary for one who wishes to write with effect is that he have no consideration for the reader and show him no mercy." ". . . to be able to accomplish this, he will stick you with a hot needle, in order to hear you yell." ". . . to irritate the public may become an obligation in conscience." Unamuno is a social author, he is aggressively so: "To be fought against is one way of being sustained and stimulated"; yet we would not say that Unamuno is the "voice" of his people.

The public can influence and modify a literary work, even to the point of endangering its quality; a writer receives this influence as a demand, a provocation, and a threat. If he knows how to apply concession and self-defense in the proper doses, then society plays a positive role of collaboration. In the activity of the prophets, the community is a conditioning factor in the literary work, at least in the way it reacts to the prophet. This social dimension may be prior to the process of inspiration, or it may permeate the whole process itself.

(3) We have in our culture the literary man of the ivory tower or the garret, the accursed poet, sealed off, fit only for initiates, a stranger to society and contemptuous of average people. This species of hot-house poet, removed or indifferent, is not found in the biblical garden. Not even the author of Ecclesiastes—an extreme case—can be classified in this category; he is thinking out loud and challenging the secure routine of the reader.

This is all we can find of a social dimension to inspiration. We cannot offer any more. Yet what we have seen is a true complementary factor in the realm, always open and attainable, of the individual. The explanations of Schleiermacher and Rahner fall principally in the first of our divisions, the author who gives expression to the sentiments of the community and in whose writings the community recognizes itself. Benoit's description does not extend beyond a consideration of the materials which are to enter into the work. McCarthy insists primarily on the living reception and use of the work on the part of the community.

We will treat of other social aspects of inspiration in Chapter 10, in the discussion of a literary work as such. We may say in this connection, however, that the greatest influence that society exercises on a writer is found in its character of audience or public. In a reality such as literature, whose very nature implies reference to another, the term of that reference is a constitutive factor in its production and finds concrete expression in the work itself. However, it is not exact to say that the charism of inspiration moves and directs the activity of the people in its capacity as audience. We should rather say that the sacred author was inspired to write his work with reference to the community. There is a parallel and complementary charism possessed by the society which receives the work; they are the people of God, the Church.

Bibliography for Chapter 8

The Opinions. The best account of the opinions is found in the authors themselves: Schleiermacher's *Der Christliche Glaube* is now translated into English: *The Christian Faith*, 2 vols., New York, 1963. Rahner's work on inspiration is in the English "Quaestiones Disputatae" series of Herder and Herder, *Inspiration in the Bible*, New York, 1961 (the German original is reviewed by M. Zerwick in VD 36, 1958, pp. 357–365 and by A. M. Dubarle in *RevScPhTh* 24, 1959, p. 106). The articles discussed in this chapter are J. L. McKenzie, "The Social Character of Inspiration," *CBQ* 24, 1962, pp. 115–124; D. J. McCarthy, "Personality, Society, and Inspiration" *TS* 24, 1963, pp. 553–576.

Form Criticism. Most of the discussions about form criticism are concerned with its historical and literary conclusions rather than with its sociological presuppositions. There is a good evaluation by P. Benoit, "Reflexions sur la 'Formgeschichtliche Methode,'" *RB* 53, 1946, pp. 481–512 (*Exégèse et Théologie*, Paris, 1961, pp. 25ff.), and a chapter in Wikenhauser's *New Testament Introduction*, New York, 1958, pp. 253–276; R. Schnackenburg wrote an article on form criticism in

ZKT 85, 1963, pp. 16-32, which is summarized in *TD* 12, 1964, pp. 147–152. The Instruction of the Pontifical Biblical Commission, *On the Historical Truth of the Gospels* (April 21, 1964), contains some positive statements in regard to form criticism. The article by J. Fitzmyer is very helpful as a commentary: "The Biblical Commission's Instruction on the Historical Truth of the Gospels," *TS* 25, 1964, pp. 386–408. A slightly different orientation can be found in C. Kearns, "The Instruction on the Historical Truth of the Gospels," *Ang* 41, 1964, pp. 218–234.

Sociology and Language. The book of Weisgerber, *Das Gesetz der Sprache*, mentioned previously, though it exaggerates certain positions, can be used here, especially section 1, which deals with the sociology of language. Weisgerber cites A. Sommerfelt, *La Langue et la Société*, Paris, 1938.

Sociology and Literature. A good treatment and an ample bibliography can be found in Wellek and Warren, *Theory of Literature*, ch. 9, "Literature and Society."

9. Speech and Writing

So far, we have usually avoided using the term "writer" when speaking of the biblical authors. But why this hesitation in using a formula already universally accepted?

There is no doubt that the formula is current in theology, and widely accepted by tradition. If, for example, we read the description of Leo XIII,[1] we find that in eight lines of text, words deriving from the root *"scribere"* occur five times: The Holy Spirit "took up men as His instruments for writing"; the sacred writers are contrasted with God, the author; God moved them to write; He assisted them while writing; the author willed faithfully to write down. . . . Someone might want to capitalize on the distinction made by the Pope between God as author and man as writer, resurrecting once again the view that human activity should be restricted to that of a secretary. But such a position would be opposed to the whole tenor of the encyclical. Nevertheless, it is true that in this description, the hagiographers are looked on simply as being writers. (Hagiographer means sacred writer.)

Pesch's description of the four stages in the hagiographer's activity is a good example of the classical view of the matter:

---

[1] *"Quare nihil admodum refert, Spiritum Sanctum assumpsisse homines tamquam instrumenta ad* scribendum, *quasi, non quidem primario auctori, sed* scriptoribus *inspiratis quidpiam falsi elabi potuerit. Nam supernaturali ipse virtute ita eos ad* scribendum *excitavit et movit, ita* scribentibus *adstitit, ut ea omnia eaque sola, quae ipse iuberet, et recte mente conciperent, et fideliter* conscribere *vellent, et apte infalibili veritate exprimerent."* EB 125; cf. RSS, p. 24. Emphasis added.

. . . *first*, he must conceive the idea of writing a book, that is, he must make a judgment as to what is to be written; *second*, he must consider how those things which he thinks should be written, ought to be expressed in words; *third*, he must decide to commit to writing those things which he has mentally conceived; *fourth*, he must carry out his decision either himself or through another. That these are the necessary steps is obvious without more consideration.[2]

The word "write" is absent from step four of the above description, in order to allow for the presence of a secretary, at least in those cases where inspiration does not require that the inspired writer be himself an amanuensis. In the rest of his study, Pesch never considers the sacred authors anything but writers. For him, the matter is so clear as to need no discussion.

Among recent studies, Rahner uses this terminology when he refers to the situations in the life of the Church which occasioned the writing of the text; he admits without difficulty that there is a distinction when he elaborates his theory of the Church speaking and expressing herself, and then concretizing this expression in the fact of writing.

Actually, this manner of speaking is very ancient and has its roots in the Bible itself: The New Testament authors cite or comment on the Old Testament, calling it "the writings," "what is written," etc., and we can read in the New Testament the statement that Moses wrote (Mk 10:5; Lk 20:28; Jn 1:45; 5:46). The Fathers, as we have already noted, were familiar with the term "hagiographer."

THE PROBLEM

The outlook and the terminology of the manuals generally reflect a view of the Scriptures which considers them as the result of a writing process: for each book there was an act of writing. Moses wrote the Pentateuch, Isaiah the work which bears his name, David wrote the Book of Psalms, and so forth. Though the act may have extended over a long period of time, it can be considered a psycho-

---

2 ". . . *debet* IMPRIMIS *mente concipere ideam libri scribendi seu debet iudicare, quid scribendum sit; debet* SECUNDO *considerare, quomodo res illas, quas scribendas iudicat, verbis exprimere velit; debet* TERTIO *habere voluntatem ea, quae mente concepit, scripto mandandi: debet* QUARTO *hoc consilium exsecutioni mandare aut per se aut per alium. Haec esse necessaria est per se evidens.*" No. 414.

logical unity, and it pertains culturally to that type of activity familiar to us, the very activity by which the author of the manual produced his own book.

However, modern historical and critical studies have done away with such a simple view of the matter: we can no longer envisage one act, there were many acts on the part of different and successive authors, and not all of these acts consisted in writing strictly so called —a large place was occupied by oral activity both in composing and in transmitting the material now found in the Scriptures. The New Testament itself often uses the word "speak," avoiding, in regard to the prophets, the use of the word "write."

> Heb 1:1: God spoke to our forefathers . . .
>
> 2 Pt 1:21: Men, moved by the Holy Spirit, spoke in behalf of God.
>
> Lk 1:70: . . . He proclaimed by the lips of His prophets. . . .
>
> Acts 3:21: . . . of which God spoke by His holy prophets (cf. Acts 4:29, 31).
>
> Acts 8:25: . . . giving their testimony and speaking the word of the Lord.
>
> Acts 28:25: How well the Holy Spirit spoke to your fathers through the prophet Isaiah. . . .
>
> Rom 3:19: All that the law says, it addresses to those who are under its authority.
>
> Heb 7:14: Moses said nothing in regard to priests of this tribe. . . .
>
> Jas 5:10: Take the prophets who spoke in the name of the Lord.

In all of these texts, we find a preference for words relating to speech when they describe the prophets, as well as some references to Moses' activity as being one of speech, and there is a description of the apostles "speaking the word of the Lord."

Oral composition and oral transmission are among the facts commonly accepted today in biblical studies. However, it is much easier to admit a change in the factual situation which a theory is considering, than to change the formulas in which the theory expresses itself. In our case, the formula is found in the phrase "the inspiration of the Scriptures." Formerly, the word "write" covered the whole process and was considered as one act; now we see that the writing of the text is only one step in the process by which it was produced, and this raises a new question: Is the oral activity inspired or is the written activity inspired, or are both inspired?

One either extends the charism of inspiration to cover all the phases of the process—and they are analogous—or restricts it to the moment of writing.

The second alternative has the appearance of fidelity to the commonly held view, yet it must be admitted that once the meaning of a term has been changed, the continued use of a formula is a change in its sense, and is a departure from what is considered common doctrine. Moreover, this second alternative runs the risk sometimes of considering inspiration as an act which enters in only after the word of God has been constituted and fixed in expression, and thus could seem to be a reversion to the view, already rejected, which holds that inspiration consists in a "subsequent approval."

On the other hand, the moment in which the act of writing takes place is indispensable and cannot be left outside the role of charismatic influence. If we are to possess sacred writings, then they must be written; and if they are to be written, there must be someone to write them; if the Holy Spirit wished to give to us the Scriptures, He had to move, in some way, the men who wrote them. All of this is so obvious as to be almost tautology; so obvious, in fact, that we dispense ourselves from thinking about it. We should reflect, however, that from this fact alone we cannot conclude that the technique and process of composition were also accomplished by writing.

It is nearly a century and a half since a theologian of Tübingen, John Baptist Drey, posed the problem quite precisely:

A curious thing: Was that not the work of God which the apostles, daily, and in many places and for many years, preached by word of mouth before it occurred to them to write any of it down? That first community of Jerusalem, and the others, and the early Christians in general, did they only hear the word of the apostles and not the word of God; did it only become the word of God when they read it? [3]

Drey's articles were published in 1820 and 1821. The problem that he posed went by unnoticed and disappeared. Today, now

---

[3] "*Sonderbar! War denn das kein Wort Gottes, das die Apostel täglich und aller Orten und viele Jahre lang mündlich predigten, ehe es ihnen einfield, auch darüber zu schreiben? Jene erste Gemeinde von Jerusalem und die andern alle, überhaupt die ersten Christen hörten also nur das Wort der Apostel, kein Wort Gottes; dies ward erst, als sie es geschrieben lasen.*" P. Dausch, *Die Schriftinspiration* . . . , p. 188; cf. ch. 8, no. 2.

that our knowledge of the process by which the Old and New Testaments were composed is much more developed, the problem returns and demands a solution.

It is an incontestable fact that a good proportion of the Old Testament existed and was transmitted largely through oral tradition before being fixed in a written form (though there are some who go to extremes in this regard). In the New Testament, an oral tradition preceded the redaction of the synoptics: The Gospel came before the Gospels. Where, then, should we locate the charism of inspiration?

SOLUTIONS

Benoit has devoted a great deal of consideration to this question. In his first study, composed as notes and commentary on St. Thomas's tract on prophecy, he distinguishes between a prophetic inspiration, moving a man to pronounce an oracle, and a literary inspiration, by which a man is moved to compose a book.

In this regard, we might distinguish two distinct vocations, as it were: the first one impels one to *repeat an oracle* which has come down from heaven; the other compels one to *compose a book*. We shall designate them by the two standard terms, "prophet" and "sacred writer." . . . For the *prophet,* who receives from God a message to deliver, the speculative judgment occupies the foreground. . . . The case of the *sacred writer* is quite different. He receives from God an impulse to compose a book. . . . This time the action of inspiration will first affect his practical reason and will have for its primary object the practical judgment. . . .[4]

Benoit wrote this in 1947. Twelve years later, he modified this distinction, and this modification also is apparent in the English

---

[4] "*On peut à ce sujet distinguer comme deux vocations distinctes: celle qui fait* RÉCITER UN ORACLE *descendu du ciel et celle qui pousse à* COMPOSER UN LIVRE. *Nous les désignerons par les deux noms typiques du* "PROPHÈTE" *et de l'* "ÉCRIVAIN SACRÉ." . . . . *Dans le cas du* PROPHÈTE *qui recoit de Dieu un message à délivrer, c'est le jugement qui occupe le premier plan.* . . . *Il en va autrement de l'* ÉCRIVAIN SACRÉ *qui recoit de Dieu l'impulsion de composer un livre.* . . . *Cette fois la motion inspiratrice atteindra d'abord la raison pratique de l'écrivain et aura pour objet premier le jugement pratique.* . . ." *La Prophétie,* by P. Benoit and P. Synave, New York, 1947, pp. 317–318. The English translation above is *Prophecy and Inspiration,* New York, 1960, pp. 106–107.

translation of *La Prophétie*.[5] On the psychological level, we find: inspiration in the order of knowledge—cognitive; inspiration in the order of speech—prophetic, apostolic, oratorical; and inspiration in the order of writing—hagiographical, scriptural. On the social level, we may distinguish between inspiration in the order of speech or action (dramatic, prophetic, apostolic) and scriptural inspiration, which is an attempt to overcome the limitations of time. These distinctions need to be developed more fully, but Benoit has the merit of at least discerning their necessity and situating them correctly.

Grelot's treatment is much clearer and better developed:

We should, then, first examine fully the question of the charisms which are related to the word of God before going on to the study of scriptural inspiration.[6]

In the Old Testament, prophecy (in the strict sense of the term) founded the community, as it were, by bringing to it the word of God. Then, other charisms followed which structured the community, in order to allow the word to maintain its existence there and to develop its potentialities. Throughout the whole of this process of development, scriptural inspiration gave to the word, from time to time, a written form, so that the community could refer to this writing as to the norm of its faith. At the end of this period, Christ, the Word of God made flesh, brought to men the fullness of revelation, by His words and by His acts; by that very fact, He showed forth the ultimate meaning of the ancient writings. But this revelation is made explicit in the message of the Gospel; and thus we see the role accorded to the apostolic charism in founding the Church . . . to which it brings the word. After this charism, there come other charisms to structure the living tradition of the Church, so that the word will maintain itself there and bear fruit throughout the course of time. This is the meaning of the hierarchical magisterium which, with the aid of the Holy Spirit, continues to watch over the apostolic deposit of faith. At the same time, this deposit has received a written and fixed expression which is due to the scriptural inspiration conferred on certain of its early recipients

[5] The modification appears in the 1959 article in *Sacra Pagina* cited above (ch. 8 no. 6); the modifications in the English of *La Prophétie* can be seen on pp. 125–127, esp. of *Prophecy and Inspiration*.

[6] "*Il sera donc utile d'examiner dans toute son ampleur la question des charismes relatifs à la Parole de Dieu avant de passer à l'étude de l'inspiration scripturaire.*" RSR 51, 1963, p. 349.

endowed with charismatic functions, who were sufficiently close to the apostles to be able to witness directly to their legacy.[7]

The term "inspiration" is qualified by the adjective "scriptural": It is a subsequent charism whose function it is to fix the message in writing, and as such it is subordinate to other charisms which have to do with the preservation and development of the word, and these in turn are completely dependent on the prophetic and apostolic word. In this way, we have a unified context: the word, a differentiation of charismatic gifts, and inspiration in the strict sense for the written expression of the word. It is obvious that this type of scriptural inspiration cannot be treated by utilizing the categories of the manuals without any recognition of the change in their content.

It is not so easy to see in Grelot's description how the charismatic activity of some of the authors in the sapiential tradition is at the service of the prophetic word, nor is there any well-developed consideration of what is involved in the literary stability given to the word by writing.

We see in Benoit and Grelot an effort to distinguish the activity of speaking from that of writing in their analysis of the charism of inspiration. But is it legitimate to make a problem out of something which is so simple and clear? Everyone talks of the Bible as the sacred books, the sacred writings, the *sacra pagina*; the term "Bible" itself signifies book or books, its authors are called hagiog-

---

[7] "*Dans l'ancien Testament, la prophétie (au sens fort du terme) fondait en quelque sorte la communauté de salut en lui apportant la Parole de Dieu. Ensuite d'autres charismes venaient structurer cette communauté, pour permettre à la Parole de s'y conserver et de développer ses virtualités. Tout au cours du développement, l'inspiration scripturaire donnait occasionellement à la Parole une forme écrite, pour que la communauté puisse se référer à cette Ecriture comme à sa règle de foi. Au term des temps, le Christ, Parole de Dieu faite chair, a apporté aux hommes la révélation totale par ses paroles et par ses actes; du même coup il a dévoilé le sens définitif des anciennes Ecritures. Mais c'est par le message évangélique que cette révélation s'est explicitée; de là le rôle du charisme apostolique, comme fondement de l'Eglise . . . . , à qu'il apporte la Parole. Après lui, d'autres charismes viennent structurer la tradition vivante de l'Eglise, pour que la Parole s'y conserve et y fructifie au cours de temps. Tel est le sens du magistère hiérarchisé qui, avec l'assistance de l'Esprit Saint, continue encore de veiller sur le dépôt apostolique. Celui-ci cependant a fait l'objet d'une fixation écrite, grâce à l'inspiration scripturaire dont on bénéficié certains dépositaires des fonctions charismatiques, encore assez rapprochés des apôtres pour pouvoir témoigner directement du dépôt légué par eux.*" Ibid., pp. 364–365.

raphers (sacred writers), and the Old Testament itself is often cited in the New Testament simply as "the writings." This tradition had existed for millenniums; what basis can there be for trying to qualify it?

Before approaching the biblical problem directly, we will first consider the fact of language in general, without trying to make any immediate applications.

SPEECH AND WRITING

Language is primarily spoken; word is primarily sound. A lack of the ability to read or write is a perfectly human thing; it existed for thousands of years, though now it is only the inheritance of small children.

Writing is a secondary and simplified means of recording. Even speech is a stylized and simplified "mimesis" of reality, both interior and exterior, but at least it has the dimensions of tone, inflection, and rhythm which our system of notation does not register. Compare, for instance, the system we use for registering speech with that which we use for the notation of music: in this latter, we indicate movement—allegro, andante, presto; intensity—piano, forte; changes in speed—rallentando, accelerando, crescendo, diminuendo; the nature of the rhythm—staccato, legato, etc. Actually, our system of speech notation is quite primitive, and the reason, at least partially, is that we have neglected the primary word.

Writing is a system of symbols, three times removed from the reality it expresses—it is the graphic notation of sound which itself represents an interior word. The primary function of writing is the conservation of the spoken word.

Once a culture has developed the art of writing, the written notation begins to develop a series of functions of its own, and can exercise a reciprocal influence on the spoken language. Some writers speak in a style characteristic of written literature;[8] and one of the psalmists compares his tongue to the quick pen of a scribe (Ps 45).

[8] A. Maurois recalls his conversation with Rudyard Kipling: his mannerisms, his subtle capacity to insinuate, and the general impression he gave of a man possessed of ancient wisdom, or like some prophet of the Old Testament. *The Writer's Craft*, p. 18; cf. ch. 8, n. 16.

Writing can give to the spoken word a juridical value: there have been contracts since the culture of Sumeria. A text can assume a magical function, as in the Egyptian execration texts. Writing stabilizes the fluid process of oral tradition; it inhibits the process by which phonetic and semantic changes are introduced into a language, and it tends to become the norm for speech: Good writers set the pace for good speakers. Writing even has an influence on the pronunciation of a language, for the reading or writing of a language can be mastered by those who cannot pronounce it correctly ("I read French, but I cannot speak it"). The literary existence of a thing facilitates repetition and diffusion, while maintaining a normative standard.

In our day, we have reached the stage where we think in terms of a series of books: Huge machines devour paper and ink and turn out mountains of literature, new "series" or "collections" are begun every day, and editors pursue authors—at least some authors. But then, at the other extreme, we have, happily, a rebirth of interest in the spoken word, captured on phonograph records and tapes, which are able to be repeated without the intermediary of a written medium and the impoverishment of being contained within some thirty or so graphic characters and ten signs of punctuation.

In a culture in which writing is already prevalent and predominant, there is a danger that some authors will lose awareness and feeling for the primary reality of the spoken word. They think in terms of letters, rather than in terms of sound, and they imagine that others near them or far from them in time or distance think, or thought, as they do.

O. Jespersen makes the very penetrating observation that the majority of linguists are helpless in the face of a living language because, unknowingly, they take writing for speech, and they are incapable of thinking in a context of sound rather than in one of written characters.[9]

Edward Sievers opposed this tendency toward "literalism" with his analyses of the sound quality of literature (in the Bible as well), and the new structural analyses take the sound patterns of a piece

---

[9] *"Noch eindringlicher legt O. Jespersen dar, dass ein grosser Teil der Linguisten der lebendigen Sprache hilflos gegenüberstehen, weil sie unbedenklich die Schrieft für die Sprache nehmen und unfähig sind, in Lauten statt in Buchstaben zu denken."* F. Kainz, *Psychologie der Sprache,* vol. 6, pp. 30–31.

as their point of departure. Jespersen's indictment of literary critics is also valid in regard to much of the thought on biblical inspiration. We ought, then, to rethink the problem, bearing in mind this central fact which has been all too often disregarded: the spoken word is primary.

THE TECHNIQUES OF COMPOSITION

In our culture, the art of writing has been well developed and printing has correspondingly been made easier by the reduction in the cost of paper (compare the ancients' esteem for writing materials—palimpsests, papyrus, etc.—with our modern phenomenon, the waste basket). As a result, there is a clearer distinction made between the two methods of composition—oral and written—which corresponds more or less to the temporal distinction between ancient and modern techniques.

In ancient times, oral composition was the normal procedure. This technique employs a great number of stereotyped formulas and artificial mnemonic devices. Because of these, the composition possesses a certain rigidity, which oral tradition undertakes to soften: In our own times, the relation is much the same as that which exists between folk songs and recorded music. Concomitant with this type of composition there arises a body of professional bards, storytellers, or ballad singers, who have their own techniques of memory and recitation while maintaining a basic respect for and fidelity to a normative version of their material.

To the stage of primitive oral composition and its oral transmission, which usually lasts for some time, there succeeds the written stage in which the work is stabilized. This implies that that which is known orally is appreciated enough to be conserved; we have the example of the enthusiasm of the romantics for folklore which has become an organized movement in our own day.[10] This literary stabilization is a service to society: Tradition is given a wider diffusion thereby, while maintaining a fixed form; variants are reduced and the text becomes normative.

Written composition is both more rigid than oral and more free: There is a fixed text which is regarded as unchangeable, but

[10] There is a society dedicated to the study of folklore, called "The Folklore Fellows," with its own periodical, *Folklore Fellows' Communications*.

there is a greater freedom from stereotyped formulas and other devices to aid the memory. It is easy in this mode of composition to utilize the written works of others; our modern scholarly works derive in large part from contact with other books (sometimes involving the cult of footnotes to the point of fetishism).

Even the very method of writing itself can have an influence in turn on the process of composition: When one composes at a typewriter, he usually settles more quickly for the formulation of his expression, especially in regard to word order. One scholar will compose the outlines of his conferences or class lecture by hand, but he will use a typewriter when he writes an article, while another will first work out the formulation of everything by hand before typing it out. Others, gifted with a facility for expression, have, with the aid of modern dictating machines, returned to the methods of an earlier age. Since the written word lacks many possibilities of expression, there have been attempts to give this medium another dimension: We find extreme examples of this in the efforts of some to convey effects with the printed lines of their poetry—in some of the work of George Herbert, e. e. cummings, Apollinaire, etc.

There are some authors, mostly poets, who compose mentally; this is a form of oral composition, or at least non-written composition. When the poem is complete, they commit it to paper. However, the ordinary method of composition, which has been in use for centuries, is to use paper as a testing ground, writing and rewriting until the final form is achieved.

LITERARY COMPOSITION OF THE BIBLE

The art of writing was already well known (cf. Jg 8:14); there was a functionary known as a scribe, and court records were kept. Papyrus was imported, and parchment and vellum were produced; often texts were partially scraped off a hide, so that it could be used again (the original of a palimpsest found at Qumran dates from the eighth century B.C.). Wood or metal tablets inscribed with a stylus were also employed, and in some cases potsherds were used, the characters being painted on rapidly with a small brush (Lachish letters). Yet the excavations in Palestine reveal hardly any written documents: This may be due to the fact that the climate is hard on any papyrus (only a dry climate, such as that in Egypt or the caves of Qumran or Murabbaat, is able to preserve papyrus), or it may be that written material tended to be concentrated in official quarters, such as the palace or temple.

Other data point to the fact that certain biblical poems were written down as early as the eleventh or tenth centuries B.C. This is indicated by the traces of an ancient system of writings still found, though not always understood, in the Massoretic text. (This has been established by the work of Albright, Cross, and Freedman.)

The Bible itself has many things to say about the way it views writing. The Covenant, laws, the Decalogue, the blessings and curses, must be written (Nm 5:23; Ex 24; Dt 4–5). According to ancient custom, the writing of a contract conferred on it a juridical status, and we may suppose that this custom prevailed in Israel. Also, writing made possible a fixed and authoritative text, to be used at the annual renewal of the Covenant. Thus the writing of a text is not merely the graphic notation of what is spoken: it is a new act constitutive and meaningful, which makes a word into a juridical instrument, an immutable norm, or a witness for the future.

A census is the same type of thing. The Book of Joshua (ch. 18) describes the distribution by lot of the Promised Land, and adds that this distribution was registered in a sort of property list. As the story stands, the act by which ownership was conferred consisted in a divine allotment by which God gave portions of his land to his people. Yet this divine act had to be juridically recorded. In this case, the act of writing did not constitute the act of allotment, but was the subsequent juridical instrument, ensuring the right to property already possessed. However, in Psalm 86 it seems that the act of writing was constitutive of the juridical effects which followed from the fact that someone "was born here." From the moment that his name was inscribed, a person was formally incorporated into the people with equal rights of citizenship, and by this act the city of Sion was constituted the mother of the nations.

Writing is often employed simply to overcome the barriers of distance and time. Letters are the means men use to extend their words a great distance: There are examples of these in the Old Testament, and a good proportion of the New Testament is made up of letters. When men attempt to overcome the dimension of time, they are looking to the continuity of their community: This motive is operative in the People of God, and in such a situation the act of writing easily confers upon the word the role of witness. Psalm 102 expressly recognizes this function of writing, which preserves the message against time and serves as a sort of testimony:

> For Yahweh rebuilds Sion,
> and is seen amidst his glory.
> He regards the prayer of the needy,
> and does not contemn their prayer.
>
> Let this be written for a generation to follow,
> a people then created will sing Yahweh's praise.
>   (Ps 102:17–19)

The future generation, which was yet to be created, had not been witness of these salvific acts of Yahweh. In times gone by it was the function of the cult to actualize the past events of salvation history, and we can hear the echo of the ancient preaching style in such phrases as: "Yahweh our God made with us a Covenant at Horeb. Not with our Fathers did he make this Covenant, but with us, we ourselves, who are here today, all of us the living" (Dt 5:2-3). This function is attributed to the written word in the Psalm we have just seen: The written fact will incite the people to praise. In verse 9 of Psalm 149 we seem to have an allusion to a written judicial sentence: "To execute on them the written sentence, this is the glory of all his faithful." Perhaps in this case the written text was looked upon as the juridical act necessary for the validity of the sentence.

The testimonial quality of a written document stands out clearly in Chapter 8 of Isaiah: "The record is to be folded and the sealed instruction kept among my disciples" (8:16; cf. v. 20). Jeremiah, Chapter 36, is an interesting example of the prevalent attitude in regard to the preservative function of writing. There we see the king attempting to obliterate the prophetic word, by cutting up the scroll Jeremiah had dictated, and throwing it into the fire. But the word was greater than the king's scheming, and because it was alive in the memory of Jeremiah, it was written again and preserved for future generations.

The sapiential literature contains references to the art of writing. In the case of the Proverbs, we see a very academic activity by which the sayings of the sages were collected, compared with variants, and included in collections which, at times, were composed outside Israel. The activity by which these collections were formed reminds us of our present-day specialists in folklore, though the efforts of these ancients seem to have been motivated by more religious considerations. And, as we will see in the following chapter, this activity had about it the literary qualities characteristic of any anthology. At the end of the Book of Ecclesiastes, we read this statement made by a disciple in regard to the master's technique of composition:

Besides being wise, Qoheleth taught the people knowledge, and weighed, scrutinized and arranged many proverbs. Qoheleth sought to find pleasing sayings, and to write down true sayings with precision.

We may sum up our survey of the biblical information in regard to writing by saying that writing is not always a mere graphic notation of the spoken word for the sake of preservation. It may also serve to add a juridical value to a word, either by constituting the juridical fact, or as a subsequent instrument, and it may also be a testimony or a norm.

Another series of facts indicate that part of the biblical literature had a prehistory in which it existed in oral form. The basic task of the prophets was that of proclaiming the word, and we see this in the accounts they leave of their vocation and in descriptions such as that of the "evangelist" or herald of good news in Is 40:9, who is bidden to "cry out at the top of your voice." However, I do not think that we can conclude from the command given to Jeremiah in Chapter 36 to write his oracles, that he had not written anything before. It is possible, but such a conclusion seems a bit oversimplified. In regard to the New Testament, we have the witness of the text itself to the intense oral activity which was carried on prior to and contemporaneous with the activity of writing.[11]

An analysis of the sound factors in some prophetic oracles and in other poetic passages demonstrates clearly that they were com-

---

[11] This is, as we have seen, the principal argument of J. B. Drey. Cf. A. H. J. Gunnweg, "Mündliche und Schriftliche Tradition der vorexilischen Propheten als Problem der neueren Prophetenforschung," *FRLANT* 73, 1958. B. Gerhardsohn, *Memory and Manuscript. Oral and Written Transmission in Rabbinic Judaism and Early Christianity*, Uppsala, 1961. For another aspect of the question, cf. B. S. Childs, *Memory and Tradition in Israel*, "Studies in Biblical Theology," no. 37, London, 1962.

posed to be recited aloud: They were poems made expressly to sound and resound.[12] At the same time the exquisite care in regard to the sound dimension of language and to rhythm which is often manifest in these poems indicates that they had already attained a literary stability before they were written down. In such cases, the process by which they finally achieved written form was often little more than a simple recording, or consisted merely in adding some verses or glosses. Sometimes this literary activity lay in constructing larger harmonic unities, utilizing and respecting the individuality of "bells" which had already been cast (the image is Gunkel's). Analysis also shows that there were often successive stages of written composition in which a similar process was operative in regard to preëxisting written material. We sometimes get the impression that this material was handled with greater freedom than were some of the oral sources.

Thus, we cannot automatically identify the fact of being written with the ultimate stage of literary fixity. Some pieces were already fixed in an oral stage of composition, while there were written documents which were reworked many times before achieving literary stability. The type of literature in question is often as important as the technique of composition, be it oral or written, in determining the point at which a piece receives a final and fixed form. There are some genres which by their nature are fixed once and for all, they are untouchable. "Do not touch it any more, the rose is like that" (Juan Ramón). Then there are other types of literature which demand that the climax be in a fixed form, a play on words or something similar, but which leave a good deal of liberty to the creative capacity of the narrator. And there is the literary form of improvisation which finds a place at times in the dramatic arts (*"recitare a soggeto"*).[13] There are times when we have in the Bible two versions of the same text: There are instances of this in the Psalms, and the Proverbs provide many examples. At other times, it seems as though the cult fixed the final form of a text, while it was still in

---

[12] See our *Estudios de Poética Hebrea*, ch. 5, "Estilística del material sonoro."

[13] Modern study in folk songs has served to illustrate both the fixity of certain formulas, referred to as "floating verses" or "floating lyric material," and the extreme variability and adaptability of verbal expression. Cf. A. Lomax, *The Folk Songs of North America*, New York, 1960; *The Folk Songs of Peggy Seeger*, New York, 1964.

the oral stage. Thus we see that the fixity of a work of literature can result from many causes and can have many results.

THE WORD

These facts, which indicate a very complex possibility of relations between speaking and writing, have caused modern authors to differ widely in their theories about inspiration, or at least in their terminology, when speaking about it. Benoit uses as his generic term the word "inspiration," which he subdistinguishes as being "oratorical" (prophetic or apostolic), "scriptural," and that which is commonly called the inspiration of the Bible, which is, "cognitive plus scriptural" or "oratorical plus scriptural." Grelot takes the concept "word" as his central consideration, and uses the word "charism" as his generic term, reserving "inspiration" to designate the last stage in which the text is given written form, though he affirms the existence of other charisms which produce, preserve, and develop the word.

I also have preferred (independently) to take "word" as the central consideration, and this is the principal reason why I have chosen to write about "The Inspired word," rather than "Inspiration."

His Excellency Neophytus Edelby, Titular Archbishop of Edessa, expressed the Eastern view of scriptural inspiration in his intervention of October 5, 1964, at the third session of Vatican II:

Scripture is a prophetic and liturgical reality; it is a proclamation more than a book, it is the testimony of the Spirit in regard to the Christ-Event whose privileged moment is the Eucharistic Liturgy. By this testimony of the Spirit, all of the plan in regard to the Son reveals the Father. The post-Tridentine controversy has tended to view Scripture almost exclusively as a written norm, whereas the Oriental Churches see in Scripture a consecration of Salvation History under the species of the human word, and they consider this consecration as inseparable from the consecration of the Eucharist in which all history is summed up in the Body of Christ.

We are going to concentrate on this theme of "consecration," transposing it back into the past. History is revelation which prepared the coming of Christ, made it actual, and prolongs it. In a wide sense, history is anything that has happened: events, words, religious experiences . . . All of this first existed as event until, as the result of a choice, certain of these events became language in an oracle or a psalm, a story or a prayer. The activity by which event becomes word, is an activity of language in an inclusive sense. This activity transpires under the charismatic influence of the Holy Spirit, whose overshadowing makes it fruitful. The "holy" offspring which is thus born "is called" the word of God, just as that which is born of Mary as a result of the Spirit's overshadowing is called the Son of God. That transcendent moment in which event becomes word is the same moment at which the word becomes the word of God.

However, since in the generation of a word the process is more varied than in the generation of a man, the fundamental reality comes about differently in different situations. In the abstract, our main interest in concentrated on that moment in which event becomes word, and it is to this moment that the charism principally has reference. In the concrete, this moment is found or is developed within differing activities.

Sometimes[14] oral composition results in a finished work, and the written notation merely gives to it a literary stability. In this case, the oral process of composition must be considered inspired.

Sometimes the oral composition results in a work which is substantially fixed, but which undergoes a series of adaptations and changes within a controlled oral tradition, until it reaches a stage of literary fixity. In this case, inspiration would have been present in all those who made a real literary contribution to the work, including, of course, the original author. It may be that all of the previous process was but preëxisting material for a true literary creator who then brings it to its final stage; then we would have the following case.

Sometimes the composition is a written process which utilizes preëxisting materials either oral or written. This true process of composition, not merely a work of edition or collection, is inspired. It is difficult to decide in each individual case how much of the preëxisting material is inspired. Sometimes the entire process of

[14] The examples that we give here indicate the minimum. We cannot exclude the action of the Holy Spirit at other stages in the composition, yet neither can we demand it.

composition is effected through writing. This composition is inspired, and it is the type of inspired activity usually envisaged by the manuals.

In these cases, and we could add others, we must posit an action of the Holy Spirit which governs the activity by which the text is written, since in the concrete order of salvation, God has willed that His word be preserved and transmitted to us by writing: "All these things happened to them by way of symbol, and they were written for our instruction" (1 Cor 10:11). The fact of writing is at least an integral part of the total process of inspiration, since without this final activity we should not have the Scriptures in the Church. And this activity makes present the "testimony," as it were, of the Spirit.

The fact of writing adds, or can add, to the meaning of words, by making them a definitive norm or by incorporating them into a larger, sacred, and all-embracing context. This substantial addition of meaning really affects the concrete being of a word, and as such it is brought about by the charismatic activity of the Spirit.

Let us recall here once again the words of Tertullian:

The words [of the prophets] and the miracles they performed in order to lead men to faith in the divinity, are now kept in the treasury of literature.[15]

And those of St. Augustine:

God has spoken first by the prophets, and then by Himself, and then by the apostles what he judged sufficient; and he has provided those writings which are called canonical, and which are of the highest authority.[16]

Those things which are actually written bring to us the guarantee of their inspiration: "As such, they have been confided to the Church" (Vatican I). The Church receives them as written and hands them on. With all tradition, we can reverently use the formula "sacred writings" in connection with this other venerable phrase: "He has spoken through the prophets."

When the process of literary stabilization is finished, there then begins or continues the process of recitation, application, and in-

---

[15] *PL* 1, 435; cf. ch. 4, n. 7.
[16] *PL* 41, 318; cf. ch. 3, n. 24.

terpretation; this process may itself be oral or written, it is always living and free. Since the object of this process is the work already completed, we will reserve to the next chapter a closer study of its nature.

When the question of speech and writing is posed in this way and applied to the notion of inspiration, there arises a whole series of questions: What is the relation between Scripture and tradition? Is it possible that there are fragments or formulas truly inspired, which never achieved the final stage of written expression? If there are, is it possible to find and recover them? For the moment, we will restrict ourself to the simple enunciation of the questions.

Bibliography for Chapter 9

Speech and Writing. The fundamentals of the problem can be found in Kainz's *Psychologie der Sprache,* vol. 4, ch. 1; cf. also L. Lavelle, *La parole et l'écriture,* Paris, 1947.

The Techniques. The works referred to in the bibliography of Chapter 7 under "An Artist with Language" are relevant also here, especially the discussions of technique in A. Maurois, *The Art of Writing,* ch. 1, "The Writer's Craft," and M. Cowley, *Writers at Work, op. cit.*

IV
THE INSPIRED WORK

ΠΑΣΑ ΓΡΑΦΗ ΘΕΟΠΝΕΥΣΤΟΣ

10. The Inspired Work

THE WORK OR THE AUTHOR?

Of the two biblical texts which are classical in the tract on inspiration, one (2 Pt 1:21) refers to the authors—"borne along by the Holy Spirit, men spoke in behalf of God," while the other text (2 Tim 3:16) refers to the written works themselves—"All of Scripture is inspired." Which of these two affirmations is the more basic?

The Fathers seem to have preferred the second formula, though, of course, not exclusively:

The Scriptures are perfect because they were pronounced by the Word of God and by His Spirit.[1]

How could all the Scripture bear witness to Him, unless it proceed from the one and the same Father? . . . The Son of God is sown throughout all the Scriptures.[2]

It is impossible that those letters be not sacred, which not only sanctify but divinize. And so the sacred writings, or the volumes which are made up of these sacred letters and syllables, the Apostle designates as inspired.[3]

The New Testament itself, when it cites the Old Testament, usually refers to it as "the Scripture" rather than naming individual authors, though again this is not an invariable practice.

---

[1] Cf. ch. 2, n. 56.

[2] "Quomodo igitur testabantur de eo Scripturae, nisi ab uno et eodem essent Patre. . . . Scilicet quod inseminatus est ubique in Scripturis ejus Filius Dei." St. Irenaeus, "Adv. Haer.," PG 7, 1000.

[3] ἱερὰ γάρ ὡς ἀληθῶς τὰ ἱεροποιοῦντα καὶ θεοποιοῦντα γράμματα ἐξ ὧν γραμμάτων καὶ συλλαβῶν τῶν ἱερῶν τὰς συγκειμένας γραφὰς τὰ συντάγματα ὁ αὐτὸς ἀκολούθως ἀπόστολος θεοπνεύστους καλεῖ. St. Clement of Alex., "Exhortation to the Greeks," ch. 9, PG 8, 197, 200.

The medieval commentators also preferred the second formula. The whole theory of the four senses was not applied by the Middle Ages to the authors of Scripture, but to the books, to the works themselves: the allegorical sense, and the tropological and anagogic senses, were there in the text, visible to the Christian who read with faith. They never asked whether or not the author of this or that book of the Old Testament perceived these senses with the same precision that they did.

When scholastic speculation began on the prophetic charism, the problem was discussed from the point of view of the mind of the prophet, more especially his knowledge. The tract was usually referred to as "Concerning the Prophetic Knowledge." The neo-scholastic movement of the last century concentrated on the psychological aspect of the problem, situating the discussion within the head of the author; this exclusive concentration has not been without its dangers.

The object of the definition of Vatican I is the books themselves, which are "holy and canonical . . . because, being written under the inspiration of the Spirit, they have God for their author, and as such they have been confided to the Church."[4] Note the last phrase: It is not the authors which have been confided to the Church, but their books; and this is the reality which continues to live in the Church.

The manuals which treat of inspiration, preoccupied as they are with the question of the "motion of the Holy Spirit," hardly ever considered this question. If we wish to gain an integral view of the mystery, we must combine the psychological view with one that is more literary.[5]

> Be not like your fathers whom the former prophets warned:
> "Thus says the Lord of Hosts:
> Turn away from your evil ways and from your wicked deeds."
> But they would not listen or pay attention to me, says the Lord.
> Your Fathers, where are they?
> And the prophets, can they live forever?

[4] D-S 3006; cf. ch. 2, n. 48.

[5] *"Olim dicebant sic: hic est liber a Deo conscriptus. Atqui liber constat non solis rebus seu veritatibus expressis, sed etiam expressione verbali. Ergo Deus ut sit auctor libri censendus est non res tantum scribendas sed etiam verba quibus exprimerentur, in individuo determinasse. Nunc vero solent ab inspiratione personali procedere."* Pesch, no. 468.

But my words and my decrees, which I have entrusted to my
    servants, the prophets,
Did not these overtake your fathers?
Then they repented and admitted:
"The Lord of Hosts has treated us according to our ways and
    deeds,
Just as He determined he would." [6]

*We may make an accommodation of these words and apply
them to our question: Where are the sacred authors now? Are
they alive now, here in the Church of God on earth? No, but their
words still reach us, their books still live on in the Church.*

*When the theologians say that inspiration refers primarily to the
authors and secondarily to their books, they are speaking of temporal priority, and are taking care to reject anything that might appear to favor the theory of subsequent approval.*

Theopnuestos is said primarily of the man, secondarily it is said also of
the book composed by such a man.[7]

*In the order of intention, and therefore of importance, the
works are primary, and all the effort of the authors and their vocation is orientated toward the work to be produced. We might say,
though with some exaggeration, that Jeremiah means nothing to
us; what interests us is his work, because his work is the word of
God.*

*In this preoccupation, we find ourselves in agreement with the
modern tendency in literary criticism.[8] There was a time when the
science of literary investigation consisted in studying the life and
times of the author; the work was reduced to a symptom, included
for its value in the depth analysis of the writer, and at times as
proof of his pathological state. Some rationalists even applied these*

[6] Za 1:4–6.

[7] *"Theopneustos est igitur primario* homo; *secundario autem ita vocatur
scriptum a tali homine compositum."* Bea, *op. cit.,* p. 6 (cf. ch. 1, n. 26).

[8] This is the orientation of the work mentioned before of Wellek and
Warren, *Theory of Literature* (ch. 4, n. 18). The two principal parts of the
book are concerned with "The Extrinsic Approach to the Study of Literature"
and "The Intrinsic Study of Literature." This is also the approach of Leo
Spitzer, and in general of the Stylistic Analysis School of literary criticism.
For a study of the various tendencies, cf. M. Wehrli, *Allgemeine Literatur-
wissenschaft,* Zurich, 1951. For a treatment of the methods of analysis, cf.
S. E. Hyman, *The Armed Vision,* New York, 1947.

methods to a study of "The Strange Experiences of the Prophets." Today, however, scholars are agreed that the proper object of literary science is the work itself, and that a study of the author and his epoch in the light of sociology, psychology, the history of ideas, etc., has a place only insofar as it aids in understanding the work.

In some circles, it used to be considered a great achievement if one could show that a work usually attributed to Smith was really the work of Jones, and with this triumph the investigation rested. But we are yet entitled to insist: Very well, the work was written by Jones and not Smith, nevertheless it still deserves to be studied in its own right.

These considerations, both of the biblical text itself and of the modern tendency of literary criticism, have prompted us to devote a separate chapter to a study of the inspired works.

WHAT IS A LITERARY WORK?

Usually, literary language is actualized in a literary work. Outside of a literary work, such language may do service in some other capacity—a conversation, a technical work, etc. Thus, it may happen that a conversation is a work of art—as was said of the conversations of Cocteau, though it may also come about that literary forms become common and thereby lose their elevation. There are works of a pedagogical nature whose main purpose is to impart technical knowledge, which still deserve a place among the works of literature—*L'Histoire naturelle* of Buffon, for example.

The intuition of the poet, or novelist, or dramatist, along with his subjective participation in reality, and the experiences he chooses to relate, acquire objective consistency in his work. This consistency is made up of words, of language forms whose own existence is in their signification, and which are communicable.

Is this true also of the Bible? We have already said that a large proportion of the Bible employs literary language. Is this language used to produce a series of individual works? Before proceeding to a comparison of the literature of the Bible and that of other literary works, it will be helpful to delineate the area of our analogy.

A work in the Old Testament may differ greatly from a modern work in the manner of its production; a work which has undergone successive elaborations at the hands of successive authors, and which achieves its final form by being incorporated into the work of yet another author, has not known the same process of composition as a novel by Mauriac. However, the process ought not to be identified with the work, and it is possible for the biblical processes to result in a true literary unity. We might recall, for instance that some sections of Macbeth seem to derive from the work of Thomas Middleton, and recall also the literary process we saw in St. John of the Cross's poem, "The Shepherd Boy," or that which produced the epic narrative of the ten plagues.

It might also be objected that there is a real divergence in the intention of a biblical author. It is usually said that a literary work is disinterested; it attempts to present reality for our contemplation and not primarily to stir us to action. Moreover, that which it would have us contemplate is found within the work itself, which is a self-contained, self-justified world.[9] The biblical authors, on the

---

[9] We must, however, maintain some presence of the intention of the author in his work. When Valéry protests that he desires not to "say" but to "make" (poiema, poiesis), he is reacting against an excessive expressionism which can degenerate into an absence of form. But in his reaction, Valéry goes too far. Could anyone seriously think that "The Graveyard by the Sea" says nothing? Rilke expresses himself more subtly when he asks of poets that they "say instead of feeling sorry for themselves," and that they "transmute into words those selves of theirs, as imperturbable cathedral carvers transposed themselves into the constant stone." In general, we might say that the poet or the artist gives himself up to his work and to its fashioning in such a way that the work is foremost in his mind and perhaps occupies all his conscious attention. But this immediate intention does not exclude the presence, albeit temporarily hidden, of a greater and more far reaching intention which reasserts its claim to conscious ratification at the proper time. It is this general intention to be of service to mankind, to the truth, or to God which in actual fact exercises its influence in the consummation of the work.

St. John of the Cross wrote poetry very well; whether it cost him much labor or little is not important. It is quite possible that in his case the presence of God dominated him even during the composition of the poem. What is important is that this presence did not destroy, but rather elevated and intensified the poetic and technical capacities of the author. Great poets, in their dedication to the work which they create, realize a great ambition to know, to say, and to reveal.

"Art for art's sake," as an explicit program of activity, can be a reaction against romanticism, but it is a perversion of something human. It effects its own retribution in the artistic destitution, insincerity, and lack of fidelity to art itself which follow in its train.

What we mean to say is that the supposed opposition between literary and biblical writings on the basis of their "intention" is groundless. In some cases, it is the product of a mentality which seeks to preserve Scripture from

other hand, are preoccupied with the necessity of proclaiming their message; they desire above all to influence and stir to action; thus, their intention is not truly literary. What this objection is really saying, is that the works of the Bible should be compared with another type of literature which is also capable of producing real literary entities: It is the literature of commitment, of message, of action; the literature of a "movement," but it is still literature. Again, we can take the example of St. John of the Cross: "Art for the sake of art, or even art pared to the bone, had no interest for him." [10] He had no intention of producing "works of art," yet what other Christian poetry can approach his?

It is possible to discuss this question on another plane. In a work of language, the human spirit reveals itself as it creates, and it manifests the world as re-created. Every work of art is the creation of a world achieved by imposing a form; every human creation effects something new and is a revelation. In this sense, art is essentially expression (though not precisely expressive); it is language. A work of literature as it transposes the practical or cosmic world to the world of representation, strips it of its bounded quality and makes it deeply significant; it shows forth clearly the truth of the being of this world, not by a series of statements (though these are not excluded), but by a process of re-presentation. When we say that a work is false, we do not refer to its propositions. Thus, to classify Scripture as a work of art is not to deny that it conveys meaning; it is rather to penetrate into the manner in which it intends to signify. The Emperor of Assyria, the proud, self-satisfied conqueror, is presented to us, and his reality, unforgettably experienced in the light of God, when we enter into the "mimesis" effected by Isaiah.

> Are not my commanders all kings?
> Is not Chalane like Charchamis,
> Or Hamath like Arphad,
> or Samaria like Damascus?

---

the slightest taint of "art for art's sake"; but this puritanism is itself occasioned by the contrary exaggeration. What mattered to the prophet was the proclamation of the message of God, and so he wished to compose a poem. His logic is admirable. It was precisely because the divine oracle meant so much to him that he was intent on its literary perfection.

[10] ". . . le tenía sin cuidado el arte por el arte y aun el arte a secas." D. Alonso, Poesía Española (cf. ch. 7, n. 23), p. 280.

Just as my hand reached out to idolatrous kingdoms
that had more images than Jerusalem and Samaria,
Just as I treated Samaria and her idols,
shall I not do to Jerusalem and her graven images?

By my own power I have done it,
and by my wisdom, for I am shrewd.
I have moved the boundaries of peoples,
their treasures I have pillaged,
and, like a giant, I have put down the enthroned.
My hand has seized like a nest
the riches of nations;
As one takes eggs left alone,
so I took in all the earth;
No one fluttered a wing,
or opened a mouth, or chirped! [11]

There are some who imagine that to speak of biblical poetry or of literary works in the Bible is to render the Scriptures worthless. It means, they think, that the Bible thereby loses its importance as revelation, and therefore any importance whatsoever. It is true that methodologically one may institute a stylistic analysis of the text, prescinding for the moment from its total meaning, but to speak of the Bible as literature is not to restrict it to this specialized field. To say that the Bible is literature is not to say that it is unimportant.

But is not such an opinion a distortion of the facts? It is difficult to read the Epistle of St. James as a work of literature, and the same can be said of many of St. Paul's exhortations. We can still speak of such examples as "works," though we may doubt their aesthetic qualities. The liturgy continues to use such texts, not simply in order to discharge a duty toward them, but to reveal to us the Church in and through a moment of her existence. These passages or books were not taken up by the Church merely to satisfy some obligation.

All of this implies that we must accord to the term "work" an ample connotation, one that will extend from a sermon to a covenant. Having thus qualified the limits of our investigation, we are entitled to begin a description of a literary work, concentrating on

11 Is 10:8–14. Cf. "Tres imagines de Isaías," *EstBib* 15, 1956, pp. 74–79.

its most characteristic factors. We will then pass on to apply the analogy to the Bible, respecting the reservations necessarily implied.

The Literary Work

What is the nature of a literary work? There is an excellent treatment of this question in Chapter 12 of *Theory of Literature* by Wellek and Warren;[12] we will content ourself here, therefore, with giving a summation of their analysis. A literary work does not exist in the material dimension of writing—the paper, the type, the ink, etc.; nor in the written text, which is only a graphic notation, nor in the sequence of sounds uttered by the speaker or reciter, since this would result in making the work non-existent when it was not actually being recited. We cannot place the work of literature in the experience of the reader, which is manifold and changeable; nor in the experience of the author, which may be only partially objectified; nor in his intention, which may remain little more than that; and it is to no avail to seek the existence of a work in a certain amalgam of experiences on the part of society.

A literary work is a precise system of words, ordered one to another and having meaning; it is a structure or a system of structures. As a structure already accomplished, it is a realized act, and at the same time it is a potentiality which can be actualized. It is to this system that the graphic notation, as well as its readers and reciters, must have reference.

This description is applicable not only to a unified work which was born of a single dominant intuition, but also to a work of composition which utilized preëxisting materials, and even to a collaborative work in which one mind is principally directive and others coöperate. It applies in varying degrees to a proverb, a poem of two verses (Juan Ramón, Montale), a novel such as *War and Peace*, or an intricate drama, such as some of Calderón's mystery plays.

Multiple Structure

A literary work possesses a multiple structure. That is, it has various levels of existence. In an ideal instance, these various levels are

[12] Cf. ch. 4, no. 18.

interrelated in harmony or counterpoint, in coördination or in designed dissonance.

There is first of all the level of sound with its various possibilities of expression, linked to the meaning of the words and giving pleasure to the ear; then there is the level of rhythm with its power to form and express; this is an ordering factor, providing a scheme for order, but it is also flexible, registering and conveying the tempo of the emotions. Built on these, and permeating them, there is the stratum of meaning with its concentric circles of connotation and resonance evoked by juxtaposition and association; this gives rise to the image level, embodying and reflecting the analogies of being, and producing fruitful and unsuspected insights. The image level gravitates toward small dynamic constellations whose structure is more or less actively determined by the inherited culture of the author. Moreover, these partial literary forms even exist in certain more generic structures, known as literary genres or types. Then there is the level of concept or idea or thought, virtually activating the whole structure, though actually existing in varying degrees of explicitness and conscious ratification.

These various strata realize and manifest the intellectual, imaginative, and emotional levels of man's existence, and thus actualize the three functions of language which we have seen before.[13] Dámaso Alonso has described this interweaving verbal structure with great sensitivity and literary experience; he finds outstanding examples of it in poetry. If we wish to extend and apply his description, we will be obliged to restrict the field of investigation and concentrate on certain aspects according to the nature of the work we are studying: poetry, prose, hymn, doctrinal treatise, narration, etc. We ought to allow room for the introduction of factors which can affect, either positively or negatively, the total meaning of a work, and we must allow for those cases in which the composition, especially of preëxisting material, has not resulted in a perfect interrelation of the various levels. The advantage of studying an ideal case lies in the fact that it allows us to

---

13 " 'Sit quidvis simplex dumtaxat et unum,' said Horace. It seems almost the reverse of the truth. 'Complex dumtaxat et unum' would be better. Every real poem is a complex poem, and only in virtue of its complexity does it have artistic unity." W. K. Wimsatt, The Verbal Icon. Studies in the Meaning of Poetry, Lexington, 1954, p. 81.

describe the reality more fully, and alerts our receptivity and critical sense to the whole gamut of possibilities. If we begin with instances in which the possibilities are only minimally realized, we may develop a certain deafness or color-blindness with regard to some dimensions of literary reality. If someone were to study music only from the aspect of melody, he would undoubtedly be able to appreciate, say, monodic compositions, but he could not very well raise them to the position of a general norm for all music. He must also study harmony, counterpoint, tone, etc.

From what we have said about plurality, certain conclusions present themselves spontaneously. It is impossible to exhaust the appreciation and the analysis of a work by taking only one aspect of it, be this its conceptual level, the emotional or imaginative strata, the literary personality created, the action or plot, the desire to influence, etc. The necessities of method or the requirements of training may require that we concentrate on one aspect or another, but we must remember that it is but one aspect and nothing more, and that by isolating this aspect we have changed it somewhat, divorcing it from the total system in which it exists. I may extract from the rich complexity of an existing work an aspect that appeals to my temperament or state of soul, or present scholarly preoccupation; but I can never legitimately identify the aspect of my choice with the totality of the literary work.

When speaking about inspiration, we said that the inspired process was ordered to and reached fulfillment in the work. Now, if we take the case of a biblical work which actually and fully possesses all the levels of existence we have been describing, we are forced to ask ourselves whether or not inspiration extends to all of them. Should we consider that inspiration affects only certain strata of a biblical work? May we exclude, for instance, the expressive function of language as this is actualized by rhythm? Must we eliminate the resonances of a turn of phrase, and restrict its allusions in order to arrive at its purely conceptual significance as being the only one inspired? Or should we not rather consider as inspired the work as a whole in its total concretization with every level of its existence according to its own nature and the role it plays in the over-all language system?

We should note, however, that to affirm that all the levels of an inspired work are influenced by the motion of the Holy Spirit is not the same thing as to make all of them of equal importance: We cannot raise a rhythmic pattern to the status of an infallible proposition. When we say that the human nature of Christ was assumed by the Person of the Word, we do not exclude from the Incarnation any corporal member or organ or tissue, yet neither do we reduce the complete human organism of the man Christ to a uniform mass of "humanity." Each member, and organ, and tissue is assumed according to its particular function: the tongue for speaking, the hand for curing, the feet for walking, the nerves for receptivity and suffering, the blood for life and death. The same applies also to Our Lord's emotional life: weariness and fear, tenderness and compassion, anger and pity. We ought to regard the works of literature in the Bible in a similar way, for they are an image of man. The work in its totality is inspired, and this affects each element and stratum according to its nature and function; thus, the revelation of God gains entrance to us by every facet of our being which can be influenced by reality. If it seems to us that the simple, spiritual, and most pure knowledge of God is thereby humiliated, we should accept this mystery of self-abasement as a revelation of love. The Fathers liked to join together the mysteries of the "self-emptying" realized in the Incarnation with that of the divine condescension embodied in the Scriptures.

These same Fathers also delighted in the manifold wealth of the sacred text, and in this, too, their views were echoed by a unanimous choir of medieval commentators: Scripture is a forest, an ocean, a banquet, a heaven with ever-widening frontiers:

"An infinite forest of meanings." —"The deep forest of Scripture." —"With such depth as the deepest ocean." —"Sacred Scripture is the table of a rich man . . . the extent of whose riches cannot be measured." —"It is as impossible to enumerate all the delights which this table contains, as it is to dry up the whole ocean." —"Sacred Scripture is like a swift-flowing river; it fills the depths of the human mind, and still flows on, it satisfies him who draws from it, yet it remains inexhaustible." —"It is measured by the immensity of its mysteries." —"O the marvellous depths of your utterances!" [14]

14 "*Infinita sensuum silva* —*latissimam scripturae silvam* —*in tanta profunditate, velut altissimo pelago* —*Mensa divitis sacra Scriptura est . . . cuius divitiarum altitudinis non est finis.* —*Huius mensae deliciae tam impossibile est explicare, quam universum abyssi pelagum absorbere—Scriptura sacra, morem rapidissimi fluminis tenes, sic humanarum mentium profunda replet,*

The Fathers and the medieval theologians attributed this plenitude of the Bible to the fact of its inspiration, its divine origin. But
we should not take this to mean that the wealth of the sacred text
is found there despite human activity; it is not some treasure hidden there by God, while the human author was asleep or distracted; it is, rather, incarnated in the text in the process by which
the text was written. We could say, in keeping with the thought of
the Fathers, that the plurality of the work was assumed by the
charism of inspiration in order to reveal the plurality of the divine
revelation. It is in this context that the medieval authors elaborated their theory of the four senses of Scripture. The following
text of St. Bonaventure is representative of their thought:

The breadth of the Scriptures refers to the number of their parts; the
length, to their account of the times and periods; the height, to their
description of the orderly levels of hierarchies; and the depth, to their
abundant allegorical senses and interpretations. . . . It is entirely
logical for Scripture to have a threefold sense in addition to the literal:
such amplitude consorts with its content, its hearer or disciple, its
origin, and its end. It consorts with its content, for scriptural teaching
is concerned with God, with Christ, with the works of salvation, and
with the things of faith. God is the Being covered by the Scriptures;
Christ is the power; the works of salvation are the action: and the
things of faith are the sum of all three aspects. Scripture's manifold
meaning consorts with its hearer. None but the humble, pure, faithful,
and attentive can hear it properly. As a deterrent to pride, a mysterious and profound signification is hidden under the shell of its obvious meaning. The very depth that lies beneath the humble word re-
proves the proud, chases out the unclean, drives away the insincere,
and awakens the slothful to search the mysteries. . . . Scripture's
manifold sense is proper to the source whence it comes: God, through
Christ and the Holy Spirit speaking by the mouth of the prophets and
of the others who committed its doctrine to writing. Now, God speaks
not with words alone, but also with deeds, for with Him saying is
doing and doing is saying; moreover, all creatures are the effects of
God's action, and, as such, point to their Cause. Therefore, in Scripture, which is received from God, both words and deeds are meaningful. Again, Christ the Teacher, lowly as He was in the flesh, remained

---

ut semper exundet; sic hauriente satiat ut inexhausta permaneat —mysteriorum immensitate extenditur. —Mira profunditas eloquiorum tuorum!" H.
de Lubac, Exégèse Médiévale, Paris, 1959–1961, vol. 1, pp. 119ff.

lofty in His divinity. It was fitting, therefore, that He and His teachings should be humble in word and profound in meaning: Even as the Infant Christ was wrapped in swaddling clothes, so God's wisdom is wrapped in humble images. Finally, there was variety in the manner whereby the Holy Spirit brought enlightenment and revelation to the hearts of the prophets. As no mind is able to hide from Him, and as He was sent to teach all truth, it was fitting that His doctrine should harbor several meanings within a single utterance. Scripture's manifold sense also accords with its End. It was given to guide man's thoughts and actions so that he might arrive at his true goal; and since all the rest of creation was designed to serve him in his ascent toward his heavenly home, Scripture takes on the very diversity of created things, to teach us through them that wisdom which leads to eternal life.[15]

The text of St. Bonaventure with its orientation toward the "four senses" is the usual expression of what was the accepted method for drawing out the riches of the sacred text. As he moves from the realm of practice to a consideration of the fittingness of these four dimensions, he presents a theological view of Scripture.[16]

[15] "Consistit autem ipsius latitudo in multitudine suarum partium, longitudo vero in descriptione temporum et aetatum, altitudo in descriptione hierarchiarum gradatim ordinatarum, profunditas in multitudine mysticorum sensuum et intelligentiarum." . . . Subiecto inquam competit, quia ipsa est doctrina quae est de Deo, de Christo, de operibus reparationis et de credibile. Subiectum enim illius quoad substantiam est Deus; quoad virtutem, Christus; quoad operationem, reparationis opus; quoad omnia haec est ipsum credibile. . . . Competit etiam hoc auditori . . . ut ipsius profunditate in humilitate litterae latente, et superbi comprimantur, et immundi repellantur, et fraudulenti declinentur, et negligentes excitentur ad intelligentiam mysteriorum. . . . Competit etiam principio a quo est: quia est a Deo, per Christum et Spiritum Sanctum loquentem per ora prophetarum et aliorum qui hanc doctrinam scripserunt. Quoniam autem Deus non tantum loquitur per verba, verum etiam per facta, quia ipsius dicere facere est, et ipsius facere dicere; et omnia creata tamquam Dei effectus innunt suam causam; ideo in Scriptura divinitus tradita non tantum debent significare verba, verum etiam facta. —Christus etiam doctor, licet humilis esset in carne, altus tamen erat in deitate: ideo decebat ipsum et eius doctrinam habere humilitatem in sermone cum profunditate sententiae. . . . Spiritus etiam sanctus diversimodo illustrabat et revelationes faciebat in cordibus prophetarum: ipsum etiam nullus latere potest intellectus, et missu erat omnem docere veritatem; ideo competebat eius doctrinae, ut in uno sermone multiplices laterent intelligentiae. Competit nihilominus ipsi fini: quia Scriptura data est ut per ipsam dirigatur homo in cognoscendis et agendis, ut tandem perveniat ad optanda." Breviloquium, pp. 202–206 (cf. ch. 3, n. 13).

[16] This wealth or fruitfulness is not exclusively due to the literary nature of a work. A simple formula or statement of the truth can contain a world:

We should also note, however, that this notion of the abundant riches of the sacred text is applied to the Bible as a whole. It cannot be predicated indiscriminately of every single part. There are sections which have a very modest role in the over-all context; there are others which, if divorced from their context, would seem poor indeed. A book of ceremonies makes no pretensions at being a complete literary work, fully activating all the levels of its existence; nor does it present itself as the most apt means of inspiring sublime sentiments. But a book of ceremonies, seen in relation to the cult, which is its frame of reference, assumes new dimensions of meaning, and can reveal unsuspected depths of theological insight. This is the case with the Book of Leviticus. An experience and a good piece of advice can soon be depleted; yet, when integrated in a whole series, such sayings can shed light on the meaning of human existence. This is exemplified by a work such as the Book of Proverbs.

Either extreme in this regard is dangerous. There is an enthusiasm which sees profundity everywhere, and a skepticism that hesitates to see it anywhere. Neither is correct, but it is foolish to imagine that skepticism is a better guide to the meaning of a text than enthusiasm.

Much can be said in a few words. This is especially true when the statement embraces a wide horizon of human experience. In such a case, the depth of the original formula is made explicit in successive articulations. This is exemplified in the simple formulation of some great intuitive insight which then becomes the principle of multiple and repeated reflection.

On the other hand, that quality of a literary work in virtue of which it embodies such wealth, can be shared by works which are not, in the strict sense, literary compositions. We see this verified in those great intellectual constructions which are embued with an immense spiritual fecundity—despite some errors—that cannot be simply equated with the sum total of their propositions. The *Summa Theologica* of St. Thomas, St. Augustine's *City of God*, Hegel's *The Philosophy of History*, a play by Calderón or Shakespeare, all of these must certainly be classified as "rich," and all of them possess a similar intellectual beauty.

There is no doubt that such compositions as the Epistle to the Romans, or to the Hebrews, fall within the category of literary work in the wide sense. The modern analytical technique known as *Redaktionsgeschichte* tends to accord the same judgment in regard to the Gospels. There are some books, such as Ben Sira, whose quality as a literary work still escapes us; but perhaps future study in this direction may yield some agreeable surprises.

STRUCTURED PLURALITY

The second thing we ought to note about this plurality is that it is structured. A literary work is a dynamically interrelated unity whose parts can be determined by analysis, but which cannot be truly understood without that which Dámaso Alonso calls "a total intuition." [17] Alonso applies this term especially to poetry, which, as he notes, proceeds from just such an intuition. We can, however, extend its application by analogy to any kind of literary work, including those which have resulted from a carefully designed plan or composition, or even those which are conscious imitations. If there exists such a thing as a merely juxtaposed series of phrases, then, of course, we would have to read it that way, allowing each statement to be autonomous and separate.

This raises the delicate question of context. An anthology which a good poet makes of his own verses is, theoretically, the juxtaposition of autonomous poems, written and conceived separately. Nevertheless, the selection of these poems and their organization creates an over-all context which is capable of shedding light on each individual poem by highlighting resemblances, antinomies, key words, similarity of structure, etc. If I pick up the collected poems of T. S. Eliot, read them through, and then return to the first poem, I see it in a new light. I experience the two factors which unify the collection: the fact that one man wrote all these poems, and the secondary fact of their being chosen and organized in an anthology.

Then there is the example of an anthology created from the works of a school of poetry, or of a period or theme. The context thus created becomes a secondary unifying factor whose worth depends primarily on the capacities of the compiler. If done well, this context allows the individual works mutually to shed light on one another. If, however, the compiler be an irresponsible dunce, he will produce not a context, but confusion: if, for all practical purposes, he takes lines, stanzas, titles, and notes, and tosses them in a hat, shakes it, and then sets them down in the order in which he draws them out, we hardly think it worthwhile to read or study his work. The Bible did not come about in this manner, though there

[17] *Op. cit.* (n. 10, and ch. 7). Cf. also Leo Spitzer, *Linguistics and Literary History*, New York, 1962, esp. ch. 1.

was undoubtedly a series of successive anthologies, giving rise to the final unity.

Would we be entitled to call this anthology a "work" of literature? Yes, analogically; it possesses structure and plurality and can be read and analyzed as such. This is what exegesis does when it compares passages, formulas, schemata, and themes. And this is what the liturgy does when it selects and reorganizes a series of smaller units.

The total view of a work is obtained by reading it through completely, since a literary work is essentially temporal, as is its medium, language. This temporality is not the sum of its moments, nor a series of partial and autonomous readings. However much we analyze a text, separating unities and studying them, we must return to a total vision of the work in order to make a synthesis. Thus, in New Testament study there is first the discipline of form criticism, by which individual units are isolated and explained in virtue of their genesis within the early community; this is followed by "redaction criticism," in which the units are seen within the structure of one of the Gospels, and their mutual relations are studied in this dimension, as well as in comparison with the other Gospels; then there is the further synthesis which presents the theology of the synoptics or of all the Gospels on one theme or aspect of New Testament teaching. This can be further integrated into an over-all "theology of the New Testament." In the liturgy, on the other hand, the predominant emphasis is on the over-all unity which is presented in the liturgical cycle: the history of salvation and the mystery of Christ. As we will see further on, this sense of unity is achieved in large part by the power of the liturgy to repeat and re-present.

Thus, it appears that the unity achieved in the Bible is variable and does not always coincide with our norms and procedures. Because of its character as public revelation, its over-all unity by which it transcends the individual work of each author is its most important aspect. This unified structure is derived from the plan of God to which it bears witness and of which it is itself a part; there is also the unity of tradition extending over millenniums, which it sums up and which finds expression in the process by which one inspired theologian accepts and builds on the work of his predecessors, as well as in the process by which individual units and strands were united and transposed, as they were incorporated in ever larger anthologies. Finally, there is the unity achieved by the Scriptures within that process by which the Church took the Scriptures to herself, added to them, and used them to effect and express her own crystallization. This whole objective process is one more reason why we cannot be content with a psychological exegesis which restricts itself entirely to the mind of the author as the only norm for determining the meaning of the text. The transcendent unity of the Bible does not suppress its lesser structural unities; rather, it enshrines them. Thus, the various types and levels of unity which are to be found therein become themselves a vehicle of revelation and facilitate understanding.

The structural unity of a work gives rise to another interesting consequence: It is possible to arrive at the life center of a piece of literature by many different roads, and having once arrived there, it is possible to view the whole from within this center. The center we are referring to is the center of the work, not that of the author. Tolstoy describes this phenomenon by using the image of converging lines: "In a work of art, the important thing is to achieve a focal point wherein all the lines converge and from which they emanate." Maritain speaks in this connection of the "immanent action" of a poem.

Sometimes the work itself indicates avenues of access to its life center; at other times it seems closed, and some minor level of its existence provides the key. Then there are times when the particular temperament or sensibilities of the reader dictate the means of entrance. A scholar may work for long periods of time and finally announce that he has found the key; this is not pride, but only the enthusiasm of the specialist. The Bible in its totality leaves many doors open so that the people of God may enter into its Holy of Holies. It is a pastoral duty to keep these doors open and to point them out to God's people.

What we have said about avenues of approach must be applied variously according to the nature of the work in question: There are some works which seem to have only one door, and this is not only hard to find, but also does not allow everyone to pass through without distinction. In the Bible, there are sections and even whole works which are difficult to understand; not everything is equally accessible and uniformly easy to expose. This is why the liturgy of the cathedrals (as distinct from that of monasteries) has always favored a selective reading.

CONSISTENCY

Another characteristic of a literary work is its inner consistency, its capacity as a self-enclosed entity to maintain its individuality (an individual according to the philosophers is something which is "one in itself and distinct from other things"). But this distinction does not mean that it is "closed to the public," or that it cannot be received and used by society. What gives this consistency to a work is its form. As Henry James puts it: "Form alone takes, and holds and preserves substance." [18]

Let us recall what we said about the language of conversation. When it is true dialogue and not technical discussion, conversation is completely realized in its passage. Its influence may be profound, even decisive in someone's life, still conversation exists by and for its passing (even if it is indiscreetly taped on a recorder). An interview for a periodical or for a television program is not a simple conversation, but a conventional form of "literature," and in this sense approaches the nature of a "work"; the same can be said, for example, of the conversations between Eckermann and Goethe.

A conversation exists in passing, but a literary work seeks to subsist, and it achieves this in an organized language system. The medium here becomes constitutive as well as revealing, and this is the meaning of Lützeler's phrase, "In science, language is at the service of meaning [sinndienend], in poetry language makes meaning [sinnbildend]." [19] While a dialogue unites two people by its flow, a literary work stays there like solidified concrete. Such things as light literature or writings entirely committed to the moment, may be exceptions to this, but these do not nullify the standard norms, nor are such things found in the Bible.

In the plan of revelation, God has willed to make Himself known in artifacts of language which are not completely grasped in a day, but are meant to last "from generation to generation." This fact was appreciated by the Fathers when they instinctively preferred to

[18] In a letter to Hugh Walpole, May 19th, 1912. *The Letters of Henry James*, selected and edited by P. Lubbock, New York, 1929, vol. 2, p. 237.
[19] *Einführung in die Philosophie der Kunst*, Bonn, 1934, p. 10.

speak of the work rather than of the author, when they discussed the Scriptures.

But was it always so? Have all the inspired works lasted down to our times? Theoretically, of course, we cannot put limits on the Holy Spirit; He could very well have inspired works which were only destined for their time. How many prophets spoke the word of God, and never wrote it? When St. Paul says that "All these things happened to them by way of symbol, and they were written for our instruction, on whom the terminal point of the ages has come," he said that of all the things which are in the Scriptures, but he did not necessarily mean that everything that happened to the people of old was written down, or that once having been written it was preserved for us. Admitting this possibility, we can go on to ask whether or not it is probable that the Holy Spirit acted in this way. In Geiselmann's theory of the canon, such a procedure is presumed:[20] The Church has chosen from among inspired works those which she found necessary or fitting—nature is prodigal in the abundant production of life, and the Holy Spirit is prodigal in His gift of inspiration. On the other hand, there are authors who deduce from the nature of inspiration the fact that it must be rare.

From what we know today about the formation of the Bible, it is reasonable to suppose that there were other inspired works which did not endure; the evidence does not allow us to go further than this probability. The whole question is, as a matter of fact, a bit academic, since, when we speak of sacred Scripture, we are referring to those books which have been "confided to the Church."

WRITING

A literary work possesses consistency because of its realization in a structured system of words, but not precisely because it is written. I might preserve a conversation by means of a tape recorder, but this adds nothing to its nature as a passing reality; a great work of drama might be lost, and then instinctively we feel that violence has been done to something which by its nature ought to endure (recall the efforts of the literary school of ancient Alexandria to form a canon).

The way in which a literary work is preserved is secondary. The

20 *Die Heilige Schrift und die Tradition* (cf. ch. 5, n. 20).

bards relied on their memory, our culture has developed the written word with its various ideograms, sign systems, etc. God has chosen writing as the means of preserving and transmitting the words He has inspired, and this is why we call them the Scriptures.

It is interesting to reflect, however, that what we actually conserve is not the work, but its notation. If I look at a score of Beethoven, I cannot say that it is his *Pastoral*. A symphony is a system of orchestrated sounds, whereas what I hold in my hand is nothing but sheets of lined paper with little black dots on them. I cannot put my ear to the paper in order to hear the symphony. In the same way, writing only preserves the "score" of a literary work; it is, however, the means of access to the work itself.[21]

Since we live in a culture which abounds in written texts, and since the technique of writing and printing has a reciprocal influence on the techniques of composing, we have reached the point where we have identified the work with its written expression. We read poems in a subdued voice (that is, we don't read them), and we conceive of language in terms of letters and not sounds. Imagination can supply; orchestra directors read a new score, and hear the music without sound, but the majority of men must hear the music if they are to know the work; and there are some who read the score, even as they listen to the piece.

In the field of literature, however, the majority of readers feel no need to hear what they are looking at, even going so far as to read a play silently.

The sacred books are merely the notation of the word of the inspired message; they are nothing more, and nothing less.

This consideration of the consistency of a literary work and of the relation it bears to written expression, brings us to another of its qualities which we would like to describe.

REPETITION

A literary work can and indeed must be repeated. In a conversation, we only repeat something or ask to have something repeated when it was not understood; we repeat a poem, either reading or

---

[21] Cf. L. Lavelle, *La parole et l'écriture*, Paris, 1947, and Gadamer's *Wahrheit und Methode* (cf. ch. 6, n.7), II, 1, b, "Die Verwandlung ins Gebilde und die totale Vermittlung."

reciting it, precisely because we have understood it, and as our understanding grows so does our joy in repeating the experience.

In literature, a work only conveys its message when it is actualized in the process by which a reader or listener creates it once again. Many readers repeat a work, but it remains inexhaustible. The reader or reciter actively re-creates the work, yet it remains intact. The work is changed slightly under the active influence of the one who recites it, yet it always maintains its identity; it is repeated indefinitely, but it is not multiplied.

This is the paradox of a poem which subsists in its written expression. It does not actully exist when it is not being repeated; it is not truly repeated, unless the reader creates once again its unifying life principle, but it is never repeated identically in the same way.

A literary work is a presentation which is only actualized in its re-presentation: this re-presentation (in the broad sense of that word) makes the work present again, and thus allows the work to actualize its own re-presentation. Repetition presents the work in the act of expressing something and of thus realizing its meaning. Actualization implies presence, the real repetition of a work, and not the simple act by which its existence is remembered; it is a vision being lived in the present.

This is the way that the Church receives and keeps the sacred writings. It is not a question of a mere material conservation, but of a handing on, a tradition, of the works of the Bible, so that the faithful may repeat and relive them, actualizing and ratifying the intuition which gave them birth. This is the meaning of the ancient adage that meditation on the sacred text reaches perfection *quando lector fit auctor* (when the reader becomes the author), and it is the source of that privileged position which the Scriptures hold in the liturgy, the whole purpose of which is to "recall" and "re-present" the salvific acts of God in history.

Let us imagine these two possibilities: A community of monks knows all the Psalms by heart and recites them every day; then, during a persecution, they are deprived of any written exemplar of the Psalter. A Christian has a lovely bound copy of the Psalms in a deluxe edition, but he never reads it. In the first instance, the inspired words are not lost; in the second, they never existed.

FIDELITY

The necessity that a literary work has of being repeated, poses the question of fidelity. Because of the fact that a work only actually exists as repetition, which necessarily implies multiplicity and variability, there is a permanent norm and certain limits of tolerance in which the variations must move. For the sake of clarity, we will illustrate this with examples taken from the world of music and the theatre.

Ought there to be a stable tradition governing the manner in which the Baroque theatre of Calderón should be presented? Is the stage setting now used by Wagner's grandsons faithful to the work of the master? How quickly should we perform the works of da Vittoria or di Lasso? In order to provide practically for these types of questions, our culture has formed two groups of men to whom, in a certain sense, the works have been confided. First, there is the corps of interpreters: the pianists, the directors, the actors, the poetry readers, etc. Then there is the corps of critics, historians, theorists, etc. These groups sustain a force and are, in turn, sustained by it; it is the force of living tradition. In this force, as it is kept alive, there resides the control exercised by society in receiving and appreciating the re-creation of the works of art. Every pianist gives a personal interpretation to a work by Beethoven, while remaining within the limits of substantial fidelity. By means of these repetitions, we possess a living and uninterrupted tradition. An orchestra director is expected to have passed through a very demanding technical formation—counterpoint, composition, the theory of music, etc. However, in the last analysis it is up to him to re-create the work in each concrete performance. He himself finds it very helpful to listen to recordings of a symphony directed by the composer.

This interpretative tradition is transmitted in our Western culture with a great measure of fidelity; still, the differences in sensibility and outlook necessarily bring with them changes in the manner of interpreting each work. It pertains to the corps of critics and scholars to see that the modifications do not exceed the limits of a substantial fidelity to the original.

We have concentrated on the example of music, because there our experience of successive interpretation is undeniable. It is another matter in literature, so long as we think that every silent reading of the text is valid. It is fashionable today to consider as ideal that type of reading which moves as fast as possible, and there are even courses advertised to teach people to read three pages a minute. This is all right for periodicals and for the mountains of paper passing over the desk of an administrator, supplying him with background and committee reports. But I cannot speed up an adagio of Bach; no one will admit the theory that if I play the tape recorder twice as fast as I ought to, I can hear twice as many symphonies in the same time—in fact, I will have heard nothing. But this is the kind of thing that is often said about the repetition of literature in general, and even of poetry. If we are so pressed for time that we have only half an hour, at least let us not waste it completely by trying to "read" thirty pages of poetry or sixty of narrative.

One of the functions of a liturgical recitation of the Scriptures will be to maintain a moderate tempo. It is certainly to be hoped that the new techniques of recording poetry readings, plays, etc., will create once again a sense of the sound dimension of these works, and impart a feeling for their tone and rhythm.

In the Church

Since the sacred text only actually exists when it is repeated, and since this text has been confided to the Church, it follows that it is the Church's responsibility to have certain groups who devote themselves to maintaining the living tradition and assuring fidelity to the works received. In this case, however, the normal, human reality of a group of critics and scholars is raised to a higher sphere, that of the Spirit. What is a simple fact of human culture is also in this context a charismatic reality.

First, there must be a body of men who can authoritatively interpret the sense of the sacred text and set the limits of tolerance within which personal variations will remain authentic throughout the generations of readers and reciters. This corps, invested with authority, will be able to perform its task with much greater security and deep fidelity than any purely human institution, since it possesses within it, still active and dynamic, the same Spirit who first inspired the works. We call this body the magisterium.

This first group usually works in collaboration with another subordinate body: that of the technical experts who apply the methods of analysis and criticism, as well as other techniques of human science, to the text, in order to remove the obstacles and prepare the way for a deeper and more vital appreciation of the sacred books. They correct interpretations that have wandered from the right path, though not, of course, with the authority proper to the magisterium. Since they apply the methods of the human sciences to a book which is also human, it is possible and even normal that they will discover new aspects, even though they may not be charismatically enlightened by the Holy Spirit. In this case, the human contribution of technique leads to a greater understanding of the message of God, since all the levels of the literary work, each according to its own nature and function, have been permeated by the Holy Spirit. Then, too, these experts, as good Christians, enter into the life center of the sacred text, and participate in their own way in the activity of the Spirit within the Church. Thus, the scholars prolong and refine the interpretations of the magisterium, and prepare for those of the future.

A wide field is still left open to the private student, in which his hermeneutical skill may display itself with signal effect and to the advantage of the Church. On the one hand, in those passages of Holy Scripture which have not as yet received a certain and definite interpretation, such labors may, in the benignant providence of God, prepare for and bring to maturity the judgment of the Church; on the other, in passages already defined, the private student may do work equally valuable, either by setting them forth more clearly to the flock and more skillfully to scholars, or by defending them more powerfully from hostile attack.[22]

A third group in the Church who actively receive and transmit the living tradition in regard to the text are those who recite it. Their usual place is within the liturgical action. The scope of their

[22] "Nam privato cuique doctori magnus patet campus, in quo, tutis vestigiis, sua interpretandi industria praeclare certet Ecclesiaeque utiliter. In locis quidem Divinae Scripturae, qui expositionem certam et definitam adhuc desiderant, effici ita potest, ex suavi Dei providentis consilio, ut, quasi praeparato studio iudicium Ecclesiae maturetur; in locis vero iam definitis potest privatus doctor aeque prodesse, si eos vel enucleatius apud fidelium plebem et ingeniosius apud doctos edisserat, vel insignius evincat ab adversariis." Providentissimus Deus, EB 109; RSS, p. 15.

activity has been greatly reduced over the centuries, but in our day, due to the great liturgical renewal and the restored prominence of the word of God, this office in the Church will become correspondingly important.

We call his third group the "Order of Readers" (*Lectores*). In the light of what we have said about the interpretative and actualizing functions of repetition, it is easy to see what an important role this is, and how necessary it is to form good readers. They must be men whose character and training will enable them worthily to "re-present" the sacred text, not only in its intellectual content, but at every level of its plurality and structure. But this is a question of something more than dignity in the sense of splendor; the very being of the inspired work is, or ought to be, made actual in its repetition. The authentic existence of the word of God depends for its reality not only on the magisterium and the scholars, but also on the readers at the liturgy. This is not the place to excuse negligence by an appeal to the omnipotence of God; we are here in the realm of the mystery of word of God, a mystery which is made present in and through men, and which reaches its culmination in the Incarnation. The word of God addressed to men becomes human once again in the intelligible and expressive voice of the reader, as the people of God assemble to listen to the voice of God. In this message, addressed at this moment to this community, the whole chain of authors, editors, and scribes is brought to fruition.

The authority of the magisterium, the *sensus fidelium*, and the labor of the exegetes, are not divergent forces variously applied to the text; they make up that one hierarchic unity in which tradition is alive and active, one force, sustained by the Spirit, which flows out from the Word and returns to the Word.

Bibliography for Chapter 10

What Is a Literary Work? The best treatment in English is found in Wellek and Warren, *Theory of Literature*, ch. 12, "The Mode of Existence of a Literary Work of Art." In this chapter, the authors cite the fundamental work of R. Ingarden, *Das literarische Kunstwerk*, Halle, 1931, in which a phenomenological approach is applied to the problem of the existence of a literary work, and various levels or "strata" are distinguished. Cf. also H. G. Gadner, *Wahrheit und Methode*, Tübingen, 1960, and Dámaso Alonso, *Poesía Española. Ensayo de metodos y limites estilisticos*, Madrid, 1950. A phenomenological view of a literary work seems presupposed to the method outlined by L. Spitzer in ch. 1, "Linguistics and Literary History," in the book of the same name.

11. The Work and Its Translation

All that we have said about a literary work forces us to raise the question of translation. If the work only exists in its repetition as being its actualization and re-presentation, are we entitled to say that it receives an authentic repetition when it is translated?

God has spoken to us in very definite human languages, and He has respected the fact that language is not a medium through which we receive disembodied ideas, but a real medium of communication. If, then, I do not understand those languages, what good is it to me that God has spoken?—He has not spoken to me.

We have accepted the two terms "interpret" and "re-present" as synonymous in some areas of meaning, especially as applied to drama. To re-present is to interpret; to interpret something is to render it present once again. Can we say of that particular kind of interpretation which is called translation that it truly re-presents the work? We might note in passing that in many languages there is a semantic interpenetration between "interpret" and "translate." Greek has the word "ermeneuein," and in medieval Latin there was "interpretari," which was contrasted with "exponere" or "comment on the text." Translation is such an established art in our culture that we take it for granted; the average reader of Dostoevski or Mauriac never gives it a thought.

When we come to the problem of holy Scripture, the best procedure seems to be to accept the fact as it is, and then begin our reflection on it with the help of some background considerations.

The primary and immediate fact of our religious life ought to be the fact of the liturgy; now, the liturgy proclaims the word of God, and I either do not understand this word, or I understand it in a *translation. Beginning from this fundamental experience, we will cast a look backwards over the history of biblical translations.*

An Historical Review

The apostles were not totally unfamiliar with Hebrew, though the language they spoke was Aramaic. When they went to preach to the Gentiles—whose language and culture were Greek—and when they began to write, they cited the Old Testament according to the ancient Greek translation, known as the Septuagint. The one Gospel which, according to tradition, was written in Aramaic, was very soon translated and adapted for a Greek audience, and this translation is our canonical text. Following this example, the majority of the Fathers used the Septuagint, and, of course, read the New Testament in Greek, as they did the later books of the Old Testament (when they were considered canonical), which were composed in Greek. Some of the Fathers studied Hebrew, in order to penetrate the Scriptures more deeply; Origen, in his famous Hexapla, arranged the Hebrew text, its transliteration, and the then known Greek translations, in parallel columns for easy reference and comparison.

In the second century, culture began to center on Rome, becoming more explicitly Latin, so that Greek was no longer the language of the Western part of the Empire. A product of this Romanization was a series of Latin translations, and Pope Damasus, desirous of having a normative version, entrusted this work to St. Jerome. A scholar, thoroughly versed in the literary and rhetorical traditions of Greek and Latin, St. Jerome had undertaken the study of Hebrew and Aramaic in order to read the Scriptures for himself in his beloved *"hebraica veritas."* By correcting previous translations (with varying degrees of thoroughness), and by producing new translations, he finally achieved a vernacular translation for the people— in Latin, of course. (Every language is vernacular, during the time that it is actually in use; after that, it becomes either a foreign language or a dead one.)

Throughout the centuries in which the Latin culture predominated in the West, St. Jerome's translation became more and more widespread, until it eventually came to be considered the popular (*vulgaris*) Bible, the Vulgate. When non-Latin European cultures began to emerge, however, translations were soon made into their languages. Sometimes the whole Bible was translated, and sometimes only passages: liturgical pericopes, the Gospels, the Psalter, were all put into these new cultural media.

The Reformation gave a new impulse to the movement toward vernacular translations; some were made from the original languages, some were translations of the Vulgate, and Luther's translation was put into other European languages. This movement had a profound influence on the literary development of the various national languages. In some countries, Catholics reacted by producing their own vernacular translations of the Vulgate, though at times utilizing the translations of their enemies, the Protestants.

The Renaissance introduced a new emphasis on classical Latin and fostered the study of languages. This resulted in new translations in Latin which were more elegant or more literal (including interlinear translations); these new versions were made both from the original and from other ancient versions. In order to reduce the danger of confusion, however, the Council of Trent chose from among all the Latin translations the one called the Vulgate, and imposed this as normative for the Western Church; at the same time, certain limits were set for translation into the vernacular. These two Tridentine decisions received a rigorist interpretation in some countries.

Toward the end of the eighteenth century, as the Enlightenment was flourishing, Benedict XIV urged that translations be made of the Vulgate, and various writers in different countries responded by producing works of genuine literary merit (Petisco, Martini, et al.).

In our times, the directives of Pius XII have given an extraordinary impetus to modern translations from the original languages, so much so that publishing of the Scriptures has taken on some of the aspects of a business with the inevitable danger to quality.

These few facts can help to provide a background for the experience of any modern reader of the Bible who finds himself confronted with a wealth of translations to choose from. I read the Confraternity of Christian Doctrine translation; my friend reads Knox; the new curate likes the "RSV," the pastor still reads the Vulgate. But who is reading the word of God? Wouldn't it be better to make one English translation for everybody? Or perhaps we ought to insist on Latin for the whole Western Church, or teach everyone Greek and Hebrew. Isn't there any translation which is considered more reliable than another for those who cannot read the original languages? Well, there are two ancient translations which have always been regarded by tradition as specially privileged.

THE GREEK TRANSLATION KNOWN AS THE SEPTUAGINT

Recently, scholars have been airing the problem of the Septuagint: Is the Septuagint, they ask, part of the inspired corpus of the Scriptures, or is it merely a translation of the inspired books?

Some authors argue in this manner: The writers of the New Testament cite the Septuagint version as "the Scripture," that is, as the word of God; but in some instances, the Greek text differs from the Hebrew original. Therefore, it should either not be cited as Scripture, or it should be considered inspired.

So long as the translation is faithful, there is no difficulty, but when the Greek text does not correspond with the original, I cannot cite it as Scripture or as a translation of Scripture, unless, of course, this Greek text is itself inspired. But there are such citations, as a matter of fact, made by the authors of the New Testament; what right, then, do we have to say that just these verses are inspired?

The Septuagint translates the original quite well in some places; in other places, however, it does not render the Hebrew text at all, simply because the translator did not understand it. Then again, there are passages which transform the original, continuing or initiating a semantic evolution and transposing the whole to a new mentality and culture.

In the case of a simple misunderstanding, it seems somewhat hardy to maintain that the Holy Spirit has effected the deformation of a text He once inspired in order now to present it to the Church. It would be more in keeping with the general nature of the divine salvific providence to say that he permitted human imperfections, which do not substantially alter the message, as the text was transmitted or interpreted. Such things are already found in the Hebrew text.

There are instances when the text is transformed or transposed, and here we have an example of a new interpretation or re-presentation. It is certainly wrong to think that all the recitations and readings of the original were perfectly equal and faithful to the point of identity. This would be to deny the nature of the work as something which needs to be repeated and finds it existence in repetition. A translation which transforms (as opposed to one which deforms) is but one more step in this direction. It involves the selection of one aspect of the original with a subsequent emphasis on it. Thus, there may occur a concentration on the conceptual aspect of a work, a minimizing of its symbolic quality, a spiritualization of the image, etc. This is the same sort of thing that we find in the various recitations of a work; there are those which are reserved and intellectual, others which are impassioned, still others which are contemplative, or dedicated to action, etc. Such variations in recitation and transpositions in translation are not opposed or foreign to the original which is present under that aspect of its total potentiality which has been actualized. In all these cases, however, we must maintain that the ultimate norm is not the translation, but the original. If the sacred writers cite a translation in this way, they are citing a possible interpretation of sacred Scripture.

But there are times when the New Testament authors invoke a text which departs from the meaning of the original. In these instances, a new element enters in: It is that activity which we call "making use of a text." This process is subsequent to and distinct from the purely interpretative function of repetition.[1] We can use a text to illustrate something, to support an argument, to stimulate reflection, or by way of allusion and ornamentation. We do not enter into the work, but rather subject it to another intention which is foreign to its own, but which is not necessarily opposed to it. A literary man knows how to use the words, phrases, and images of another in a way which is neither a simple citation nor an interpretation.

The authors of the New Testament can use the Old Testament in much the same way: developing an argument according to the rabbinic standards of the day, introducing an allusion or reflection which sheds light on the mystery of Christ, etc. This use of another

---

[1] Cf. C. H. Giblin, "As It Is Written. A Basic Problem in Noematics and Its Relevance to Biblical Theology," *CBQ* 20, 1958, pp. 327–353, 477–498.

text, since it is a literary activity which achieves objective existence in the work, is an inspired process. However, inspiration does not convert the free use of a text into a citation or interpretation. It is a literary procedure in its own right, one that is inspired, and one that allows more liberty to the author who uses the text.

Such are the possibilities. We are, after all, confronted with the inspired text, not with its authors. That which transpired in the mind of the author as he wrote with attention and conscious reflection, does not exactly adequate the reality of his work, especially if the work enters into the stream of a living tradition. In a certain sense, the work exceeds the author. As Kainz has remarked of this problem:

The statement of a theorem can develop a fecundity never foreseen by the scholar who first chose or found the words to express his new insight, and this fecundity may well go far beyond the initial intention of its author. A capacity for being exploited may attach itself to the original formula in such a way that it takes a direction quite other than that which was intended and for the sake of which it was conceived. Or, later on, there can occur some play on words or gloss which brings to light a real fecundity never even imagined at the beginning. . . . The formula has proved once again to be more intelligent than its creator.[2]

What Kainz says of scientific thought is all the more applicable to literary work wherein repetition, interpretation, and use have a much greater legitimate ambiance.

Returning now to the Septuagint, we may distinguish three different levels: the meaning of the Hebrew original, the meaning of the Greek translation, and the literary use made of this latter in the New Testament. Benoit and Auvray defend the inspiration of the first two levels as being the only way that we can understand

[2] "Ein Lehrsatz kann eine Fruchtbarkeit entfalten, an die der betreffende Forscher gar nicht gedacht hatte, als er eben diese Worte für seine neue Erkenntnis wählte oder fand, eine Fruchbarkeit also, die über die Ausgangs-intention ihres Schöpfers weit hinausreicht. An die vorhandene Formulierung kann sich eine Auswertbarkeit schliessen, die in ganz anderer Richtung liegt als der, auf die der Satz ursprünglich zielte, um derentwillen er konzipiert war. Ja es kann ein wortspielhaft erlebter, ein glossomorpher Einfall im weitern Verlauf eine sachliche Fruchtbarkeit erweisen, die anfänglich nicht zu vermuten stand. . . . Die Formel war wieder einmal gescheiter als ihr Schöpfer." Kainz, Psychologie der Sprache, vol. 1, pp. 259–260.

the citation in the New Testament.[3] But we believe that there is another alternative—to place the inspiration in the first and the third levels. The Hebrew original is inspired, and the New Testament use made of its Greek version is also inspired. It then follows that St. John had no intention of defining for us, with the help of faultless philology, what Isaiah meant in a given text.

We do not pretend to close the discussion once and for all with the solution we have proposed; there is no definition of the magisterium which settles the issue. The majority of scholars do not consider that the Septuagint is inspired, and the articles of Benoit and Auvray have not met with wide acceptance.

However, the ancient Greek version of the Old Testament will always retain the privilege of having been for all practical purposes the Bible of the writers of the New Testament and of the Church during her period of formation. This privileged position is still actively accorded to the Septuagint by the Oriental Church.

The Vulgate

The other translation which commands our special reverence is the Vulgate. It was the text of the Western liturgy for more than a thousand years; centuries of theologians have studied it, and generations of Christians received from it their faith and devotion, and in turn gave these expression through its phrases.

No one ever thought of calling the Vulgate inspired, but there have been those who considered it the only reliable text from which to receive the word of God. It will suffice in this regard to cite the post-Tridentine theologian Melchior Cano, who has exercised a vast influence on later ages through his *De locis theologicis*.

CHAPTER 12 In which are set forth the arguments of those who wish to maintain that for the understanding of sacred Scripture recourse must be had to the Hebrew and Greek sources.

CHAPTER 13 In which there is proved the authority of the ancient Vulgate edition, and that recourse is not to be had now to the Hebrew and Greek Text.

CHAPTER 14 In which the arguments in Chapter 12 are refuted.

Among Cano's own arguments, one finds this polemical position:

[3] Cf. the works referred to in the bibliography.

The scholars among the Hebrews, that is, our enemies, strive with great effort to corrupt the Hebrew text, in order to render it contrary to our exemplars, as Eusebius relates in his *Ecclesiastical History*, Book 4, Chapter 18. And the Greeks do the same thing in many places; in order to twist the Scriptures to fit their theories, they violate the New Testament.[4]

When responding to the arguments of those who wish to have recourse to the original languages, Cano supposes that the translator who produced the Vulgate was endowed with a charism similar to the prophetic charism, but he does not go on to make this declaration of his more precise:

. . . either the ancient translator rendered the sacred writings through a special grace of the Holy Spirit, or the Latin Church has not possessed for all these centuries the Gospel of God, but of man. You may object that the translator was not a prophet. Certainly, he was not a true prophet, but he possessed a charism very closely approximating that of prophecy (as Titelmann has rightly asserted) which I have shown to be necessary for the translating of the sacred text. Especially was this necessary, so that the Latin Church would have an edition of the sacred books which it could safely follow in matters of faith and morals.[5]

Finally, in Chapter 15, Cano recognizes the utility of knowing Hebrew and Greek: in order the better to converse with infidels, when the Latin text is not as strong; in order to get various mean-

---

[4] LIBER II CAP 12 "*Ubi eorum argumenta ponuntur, qui suadere volunt, in sacrarum intelligentia Scripturarum, ad fontes Hebraicum et Graecum recurrendum.*"

CAP 13 "*In quo veteris vulgatae editiones autoritas demonstratur, et quod non est nunc ad Hebraeos Graecosve recurrendum.*"

CAP 14 "*In quo argumenta capitis duodecimi refutantur.*"

"*Item Hebraeorum doctores, nostri videlicet inimici, multo studio contenderunt textum Hebraicum corrumpere, ut vetus testamentum nostris exemplaribus facerent esse contrarium, ut Euseb. lib. 4. eccl. hist. 18. refert. Graeci quoque eadem contentione multis locis, ut scripturam ad suum sensum traherent, novum testam. violarunt.*" Liber II, Cap 13.

[5] "*. . . aut veterem interpretem Spiritus sancti peculiari dono sacras literas convertisse, aut ecclesiam Latinam multis retro seculis non Dei habuisse Evangelium, sed hominis. Cum igitur objicit, interpretem non fuisse Prophetam. Sane vero propheta non fuit, habuit tamen (ut Titelmannus recte asseverat) spiritum quendam prophetico vicinum & proximum: qualem necessarium esse ostendimus sacris literis interpretandis. Imo qualis erat necessarius, ut ecclesia Latina editionem sacrorum librorum haberet, quam tuto in fide & moribus sequeretur.*" Liber II, Cap 14.

ings from the same passage, so that one may understand idioms, turns of phrase, and proverbs; and in order to understand the Hebrew and Greek words incorporated in the Latin text.

This position was common doctrine, at least in practice, for many centuries. When the acts of the Council of Trent were published, it was evident that zealous theologians of subsequent periods, in their polemic preoccupation, had exaggerated and solidified an extreme position. In his encyclical, *Divino afflante Spiritu*, Pius XII authoritatively interpreted the Tridentine decree:

Nor should anyone think that this use of the original texts, in accordance with the methods of criticism, in any way derogates from those decrees so wisely enacted by the Council of Trent concerning the Latin Vulgate. It is historically certain that the Presidents of the Council received a commission, which they duly carried out, to beg, that is, the Sovereign Pontiff in the name of the Council that he should have corrected, as far as possible, first a Latin, and then a Greek, and Hebrew edition, which eventually would be published for the benefit of the Holy Church of God. If this desire could not then be fully realized, owing to the difficulties of the times and other obstacles, at present it can, we earnestly hope, be more perfectly and entirely fulfilled by the united efforts of Catholic scholars.

And if the Tridentine Synod wished "that all should use as authentic" the Vulgate Latin version, this, as all know, applies only to the Latin Church and to the public use of the same Scriptures; nor does it, doubtless, in any way diminish the authority and value of the original texts. For there was no question then of these texts, but of the Latin versions, which were in circulation at that time, and of these the same Council rightly declared to be preferable that which "had been approved by its long-continued use for so many centuries in the Church." Hence, this special authority, or, as they say, *authenticity* of the Vulgate was not affirmed by the Council particularly for critical reasons, but rather because of its legitimate use in the Churches throughout so many centuries; by which use, indeed, the same is shown, in the sense in which the Church has understood and understands it, to be free from any error whatsoever in matters of faith and morals; so that, as the Church herself testifies and affirms, it may be quoted safely and without fear of error in disputations, in lectures, and in preaching; and so its authenticity is not specified primarily as *critical*, but rather as *juridical*.[6]

[6] "*Neque arbitretur quisquam hunc primorum textuum usum, ad critices rationem habitum, praescriptis illis quae de Vulgata Latina Concilium Triden-*

Among all the diverse Latin translations in the Latin Church, for public use, the Vulgate is to be preferred. This is the moderate scope of the Tridentine decree.

As a matter of fact, anyone who wants to become directly acquainted with our rich theological tradition has to know the Vulgate, since it was the dogmatic basis for centuries of theological thought in the West. But that does not mean that the Vulgate must always retain this position, nor can it continue to be a sincere expression of faith and devotion for those who cannot understand its language, except in the sense that these people make a global act of faith in the contents of the sacred writings. It has even less right to be considered the ultimate norm of interpretation and re-presentation.

Just as a director of an orchestra or theatrical production, as he strives to produce his own interpretation, must take into account interpretations of the masters and other recognized authorities, so, too, future interpreters of the Bible must always accord to the Vulgate the respect and authority due to a magisterial performance.

---

tinum sapienter statuit, ullo modo officere. Constat enim e litterarum monumentis Concilii Praesidibus fuisse creditum, ut ipsius Sacrae Synodi nomine Summum Pontificem rogarent—quod illi quidem fecerunt—ut Latina primum editio, dein vero et Graeca et Hebraica, quoad fieri posset, corrigerentur, in Ecclesiae Sanctae Dei utilitatem tandem aliquando vulgandae. Cui voto, si tunc propter temporum difficultates aliaque impedimenta non plene responderi potuit, in praesens, ut fore confidimus, doctorum catholicorum collatis viribus perfectius ampliusque satisfieri potest. Quod autem Vulgatam Tridentina Synodus esse voluit latinam conversionem, 'qua omnes pro authentica uterentur', id quidem, ut omnes norunt, latinam solummodo respicit Ecclesiam, eiusdemque publicum Scripturae usum, ac nequaquam, procul dubio, primigeniorum textuum auctoritatem et vim minuit. Neque enim de primigeniis textibus tunc agebatur, sed de latinis, quae illa aetate circumferebantur conversionibus, inter quas idem Concilium illam jure praeferendam edixit, quae 'longo tot saeculorum usu in ipsa Ecclesia probata est.' Haec igitur praecellens Vulgatae auctoritas seu, ut aiunt, AUTHENTIA *non ob criticas praesertim rationes a Concilio statuta est, sed ob illius potius legitimum in Ecclesiis usum, per tot saeculorum decursum habitum; quo quidem usu demonstratur eamdem, prout intellexit et intellegit Ecclesia, in rebus fidei ac morum ab omni prorsus esse errore immunem; ita ut, ipsa Ecclesia testante et confirmante, in disputationibus, lectionibus concionibusque tuto ac sine errandi periculo, proferri possit; atque adeo eiusmodi* AUTHENTIA *non primario nomine* CRITICA, *sed* IURIDICA *potius vocatur." EB 549; RSS, pp. 91–92.*

MODERN TRANSLATIONS

Having considered the qualities of the two privileged translations, we may now go on to discuss modern translations.

Every translation must answer the needs of its age. The Vulgate itself was a vernacular translation, made into the language which was currently spoken and written in the Western world of that time. Just as the Septuagint and the Vulgate exercised a great influence on the formation of the language of Christians, so the new translations will influence the religious language, both cultic and theological, of their epoch.

The principal object of this task is to achieve an "interpretation" or "repetition" of the original work in such a way that when the translation is recited, the whole structured language system exists again here and now.

But is this possible? If the work is a structured system, how is it possible that in a new language the same interrelations and structure will exist again? It is impossible to be equally faithful to all the levels of the original. The better one knows the original language, the more difficult translation appears; the more deeply one has penetrated the original, by intuition or by analysis, the more does one despair of translating its riches. Croce declares that a literary work of art can never be translated; Edward Sapir, however, himself a master in the study of language, recognizes the fact that, "nevertheless, literature does get itself translated, sometimes with astonishing adequacy." [7] His explanation of this fact is, however, disputable.

Because of the plurality of the work itself, and because of its need to be repeated, it is possible and even necessary to have many translations in order that all the aspects of the original may be the better appreciated. Just as the Septuagint effected a spiritualization of certain symbols and images, so we may continue this process of conceptualization as long as we keep in mind the grave danger of transposing a literary work into the realm of technical language. This would only serve to obstruct the authentic actualization of the inspired work. Along this road there lies in wait the "logical fal-

---

[7] *Language*, p. 222.

lacy" which we have already treated of in an article dealing with the techniques of translating Hebrew poetry.[8]

Though we admit the possibility of various translations existing at the same time, due to the mutual inadequacy of the languages, still there is an ideal toward which all must strive: The text must approach as far as possible a real capacity to repeat and actualize the original with immediacy and unity.

A theatrical work should be translated primarily for the stage, a piece of lyric poetry for recitation, and the translation of the Bible should look towards its liturgical proclamation. We would like to point out here two principles of rather ample scope which must be operative in order to achieve this ideal.[9]

(1) The principle of stylistic level means that we must pay attention to the plane on which the original moves; we must note its "tone": It may be that of conversation, lyric, oratory, or of elevated prose. We may allow poetry to lose its rhythm in translation, but we cannot permit poetry to become prose. A prosaic translation of poetry is not a translation, but a betrayal (unless, of course, one is only preparing a "trot" for those who are going to consult the original). In order to render the tone of the original, logic will not suffice; there must be a feeling for the work, born of familiarity.

(2) The principle of stylistic system means that the original work must show forth its own system, in order to become the life center of the translation. The translator discovers this system and its "soul" by intuition, trial, and analysis. If in a particular poem the factor of sound is predominant, then the translation must also make this its central consideration, even to the point of subordinating an imagined terminological exactitude. Thus, if the name of a tree mentioned in a poem were selected, not for botanical reasons but for alliteration, then it would be unfaithful to the original to abide by the botany and neglect the alliteration. The same can be said for factors of rhythm, image, plasticity, idea, etc.

A frequent temptation of Western minds, especially of professors, is to make the translation more precise than the original; as

[8] "Traducción de textos poéticos biblicos," *EstBíb* 19, 1960, pp. 311-328.
[9] We have treated of the technique of translation, giving examples in a series of articles: (1) "Traducción de textos poéticos hebreos," *CB* 17, 1960, pp. 170-176. (2) "Traducción de textos poéticos," *CB* 17, 1960, pp. 257-265. (3) "Traducción de textos poéticos," *CB* 18, 1961, pp. 336-346. (4) "Textos poéticos: análisis y traducción," *CB* 19, 1962, pp. 282-294.

though the original were a system of genera which must be reduced to species. The symbol becomes a concept; a suggestion becomes an affirmation, and so forth. Another temptation is that of trying to have the translation explicitly convey all the resonances which the original owes to its general context. An integral translation will strive to realize the total context, so that the resonances will be heard and felt as contextual, rather than as completely explicit in the one passage.

There is always the temptation to regard literal translation as the best, and though this can be useful, it is not faithful. It is a temptation to demand that the translation be always harmonious and smooth; many times it is in the dissonance or erratic rhythm of the original that the expression consists. Paraphrase always offers a great temptation. There are many more temptations that beset the translator, but this is not the place to enumerate or develop them, since this is not a practical treatise on the art of translation.

It was the fact itself of biblical translation that interested us. It is the unavoidable consequence of the fact that the divine word has become incarnate in human speech. Since its original concretization in one language, one author, one work, the word of God seeks wider scopes for its energy—it seeks to reach every man. "St. Paul wrote to one city; through St. Paul and through that city the Holy Spirit has written to all" (Chrysostom).

The inspired word demands translation by its very nature, and translation is an exalted and arduous service of the Word.

Bibliography for Chapter 11

The fact of translation in regard to the Bible is vividly brought home to anyone who consults the "Elenchus Bibliographicus" in *Biblica*. In part 3, "Textus et Versiones," which prolongs as it were the corresponding treatment in any standard introduction, there are often as many as one hundred and twenty titles. Among the ancient versions, we find: the Targums, the Septuagint and other Greek versions, the Vetus Latina, the Vulgate, Ethiopian, Armenian, Coptic, Georgian, Gothic, Old

Slavic, and Syriac. The ancient translations are valuable in attempts to restore a faulty passage in the original, but their interest here lies in the witness they give to the diffusion of the word of God by means of translation. In regard to the art of translation in general, there is the work edited by W. Arrowsmith and R. Shattuck, *The Craft and Context of Translation*, Austin, 1961; most of the articles are concerned with translations of the classics, but the Introduction and the chapter "Impossibilities of Translation" by W. Winter are of a more general orientation. There is an appendix of twenty-two pages in which the observations of various Latin and English authors (including St. Jerome and the translators of the King James version) are presented. A more technical treatment of the same problem can be found in G. Mounin, *Les problèmes théoriques de la traduction*, Paris, 1963.

A discussion of the modern translations made by the translators themselves can be found in their introductions or in separate articles and books, as in the case of R. Knox, *Trials of a Translator*, New York, 1949; Theophile Meek, who did so much of the work in the *Chicago Bible*, propounds some of his principles in "Old Testament Translation Principles," *JBL* 81, 1962, pp. 143–154.

The Septuagint. P. Benoit has two articles on the inspiration of the Septuagint: "La Septante est elle inspirée?" in *Vom Wort des Lebens* (Festschr. für M. Meinertz), Münster, 1951, pp. 41ff.; (*Exégèse et Théologie*, vol. 1, pp. 1ff.), and "L'inspiration des Septante d'après les Pères," in *L'Homme devant Dieu. Mélanges offerts au Père Henri de Lubac, Exégèse et Patristique*, Paris, 1963, pp. 169–187. And P. Auvray has an article in *RB* 59, 1953, pp. 321ff, "Comment se poser le problème des Septante." A. Vaccari treats of the citations of the Septuagint in "Las citas del Antiquo Testamento en la epístola ad Hebraeos," *CB* 13, 1956, pp. 239ff. Recently, P. Grelot has expressed his approval of the position of Benoit and Auvray: "Sur l'inspiration et la canonicite de la Septante," *Sciences Ecclesiastiques*, 17, 1964, pp. 387–418.

The Vulgate. In addition to the standard treatment in the introductions, there is the work of Dom Chapman, *Notes on the Early History of the Vulgate Gospels*, New York, 1908. The study most relevant to our purpose is A. Allgeier "Haec vetus et vulgata editio. Neue worte und begriffesgeschichtliche Beiträge zur Bibel auf dem Tridentinum," *Historisches Jahrbuch* 60, 1940, pp. 142–158; *Bib* 29, 1948, pp. 253–290.

Modern Translations. The fundamental article is the collaborative work edited by J. Schmid, "Moderne Bibelübersetzungen. Eine Übersicht," *ZKT* 82, 1960, pp. 290–332. There is a discussion of various modern translations by way of review in the biblical periodicals (cf., for example, the reviews of *The New English Bible* in the "Elenchus Bibl.," *Bib*, 1962, nos. 703–705; 1963, nos. 763–764). R. Nida's long interest in this field is summed up in his *Toward a Science of Translating*, Leiden, 1964.

12. The Reception of the Work

RECEPTION

When, by means of translation, we have achieved an actualization of the inspired work, it still remains only potentially actualized until the moment when it is recited publicly or read privately.

When the people of God are united in the liturgy to hear the word of God being proclaimed out loud in a language they can understand, there above all the word of God finds full existence. To the profession of faith which declares that "He spoke through the prophets," we can add this other profession: "Who now comes to speak to me in the reader at the liturgy."

. . . Christ is always present in His Church, especially in her liturgical celebrations. . . . He is present in His word, since it is He Himself Who speaks when the holy Scriptures are read in the Church.[1]

In the liturgy, God speaks to His people and Christ is still proclaiming His Gospel.[2]

The act of understanding consummates and completes the process of language. That which has been given objective existence is once again made subjective. Language actualizes and manifests what is interior, a work actualizes an experience by means of language, and repetition actualizes the word-system of a work; but all these still remain somehow in potency, and the potency receives its definitive actualization when the reader or listener receive it.

A re-presentation is for others, otherwise it remains an abortive

[1] ". . . *Christus Ecclesiae suae semper adest, praesertim in actionibus liturgicis. . . . Praesens adest in verbo suo, siquidem ipse loquitur dum sacrae Scripturae in Ecclesia legentur.*" *Const.*, no. 7.

[2] "*In Liturgia enim Deus ad populum suum loquitur; Christus adhuc Evangelium annuntiat.*" *Const.*, no. 33.

effort or play. In private reading, the reader is the audience, and if he reads out loud, he becomes both spectator and actor.

The reception of an act of language is not a passive operation, as though the spectator or listener can give themselves up to a blissful inertia. It is, rather, in every phase of the process, an intense spiritual activity. This complete activity transpires without our being fully aware of it, in the simple act by which we understand something expressed in language. It is more intense in dialogue, still more so perhaps in the reception of a complete literary work. This activity, like so many other human operations, can become a real pleasure, whether it be the pure activity of reception or the reciprocal activity of communication with another person. Dialogue demands response, and this is what consummates the act of listening. If the words of the one speaking to us are meant to influence us, then our response must be in acting. These are the two fundamental forms of response—in word and in act.

A literary work also requires these two types of response. A work which poses problems and communicates the author's reflections, demands of me that I also reflect and take a stand; a work which challenges, demands that I act.

In the liturgical action, the whole community, except for the onlookers, takes part in the act of re-presentation. But are there really spectators? In a certain sense, no. Someone who comes only to watch, to look on, does not enter into the reality, and therefore does not receive the liturgical action, since this can be appreciated only from within. Would we say, then, that the liturgy is a play? Insofar as it is a re-presentation which wishes no one to be really an onlooker, it can be called play. Guardini, in his classic book on the spirit of the liturgy, has a whole chapter on the liturgy as play. He saw the total meaning of this notion: The liturgy is a sacred reënactment presented before God. God is, in a certain way, the onlooker of the play which men enact in order to praise and glorify Him.

Such is the wonderful fact which the liturgy demonstrates; it unites art and reality in a supernatural childhood before God. That which formerly existed in the world of unreality only, and was rendered in art as the expression of mature human life, has here become reality. These forms are the vital expression of real and frankly supernatural life. But this has one thing in common with the play of the child and the life of art—it has no purpose, but it is full of profound meaning. It is not work, but play. To be at play, or to fashion a work of art in God's sight—not to create, but to exist—such is the essence of liturgy. From this is derived its sublime mingling of profound earnestness and divine joyfulness.[3]

The whole assembly sings a Psalm and the word, the inspired word, comes into play, achieving through the community its full actualization. The whole assembly hears the word of God proclaimed, and they must respond with word and action: Not only with the liturgical action, but with the action of the whole of their lives, which then becomes energized and enlightened by the power of the Word.

In a secondary sense, the liturgical action can be of interest to a non-believer or a Christian of another community, and it thus acquires another value added to its primary meaning. But when this aspect of being a play becomes commercialized and looks for tourists, God leaves, and the play is no longer sacred. The work does not now receive its consummating actualization, and becomes instead a falsehood.

The liturgical actuation gives the work a new dimension of actuality: The re-presentation is a presence of the Word. Not the contents of the work, insofar as they are different from and anterior to it, but the meaning of the work itself which is revealed in the re-presentation—this is the vehicle for the word. We are referring here to the word as it is present in the liturgy.

Since the actualization of the inspired work is effected by the active participation of the community entering thus into the reality, it is easy to understand why the *Constitution on the Sacred Liturgy* makes such great efforts to restore this aspect of the liturgical action: not only in the Eucharistic action itself, but also in the liturgy of the Word:

Pastors of souls must realize that, when the liturgy is celebrated, something more is required than the mere observation of the laws governing valid and licit celebration; it is their duty also to insure that the faithful take part fully aware of what they are doing, actively engaged in the rite, and enriched by its effects.[4]

[3] R. Guardini, *The Church and the Catholic, and the Spirit of the Liturgy*, New York, 1935, p. 181.

[4] "*Ideo sacris pastoribus advigilandum est ut in actione liturgica non solum*

Mother Church earnestly desires that all the faithful should be led to that full, conscious, and active participation in liturgical celebrations which is demanded by the very nature of the liturgy. Such participation by the Christian people as "a chosen race, a royal priesthood, a holy nation, a redeemed people (1 Pt 2:9; cf. 2:4–5) is their right and duty by reason of their Baptism." [5]

The Work as Mediator

When we insist on the importance of the work, on its structured consistency and inner dynamic unity, we do not mean that it is living in the formal sense of that term. A literary work is the manifestation of a meaningful reality, it subsists in itself, yet its subsistence lies in its meaning.

Artists themselves often witness to this enduring, independent existence of a literary work. From among the many possible testimonies, we adduce these lines of W. K. Wimsatt:

The poem is not the critic's own and not the author's (it is detached from the author at birth and goes about the world beyond his power to intend it or control it). [6]

A poem should not mean but be. It is an epigram worth quoting in every essay on poetry. [7]

Rilke's "Requiem for Wolf Graf von Kalckreuth" contains the same thought in a more nuanced form:

We only watch the poems that still climb,
still cross, the inclination of your feeling,
carrying the words that you had chosen. No,
you did not choose all; often a beginning
was given you in full, and you'd repeat it
like some commission. And you thought it sad.
Ah, would you had never heard it from yourself!

---

observentur leges ad validam et licitam celebrationem, sed ut fideles scienter, actuose et fructuose eandem participent." Const., no. 11.

[5] "Valde cupit Mater Ecclesia ut fideles universi ad plenam illam, consciam atque actuosam liturgicarum celebrationum participationem ducantur, quae ab ipsius Liturgiae natura postulatur et ad quam populus christianus, 'genus electum, regale sacerdotium, gens sancta, populus adquisitionis' (1 Pt 2:9; cf. 2:4–5), vi Baptismatis ius habet et officium." Const., no. 14.

[6] The Verbal Icon, p. 5 (cf. ch. 10, n. 13).

[7] Ibid., p. 81.

Your angel sounds on, uttering the same
text with a different accent, and rejoicing
breaks out in me to hear his recitation,
rejoicing over you: for this was yours.[8]

In a work, I live somehow with other persons, I come to know
events and things, and often I feel myself in the company of the
author as he speaks. We might say that in the work and through
the work we come into contact with things and events and with
the author. Some prefer the formula "in the work," others prefer
to describe this contact as taking place "through the work." Without any pretensions at settling the question, we would tend to
choose the first formula.

Contacting Events in the Work

Events, which are by their nature passing, limited, and irreversible,
achieve stability in a system of words which we call a literary work.
This is the principle underlying all narration, which, in its turn, is
the subsisting memory of a community. When event becomes
word, it is not merely repeated, but receives in the process a human
and personal interpretation. To interpret is not to falsify; as a matter of fact, it is just the opposite. It means to penetrate into the
meaning of an event and transpose superficial appearances to the
level of intelligibility (there can, of course, be false interpretations).

There is a school of painting which attempts to interpret and
manifest the interior meaning of things by distorting their external
appearances, simplifying lines, changing colors and shapes, etc.
This is a form of expressionism, and it has more truth in it than the
naïve preoccupation with what "things really look like." Thus,

[8] *Nur den Gedichten sehn wir zu, die noch*
über die Neigung deines Fühlens abwärts
die Worte tragen, die du wähltest. Nein,
nicht alle wähltest du; oft ward ein Anfang
dir auferlegt als Ganzes, den du nachsprachst
wie einen Auftrag. Und er schein dir traurig.
Ach hättest du ihn nie von dir gehört.
Dein Engel lautet jetzt noch und betont
denselben Wortlaut anders, und mir bricht
der Jubel aus bei seiner Art zu sagen,
der Jubel über dich: denn dies war dein.
Sämtliche Werke, p. 662; Translation by Leishman (cf. ch. 7, n. 7).

van Gogh pictures the sun as a great gyrating power which imparts its movement to all the beings on the earth. Is the monochromatic sun of a "realist" painter actually more true? (We once saw in *The Illustrated London News*, pictures of the sun taken from high altitude balloons, and they bore a striking resemblance to the sun envisaged by van Gogh.)

In order to interpret an event, a narration may highlight one aspect and neglect others, liberating the event from its bounded temporal existence, making it capable of being remembered and recited, and raising it to the level of a universal reality without being false to the deepest concrete meaning of the event.

In sacred Scripture, we meet many events which are interpreted and transmitted in a structured system of words. Inspiration guarantees for us that this interpretation is profoundly correct. A scholar could go to the Bible and abstract from it the facts and events he needs to reconstruct a critical history; his reorganized series of extracts is not inspired, neither is his interpretation. What he has gained in his recapturing of "things as they really were," he has lost in the inspired "expressionism" which revealed the deepest meaning of the events. For while these happenings were, undoubtedly, human actions, they were also the actions of God, and by that fact revelations of God in history. As they took place on this globe, they looked like any other events, but the sacred author saw their inner significance, and this was the living intuition which dominated the whole process by which his work was realized.

In the work, we come into contact with events as interpreted; in order to repeat or re-present the work, this transcendent dimension which constitutes the revelation of God must be preserved. It is not the simple empirical fact, which is unrepeatable by its nature, not is it a pure poetical repetition, even though this might possess validity and depth; it is, rather, that which in the event made it salvation history and thus is deeply relevant to our lives. These sacred events reach us in the biblical "work" as re-presented in the liturgy. As events, their deepest meaning is in the fact that God acted in them. As present in the work, and actualized in the liturgy, they are the events in which God acts now.

> For Yahweh rebuilds Sion,
> and is seen amidst his glory.

> He regards the prayer of the needy,
> and does not contemn their prayer.

> Let this be written for a generation to follow,
> a people then created will sing Yahweh's praise.[9]

Contacting the Author in the Work

We do not wish to consider the work of an author as a symptom by which we can classify him as "introverted," "psychotic," or "neurotic." This would be to look on the author as an object of scientific investigation (if such procedures can be called scientific), but it is not knowing him as a person. We wish instead to have a dialogue which is truly human and not merely utilitarian. But is it possible to have such access to an author by means of his work? Does he desire it? Or is the work a total presence, meant once for all to relegate the author to a dignified aloofness?

It is sometimes said that present literary investigation concentrates on the work and nothing but the work, and that the author is not of any interest. This reaction against the psychologism of an earlier generation has led, in turn, to some exaggeration. It is perfectly true that our literary analyses are not primarily concerned with the private life of the author: how he dressed, what kind of whiskey he drank, the name of the woman who presently caught his fancy and to whom he dedicated a sonnet, etc. To know the family name, the social class, and the dates of birth and death of Laura is not exactly the overriding preoccupation of a literary study of Petrarch. Personal information about the author only interests us insofar as it has influenced his work and left its mark there.

But it is no less certain that a reader can relive the intuition of the author, and can thus approach him as a person, stand by his side, and share his vision for a few moments. Both men may now repeat the same words and in them find themselves united in joy or pain, or it may be that the reader follows the author, dimly aware that he is approaching something, but not quite reaching it. A literary work can be a real manifestation of an author; and this is true not only of lyric, but also of epic poetry and drama.

This capacity to manifest the author is obvious in the case of lyric poetry, but there are two things that we must bear in mind: At times, a poet is moved to create by way of reaction against his

[9] Ps 102:17–19.

experience, as a form of compensation or liberation, and in this case it is important to be able to sense the nature of the revelation being made through the work. At other times, the author puts himself in the place of someone else, and then his self-revelation is "once removed," so to speak; it is conveyed through the person he has assumed.[10]

An epic can also manifest its author. We must look to the selection, disposition, and interpretation he has given to the events he narrates. The selective process is most significant in what it leaves out, for often an omission is more motivated than the decision to include something. There may be some philosophical or theological principle at the center of a narrative composition, even though it never be formulated. An author may manifest a tendency toward apologetics, a penchant for storytelling, an enthusiasm for ideals, a preoccupation with exactitude, etc. The mentality of the author is there concretely in the work; it is not necessary nor even possible to contact it by a series of inferences or syllogisms.

An author may speak through the characters he creates (here, though we will be repeating concepts which we saw in Chapter 2, we are not repeating the analogy we used there to help us understand inspiration). In some rare cases, an author can make his characters speak with Sophoclean ambiguity—Oedipus Rex, Caiaphas in St. John's Gospel, etc. There is also the other extreme in which an author enters into his own work by means of one of his characters, and addresses his audience directly; he may do this boldly, and make it apparent to all, or he may choose to disguise it, leaving only a clue. Between these two extremes, there is the whole gamut of possibilities: An author may keep his distance from characters, and he may by the force of the context in which he puts them convey to us his personal feelings about them. This is clearly seen, for instance, in the novel with a thesis: as when an author condemns a "bad" person to defeat and frustration, and when he crowns the efforts of the "good" character with success and happiness. Other authors surround their characters with affection and intuitive understanding—think of the relation between Cervantes and Don Quixote—and this show of paternal affection is itself a way the author has of speaking to us. The average reader enters right into the world of the novel and never gives the author

[10] Cf. W. Kayser, *Das sprachliche Kunstwerk*, Berne, 1954, pp. 191ff.

a thought. Then at the end there may come a flash of insight or a moment of deep reflection, and he realizes that the author was there all the time, there in the novel, living along with the reader in his contemplation of reality as it presented itself to him in the re-creation effected by the author.

We do not wish to discuss here whether or not this experience of the living presence of the author is of a purely aesthetic or literary nature. We personally think that it really belongs to language. Nor do we wish to maintain that this experience is absolutely universal: that it happens to all readers, whenever they read any book. We wish only to appeal to the experience of many readers. We know some who have a real love for Antonio Machado, Dostoevski, the author of Ecclesiastes—a lyricist, a novelist, and an essayist. And this experience is sufficient to warrant our going on to ask the cardinal question.

Contacting God

In the work, we contact the author. Is it possible, then, in the Bible to contact God? We do not, of course, refer here to the modes of syllogistic and inferential thought. It is true that God has willed that this human author tell me this or that event, this or that way, and that what is written here is a manifestation of the will of God. But is that all that I can find there? Is it only a witness to a decree of God?

The Fathers understood this aspect in a deeper and more immediate way (though, of course, they respected the analogy they were dealing with). God has initiated a dialogue, and He allows me to enter into His heart.

Let each one consider that through the tongue of the prophets we hear God speaking to us.[11]

What is Scripture, but a letter from Almighty God to His creature? . . . Strive then each day to meditate on the words of your Creator. Come to know the heart of God in the words of God.[12]

[11] St. John Chrys. Cf. ch. 5, n. 7.
[12] "*Quid est autem Scriptura sacra, nisi quaedam epistola omnipotentis Dei ad creaturam suam? . . . Stude ergo, quaeso, et quotidie Creatoris tui verba meditare. Disce cor Dei in verbis Dei, ut ardentius ad aeterna suspires, ut mens vestra ad coelestia gaudia majoribus desideriis accendatur.*" St. Gregory, "Letter 31, Ad Theodorum," PL 77, 706.

Through the sacred writers who composed the text, and by means of the world of narrative, God really speaks to me. In the work, I contact God because the work itself is a sort of incarnation in which God has concretized his self-revelation. It is a new creation through a medium, "through the prophets," and yet it is direct: "He spoke."

We have already seen these words of Pesch:

. . . and, therefore, God speaks to us immediately in Scripture, because Scripture is the word of God in the formal and proper sense. The sacred writers are intermediaries between us and God; they are intermediaries, not in the sense that they are objects by whom we know God, but in a subjective sense, as being the mouth of God, by which He speaks to us.[13]

[13] "*Eatenus igitur* DEUS NOBIS IN SCRIPTURA IMMEDIATE LOQUITUR, *quia Scriptura est verbum Dei formale et proprie dictum. Sunt quidem intermedii inter nos et Deum scriptores sacri; at sunt intermedii non ut objecta, ex quibus Deum cognoscimus, sed sensu subiectivo ut os Dei, per quod Deus ad nos loquitur.*" No. 411.

V
THE CONSEQUENCES
OF INSPIRATION

ἀκούσαντες τὸν λόγον τῆς
ἀληθείας

ζῶν ὁ λόγος τοῦ Θεοῦ
καὶ ἐνεργὴς

13. The Context of the Word: Truth

*There are some who prefer to speak of the "effects of inspiration,"
but actually the effect of inspiration is to make of the human word
the word of God, just as the effect of the action of the Spirit in the
Incarnation is the God-Man Christ: "The Holy Spirit will come
upon you and the power of the Most High will overshadow you;
and for that reason the holy child to be born will be called 'Son of
God.'" Because of the action of the Spirit on Mary, because of the
power and the overshadowing, the Child which will be born of her
is really God. Because of the action of the Spirit on the sacred
writer, that structured reality of human words which will emerge is
really the word of God.*

*From this effect there follow many consequences. But once the
terminology has been agreed on, there is no difficulty in adopting
the more usual designation, "the effects of inspiration."*

*It is much more difficult to reach an agreement in another sense
about a final "s" which, though it may appear to be insignificant,
reveals a whole difference of concept. The manuals speak not of the
effects of inspiration, but of its effect, in the singular. From the
action of the Spirit and from the nature of the Word of God, there
is only one "effect"—inerrancy. This one aspect is considered so
important that it occupies half the tract; so fundamental that it
dominates the whole treatment of hermeneutics to such a degree
that hermeneutics becomes the art of saving the Bible from error.[1]*

[1] Pesch does not speak of inerrancy as an effect of inspiration, but he
devotes a great deal of attention to it. Van Laak (1911), after having
proved the existence of inspiration, derives one consequence: inerrancy.
Billot (4th ed., 1929) proposes various consequences: the spiritual sense,
inerrancy, the rules for interpretation. Tromp treats of the question affirming the infallible truth of the Scriptures which he considers under two head-

Imagine, for example, a tract "De Verbo Incarnato," divided into two equal parts: part one—"The Incarnation"; the fact and the mode of its existence—one Person in two natures. Part two— "The Effect of the Incarnation"; the impeccability of Christ. The impeccability of Christ could be proved from Scripture—"which of you can convict me of sin," and by a metaphysical deduction—it is contrary to the nature of the divine sanctity. Then the theory would be applied to answering objections: As a boy, Christ stayed behind in the temple (disobedience); later, He cast out the buyers and sellers from the temple (anger); He exposed the Pharisees (revenge); He slipped away from a threatening crowd (cowardice); He went to banquets and dinners, let Himself be touched by a prostitute, etc., etc. None of these is a new accusation, but they could easily occupy half our tract on the Incarnation.

Would we accept such a treatise? We can already hear the objections: What has happened to the solidarity of all men in Christ, the consideration of our adoptive sonship, the example of His life, His revelation of the Father? Though most of our modern manuals have done away with the classical tract on "The Mysteries of the Life of Christ," still they have not reduced themselves to the narrow limits of the tract we have just made up.

Why, then, has there been such a narrowing of the tract on inspiration, which should follow a structure parallel to that on the Incarnation? The reason is to be found in the history of the last half century or so.

What purpose do the medieval castles and walls serve? Why are there such great walls around Avila or Avignon? Now, because the tourists visit them, and because they are historical and artistic monuments. But castles and walls are built in order to provide habitation and defense during times when there is open hostility or uneasy peace. The building of a castle is an assurance of power; to make a breach in the wall is the first decisive step in conquering a city.

Until the end of the last century, Scripture found itself in a state of war, confronted with open hostility. In an age now remote from us, persecutors demanded that the sacred books be handed over so

---

ings: inerrancy, and the truth within the meaning of the text (literary types). Höpfl-Gut speak of one effect of inspiration: inerrancy.

*that they could destroy them, and Christians died heroically in or-
der to save the inspired text. In an age when culture was nearly
extinct, the enemy was decadence and negligence, and the monks
labored to preserve and multiply copies of the Bible. Toward the
end of the last century, the arms of the enemy were directed against
the supposed errors of the Bible in an effort to force a breach and
enter the sanctuary of inspiration in order to destroy it. The Bible
had to be defended; and this is the time when our manuals on
inspiration were conceived and constructed. It is not strange, then,
that they were surrounded by such great walls of arguments and
replies in those sections which dealt with inerrancy.*

*It would be disrespectful and unfitting to dismantle these walls
which still have a function, but we must stop to consider whether
or not the wall is the essence of the city, or whether peaceful habitation of the city is not something more important. Certainly, the
centuries' long tradition of the Church has regarded the Scriptures
with much greater breadth of view, and it seems to me that it is
healthier and more balanced to follow this ancient tradition, especially in these times of such wonderful renewal in the appreciation
of the Bible.*

*This is why we return to the division made in Chapter 1—the
context of the Word and the context of the Spirit. In the context
of the Word, "Truth"; in the context of the Spirit, "Power." Not
that these are the unique consequences of inspiration; they are,
rather, headings under which we may group the other consequences, while clearly asserting that Truth and Power are found
intimately united in the multiple unity of the divine action.*

*The Fathers of the Church often spoke of the action of the
Trinity in the Scriptures, either naming all three Persons explicitly,
or uniting the Word with the Father or with the Holy Spirit.*

The holy books were written under the inspiration of the Holy Spirit,
by the will of the Father of all, through Jesus Christ.[2]

One God, the Father, the Lord of the Old Testament and the New;
One Lord, Jesus Christ, Who was foretold in the Old Testament and

[2] Διόπερ τοῖς πειθομένοις μὴ ἀνθρώπων εἶναι συγγράμματα τὰς ἱερὰς βίβλους
ἀλλ' ἐξ ἐπιπνοίας τοῦ ἁγίου Πνεύματος βουλήματι τοῦ Πατρὸς τῶν ὅλων διὰ Ἰησοῦ
Χριστοῦ ταύτας ἀναγέγραφθαι καὶ εἰς ἡμᾶς ἐληλυθέναι. Origen, "De Princ., bk.
4," PG 11, 359. Cf. R. Gögler, *Zur Theologie des Biblischen Wortes bei
Origenes,* Düsseldorf, 1963, "Logos und Pneuma," pp. 282-298.

came in the New; and one Holy Spirit, Who through the prophets preached concerning Christ, and when Christ had come, descended on Him and made Him known. Thus, no one should separate the Old Testament from the New, nor should anyone say that there is one Spirit in the first and another in the second, otherwise he will offend against that Holy Spirit Who is honored along with the Father and the Son.[3]

The Scriptures are perfect, because they were pronounced by the Word of God and by His Spirit.[4]

All these [prophets] were endowed with the Spirit of prophecy and honored by the Word . . .[5]

REVELATION OF A MYSTERY

In the context of the word "Truth," Christ, Who has revealed God, is the Truth. Not only does He speak the truth, He causes it to be and is Himself the Truth. In an analogous and participated way, sacred Scripture, insofar as it is the revelation of God, is the truth.

We can think of this in terms of ontological truth: the manifestation of being and of its meaning; and we can think of it as reflective logical truth, enunciated in propositional form. In the Scriptures, we find a manifestation of being, and its meaning within salvation; we also find many statements made about salvation. In regard to the manifestation of being, we can say that the Scriptures are true; in regard to its statements, we can say that the Scriptures contain truth.

Truth can be considered in its total unity or in its relative unity, as it relates to a point of view (not relative truth, but relative unity); revelation, too, may be considered either in its total unity or in terms of the units of revelation. When we know a person, we possess the truth of that person in a unified way: We express this

---

[3] Εἷς Θεὸς, ὁ Πατὴρ, Παλαιᾶς καὶ Καινῆς διαθήκης Δεσπότης. καὶ εἷς Κύριος, Ἰησοῦς Χριστὸς, ὁ ἐν Παλαιᾷ προφητευθεὶς καὶ ἐν Καινῇ παραγενόμενος. καὶ ἕν Πνεῦμα ἅγιον, διὰ προφητῶν μὲν περὶ Χριστοῦ κηρύξαν. ἐλθόντος δὲ τοῦ Χριστοῦ καταβὰν, καὶ ἐπιδείξαν αὐτόν. Μηδεὶς οὖν χωριζέτω τὴν Παλαιὰν ἀπὸ τῆς Καινῆς Διαθήκης. μηδεὶς λεγέτω, ὅτι ἄλλο τὸ Πνεῦμα ἐκεῖ, καὶ ἄλλο ὧδε. ἐπεὶ προσκρούει αὐτῷ τῷ ἁγίῳ Πνεύματι, τῷ μετὰ Πατρὸς καὶ Ἱοῦ τετιμημένῳ. St. Cyril of Jer., "Catech. 16, On the Holy Spirit," PG 33, 920–21.
[4] St. Irenaeus; cf. ch. 2, n. 56.
[5] St. Hippolytus; cf. ch. 2, n. 19.

unity by dividing and differentiating it in a series of things we know about him—his opinions, his plans, his character, his reactions, his attitudes, tastes, and ideals. Since a person does not manifest himself to us in one total act by which we enter into the simplicity of his life center, we get to know him through a series of truths, or, better, units of truth about him. These we can repeat in statement form, when someone asks us about him. Behind all these manifestations and in them, we catch a glimpse of the radical unity of a person. This is his highest truth.[6]

In the same way, God wishes to reveal Himself to us as a Person, inviting us to friendship. He divides His self-manifestation into a long series of salvific acts which give understanding of diverse aspects of His unity. These we call His decisions, His actions, His precepts, or His counsels. We are able to reduce this multiple series to a synthesis, to a higher unity; we can also perceive in these manifestations the presence of the Person Who is revealing Himself.

The unity of revelation is the mystery of salvation in Christ. This is our highest truth,[7] and in itself it is a totality. This one truth can be articulated and divided into a whole series of truths or units of truth. Usually, when we speak of aspects of truths, we think immediately of a series of theoretical propositions: the tract on soteriology—Christ, His activity, His unity, His operations, the sacraments, and these are broken down into a series of theses. Actually, the mystery of Christ is articulated in a series of ordered events, which sum up salvation history. Since we are in the context of truth, we must consider these events in their ultimate meaning. They are significant events; their relation to salvation is their ultimate meaning; their unfolding of the mystery of truth is their ultimate truth. We should here take the term "events" in a wide sense, as including happenings, experiences, and even words, but the predominant medium of revelation for God is in event as a happening. To set forth the meaning of these events is to manifest their transcendent truth. This is fundamentally the truth of Scripture: It is one in the mystery of Christ revealed; it is manifold in that series of events which manifest its meaning as they reveal their own.

[6] The process of getting to know a person resembles the "hermeneutic circle." From the parts to the whole, from the whole to the parts.

[7] "*Jesu corona celsior et veritas sublimior.*" From the hymn for Confessors.

Since the sacred writers reveal this truth, they teach us and convey understanding. In this general sense, we may speak of the Bible as a teaching, an instruction or doctrine. Some describe Scripture as the doctrine of salvation; others say that it contains this doctrine. The question is largely one of terminology. However, in neither view are we allowed to take the term in the sense of "ideology" or "theory." We use the word in its wider meaning when we say that life teaches us, or history, or failure.

In some books of the Bible, especially in the New Testament, teaching takes on an obviously didactic aspect, which includes doctrine. But this is not so in the Old Testament, not even in the sapiental books, which are not really very "doctrinal." These were the reasons which led the scholastics to discuss the question of the "modes" of Scripture, which, while they are not those of the scientist, still are more certain. Thus, Scripture is the source and norm for theological truth, even though it does not present itself exclusively as doctrine. Its literary "modes" convey the highest truth.

"God is Love"; "God loved the world so much that He gave His only Son that everyone who has faith in Him may not die, but have eternal life." The first statement is quite simple; the second is complex. Both enunciate and affirm something. They teach with sufficient clarity though their terminology is not conceptual, but symbolic and mysterious. Still, they both retain their character as propositional teaching, as teaching by statement.

In such cases, which are frequent in the Bible, this question of truth is not difficult. The truth is proposed as a manifestation of the mystery which reveals and veils, and thus stimulates the search for greater understanding. This kind of biblical truth is simple, and it suffices to note and affirm its existence. On the other hand, the truth of the literary "modes" of the Bible is more difficult. Following the example of the medieval theologians, we will treat of this aspect separately, and for this purpose will use the categories of our Western culture, since they are more easily understood.

LITERARY TRUTH

Just as life is a teacher, so is literature. Literature, in the full sense, is not a doctrinal treatise. How, then, does literature teach? What is the truth of literature? In this section, we are going to follow

Hans Meyerhoff, whose treatment in Chapter 4 of his *Time in Literature* is especially clear and well-balanced.[8]

Information Is Accidental

A literary work contains a good deal of information: elements of description which touch on life or history, the arts, work, etc. This data, which is integrated accidentally into the work, can be controlled by like information from other sources. It is the object which an historian, sociologist, or archeologist has in mind when he consults the literature of the past. We can learn from the *Iliad* a good deal about the customs of the Mycenaean age and of the epoch in which the poem itself was fixed (eighth century B.C.). In the *Odyssey*, we can learn a good deal about the sailing techniques of that age. All this information does not constitute the specific truth of the literary work, and the specialist who goes to the text only for the sake of its data, never comes in contact with the work as literature.

The Scriptures can also supply us with a good deal of information about the customs and concepts of the ancient Near East. There were two-story houses with pillars supporting the upper story; there were hand mills, operated by two women; the heavens were looked upon as a solid dome; shepherds used slings; people thought that there was a great supply of hail up in the heavens, etc. None of this information constitutes the specific truth of the Scriptures. St. Augustine had already pointed out this fact, and Cardinal Baronius (according to the testimony of Galileo) formulated it this way: "The Holy Spirit wishes to teach us not how the heavens go, but how to go to heaven." (Yet about sixty years ago, L. Murillo tried to find scientific information revealed in Genesis.)

This type of data is not the truth of the Scriptures, and the sacred author may utilize such information with a certain liberty, subordinating it to the truth of his work. He can simplify the facts, he can accept the information without troubling to find out if it is completely exact, he can make up some of the information and use it in his work, he can distort things in the interest of narrative or expression, or he can exaggerate them. This is neither trickery nor whim, but a functional judgment made in virtue of the

[8] H. Myerhoff, *Time in Literature*, ch. 4, "Literature, Science, and Philosophy."

overriding truth of the work. If the scholar uses the work as a reliable source of information, he must assume responsibility for his own errors and not attribute them to the literary author. We cannot exclude beforehand the possibility that the sacred author made such functional judgments and exercised liberty with the information available to him; he was not writing an encyclopedia.[9]

Theories and Doctrines

Another truth of a literary work is found in the theories or doctrines propounded by the author within the work, either through the mouth of a fictional character or in the form of reflections which interrupt the flow of the narrative. This is not the ideal of literature, but it exists. In the Bible, which is not pure literature, this form of teaching is often found: A reflection on the meaning of a life or an event can be expressed through one of the people in the narrative. Thus, the "Deuteronomist" author puts speeches in the mouths of Joshua, Samuel, and Solomon at turning points in his account of the history of Israel. This obvious literary device proved very helpful to the author as a means of inculcating his thesis, his truth. When he relates the fall of Samaria, and can find no one prominent enough to deliver his message, the author himself takes the stage to explain the meaning of the tragedy.[10]

Truth Properly Literary

Meyerhoff distinguishes between a primary truth and a secondary truth of literature. He calls this latter truth one of "inference." *The primary truth* is the internal coherence of the work which reveals truth to us as a property of being, and as such makes an

[9] This is, we think, what Benoit develops under title of "practical judgment." It would be risky for instance to use the Book of Judith as a source for historical information: Nebuchadnezzar, King of the Assyrians in Nineveh. On the other hand, in a work which sets out to be historical, its truth is the facts themselves along with their interpretation. The way that this interpretation is given can determine the literary type of the work: epic, religious, "causal," etc. But even here the facts are not presented in a list, but are incorporated and used according to the purpose of the author.

[10] In the Book of Judith, the author places the discourse in the mouth of Achior, the Ammonite. There is a certain irony in this procedure, as well as a dialectical purpose and a desire to highlight the nature of the religious confession. Though often these speeches are intruded into the narrative with a certain lack of literary finesse, they are valuable since they are frequently a key to the meaning of the whole composition.

316

appeal to the person. Some critics speak of such a work as "convincing," not in the oratorical sense of persuasion, but in the sense that the work has consistency and reality.

There are many passages in Scripture which are convincing in this sense. Take the description of the drunkard in Proverbs 23:

> Who scream? Who shriek?
> Who have strife? Who have anxiety?
> Who have wounds for nothing?
> Who have black eyes?
> Those who linger long over wine,
> those who engage in trials of blended wine,
> Look not on the wine when it is red,
> when it sparkles in the glass.
> It goes down smoothly;
> But in the end it bites like a serpent,
> or like a poisonous adder.
> Your eyes behold strange sights,
> and your heart utters disordered thoughts;
> You are like one now lying in the depths of the sea,
> now sprawled at the top of the mast.
> They struck me, but it pained me not;
> They beat me, but I felt it not;
> When shall I awake
> to seek wine once again?

Readers instinctively apply such adjectives as "real," "authentic," "convincing" to a passage such as this. In Meyerhoff's terminology, we have here a true artistic presentation, one that is authentic; and there is a true communication with the reader, one that elicits a true response. The text incorporates an experience, personal or otherwise, presents it authentically or truly, and is able to evoke an authentic decision.[11]

But not all of Scripture has this power to convince, especially when the author simplifies events to the point of schematization. Many of the kings appear unconvincing literarily, even though the teaching of the writer be true.

The secondary truth of inference involves a certain generaliza-

[11] Ordinarily, this kind of truth involves a moment of recognition in which there is a new perception or a deeper insight. In this act of "re-cognition," there is an increase of knowledge in one way or another. As the reality is presented, it reveals itself manifesting its own truth.

tion. A literary work presents to us new aspects of reality and experience, broadening our knowledge by acquaintance. When discussing the first kind of literary truth, we spoke of the knowledge which can be gained from it by accident, as it were: all the information which the work may contain, but which does not constitute its specific truth. Knowledge which is gained by familiarity is a different thing altogether, and one which is much more integrally human. This type of knowledge is transmitted by literature. The high point of such knowledge is found in the knowledge conveyed of another person, but we can also acquire knowledge of this type with regard to the objects which form part of our life.

The Scriptures often provide us with a knowledge born of familiarity; this is the way we come to know God as Someone Who comes and associates with men. Many other beings then enter the context of our lives as a result of this condescension, and they become familiar to us. This most important aspect of the truth of the Scriptures can never be adequately conveyed in propositional form.

Knowledge by familiarity is the basis of that contemplative activity by which Christians reflect on a passage of the sacred text: As the text is read slowly and its actualization often repeated, it begins to yield its deep truth, until finally he who gazes into it is penetrated by it. The life of Christ reveals the mystery of Christ to those who know it by familiar contact. This is the principle which St. Ignatius proposes to him who would "exercise himself" in the knowledge of Christ, and it is a method far superior to that in which cerebral meditation gives rise to voluntarist decisions. In meditation, the understanding operates according to the laws of deduction and analogy, the truth with which it is concerned is contained in a proposition; in contemplation, the predominant factor is presence, somehow perceived—the mind is free and receptive and thus dynamically active.

A work of literature reveals our own inner meaning and depth, and makes us conscious of ourselves. As we read, we see ourselves in the light of the author or of his work, and in virtue of this knowledge we can respond by acting to change ourselves. This is the meaning of the last line of Rilke's sonnet, ". . . you must change your life." [12]

[12] "Du musst dein Leben ändern." Last line of "Archaïscher Torso Appolos"; cf. Sämtliche Werke, vol. 1, p. 557 (op. cit., ch. 7, n. 7).

The Epistle to the Hebrews says that the word of God "pierces as far as the place where life and spirit, joints and marrow, divide. It sifts the purposes and thoughts of the heart." The Scriptures are true in the sense that they reveal to us what we are in the sight of God. In Psalm 50, God comes to confront the sinner in a vivid litigation:

> When you do these things, shall I be silent?
> Or do you think that I am like yourself?
> I will correct you by drawing them up before your eyes.

And man responds to God:

> I acknowledge my offense,
> and my sin is before me always (Ps 51).

What God effects in the Psalm by direct accusation, He can also do indirectly by showing us someone else, David for instance, in his sin and repentance. Without having formulated any proposition, I have been shown the truth about myself, that is, I see what I am before God, and this impels me to repentance and a deeper conversion. The truth of Scripture is "con-vincing" in this sense also; it is the deep and active truth of the inspired word.

A literary work can reveal the structure of a being, of our own being, as we have just seen. An event presented in this way unlocks the mystery of its meaning, and transcends its own limitations.

In the Scriptures an historical event, unique and irreversible, is presented in its inner meaning in such a way that this meaning sheds light on other events. By recounting happenings which can never be repeated, the sacred writer reveals the structure of the history dominated by God; he writes a theology of history, or, at least, one chapter of it. Book two, or part two, of St. Luke's work recounts the life of the early Church. The Church's structure is revealed as an historical institution with an existence in time. Though the Acts of the Apostles is not a treatise on ecclesiology, it gives us the light by which we understand the dynamic reality of the Church.

Meyerhoff concludes by showing the similarity in theme and method between existential philosophy and literature. The principal existentialist authors study and freely quote literary works as a source of knowledge which can shed light on the meaning of existence.[13]

Though the Scriptures do not fit in this category exactly, Meyerhoff's observations can help in understanding what kind of truth, what kind of authenticity and power, we are to find in the Scriptures. In doing so, we will not be far from those medieval thinkers who saw in the "modes" of Scripture a knowledge which exceeds all others in certainty and sublimity.

The Truth of Witness

We can add to Meyerhoff's categories another type of truth—that of the witness. It is a truth which has a juridical quality, but also an existential quality, capable of engaging the whole man. We are not speaking here of the account of an eyewitness which he relates for the pleasure of telling it; this is not testimony in the strict sense of the term. The testimony demanded by the law is an instrument of justice; this is the source of the gravity of false testimony. The testimony demanded and inspired by faith, therefore, must be carried even as far as martyrdom (*martys* in Greek means witness, and in Christian antiquity the Latin designation for a martyr was "*confessor fidei*"). This quality of truth with its juridical element and existential commitment constitutes the prophetic and apostolic vocation.

Sacred Scripture in its more important sections presents the truth in all its power as ineluctably present, forcing its way in. In a wide sense, since all Scripture is salvation history, and a presentation of the mystery of Christ, it can be considered a witness to this mysterious reality. This brings us back once again to the substantial truth of the Scriptures, which we discussed above.

Christ is the Truth (Jn 14:6), and He is a witness to the truth (Jn 18:37). His words bear witness to Himself and to His mission. Christ staked His life on bearing this witness when He was judged. In thus committing Himself to death, He gave His testimony an unshakable authenticity. The whole validity of biblical truth as a testimony rests on this fact, and draws its strength from it. The

[13] This is especially true of Heidegger and Jaspers. Sartre not only quotes literature, he writes it.

law and the prophets bore witness in the past (Rom 3:21), and the apostles are to continue it (1 Jn 4:14).

TRUTH IN DIALOGUE

Finite, human truth often resides in a quest. This is so because none of our truths is the whole truth, even though each of them may be complete in itself. The search for truth may take the form of a solitary meditation or of a friendly dialogue. A deduction is truth in the process of becoming; a syllogism is part of a dialectic. The truth is also sought in the clash of opinions, and this itself is a form of dialectic, a "disputed question." A dialectical dispute may mobilize the energies of two individuals or groups or schools of thought, and thus acquire a true historical dimension.

In a didactic or literary treatment, one can adopt either of two methods: He can present the results of his investigation, the conclusion of a syllogism, the accepted text, the correct formula, etc., or he can present the process of investigation as a sort of intellectual lyric or perhaps a drama. This second method was exploited by the unrivaled genius of Plato. His dialogues are "dramatic," and this dynamic quality was not without its effect on the thought of the philosopher. (We can hardly imagine that it made no difference to Plato whether he exposed his thought dynamically or in a series of static, objective propositions.)

Does Scripture ever employ the same method? If it is revelation, it would seem that it should present me with the truth as already realized, proposed by God or in the name of God; revelation is not the product of human searching, and searching is not possible to God. Thus, it seems that there is no room for personal investigation or an inquiry in dialogue.

But the facts contradict this theory. Because revelation is progressive, challenging man and stimulating him to ask questions, it cannot be a block of truth which descends abruptly from heaven. A revelation awakens man, forcing him to search more deeply, and so prepares him for future revelations.

If one of the functions of language—that of monologue—is to sustain the process of thought, and if another function—that of dialogue—is the contrast of opinions as a means of finding and possessing truth in common, then there does not seem to be any reason why this dimension of language must be a stranger to inspiration. Dialogue is too human a thing and too noble to be excluded *a priori* from the Bible.

One Easter day two disciples of Jesus were making their way to Emmaus. As they walked, they discussed the events of Friday. And so they talked over these things and inquired together. St. Luke's term here is provocative: they went along inquiring between themselves— this is the dialogue of Easter morning. And in the midst of their joint inquiry, the Truth joined them; it was Jesus, but they did not recognize Him yet.

The scene here from the Gospel is charged with emotion and with potential. We should not forget this Greek word *"suzetein"*—"to inquire together." The best definition of dialogue would be just that: two persons searching out between themselves the truth and the Truth.[14]

The author of Ecclesiastes includes in his book the process itself of his meditation, that is, he sets about presenting his truth dynamically. It is impossible to understand this book, or the Book of Job, unless we grant that they are dialectical pieces, concerned with the great problem of retribution—they are "disputed questions," and the problem discussed by these two was only satisfactorily answered by Christ. The dialectic preoccupation of the Epistle of St. James is manifest, and the Book of Wisdom seems to be a reply to Ecclesiastes. The Deuteronomist sought out the meaning of events and tried to establish their inner consistency; his was a *"fides quaerens intellectum."*

We see, then, that the Scriptures, especially the Old Testament, also contain the truth by way of inquiry, and that is part of their drama. It shows man faced with the obscure light of mystery, endowed and challenged by the word. Since the sacred text does not present us with all truth in the form of a definitive answer, it remains open to the inquiry and ever deeper penetration of the faithful. It is the Word, imposing on us the obligation to ask questions, directing our inquiry, and, by means of the Spirit, bringing us into the fullness of the truth.

One might, in virtue of some epistemological theory, condemn

[14] L. Alonso Schökel, *Pedagogía de la comprensión*, 2nd ed., Barcelona, 1961, pp. 117–118.

the above exposition as being too complicated, and wish to substitute another series of categories which would be much simpler. Frankly, our intention was rather to point out various aspects of biblical truth which seem to fit badly into the usual compartments. Sacred Scripture possesses a transcendental truth manifesting the Mystery as being, and it contains many logical truths of judgment and statement, in and through which transcendental truth finds articulation.

Logical Truth

This one aspect of truth has assumed a great importance in the history of our tract. This truth, which we call logical, is that of a formal statement or proposition. Its contrary, logical error, is the error of a formal statement. Logical truth and logical error are thus found in the well-defined and limited area of proposition, whose structure will allow of only contradictory judgments, affirming or denying the relation between subject and predicate. When confronted by a proposition, we are fully justified in examining its validity with the presupposition that it must be either true or false. In some cases, a distinction may be employed which divides the proposition in two, delimiting the extension of the subject or the predicate. Before such a distinction is made, in strict logic the proposition is not true and false at the same time, but is rather an imperfect proposition, since it does not clearly affirm or deny one thing. The technique of distinguishing, both in the art of dialectic and in everyday life, shows us that not everything which is a proposition linguistically is a strict logical proposition.

So, then, if I go to the Bible preoccupied with questions of logical truth and error, I have prejudiced the issue and have no right indiscriminately to confront every verse of the Bible with my dilemma. To pose the queston in such a way is to limit, at least methodologically, the extent and type of truth to be found in the Scriptures, and to exclude in principle all truth which is not propositional. This narrow view of the question was aggressively put forward by the rationalists, and meekly accepted by a good number of Catholic theologians.

Is it possible, then, to make universal statements in regard to logical truth? We can do so if we put our statements in a negative form, since a negation has universal dimensions. Some verses of the Bible contain truth; no verse of the Bible contains error. Just as, for instance, a positive precept does not bind always and everywhere: "Give alms" does not mean that I must give to every poor man at every moment. A negative precept is universally binding: "Do not blaspheme."

I cannot affirm universally that all the Bible contains logical truth: interjections, questions, commands, suggestions, allusions, images are not propositions and cannot, by definition, be the expression of logical truth. But I can frame this universal negative: No part of the Bible contains error, since the above figures of speech are equally incapable of expressing logical error. This is the significance of the negative formula, "inerrancy." And though it is universally applicable to the Bible, it presupposes a very restricted view of biblical truth. It has the advantage of all such specific formulas of being precise, but the danger begins when it is allowed to dominate the whole consideration of truth in the Bible, thus reducing the Scriptures to a catalogue of formal propositions. Such an attitude in its zeal to defend the inerrancy of the Bible finds that it has dumped into the text truckloads of "logical errors." In order to avoid this, we must put the question of inerrancy in the larger context of the truth of the Bible. Then the negative universality and precision of the term "inerrancy" will work to best advantage.

The principle of inerrancy is easy to understand: God cannot be deceived, nor can he deceive us. If God proposes something in the Scriptures, it is true and cannot be false.

. . . and so far is it from being possible that any error can coexist with inspiration, that inspiration not only is essentially incompatible with error, but excludes and rejects it as absolutely and necessarily as it is impossible that God Himself, the supreme Truth, can utter that which is not true.[15]

The deduction is simple. God has spoken, and God cannot utter falsehood. It does no good to take refuge in the distinction between the divine and the human in the Scriptures; the truth is

---

[15] ". . . *tantum vero abest ut divinae inspirationi error ullus subesse possit, ut ea per se ipsa, non modo errorem excludat omnem, sed tam necessario excludat et respuat, quam necessarium est, Deum, summam Veritatem, nullius omnino erroris auctorem esse.*" *Providentissimus Deus*, EB 124; RSS, p. 24.

divine, the error human—such a distinction has no basis in the nature of the inspired text:

Hence, the fact that it was men whom the Holy Spirit took up as His instruments for writing does not mean that it was these inspired instruments—but not the primary author—who might have made an error.[16]

But the following deduction is false: God has spoken; therefore He has pronounced a series of propositions. God has rather assumed all the dimensions of human language.

The general principle which follows quite simply from the veracity of God, can get quite complicated when we start to apply it. The situation has been aggravated by the half-century of discussion which was carried on in Catholic circles on the subject of inerrancy. This is not the place to give an historical synthesis of those battles (the maneuvers of which can be studied in the older manuals); we wish simply to note a few of the opinions. There was Salvatore di Bartolo, who restricted inerrancy to matters of faith and morals; Cardinal Newman, who proposed that along with the inspired message there were other things *"obiter dicta"*; Lenormant distinguished between inspiration and revelation: All of Scripture is inspired, not all of it is revelation; only revelation demands our assent to its infallibility.

Leo XIII refused to admit any limitation to inerrancy, and proposed some principles which could be used in resolving diffiulties. His counsels, which extended to the realm of interpretation, can be summed up in this "golden rule" of St. Augustine, quoted by the Pontiff himself:

And if in these books I meet anything which seems contrary to truth, I shall not hesitate to conclude either that the text is faulty, or that the translator has not expressed the meaning of the passage, or that I myself do not understand.[17]

[16] "*Quare nihil admodum refert, Spiritum Sanctum assumpsisse homines tamquam instrumenta ad scribendum, quasi, non quidem primario auctori, sed scriptoribus inspiratis quidpiam falsi elabi potuerit.*" Ibid., EB 125; RSS, p. 25.

[17] "*Ego fateor caritati tuae, solis eis Scripturarum libris, qui iam canonici appellantur, didici hunc timorem honoremque deferre, ut nullum eorum auctorum scribendo aliquid errasse firmissime credam. Ac si aliquid in eis offendero litteris, quod videatur contrarium veritati, nihil aliud quam vel mendosum esse codicem, vel interpretem non assecutum esse quod dictum est, vel*

The Pope then explains how we should understand what the Scriptures have to say on matters dealing with the physical sciences, and he goes on to suggest that a similar solution be applied to historical questions.

Other attempts to understand the Bible in the context of inerrancy proved unfortunate: There were the notions of "history according to appearances," implicit citations, an immature version of "literary genres," etc. All of these attempts were well-intentioned and contained an element of truth, namely, that once the Scriptures are understood, the question of their being in error disappears. However, good intentions cannot save a defective theory.

Pius XII, in his encyclical, *Divino afflante Spiritu*, repeated the same principle, which we may paraphrase roughly: If we can understand the Scriptures correctly, the errors they supposedly contain will disappear; however, let us have humility to admit that we cannot resolve all the difficulties.

By this knowledge and exact appreciation of the modes of speaking and writing in use among the ancients can be solved many difficulties, which are raised against the veracity and historical value of the divine Scriptures, and no less efficaciously does this study contribute to a fuller and more luminous understanding of the mind of the sacred writer. . . . Nevertheless, no one will be surprised if all difficulties are not yet solved and overcome, but that even today serious problems greatly exercise the minds of Catholic exegetes.[18]

In this way, the principle of inerrancy becomes a negative canon of hermeneutics: There can be no interpretation which implicates the Bible in error. This norm is particularly relevant when dealing with the synoptic question and the frequent discrepancies found in their narratives.

Pesch dedicated sixty-three pages to inerrancy in the second part of his book, which he followed with a supplement in 1926. For

---

me minime intellexisse, non ambigam." "Letter 82, to St. Jerome," cf. *EB* 127; *RSS*, p. 25.

[18] *"Cognitis igitur accurateque aestimatis antiquorum loquendi scribendique modis et artibus, multa dissolvi poterunt, quae contra Divinarum Litterarum veritatem fidemque historicam opponuntur; neque minus apte eiusmodi studium ad Sacri Auctoris mentem plenius illustriusque perspiciendam conducet.* . . . *Nemo tamen miretur non omnes adhuc esse difficultates expeditas atque evictas, sed graves etiam hodie quaestiones catholicorum exegetarum mentes non parum agitare."* *EB* 560, 563; *RSS*, pp. 99, 101.

thirty years, there were no new efforts in this direction; the encyclical of Pius XII was more a change of outlook and approach than a speculative contribution to the problem. In regard to modern opinions, we will merely list some of the recent work which has been done in the field.

Benoit made a real contribution with his notions on speculative and practical judgment.[19] The speculative judgment has the truth for its object and thus, as a human operation, it is open to error. In inspiration, God guarantees the truth of such a judgment. The object of the practical judgment is the good, and as such is not subject to error or truth, but is judged by whether or not it corresponds to what was intended. When a practical judgment enlists speculative judgments for its own purpose, these latter are conditioned by their context. In other words, Benoit insists that before one can inquire as to whether or not a judgment is true or false—in order either to defend or attack it—we must first inquire whether or not that judgment moves exclusively in the realm of logic.

A. Moretti[20] proposes a theory based on the notion of opinion. Opinion, by its nature, pertains to the intermediate zone of probability; it is only an error when, being erroneous itself, it is proposed as true. When we say: "I think . . . ," "I believe . . . ," "It seems to me . . . ," "I would say . . . ," we have explicitly declared that what we are saying pertains to the area of opinion, and we cannot be guilty of error, since we have formally stated that our adherence to what we say is conditioned. In the Book of Ecclesiastes, opinions are put forth explicitly as such, even though the Hebrew terminology is not as neatly categorized. In normal speech, and in much of what we write or give in conferences, there are many implicit statements of opinion which may take the verbal form of a proposition, though they are not really such at all. Usually, the general or specific context suffices to indicate this implicit quality of our statement as an opinion. We cannot exclude beforehand the possibility that the Bible also contains this way of proposing an opinion. The Bible is a human book, and it is not human always to express oneself in a pondered true or false proposition. Our theology manuals are accustomed to gradate carefully the de-

---

[19] Cf. ch. 9.
[20] "De Scripturarum inerrantia et de hagiographis opinantibus." *DivTh* 62, 1959, pp. 32–68.

gree of certitude of each thesis: "Of defined faith," "of faith," "ecclesiastical doctrine," "theologically certain," "common doctrine," "more probable opinion". . . . The language of conversation and that of literature could not do the same without pedantry.

N. Lohfink[21] has lately studied the problem from another angle, and has taken a significant step forward. His primary concern is to provide a formula that will be faithful to tradition, and at the same time be pastoral. In keeping with tradition, we must widen the psychologically preoccupied horizons of the last century, which situated problems and sought their solutions totally within the mind of the author. We must consider the work as a literary reality. This reality is not to be found in a single granulated verse, obtained by artificially pulverizing the context. One may ask whether or not the Bible really contains "books" in our modern sense of the term. Modern study has shown us the organic growth and successive transpositions and integrations which finally culminated in the transposition effected by Christ, Who then confided the Scriptures to the Church. From this it appears that the formula "inspired books" is too vague and problematic. Inerrancy should be predicated of the Scriptures as they have been entrusted to the Church, "and which as such have been confided to the Church." This is the integral and primary meaning of the Scriptures, within which we must find the meaning of its lesser units, books, oracles, verses.

CONCLUSION

If we have treated the question of inerrancy somewhat briefly, it is not because we think it secondary, but because of other positive considerations. First, every manual provides an ample treatment of the question, from both an historical and a theoretical point of view. Secondly, we have preferred to adopt the orientation of *Divino afflante Spiritu*, which has changed the center of gravity in this problem, and put the stress on hermeneutics. The lesson of the recent past has taught us that an excessive preoccupation with inerrancy can stultify exegesis, while a serene and solid exegesis eliminates most of the problems met with in the defense of inerrancy. Though, as is the case with most slogans, this one oversimplifies

[21] In the article, "Über die Irrtumslosigkeit und Einheit der Schrift," SZ 84, 1964, pp. 161–181, mentioned before (cf. ch. 2, n. 11).

the reality, still it is true to say that for the last sixty years we have been struggling to defend the Scriptures, now we are working to understand them.

One last point: It is neither legitimate nor prudent to consider hermeneutics as an appendix to the consideration of inerrancy. Thus, for example, the method which seeks and describes the literary types in the Bible is not a last desperate measure to save the Bible from error now that all other attempts have failed. It is a fruitful method in its own right, whose purpose is the appreciation and interpretation of the text. Pius XII in *Divino afflante Spiritu* deduces the need for a hermeneutical method from the divine-human nature of the Bible itself: This is the outlook which predominates in Catholic exegesis today, and it is the outlook which should prevail in a treatise on inspiration.

Bibliography for Chapter 13

Literary Truth. In addition to the work by Hans Meyerhoff, *Time in Literature*, there is the work of W. Kayser, *Die Wahrheit der Dichter. Wandlung eines Begriffes in der deutschen Literatur*, Hamburg, 1959, which develops its theme by selecting authors representative of each century. Thus, for example, we have: the truth of facts and fiction, to declare the truth while smiling (Grimmelshausen), to declare the truth in images (Gottsched), the truth of form and symbol (Goethe), etc. There is a good treatment and ample bibliographical material in Wellek and Warren, *Theory of Literature*, ch. 10, "Literature and Ideas," and ch. 3, "The Function of Literature."

The Truth of Witness. Söhngen dedicates four pages to this theme in his *Analogie und Metaphern*, vol. 4, ch. 2 ("Die Zeugnis und Bekenntnisfunktion," pp. 107–110). Cf. also R. Asting, *Die Verkündigung des Wortes Gottes im Urchristentum dargestellt an den Begriffen Wort Gottes, Evangelium und Zeugnis*, Stuttgart, 1939.

Logical Truth (Inerrancy). A. Moretti, "De Scripturarum inerrantia et de hagiographis opinantibus," *DivTh* 62, 1959, pp. 32–68; cf. also M. de Tuya, "La inerrancia bíblica y el hagiógrafo opinante," *EstEc* 34, 1960, pp. 339–347, and the article of N. Lohfink mentioned before, "Über die Irrtumslosigkeit und die Einheit der Schrift," SZ 89, 1964, pp. 161–181. There is an article of J. Coppens in which he contests the position of Benoit: "L'Inspiration et l'inerrance bibliques," ETL 33, 1957, pp. 36–57, and an interesting study by J. Forestell, "The Limitation of Inerrancy," CBQ 20, 1958, pp. 9–18. Recently, P. Zerafa discussed the topic in Ang 39, 1962, pp. 92–119, "The Limits of Biblical Inerrancy." J. Coppens has expressed some disagreement with the position of Lohfink: cf. "Comment mieux concevoir et énoncer l'inspiration et l'inerrance des Saintes Ecritures?" NRT 96, 1964, pp. 933–947. Another orientation can be found in O. Loretz, Die Wahrheit der Bibel, Freiburg, 1964.

14. Revealed Doctrine and the People of God

THE WHOLE OF REVELATION?

In *Providentissimus Deus*, Leo XIII recommended the Scriptures as an "arsenal" of doctrine:

For those whose duty it is to handle Catholic doctrine before the learned or unlearned will nowhere find more ample matter or more abundant exhortation, whether on the subject of God, the supreme Good and the All-Perfect Being, or of the works which display His glory and His Love. Nowhere is there anything more full or more express on the subject of the Savior of the world than is to be found in the whole range of the Bible.

As St. Jerome says, "to be ignorant of the Scripture is not to know Christ." In its pages His Image stands out, living and breathing; diffusing everywhere around consolation in trouble, encouragement to virtue, and attraction to the love of God. And as to the Church, her institutions, her nature, her office, and her gifts, we find in Holy Scripture so many references and so many ready and convincing arguments, that as St. Jerome again most truly says: "A man who is well-grounded in the testimonies of the Scripture is the bulwark of the Church." And if we come to morality and discipline, an apostolic man finds in the sacred writings abundant and excellent assistance: most holy precepts, gentle and strong exhortation, splendid examples of every virtue, and finally the promise of eternal reward and the threat of eternal punishment, uttered in terms of solemn import, in God's name and in God's own words.[1]

[1] "*Nam catholicae veritatis doctrinam qui habeant apud doctos vel indoctos tractandam, nulla uspiam de Deo, summo et perfectissimo bono, deque operibus gloriam caritatemque ipsius prodentibus, suppetet eis vel cumulatior copia vel amplior praedicatio. De Servatore autem humani generis nihil uberius expressiusve quam ea, quae in universo habentur Bibliorum contextu; recteque affirmavit Hieronymus, 'ignorationem Scripturarum esse*

This paragraph of Leo XIII is a summary of Christian doctrine under the four headings, "*De Deo,*" "*De Christo Salvatore,*" "*De Ecclesia,*" "*De Moribus et De Novissimis.*" According to the Pontiff, Scripture contains this doctrine in a way that is unequalled.

Does Scripture contain all the doctrine of salvation? Or to rephrase the question, is the whole of revelation contained in Scripture? Or, as it is frequently posed today, are there two parallel sources of revelation?

Formulated this way, the question has resounded throughout the whole world, and has been echoed in the discussions of Vatican II. In this question, two currents of thought confront one another.

Since we cannot list here all of the many opinions on the matter, or even summarize so lengthy a discussion, we must content ourself with giving an outline of the state of the question. All Catholics agree that there are these two—Scripture and tradition. The Protestants, as a result of the studies in form criticism, agree that there was an oral tradition in the Church before it was subsequently given literary stability; and many Protestants are seeking to discern an interpretative tradition.

Protestants understand the sufficiency of Scripture to mean that the Bible is its own norm (in regard to the canon), and that it provides its own interpretation.

The canonical Scripture, the word of God, bestowed by the Holy Spirit and proposed to the world by the prophets and apostles, is the most ancient and most perfect philosophy of all; it alone perfectly contains all piety and every norm for life. Its interpretation is to be sought from it alone, as it is its own interpreter under the guidance of charity and faith.[2]

---

ignorationem Christi': ab illis nimirum exstat, veluti viva et spirans imago eius, ex qua levatio malorum, cohortation virtutum, amoris divini invitatio mirifice prorsus diffunditur. Ad Ecclesiam vero quod attinet, institutio, natura, munera, charismata eius tam crebra ibidem mentione occurrunt, tam multa pro ea tamque firma prompta sunt argumenta, idem ut Hieronymus verissime edixerit: 'Que Sacrarum Scripturarum testimoniis roboratus est, is est propugnaculum Ecclesiae.' Quod si de vitae morumque conformatione et disciplina quaeratur, larga indidem et optima subsidia habituri sunt viri apostolici: plena sanctitatis praescripta, suavitate et vi condita hortamenta, exempla in omni virtutum genere insignia; gravissima accedit, ipsius Dei nomine et verbis, praemiorum in aeternitatem promissio, denunciatio poenarum." EB 86; RSS, p. 4.

[2] "*Scriptura canonica, verbum Dei, Spiritu Sancto tradita et per prophetas*

When a Catholic speaks of the sufficiency of Scripture, he means that the scriptures *"catholice tracta,"* as they are understood in the Church and by the Church, are enough. Geiselmann[3] gives many ancient texts which clearly affirm the sufficiency of the Scriptures. We will cite here only two:

. . . perfect in itself, and for everything sufficient (St. Vincent of Lérins).

. . . the source and summation of all our faith (Hugo of St. Victor).

THE TWO THEORIES

So far, Catholics are in unanimous agreement among themselves. Differences begin when the discussion moves to the question of the relation between Scripture and oral tradition. There are two opposing explanations, which we will characterize as establishing a quantitative or a qualitative relation.

The first position maintains that the Scripture contains a series of truths, and that tradition contains some of these same truths and others; tradition adds to Scripture quantitatively. Thus, for example, if in revelation there are 1300 truths, Scripture might contain one thousand of them, tradition another three hundred. Or it might be that revelation is contained partly in Scripture and partly in tradition (the formula *"partim-partim"* was not accepted at Trent).

The second view holds that the whole of revelation is in Scripture, but that it is there in a special way. It is fixed in literature, but it is not purely propositional; it contains some things explicitly and others implicitly; some realities it sets forth in concepts, others in symbol; some truths are given as propositions, others as possible inferences; some fully developed, others in germ. There are neat formulas and also presences existing within and sustaining aspects of the total organic structure. This fullness of revelation in the Scriptures demands by its very nature a process of reading, inter-

---

apostolosque mundo proposita, omnium perfectissima et antiquissima philosophia, pietatem omnem, omnem vitae rationem sola perfecte continet. Huius interpretatio ex ipsa sola petenda est, ut ipsa interpres sit sui, caritatis fideique regula moderante." Confessio Helvetica (1536), cited by Pesch, no. 218.

[3] *Die Heilige Schrift und die Tradition;* cf. ch. 5, n. 20.

pretation, explanation, and development which will never end; and this is tradition. Congar thus arrives at the conclusion that there is no truth revealed only in Scripture, none revealed only in tradition, with the one exception of the truth that must be outside Scripture: "These books are inspired."

These two theories represent two mentalities. The first looks on revelation primarily as proposition; it is not so much the revelation of a Person as the revelation of truths, and truths are propositions. Correspondingly, faith, rather than a total personal commitment, is more an intellectual activity whose object is framed in propositions. But it is clear that there are some dogmas of faith which are not "proposed" in Scripture. That is why the great champion of this opinion in recent times, Lennerz,[4] has requested professors of theology to refrain from their heroic efforts to find "proof texts" for certain theses. But then, a number of these dogmas are not found in propositional form in the early Fathers or in the ancient documents of the magisterium. At this point, the adherents of the propositional theory ought to have recourse to a *"disciplina arcanae"* which has been transmitted from mouth to mouth without ever leaving any traces until that moment when it is publicly proposed. If there be no such recourse, then these men must admit that they are exercising in regard to the ancient documents of tradition an interpretative activity which they refuse to concede as valid in regard to sacred Scripture. Those who maintain this position consider tradition especially in its ultimate stage, of the ordinary and and extraordinary magisterium, and attend much less to the living tradition of the *sensus fidelium* of the entire Church.

The second mentality is more integral and organic: Revelation is not only propositional, it is rather a presentation of the Person of Christ in His acts and teaching. The evangelists had already begun the task of explaining the meaning of the Christ-fact; they gave tradition a literary fixity, but they did not interrupt it. Revelation can assume many literary forms and can exist in life before being formulated. Thus the *"sensus fidelium"* is extremely important when it is joined and subordinated to the magisterium. This outlook seeks first of all to grasp the unity of the two realities in the Church, which we call Scripture and tradition.

Which of these theories is the true one? As of this moment, the

[4] Cf. bibliography.

question has not been settled, and still remains a "disputed question."[5] We should rather ask: Which theory is more probable? To answer that question, we cannot rest content with discussion and speculation; we must consult tradition. Here again, the two theories part company in the way they set about studying the problem.

The first theory bases itself to a great extent on the manuals produced during the last hundred years, and the catechisms which, in their capacity of exponents of the "common opinion," serenely propose the quantitative theory. The adherents of this view also cite the way in which certain recent encyclicals have spoken:

It was chiefly out of the sacred writings that they [the Fathers] endeavored to proclaim and establish the articles of faith and the truth connected with it, and it was *in them, together with divine tradition,* that they found the refutation of heretical error, and the reasonableness, the true meaning, and the mutual relation of the truths of Catholicism.[6]

It is also true that theologians must always return to the sources of divine revelation: for it belongs to them to point out how the doctrine of the living teaching authority is to be found either explicitly or implicitly in the Scriptures and in tradition.[7]

Finally, they cite the Tridentine decree, giving it the sense attributed to it by St. Robert Bellarmine:

. . . and seeing that this truth and discipline is contained in written books and in traditions not written . . .[8]

[5] In the volume *De Scriptura et Traditione*, one of the contributors confidently asserts that it is *de Fide* that not all of the revealed truths are contained in Scripture (Augustín Trapé, p. 326). Since he does not say whether or not he understands this of other truths besides the canon of the Scriptures, no one need disagree with the statement.

[6] "*Nam quae obiectum sunt fidei vel ab eo consequuntur, ex Divinis potissime Litteris studuerunt asserere et stabilere; atque ex ipsis,* SICUT PARITER EX DIVINA TRADITIONE, *nova haereticorum commenta refutare, catholicorum dogmatum rationem, intelligentiam, vincula exquirere.*" *Providentissimus Deus,* EB 114; RSS, p. 18; emphasis added.

[7] "*Verum [quoque] est, theologis semper redeundum esse ad divinae revelationis fontes: eorum enim est indicare qua ratione ea quae a vivo Magisterio docentur, in Sacris Litteris et in divina 'traditione,' 'sive explicite, sive implicite inveniantur.'*" *Humani generis,* EB 611; NCWC trans., p. 10.

[8] ". . . *perspiciensque hanc veritatem et disciplinam contineri in libris scriptis et sine scripto traditionibus. . . .*" Decree of the Council of Trent, sess. 4, EB 57.

The second theory[9] has extended its study of tradition to include the most ancient documents, and joined to this a consideration of the practice of the Church, as well as a study of her formulas. Three authors in particular have carried on this historical study of tradition. J. R. Geiselmann has reworked and synthesized the studies of two Tübingen theologians—Kuhn and Möller; he has studied the meaning of the Tridentine definition and its later interpretation, giving attention to the work of the theologians of the later Middle Ages. In his books and articles, which are a mine of information, he has succeeded in creating an awareness of the problem, and has orientated investigation toward a solution that is more integral and traditional. H. de Lubac does not study our problem directly, but in his great work on medieval exegesis whose roots he traces to the work of Origen, thus covering a thousand years of Catholic thought on revelation and the Bible, we are brought to the same conclusions. Y. Congar has dedicated a two-volume work to the problem, the first historical and the second systematic. The plebiscite of tradition consulted by these three men, though it is complex and nuanced, favors the theory of an organic integrated unity. Rahner, for his part, approaches the problem from a speculative point of view, and fully accords with this theory. In the same line of thought, though with variations in interpretation, we can list Beumer in his numerous articles, which are extremely well-informed and enriched with personal insight. We can also list the works of Holstein and Tavard, as well as many diverse monographs whose conclusions are in the same vein. And then, of course, the question has run the whole gamut of the popular press, because of the discussions during the first and third sessions of Vatican II.

Taking the present state of the question into account, we would propose this evaluation of the opinions: The theory and the practice of the Church, which has extended for nearly two thousand years, is not explained by the view which holds for a quantitative relation between Scripture and tradition. Such a view is not adequate to the fullness of the witness of the magisterium in its decrees and teaching, of the Fathers in their preaching and theological reflection, or of the medieval authors who looked to the Scriptures to find revelation. The quantitative theory is new: It is not what

[9] The works referred to in this paragraph are all found in the bibliography.

the Council of Trent intended to define (Geiselmann); it was born of anti-Protestant polemic (Bellarmine); it has been repeated in the manuals without any serious attempt to study the problem. It involves a devaluation of the Scriptures, which is certainly not a tradition in the Church. Now that the Scriptures are being restored to their place in the life of the Church, the problem must be met and solved.

The theory of qualitative relation or organic unity existing between Scripture and tradition explains the traditional thought and practice of the Church much more adequately; it is more consistent with a personalist view of revelation and of faith, and it is more in keeping with the unity of charismatic activity.

Some light can be shed on this question by recalling some of the things we have said in the preceding chapters: the medieval doctrine of the "literary modes" of the Bible, the structured plurality of a literary work, the various types of truth (including the truth of search), the relative autonomy of a work of literature, the work and its context, the repetition of a work as its re-presentation, symbolic thought and expression, inspiration in the context of the other charisms. These and perhaps other realities which we have discussed throughout this book easily find their place within the theory which holds for the organic and integral unity of Scripture and tradition.[10]

THE USES OF DOCTRINE

This question depends in some degree on the former. At this point in the Church's history, in the second half of the twentieth century, a Christian has many means at his disposal by which he can come to a knowledge of revealed doctrine. He can find all of the principal ecclesiastical documents arranged and catalogued in the one volume of Denzinger-Schönmetzer; and if he wishes to study a doctrine or settle a question, he need only consult the index, and then read the history of Christian thought on his point, as it is manifested in the documents of the Church; while the third index will give him an over-all view of this same teaching according to the traditional schema of the manuals. However, while it is true that all

[10] The contrary opinions expressed at the council have served to highlight the problem and have given it added interest, as well as providing a stimulus.

these documents proceed in one way or another from the Scriptures (at least according to the second theory), the reader is liable to consider himself dispensed from consulting the sacred text personally, especially since his manual (*enchiridion*) speaks a language which is more precise and better organized.

But this is not the way to hand on the Christian reality in its fullness. Bellarmine said that the Scriptures were not necessary, but this is polemic, not tradition. If God has confided His revelation in the Scriptures to the Church, the Church must make them available to her children. The Church fulfills this obligation on various levels of her existence. We will, therefore, schematize these levels somewhat, and consider them as three: liturgy, catechesis, and theology.

The Liturgy

In the context of the liturgy, Scripture becomes a teaching when it is read and understood. It is not understood, and thus cannot teach, when the language instead of being a medium of communication is a means of separation: Millions of Christians do not understand Latin. The remedy for this is either to teach everyone Latin, or translate the text:

"But since the use of the mother tongue, whether in the Mass, the administration of the sacraments, or other parts of the liturgy, frequently may be of greater advantage to the people, the limits of its employment may be extended. This will apply in the first place to the readings and directives, and to some of the prayers and chants . . .[11]

The *Constitution on the Sacred Liturgy* has opted for translation, and some think that the question is now completely resolved.

But in reality this is not so. Biblical language, even if translated well, or perhaps because it is well-translated, can seem strange and unintelligible to the people, and lose thereby its capacity to teach. Someone completely unacquainted with St. Paul will not understand him just because he is read out in English. How many peo-

---

[11] "*Cum tamen, sive in Missa, sive in Sacramentorum administratione, sive in aliis Liturgiae partibus, haud raro linguae vernaculae usurpatio valde utilis apud populum exsistere possit, amplior locus ipsi tribui valeat, imprimis autem in lectionibus et admonitionibus, in nonnullis orationibus et cantibus. . . .*" Const., no. 36:2.

ple, for instance, know the theological wealth contained in the word "Lord" (*Kyrios*) as St. Paul uses it? It has become so familiar that we unconsciously assume that St. Paul meant no more by it than we usually do. Ought we then to translate the Bible into another language that is non-biblical, or should we teach the Christian people the meaning of the biblical language? A bit of both: One of the principal tasks of the liturgical homily is precisely that of making the language of the Scriptures intelligible to the people.[12] Considering the present stage of biblical renewal, we would go so far as to say that this will be the most crucial task for a generation or so. It may be that we should have a sort of homily to precede the reading by way of preparation; or perhaps after the homily which follows the reading, the text could be read again.

Little by little the language of the Scriptures will become familiar to the people of God, and then they will understand the language of God. In this way, with time and patience, the effort at putting the biblical language into a more available medium will have the result of teaching the people the language itself. Then the simple reading of the text will become a real teaching. This teaching achieves new depths because of the liturgical contexts which establish and highlight relations between the texts as they mutually shed light on one another and orientate themselves toward the liturgical action. This is the traditional practice of the Church, somewhat obscured these last few decades.

Although the sacred liturgy is above all things the worship of the divine Majesty, it likewise contains much instruction for the faithful. For in the liturgy, God speaks to his people and Christ is still proclaiming his Gospel. And the people reply to God both by song and prayer.[13]

The sermon, moreover, should draw its content mainly from scriptural and liturgical sources. . . .[14]

[12] We intend here only to outline the problem and schematically to propose a few possible solutions insofar as they touch on the theme of the word.

[13] "*Etsi sacra Liturgia est praecipue cultus divinae maiestatis, magnam etiam continet populi fidelis eruditionem. In Liturgia enim Deus ad populum suum loquitur; Christus adhuc Evangelium annuntiat. Populus vero Deo respondet tum cantibus tum oratione.*" *Const.*, no. 33.

[14] "*Haec vero imprimis ex fonte sacrae Scripturae et Liturgiae hauriatur . . .*" *Const.*, no. 35:2.

By means of the homily, the mysteries of the faith and the guiding principles of the Christian life are expounded from the sacred text, during the course of the liturgical year; the homily, therefore, is to be highly esteemed as part of the liturgy itself; . . .[15]

Catechesis

The other means of imparting sacred doctrine are related to this principal means as preparation or prolongation. Catechesis is a preparation. The Counter-Reformation conceived of this activity as a process by which the child was taught a series of rigid and precise formulas which he did not understand, but which were meant to protect him in the future. Later, under the influence of the Enlightenment, this type of catechism seemed to answer perfectly to the ideal of intellectual precision. The biblical and liturgical renewal of our times has imposed a different orientation: Catechetical instruction as a pedagogical activity adapts itself to the intellectual development of the child; that is, it begins with the history of salvation, moving from events to expressions of a more doctrinal nature. This initiation into the language of the Scriptures brings one into a world in which God becomes familiar; it brings the child into contact with Life. The new catechetical methods spontaneously turn to the Scriptures.

Theology

The doctrine proposed by the liturgy which is prepared for by catechesis is extended and developed by the science of theology:

Most desirable is it, and most essential, that the whole teaching of theology should be pervaded and animated by the use of the divine Word of God. This is what the Fathers and the greatest theologians of all ages have desired and reduced to practice. It was chiefly out of the sacred writings that they endeavored to proclaim and establish the articles of faith and the truth connected with it, and it was in them, together with divine tradition, that they found the refutation of heretical error, and the reasonableness, the true meaning, and the mutual relation of the truths of Catholicism. Nor will anyone wonder at this who considers that the sacred books hold such an eminent position among the sources of revelation that, without their assiduous study

---

[15] "Homilia, qua per anni liturgici cursum ex textu sacro fidei mysteria et normae vitae christianae exponuntur, ut pars ipsius liturgiae valde commendatur; . . ." Const., no. 52.

and use, theology cannot be placed on its true footing, or treated as its dignity demands.

For although it is right and proper that students in academies and schools should be chiefly exercised in acquiring a scientific knowledge of dogma, by means of reasoning from the articles of faith to their consequences, according to the rules of approved and sound philosophy —nevertheless, the judicious and instructed theologian will by no means pass by that method of doctrinal demonstration which draws its proof from the authority of the Bible.[16]

The principle which the Pope proposes, and which is recommended by the teaching and practice of Christian antiquity, touches on the profound nature of theology, and it is beginning to be realized again in our teaching of sacred doctrine. Sacred Scripture must animate the study of dogma (the "articles of faith"), the exercise of theological reasoning ("their consequences"), controversy ("refutation of heretical error"), speculative theology ("the reasonableness"), and systematic theology ("the mutual relation").

The same Pontiff made restricted application of his principle in a way suited to the theological climate of his time: The student in a university course should begin from the articles of faith (creeds and dogmatic definitions), and proceed by a strict process of reasoning; the professor who does research (as opposed to his classroom work which corresponds to the duties of students just seen) cannot neglect the Scriptures in his investigation into dogma. The student who wishes to prepare himself for the study of the Bible which will be profitable and without peril, begins by studying philosophy and theology according to St. Thomas.

[16] "*Illud autem maxime optabile est et necessarium, ut eiusdem Divinae Scripturae usus in universam theologiae influat disciplinam eiusque prope sit anima: ita nimirum omni aetate Patres atque praeclarissimi quique theologi professi sunt et re praestiterunt. Nam quae obiectum sunt fidei vel ab eo consequuntur, ex Divinis potissime Litteris studuerunt asserere et stabilire; atque ex ipsis, sicut pariter ex divina traditione, nova haereticorum commenta refutare, catholicorum dogmatum rationem, intelligentiam, vincula exquirere. Neque id cuiquam fuerit mirum, qui reputet, tam insignem locum inter revelationis fontes Divinis Libris deberi, ut, nisi eorum studio usuque assiduo, nequeat theologia rite et pro dignitate tractari. Tametsi enim rectum est iuvenes in academiis et scholis ita praecipue exerceri, ut intellectum et scientiam dogmatum assequantur, ab articulis fidei argumentatione instituta ad alia ex illis, secundum normas probatae solidaeque philosophiae, concludenda; gravi tamen eruditoque theologo minime negligenda est ipsa demonstratio dogmatum ex Bibliorum auctoritatibus ducta; . . .*" Providentissimus Deus, EB 114; RSS, pp. 17-18.

At the end of the last century, St. Thomas was considered simply in his role as the author of the *Summas,* and his exegetical labors, as well as the ancient meaning of *"magister theologiae,"* were ignored.[17] At the time of Leo XIII, biblical studies were handicapped by the influence of rationalism: The statement of the Pontiff was far-reaching and courageous, but it was not the last word. Pius XII took a step forward:

. . . they should set forth in particular the theological doctrine in faith and morals of the individual books or texts so that their exposition may not only aid the professors of theology in their explanations and proofs of the dogmas of faith, but may also be of assistance to priests in their presentation of Christian doctrine to the people, and, in fine, may help all the faithful to lead a life that is holy and worthy of a Christian.[18]

The theological doctrine of Scriptures is placed at the service of the professor of theology, so that he may explain and prove dogma; it is at the service of priests, so that they may present Christian doctrine to the people. We should note here the consequences of our modern specialization: The Middle Ages (including, naturally, St. Thomas) considered the professor of theology (*magister theologiae*) as entrusted with the task of expounding the sacred text: *"legit sacram paginam"*; whereas now his task is to expound and prove dogmas. According to the ancient idea, a homily was meant to explain passages of the Bible; now it has become a process of presenting Christian doctrine, though this is not further defined. Theological doctrine expounded by an exegete (who has become a

---

[17] "St. Thomas's written work in *sacra pagina* must certainly have extended over the whole of his teaching career, since commenting on the Bible was the prime task of the master in theology." M. D. Chenu, *Toward Understanding St. Thomas,* Chicago, 1964, p. 243. Pius XII, in his allocution to the Angelicum, January 14th, 1958, first praised the commentaries of St. Thomas on Scripture, and then concluded: "Quare si quis ea [commentaria] neglegat, minime dicendus est S. Angelici Doctoris plane et plene familiaritate et notitia uti." *AAS* 50, 1958, p. 152.

[18] ". . . *ostendant potissimum quae sit singulorum librorum vel textuum theologica doctrina de rebus fidei et morum, ita ut haec eorum explanatio non modo theologos doctores adiuvet ad fidei dogmata proponenda confirmandaque, sed sacerdotibus etiam adiumento sit ad doctrinam christianam coram populo enucleandam, ac fidelibus denique omnibus ad vitam sanctam homineque christiano dignam agendam adserviat.*" *Divino afflante Spiritu,* EB 551; *RSS,* p. 93.

specialist himself) is considered auxiliary. When the encyclical speaks of "the individual books or texts," it does not take account of biblical theology as a separate discipline.

The directives of Pius XII are an advance over those of Leo XIII, and they point out a road which the concluding paragraphs of the encyclical invite us to follow.

The predominant method of using scriptural doctrine in our theology manuals is that of the "proof from Scripture." If this were only a pedagogical device, leading the student back from the dogmatic formulation to its germinal presentation in the sacred text, it would be acceptable. But the method has created an outlook which puts the reality entirely out of focus: The Bible has become a supply depot for "proofs"; its function is seen as secondary and subordinate to dogmatic theology.

In an article on this theme,[19] we attempted to point out the origin of the "intellectual mechanism" which is called the "proof": It derives from the dialectic of Aristotle, and was imposed by the treatise of Melchior Cano, De locis theologicis.[20] Its place is found only when there is question of proving a proposition which is debatable or debated (thesis); or in controversy where, as a methodological procedure, that which is denied by the adverasry (historically, the Protestants) is treated as open to discussion. This same method was used as a means for training students. The aspect of controversy or dispute ended by becoming the exclusive orientation of theology, though, as Lonergan has observed, rhetoric also served to influence the process.

It is useless now to try to improve the proofs from Scripture. What we must do, is reduce the emphasis on proof to its proper and legitimate role, and expand theology more in the direction of its expository functions, as expounding and interpreting the revealed doctrine: this is, to return to the method of the Middle Ages.[21] Such a renewal is already in progress, caused partly by the

[19] "Argument d'Ecriture et théologie biblique dans l'enseignement théologique," NRT 91, 1959, pp. 337–354.

[20] Cf. A. Lang, Die loci theologici des Melchior Cano und die Methode des theologischen Beweises, Munich, 1925.

[21] Cf. Chenu, op. cit. (n. 17). In this connection, paragraph 16 of the Constitution on the Sacred Liturgy takes on a special importance: "Curent insuper aliarum disciplinarum magistri, imprimis theologiae dogmaticae, sacrae Scripturae, theologiae spiritualis et pastoralis ita, ex intrinsecis exi-

conviction of many professors, and partly by the present dissatis-
faction of most of the students. In both groups, there is a renewed
awareness of the place of Scripture in the Church.

This renewal will draw in its train a whole world of theological
riches; men will discover wealth only dimly suspected before. In
teaching, the factor of time will, obviously, require a selection of
certain themes or aspects for fuller treatment, while others, more
vital in another age, will receive less attention.

These three channels of doctrine, liturgy (and preaching),
catechesis, and theology are not the only means by which biblical
revelation can be actualized, as though the Church in general or its
magisterium were excluded from this need of the Bible. The
Church of God as a whole, and the teaching magisterium must also
listen to the Scriptures, accept them and expound them. These
words of Pesch are still relevant:

The Scripture is a rule of faith from which the Church may not depart; she is obliged by its authority as by the authority of God Himself speaking.[22]

The Scripture has been given by God to the ecclesiastical magisterium, so that it learn from it what it should teach to both wise and
ignorant.[23]

In this activity of the magisterium, the exegete can have a subordinate function, since his labors may, in the "Providence of God,
prepare for and bring to maturity the judgment of the Church."

The exegete actualizes the doctrine of Scripture by a theological
exposition of particular passages, and by establishing a biblical theology around some theme or in a more general context. These
studies are extended by dogmatic theology, and echoed by the min-
isters of the word; however, this action is not unilateral and the
roles are not exclusive.

---

gentiis proprii uniuscuiusque obiecti, mysterium Christi et historiam salutis
excolere, ut exinde earum connexio cum Liturgia et unitas sacerdotalis
institutionis aperte clarescant." The "mysterium Christi" and the "historia
salutis" are the central theme of the Scriptures.

[22] "Scriptura fit regula fidei, a qua ecclesia recedere non potest . . ." No.
578.

[23] ". . . ipsi magisterio ecclesiastico etiam Scriptura a Deo data est, ut
ex ea discat, quae doctos et indoctos doceat." No. 579.

All human words need proof and witnesses, but the word of God is a witness to itself, because it must be that whatsoever enunciates incorruptible truth is an incorruptible witness to the truth. But since our God has willed that through the Scriptures we come to know something of His most intimate thoughts and desires, and since the very message of the sacred Scripture is, in a certain way, the mind of God, I will not be silent about anything which God has willed to be known or preached.[24]

Bibliography for Chapter 14

Scripture and Tradition. The fundamental work in this area has been done by J. R. Geiselmann whose work, *Die Heilige Schrift und die Tradition,* we have already cited. In addition, Geiselmann had dedicated other books and articles to this theme, especially "Die mündliche Überlieferung" in *Beitrag zum Begriff der Tradition,* ed. by M. Schmaus, Munich, 1962. One of Geiselmann's studies can be found in English in *Christianity Divided,* ed. by D. Callahan *et al.,* New York 1961 (cf. "Scripture, Tradition, and the Church: An Ecumenical Problem"). The work of Congar is embodied in his two volumes: *La Tradition et les Traditions. Essai historique,* Paris, 1960; *La Tradition et les Traditions. Essai Théologique,* Paris, 1963. In English, we have the excellent work of G. H. Tavard, *Holy Writ or Holy Church,* London, 1959. Lennerz has published most of his work in various articles in *Gregorianum,* and Beumer has most of his articles in *Scholastik.* The majority of authors who treat of the question put the stress on the aspect of tradition. The large volume of seven hundred pages, *De Scriptura et Traditione,* Rome, 1963, contains, in addition to articles treating of the state of the question since Trent (and therefore somewhat polemic in tone), studies from a biblical point of view (Feuillet, Rigaux), patristic doctrine (Ortiz de Urbina on the Oriental Fathers, and Holstein on the Western Fathers after St. Augus-

---

[24] *"Alia enim omnia, id est, humana dicta, argumentis ac testibus egent. Dei autem sermo ipse sibi testis, quia necesse est quidquid incorrupta veritas loquitur, incorruptum sit testimonium veritatis. Sed tamen cum per Scripturas sacras scire nos quasi de arcano animi ac mentis suae quaedam voluerit Deus noster, quia ipsum quidquid vel agnosci per suos vel praedicari Deus voluit, non tacebo."* St. Salvian, "De Gubernatione Dei, bk. 3," PL 53, 57.

tine), the doctrine of the early reformers, the Orthodox, and the Anglicans. The bibliography by Beumer on p. 85 is especially valuable. The state of the question before the Council is excellently presented by G. Moran, *Scripture and Tradition. A Survey of the Question*, New York, 1963 cf. also in *Herder Korrespondenz* 13, 1958–1959, pp. 349–353 14, 1959–1960, pp. 567–573, Über das Traditionsprinzip." For the period immediately after the Council, see the "Elenchus Bibl." in *Biblica* for 1964, especially nos. 82 and 247. There is also a good résumé of the discussion in *Herder Correspondence* 2, 1965, pp. 16–21, "The Debate on Revelation."

The Uses of Doctrine. A. Grillmeier, "Vom Symbolum zur Summa. Zum theologiegeschichtlichen Verhältnis von Patristik und Scholastik," in *Kirche und Überlieferung*, Freiburg, 1960. The recent discussions about biblical theology must necessarily consider this question. A. Lang's study on Melchior Cano is still valuable, *Die loci theologici des Melchior Cano und die Methode des theologischen Beweises*, Munich, 1925; Karl Rahner has two articles in vol. 5 of *Schriften zur Theologie*, Cologne, 1962: "Exegese und Dogmatik," pp. 82–111; and "Was ist eine dogmatische Aussage?", pp. 54–81. This volume will probably be published in English. The first of these articles can be found in *Dogmatic vs. Biblical Theology*, ed. by H. Vorgrimler, Baltimore, 1964. As mentioned earlier, Lang's study is utilized in L. Alonso Schökel, "Argument d'Ecriture et théologie biblique dans l'enseignement théologique," NRT 81, 1959, pp. 337–354. There is a good but brief discussion of biblical theology in D. Stanley's *Christ's Resurrection in Pauline Soteriology*, Rome, 1961, "Introduction." James Robinson has recently given an excellent evaluation of the problem of biblical theology, seeing the Catholic *Problematik* from a Protestant viewpoint: cf. "Scripture and Theological Method," *CBQ* 27, 1965, pp. 6–27.

Catechesis and Preaching. These subjects are treated in both Chapters 14 and 15; the bibliography given here will apply to both of them. The fundamental work is that by J. Jungmann, *Die Frohbotschaft und unsere Glaubensverkündigung*, Regensburg, 1936, which has been translated, abridged, and edited by W. Huesman as *The Good News Yesterday and Today*, New York, 1962. In regard to the liturgy and preaching, there is the work of Daniélou, *The Bible and the Liturgy*, Notre Dame, 1956, and an interesting study by A. Wilder, *The Language of the Gospel. Early Christian Rhetoric*, New York, 1964. The volume *La Parole de Dieu en Jésus Christ*, Paris, 1961, has, among others, an article by H. Holstein, "Prédication apostolique et magistère." And the papers of the Strasbourg Congress, *The Liturgy and the Word of God,* already cited, contains an article by F. Coudreau, "The Bible and the Liturgy in Catechesis," Again, the "Elenchus Bibliographicus" of *Biblica* can provide bibliographical information, as also the "Elenchus Suppletorius" in *Verbum Domini,* and the periodical *Worship* devotes many of its articles to this subject.

15. The Context of the Spirit: Saving Power

Sacred Scripture, because it is the inspired word, contains the doctrine of salvation and it possesses the power of salvation. In the context of the Logos—Truth; in the context of the Spirit—Power. Holy Scripture not only teaches us, it acts on us; it not only teaches us to act, it makes us act. This traditional doctrine has been somewhat neglected recently and stands in need of being re-affirmed.

HUMAN LANGUAGE

There is within human language a certain force and power. We have already seen something of this aspect in our discussion of the "impressive" function of language. It is this notion which we wish to develop more fully here.

Fundamentally, the energy of language derives from will and terminates in will through the medium of language expressed and understood. We will discuss now the ways in which this general pattern is realized specifically.

The power of the will is made objective in forceful, significant word forms, which can reach the area of the intellect and create conviction, or the weaker adherence of opinion, or the wider scope of a mentality. From a social point of view, a will radiating out in ever-widening circles can create a public opinion, an enormous force, a collective mentality, or a common conviction.

We call this energy residing in the one speaking authority, and it is a genuine power. But we can also consider this power as it is in language divorced from the speaker, as something significant and literarily structured. Since in human speech the two factors of speaker and thing spoken can be disassociated, we can find instances of men without authority becoming the bearers of a powerful message; and we see cases in which the message, lacking authentic power because it is wrong or evil, still acquires power because of the force of the language or the authority of him who speaks it: this is the charge that Plato laid to the Sophists. This example of evil and error being spread by the energy of agitators, at least shows the power of the word. But there can be no such distinction when God speaks. His authority is invested in his words, and through these it passes to the listener without the aid of artifice.

Secondly, the power made objective can reach the area of the will, calling forth a decision, either in the realm of action or of attitude. This second effect of language we call persuasion, just as we called the first conviction. Conviction prefers arguments, persuasion relies on values and motives. This latter may also assume a social dimension: Oratory is a large part of political activity.

Thirdly, the energy of words may extend into the realm of the emotions, effecting some change or even producing total transformation. Words console, animate, rejoice, impart sympathy, confidence, or peace. In these cases, the word does not so much proceed from authority of will as transmit a deep affective participation which is imparted to the other. The social radiation of this power of the word is more limited except where there is question of elemental feelings. In all these aspects which we have described, we are speaking of language as a medium of communication, as a signifying reality, that is, as identical with its meaning.

In dialogue, these dimensions of language may act in an "alternating current" of influence, increasing in intensity in a number of ways. In order to convince another, I redouble my own conviction; or having begun to convince another, he ends by convincing me, or perhaps we exchange convictions. We may stir one another to action which may be common, complementary or divergent. The affective power of dialogue is obvious.

Since our soul is one, the activities we have described seldom exist as separate realities; usually, one predominates and enlists the other two.

The word of God must have this energy or power in the highest degree. Because it proceeds from an infinite authority and cannot be different from what is good and true, it reaches man wholly. Since it is the word of God, it occurs in the realm of the supernatural; it is for salvation and its power is saving. The word of God is a bearer of grace; it works salvation: "In his word, God not only reveals what grace is, He also imparts grace in that word." [1]

THE DYNAMIC FORMS OF LANGUAGE

There are certain forms in a language which manifest and actualize the "energic" or dynamic quality of speech. We will treat of the principal forms briefly.

Address. The mere fact of calling someone by his name makes him attentive and disposed to listen. There is the call to arms, and the summons to witness. I can invoke the name of another and make him present to myself; I can invoke his name to another in order to obtain a favor. Invocation, when it takes on a social dimension, becomes convocation and refers to a parliament or assembly, including a cultic assembly.

Another form of address is found in the act of *naming*, which establishes someone juridically in an office. In an election, it usually suffices either to name the person in a recognized context, or to write his name on a ballot. The power of the "address" in this case resides in the accumulated naming on the part of a majority of the community.

Address can also take other forms, such as personal invitation, a slogan held in common, etc. When the address is mutual, then one call is echoed by another.

The *imperative* form is a pure expression of will intended to result in action. If it proceeds from one invested with authority in the juridical sense, then it has the force of a precept or a law. If it is based on a right, then it imposes an obligation. In other cases, it may be simply a petition. There are linguistic variations of the imperative, such as the gerundive "No Smoking," the future indicative, etc. The imperative can be mutual, social, etc.

The *question* requires a verbal response, and in this sense it is

---

[1] "*In seinem Wort offenbart Gott nicht nur, was Gnade ist, Gott erweist uns auch in seinem Wort Gnade.*" Volk, in Fries, *Handbuch Theologischer Grundbegriffe*, vol. 2, p. 868.

active or activating. It may be a tacit request or command, as in the case of a judge or a professor. There is a form of question which does not require that one respond to the questioner: this is what is called a "rhetorical question," and it can possess great power. A question of this kind can pursue a man, echoing in his soul for years in order to confront him and demand a radical decision.

The grammatical form of *statement* can also be the bearer of a particular force. There is the sentence which is not only so grammatically, but also juridically, and there are declarations which have extensive juridical effect. There are also statements of principle or policy endowed with all the force of that which they represent; and there are personal declarations which possess the power of example. A man's last will and testament is made in the form of a statement. A declaration can be mutual and can commit both parties for life ("I love you"), and mutual declarations can bind whole societies within their own structure or in relation to one another.

There are other forms of speech which can be reduced roughly to one or more of the above: counsel, exhortation, suggestion, insinuation, recommendation, intercession. Every language has many words to express this dynamic function of language.

Magic formulas pertain to another sphere altogether: These are considered powerful not for what they say, but by the fact that they are said.

Finally, there are blessings and curses, considered by many people to have an efficacy; which indeed they do, within certain religious contexts.

The Scriptures contain nearly all these forms of speech, and, obviously, they lose none of their force by being the word of God. They are, rather, brought to their maximum of intensity, and since they pertain to the plan of salvation, their energy and their action are saving.

The soul by its nature can be corrupted and saved by words. A word can drive it to anger, and again, a word can make it meek; a sordid remark can incite it to lust, and honest words can instill moderation. If, then, a mere word has such force, tell me why do you disregard the Scriptures? If an exhortation can accomplish so much, what will be the effect when the exhortations are from the Spirit? More powerful than fire to melt the heart is the good word which resounds from the divine Scriptures and prepares a man for any good work.[2]

Before studying specific dynamic forms of biblical language, we are going to listen to what the Bible has to say of itself as word, and see how the Bible represents the word in action. We are going to offer a very generous selection of texts in this section, since the doctrine of the power of the biblical word is extremely important and has been somewhat neglected lately.

THE OLD TESTAMENT

The *creative* word. The first chapter of Genesis, that glorious portico of the Bible, is really a liturgy of creation. God calls things to assemble in existence: God's initiative is a word which makes things exist, and creatures respond by their existing. God imposes names on His creatures and by this act establishes order and variety; creatures respond by taking their place within the cosmos. God's word is charged with power, it bears His will, "Let there be light, and there was light. . . . God called the light Day." Neither formless nothingness (*tohu-wa-bohu*) nor the darkness can resist the word of God. But the word of God does not confer existence as some mute and static presence; it creates activity and bestows an irrepressible dynamism:

Be fruitful, multiply, and fill the waters of the seas.

Let the earth bring forth living things; tame beasts, creeping things, creatures of the field, each according to its kind.

Be fruitful, multiply, fill the earth and master it. . . .

Covenant. God "called His son" from Egypt. The existence of the people of God is due to this "vocation," this active word of God. The mob of disparate clans and peoples who left Egypt are

---

2 Ἀπὸ γὰρ λόγων καὶ φθείρεσθαι καὶ σώζεσθαι πέφυκε. καὶ γὰρ εἰς ὀργὴν τοῦτο αὐτὴν ἐξάγει, καὶ πραύνει τὸ αὐτὸ πάλιν. καὶ πρὸς ἐπιθυμίαν ἐξῆψε ῥῆμα αἰσχρὸν, καὶ εἰς σωφροσύνην ἤγαγε λόγος σεμνότητος γέμων. Εἰ δε λόγος ἁπλῶς τοσαύτην ἔχει τὴν ἰσχὺν, πῶς τῶν Γραφῶν καταφρονεῖς; εἰπέ μοι. Εἰ γὰρ παραίνεσις τοσαῦτα δύναται, πολλῷ μᾶλλον ὅταν μετὰ πνεύματος ὦσιν αἱ παραινέσεις; καὶ γὰρ πυρὸς μᾶλλον τὴν πεπωρωμένην μαλάττει ψυχὺν, καὶ πρὸς ἅπαντα ἐπιτηδείαν κατασκευάζει τά καλά, λόγος ἀπὸ τῶν θείων ἐνηχούμενος Γραφῶν. St. John Chrys., "Homily 2, 10 on Mt," PG 57, 31.

united in their hearing of God's call, and they become a people—God's people—by continual response to the call which saved them: This is what we mean by covenant. In this case, the response to God's initiative is not the simple fact of existence and activity. Here the people must consciously accept and freely ratify the call, expressing their response by active obedience.

Commandments. The word of God which was expressed in the jussive form at creation takes the form of a categorical future in the Decalogue: "You shall not have strange gods," "you shall not kill." Language in the form of an imperative assumes the qualities of a will-act; it is possessed of a certain power which addresses itself to another person precisely as a person. That is, an imperative conveys will to another precisely in his capacity to accept or reject what is conveyed. A command is not magic; the force that it bears is a human force, it is personal and dynamic, but it is not irresistible. When a command is expressed in the future rather than as a simple imperative, it seems to acquire a new capacity and power while retaining its characteristic of being expressly directed to a second person: "Do not kill—you shall not kill . . . do not steal—you shall not steal." When a command is accepted, it achieves fulfillment and becomes capable of forming a society, sustaining a covenant by which men are joined to one another and to God. To hear this word is to obey. A man may close himself off, freely and culpably, so that "hearing he does not hear." In the final age of a new covenant, God will increase the force of His command by engraving his law on the hearts of the people, thus making it an immanent source of man's response while respecting his responsibility.

Within the vocation of the people, and deriving from it, we find the vocation of the individual: the prophets, the servant, the apostles, and this call may also include the imposition of a new name (Abram—Abraham; Simon—Peter).

The context of the covenant includes other aspects of word as dynamic: There is, for instance, the fact of *blessings* and *curses.* The law contains and expresses a whole series of benedictions and maledictions charged with a power which man unleashes not by magic but by obedience or disobedience. The prophet Zechariah has described the power of this word in "surrealist" poetry which catches the terrible and destructive force of this word set loose on the land by the people's infidelity:

Then I raised my eyes again and saw a scroll flying.

"What do you see?" he asked me.

I answered,

"I see a scroll flying; it is twenty cubits long and ten cubits wide."

Then he said to me:

"This is the curse which is to go forth over the whole earth;
in accordance with it shall every perjurer be expelled from here.
I will send it forth, says the Lord of hosts,
and it shall come into the house of the thief,
or into the house of him who perjures himself with my name;
it shall lodge within his house
consuming it, timber and stones." [3]

The Prophetic Word. Sometimes when the prophet pronounces a divine oracle, he acts as a preacher moving the wills of his audience; at other times he predicts the future. Often, this prediction of the future is a force in the present which brings it about, not by way of magic but in virtue of the dynamic power of the word of God. The oracle enters human history as an active element, not merely as a simple statement of what will happen in the future. The fact that many oracles make themselves dependent on the interplay of human wills does not derogate from their authority or reduce the respect due to an inspired prediction. These so-called "conditional prophecies," by the very fact of their being pronounced, enter into and confront human decisions, the future is different because of them, and they have fulfilled their role. The "fulfillment" of what they predict is to be judged by their power, since they are the message of a prophet, not the estimate of a news commentator.

The *declaration* of God is always valid, not because it discovers what already exists, but because it creates the situation in which it is verified; in this, God's declaration resembles a juridical decision. When David repented of his crimes of adultery and murder, he heard the oracle. "Yahweh has forgiven your sin." At other times, the same type of oracle is condemnatory: "For the three crimes of Damascus and for the fourth, I will not hold it back" (Amos 1:3).

The *name* of God (Yahweh) is also dynamic: It is the guarantee of the authority of a command: [4]

---

[3] Za 5:1–4.

[4] Cf. R. Criado, *El valor dinamico del nombre divino en el Antiguo Testamento,* Granada, 1950.

Keep, then, my statutes and decrees, for the man who carries them out will find life through them, I am Yahweh (Lv 18:5).

You shall not swear falsely by my name, thus profaning the name of your God. I am Yahweh (Lv 19:12).

You shall love your neighbor as yourself. I am Yahweh (Lev 19:18).

The name of Yahweh is a blessing:

You shall set my name upon the sons of Israel, and I will bless them (Nm 6:27).

And the imposition upon a child of a name which includes the name of Yahweh is the means of assuring for this new life God's constant protection.

Not only the juridical decision, but the whole process of litigation (*rîb*), when it is directed by God, is composed of living words: questions, proofs, objections, denunciation, threat, testimony. The word of God pursues man aggressively until it evokes a confession:

> Hear, my people, and I will speak;
> Israel, I will testify against you; . . .
> But to the wicked man God says:
> "Why do you recite my statutes,
> and profess my covenant with your mouth,
> Though you hate discipline
> and cast my words behind you?
> When you see a thief, you keep pace with him,
> and with adulterers you throw in your lot. . . .
> When you do these things, shall I be deaf to it?
> Or think you that I am like yourself?
> I will correct you by drawing them up before your eyes." [5]

At the other extreme, there is the word of the people at *prayer*. This word, possessing a power given it by God, is able to remain immanent while still having an effect in the realm of the divine, reaching to God Himself. A remarkable instance of this power is found in the intercession of Moses which finally prevails against God: "And Yahweh refrained from the evil which he had threatened to do against his people" (Ex 32:14).

[5] Ps 50.

Finally, there is the case where God swears by His own life, thus endowing His word with the very intensity of the divine existence.

In a remarkable work, known as the "Book of Consolation" and which now comprises chapters 40–55 of Isaiah, we find a meditative synthesis of all these aspects of the word of God.

There is the word of *vocation* or calling which governs events:

Who has performed these deeds? He who has called forth the generations since the beginning (41:4).

We find the process of naming by which possession is assured:

But now, thus says the Lord,
who created you, O Jacob, and formed you, O Israel:
Fear not, for I have redeemed you;
I have called you by name: you are mine (43:1).

The prophetic word announcing and effecting the future:

It is I who confirm the words of my servants,
I carry out the plan announced by my messengers;
I say to Jerusalem: Be rebuilt;
I will raise up their ruins.
It is I who said to the deep: Be dry;
I will dry up your well springs.

I say of Cyrus: My shepherd,
who fulfills my every wish (44:26–27).

The word once uttered is unchangeable:

By myself I swear,
uttering my just decree
and my unalterable word (45:23).

The word is heard by the heavens and by kings:

Yes, my hand laid the foundations of the earth;
my right hand spread out the heavens.
When I call them they stand forth at once. . . .
I myself have spoken, I have called him,
I have brought him and his way succeeds! (48:13, 15).

The word which calls confers power on the word of the prophet:

The Lord called me from birth,
from my mother's womb he gave me my name.
He has made my mouth a sharp-edged sword (49:1–2).

These texts, selected from among the more significant, are marked off by a literary device known as "inclusion"; that is, the theme with which the work begins is taken up and echoed, sometimes with the aid of the same words, at the conclusion of the work. The words contained in this Book of Consolation, which is itself a series of poems loosely joined, are active and true because they are the word of God:

> The grass withers, the flower wilts,
> when the breath of the Lord blows upon it.
> Though the grass withers and the flower wilts,
> the word of our God stands forever (40:7–8).

> For just as from the heavens
> the rain and snow come down
> and do not return there
> till they have watered the earth,
> making it fertile and fruitful,
> giving seed to him who sows
> and bread to him who eats,
> so shall my word be
> that goes forth from my mouth;
> it shall not return to me void,
> but shall do my will,
> achieving the end for which I sent it (55:10–11).

This is how the Old Testament looked on the word of God: Not only as a means of knowing, but as a force which is acting. Its sphere of activity is creation in history, especially the redemptive creation of salvation history. We tend to look on such a view as being a bit primitive, ingenuous, allegorical, or imaginative. But we should be careful. The fault lies with us and with our narrow concept and impoverished experience of word in a culture which regards it as nothing more than a conventional and ephemeral "sign." We recognize in theory the power of ideas; actually, in practice we are subject to the power of words more than we realize; to words, not as empty sounds, but as significant realities. Sincere reflection on this fact leads us to a recognition of the "energic" power of human language, and by means of this insight we are prepared to study the saving power with which God endows His word.

THE GOSPELS

The Gospels present Christ to us as speaking and acting, going through the land of Palestine preaching the Kingdom of God and working miracles. Without realizing it, or formulating it explicitly, we tend to make a division in the activity of Christ: By His words He taught us and by His deeds He saved us. [6]

But let us consider an outstanding example in the life of Christ: The raising of Lazarus as told in the Gospel of St. John. We find there the statement: "I am the resurrection and the Life"; not merely "I bring" or "I announce," but "I am." Christ reveals life and gives life because He Himself is the Life, and from Him there radiates the power of life even to the dead, because of His own resurrection from the dead. As the narrative proceeds, we catch a glimpse of the heart of Christ: "When Jesus saw them weeping, He sighed heavily and was deeply moved." In this sincere and heartfelt participation in their sorrow, Jesus manifests and ratifies His deep solidarity with humankind. In His sympathy He established a union with those who are weeping, and with His friend who has been overcome by death. The sisters, in good faith, and some of the Jews, murmuring, seemed to suppose that if Christ had been present, this death would not have taken place: "If you had only been here my brother would not have died . . ." "Could not this man, who opened the blind man's eyes, have done something to keep Lazarus from dying?" No one specifies exactly what they think Christ could have done: The sisters mention only His presence, the Jews recall a past action. Then there is another series of words uttered by Jesus in which He thanks His Father for having heard Him; He does this in a loud voice so that those present will believe in His mission. Finally, He calls out: "Lazarus come forth," and Lazarus comes forth.

What took place in this miracle? We can view it from many aspects: the personal power of Christ, His compassion, His prayer, His word. No doubt, all of these facets of the event were truly part of it: The power of Christ derives from His mission, it is actualized

[6] Cf. K. Wennemer, "Theologie des Wortes im Johannesevangelium. Das innere Verhältnis des verkündigten logos theou zum persönlichen Logos," *Schol* 38, 1963, pp. 1–17. Also O. Cullmann, *The Christology of the New Testament*, Philadelphia, 1959, ch. 9, "Jesus the Word."

in His prayer, expressed in His compassion, and realized its effect through His word. The great danger here is that we will divorce these aspects from the miracle itself, making them the mere trappings or occasion for the exercise of divine omnipotence, as though God acted immediately here, and everything else that happened had no real influence on the event, but was only occasioned by and for the people who were present.

Such a view is really not Christian. Pushed to its ultimate conclusion, it gives rise to the opinion that the omnipotence of God has saved us and that the Incarnation was not really necessary. In a mitigated form, we find such thinking behind the idea that Christ has died and God gives us life, but there is no intrinsic connection between these realities; on the occasion of a word of Christ, God worked a miracle, the word itself effected nothing. Anyone who really believes in the Incarnation cannot accept a view that makes of it and of all the activity of Christ the mere occasion for divine action which is independent of it.

We are not trying here to imagine what God could do, but what He has done. God's love does not seek us while remaining distant; Christ has wept with us. The blind man was not cured by some remote activity on the part of the divine omnipotence; he was cured by a little mud smeared on his eyes by Jesus and by the command to go and wash. We are not saved by some abstract thing we name "the will of God," but by the passion and resurrection of Christ. The Word of Life is not a beautiful Platonic theory, but something we have seen and heard and felt with our hands.

Once this principle is established, it is clear that we cannot restrict the saving power of Christ to actions alone, excluding His words. Just as all the actions of Christ are words because they speak of the Father, so too all the words of Christ are actions and are endowed with power. In the case of Lazarus, the power of Life was in the words, "Lazarus, come forth!"; the words wrought the miracle and at the same time manifested its meaning. It was a power of salvation because, through the word of Christ, His resurrection was present by anticipation. This power of Christ's words is not restricted to miracles, but is found in all His words. It will suffice here to mention instances already known.

Christ's *teaching* was characterized by authority and power: "When Jesus finished this discourse, the people were astounded at

His teaching; unlike their own teachers, He taught with a note of authority" (Mt 7:28; cf. Mk 1:27 and Lk 4:32). The people were struck, not only by the depth and beauty of this new teaching, but even more by the power it held, and which they had experienced. We might give a free translation of the Greek word "*exousia*" by saying that Christ's teaching was "convincing."

Christ's *call* was efficacious: It was a vocation. He repeated this call, and vocation became convocation. He chose twelve of His disciples, and, according to St. Luke (6:13), "named" them apostles; Simon, their leader, He named Peter.

The *command* of Christ held sway over wind and water, over fever and demons; when He willed it, His words were irresistible. The miracles that He worked without words are very few in number; such as the power that "went out from Him" to cure the woman who touched the hem of His robe. A leper made a simple appeal to His will: "If You will it, you can make me clean"; Christ gave expression to His will in an imperative: "I will it, be clean," and "immediately the leprosy left him."

Christ *promulgated* His law with His own authority: "You have learned that they were told . . . But what I tell you is this . . ." And this law can even become beatitude.

Christ's word expresses and effects *forgiveness:* "The Son of Man has the power to forgive sins." And this power is realized in a declaration which saves: "Your sins are forgiven. Go in peace."

Christ pronounced His *prophetic* word over bread and wine and the imminent sacrifice becomes present; bread and wine become body and blood establishing a covenant which is at the same time a testament. By our repeating these words of Christ, His memory and His sacrifice are once again made present.

Christ *prays* to His Father, and the Father hears Him.

The words of Christ are not merely the medium of knowledge; they are themselves spirit and life.

This power of Christ's word is rooted in His person and His mission, and cannot be conceived as something apart from the work of redemption. His words acquire a new force after the resurrection, since they somehow endured along with Him a kind of death, accepting fully the human dimension of limitation and destruction. The words of Christ, even during His life, were powerful, but since the resurrection they have shared in the glory of His risen state, free of the limitations and corruptions of this life and endowed with the fullness of power by the Spirit: "The Word of God is not bound." This is the word which reaches us as Christians. Though it sounds paradoxical, it is still true that as we read the Gospels we perceive the word of Christ more perfectly than did the Apostles who heard them during the earthly life of Jesus. Just as the Eucharist is the body of the Lord, the Kyrios, the Glorified, the Christ, so too the Gospel is the message of Christ in glory. Jesus has traversed the valley of death and emerged to abide now forever glorious and free; His words, too, "will not pass away." Not only are Christ's words more intelligible now that He is risen, they are also more powerful, more capable of imparting life.

In the light of these principles, and in view of the fact that all the power of the inspired word is rooted in Christ, we are going now to consider the rest of the New Testament writings in which the word bears witness to itself.

THE NEW TESTAMENT WRITINGS

The New Testament refers to the word of God as Scripture, first applying this to the Old Testament and then by implication to the New Testament.

The Epistle to the Hebrews contains a fundamental passage in regard to the inspired word which, interestingly enough, stresses the effectiveness of this word:

The word of God is alive and active. It cuts more keenly than any two-edged sword, piercing as far as the place where life and spirit, joints and marrow divide. It sifts the purposes and thoughts of the heart (4:12).

In the original Greek of this passage, the word "alive" or "living" is in the emphatic position as the first word of the sentence: We could translate the first line somewhat rhetorically as: "Living is the word of God and active." It is living, as God is the living God, and its activity is the actualization of the power of God: it penetrates into the most intimate depths of a being, reaching that mysterious point of our vital and psychic principle which is touched and permeated by the Spirit. From within, it can judge and condemn because it forces man to take up a position, to make a decision. Faced with this word, it is useless to try to dissimulate or compromise.

Let us look again at the four descriptive words used in this passage to characterize the word of God: alive, active, cutting, piercing. Whoever, in the name of inerrancy, refuses to accept all these terms as valid is accusing the Bible of error. Whoever, in the name of inerrancy, forgets these adjectives is insulating himself from the piercing power of God's word. Let us hope that the living word will not let itself be overcome.

One of the two texts which we have already called "classical" in the tract on inspiration is, when cited in its entire context, a testimony also to the power of the inspired word. The general context is that of a pastoral letter: a series of counsels and doctrines given to a man charged with the care of souls. The "man of God" referred to in the text applies to this type of office, and for such a person the Scriptures are an instrument by which he carries out his task. However, though the text is concentrating on the pastoral duties of a bishop, the realities that it describes are applicable to the life of every Christian.

But for your part, stand by the truths you have learned and are assured of. Remember from whom you have learned them; remember that from early childhood you have been familiar with the sacred writings which have power to make you wise and lead you to salvation through faith in Christ Jesus. Every inspired scripture has its use for teaching the truth and refuting error, or for reformation of manners and discipline in right living, so that the man who belongs to God may be efficient and equipped for good work of every kind (2 Tim 3:14-17).

In the work of salvation which comes about through faith in Christ, that is, by accepting Him and committing oneself to Him, sacred Scripture has a very special role to play: It has the power to make a man wise with a wisdom that is not a theoretical mastery of a science or practical competence in a craft, but rather personal knowledge of God. Timothy has known the Scriptures familiarly since childhood; there is no need to convince him of their power: The sacred writings possess a "spirit" which makes them uniquely apt and efficacious in the apostolic ministry.

There is in St. Paul's description a certain sense of integrity and fullness conveyed by the descriptive words he has chosen and by the broadening rhythm in the last phrase. He mentions the inspiration of the Scriptures because he wants to stress their power. Obviously, they would not possess such a power if they were false or mistaken. Immediately before the passage we quoted, St. Paul had said: "Wicked men and charlatans will make progress from bad to worse, deceiving and deceived." Thus, the first consequence, the very reason for inspiration at all, is that the word of God may act effectively in the Christian life and in apostolic activity.

St. Thomas, commenting on this passage, has this to say about the power of the word:

Thus, the effects of Scripture are fourfold: in the speculative order, to teach the truth and to refute error; in the practical order, to take from evil and to incite to good. Its ultimate effect is to bring men to perfection.[7]

There is another very interesting passage in this same letter. St. Paul is speaking of his "Gospel," of the message he proclaims whose substance is Christ, risen and glorified. But this message is not something in the order of a mere fact that can allow itself to be silenced or suppressed, or even opposed by contrary propaganda. What St. Paul preaches is the message concerning the risen Lord, and as such it cannot be imprisoned:

Remember Jesus Christ, risen from the dead, born of David's line. This is the theme of my gospel, in whose service I am exposed to hardship, even to the point of being shut up (2 Tim 2:8-9).

The earliest letter of St. Paul which we possess is his First Epistle to the Thessalonians. St. Paul had preached at Thessalonica and his word had been the word of God; God had spoken through him. The Thessalonians had accepted this preaching, knowing that it was the word of God. They did not receive it as some merely human word, but, aided by the Spirit, they accepted it in all its reality. This word which the believers received was not a simple statement of fact or theory, but an active and living power:

---

[7] "Sic ergo quadruplex est effectus sacrae scripturae, scilicet docere veritatem, arguere falsitatem, quantum ad speculativam: eripere a malo, et inducere ad bonum, quantum ad practicam. Ultimus effectus eius est, ut perducat homines ad perfectum." "Comm. on 2 Tim 3:16, 17" (in Marietti ed., nos. 127–128).

This is why we thank God continually, because when we handed on God's message, you received it, not as the word of men, but as what it truly is, the very word of God at work in you who hold the faith (1 Th 2:13).

The Epistle to the Romans contains two passages which are very instructive in regard to this theme of the power of God's word. The first is found at the beginning of the letter and provides an outline of all that is to follow:

I am not ashamed of the Gospel. It is the saving power of God for everyone who has faith. . . . (1:16).

The Gospel here is the preaching of St. Paul, the message which he brings of the mystery of Christ: This Gospel is not merely concerned with the saving power of God, it is that power in action. And, as is the case with the whole of salvation, the sphere of this power is faith. There is nothing mechanical or magical about this: Man can freely refuse it. But he who receives this Gospel, receives salvation.

The other passage is found at the end of the letter, and is a synthesis of the Christian life. The mystery of Christ has its center in His death and resurrection. Christ suffered and died, and the Father raised Him up and glorified Him. We must die and rise with Christ, sharing the sufferings of His life, and His glory. We share His death when we suffer as Christians, we share His resurrection when we are strengthened and consoled. The marvelous thing about this mystery is that it is precisely in suffering that we come to know this consolation and encouragement. It is through fellowship in His sufferings that we experience the power of His resurrection, and this experience strengthens our hope of final glory, which will itself be a full participation in the glory of the risen Jesus. To suffer with endurance is a grace; to experience Christ's consolation is part of the same grace, and this encouragement is given to us by the Scriptures:

All that was written of old, was written for our instruction; so that by the endurance and encouragement of the Scriptures, we might have hope (Rom 15:4).

The word translated as "encouragement" is, in Greek, "*paraklesis*," which contains an inevitable allusion to the Paraclete, the

Spirit who consoles, instructs, and encourages, the Spirit sent by the glorified Christ, the Spirit Who inspired the Scriptures.

There is a similar thought in the first book of Maccabees:

. . . So, though we have no need of these, since we find our encouragement in the sacred books that are in our keeping . . . (1 Mac 12:9).

In the First Epistle of St. Peter, we find an exhortation to fraternal charity: This mutual love must be based on the fact that we share a common birth. We are related spiritually, and should maintain and express the family ties that bind us together. This spiritual birth was not brought about by corruptible seed, but by a seed that is incorruptible, the word of God, living and abiding. God lives and imparts His life to others; His life is eternal, and thus He can impart eternal life. He does this through the medium of His Word, Who likewise is eternal. The word of God referred to in the passage below is the Old Testament, which, since it is from God, must abide; it does not pass away, but is consummated and realized in the word of the Gospel.

Having purified your souls by obedience to the truth so that you love your brothers sincerely, love one another deeply and purely. You have been reborn, not from a corruptible seed, but from one that is incorruptible; by the living and enduring word of God. For

"All flesh is grass
and all its glory like the flowers of grass.
The grass withers,
the flower fails.
But the word of the Lord endures forever."

And this word is the Gospel announced to you (1 Pt 1:22-25).

The progress of this word of God is told in the Acts of the Apostles, which traces the growth and consolidation of the Church. We should note this ecclesial function of the word: When the Church was being formed, it entered into her very structure, and now it remains there vital and active.

The word of God now spread more and more widely; the number of disciples in Jerusalem went on increasing rapidly . . . (6:7).

Meanwhile, the word of God continued to grow and spread (12:24).

In such ways the word of the Lord showed its power, spreading more and more widely and effectively (19:20).

Not only the man who believes, but even inanimate creation can be sanctified by the word of God. It was created by the word of God and is good and beautiful; eating and drinking, matrimony, and all the goods of the earth should be received with gratitude:

For everything that God created is good, and nothing is to be rejected when it is taken with thanksgiving, since it is hallowed by God's own word and prayer (1 Tm 4:4).

God takes the initiative in the work of salvation; just as at creation His powerful word called all things into existence, so now His word calls to the true life the chosen part of His creation, the Christians. Our response must be the humble acceptance of the word which God sows within us, in order that it may produce our salvation.

On his own initiative He has brought us to birth by the word of truth, so that we might be a sort of first fruits of His creatures. . . . Away, then, with all that is sordid and the malice that hurries to excess, and quietly accept the message [Logos] planted in your hearts, which can bring you salvation (Jas 1:18, 21).

By way of conclusion to this section, let us hear the moving words of St. Paul's farewell address to the elders of Ephesus. They could well form the basis for a meditation on this mysterious aspect of the word of God:

You know how, from the day that I first set foot in the province of Asia, for the whole time that I was with you, I served the Lord in all humility amid the sorrows and trials that came upon me through the machinations of the Jews. . . . And now, as you see, I am on my way to Jerusalem, under the constraint of the Spirit. Of what will befall me there I know nothing, except that in city after city the Holy Spirit assures me that imprisonment and hardships await me. For myself, I set no store by my life; I only want to finish the race, and complete the task which the Lord Jesus assigned to me, of bearing my testimony to the gospel of God's grace. . . . I know that none of you will see my face again. . . . And now I commend you to God and to his gracious word, which has power to build you up and give you your heritage among all who are dedicated to him. . . . (Acts 20:17–32).

All of St. Paul's apostolic activity had for its purpose the building up of the Church of Christ in order to impart a share in the
inheritance of heaven by his proclamation of the good news. This
activity was coming to an end in one area of the Church, and the
Apostle could not leave until he had provided for the continuance
of his work. He commends the Church at Ephesus to its pastors,
and he commends the pastors to God and to the word of God:
This word will continue to build up the Church, and confer on it
the heritage of the Kingdom of God.

We never knew St. Paul personally, we did not follow him in
sadness as he boarded the ship; yet he has left us his word, and we
have received it for what it really is—the word of God. This word
continues to build up within us, and through us, the Church of
God.

The Fathers

The Fathers of the Church well understood this farewell message
of St. Paul: They continued to build up the Church with the word
and to profess their faith in its saving power.[8]

Therefore, brothers and sisters, following the God of truth, I am
reading you an exhortation to pay attention to that which is written,
that you may both save yourselves and him who is the reader among
you.[9]

The holy Scriptures, and wise rules for conduct, are the high roads
of salvation.[10]

Truly, these letters are holy and divinizing.[11]

We say that the sources of salvation are the holy prophets, evangelists, and apostles; for these, with the assistance of the Holy Spirit,

[8] Cf. the work of Gögler which we have cited frequently (e.g., ch. 13, n.
2), esp. the section, "Die Macht des Wortes," pp. 270–274.

[9] "Ὥστε, ἀδελφοὶ καὶ ἀδελφαί, μετὰ τὸν Θεὸν τῆς ἀληθείας ἀναγινώσκω ὑμῖν
ἔντευξιν εἰς τὸ προσέχειν τοῖς γεγραμμένοις, ἵνα καὶ ἑαυτοὺς σώσητε καὶ τὸν
ἀναγινώσκοντα ἐν ὑμῖν. 2 Clem 19:1. Greek and English both taken from
Loeb Classical Library, *The Apostolic Fathers*, vol. 1.

[10] Γραφαὶ δὲ αἱ θεῖαι, καὶ πολιτεῖαι σώφρονες, σύντομοι σωτηρίας ὁδοί. St.
Clement of Alex., "Exhortation to the Greeks, 8," PG 8, 188.

[11] *Ibid.*, ch. 9 (cf. ch. 10, n. 3).

have communicated to the world the sublime and heavenly saving word.[12]

From the field we derive the comfort of wheat, from the vine the fruit which sustains us, from the Scriptures the doctrine which gives life.[13]

Drink of Christ that you may drink His words. His word is the Old Testament, His word is the New Testament. The divine Scriptures are taken as drink and consumed as food when the sweetness of the Eternal Word sinks into the very marrow and powers of the soul.[14]

The ancients used the Scriptures to drive out demons, to bless infants, and to cure the sick; and these practices are not totally unknown in the Church of our own day.

THE MAGISTERIUM

And it is this peculiar and singular power of Holy Scripture, arising from the inspiration of the Holy Spirit, which gives authority to the sacred orator, fills him with apostolic liberty of speech, and communicates force and power to his eloquence. For those who infuse into their efforts the spirit and strength of the Word of God speak "not in word only, but in power also, and in the Holy Spirit, and in much fullness" (1 Th 1:15).[15]

Nor does "the word of God, living and effectual and more piercing than any two-edged sword and reaching unto the division of the soul and the spirit, of the joints also and the marrow, and a discerner of the thoughts and intents of the heart" (Heb 4:12), need artificial devices and human adaptation to move and impress souls; for the Sa-

---

[12] Σωτηρίου δὲ πηγὰς εἶναί φαμεν τοὺς ἁγίους προφήτας, εὐαγγελιστάς τε καὶ ἀποστόλους, οἳ τὸν ἄνωθεν καὶ ἐξ οὐρανοῦ καὶ σωτήριον τῷ κόσμῳ βρύουσι λόγον, χορηγοῦντος αὐτοῖς τοῦ ἁγίου Πνεύματος ἅπασάν τε οὕτω κατευφραίνουσι τὴν ὑπ' οὐρανόν. St. Cyril of Alex., "On the Orthodox Faith, 2, 1," PG 76, 1337.

[13] St. Ephrem, Opera, Rome, 1743, p. 41.

[14] St. Ambrose (cf. ch. 2, n. 2).

[15] "Atque haec propria et singularis Scripturarum virtus, a divino afflatu Spiritus Sancti profecta, ea est, quae oratori sacro auctoritatem addit, apostolicam praebet dicendi libertatem, nervosam victricemque tribuit eloquentiam. Quisquis enim divini verbi spiritum et robur eloquendo refert, ille, non loquitur in sermone tantum, sed et in virtute et in Spiritu Sancto et in plenitudine multa." Providentissimus Deus, EB 87; RSS, pp. 4–5.

cred Pages, written under the inspiration of the Spirit of God, are of themselves rich in original meaning; endowed with a divine power, they have their own value; adorned with heavenly beauty, they radiate of themselves light and splendor, provided they are so fully and accurately explained by the interpreter, that all the treasures of wisdom and prudence therein contained are brought to light.[16]

The *Constitution on the Sacred Liturgy* teaches that Christ is actively present in His word when it is read in the Church. The paragraph which contains this statement places the word in the series: sacrifice—Eucharist—sacraments—word—prayer. The *Constitution* then goes on to say of this series it has just enumerated that it is part of "that great work wherein God is perfectly glorified and men are sanctified." This sanctification is brought about by "signs that are perceptible to the senses, and is effected in a way which corresponds with each of these signs." The word is one of these signs; let us read the whole paragraph attentively.

To accomplish so great a work, Christ is always present in his Church, especially in her liturgical celebrations. He is present in the sacrifice of the Mass, not only in the person of his minister, "the same now offering, through the ministry of priests, who formerly offered himself on the cross," but especially under the eucharistic species. By his power, he is present in the sacraments, so that when a man baptizes it is really Christ himself who baptizes. He is present in his word, since it is he himself who speaks when the holy scriptures are read in the Church. He is present, lastly, when the Church prays and sings, for he promised: "Where two or three are gathered together in My name, there am I in the midst of them" (Mt 18:20).

Christ indeed always associates the Church with himself in this great work wherein God is perfectly glorified and men are sanctified. The Church is his beloved Bride who calls to her Lord, and through him offers worship to the Eternal Father.

Rightly, then, the liturgy is considered as an exercise of the priestly

[16] "*Nec 'vivus sermo Dei et efficax et penetrabilior omni gladio ancipiti et pertingens usque ad divisionem animae ac spiritus, compagum quoque ac medullarum, et discretor cogitationum et intentionum cordis' (Heb 4:12), calamistris indiget, vel humana accommodatione, ut animos moveat ac percellat; ipsae enim Sacrae Paginae, Dei afflante Spiritu exaratae, per se nativo abundant sensu; divina virtute ditatae, per se valent; superno decore ornatae, per se lucent ac splendent, dummodo ab interprete tam integre et accurate explicentur, ut omnes thesauri sapientiae et prudentiae, quae in eis latent, in lucem proferantur.*" Divino afflante Spiritu, EB 553; RSS, p. 94.

office of Jesus Christ. In the liturgy, the sanctification of man is signified by signs perceptible to the senses, and is effected in a way which corresponds with each of these signs; in the liturgy, the whole public worship is performed by the mystical body of Jesus Christ, that is, by the head and his members.

From this it follows that every liturgical celebration, because it is an action of Christ the priest and of his body which is the Church, is a sacred action surpassing all others; no other action of the Church can equal its efficacy by the same title and to the same degree.[17]

By the ministry of the word they [the bishops] communicate God's power to those who believe unto salvation (cf. Rom 1:16), and through the sacraments, the regular and fruitful distribution of which they regulate by their authority, they sanctify the faithful.[18]

This series of texts is sufficient to indicate that we are dealing here with a traditional doctrine. It now remains for us to determine how we should understand the repeated testimonies of tradition in regard to the saving power of the word.

The word of God exercises its saving power as a word. It does not act by magic, as though it were some ancient execration text, or by some mysterious power of repetition as is attributed to certain magical formulas. A human word is endowed with a power which

---

[17] "Ad tantum vero opus perficiendum, Christus Ecclesiae suae semper adest, praesertim in actionibus liturgicis. Praesens adest in Missae Sacrificio cum in ministri persona, 'idem nunc offerens sacerdotum ministerio, qui seipsum tunc in cruce obtulit,' tum maxime sub speciebus eucharisticis. Praesens adest virtute sua in Sacramentis, ita ut cum aliquis baptizat, Christus ipse baptizet. Praesens adest in verbo suo, siquidem ipse loquitur dum sacrae Scripturae in Ecclesia leguntur. Praesens adest denique dum supplicat et psallit Ecclesia, ipse qui promisit: 'Ubi sunt duo vel tres congregati in nomine meo, ibi sum in medio eorum' (Mt 18:20).

"Reapse tanto in opere, quo Deus perfecte glorificatur, et homines sanctificantur, Christus Ecclesiam, sponsam suam dilectissimam, sibi semper consociat, quae Dominum suum invocat er per ipsum Aeterno Patri cultum tribuit.

"Merito igitur Liturgia habetur veluti Jesu Christi sacerdotalis muneris exercitatio, in qua per signa sensibilia significatur et modo singulis proprio efficitur sanctificatio hominis, et a mystico Jesu Christi Corpore, Capite nempe ejusque membris, integer cultus publicus exercetur.

"Proinde omnis liturgica celebratio, utpote opus Christi sacerdotis, ejusque Corporis, quod est Ecclesia, est actio sacra praecellenter, cujus efficacitatem eodem titulo eodemque gradu nulla alia actio Ecclesiae adaequat." Const., no. 7.

[18] Constitution of Vatican II, De Ecclesia, from the "unofficial Latin translation" The New York Times, November 23rd, 1964, p. 20.

370

it exercises precisely as a word, that is, when it is understood and accepted; even sometimes when it is knowingly rejected, it has a power by way of reaction. The divine word possesses a saving power which is operative when it is understood and accepted in faith; if it is rejected, then it still has power: that of passing judgment.

One indication that the word of God is the actual salvific activity of God can be seen in the fact that God's word leads to judgment. Judgment here has the biblical meaning of a decisive situation. The word of God is both judgment and grace, since it both reveals our state of sinfulness and offers us salvation in Christ. It produces a crisis since man must now decide whether or not to acknowledge his state of sin and accept Christ as his salvation (cf. Jn 12:31; Heb 4:12–13). This sort of decisive situation cannot be brought about by just any kind of truth, but only by an actual confrontation with God Himself which takes place in the word of God. And since the decision effected by the word of God must necessarily come to pass, this word itself is more than a mere statement about something; in the word of God there is present the grace of God, and, in a certain sense, God Himself.[19]

The modern custom of listening to the Epistle and Gospel being read out in a language which is unintelligible, may lead some to think that all this talk about the power of the word is a bit exaggerated, or it may foster the notion that the power has something to do with magic. But the situation in which we have found ourselves until recently is not the usual one. The word that I do not understand is not for me a word at all, but only sound, perhaps music; it does not have in me the proper effect of language. This is why the liturgical renewal being promoted by the conciliar con-

---

[19] "*Ein Kennzeichen dafür, dass das Wort Gottes aktuelles Heilshandeln Gottes ist, muss man darin sehen, dass das Wort in die Krisis, in das Gericht führt. Gericht hat hier die biblische Bedeutung einer entscheidenden Entscheidungssituation. Das Wort Gottes ist Gericht und Gnade zugleich weil es zugleich unsere Sündigkeit aufdeckt und das Heil in Christus anbietet. Dadurch ensteht Krisis, weil der Mensch sich nun entscheiden muss, ob er seine Sündigkeit anergennt und Christus als sein Heil annimmt. (Jn 12:31; Heb 4:12–13). Diese Art von Entscheidungssituation kann für den Menschen nicht durch beliebige Wahrheiten herbeigeführt werden, sondern nur durch eine aktuelle Konfrontation mit Gott selbst, welche sich im Wort Gottes ereignet. Da Entscheidung durch das Wort Gottes notwendig wird, ist Wort Gottes mehr als ein Reden über etwas; in dem Wort Gottes wird Gottes Gnade und darin in gewisser Weise Gott selbst präsent.*" Volk, in Fries, Handbuch Theologische Grundbegriffe, vol. 2, p. 868.

stitution wishes to have the proclamation of the word of God in the vernacular so that it will be once again a true word in the Church.

We are dealing here with a supernatural power, one that must be received in faith. At the outset, the preaching of the Gospel may engender faith: "Faith is from hearing, and that hearing comes about by the word of Christ" (Rom 10:17); ". . . in Christ, by the Gospel, I fathered you" (1 Cor 4:15); this is the new creation called into being by the saving word. The Christian who already possesses the faith should listen to the word of God in an explicit attitude of faith. He should hear it as the word of God—for such it is—and then this word releases its energy in the hearts of those who believe. This attitude of faith, as something radical and total, as something derived from grace, gives rise to a new spiritual atmosphere in which the inspired word can resound to the fullness of its potentiality. Outside of such a context, the bible degenerates into an object of study, a source of distraction or delight, as though it were but a human word. The Scriptures cannot be read as though they were just another book, even a spiritual book. In the liturgical action, the atmosphere of faith and grace is created and then the word of God is proclaimed. In all rites, the proclamation of the word is preceded by a call to attention, meant to stir the people to an awareness in faith of what is going to take place; and at this point, the designation of Christians as "hearers" finds its fullest application.

The saving action of the Scriptures is not mediate, or parallel, or consequent in relation to the word. Some seem to think this way: Man hears the word of God, and this is a human act performed with a good intention, and at the same time God gives His grace. The grace comes immediately from God; the word is only the occasion of its being given. But such a theory is simply unacceptable: It denies that the word of God is an action of God; it refuses to accord to God the power of acting through His word. Such thinking, which we have met before when discussing the words of Christ, does not do justice to the many passages of Scripture in which the word bears witness to itself. The words of Jesus were not merely the occasion for an immediate and miraculous activity on the part of the Father; Christ really acted through His word. But the Scriptures are the word of Christ abiding in the Church.

Nor is it sufficient to say that the word of God operates mediately through the doctrine it conveys: The Scriptures provide me with instruction, and this instruction has an influence on my actions as a man and as a Christian. In the same way, for instance, I acquire a knowledge of doctrine from a treatise in theology, and this has its influence on my life. All this is true, but it is not enough. We cannot lower the word of God to the level of just one more theology manual. This point is crucial: It is not simply that the inspired word speaks about Christ; it is rather Christ Who speaks, and "with authority"; the text of the bible does not only speak about grace, it is itself an act of grace. The word of God is not only a font of truth, it is also a source of life. St. Thomas poses to himself this question:

. . . why is not every writing inspired, since according to Ambrose, "anything that is true, no matter by whom said, is from the Holy Spirit"? I answer that God works in two ways: He works immediately, and then the work is uniquely His own; and He also works through the mediation of inferior causes, such as the operations of nature. Thus, we read in Job (10:8): "Your hands, O Lord, have formed me," though this activity was accomplished by a natural operation. And so, with regard to man, God instructs the intellect, both immediately through the sacred writings, and mediately through other writings.[20]

(Notice that St. Thomas envisages the immediate activity of God as taking place through the sacred text, not parallel to it.)

Even less satisfactory is the view which holds that Scripture, or rather God, dispenses grace as a reward for having read the text: This would be to reduce reading the Bible to the level of any good work. Though the Spirit can give grace as He wills, His word is still objectively greater than any good work on the part of man, just as the Eucharist is objectively greater than any well-intentioned human activity. It seems strange, indeed, to maintain that the Spirit can confer as He wills except through the medium of His word

---

[20] "Sed dices: quomodo non alia omnis scriptura divinitus inspiratur, cum secundum Ambrosianum, omne verum a quocumque dicatur a Spiritu Sancto est? Dicundum est quod Deus dupliciter aliquid operatur, scilicet immediate, ut proprium opus, sicut miracula; aliquid mediantibus causis inferioribus, ut opera naturalia ut in Job (10:8), 'Manus tuae, Domine, fecerunt me . . .'; quae tamen fiunt operatione naturae. Et sic in homine instruit intellectum et immediate per sacras litteras, et mediate per alias scripturas." "Comm. on 2 Tim 3:16" (cf. n. 7).

(the burden of the proof for such a view rests with him who holds it).

The saving activity of the inspired word is not a sacrament: In a sacrament, in addition to the word, there is a thing or an action which concurs in making up the symbol. A sacrament, in its capacity of symbolic sign, really "does what it signifies." But on the other hand, the Scriptures are much more than a sacramental.

Semmelroth[21] distinguishes and unites the two activities in the following way: Christ effected salvation by His death and resurrection and by the preaching of His message. These two realities both derive their subsistence and divine quality from the same divine personality; they complement one another: The word, besides being an explanation, is an action, and the action is explained in the word. We can neither understand nor possess Christ if we divide these two elements of his life: action and word. These two realities are prolonged in the Church: Christ's action is contained in the sacrifice of the Mass and in the other sacraments which are centered in the Eucharist. The word of Christ is in the Scriptures, which have been confided to the Church and are proclaimed within her. Action and word still operate in unity: The word is also action when it is proclaimed or read; and action reveals its meaning in word. The union between these two elements in the liturgy is not something haphazard or arbitrary:

The two parts which, in a certain sense, go to make up the Mass, namely, the liturgy of the word and the Eucharistic liturgy, are so closely connected with each other that they form but one single act of worship.[22]

Our efforts to understand this doctrine of the saving power of the word can be greatly hindered by too "corporeal" an idea of grace and too ritualistic an idea of the sacraments. People insist a great deal on the fact that grace is a created entity which is given by God according to His generosity and our merit; but perhaps they

[21] O. Semmelroth, S.J., *The Preaching Word*, New York, 1965, esp. "God's Word and Man's Reply," pp. 55–71.

[22] "*Duae partes e quibus Missa quodammodo constat, liturgia nempe verbi et eucharistica, tam arcte inter se coniunguntur, ut unum actum cultus efficiant. Sacra proinde Synodus vehementer hortatur animarum pastores ut, in catechesi tradenda, fideles sedulo doceant de integra Missa participanda, praesertim diebus dominicis et festis de praecepto.*" Const., no. 56.

neglect another aspect of grace, namely, that God is personal, and that grace is the basis of our friendship, of our "common life" with God. Karl Rahner has posed the question in terms of eternal glory:[23] In heaven, God does not communicate Himself through the medium of a created entity but directly and intimately. Grace, too, can be looked on as a mystery of communication and union. This is not to deny that the soul is really changed by grace, or to make of grace something purely extrinsic; on the contrary, it is to see that the change which is effected within the soul comes about through a participation in the life of God. Just as in a human dialogue, man turns to another person, so too, God turns toward us and speaks to us in an act of self-communication; and communication with God is grace: "Through the tongue of the prophets, we hear God speaking with us" (Chrysostom).

In His word, God gives us knowledge of Himself, introducing us into His mystery; and to know God is grace: "This is eternal life, to know You, the only true God, and Jesus Christ, Whom You have sent" (Jn 17:3). According to St. Gregory, "we know the heart of God in the words of God"; and St. Jerome says that "to be ignorant of the Scriptures is to know not Christ."

What we have said above is not intended to deny other aspects of grace, such as its reality as gift or merit; our intention has been to show the place of word in the work of salvation.[24]

In regard to the sacraments, the study of E. Schillebeeckx has served to highlight their character as an encounter with Christ:[25] They are an encounter which is less than that of heaven, since it takes place in signs and symbols; yet they are more intimate by far than that which is open to us naturally by inference and deduction. In this sense, the word is classified along with the sacraments without there begin an increase in their number. The parallelism Eucharist—Scripture, derives ultimately from Chapter 6 of St. John's Gospel.

Given the very nature of a word, it seems reasonable to admit

[23] Cf. *Theological Investigations*, vol. 1, 2nd ed., Baltimore, 1963, ch. 10, "Some Implications of the Scholastic Concept of Uncreated Grace," pp. 319–346.
[24] Cf. O. Schilling, *Das Wort Gottes im Alten Testament. Zur Diskussion um die Sakramentalität des Wortes Gottes*, Miscellanea Erfordiana, Leipzig, 1962.
[25] *Christ the Sacrament of the Encounter with God*, New York, 1963.

variations in intensity or concentration of salvific power; just as it is possible that the same word can have various degrees of effectiveness proportionate to the degree that it is understood, or according to the dispositions of the one receiving the word. Under this aspect of intensity, the Gospels hold a privileged and central position.

When Origen speaks of the "inspiring power" of the sacred text, he has no intention of defining "*theopneustos*," or of establishing its primary meaning in Second Timothy; he wishes only to describe a real quality of the inspired word:

Having received of His fullness, the prophets sang of that which they received of the fullness; and therefore, the sacred books breathe forth the fullness of the Spirit, and there is nothing in the prophets, the law, or the Gospel which has not descended from the fullness of the divine majesty. That is why the words of fullness found in the Scriptures are inspiring today. They are inspiring for those who have eyes to see what is heavenly, ears to hear what is divine, and nostrils able to detect the scent of fullness.[26]

THE POWER IN ACTION

The saving power of the Scriptures is a potentiality which must be actualized, and this actualization occurs in various contexts which are like so many concentric circles radiating out from the liturgy.

Liturgy. The central circle, which is proportionately more intense in its actualizing power, is the liturgy. This principle governed the use of Scripture in the Israelite community: Not only the Psalms, but many other texts besides had a liturgical function and were read in the context of the liturgy. In the early Christian community, the letters of St. Paul were read at the liturgy, as were the Gospels, and often the practical norm of canonicity was simply "those books which are read at the liturgy"; this explains why we find prohibitions against certain works being read at the liturgical assembly. During a time when the reading of the

---

[26] "Ex plenitudine ejus accipientes prophetae ea quae erant de plenitudine sumpta cecinerunt; et idcirco sacra volumina Spiritus plenitudinem spirant, nihilque est sive in prophetia, sive in lege, sive in Evangelio, sive in apostolo, quod non a plenitudine divinae majestatis descendat. Quamobrem spirant in Scripturis Sanctis hodieque plenitudinis verba. Spirant autem his qui habent et oculos ad videnda coelestia, et aures ad audienda divina, et nares ad ea quae sunt plenitudinis sentienda." "Homily on Jer 21, 2," PG 13, 536.

376

Scriptures was a rare practice among Catholics, the liturgy managed to preserve at least some measure of the traditional practice.

In the liturgy, the inspired word is read as a source of instruction and of grace. It is not a question simply of recalling what Christ said on one occasion, but of what He is saying now, speaking as one having authority and power: "Who spoke through the prophets," "Who is speaking now through the reader."

Christ is present in word, since it is he Himself who speaks when the holy scriptures are read in the Church.

In the liturgy, God speaks to his people and Christ is still proclaiming his gospel.[27]

The initial formula "At that time" can have the effect of reducing the reading to a mere historical remembrance, but it ought to be taken as an affirmation of the historical dimension of Christ Who, in His Incarnation and His speaking, assumed the limitations of time and space. It is not the memory of the word which "abides forever," but the word itself, because in the liturgical action the transcendent dimension of the historical event is made present once again.

From what we have said, it is easy to see the importance of the reading or proclamation of the word which takes place at the liturgy. We need only recall what was said in our discussion of the actualization and re-presentation of a literary work, which through a reader or a body of interpreters receives once again the fullness of the only type of existence possible to it.

We should apply here what we have said about the representation of a work before a public, and the integral "play" of complete community participation without a public. The reader lends his voice and his sensibilities to the mute notation on the page, and once again the word exists and is actual.

A reader must not hide himself behind a recitation which is frigid, impersonal, or "hieratic." There have been times when an attitude of sacred elevation was extremely effective; the reader was an impersonal herald. Nowadays, however, we prefer to have all the expressive possibilities of the original text re-presented in its actualization, so that in the voice of the reader there is a sort of new incarnation: "He is speaking through the reader." This means that

27 *Const.*, no. 7 (cf. n. 17), and no. 33 (cf. ch. 14, n. 13).

the readers must be well-trained and should, perhaps, be promoted to an order for the service of the liturgy. But even without this special ordination, the *Constitution on the Sacred Liturgy* declares expressly that readers fulfill a liturgical function (cf. no. 29).

An actor in the theatre commits his whole life to the literary text, to make it come alive on the stage and in the souls of his audience; and as he gives life to the text, he himself lives both spiritually and physically. So, too, a reader must commit himself to the text—without histrionics, imparting to it his own life in the service of the community. Then the text will become alive, and will impart in its turn a life greater than that of him who reads and of those who listen. "Consider carefully that which is written, that you may save yourselves and him who is the reader among you" (St. Clement).

The assembly must truly listen. So long as the liturgical readings were proclaimed in a language that was not understood, the best solution was to read the text simultaneously in a missal. But now that the readings are truly such, the situation is completely different. Let us imagine that there was some new bestseller which had achieved a great success, and all the members of the Russian reading club got together to enjoy the original. There they were, each one deep in his own arm chair reading a copy of the same book: We could not really call it a community activity, except accidentally in that they were all reading the same story. Something similar happens at the liturgy if those present, rather than listen to the reader, attend each one to his own missal. If the community is to act as such, then its activity must be centered on the same reality; there must be a real participation if there is to be union in the word. The word is one yet multiple, it is given to all and joins all together, causing them to share in the same life. And thus united in the passive activity of listening, the community passes to the "play" of song and prayer in which it expresses its response to the word by actualizing the word.

Often, this common prayer of the faithful will itself be an inspired word, a Psalm for instance. In this case, the actualization occurs in choral singing: A psalm written in the plural is only represented wholly when it is sung in common; when it is said privately, the adaptation is legitimate, but something of its full extent is limited. This inspired word possesses power as prayer: Christ is

378

joined to us in this prayer in a very special way; He is praying with us and in us, and His prayer is efficacious:

He is present, lastly, when the Church prays and sings, for he promised: Where two or three are gathered together in my name, there am I in the midst of them" (Mt. 18:20).[28]

If someone were to say that this Psalm is written for us, he would not be missing the truth. For the divine words belong to us, and to the whole Church of God as gifts from God; they are read out loud at every assembly as spiritual food provided by the Spirit.[29]

Obviously, the liturgical reading of the text does not re-present it exactly as it was first composed; the text receives a new interpretation both from the fact that it is recited, and from the new context and combination of texts in which it finds itself. The context is not something peripheral to the work, some decorative addition; it is part of the re-presentation and affects the concrete meaning of the texts selected. Such a process in principle is not an infidelity to the text, but derives ultimately from the nature of a literary work—especially one that is inspired—which, as we have seen, cannot be exhausted by one re-presentation or translation.

We say that this is true "in principle"; we cannot expect a special divine assistance to protect the text from every error or exaggeration in interpretation. We know that there is no deformation in the essentials; in regard to the accidentals, there is a good deal of latitude, and each generation must seek a form of expression which is ever more faithful and more effective.

Homily. The second sphere pertains to the same context as the first and is intimately related to it: It is the liturgical homily.

Because the sermon is part of the liturgical service, the best place for it is to be indicated even in the rubrics, as far as the nature of the rite will allow; the ministry of preaching is to be fulfilled with exactitude and fidelity. The sermon, moreover, should draw its content mainly from scriptural and liturgical sources, and its character should be that of a proclamation of God's wonderful works in the history of salva-

---

[28] *Const.* no. 7 (cf. n. 17).

[29] Ἡμῖν οὖν γεγράφθαι τὸν ψαλμὸν εἰπών τις, οὐκ ἂν ἁμάρτοι τῆς ἀληθείας. Διὸ καὶ ἡμέτερά ἐστι τὰ θεῖα λόγια καὶ τῇ τοῦ Θεοῦ ἐκκλησίᾳ ὡς θεόπεμπτα δῶρα, καθ᾽ἕκαστον σύλλογον ὑπαναγινώσκεται, οἷόν τις τροφὴ ψυχῶν χορηγουμένη διὰ τοῦ πνεύματος. St. Basil, "On Ps 59," PG 29, 464.

tion, the mystery of Christ, ever made present and active within us, especially in the celebration of the liturgy.[30]

By means of the homily, the mysteries of the faith and the guiding principles of the Christian life are expounded from the sacred text, during the course of the liturgical year; the homily, therefore, is to be highly esteemed as part of the liturgy itself; in fact, at those Masses which are celebrated with the assistance of the people on Sundays and feasts of obligation, it should not be omitted except for a serious reason.[31]

The homily should base itself on the sacred text and expound the mysteries of faith and the principles of the Christian life. For centuries, the homily was a form of living theology, dogmatic, moral, and ascetic. Rather than proofs it presented mysteries, rather than ethics it presented the Christian life. There are examples even in the sacred text of homiletic style: The Book of Deuteronomy presents Moses in the role of a northern Levite preaching to the people, and many passages in St. Paul's letters are paraenetic.

The homily must explain, that is, it must unfold for the people the riches contained in the inspired text; it must break the bread of the word, spreading out its treasures for all to contemplate.[32] The liturgical homily is an extension of the inspired word: The word increases in breadth and loses in concentration. We cannot maintain that whatever the priest says is the word of God in the strict sense of the term, but a homily should share in the nature of the inspired word. This means that a true homily participates somehow in the veracity and dynamism of the word of God, and it is another way of actualizing its power.

There is another type of instruction, which, though it is not a

---

[30] "*Locus aptior sermonis, utpote partis actionis liturgicae, prout ritus patitur, etiam in rubricis notetur; et fidelissime ac rite adimpleatur ministerium praedicationis. Haec vero imprimis ex fonte sacrae Scripturae et Liturgiae hauriatur, quasi annuntiatio mirabilium Dei in historia salutis seu mysterio Christi, quod in nobis praesens semper adest et operatur, praesertim in celebrationibus liturgicis.*" Const., no. 35:2.

[31] "*Homilia, qua per anni liturgici cursum ex textu sacro fidei mysteria et normae vitae christianae exponuntur, ut pars ipsius liturgiae valde commendatur; quinimmo in Missis quae diebus dominicis et festis de praecepto concurrente populo celebrantur, ne omittatur, nisi gravi de causa.*" Const., no. 52.

[32] Cf. *Divino afflante Spiritu*, esp. EB 553 and 566.

homily strictly so called, can fulfill an important function: We refer to an introductory explanation of the reading. The homily presupposes that the text was understood when it was read, and goes on from this point to expound the message. The introductory instruction starts from the fact that text itself is very imperfectly understood, and goes on to prepare the people to hear the reading profitably. There is nothing strange in such a procedure; many plays and operas take care to prepare their audiences to understand and share their message.

In our day, in many countries, the people have become strangers to the inspired word. In such a situation, they need to be introduced to the language of the Bible, to its style and to its world. An introduction of the type we have been describing would logically conclude with a reading of the sacred text: Such preparation could be an important feature of a Bible service. We have to set up a certain dialectic in order to penetrate the text; its schema would be either introduction→reading→commentary; or reading→homily →reading. In the liturgy itself, the proper form is proclamation→ homily; but special circumstances can dictate another form until the people are ready to profit fully from the traditional arrangement.

Bible Services. The inspired word can achieve actualization in a form of liturgy which is only mediately related to the Eucharistic sacrifice:

Bible services should be encouraged, especially on the vigils of the more solemn feasts, on some weekdays in Advent and Lent, and on Sundays and feast days. They are particularly to be commended in places where no priest is available; when this is so, a deacon or some other person authorized by the bishop should preside over the celebration.[33]

In order to be liturgical, and to actualize the word in the Christian community, these services must have some reference to the Eucharistic sacrifice; and thus they form another concentric circle

---

[33] *"Foveatur sacra Verbi Dei celebratio in solemniorum festorum pervigiliis, in aliquibus feriis Adventus et Quadragesimae, atque in dominicis et diebus festis, maxime in locis quae sacerdote carent: quo in casu celebrationem diaconus vel alius ab Episcopo delegatus dirigat."* Const., no. 35:4.

flowing out from this life center. Since they have the word as their specific object, such services can make use of reading, reciting, or representation. There is ample room for an introduction and commentary, for a repetition of the reading, pauses for personal reflection, etc. The greater liberty allowed in the manner in which the text is actualized can have many advantages both didactic and spiritual, though we cannot automatically conclude that such procedures constitute the ideal of the Christian life: The high point of the Christian life is the Eucharist. But it is true that insofar as they make the word actual and cause people to participate in it, these services actualize the saving power of the word: Christ really speaks to His people, and just as in the Eucharistic blessing, so here, too, Christ really blesses His people.

Another concentric circle is formed by preaching done in the name of the Church. This should also draw its power from the inspired word. All Christian preaching centers on the mystery of Christ, that is, on revelation; and this revelation is contained in Scripture. Preaching should derive from the sacred text first in regard to the doctrine it proposes, second in regard to the language it uses, and third in regard to the power it dispenses.

Tradition has always recognized the value of placing rhetoric at the service of the word; many of the Fathers are prime examples of this. The use of eloquence to prepare a conversion is itself a sort of *"praeparatio evangelica"*; however, the power of Christian preaching does not reside precisely in the force of persuasion, but is contained within the inspired word.[34]

There are some who seem to consider preaching as nothing more than an exercise of eloquence: As a result of the artillery fire of arguments, we force the surrender of the will to God, and once the gates of liberty have been opened, God enters and acts immediately with His grace. This makes of a sermon a purely human activity: It is a battle of persuasion which prepares for grace, but which does not itself pertain to the sphere of grace. Such a thing is possible, but it is not specifically Christian. When preaching really derives from the word of God and is an extension of it, then the preaching itself is an instrument of grace, because it actualizes the

[34] Cf. P. Duployé, *Rhétorique et Parole de Dieu,"* Paris, 1955.

saving power of the inspired word. In this sense, and only in this sense, can rhetoric and eloquence be considered a prolongation of the word of Christ.[35]

There is another concentric circle, which we have reserved for last, though not because we considered it to be peripheral or unimportant: We refer to the private reading of the Bible. Private does not mean independent; it has reference, rather, to that type of reading in which one's relation to community is not given expression, and in which the individual dimension of the personal search for God is accentuated. Such reading can never be completely private: The Christian has received the Bible from the Church (it would be a really beautiful liturgical ceremony if the head of a family or an individual Christian were actually to receive the sacred book during an assembly of the community). The fundamental fact makes every devout reading of the Bible a "Catholic action," one which finds its wellsprings within the community, and which can never lose its ecclesial dimension.

But we wish here to concentrate on the individual aspect of the reading: that kind of activity in which I go to my room, or to the Church, and open the Bible to read it by myself. Here, too, in secret, the inspired word begins to exist anew, God speaks once again, He reaches me with His word in order to save me: "Thus speaking, He looks for us" (St. Augustine).

The life of a good Christian is grafted on to that of Christ, and the Spirit dwells actively within him. When such a person reads the word of the Spirit, we cannot imagine that He Who inspired the text will withdraw or remain inactive. A real Christian does not, of course, exclude the teaching of the Church from his own private reading of the sacred text; rather, he approaches the inspired word with his Christian faith and formation, his Christian life and outlook; he possesses already within him a predisposition toward hearing the word of God and a connaturality with it. None of this dispenses him from diligent application and from the humility which is able to seek and accept advice, but it does provide him with a fundamental security. The Fathers constantly recommend this kind of personal reading:

[35] Cf. A. Wilder, *The Language of the Gospel*, New York, 1964, ch. 1, "The New Utterance."

Since you have the consolation of the divine writings, there is no need for me or for anyone else in order that you may know what is proper. You yourself have the counsel and guidance of the Holy Spirit to show you what to do [36]

But this is what has ruined everything, your thinking that the reading of Scripture is for monks only, when you need it more than they do. Those who are placed in the world, and who receive wounds every day, have the most need of medicine. So, far worse even than not reading the Scriptures is the idea that they are supererogatory. Such things were invented by the devil.[37]

And therefore, I ask that we do not approach the content of the Scriptures thoughtlessly, but rather read carefully what we find there, so that the fruit we gather may be profitable, and sometime later we may be able to receive in turn the virtue which pleases God.[38]

We should imitate sailors who arrive safely in port after a storm. Just lately freed from the tumult and roar of the waves, let us moor our souls in the reading of the Scriptures as in a quiet harbor. The Scriptures are a tranquil port, an impregnable wall, an unshakable tower, a glory which cannot be carried off, armor impregnable, unfailing cheer, constant delight, whatever good may be thought of, this you will find in the assembly of the divine Scriptures.[39]

---

[36] Ἔχουσα δὲ τὴν ἐκ τῶν Θείων Γραφῶν παράκλησιν, οὔτε ἡμῶν οὔτε ἄλλου τινὸς δεηθήσῃ πρὸς τὸ τὰ δέντα, συνορᾶν αὐτάρκη τὴν ἐκ τοῦ ἁγίου Πνεύματος ἔχουσα συμβουλίαν καὶ ὁδηγίαν πρὸς τὸ συμφέρον. St. Basil, "Letter 283," PG 32, 1020.

[37] Τοῦτο γάρ ἐστιν ὃ πάντα ἐλυμήνατο ὅτι ἐκείνοις (μοναχοῖς) μόνοις νομίζετε προσήκειν τὴν ἀνάγνωσιν τῶν Θείων Γραφῶν, πολλῷ πλέον ἐκείνων ὑμεῖς δεόμενοι. Τοῖς γὰρ ἐν μέσῳ στρεφομένοις καὶ καθ' ἑκάστην ἡμέραν τραύματα δεχομένοις, τούτοις μάλιστα δεῖ φαρμάκων. Ὥστε τοῦ μὴ ἀναγινώσκειν πολλῷ χεῖρον τὸ καὶ περιττὸν εἶναι τὸ πρᾶγμα νομίζειν. Ταῦτα γὰρ σατανικῆς μελέτης τὰ ῥήματα. St. John Chrys., "Homily 2, 5 on Mt," PG 57, 30.

[38] Διὸ, παρακαλῶ, μὴ ἁπλῶς ἐπερχώμεθα τὰ ἐν ταῖς Θείαις Γραφαῖς κείμενα, ἀλλὰ μετὰ προσοχῆς ἀναγινώσκωμεν τὰ ἐγκείμενα, ἵνα τὴν ἐξ αὐτῶν ὠφέλειαν καρπούμενοι, ὀψὲ γοῦν ποτε τῆς κατὰ Θεὸν ἀρετῆς ἀντιλαβέσθαι δυνηθῶμεν. St. John Chrys., "Homily 21 on Gn," PG 53, 183.

[39] Τούτους (ναύτας) δὴ ἡμεῖς μεμησώμεθα, καὶ τῆς πρώην ταραχῆς ἀπαλλαγέντες, καὶ τοῦ θορύβου, καὶ τῶν κυμάτων, ὥσπερ εἴς τινα λιμένα εὔδιον, τῶν Γραφῶν τὴν ἀνάγνωσιν τὴν ψυχὴν τὴν ἡμετέραν ὁρμίσωμεν. Καὶ γὰρ λιμὴν ἀκύμαντος, καὶ τεῖχος ἀρραγές, καὶ πύργος ἄσειστος, καὶ δόξα ἀναφαίρετος, καὶ ὅπλον ἄτρωτον, καὶ εὐθυμία ἀμάραντος, καὶ ἡδονὴ διηνεκής, καὶ πάντα ὅσα ἄν εἴποι τις καλά, τῶν Θείων Γραφῶν ἡ συνουσία. St. John Chrys., "Homily on Ps 48," PG 55, 513.

All of the instances we have discussed—liturgical reading, homily, Bible service, preaching, private reading—open out into the last circle in which the word resounds—meditation. Every human word possesses or creates a resonant space within the soul: "I have to think about that for a while," a word has impressed us deeply, or a poem imposes silence as it ends. "To ponder in one's heart" is to allow a word the tranquillity and space that it needs to resound in our souls so that it penetrates, reaching to the division of joints and marrow, seeping down into the depths of our soul. Sometimes a piece of music stays with us, echoing within us; unconsciously, we hear its ebb and flow, its themes return and combine anew; we treasure its sweetness and accept its insistence. There are times when, after having heard a piece of music, we want to hear no more; we wish only to be quiet and recollected.

The phrase is brief, yet its power great. . . . through tiny words the grace of the Spirit plants wisdom within those who are attentive; and sometimes one sentence provides those who receive it with nourishment sufficient for the whole journey of life.[40]

Such resonances are not, strictly speaking, repetitions, yet they are actualizations of the word.

Let us keep within our souls a space wherein the word of God can resound; as it echoes and returns, its grace will reach and touch us. As one word fully resounds, our soul expands and allows greater scope for melody. In this vast expanse which we find within us, God is present in His word. And then our soul receives another word, a word of song and praise and prayer; and the first word of God is answered by another. The answer reaches God somehow as it resounds within us and becomes our own. This is the dialogue of grace and of salvation; persons are united in a word which is divine and human. God has spoken our language in a human way, He has searched for us and found us; in order to find us, He has let us find Him in the mystery of His Word.

[40] Εἰ γὰρ καὶ βραχεῖα ἡ ῥῆσις, ἀλλὰ πολλὴ ἡ δύναμις. . . . ἡ δὲ τοῦ Πνεύνατος χάρις οὐχ οὕτως, ἀλλὰ τοὐναντίον ἅπαν διὰ μικρῶν ῥημάτων πᾶσι τοῖς προσέχουσι φιλοσοφίαν ἐντίθησι: καὶ ἀρκεῖ ῥῆμα πολλάκις ἕν λαβόντας ἐντεῦθεν, πάσης τῆς ζωῆς ἔχειν ἐφόδιον. St. John Chrys., "Homily 1, 3 on the Statues," PG 49, 18.

Bibliography for Chapter 15

As was mentioned before, the bibliography given in Chapter 14 is relevant to the topic treated here. The fundamental work on the power of the word is that by O. Semmelroth, *The Preaching Word*, New York, 1965 (cf. the review of the original German by M. Zerwick in VD 40, 1962, pp. 153–157). The articles by Rahner and Semmelroth in *The Word*, compiled at the Canisianum, New York, 1964, also treats aspects of this question. There is also the book by H. Volk, *Zur Theologie des Wortes Gottes*, Münster, 1962.

In regard to the reading of Scripture, there is the work of C. Charlier, *The Christian Approach to the Bible*, Westminster, 1958; L. Bouyer's *The Meaning of Sacred Scripture*, Notre Dame, 1958; and the beautiful pamphlet by Pierre-Yves Emery, *La méditation de l'Écriture*, Taizé, as well as some interesting pages in Dom J. Leclercq, *The Love of Learning and the Desire for God*, New York, 1961. There are any number of articles and books which are designed to help in the reading of the sacred text: the articles in the periodical *The Bible Today* are excellent.

Appendix

A Résumé of the Dogmatic Section of Christian Pesch's
De Inspiratione Sacrae Scripturae, Numbers 373-636

I present here a *précis* of the dogmatic section of Pesch by way of homage to his great work. His manual has been replaced by others in most lecture rooms, but this is unfortunate. No one had or has at his disposal the wealth of information, scriptural, patristic, and theological, that he had; and this not only in the historical section, but also in the systematic analysis.

I hope that my act of homage will also be of use. Pesch offers us the classical systematic treatment, and thus the synthesis of his work which follows will serve to put my study in the larger context of the *"doctrina communis,"* and to indicate those areas in which I have intended to make a contribution.

It is true that many of Pesch's opinions were conditioned by the historical situation in which he lived and are highly influenced by motives of an apologetic nature. As such, they are interesting for the light they throw on that epoch. Nevertheless, many problems are posed quite exactly and formulated with precision, and the author himself offers us material for new solutions provided that we study it critically. Then again, there are solutions proposed here which are just as valid now as when they were first formulated.

I hope, then, that these pages will be of service to students. The professor may make use of them as a basis for commentary, availing himself of the work itself.

The synthesis which follows is an English translation of an outline composed almost entirely of the words of the author himself, and relying for the most part on the italicized words in his text.

Christian Pesch, *On the Inspiration of Sacred Scripture*

PART II. DOGMATIC TREATISE

CHAPTER I. THE EXISTENCE OF INSPIRATION

Article I. The Testimony of Scripture

1. The Old Testament

The Law: Dt 34:10; Nm 12:6ff. The Psalmist (David): 2 K 23:1; Ps 45:2. The Prophets: The word "prophet" includes the notion of a man who is moved by God to speak, and who, in the name of God and not in his own, speaks to the people: Ex 7:1, 4:15–16; Jer 15:19, 1:9; 1 K 2:27; 9:6; Hos 9:7.

The prophets, so as to be able to be legates of God to men, receive into their intellects and wills the divine motion, by which they are made living instruments of God: 1 K 10:10, 19:20; 2 Chr 20:14; Ezr 3:12; 2 Chr 24:10; Za 7:12.

By reason of their more elevated knowledge, they are often called "seers": 1 S 3:1, 9:9, 11, 18, 19; Is 29:20, 30:10.

The motion of the will: Is 6:9; Jer 1:7.

Unwillingness to receive the words of the prophets is the same as rebellion against God: Jer 7:25; Ezr 3:7; Za 7:13.

In receiving divine influence, the prophets are not necessarily deprived of the use of the external senses, still less of the use of reason: Ex 4:10; Jer 1:6; Jon 1:3; 1 K 19:4, 10, 14. True and false prophets: 2 K 9:11; Jer 29:26; Hos 9:7; Ct 3:4. Special cases: Ezr 2:1; Dn 10:4; Nm 22ff.

God sometimes orders the prophets to write: Ex 17:14, 34:27; Is 8:1, 30:8, 34:16; Hb 2:2, 3; Dn 8:26, 12:4; Jer 36.

2. The New Testament

In the New Testament, the sacred books of the Old Testament are considered prophetic books: Mt 1:22, 2:5, 15, 17, 23; Lk 24:44.

A collection of sacred books, called the Scripture, was in existence: Jn 2:22, 10:35; Gal 3:22; Jn 5:39, 7:42; 1 Pt 2:6; Rom 3:10.

This was divided into "The Law," "The Prophets," and "The Psalms": Lk 24:44; Mt 5:17; Jn 10:34, 12:34; 1 Cor 14:21. Individual passages were also called "The Scripture": Jn 19:36; Mk 12:10; Lk 4:21; Acts 8:35; 2 Pt 3:16.

Sacred Scripture was endowed with supreme authority: Mt 4:14; Jn 10:34; Acts 15:15; Rom 1:17; 1 Pt 2:6. Individual passages were as well: Gal 3:16; Heb 8:8, 13; Jn 10:35; Acts 1:16; Lk 24:44; Mt 5:18.

The reason for this authoritativeness was that God spoke through the sacred writers as through the prophets: Mt 1:22, 2:15; Jn 5:45; Mt 22:31, 41.

And the apostles of Christ spoke in the same fashion: Acts 1:16, 2:30; Heb 4:4, 10:15; Gal 3:8.

Inspiration is explicitly taught: 2 Tim 3:14, 15, 16; 2 Pt 1:19.

Scholion 1. Is it possible to prove the divine inspiration of Scripture by means of the typical sense? —It is not proved, but confirmed. Types are such as they are set forth.

Scholion 2. Is it possible to prove the inspiration of the New Testament by means of Scripture? —Not of the whole of the New Testament.

Article II. *The Testimony of Tradition*

1. Practical

An argument cannot be found in the word "inspiration" alone.

The sacred books of Scripture were everywhere read and explained in the public liturgy; apocryphal books were forbidden.

The holy Fathers sought, with the greatest zeal, to discover the meaning of Scripture and to explain it to others.

The Gentiles, well aware of the honor in which the sacred books were held by the Christians, considered it a great triumph if they were able to elicit scriptural traditions from them by force.

2. Theoretical

The Fathers customarily speak of "the divine Scripture," by reason of the fact that its authors are prophets through whom God spoke to men. Scripture is the word of God; letters sent from God to men through prophets, the Scriptures are said to be written by the Holy Spirit.

The Scriptures must be held to be so inspired by God that He is their true and proper author: councils of Florence, Trent, Vatican I.

CHAPTER II. THE ESSENCE OF INSPIRATION

Article I. What Must Not Be Confused with the Dogma of Inspiration

Article II. On Divine and Human Authorship

Article III. What Is Insufficient for Inspiration

Article IV. What Is Not Required for Inspiration

Article V. The Influence of God on the Intellect

Article VI. The Influence of God on the Will and Executive Faculties

Article I. What Must Not Be Confused with the Dogma of Inspiration

The question of the identity of the human authors of the individual sacred books cannot be answered by the doctrine of inspiration; neither does the judgment of the inspiration or non-inspiration of an individual book depend on the doctrine of inspiration.

Nor is it possible to determine, on the basis of the dogma of inspiration, whether a book attributed in our canon to one author may not perhaps have been composed by a number of authors, or reworded by some editor and enlarged by certain additions.

Moreover, no literary genre is excluded from the ambit of inspiration.

Still less can there be any question here of the preservation of the sacred text, or any question of the versions.

The only thing which is to be considered here is the inspirative influence by which God is made the author of the sacred books. Personal inspiration can and does have various species and degrees. The inspiration involved here is that which is equally shared by all the sacred books and which distinguishes them from all other books. It is, quite simply, the inspiration to write. This is a question of dogma which looks of itself to some universal concept, and seeks to define that essential note which makes all the sacred books, however different one from another, inspired.

Article II. On Divine and Human Authorship

There are some who distinguish between the human writers and the divine author. Since the human writers are authors, though, it became customary to speak of the primary author and the secondary authors.

God is the principal cause, while the sacred writer is an instrumental cause.

It may be asked how it is possible for the principal author to use secondary authors as instruments and still remain truly and properly the principal author.

The sacred writers are living, rational instruments.

To answer the question, recourse must be had to that extraordinary supernatural influence called charismatic.

God, in His wisdom and power, habitually makes use of creatures in such a way as not to suppress their nature and faculties, but rather to apply them to the task which He wishes done. God employs the sacred writers for the purpose of writing, inasmuch as they possess the faculties apt for producing the books He intends. God elevates and moves these faculties.

Article III. What Is Insufficient for Inspiration

Preservation from error is not enough: *contra* Chrismann, Jahn, others.

The subsequent approval of the Church is not enough. Nor is it enough that God by subsequent approbation render divinely inspired books which were composed solely as human works. Opinion of Lessius.

Insufficient also are: divine counsel, command, initial excitation to write and direction in execution, a general suggestion of the matter.

Still less sufficient is that personal inspiration, of which recent Protestants often speak, as of a particular kind of personal religious experience.

Article IV. What Is Not Required for Inspiration

Revelation, strictly speaking, does not enter into the formal concept of inspiration. On the other hand, the language of the inspired books, because and to the extent that it is affirmed by God, can be believed with divine faith.

A distinction must be made between revelation broadly speaking and revelation strictly speaking. A distinction must also be made between the revelation made to the hagiographers themselves and the revelation made to us, through the hagiographers, by God. It is certain that the hagiographers did not receive through divine revelation the knowledge of all those things of which they wrote. Furthermore, where there is question of treating in writing those things which could be learned by supernatural revelation alone, the hagiographers themselves need not have received that revelation.

The sense in which everything is inspired can be said to be revealed. *Contra* Bonaccorsi. God speaks to us immediately in sacred Scripture, because the words of Scripture are the immediate communications of God to us; therefore, all that is inspired is revealed to us.

Nothing, however, prevents a man from being inspired to write those things which he already knew, independently of any extraordinary divine influence, or even such things as were known to other men and may already have been written by them as purely human works.

But with regard to the subsequent inspiration itself, revelation is necessary.

It is not necessary for inspiration that the man write in an ecstatic state.

Nor is it required that God predetermine the writer to write in such a way as to destroy human liberty.

Article V. The Influence of God on the Intellect of the Hagiographer

When one already possessed of the necessary knowledge comes to write the book, he must have four qualifications: He must conceive in his mind the idea of the book, he must consider the mode of expression, he must have the will to write, he must put counsel into execution. These are distinct qualifications, separable from one another. Some sacred writers expressly affirm that they wrote their books in this fashion.

If God is to be the principal author of the book, he must be the principal agent of those things by which men become authors.

The idea of the book must exist principally in the divine mind and be derived from it to the human mind. The divine idea is the exemplary cause of the writing of the book; the divine influence on the mind of the man pertains to the order of efficient causality.

This action is the light of judgment by which the man puts together sentences in such a way as fully to express everything in the order intended by God.

And the object of the supernatural judgments? It is not precisely the knowledge already possessed by the man, but theoretical judgments, whether natural or supernatural as to object, are prerequisite.

God illumines the writer by a supernatural light, in virtue of which he judges those things and in that order to be written which God wills to be written, as God wills them to be written.

Scholion 1. Were the hagiographers conscious of the fact that they were inspired? —Not always.

Scholion 2. And was the Second Book of Maccabees taken from the books of Jason? —Certainly.

Article VI. Regarding the Influence of God on the Will and Executive Faculties of the Hagiographer; the Divine Assistance and the Transmission of the Books to the Church

Since God as principal author wishes that the man himself decide to write the book, a corresponding charismatic motion of the will is called for.

A double influence of God on the will of the writer must be acknowledged: One is moral, from which the practical judgments proceed; the other is physical.

On the point that it is not necessary for authorship that the writing be done by the physical operation of the author himself: 1 Pt 5:12; Rom 16:22; 1 Cor 16:21; 2 Th 2:2; Gal 6:11.

For God to be author and co-writer of the sacred books, it is not required that there be an immediate charismatic influence, physical as regards the executive or writing faculties and the actual writing itself. But divine assistance is required.

From this becomes evident the difference between sacred Scripture and conciliar or pontifical definitions: Divine assistance pertains to the latter only to the extent that they are infallibly proposed as revealed.

God, when He inspired the sacred books, intended that they be handed down to the Church in the name of God as the written word and as the source and rule of faith.

Conclusion. Definition and Degrees of Biblical Inspiration

Biblical inspiration is a charismatic illumination of the intellect, motion of the will, and divine assistance bestowed on the hagiographer for the purpose of writing those things, and only those things, which God, in His own name, wishes to be written and to be handed on to the Church.

The inspiration of the sacred writer, because it is a finite motion, can admit of degrees.

Degrees of inspiration are not to be distinguished among the inspired books themselves, as if one were more the word of God than another or have greater authority to command theological faith.

Chapter III. The Extent of Inspiration

Article I. Generally
Article II. Individual Expressions
Article III. Specific Words

Article I. The Extent of Inspiration to All Things Contained in Scripture

Restrictive opinions: Newman, Holden.
  The testimony of Scripture: 2 Tim 3:16.
  The testimony of the Fathers.
  The Fathers often discovered the most exalted meanings in the slightest phrases.

Article II. The Sense in which the Individual Expressions of Scripture Are the Words of God.

What God says is so, without doubt is so; but what God says is said by others, is not necessarily so.

Sometimes human expressions are involved which are approved or disapproved explicitly, either by God, by Christ, or by the hagiographers. In regard to these, we have the infallible judgment of God: Mt 16:16; Tit 1:12; Jn 11:50; Acts 17:28.

If a rather long passage is commended as true, that surely is true which is intended and affirmed by the passage as a whole; but each and every word which occurs in the passage is not necessarily true, where these have no necessary relationship to the principal intent: Jb 42:7, 42:3; Acts 6-7 (Stephen's discourse).

If certain men are praised in sacred Scripture for having done some good thing or even for having notably accomplished many deeds, it does not follow from that fact alone that all their words are said to have been true: Ex 1:19–20; Jud 10:12. Approval can be given without specific words: 2 Mac 7:18ff.

From those words which are related in historical fashion must be distinguished the words of imaginary persons which are employed, by the intention of the sacred writer, to represent certain teaching or opinions: Wis 2, 5:4.

Relation in the Bible of words said by others confers no canonical dignity on such words, but leaves to them that dignity which they have independently of the inspired writing: 2 Mac 1:15ff., 9:1ff.; Jn 9:31; Acts 5:34.

When the words of the apostles in their apostolic activity are set forth, their doctrine on matters of faith and morals must be believed, not because what they say has been written down by an inspired author, but because they received from Christ the gift of infallibility when exercising their apostolic task: Acts 20:25; 2 Tim 4:20; Acts 21:29. What holds true of the apostles holds true of the prophets: 2 K 7:1.

If angels are sent as envoys of God to announce certain things to men, their words are to be believed with divine faith: Lk 1:20; Acts 7:53; Gal 3:19.

If the hagiographer proposes a doctrine pertaining to faith and morals, God himself proposes this doctrine: Gal 5:2; 2 Cor 13:3; Sir 12:12.

Within the limits of those things which by divine law are licit and open to men, the sacred writer can give counsel in temporal as well as in spiritual matters. Through inspiration, God witnesses that this counsel is reasonable: 1 Cor 7:10.

In the historical books, the sacred writers sometimes relate what they themselves said. In virtue of inspiration, it is certain that they once said such things; but words once said are hardly made divine by the mere fact that they are narrated by a sacred writer: Ex 2.

If the hagiographer speaks vaguely or doubtfully, it is certain that God is neither doubtful nor ignorant, but affirms the doubt or even the ignorance of the hagiographer: 1 Cor 1:14; Acts 25:6; Jn 2:6.

The sacred writers often express the feeling they experienced while writing: Rom 1:11, 9:1; 2 Cor 6:11; Gal 1:6, 3:1, 4:19, 5:12. These are words of God by which God does not express His feelings, but by which He witnesses to the emotions which St. Paul had while writing under inspiration. These emotions were morally good.

Difficulty regarding curses. These put into words the law of God against the enemies of God; they are often prophetic; they invoke a sanction already promulgated by God.

Sometimes the hagiographers not only propose a doctrine, but also strengthen it by arguments. These arguments, since they are inspired by God, cannot be false and ineffectual. Arguments *ad hominem* are not excluded: 1 Cor 15.

New Testament writers frequently argue from the words of the Old Testament according to the Septuagint translation, and not according to the original text. Such an argument is not an argument from Scripture.

Another case is presented by the accommodation of the words of Scripture to mean something rightly expressed by the words themselves, even though they had, in their original context, another meaning: Rom 10:18; 2 Cor 8:14.

Conclusion: Whatever things are said by the hagiographers are by that reason alone the words of God, for God bears witness to the truth and correctness of the individual expressions according to the sense intended by the hagiographers.

Article III. The Extent of Inspiration to the Individual Words of Scripture

The state of the question: Inspiration must be extended also to the very words themselves in some fashion. But how? A distinction is to be made between mental or formal words, imaginative words, external material words. Our question concerns the influence of God on the words of the imagination: How do they depend on charismatic influence?

Opinions: external dictation: orthodox Protestants; internal dictation: by which God would stir up individual images of individual words and would impel them to be written. Supernatural illumination for the apt expression of the matters involved.

Arguments: Ps 54:2; Jer 36:18. The prophetic formula "to speak the words of God." Certain of the letters of St. Paul (Heb, Cor): The ideas are St. Paul's, but the words and style are the secretary's. The hagiographers cite Scripture in somewhat changed words, in the style of Rom 9:33. Two variants of a single text can be found: 2 K 22 and Ps 18. There are variations in style as well as imperfections: 2 Cor 11:6; 2 Mac 15. Inspired words have perished: the Aramic version of St. Matthew; textual corruptions; versions . . . the Fathers sometimes make a distinction between words and meaning.

One recent explanation: God so supernaturally elevates and moves the whole man, as an instrument for writing, that He determines the book to be produced, with all its perfections and imperfections; and, since inspiration consists in this very elevation and motion, everything must be recognized as inspired which is produced by the writer, supernaturally elevated and moved.

The opinion of Pesch himself: Although it is psychologically impossible that the material execution be completely uninfluenced by the judgment, formed by a charismatically illumined and moved writer, of what is to be written, still there is no solid argument by which it can be proved that each and every material word of Scripture is determined in the individual by God; indeed, there are reasons which suggest that this is by no means the case.

Scholion: The opinion of Augustine on the special majesty of biblical rhetoric.

CHAPTER IV. THE INERRANCY OF SACRED SCRIPTURE

Article I. The Fact
Article II. The Allegorical Interpretation of the Fathers
Article III. Standards of Truth
Article IV. Physical Matters
Article V. History
Article VI. Myths and Legends
Article VII. The Fathers on History
Article VIII. Implicit Citations
Article IX. Popular Traditions

Article I. Sacred Scripture Is Immune from Errors

By the inerrancy of the sacred books is meant that property by reason of which whatever is taught in Scripture is true and utterly excludes all error.

Opinions: The ancients were unanimous on this point. Orthodox thinkers remain so. Rationalists reject the position. Some Catholics restrict it to religious matters.

Arguments: Jn 10:35; Acts 1:16; Lk 24:44; Mt 5:18. The Fathers. The theologians. The popes.

Article II. May Not the Patristic Argument for Inerrancy Be Weakened by the Allegorical Interpretations of the Fathers Themselves?

Objection: The Fathers of the Church either failed to see our difficulties or, if they saw them, hid behind an allegorical interpretation.

Response: The Fathers affirmed the principle of inerrancy not inductively, from ignorance, but dogmatically; those who held tenaciously to the literal sense held the same principle; they often explained metaphorically; but they always supposed a literal sense.

Article III. The Same Standard of Truth Is Not To Be Applied to All Parts of Scripture

Moral truth or veracity. Pseudonyms.

Logical truth: the conformity of what the hagiographers experienced and what they wrote with objective truth. The truth of history, of parable; fictional tales can be inspired. The truth of song in description or in prophecy; conditional predictions.

All the expressions of Scripture are certainly true, but according to that standard of truth which is appropriate to the genus of the individual books, be they historical, prophetic, poetic, or didactic.

The question of critical historiography must not be confused with this one. Is it possible that there pertain to the words of Sacred Scripture more truth than the hagiographers themselves understood and intended? Some say that whatever the sacred author did not will to say, God did not will to say. Pesch's reply is that the hagiographers did not perfectly understand all the things which God wished to express by their words. The testimony of the authors on this point: St. Augustine, St. Jerome, St. Thomas Aquinas, Suarez, Leo XIII.

Conclusion: There frequently underlies the words of Scripture a higher meaning than that which can be discovered by the common rules of interpretation, and this full breadth of meaning of the inspired words was not always grasped by the hagiographers themselves.

Article IV. The Relation of the Truth of Scripture to the Sciences

God gave Scripture to men for the purpose of furthering the way of salvation, and not for communicating secular instruction: 2 Tim 3:16–17.

A distinction must be made between that which is revealed *per se* (mysteries) and that which is revealed *per accidens* (history).

Whatever has been revealed, in the way in which it has been revealed, is the word of God, which the faithful may not deny. It is possible for that which has been revealed *per accidens* to be corrupted (numbers, e.g.). From the very fact that they can have a common object, a certain tension exists between the theologian and the natural scientist. St. Augustine, St. Thomas Aquinas, Leo XIII. But no contradiction is possible. Note the existence of popular or common speech, which goes by appearances.

Article V. The Difference between Physical Matters and Historical Matters

History as such either narrates facts or it is false. Yet it remains possible for the narrator to set forth fictitious material or to quote extraneous material.

1. Popular science speaks of things known to all; history does otherwise.

2. Nature does not pertain to salvation *per se*, whereas the history of salvation certainly does.

3. Many historical facts have been revealed and must be believed: the Creed.

Discussions of what is called "history according to appearances."

Sacred history is true with respect to extent: inasmuch as it does not tell all that was known to the hagiographers and others: Jn 21:25.

It is true with respect to manner: inasmuch as it uses indeterminate or summary expressions. It is true with respect to intent: inasmuch as the author's sole intention is to refer to what he has found in the sources.

The substance of sacred history is true; the manner of describing historical matters is that which was employed by the ancients, not that which is customary among moderns.

Article VI. Are There Myths or Legends in the Historical Books of Scripture?

Pesch means by this (he mentions no names) a narration which, under the guise of history, tells things which are substantially false. This is something essentially different from an historical allegory, which proposes abstract ideas in fictional narrative form. Texts of the Fathers.

Article VII. Did Some of the Fathers Teach that the Historical Narrations of Scripture Were Not Always Truly Historical?

Texts and discussion.

Article VIII. Implicit Citations from Sacred Scripture

The truth of the citation and the truth of the matter cited.

Explicit citations: Neh 7:4ff.; Jer 28:2ff. (reproving); Tim 1:12 (approving).

Implicit citations: 2 Chr 5:9, 8:8; 2 K 24:9 with 1 Chr 21:5; Gn 46:21 with 1 Chr 7:6; 1 Chr 2:3 with 4:1; 1 Chr 8:29 with 9:35; Ezr 2 with Neh 7; 1 Mac 3:39 with 2 Mac 8:9.

At times recourse is rather to be had to corruption of numbers.

Some are certainly present, others not arbitrarily to be supposed; nor can the whole of the Old Testament be reduced to them.

Citations of the Old Testament in the New Testament according to the version of the Septuagint. Some consider the Septuagint to be inspired. Where the meaning is the same, there is no difficulty. Where the meaning is different.

Article IX. Popular Traditions

These are handed on orally, not by a canon; likewise, religious tradition, even revealed.

There is nothing to prevent the sacred authors of the Old Testament from drawing, among their sources, from what we would call popular traditions. But within popular tradition, truth is preserved and handed on in a way different from that proper to what is written according to artistic rules: poetically and concretely, by proverb and metaphor, on the basis of appearance and opinion; little by little it may come about that the true becomes mingled with what is false.

The sacred author can take what is true from these traditions, even retaining the popular style; but he cannot retain the false without disapproving of it.

CHAPTER V. THE MEANING OF SACRED SCRIPTURE

Article I. Literal Meaning
Article II. Typical Meaning

CHAPTER VI. THE CLARITY AND SUFFICIENCY OF SACRED SCRIPTURE

Article I. The Clarity of Scripture
Article II. The Sufficiency of Scripture

Article I. The Clarity of Scripture

The opinion of Protestants on the clarity of Scripture as a norm.

Certain Scriptural expressions are clear, while others are obscure.

The whole of Scripture, taken as a single book, must be called obscure and difficult rather than clear and easily understood: remoteness of cultural milieu, frequently unknown circumstances, mysteries, corruption of the text.

Why the Holy Spirit wished His books to be obscure: historical condition, variations among men; He demands the reader's coöperation and effort.

Article II. The Sufficiency of Scripture

Opinion of Protestants.

It is not adequate to prove its own authority.

Nor is it sufficient to prove that it has been preserved incorrupt.

Its insufficiency is due to the nature of those who had to be instructed: They neither knew how to read, nor did they know languages.

A priori, it is improbable that God, by giving men a book, would have imposed on all men the obligation of reading it and of gathering from it all that was necessary for salvation.

Christ provided in a better way for the preservation of revealed truth: Mt 28:18; Mk 16:16, 20; 2 Tim 1:13–14, 2:2; Tit 1:5, 7, 9. Patristic doctrine.

Christ instituted oral tradition as the principal and universal means of preserving and handing on revealed doctrine.

Scripture depends on tradition inasmuch as its authority is known from tradition.

The books of the New Testament infallibly assert the magisterium instituted by Christ.

Scripture, inasmuch as it declares that Christ instituted a living magisterium from which it was necessary to learn all truth, can rightly be said to be sufficient to show us the way of salvation.

Scripture depends on the Church inasmuch as only the infallible magisterium of the Church can make known the inspiration of the whole of Scripture.

Scripture sets down a rule of faith from which the Church cannot withdraw.

Further, Scripture was given to the magisterium of the Church that it might learn from Scripture what was to be taught learned and unlearned alike. Inasmuch as God willed to provide for the needs of the teaching Church by means of Scripture, Scripture is undoubtedly sufficient for the purpose intended by God.

Scripture is sufficient to demonstrate the dogmas which are contained in the Creed and which must be believed by all without exception.

Scripture is sufficient to resolve many controversies with those heretics who, along with Catholics, recognize the sacred books as inspired.

Scripture does not suffice to make all capable of rightly explaining it.

The Church does not bestow dignity on Scripture, but recognizes and affirms it.

The Church does not subject Scripture to herself, but interprets it.

The excellence of Scripture consists in its being formally the word of God.

CHAPTER VII. THE CRITERIA OF INSPIRATION

Article I. The Universal Criterion: Tradition
Article II. Internal Criteria
Article III. The Testimony of Scripture about Itself
Article IV. The Apostolate

Article I. The Universal Criterion of Inspiration Is Sacred Tradition

The testimonies of tradition.

From the nature of the thing: since it is a divine operation, not immediately perceptible.

Are only those books inspired which have been handed down in the canon?

What of those books already in existence in apostolic times and considered by some as inspired, but not received into the canon?

Have some inspired books perished? 1 Cor 5:9; Col 4:6.

Article II. What Internal Criteria Are of Value in Establishing the Fact of Inspiration?

According to Protestants: antiquity, majesty, efficacity, attacks, miracles.

Internal criteria are not sufficient; nonetheless, they are of worth in recommending Scripture.

Negative criteria: these are applied only with difficulty to Scripture.

Positive criteria: unity, inerrancy. These are valuable, but not sufficient to convince. Prophecies fulfilled. The authority with which it speaks. The "feel" of Scripture.

Article III. The Value of the Testimony of Scripture Regarding Its Inspiration

Once the Hebrew canon has been historically established, the testimony of the New Testament regarding the Old Testament becomes valuable. Similarly, the collection of Old Testament citations in the New Testament. But there is no mention in the New Testament of the following books: Ru, Ezr, Neh, Est, Ct, Ob, Na, Ct, Eccl.

The testimony of the New Testament is not a sufficient and universal criterion to establish the inspiration of the whole of the Old Testament, much less of the New Testament itself.

Article IV. May Not the Apostolate Be a Criterion of Inspiration?

It is a negative criterion by reason of time.

Opinions.

What tradition tells us.

Controversies.

Index of Names

Alan of Lille, 27
Aland, K., 223
Albright, W. F., 245
Alexander of Hales, 104
Allen, W., 90, 215
Allgrier, A., 294
Allo, E. B., 45
Alonso, A., 38
Alonso, D., 173, 202, 263, 269, 280
Alonso Schökel, L., 102, 103, 117, 130, 135, 170, 212, 248, 322, 346
Alt, A., 156
Ambrose, St., 50, 51, 114, 115, 368, 373
Anderson, B. W., 89, 118
Apollinaire, G., 244
Aristotle, 123, 170, 214, 343
Arrowsmith, W., 294
Ashe, S. K., 214
Asting, R., 329
Athenagoras, St., 59
Auerbach, E., 90
Augustine, St., 25, 26, 60, 61, 63, 67, 82, 106, 115, 116, 122, 251, 268, 315, 325, 345, 383
Autolycus, 59
Auvray, P., 286, 294

Bach, J., 277
Bacon, R., 170
Balthasar, H. Urs von, 46, 88, 126, 132, 133, 144
Baltzer, K., 157
Bañez, D., 68
Baronius, C., 315
Bartolo, S. di, 325

Basil, St., 142, 384
Baumgartner, W., 117
Bea, A., 45, 81, 82, 89, 90, 183, 257
Beauchamp, P., 117
Bellarmine, St. Robert, 148, 335, 337, 338
Bellet, P., 53
Bendrix, Maurice, 35
Benedict XIV, 283
Benoit, P., 22, 23, 64, 81, 150, 180, 182, 183, 193, 213, 214, 221, 222, 231, 232, 238, 240, 249, 286, 294, 316, 327, 330
Bergson, H., 167
Bernard, St., 137
Bernheim, E., 34
Bertram, R., 219
Beethoven, L. van, 274, 276
Beumer, J., 336, 345, 346
Billot, 214, 309
Billuart, C. R., 68
Blake, W., 160
Block, H., 215
Boileau, N., 214
Bonaventure, St., 27, 104, 267
Bonsirven, J., 45
Bourke, M., 47
Bouyer, L., 386
Bovary, Madame, 76
Bromiley, G. W., 46
Brown, R., 149
Brunner, A., 89
Buffon, 258
Bühler, K., 134, 150
Bultmann, R., 47, 149, 219
Burrell, D., 89
Buttrick, G. A., 118

Index of Subjects

Biblical References

414